Illustrated Library Edition

JACOB FAITHFUL

THE MISSION
OR
SCENES IN AFRICA

BY
CAPTAIN FREDERICK MARRYAT

With Introduction by
W. L. COURTNEY, M. A., LL. D.

BOSTON
COLONIAL PRESS COMPANY
PUBLISHERS

INTRODUCTION

"JACOB FAITHFUL" is the first of a trio of novels which · Captain Marryat wrote in the course of the year 1834, the other two being "Mr. Midshipman Easy" and "Japhet in Search of a Father." They did not appear consecutively in three-volume form, for the collection of stories entitled "The Pacha of Many Tales" was the immediate successor of "Jacob Faithful," while the publication of "Midshipman Easy" and "Japhet" was deferred until 1836. Nevertheless the pages of the *Metropolitan Magazine* bore witness during the course of 1834 to the enormous industry of our author, perhaps accounted for by the expense to which he had been put in standing for Tower Hamlets, as already narrated in the introduction to "Peter Simple." Now that Captain Marryat is really launched on his literary career, he has no time or inclination to quarrel with his critics, or to give us those personal disquisitions as to his motives and his meanings which appeared in the earlier volumes. He goes in a straightforward way to the execution of his business, occupied solely with the adventures of his hero, and never allowing the course of his narrative to be embarrassed with explanatory or exculpatory passages. Moreover, he has learnt better than before the principles of his profession ; his object is to interest the reader and carry out his novelistic design—the result being that "Jacob Faithful" is, from a technical standpoint, one of the best of his books, now and again reminding us of Smollett, and in the opinion of some critics representing a high-water mark in Marryat's literary career.

INTRODUCTION

For the nonce the author deserts the sea, and occupies himself with the Thames instead. Jacob Faithful is born on a lighter, and has early acquaintance with the Thames mud. It may, of course, be an individual opinion, but to me there is a sense of effort, of artificiality, of something like make-believe, whenever Captain Marryat takes us away from the high seas. The story is no doubt an excellent one, as Thackeray declared, adorned with a wonderful wealth of incidents and occasional narratives, and developed from the first page to the last with unfailing *verve* and good spirits. But every reader will observe that whenever he can make to himself a convenient excuse, and introduce a yarn told by one of his characters, Captain Marryat forgets all about the river Thames, and makes us breathe the keen air of the ocean. Turnbull is full of tales of high latitudes; so, too, is Stapleton, and to some extent old Tom. They are condemned to the unexciting life of the river, but their hearts are elsewhere, full of recollections of stormy scenes and hair-breadth escapes, far from the monotonous landscape and muddy banks on which they temporarily find a home. So, too, towards the end of the book, both Jacob Faithful and his friend young Tom Beazeley are pressed into his Majesty's service, and enjoy all the fearful delights of chasing a French privateer. The chapters which detail this adventure—Chapters xxxviii. and xxxix.—contrast very significantly with many of their predecessors in the easy swing of their spirited narrative.

En revanche for whatever may be lacking in a story of the river, Captain Marryat pays great care and attention to his characters. Old Tom Beazeley on his wooden stumps, blessed as he is with a melodious voice and an unusual acquaintance with romantic ballads and nautical ditties; young Tom, his son, ready with quip and repartee, careless, gallant, debonair; old Stapleton, with his eternal reference to "human natur" as the sole solution for all the problems of sex relationship; Domine Dobbs, the erudite old scholar with the big nose, prolific in his allusions to the classics, a walking encyclopædia of useless and forgotten culture—figures like these stand out from the pages with inimitable force and truth. The hero himself, Jacob Faithful, as usually happens in the case of an autobiography, is a good deal less interesting than some of those with whom he is brought into contact. He serves, in fact, in many ways as a sort of conducting-pipe to the gaiety and cleverness of others, a background on which Captain Marryat paints a series of eccentric portraits. As the narrative proceeds he begins to be an example in morals—the honest and trustworthy man whose pride and independence stands in the light of his own appropriate advancement. So at least Captain Marryat tells us in his last paragraph, although, fortunately for his reader, he constantly forgets this assumed didactic purpose. Mary Stapleton, too, the fickle and sometimes heartless coquette, appears quite as much for the object of pointing the moral as for adorning the tale ; while the gracious little lady whom Jacob Faithful ultimately marries, Sarah Drummond, is an almost colourless character.

For the rest, the only point which seems worthy of remark is Captain Marryat's lavish use of puns. The conversation of Tom the father and Tom the son is almost entirely occupied with verbal quips and cranks of the form which we now associate with the Christmas pantomime rather than with the novel. The effect is wearisome to the last degree, although doubtless the author supposed that he was thereby illustrating some of the idiosyncrasies of character. The Domine's Latin quotations are so voluminous that they seem to be extracted from a classical phrase-book ; albeit that now and again the allusions are happy and well-placed. But in this, as perhaps also in some other qualities of his novelistic art, Captain Marryat is too exuberant, spoiling his effect by over-emphasis. There is one passage at the end of the eighteenth chapter which, in this book at all events, is a rare instance of a homily or moral reflection. Perhaps Captain Marryat was thinking

INTRODUCTION

of his own youthful experiences, not, so far as we can learn, very happy, when he was a boy at school, and ran away three times with the intention of getting to sea. " How dangerous, how foolish, how presumptuous it is in adults," he says, " to suppose that they can read the thoughts and the feelings of those of a tender age." " Youth," he adds, " should never be judged harshly, and even when judged correctly, should it be in an evil course, may always be reclaimed ; those who decide otherwise and leave it to drift about the world have to answer for the castaway."

W. L. C.

June 1896.

CONTENTS

ix

CONTENTS

CHAPTER V

CHAPTER VI

CHAPTER VII

CHAPTER VIII

CHAPTER IX

CHAPTER X

CONTENTS

CHAPTER XI

CHAPTER XII

CHAPTER XIII

CHAPTER XIV

CHAPTER XV

CHAPTER XVI

CONTENTS

CHAPTER XVII

PAGE

CHAPTER XVIII

CHAPTER XIX

CHAPTER XX

CHAPTER XXI

CHAPTER XXII

CONTENTS

CONTENTS

CHAPTER XXIX

CHAPTER XXX

CHAPTER XXXI

CHAPTER XXXII

CHAPTER XXXIII

CHAPTER XXXIV

CONTENTS

CHAPTER XXXV

CHAPTER XXXVI

CHAPTER XXXVII

CHAPTER XXXVIII

CHAPTER XXXIX

CONTENTS

CHAPTER XL

CHAPTER XLI

CHAPTER XLII

CHAPTER XLIII

CHAPTER XLIV

CHAPTER XLV

CHAPTER XLVI

LIST OF ILLUSTRATIONS

JACOB FAITHFUL

THE MISSION; OR, SCENES IN AFRICA

JACOB FAITHFUL

CHAPTER I

*My birth, parentage, and family pretensions—Unfortunately
I prove to be a detrimental or younger son, which is remedied
by a trifling accident—I hardly receive the first elements of
science from my father, when the elements conspire against me,
and I am left an orphan.*

GENTLE reader, I was born upon the water—not upon
the salt and angry ocean, but upon the fresh and rapid-flowing
river. It was in a floating sort of box, called a lighter, and
upon the river Thames, at low water, that I first smelt the
mud. This lighter was manned (an expression amounting to
bullism, if not construed *kind*-ly) by my father, my mother,
and your humble servant. My father had the sole charge—
he was monarch of the deck ; my mother of course was queen,
and I was the heir-apparent.

Before I say one word about myself, allow me dutifully to
describe my parents. First, then, I will portray my queen
mother. Report says that when first she came on board of
the lighter, a lighter figure and a lighter step never pressed a
plank ; but as far as I can tax my recollection, she was always
a fat, unwieldy woman. Locomotion was not to her taste—gin
was. She seldom quitted the cabin—never quitted the lighter ;
a pair of shoes may have lasted her for five years, for the wear
and tear that she took out of them. Being of this domestic
habit, as all married women ought to be, she was always to be
found when wanted ; but although always at hand, she was
not always on her feet. Towards the close of the day she lay
down upon her bed—a wise precaution when a person can no
longer stand. The fact was, that my honoured mother, although

her virtue was unimpeachable, was frequently seduced by liquor; and although constant to my father, was debauched and to be found in bed with that insiduous assailer of female uprightness—*gin*. The lighter, which might have been compared to another Garden of Eden, of which my mother was the Eve, and my father the Adam to consort with, was entered by this serpent who tempted her; and if she did not eat, she drank, which was even worse. At first, indeed—and I may mention it to prove how the enemy always gains admittance under a specious form—she drank it only to keep the cold out of her stomach, which the humid atmosphere from the surrounding water appeared to warrant. My father took his pipe for the same reason; but, at the time that I was born, he smoked and she drank from morning to night, because habit had rendered it almost necessary to their existence. The pipe was always to his lips, the glass incessantly to hers. I would have defied any cold ever to have penetrated into their stomachs;—but I have said enough of my mother for the present, I will now pass on to my father.

My father was a puffy, round-bellied, long-armed, little man, admirably calculated for his station in, or rather out of society. He could manage a lighter as well as anybody, but he could do no more. He had been brought up to it from his infancy. He went on shore for my mother, and came on board again— the only remarkable event in his life. His whole amusement was his pipe; and as there is a certain indefinable link between smoking and philosophy, my father by dint of smoking had become a perfect philosopher. It is no less strange than true that we can puff away our cares with tobacco, when without it they remain an oppressive burthen to existence. There is no composing-draught like the draught through the tube of a pipe. The savage warriors of North America enjoyed the blessing before we did; and to the pipe is to be ascribed the wisdom of their councils, and the laconic delivery of their sentiments. It would be well introduced into our own legislative assembly. Ladies, indeed, would no longer peep down through the ventilator; but we should have more sense and fewer words. It is also to tobacco that is to be ascribed the stoical firmness of those American warriors who, satisfied with the pipe in their mouths, submitted with perfect indifference to the torture of their enemies. From the well-known virtues

2

of this weed arose that peculiar expression, when you irritate another, that you "put his pipe out."

My father's pipe, literally and metaphorically, was never put out. He had a few apophthegms which brought every disaster to a happy conclusion ; and, as he seldom or never indulged in words, these sayings were deeply impressed upon my infant memory. One was, " It's no use crying ; what's done can't be helped." When once these words escaped his lips, the subject was never renewed. Nothing appeared to move him ; the abjurations of those employed in the other lighters, barges, vessels, and boats of every description, who were contending with us for the extra foot of water, as we drifted up or down with the tide, affected him not, further than an extra column or two of smoke rising from the bowl of his pipe. To my mother he used but one expression, " Take it coolly ; " but it always had the contrary effect with my mother, as it put her more in a passion. It was like pouring oil upon flame ; nevertheless the advice was good, had it ever been followed. Another favourite expression of my father's when anything went wrong, and which was of the same pattern as the rest of his philosophy, was, " Better luck next time." These aphorisms were deeply impressed upon my memory ; I continually recalled them to mind, and thus I became a philosopher long before my wise teeth were in embryo, or I had even shed the first set with which kind Nature presents us, that in the petticoat age we may fearlessly indulge in lollipop.

My father's education had been neglected. He could neither write nor read ; but although he did not exactly, like Cadmus, invent letters, he had accustomed himself to certain hieroglyphics, generally speaking sufficient for his purposes, and which might be considered as an artificial memory. " I can't write nor read, Jacob," he would say ; " I wish I could ; but look, boy, I means this mark for three-quarters of a bushel. Mind you recollects it when I axes you, or I'll be blowed if I don't wallop you." But it was only a case of peculiar difficulty which would require a new hieroglyphic, or extract such a long speech from my father. I was well acquainted with his usual scratches and dots, and having a good memory, could put him right when he was puzzled with some misshapen x or z, representing some unknown quantity, like the same letters in algebra.

I have said that I was heir-apparent, but I did not say that I was the only child born to my father in his wedlock. My honoured mother had had two more children; but the first, who was a girl, had been provided for by a fit of the measles; and the second, my elder brother, by tumbling over the stern of the lighter when he was three years old. At the time of the accident, my mother had retired to her bed, a little the worse for liquor; my father was on deck forward, leaning against the windlass, soberly smoking his evening pipe. "What was that?" exclaimed my father, taking his pipe out of his mouth, and listening; "I shouldn't wonder if it wasn't Joe." And my father put in his pipe again, and smoked away as before.

My father was correct in his surmises. It was Joe—who had made the splash which roused him from his meditations, for the next morning Joe was nowhere to be found. He was, however, found some days afterwards; but, as the newspapers say, and as may well be imagined, the "vital spark was extinct;" and, moreover, the eels and chubs had eaten off his nose and a portion of his chubby face, so that, as my father said, "he was of no use to nobody." The morning after the accident, my father was up early and had missed poor little Joe. He went into the cabin, smoked his pipe, and said nothing. As my brother did not appear as usual for his breakfast, my mother called out for him in a harsh voice; but Joe was out of hearing, and as mute as a fish. Joe opened not his mouth in reply, neither did my father. My mother then quitted the cabin, and walked round the lighter, looked into the dog-kennel to ascertain if he was asleep with the great mastiff—but Joe was nowhere to be found.

"Why, what can have become of Joe?" cried my mother, with maternal alarm in her countenance, appealing to my father, as she hastened back to the cabin. My father spoke not, but taking his pipe out of his mouth, dropped the bowl of it in a perpendicular direction till it landed softly on the deck, then put it into his mouth again, and puffed mournfully. "Why, you don't mean to say that he is overboard?" screamed my mother.

My father nodded his head, and puffed away at an accumulated rate. A torrent of tears, exclamations, and revilings succeeded to this characteristic announcement. My father allowed my mother to exhaust herself. By the time when she had finished, so was his pipe; he then knocked out the ashes, and quietly observed, "It's no use crying; what's done can't be helped," and proceeded to refill the bowl.

"Can't be helped!" cried my mother; "but it might have been helped."

"Take it coolly," replied my father.

"Take it coolly!" replied my mother, in a rage; "take it coolly! Yes, you're for taking everything coolly; I presume, if I fell overboard, you would be taking it coolly."

"You would be taking it coolly, at all events," replied my imperturbable father.

"O dear! O dear!" cried my poor mother; "two poor children, and lost them both!"

"Better luck next time," rejoined my father; "so, Sall, say no more about it."

My father continued for some time to smoke his pipe, and my mother to pipe her eye, until at last my father, who was really a kind-hearted man, rose from the chest upon which he was seated, went to the cupboard, poured out a teacupful of gin, and handed it to my mother. It was kindly done of him, and my mother was to be won by kindness. It was a pure offering in the spirit, and taken in the spirit in which it was offered. After a few repetitions, which were rendered necessary from its potency being diluted with her tears, grief and recollection were drowned together, and disappeared like two lovers who sink down entwined in each other's arms.

With this beautiful metaphor, I shall wind up the episode of my unfortunate brother Joe.

It was about a year after the loss of my brother that I was ushered into the world without any other assistants or spectators than my father and Dame Nature, who I believe to be a very clever midwife, if not interfered with. My father, who had some faint ideas of Christianity, performed the baptismal rites by crossing me on the forehead with the end of his pipe, and calling me Jacob; as for my mother being churched, she had never been but once to church in her life. In fact, my father and mother never quitted the lighter, unless when the former was called out by the superintendent or proprietor, at the delivery or shipment of a cargo, or was once a month for a few minutes or shore to purchase necessaries. I cannot

5

recall much of my infancy; but I recollect that the lighter was often very brilliant with blue and red paint, and that my mother used to point it out to me as "so pretty," to keep me quiet. I shall therefore pass it over, and commence at the age of five years, at which early period I was of some little use to my father. Indeed, I was almost as forward as some boys at ten. This may appear strange; but the fact is, that my ideas, although bounded, were concentrated. The lighter, its equipments, and its destination were the microcosm of my infant imagination; and my ideas and thoughts being directed to so few objects, these objects were deeply impressed, and their value fully understood. Up to the time that I quitted the lighter, at eleven years old, the banks of the river were the boundaries of my speculations. I certainly comprehended something of the nature of trees and houses; but I do not think that I was aware that the former *grew*. From the time that I could recollect them on the banks of the river, they appeared to be exactly of the same size as they were when first I saw them, and I asked no questions. But by the time that I was ten years old, I knew the name of every reach of the river, and every point—the depth of water, and the shallows, the drift of the current, and the ebb and flow of the tide itself. I was able to manage the lighter as it floated down with the tide; for what I lacked in strength I made up with the dexterity arising from constant practice.

It was at the age of eleven years that a catastrophe took place which changed my prospects in life, and I must therefore say a little more about my father and mother, bringing up their history to that period. The propensity of my mother to ardent spirits had, as always is the case, greatly increased upon her, and her corpulence had increased in the same ratio. She was now a most unwieldy, bloated mountain of flesh, such a form as I have never since beheld, although, at the time, she did not appear to me to be disgusting, accustomed to witness imperceptibly her increase, and not seeing any other females, except at a distance. For the last two years she had seldom quitted her bed—certainly she did not crawl out of the cabin more than five minutes during the week—indeed her obesity and habitual intoxication rendered her incapable. My father went on shore for a quarter of an hour once a month, to purchase gin, tobacco, red herrings and decayed ship-biscuits—the latter was my principal fare, except when I could catch a fish over the sides, as we lay at anchor. I was therefore a great water-drinker, not altogether from choice, but from the salt nature of my food, and because my mother had still sense enough left to discern that "gin wasn't good for little boys." But a great change had taken place in my father. I was now left almost altogether in charge of the deck, my father seldom coming up except to assist me in shooting the bridges, or when it required more than my exertions to steer clear of the crowds of vessels which we encountered when between them. In fact, as I grew more capable, my father became more incapable, and passed most of his time in the cabin, assisting my mother in emptying the great stone bottle. The woman had prevailed upon the man, and now both were guilty in partaking of the forbidden fruit of the Juniper Tree. Such was the state of affairs in our little kingdom when the catastrophe occurred which I am now about to relate.

One fine summer's evening we were floating up with the tide, deeply laden with coals, to be delivered at the proprietor's wharf, some distance above Putney Bridge; a strong breeze sprang up and checked our progress, and we could not, as we expected, gain the wharf that night. We were about a mile and a half above the bridge when the tide turned against us, and we dropped our anchor. My father, who, expecting to arrive that evening, had very unwillingly remained sober, waiting until the lighter had swung to the stream, and then saying to me, " Remember, Jacob, we must be at the wharf early to-morrow morning, so keep alive," went into the cabin to indulge in his potations, leaving me in possession of the deck, and also of my supper, which I never ate below, the little cabin being so unpleasantly close. Indeed, I took all my meals *al fresco*, and unless the nights were intensely cold slept on deck, in the capacious dog-kennel abaft, which had once been tenanted by the large mastiff; but he had been dead some years, was thrown overboard, and in all probability had been converted into savoury sausages, at 1s. per lb. Some time after his decease, I had taken possession of his apartment and had performed his duty. I had finished my supper, which I washed down with a considerable portion of Thames water, for I always drank more when above the bridges, having an idea that it tasted

7

more pure and fresh. I had walked forward and looked at
the cable to see if all was right, and then having nothing
more to do I lay down on the deck, and indulged in the
profound speculations of a boy of eleven years old. I was
watching the stars above me, which twinkled faintly, and
appeared to me ever and anon to be extinguished and then
relighted. I was wondering what they could be made of,
and how they came there, when of a sudden I was interrupted in my reveries by a loud shriek, and perceived a
strong smell of something burning. The shrieks were renewed again and again, and I had hardly time to get upon
my legs when my father burst up from the cabin, rushed
over the side of the lighter, and disappeared under the
water. I caught a glimpse of his features as he passed me,
and observed fright and intoxication blended together. I
ran to the side where he had disappeared, but could see
nothing but a few eddying circles as the tide rushed quickly
past. For a few seconds I remained staggered and stupefied
at his sudden disappearance and evident death, but I was
recalled to recollection by the smoke which encompassed
me, and the shrieks of my mother, which were now fainter
and fainter, and I hastened to her assistance.

A strong, empyreumatic, thick smoke ascended from the
hatchway of the cabin, and, as it had now fallen calm, it
mounted straight up the air in a dense column. I attempted
to go in, but so soon as I encountered the smoke I found
that it was impossible; it would have suffocated me in half
a minute. I did what most children would have done in
such a situation of excitement and distress—I sat down and
cried bitterly. In about ten minutes I removed my hands,
with which I had covered up my face, and looked at the
cabin hatch. The smoke had disappeared, and all was silent.
I went to the hatchway, and although the smell was still
overpowering, I found that I could bear it. I descended the
little ladder of three steps, and called, "Mother!" but there
was no answer. The lamp fixed against the after bulk-head,
with a glass before it, was still alight, and I could see plainly
to every corner of the cabin. Nothing was burning—not
even the curtains to my mother's bed appeared to be singed.
I was astonished; breathless with fear, with a trembling
voice, I again called out, "Mother!" I remained more than

a minute panting for breath, and then ventured to draw back the curtains of the bed—my mother was not there! but there appeared to be a black mass in the centre of the bed. I put my hand fearfully upon it—it was a sort of unctuous pitchy cinder. I screamed with horror—my little senses reeled—I staggered from the cabin, and fell down on the deck in a state amounting almost to insanity; it was followed by a sort of stupor, which lasted for many hours.

As the reader may be in some doubt as to the occasion of my mother's death, I must inform him that she perished in that very peculiar and dreadful manner which does sometimes, although rarely, occur to those who indulge in an immoderate use of spirituous liquors. Cases of this kind do indeed present themselves but once in a century, but the occurrence of them is too well authenticated. She perished from what is termed *spontaneous combustion,* an inflammation of the gases generated from the spirits absorbed into the system. It is to be presumed that the flames issuing from my mother's body completely frightened out of his senses my father, who had been drinking freely; and thus did I lose both my parents, one by fire and the other by water, at one and the same time.

CHAPTER II

I fulfil the last injunctions of my father, and I am embarked upon a new element—First bargain in my life very profitable —First parting with old friends very painful—First intro- duction into civilised life very unsatisfactory to all parties.

IT was broad daylight when I awoke from my state of bodily and mental imbecility. For some time I could not recall to my mind all that had happened: the weight which pressed upon my feelings told me that it was something dreadful. At length the cabin hatch, still open, caught my eye; I recalled all the horrors of the preceding evening, and recollected that I was left alone in the lighter. I got up and stood upon my feet in mute despair. I looked around me—the mist of the morning was hanging over the river, and the objects on shore were with difficulty to be distinguished. I was chilled from lying all night in the heavy dew, and perhaps still more from

9

previous and extraordinary excitement. Venture to go down into the cabin I dare not. I had an indescribable awe, a degree of horror at what I had seen, that made it impossible; still I was unsatisfied, and would have given worlds, if I had had them, to explain the mystery. I turned my eyes from the cabin hatch to the water, thought of my father, and then for more than half-an-hour watched the tide as it ran up—my mind in a state of vacancy. As the sun rose, the mist gradually cleared away; trees, houses, and green fields, other barges coming up with the tide, boats passing and repassing, the barking of dogs, the smoke issuing from the various chimneys, all broke upon me by degrees; and I was recalled to the sense that I was in a busy world, and had my own task to perform. The last words of my father—and his injunctions . had ever been a law to me—were, " Mind, Jacob, we must be up at the wharf early to-morrow morning." I prepared to obey him. Purchase the anchor I could not; I therefore slipped the cable, lashing a broken sweep to the end of it, as a buoy-rope, and once more the lighter was at the mercy of the stream, guided by a boy of eleven years old. In about two hours I was within a hundred yards of the wharf and well in-shore. I hailed for assistance, and two men who were on board of the lighters moored at the wharf pushed off in a skiff to know what it was that I wanted. I told them that I was alone in the lighter, without anchor or cable, and requested them to secure her. They came on board, and in a few minutes the lighter was safe alongside of the others. As soon as the lashings were passed, they interrogated me as to what had happened, but although the fulfilling of my father's last injunctions had borne up my spirits, now that they were obeyed a reaction took place. I could not answer them; I threw myself down on the deck in a paroxysm of grief, and cried as if my heart would break.

The men, who were astonished not only at my conduct but at finding me alone in the lighter, went on shore to the clerk, and stated the circumstances. He returned with them, and would have interrogated me, but my paroxysm was not yet over, and my replies, broken by my sobs, were unintelligible. The clerk and the two men went down into the cabin, returned hastily, and quitted the lighter. In about a quarter of an hour I was sent for, and conducted to the house of the proprietor—the first time in my life that I had ever put my foot on *terra firma*. I was led into the parlour, where I found the proprietor at breakfast with his wife and his daughter, a little girl nine years old. By this time I had recovered myself, and on being interrogated, told my story clearly and succinctly, while the big tears coursed each other down my dirty face.

"How strange and how horrible!" said the lady to her husband; "I cannot understand it even now."

"Nor can I; but still it is true, from what Johnson, the clerk, has witnessed."

In the meantime my eyes were directed to every part of the room, which appeared to my ignorance as a Golconda of wealth and luxury. There were few things which I had seen before, but I had an innate idea that they were of value. The silver teapot, the hissing urn, the spoons, the pictures in their frames, every article of furniture, caught my wondering eye, and for a short time I had forgotten my father and my mother; but I was recalled from my musing speculations by the proprietor inquiring how far I had brought the lighter without assistance.

"Have you any friends, my poor boy?" inquired the lady.

"No."

"What, no relations on shore?"

"I never was on shore before in my life."

"Do you know that you are a destitute orphan?"

"What's that?"

"That you have no father or mother," said the little girl.

"Well," replied I, in my father's words, having no answer more appropriate, "it's no use crying; what's done can't be helped."

"But what do you intend to do now?" inquired the proprietor, looking hard at me after my previous answer

"Don't know, I'm sure. Take it coolly," replied I, whimpering.

"What a very odd child!" observed the lady. "Is he aware of the extent of his misfortune?"

"Better luck next time, missus," replied I, wiping my eyes with the back of my hand.

"What strange answers from a child who has shown so much feeling," observed the proprietor to his wife. "What is your name?"

11

" Jacob Faithful."

" Can you write or read ? "

" No," replied I, again using my father's words. " No, I can't; I wish I could."

" Very well, my poor boy, we'll see what's to be done," said the proprietor.

" I know what's to be done," rejoined I ; " you must send a couple of hands to get the anchor and cable, afore they cut the buoy adrift."

" You are right, my lad, that must be done immediately," said the proprietor ; " but now you had better go down with Sarah into the kitchen—cook will take care of you. Sarah, my love, take him down to cook."

The little girl beckoned me to follow her. I was astonished at the length and variety of the companion-ladders, for such I considered the stairs, and was at last landed below, when little Sarah, giving cook the injunction to take care of me, again tripped lightly up to her mother.

I found the signification of "take care of any one " very different on shore from what it was on the river, where taking care of you means getting out of your way, and giving you a wide berth ; and I found the shore-reading much more agreeable. Cook did take care of me: she was a kind-hearted, fat woman, who melted at a tale of woe, although the fire made no impression on her. I not only beheld but I devoured such things as never before entered into my mouth or my imagination. Grief had not taken away my appetite. I stopped occasionally to cry a little, wiped my eyes, and sat down again. It was more than two hours before I laid down my knife, and not until strong symptoms of suffocation played round the regions of my trachea did I cry out, "Hold, enough." Somebody has made an epigram about the vast ideas which a. miser's horse must have had of corn. I doubt, if such ideas were existent, whether they were at all equal to my astonishment at a leg of mutton. I had never seen such a piece of meat before, and wondered if it were fresh or otherwise. After such reflection I naturally felt inclined to sleep ; in a few minutes I was snoring upon two chairs, cook having covered me up with her apron to keep away the flies. Thus was I fairly embarked upon an element new to me — my mother earth ; and it may be just as well to

examine now into the capital I possessed for my novel enter-
prise. In person I was well-looking; I was well-made,
strong, and active. Of my habiliments the less said the
better. I had a pair of trousers with no seat to them; but
this defect when I stood up was hid by my jacket, composed
of an old waistcoat of my father's, which reached down as low
as the morning frocks worn in those days. A shirt of coarse
duck, and a fur cap, which was as rough and ragged as if it
had been the hide of a cat pulled to pieces by dogs, completed my attire. Shoes and stockings I had none; these
supernumerary appendages had never confined the action of my
feet. My mental acquisitions were not much more valuable;
—they consisted of a tolerable knowledge of the depth of
water, names of points and reaches in the river Thames, all
of which was not very available on dry land—of a few hieroglyphics of my father's which, as the crier says sometimes,
winding up his oration, were of "no use to nobody but the
owner." Add to the above, the three favourite maxims of
my taciturn father, which were indelibly imprinted upon my
memory, and you have the whole inventory of my stock-in-
trade. These three maxims were, I may say, incorporated
into my very system, so continually had they been quoted to
me during my life; and before I went to sleep that night,
they were again conned over. "What's done, can't be
helped," consoled me for the mishaps of my life; "Better
luck next time," made me look forward with hope; and
"Take it coolly," was a subject of deep reflection, until I fell
into a deep sleep; for I had sufficient penetration to observe
that my father had lost his life by not adhering to his own
principles; and this perception only rendered my belief in the
infallibility of these maxims to be even still more steadfast.

I have stated what was my father's legacy, and the reader
will suppose that from the maternal side the acquisition was
nil. Directly such was the case, but indirectly she proved a
very good mother to me, and that was by the very extraordinary way in which she had quitted the world. Had she
met with a common death, she would have been worth
nothing. Burke himself would not have been able to dis-
pose of her; but dying as she did, her ashes were the source
of wealth. The bed, with her remains lying in the centre,
even the curtains of the bed, were all brought on shore, and

locked up in an outhouse. The coroner came down in a post-chaise and four, charged to the county; the jury was empanneled, my evidence was taken, surgeons and apothecaries attended from far and near to give their opinions, and after much examination, much arguing, and much disagreement, the verdict was brought in that she "Died by the visitation of God." As this, in other phraseology, implies that "God only knows how she died," it was agreed to *nem. con.*, and gave universal satisfaction. But the extraordinary circumstance was spread everywhere, with all due amplifications, and thousands flocked to the wharfinger's yard to witness the effects of spontaneous combustion. The proprietor immediately perceived that he could avail himself of the public curiosity to my advantage. A plate, with some silver and gold, was placed at the foot of my poor mother's flock mattress, with "For the benefit of the orphan," in capital text, placarded above it; and many were the shillings, half-crowns, and even larger sums which were dropped into it by the spectators, who shuddered as they turned away from this awful specimen of the effects of habitual intoxication. For many days did the exhibition continue, during which time I was domiciled with the cook, who employed me in scouring her saucepans, and any other employment in which my slender services might be useful, little thinking at the time that my poor mother was holding her levee for my advantage. On the eleventh day the exhibition was closed, and I was summoned upstairs by the proprietor, whom I found in company with a little gentleman in black. This was a surgeon, who had offered a sum of money for my mother's remains, bed and curtains, in a lot. The proprietor was willing to get rid of them in so advantageous a manner, but did not conceive that he was justified in taking this step, although for my benefit, without first consulting me, as heir-at-law.

"Jacob," said he, "this gentleman offers £20, which is a great deal of money, for the ashes of your poor mother. Have you any objection to let him have them?"

"What do you want 'em for?" inquired I.

"I wish to keep them, and take great care of them," answered he.

"Well," replied I, after a little consideration, "if you'll take care of the old woman, you may have her;" and the bargain was concluded. Singular that the first bargain I ever made in my life should be that of selling my own mother. The proceeds of the exhibition and sale amounted to £47 odd, which the worthy proprietor of the lighter, after deducting for a suit of clothes, laid up for my use. Thus ends the history of my mother's remains, which proved more valuable to me than ever she did when living. In her career she somewhat reversed the case of Semele, who was first visited in a shower of gold, and eventually perished in the fiery embraces of the god; whereas my poor mother perished first by the same element, and the shower of gold descended to her only son. But this is easily explained. Semele was very lovely and did not drink gin—my mother was her complete antithesis.

When I was summoned to my master's presence to arrange the contract with the surgeon, I had taken off the waistcoat which I wore as a garment over all, that I might be more at my ease in chopping some wood for the cook, and the servant led me up at once, without giving me time to put it on. After I had given my consent, I turned away to go down-stairs again, when having, as I before observed, no seat to my trousers, the solution of continuity was observed by a little spaniel, who jumped from the sofa, and arriving at a certain distance, stood at bay, and barked most furiously at the exposure. He had been bred up among respectable people, and had never seen such an *exposé*. Mr. Drummond, the proprietor, observed the defect pointed out by the dog, and forthwith I was ordered to be suited with a new suit— certainly not before they were required. In twenty-four hours I was thrust into a new garment by a bandy-legged tailor, assisted by my friend the cook, and turn or twist whichever way I pleased, decency was never violated. A new suit of clothes is generally an object of ambition, and flatters the vanity of young and old; but with me it was far otherwise. Encumbered with my novel apparel, I experienced at once feelings of restraint and sorrow. My shoes hurt me, my worsted stockings irritated the skin; and as I had been accustomed to hereditarily succeed to my father's cast-off skins, which were a world too wide for my shanks, having but few ideas, it appeared to me as if I had swelled out to the size of the clothes which I had been unaccustomed

15

to wear, not that they had been reduced to my dimensions. I fancied myself a man, but was very much embarrassed with my manhood. Every step that I took I felt as if I was checked back by strings. I could not swing my arms as I was wont to do, and tottered in my shoes like a rickety child. My old apparel had been consigned to the dust-hole by cook, and often during the day would I pass, casting a longing eye at it, wishing that I dare recover it, and exchange it for that which I wore. I knew the value of it, and, like the magician in Aladdin's tale, would have offered new lamps for old ones, cheerfully submitting to ridicule, that I might have repossessed my treasure.

With the kitchen and its apparatus I was now quite at home; but at every other part of the house and furniture I was completely puzzled. Everything appeared to me foreign, strange, and unnatural, and Prince Le Boo or any other savage never stared or wondered more than I did. Of most things I knew not the use, of many not even the names. I was literally a savage, but still a kind and docile one. The day after my new clothes had been put on, I was summoned into the parlour. Mr. Drummond and his wife surveyed me in my altered habiliments, and amused themselves at my awkwardness, at the same time that they admired my well-knit, compact, and straight figure, set off by a fit, in my opinion, much too strait. Their little daughter, Sarah, who often spoke to me, went up and whispered to her mother. "You must ask papa," was the reply. Another whisper, and a kiss, and Mr. Drummond told me that I should dine with them. In a few minutes I followed them into the dining-room, and for the first time I was seated to a repast which could boast of some of the supernumerary comforts of civilised life. There I sat, perched on a chair, with my feet swinging close to the carpet, glowing with heat from the compression of my clothes, and the novelty of my situation, and all that was around me. Mr. Drummond helped me to some scalding soup, a silver spoon was put into my hand, which I twisted round and round, looking at my face reflected in miniature on its polish.

"Now, Jacob, you must eat the soup with the spoon," said little Sarah, laughing; "we shall all be done. Be quick."

"Take it coolly," replied I, digging my spoon into the burning preparation, and tossing it into my mouth. It burst forth from my tortured throat in a diverging shower, accompanied with a howl of pain.

"The poor boy has scalded his mouth," cried the lady, pouring out a tumbler of water.

"It's no use crying," replied I, blubbering with all my might; "what's done can't be helped."

"Better that you had not been helped," observed Mr. Drummond, wiping off his share of my liberal spargefication from his coat and waistcoat.

"The poor boy has been shamefully neglected," observed the good-natured Mrs. Drummond. "Come, Jacob, sit down and try it again; it will not burn you now."

"Better luck next time," said I, shoving in a portion of it, with a great deal of tremulous hesitation, and spilling one-half of it in its transit. It was now cool, but I did not get on very fast; I held my spoon awry, and soiled my clothes.

Mrs. Drummond interfered, and kindly showed me how to proceed; when Mr. Drummond said, "Let the boy eat it after his own fashion, my dear—only be quick, Jacob, for we are waiting."

"Then I see no good losing so much of it, taking it in tale," observed I, "when I can ship it all in bulk in a minute." I laid down my spoon, and stooping my head, applied my mouth to the edge of the plate, and sucked the remainder down my throat without spilling a drop. I looked up for approbation, and was very much astounded to hear Mrs. Drummond quietly observe, "That is not the way to eat soup."

I made so many blunders during the meal, that little Sarah was in a continued roar of laughter; and I felt so miserable, that I heartily wished myself again in my dog-kennel on board of the lighter, gnawing biscuit in all the happiness of content, and dignity of simplicity. For the first time I felt the pangs of humiliation. Ignorance is not always debasing. On board of the lighter I was sufficient for myself, my company, and my duties. I felt an elasticity of mind, a respect for myself, and a consciousness of power, as the immense mass was guided through the waters by my single arm. There, without being able to analyse my feelings, I was a spirit guiding a little world; and now, at this table, and in company with rational and well-informed beings, I felt humiliated and degraded; my heart was overflowing with shame, and at one unusually loud laugh of the little Sarah, the heaped-up measure of my anguish overflowed, and I burst into a passion of tears. As I lay with my head upon the tablecloth, regardless of those decencies I had so much feared, and awake only to a deep sense of wounded pride, each sob coming from the very core of my heart, I felt a soft breathing warm upon my cheek, that caused me to look up timidly, and I beheld the glowing and beautiful face of little Sarah, her eyes filled with tears, looking so softly and beseechingly at me, that I felt at once I was of some value, and panted to be of more.

"I won't laugh at you any more," said she; "so don't cry, Jacob."

"No more I will," replied I, cheering up. She remained standing by me, and I felt grateful. "The first time I get a piece of wood," whispered I, "I'll cut you out a barge."

"O papa, Jacob says he'll cut me out a barge."

"That boy has a heart," said Mr. Drummond to his wife.

"But will it swim, Jacob?" inquired the little girl.

"Yes, and if it's lopsided, call me a lubber."

"What's lopsided, and what's a lubber?" replied Sarah.

"Why, don't you know?" cried I; and I felt my confidence return when I found that in this little instance I knew more than she did.

CHAPTER III

I am sent to a charity-school, where the boys do not consider charity as a part of their education—The peculiarities of the master, and the magical effects of a blow of the nose—A disquisition upon the letter A, from which I find all my previous learning thrown away.

BEFORE I quitted the room, Sarah and I were in deep converse at the window, and Mr. and Mrs. Drummond employed likewise at the table. The result of the conversation between Sarah and me was the intimacy of children; that of Mr. and Mrs. Drummond, that the sooner I was disposed of, the more it would be for my own advantage. Having some interest with the governors of a charity-school near Brentford, Mr. Drummond lost no time in procuring me admission; and before I had quite spoiled my new clothes, having worn them nearly three weeks, I was suited afresh in a formal attire— a long coat of pepper and salt, yellow leather breeches tied at the knees, a worsted cap with a tuft on the top of it, stockings and shoes to match, and a large pewter plate upon my breast, marked with No. 63, which, as I was the last entered boy, indicated the sum total of the school. It was with regret that I left the abode of the Drummonds, who did not think it advisable to wait for the completion of the barge, much to the annoyance of Miss Sarah and myself. I was conducted to the school by Mr. Drummond, and before we arrived met them all out walking. I was put into the ranks, received a little good advice from my worthy patron, who then walked away one way, while we walked another, looking like a regiment of yellow-thighed fieldfares straight- ened into human perpendiculars. Behold, then, the last scion of the Faithfuls, peppered, salted, and plated, that all the world might know that he was a charity-boy, and that there was charity in this world. But if heroes, kings, great and grave men must yield to destiny, lighter-boys cannot be expected to escape ; and I was doomed to receive an educa- tion, board, lodging, raiment, &c., free, gratis, and for nothing.

Every society has its chief; and I was about to observe that every circle has its centre, which certainly would have been true enough, but the comparison is of no use to me, as our circle had two centres, or, to follow up the first idea, had two chiefs — the chief schoolmaster, and the chief domestic—the chief masculine, and the chief feminine—the chief with the ferula, and the chief with the brimstone and treacle—the master and the matron, each of whom had their appendages—the one in the usher, the other in the assistant housemaid. But of this quartette, the master was not only the most important, but the most worthy of de- scription ; and, as he will often appear in the pages of my narrative long after my education was complete, I shall be very particular in my description of Domine Dobiensis, as he delighted to be called, or Dreary Dobs, as his dutiful scholars delighted to call him. As, in our school, it was necessary that we should be instructed in reading, writing, and cipher- ing, the governors had selected the Domine as the most fitting person that had offered for the employment, because

19

he had, in the first place, written a work that nobody could understand upon the Greek particles; secondly, he had proved himself a great mathematician, having, it is said, squared the circle by algebraical false quantities, but would never show the operation for fear of losing the honour by treachery. He had also discovered as many errors in the demonstrations of Euclid, as ever did Joey Hume in army and navy estimates, and with as much benefit to the country at large. He was a man who breathed certainly in the present age, but the half of his life was spent in antiquity or algebra. Once carried away by a problem, or a Greek reminiscence, he passed away, as it were, from his present existence, and everything was unheeded. His body remained, and breathed on his desk, but his soul was absent. This peculiarity was well known to the boys, who used to say, " Domine is in his dreams, and talks in his sleep."

Domine Dobiensis left reading and writing to the usher, contrary to the regulations of the school, putting the boys, if possible, into mathematics, Latin, and Greek. The usher was not over-competent to teach the two first; the boys not over-willing to learn the latter. The master was too clever, the usher too ignorant; hence the scholars profited little. The Domine was grave and irascible, but he possessed a fund of drollery and the kindest heart. His features could not laugh, but his trachea did. The chuckle rose no higher than the rings of the windpipe, and then it was vigorously thrust back again by the impulse of gravity into the region of his heart, and gladdened it with hidden mirth in its dark centre. The Domine loved a pun, whether it was let off in English, Greek, or Latin. The last two were made by nobody but himself, and not being understood, were of course relished by himself alone. But his love of a pun was a serious attachment: he loved it with a solemn affection—with him it was no laughing matter.

In person, Domine Dobiensis was above six feet, all bone and sinews. His face was long, and his lineaments large; but his predominant feature was his nose, which, large as were the others, bore them down into insignificance. It was a prodigy—a ridicule; but he consoled himself—Ovid was called Naso. It was not an aquiline nose, nor was it an aquiline nose reversed. It was not a nose snubbed at the extremity, gross, heavy, or carbuncled, or fluting. In all its magnitude of proportions, it was an intellectual nose. It was thin, horny, transparent, and sonorous. Its snuffle was consequential, and its sneeze oracular. The very sight of it was impressive, its sound, when blown in school hours, was ominous. But the scholars loved the nose for the warning which it gave : like the rattle of the dreaded snake, which announces its presence, so did the nose indicate to the scholars that they were to be on their guard. The Domine would attend to this world and its duties for an hour or two, and then forget his scholars and his schoolroom, while he took a journey into the world of Greek or algebra. Then, when he marked x, y, and z, in his calculations, the boys knew that he was safe, and their studies were neglected.

Reader, did you ever witness the magic effects of a drum in a small village, when the recruiting-party, with many-coloured ribands, rouse it up with a spirit-stirring tattoo? Matrons leave their domestic cares, and run to the cottage-door; peeping over their shoulders, the maidens admire and fear. The shuffling clowns raise up their heads gradually, until they stand erect and proud; the slouch in the back is taken out, their heavy walk is changed to a firm yet elastic tread, every muscle appears more braced, every nerve, by degrees, new strung ; the blood circulates rapidly ; pulses quicken, hearts throb, eyes brighten, and as the martial sound pervades their rustic frames, the Cimons of the plough are converted, as if by magic, into incipient heroes for the field—and all this is produced by beating the skin of the most gentle, most harmless animal of creation.

Not having at hand the simile synthetical, we have resorted to the antithetical. The blowing of the Domine's nose produced the very contrary effect. It was a signal that he had returned from his intellectual journey, and was once more in his schoolroom—that the master had finished with his x, y, z's, and it was time for the scholars to mind their p's and q's. At this note of warning, like the minute roll among the troops, every one fell into his place ; half-munched apples were thrust into the first pocket ; popguns disappeared ; battles were left to be decided elsewhere ; books were opened, and eyes directed to them ; forms that were fidgeting and twisting in all directions now took one regimental inclined position over the desk ; silence was restored ; order resumed her reign; and Mr. Knapps, the usher, who always availed himself of these interregnums, as well as the scholars, by deserting to the matron's room, warned by the well-known sound, hastened to the desk of toil; such were the astonishing effects of a blow from Domine Dobiensis' sonorous and peace-restoring nose.

"Jacob Faithful, draw near," were the first words which struck upon my tympanum the next morning, when I had taken my seat at the further end of the schoolroom. I rose and threaded my way through two lines of boys, who put out their legs to trip me up in my passage through their ranks; and, surmounting all difficulties, found myself within three feet of the master's high desk, or pulpit, from which he looked down upon me like the Olympian Jupiter upon mortals in ancient time.

"Jacob Faithful, canst thou read?"

"No, I can't," replied I. "I wish I could."

"A well-disposed answer, Jacob; thy wishes shall be gratified. Knowest thou thine alphabet?"

"I don't know what that is."

"Then thou knowest it not. Mr. Knapps shall forthwith instruct thee. Thou shalt forthwith go to Mr. Knapps, who inculcateth the rudiments. *Levior puer*, lighter-boy, thou hast a *crafty* look." And then I heard a noise in his thorax that resembled the "cluck, cluck," when my poor mother poured the gin out of the great stone bottle.

"My little navilculator," continued he, "thou art a weed washed on shore, one of Father Thames' cast-up wrecks. '*Fluviorum rex Eridanus.*' [Cluck, cluck.] To thy studies; be thyself—that is, be Faithful. Mr. Knapps, let the Cadmean art proceed forthwith." So saying, Domine Dobiensis thrust his large hand into his right coat pocket, in which he kept his snuff loose, and taking a large pinch (the major part of which, the stock being low, was composed of hair and cotton abrasions, which had collected in the corner of his pocket), he called up the first class, while Mr. Knapps called me to my first lesson.

Mr. Knapps was a thin, hectic-looking young man, apparently nineteen or twenty years of age, very small in all his proportions, red ferret eyes, and without the least sign of incipient manhood; but he was very savage, nevertheless. Not being permitted to pummel the boys when the Domine was in the schoolroom, he played the tyrant most effectually when he was

22

left commanding officer. The noise and hubbub certainly warranted his interference—the respect paid to him was positively nil. His practice was to select the most glaring delinquent, and let fly his ruler at him, with immediate orders to bring it back. These orders were complied with for more than one reason; in the first place, was the offender hit, he was glad that another should have his turn; in the second, Mr. Knapps being a very bad shot (never having drove a Kamschatdale team of dogs), he generally missed the one he aimed at and hit some other, who, if he did not exactly deserve it at that moment, certainly did for previous, or would for subsequent delinquencies. In the latter case, the ruler was brought back to him because there was no injury inflicted, although intended. However, be it as it may, the ruler was always returned to him; and thus did Mr. Knapps pelt the boys as if they were cocks on Shrove Tuesday, to the great risk of their heads and limbs. I have little further to say of Mr. Knapps, except that he wore a black shalloon loose coat, on the left sleeve of which he wiped his pen, and upon the right, but too often, his ever-snivelling nose.

"What is that, boy?" said Mr. Knapps, pointing to the letter A.

I looked attentively, and recognising, as I thought, one of my father's hieroglyphics, replied, "That's half a bushel;" and I was certainly warranted in my supposition.

"Half a bushel! You're more than half a fool. That's the letter A."

"No; it's half a bushel; father told me so."

"Then your father was as big a fool as yourself."

"Father knew what half a bushel was, and so do I; that's half a bushel."

"I tell you it's the letter A," cried Mr. Knapps, in a rage.

"It's half a bushel," replied I doggedly. I persisted in my assertion, and Mr. Knapps, who dared not punish me while the Domine was present, descended his throne of one step, and led me up to the master.

"I can do nothing with this boy, sir," said he, red as fire; "he denies the first letter in the alphabet, and insists upon it that the letter A is not A, but half a bushel."

"Dost thou, in thine ignorance, pretend to teach when thou comest here to learn, Jacob Faithful?"

"Father always told me that that thing there meant half a bushel."

"Thy father might, perhaps, have used that letter to signify the measure which thou speakest of, in the same way as I, in my mathematics, use divers letters for known and unknown quantities; but thou must forget that which thy father taught thee, and commence *de novo.* Dost thou understand?"

"No, I don't."

"Then, little Jacob, that represents the letter A, and whatever else Mr. Knapps may tell thee, thou wilt believe. Return, Jacob, and be docile."

CHAPTER IV

Sleight of hand at the expense of my feet—Filling a man's pockets as great an offence as picking them, and punished accordingly—A turn out, a turn up, and a turn in—Early impressions removed, and redundancy of feeling corrected by a spell of the rattan.

I DID not quit Mr. Knapps until I had run through the alphabet, and then returned to my place, that I might con it over at my leisure, puzzling myself with the strange complexity of forms of which the alphabet was composed. I felt heated and annoyed by the constraint of my shoes, always an object of aversion from the time I had put them on. I drew my foot out of one, then out of the other, and thought no more of them for some time. In the meanwhile the boys next me had passed them on with their feet to the others, and thus were they shuffled along until they were right up to the master's desk. I missed them, and perceiving that there was mirth at my expense, I narrowly and quietly watched up and down, until I perceived one of the head boys of the school, who sat nearest to the Domine, catch up one of my shoes, and the Domine being then in an absent fit, drop it into his coat pocket. A short time afterwards he got up, went to Mr. Knapps, put a question to him, and while it was being answered, he dropped the other into the pocket of the usher, and tittering to the other boys returned to his seat. I said nothing, but when the hours of school were over, the Domine looked at his watch, blew his nose, which made the whole of the boys pop up their heads, like the clansmen of Roderick Dhu when summoned by his horn, folded up his large pocket-handkerchief slowly and reverently, as if it were a banner, put it into his pocket, and uttered in a solemn tone, *"Tempus est ludendi."* As this Latin phrase was used every day at the same hour, every boy in the school understood so much Latin. A rush from all the desks ensued, and amidst shouting, yelling, and leaping, every soul disappeared except myself, who remained fixed to my form. The Domine rose from his pulpit and descended, the usher did the same, and both approached me on their way to their respective apartments.

"Jacob Faithful, why still porest thou over thy book—didst thou not understand that the hours of recreation had arrived? Why risest thou not upon thy feet like the others?"

"'Cause I've got no shoes."

"And where are thy shoes, Jacob?"

"One's in your pocket," replied I, "and t'other's in his'n."

Each party placed their hands behind, and felt the truth of the assertion.

"Expound, Jacob," said the Domine, "who hath done this?"

"The big boy with the red hair, and a face picked all over with holes like the strainers in master's kitchen," replied I.

"Mr. Knapps, it would be *infra dig.* on my part, and also on yours, to suffer this disrespect to pass unnoticed. Ring in the boys."

The boys were rung in, and I was desired to point out the offender, which I immediately did, and who as stoutly denied the offence; but he had abstracted my shoe-strings, and put them into his own shoes. I recognised them, and it was sufficient.

"Barnaby Bracegirdle," said the Domine, "thou art convicted, not only of disrespect towards me and Mr. Knapps, but further, of the grievous sin of lying. Simon Swapps, let him be hoisted."

He was hoisted: his nether garments descended, and then the birch descended with all the vigour of the Domine's muscular arm. Barnaby Bracegirdle showed every symptom of his disapproval of the measures taken, but Simon Swapps held fast, and the Domine flogged fast. After a minute's flagellation, Barnaby was let down, his yellow tights pulled up, and the boys dismissed. Barnaby's face was red, but the antipodes were redder. The Domine departed, leaving us together—he adjusting his inexpressibles, I putting in my shoe-strings. By the time Barnaby had buttoned up, and wiped his eyes, I had succeeded in standing in my shoes. There we were *tête-à-tête*.

"Now, then," said Barnaby, holding one fist to my face, while with the other open hand he rubbed behind, "come out in the playground, Mr. *Cinderella*, and see if I won't drub you within an inch of your life."

"It's no use crying," said I soothingly; for I had not wished him to be flogged. "What's done can't be helped. Did it hurt you much?"

This intended consolation was taken for sarcasm. Barnaby stormed.

"Take it coolly," observed I.

Barnaby waxed even more wroth.

"Better luck next time," continued I, trying to soothe him.

Barnaby was outrageous—he shook his fist and ran into the playground, daring me to follow him. His threats had no weight with me. Not wishing to remain indoors, I followed him in a minute or two, when I found him surrounded by the other boys, to whom he was in loud and vehement harangue.

"Cinderella, where's your glass slippers?" cried the boys, as I made my appearance.

"Come out, you water-rat," cried Barnaby; "you son of a cinder!"

"Come out and fight him, or else you're a coward!" exclaimed the whole host, from No. 1 to No. 62 inclusive.

"He has had beating enough already to my mind," replied I; "but he had better not touch me—I can use my arms."

A ring was formed, in the centre of which I found Barnaby and myself. He took off his clothes, and I did the same. He was much older and stronger than I, and knew something about fighting. One boy came forward as my second. Barnaby advanced and held out his hand, which I shook heartily, thinking it was all over; but immediately received a right and left on the face, which sent me reeling backwards. This was a complete mystery, but it raised my bile,

26

and I returned it with interest. I was very strong in my arms, as may be supposed, and I threw them about like sails of a windmill, never hitting straight out, but with semicircular blows, which descended on or about his ears. On the contrary, his blows were all received straightforward, and my nose and face were soon covered with blood. As I warmed with pain and rage, I flung about my arms at random, and Barnaby gave me a knockdown blow. I was picked up, and sat upon my second's knee, who whispered to me, as I spat the blood out of my mouth, "Take it coolly, and make sure when you hit."

My own—my father's maxim—coming from another, it struck with double force, and I never forgot it during the remainder of the fight. Again we were standing up face to face; again I received it right and left, and returned it upon his right and left ears. Barnaby rushed in—I was down again.

"Better luck next time," said I to my second, as cool as a cucumber.

A third and a fourth round succeeded, all apparently in Barnaby's favour, but really in mine. My face was beat to a mummy, but he was what is termed groggy, from the constant return of blows on the side of the head. Again we stood up, panting and exhausted. Barnaby rushed at me, and I avoided him; before he could return to the attack, I had again planted two severe blows upon his ears, and he reeled. He shook his head, and, with his fists in the attitude of defence, asked me whether I had had enough.

"He has," said my second; "stick to him now, Jacob, and you'll beat him."

I did stick to him; three or four more blows applied to the same part finished him, and he fell senseless on the ground.

"You've settled him," cried my second.

"What's done can't be helped," replied I. "Is he dead?"

"What's all this?" cried Mr. Knapps, pressing his way through the crowd, followed by the matron.

"Barnaby and Cinderella having it out, sir," said one of the elder boys.

The matron, who had already taken a liking for me, because I was good-looking, and because I had been recommended to her care by Mrs. Drummond, ran to me.

"Well," says she, "if the Domine don't punish that big brute for this, I'll see whether I'm anybody or not;" and

27

taking me by the hand, she led me away. In the meantime Mr. Knapps surveyed Barnaby, who was still senseless, and desired the other boys to bring him in and lay him on his bed. He breathed hard, but still remained senseless, and a surgeon was sent for, who found it necessary to bleed him copiously. He then, at the request of the matron, came to me ; my features were undistinguishable, but elsewhere I was all right. As I stripped he examined my arms.

"It seemed strange," observed he, "that the bigger boy should be so severely punished ; but this boy's arms are like little sledge-hammers. I recommend you," said he to the other boys, "not to fight with him, for some day or other he'll kill one of you."

This piece of advice was not forgotten by the other boys, and from that day I was the cock of the school. The name of Cinderella, given me by Barnaby, in ridicule of my mother's death, was immediately abandoned, and I suffered no more persecution. It was the custom of the Domine, whenever two boys fought, to flog them both ; but in this instance it was not followed up, because I was not the aggressor, and my adversary narrowly escaped with his life. I was under the matron's care for a week, and Barnaby under the surgeon's hands for about the same time.

Neither was I less successful in my studies. I learnt rapidly after I had conquered the first rudiments, but I had another difficulty to conquer, which was my habit of construing everything according to my confined ideas ; the force of association had become so strong that I could not overcome it for a considerable length of time. Mr. Knapps continually complained of my being obstinate, when, in fact, I was anxious to please, as well as to learn. For instance, in spelling, the first syllable always produced the association with something connected with my former way of life. I recollect the Domine once, and only once, gave me a caning, about a fortnight after I went to the school.

I had been brought up by Mr. Knapps as contumelious.

"Jacob Faithful, how is this? thine head is good, yet wilt thou refuse learning. Tell me now, what does *c-a-t* spell?"

It was the pitch-pipe to cat-head, and I answered accordingly.

"Nay, Jacob, it spells *cat ;* take care of thy head on the

next reply. Understand me, head is not understood. Jacob, thy head is in jeopardy. Now, Jacob, what does *m-a-t* spell?"

"Chafing-mat," replied I.

"It spells mat only, silly boy; the chafing will be on my part directly. Now, Jacob, what does *d-o-g* spell?"

"Dog-kennel."

"Dog, Jacob, without the kennel. Thou art very contumelious, and deservest to be rolled in the kennel. Now, Jacob, this is the last time that thou triflest with me; what does *h-a-t* spell?"

"Fur-cap," replied I, after some hesitation.

"Jacob, I feel the wrath rising within me, yet would I fain spare thee; if *h-a-t* spell fur-cap, pray advise me, what doth *c-a-p* spell, then?"

"Capstern."

"Indeed, Jacob, thy stern as well as thy head are in danger, and I suppose then *w-i-n-d* spells windlass, does it not?"

"Yes, sir," replied I, pleased to find that he agreed with me.

"Upon the same principle, what does *r-a-t* spell?"

"Rat, sir," replied I.

"Nay, Jacob, *r-a-t* must spell *rattan*, and as thou hast missed thine own mode of spelling, thou shalt not miss the cane." The Domine then applied it to my shoulders with considerable unction, much to the delight of Mr. Knapps, who thought the punishment was much too small for the offence. But I soon extricated myself from these associations, as my ideas extended, and was considered by the Domine as the cleverest boy in the school. Whether it were from natural intellect, or from my brain having lain fallow, as it were, for so many years, or probably from the two causes combined, I certainly learnt almost by instinct. I read my lesson once over, and threw my book aside, for I knew it all. I had not been six months at the school, before I discovered that, in a thousand instances, the affection of a father appeared towards me under the rough crust of the Domine. I think it was on the third day of the seventh month, that I afforded him a day of triumph and warming of his heart, when he took me for the first time into his little study, and put the Latin Accidence into my hands. I learnt my first lesson in a quarter of an hour; and I remember well how that unsmiling, grave man looked into my smiling eyes;

29

parting the chestnut curls, which the matron would not cut off, from my brows, and saying, *"Bene fecisti, Jacobe."* Many times afterwards, when the lesson was over, he would fix his eyes upon me, fall back in his chair, and make me recount all I could remember of my former life, which was really nothing but a record of perceptions and feelings.. He *could* attend to *me*, and as I related some early and singular impression, some conjecture of what I saw, yet could not comprehend, on the shore which I had never touched, he would rub his hands with enthusiasm, and exclaim, " I have found a new book—an album, whereon I may write the deeds of heroes and the words of sages. *Carissime Jacobe !* how happy shall we be when we get into Virgil ! " I hardly need say that I loved him—I did so from my heart, and learnt with avidity to please him. I felt that I was of consequence—my confidence in myself was unbounded. I walked proudly, yet I was not vain. My schoolfellows hated me, but they feared me as much for my own prowess as my interest with the master; but still many were the bitter gibes and innuendoes which I was obliged to hear as I sat down with them to our meals. At other times I held communion with the Domine, the worthy old matron, and my books. We walked out every day, at first attended by Mr. Knapps, the usher. The boys would not walk with me without they were ordered, and if ordered, most unwillingly. Yet I had given no cause of offence. The matron found it out, told the Domine, and ever after that the Domine attended the boys, and led me by the hand.

This was of the greatest advantage to me, as he answered all my questions, which were not few, and each day I advanced in every variety of knowledge. Before I had been eighteen months at school, the Domine was unhappy without my company, and I was equally anxious for his presence. He was a father to me, and I loved him as a son should love a father, and, as it will hereafter prove, he was my guide through life.

But although the victory over Barnaby Bracegirdle, and the idea of my prowess, procured me an enforced respect, still the Domine's goodwill towards me was the occasion of a settled hostility. Affront me, or attack me openly they dare not; but supported as the boys were by Mr. Knapps, the usher, who was equally jealous of my favour, and equally mean in spirit, they caballed to ruin me, if possible, in the good opinion of my master. Barnaby Bracegirdle had a talent for caricature, which was well known to all but the Domine. His first attempt against me was a caricature of my mother's death, in which she was represented as a lamp supplied from a gin-bottle, and giving flame out of her mouth. This was told to me, but I did not see it. It was given by Barnaby to Mr. Knapps, who highly commended it, and put it into his desk. After which, Barnaby made an oft-repeated caricature of the Domine with a vast nose, which he showed to the usher as *my* performance. The usher understood what Barnaby was at, and put it into his desk without comment. Several other ludicrous caricatures were made of the Domine, and of the matron, all of which were consigned to Mr. Knapps by the boys, as being the production of my pencil; but this was not sufficient—it was necessary I should be more clearly identified. It so happened, that one evening, when sitting with the Domine at my Latin, the matron and Mr. Knapps being in the adjoining room, the light, which had burnt close down, fell in the socket and went out. The Domine rose to get another; the matron also got up to fetch away the candlestick with the same intent. They met in the dark, and ran their heads together pretty hard. As this event was only known to Mr. Knapps and myself, he communicated it to Barnaby, wondering whether I should not make it a subject of one of my caricatures. Barnaby took the hint; in the course of a few hours, this caricature was added to the others. Mr. Knapps, to further his views, took an opportunity to mention with encomium my talent for drawing, adding that he had seen several of my performances. "The boy hath talent," replied the Domine; "he is a rich mine, from which much precious metal is to be obtained."

"I hear that thou hast the talent of drawing, Jacob," said he to me, a day or two afterwards.

"I never had in my life, sir," replied I.

"Nay, Jacob; I like modesty, but modesty should never lead to a denial of the truth. Remember, Jacob, that thou do not repeat the fault."

I made no answer, as I felt convinced that I was not in fault; but that evening I requested the Domine to lend me a pencil, as I wished to try and draw. For some days, various scraps of my performance were produced, and received commendation.

"The boy draweth well," observed the Domine to Mr. Knapps, as he examined my performance through his spectacles.

"Why should he have denied his being able to draw?" observed the usher.

"It was a fault arising from modesty or want of confidence—even a virtue, carried to excess, may lead us into error."

The next attempt of Barnaby was to obtain the Cornelius Nepos which I then studied. This was effected by Mr. Knapps, who took it out of the Domine's study, and put it into Barnaby's possession, who drew on the fly-leaf, on which was my name, a caricature head of the Domine; and under my own name, which I had written on the leaf, added, in my hand, *fecit*, so that it appeared, Jacob Faithful *fecit*. Having done this, the leaf was torn out of the book, and consigned to the usher with the rest. The plot was now ripe, and the explosion soon ensued. Mr. Knapps told the Domine that I drew caricatures of my schoolfellows. The Domine taxed me, and I denied it. "So you denied drawing," observed the usher.

A few days passed away, when Mr. Knapps informed the Domine that I had been caricaturing him and Mrs. Bately, the matron, and that he had proofs of it. I had then gone to bed; the Domine was much surprised, and thought it impossible that I could be so ungrateful. Mr. Knapps said that he should make the charge openly, and prove it the next morning in the schoolroom; and wound up the wrong by describing me, in several points, as a cunning, good-for-nothing, although clever boy.

CHAPTER V

Mr. Knapps thinks to catch me napping, but the plot is dis-covered, and Barnaby Bracegirdle is obliged to loosen his braces for the second time on my account—Drawing cari-catures ends in drawing blood—The usher is ushered out of the school, and I am very nearly ushered into the next world, but instead of being bound on so long a journey, I am bound "'prentice to a waterman."

IGNORANT of what had passed I slept soundly, and the next morning found the matron very grave with me, which I could not comprehend. The Domine also took no notice of my morning salute, but supposing him to be wrapt in Euclid at the time, I thought little of it. The breakfast passed over, and the bell rang for school. We were all assembled; the Domine walked in with a very magisterial air, followed by Mr. Knapps, who, instead of parting company when he arrived at his own desk, continued his course with the Domine to his pulpit. We all knew that there was something in the wind; but of all, perhaps I was the least alarmed. The Domine unfolded his large handkerchief, waved it, and blew his nose and the school into profound silence. "Jacob Faithful, draw near," said he, in a tone which proved that the affair was serious. I drew near, wondering. "Thou hast been accused by Mr. Knapps of caricaturing, and holding up to the ridicule of the school, me —thy master. Upon any other boy such disrespect should be visited severely, but from thee, Jacob, I must add, in the words of Cæsar, '*Et tu, Brute,*' I expected, I had a right to expect, otherwise. *In se animi ingrati crimen vitia omnia condit.* Thou understandest me, Jacob—guilty, or not guilty?"

"Not guilty, sir," replied I firmly.

"He pleadeth not guilty, Mr. Knapps; proceed, then, to prove thy charge."

Mr. Knapps then went to his desk, and brought out the drawings with which he had been supplied by Barnaby Bracegirdle and the other boys. "These drawings, sir, which you will please to look over, have been all given up to me as the performance of Jacob Faithful. At first I could not believe it to be true, but you will perceive at once that they are all by the same hand."

"That I acknowledge," said the Domine; "and all reflect upon my nose. It is true that my nose is of large dimensions, but it was the will of Heaven that I should be so endowed; yet are the noses of these figures even larger than mine own could warrant, if the limner were correct, and not malicious. Still have they merit," continued the Domine, looking at some of them; and I heard a gentle cluck, cluck, in his throat, as he laughed at his own *mis*-representations. "*Artis adumbratæ meruit ceu sedula laudem,* as Prudentius hath it. I have no time to finish the quotation."

"Here is one drawing, sir," continued Mr. Knapps, "which proves to me that Jacob Faithful is the party; in which you and Mrs. Bately are shown up to ridicule. Who would have been aware that the candle went out in your study, except Jacob Faithful?"

"I perceive," replied the Domine, looking at it through his spectacles, when put into his hand, "the arcana of the study have been violated."

"But, sir," continued Mr. Knapps, "here is a more convincing proof. You observe this caricature of yourself, with his own name put to it—his own handwriting. I recognised it immediately, and happening to turn over his Cornelius Nepos, observed the first blank leaf torn out. Here it is, sir, and you will observe that it fits on to the remainder of the leaf in the book exactly."

"I perceive that it doth, and am grieved to find that such is the case. Jacob Faithful, thou art convicted of disrespect. and of falsehood. Where is Simon Swapps?"

"If you please, sir, may I not defend myself?" replied I. "Am I to be flogged unheard?"

"Nay, that were an injustice," replied the Domine, "but what defence canst thou offer? *O puer infelix et sceleratus!*"

"May I look at those caricatures, sir?" said I.

The Domine handed them to me in silence. I looked them all over, and immediately knew them to be drawn by Barnaby Bracegirdle. The last particularly struck me. I had felt confounded and frightened with the strong evidence brought against me; but this reassured me, and I spoke boldly. "These drawings are by Barnaby Bracegirdle, sir, and not by me. I never drew a caricature in my life."

"So didst thou assert that thou couldst not draw, and afterwards provedst by thy pencil to the contrary, Jacob Faithful."

"I knew not that I was able to draw when I said so, but I wished to draw when you supposed I was able—I did not like that you should give me credit for what I could not do. It was to please you, sir, that I asked for the pencil."

"I wish it were as thou statest, Jacob—I wish from my inmost soul that thou wert not guilty."

"Will you ask Mr. Knapps from whom he had these drawings, and at what time? There are a great many of them."

"Answer, Mr. Knapps, to the question of Jacob Faithful."

"They have been given to me by the boys at different times during this last month."

34

"Well, Mr. Knapps, point out the boys who gave them."

Mr. Knapps called out eight or ten boys, who came forward.

"Did Barnaby Bracegirdle give you none of them, Mr. Knapps?" said I, perceiving that Barnaby was not summoned.

"No," replied Mr. Knapps.

"If you please, sir," said I to the Domine, "with respect to the leaf out of my Nepos, the Jacob Faithful was written on it by me on the day that you gave it to me; but the *fecit*, and the caricature of yourself, is not mine. How it came there I don't know."

"Thou hast disproved nothing, Jacob," replied the Domine.

"But I have proved something, sir. On what day was it that I asked you for the pencil to draw with? Was it not on a Saturday?"

"Last Saturday week I think it was."

"Well then, sir, Mr. Knapps told you the day before that I could draw?"

"He did; and thou deniedst it."

"How, then, does Mr. Knapps account for not producing those caricatures of mine, which he says that he has collected for a whole month? Why didn't he give them to you before?"

"Thou puttest it shrewdly," replied the Domine. "Answer, Mr. Knapps, why didst thou, for a fortnight at the least, conceal thy knowledge of his offence?"

"I wished to have more proofs," replied the usher.

"Thou hearest, Jacob Faithful."

"Pray, sir, did you ever hear me speak of my poor mother but with kindness?"

"Never, Jacob; thou hast ever appeared dutiful."

"Please, sir, to call up John Williams."

"John Williams, No. 37, draw near."

"Williams," said I, "did you not tell me that Barnaby Bracegirdle had drawn my mother flaming at the mouth?"

"Yes, I did."

My indignation now found vent in a torrent of tears. "Now, sir," cried I, "if you believe that I drew the caricatures of you and Mrs. Bately—did I draw this, which is by the same person?" And I handed up to the Domine the caricature of my mother, which Mr. Knapps had inadvertently produced at the bottom of the rest. Mr. Knapps turned white as a sheet.

The Domine looked at the caricature, and was silent for some time. At last he turned to the usher.

"From whom didst thou obtain this, Mr. Knapps?"

Mr. Knapps replied in his confusion, "From Barnaby Bracegirdle."

"It was but this moment thou didst state that thou hadst received none from Barnaby Bracegirdle. Thou hast contradicted thyself, Mr. Knapps. Jacob did not draw his mother, and the pencil is the same as that which drew the rest—*ergo*, he did not, I really believe, draw one of them. *Ite procul fraudes*. God, I thank Thee, that the innocent have been protected. Narrowly hast thou escaped these toils, O Jacob —*Cum populo et duce fraudulento*. And now for punishment. Barnaby Bracegirdle, thou gavest this caricature to Mr. Knapps; from whence hadst thou it? Lie not."

Barnaby turned red and white, and then acknowledged that the drawing was his own.

"You boys," cried the Domine, waving his rod which he had seized, "you gave these drawings to Mr. Knapps; tell me from whom they came?"

The boys, frightened at the Domine's looks, immediately replied in a breath, "From Barnaby Bracegirdle."

"Then, Barnaby Bracegirdle, from whom didst thou receive them?" inquired the Domine. Barnaby was dumfounded. "Tell the truth; didst thou not draw them thyself, since thou didst not receive them from other people?"

Barnaby fell upon his knees, and related the whole circumstances, particularly the way in which the Cornelius Nepos had been obtained through the medium of Mr. Knapps. The indignation of the Domine was now beyond all bounds. I never had seen him so moved before. He appeared to rise at least a foot more in stature; his eyes sparkled, his great nose turned red, his nostrils dilated, and his mouth was more than half open, to give vent to the ponderous breathing from his chest. His whole appearance was withering to the culprits.

"For thee, thou base, degraded, empty-headed, and venomous little abortion of a man, I have no words to signify my contempt. By the governors of this charity I leave thy conduct to be judged; but until they meet, thou shalt not pollute and contaminate the air of this school by thy presence. If thou hast one spark of good feeling in thy petty frame, beg pardon of this

36

poor boy, whom thou wouldst have ruined by thy treachery. If not, hasten to depart, lest in my wrath I apply to the teacher the punishment intended for the scholar, but of which thou art more deserving than even Barnaby Bracegirdle."

Mr. Knapps said nothing, hastened out of the school, and that evening quitted his domicile. When the governors met he was expelled with ignominy. "Simon Swapps, hoist up Barnaby Bracegirdle." Most strenuously and most indefatigably was the birch applied to Barnaby a second time through me. Barnaby howled and kicked, howled and kicked, and kicked again. At last the Domine was tired. "*Consonat omne nemus strepitu,*" (for *nemus* read schoolroom,) exclaimed the Domine, laying down the rod, and pulling out his handkerchief to wipe his face. "*Calcitrat, ardescunt germani cæde bimembres,* that last quotation is happy" [cluck, cluck]. He then blew his nose, addressed the boys in a long oration; paid me a handsome compliment upon my able defence; proved to all those who chose to listen to him that innocence would always confound guilt; intimated to Barnaby that he must leave the school; and then, finding himself worn-out with exhaustion, gave the boys a holiday, that they might reflect upon what had passed, and which they duly profited by, in playing at marbles, and peg in the ring. He then dismissed the school, took me by the hand and led me into his study, where he gave vent to his strong and affectionate feelings towards me until the matron came to tell us that dinner was ready.

After this, everything went on well. The Domine's kindness and attention were unremitting, and no one ever thought of caballing against me. My progress became most rapid; I had conquered Virgil, taken Tacitus by storm, and was reading the Odes of Horace. I had passed triumphantly through decimals, and was busily employed in mensuration of solids, when one evening I was seized with a giddiness in my head. I complained to the matron; she felt my hands, pronounced me feverish, and ordered me to bed. I passed a restless night; the next morning I attempted to rise, but a heavy burning ball rolled as it were in my head, and I fell back on my pillow. The matron came, was alarmed at my state, and sent for the surgeon, who pronounced that I had caught the typhus fever, then raging through the vicinity. This was the first time in my life that I had known a day's sickness—

it was a lesson I had yet to learn. The surgeon bled me, and giving directions to the matron, promised to call again. In a few hours I was quite delirious—my senses ran wild. One moment I thought I was with little Sarah Drummond, walking in green fields, holding her by the hand. I turned round, and she was no longer there, but I was in the lighter, and my hand grasped the cinders of my mother; my father stood before me, again jumped overboard and disappeared; again the dark black column ascended from the cabin, and I was prostrate on the deck. Then I was once more alone on the placid and noble Thames, the moon shining bright, and the sweep in my hand, tiding up the reach, and admiring the foliage which hung in dark shadows over the banks. I saw the slopes of green, so pure and so fresh by that sweet light, and in the distance counted the numerous spires of the great monster city, and beheld the various bridges spanning over the water. The faint ripple of the tide was harmony, the reflection of the moon, beauty; I felt happiness in my heart; I was no longer the charity-boy, but the pilot of the barge. Then, as I would survey the scene, there was something that invariably presented itself between my eyes and the object of my scrutiny; whichever way I looked it stood in my way, and I could not remove it. It was like a cloud, yet transparent, and with a certain undefined shape. I tried for some time, but in vain, to decipher it, but could not. At last it appeared to cohere into a form— it was the Domine's great nose, magnified into that of the Scripture, "as the tower which looketh towards Damascus." My temples throbbed with agony—I burned all over. I had no exact notions of death in bed, except that of my poor mother, and I thought that I was to die like her; the horrible fear seized me that all this burning was but prefatory to bursting out into flame and consuming into ashes. The dread hung about my young heart and turned that to ice, while the rest of my body was on fire. This was my last recollection, and then all was blank. For many days I lay unconscious of either pain or existence. When I awoke from my stupor, my wandering senses gradually returning, I opened my eyes, and dimly perceived something before me that cut across my vision in a diagonal line. As the mist cleared away, and I recovered myself, I made out that it was the nose of Domine Dobiensis, who was kneeling at the bedside, his nose adumbrating the coverlid of my bed, his spectacles dimmed with tears, and his long grey locks falling on each side, and shadowing his eyes. I was not frightened, but I was too weak to stir or speak. His prayer-book was in his hand, and he still remained on his knees. He had been praying for me. Supposing me still insensible, he broke out in the following soliloquy :—

" *Naviculator parvus pallidus*—how beautiful even in death ! My poor lighter-boy, that hath mastered the rudiments, and triumphed over the Accidence—but to die ! *Levior puer*, a puerile conceit, yet I love it, as I do thee. How my heart bleeds for thee ! The icy breath of death hath whitened thee, as the hoar-frost whitens the autumnal rose. Why wert thou transplanted from thine own element ? Young prince of the stream—lord of the lighter—' *Ratis rex et magister* '—heir-apparent to the tiller—betrothed to the sweep—wedded to the deck—how art thou laid low ! Where is the blooming cheek, ruddy with the browning air ? where the bright and swimming eye ? Alas ! where ? ' *Tum breviter diræ mortis apèrta via est*,' as sweet Tibullus hath it ; " and the Domine sobbed anew. " Had this stroke fallen upon me, the aged, the ridiculed, the little regarded, the ripe for the sickle, it would have been well (yet fain would I have instructed thee still more before I quitted the scene—fain have left thee the mantle of learning). Thou knowest, Lord, that I walk wearily, as in a desert, that I am heavily burdened, and that my infirmities are many. Must I then mourn over thee, thou promising one—must I say with the epigrammist—

> ' Hoc jacet in tumulo, raptus puerilibus annis,
> Jacob Faithful domini cura, doloroque sui ?'

True, most true. Hast thou quitted the element thou so joyously controlledst, and hast come upon the *terra firma* for thy grave ?

> ' Sis licet inde sibi tellus placata, levisque,
> Artifices levoir non potes esse manu.'

Earth, lay light upon the lighter-boy—the lotus, the water-lily, that hath been cast on shore to die. Hadst thou lived, Jacob, I would have taught thee the Humanities ; we would have conferred pleasantly together. I would have poured out my learning to thee, my Absalom, my son ! "

He rose, and stood over me; the tears coursed down his long nose from both his eyes, and from the point of it poured out like a little rain-gutter upon the coverlid. I understood not all his words, but I understood the spirit of them—it was love. I feebly stretched forth my arms, and articulated, "Domine!" The old man clasped his hands, looked upwards, and said, "O God, I thank Thee—he will live. Hush, hush, my sweet one, thou must not prate;" and he retired on tip-toe, and I heard him mutter triumphantly, as he walked away "He called me 'Domine!'"

From that hour I rapidly recovered, and in three weeks was again at my duties. I was now within six months of being fourteen years old, and Mr. Drummond, who had occasionally called to ascertain my progress, came to confer with the Domine upon my future prospects. "All that I can do for him, Mr. Dobbs," said my former master, "is to bind him apprentice to serve his time on the river Thames, and that cannot be done until he is fourteen. Will the rules of the school permit his remaining?"

"The regulations do not exactly, but I will," replied the Domine. "I have asked nothing for my long services, and the governors will not refuse me such a slight favour; should they, I will charge myself with him, that he may not lose his precious time. What sayest thou, Jacob, dost thou feel inclined to return to thy Father Thames?"

I replied in the affirmative, for the recollections of my former life were those of independence and activity.

"Thou hast decided well, Jacob—the tailor at his needle, the shoemaker at his last, the serving-boy to an exacting mis-tress, and all those apprenticed to the various trades, have no time for improvement; but afloat there are moments of quiet and of peace—the still night for reflection, the watch for medi-tation; and even the adverse wind or tide leaves moments of leisure, which may be employed to advantage. Then wilt thou call to mind the stores of learning which I have laid up in thy garner, and wilt add to them by perseverance and in-dustry. Thou hast yet six months to profit by, and, with the blessing of God, those six months shall not be thrown away."

Mr. Drummond, having received my consent to be bound apprentice, wished me farewell, and departed. During the six months, the Domine pressed me hard, almost too hard, but I worked for *love*, and to please him I was most diligent. At last the time had flown away, the six months had more than expired, and Mr. Drummond made his appearance, with a servant carrying a bundle under his arm. I slipped off my pepper-and-salt, my yellows, and my badge, dressed myself in a neat blue jacket and trousers, and, with many exhortations from the Domine, and kind wishes from the matron, I bade farewell to them and to the charity-school, and in an hour was once more under the roof of the kind Mrs. Drummond.

But how different were my sensations to those which oppressed me when I had before entered! I was no longer a little savage, uneducated or confused in my ideas. On the contrary, I was full of imagination, confident in myself, and in my own powers, cultivated in mind, and proud of my success. The finer feelings of my nature had been called into play. I felt gratitude, humility, and love, at the same time that I was aware of my own capabilities. In person I had much improved, as well as much increased in stature. I walked confident and elastic, joying in the world, hoping, anticipating, and kindly disposed towards my fellow-creatures. I knew I felt my improvement, my total change of character, and it was with sparkling eyes that I looked up at the window, where I saw Mrs. Drummond and little Sarah watching my return and reappearance, after an absence of three years.

Mrs. Drummond had been prepared by her husband to find a great change, but still she looked for a second or two with wonder as I entered the room, with my hat in my hand, and paid my obeisance. She extended her hand to me, which I took respectfully.

"I should not have known you, Jacob; you have grown quite a man," said she, smiling. Sarah held back, looking at me with pleased astonishment; but I went up to her, and she timidly accepted my hand. I had left her as my superior —I returned, and she soon perceived that I had a legitimate right to the command. It was some time before she would converse, and much longer before she would become intimate; but when she did so, it was no longer the little girl encouraging the untutored boy by kindness, or laughing at his absurdities, but looking up to him with respect and affection, and taking his opinion as a guide for her own. I had gained the *power of knowledge.*

41

By the regulations of the Watermen's Company, it is necessary that every one who wishes to ply on the river on his own account, should serve as an apprentice, from the age of fourteen to twenty-one; at all events, he must serve an apprenticeship for seven years, and be fourteen years old before he signs the articles. This apprenticeship may be served in any description of vessel which sails or works on the river, whether it be barge, lighter, fishing-smack, or a boat of larger dimensions; and it is not until that apprenticeship is served, that he can work on his own account, either in a wherry or any other craft. Mr. Drummond offered to article me on board of one of his own lighters free of all expense, leaving me at liberty to change into any other vessel that I might think proper. I gratefully accepted the proposal, went with him to Watermen's Hall, signed the papers, and thus was, at the age of fourteen, "bound 'prentice to a waterman."

CHAPTER VI

I am recommended to learn to swim, and I take the friendly advice—Heavy suspicion on board of the lighter, and a mystery, out of which Mrs. Radcliffe would have made a romance.

JACOB, this is Marables, who has charge of the *Polly* barge," said Mr. Drummond, who had sent for me into his office, a few days after my arrival at his house. "Marables," continued my protector, addressing the man, " I have told you that this lad is bound 'prentice to the *Polly;* I expect you will look after him, and treat him kindly. No blows or ill-treatment. If he does not conduct himself well (but well I'm sure he will), let me know when you come back from your trip."

During this speech, I was scrutinising the outward man of my future controller. He was stout and well-built, inclining to corpulence; his features remarkably good, although his eyes were not large. His mouth was very small, and there was a good-natured smile on his lips, as he answered, " I never treated a cat ill, master."

" I believe not," replied Mr. Drummond; " but I am anxious that Jacob should do well in the world, and therefore let you know that he will always have my protection, so long as he conducts himself properly."

"We shall be very good friends, sir, I'll answer for it, if I may judge from the cut of his jib," replied Marables, extending to me an immense hand, as broad as it was long.

After this introduction, Mr. Drummond gave him some directions, and left us together.

"Come and see the craft, boy," said Marables; and I followed him to the barge, which was one of those fitted with a mast which lowered down and hauled up again as required. She plied up and down the river as far as the Nore, sometimes extending her voyage still farther; but that was only in the summer months. She had a large cabin abaft and a cuddy forward. The cabin was locked, and I could not examine it.

"This will be your berth," said Marables, pointing to the cuddy-hatch forward; "you will have it all to yourself. The other man and I sleep abaft."

"Have you another man, then?"

"Yes, I have, Jacob," replied he; and then muttering to himself, "I wish I had not—I wish the barge was only between us, Jacob, or that you had not been sent on board," continued he gravely. "It would have been better—much better." And he walked aft, whistling in a low tone, looking down sadly on the deck.

"Is your cabin large?" inquired I, as he came forward.

"Yes, large enough; but I cannot show it to you now—he has the key."

"What, the other man under you?"

"Yes," replied Marables hastily. "I've been thinking, Jacob, that you may as well remain on shore till we start. You can be of no use here."

To this I had no objection, but I often went on board during the fortnight that the barge remained, and soon became very partial to Marables. There was a kindness about him that won me, and I was distressed to perceive that he was often very melancholy. What surprised me most was to find that during the first week the cabin was constantly locked, and that Marables had not the key; it appeared so strange that he, as master of the barge, should be locked out of his own cabin by his inferior.

One day I went early on board, and found not only the

43

cabin doors open, but the other man belonging to her walking up and down the deck with Marables. He was a well-looking, tall, active young man, apparently not thirty, with a general boldness of countenance strongly contrasted with a furtive glance of the eye. He had a sort of blue smock-frock overall, and the trousers which appeared below were of a finer texture than those usually worn by people of his condition.

"This is the lad who is bound to the barge," said Marables. "Jacob, this is Fleming."

"So, younker," said Fleming, after casting an inquiring eye upon me, "you are to sail with us, are you? It's my opinion that your room would be better than your company. However, if you keep your eyes open, I'd advise you to keep your mouth shut. When I don't like people's company, I sometimes give them a hoist into the stream—so keep a sharp look-out, my joker."

Not very well pleased with this address, I answered, "I thought Marables had charge of the craft, and that I was to look to him for orders."

"Did you, indeed!" replied Fleming, with a sneer. "I say, my lad, can you swim?"

"No, I can't," replied I; "I wish I could."

"Well then, take my advice—learn to swim as fast as you can; for I have a strong notion that one day or other I shall take you by the scruff of the neck, and send you to look after your father."

"Fleming! Fleming! pray be quiet!" said Marables, who had several times pulled him by the sleeve. "He's only joking, Jacob," continued Marables to me, as, indignant at the mention of my father's death, I was walking away to the shore, over the other lighters.

"Well," replied I, turning round, "if I am to be tossed overboard, it's just as well to let Mr. Drummond know, that if I'm missing he may guess what's become of me."

"Pooh! nonsense!" said Fleming, immediately altering his manner and coming to me where I stood, in the barge next to them. "Give us your hand, my boy; I was only trying what stuff you were made of. Come, shake hands; I wasn't in earnest."

I took the proffered hand, and went on shore. "Nevertheless," thought I, "I'll learn to swim; for I rather think he was in earnest." And I took my first lesson that day, and by dint of practice soon acquired that very necessary art. Had it not been for the threat of Fleming, I probably should not have thought of it; but it occurred to me that I might tumble, even if I were not thrown overboard, and that a knowledge of swimming would do no harm.

The day before the barge was to proceed down the river to Sheerness, with a cargo of bricks, I called upon my worthy old master, Domine Dobiensis.

"*Salve puer!*" cried the old man, who was sitting in his study. "Verily, Jacob, thou art come in good time. I am at leisure, and will give thee a lesson. Sit down, my child."

The Domine opened the Æneid of Virgil, and commenced forthwith. I was fortunate enough to please him with my offhand translation; and as he closed the book I told him that I had called to bid him farewell, as we started at daylight the next morning.

"Jacob," said he, "thou hast profited well by the lessons which I have bestowed upon thee; now take heed of that advice which I am now about to offer to thee. There are many who will tell thee that thy knowledge is of no use, for what avail can the Latin tongue be to a boy on board of a lighter? Others may think that I have done wrong thus to instruct thee, as thy knowledge may render thee vain—*nil exactius eruditiusque est*—or discontented with thy situation in life. Such is too often the case I grant; but it is because education is not as general as it ought to be. Were all educated, the superiority acquired or presumed upon by education would be lost, and the nation would not only be wiser, but happier. It would judge more rightly, would not condemn the measures of its rulers, which at present it cannot understand, and would not be led away by the clamour and misrepresentation of the disaffected. But I must not digress, as time is short. Jacob, I feel that thou wilt not be spoilt by the knowledge instilled into thee; but mark me, parade it not, for it will be vanity, and make thee enemies. Cultivate thyself as much as thou canst, but in due season— thy duties to thy employer must be first attended to—but treasure up what thou hast, and lay up more when thou canst. Consider it as hidden wealth, which may hereafter be advantageously employed. Thou art now but an apprentice in a barge, but what mayest thou not be, Jacob, if thou art diligent

45

—if thou fear God, and be honest ? I will now call to my mind some examples to stimulate thee in thy career."

Here the Domine brought forward about forty or fifty instances from history, in which people from nothing had risen to the highest rank and consideration ; but, although I listened to them very attentively, the reader will probably not regret the omission of the Domine's catalogue. Having concluded, the Domine gave me a Latin Testament, the Whole Duty of Man, and his blessing. The matron added to them a large slice of seed-cake, and by the time that I had returned to Mr. Drummond's, both the Domine's precepts and the matron's considerate addition had been well digested.

It was at six o'clock the next morning that we cast off our fastenings and pulled into the stream. The day was lovely, the sun had risen above the trees, which feathered their boughs down on the sloping lawns in front of the many beautiful retreats of the nobility and gentry which border the river, and the lamp of day poured a flood of light upon the smooth and rapidly ebbing river. The heavy dew which had fallen during the night studded the sides of the barge, and glittered like necklaces of diamonds ; the mist and the fog had ascended, except here and there, where it partially concealed the landscape; boats laden with the produce of the market-gardens in the vicinity were hastening down with the tide to supply the metropolis ; the watermen were in their wherries, cleaning and mopping them out, ready for their fares ; the smoke of the chimneys ascended in a straight line to heaven ; and the distant chirping of the birds in the trees added to the hilarity and lightness of heart with which I now commenced my career as an apprentice.

I was forward, looking down the river, when Marables called me to take the helm, while they went to breakfast. He commenced giving me instructions, but I cut them short by proving to him that I knew the river as well as he did. Pleased at the information, he joined Fleming, who was preparing the breakfast in the cabin, and I was left on the deck by myself. There, as we glided by every object which for years I had not seen, but which was immediately recognised, and welcomed as an old friend, with what rapidity did former scenes connected with them flash into my memory ! There was the inn at the water-side, where my father used to replenish the stone bottle;

46

it was just where the barge now was, that I had hooked and pulled up the largest chub I had ever caught. Now I arrived at the spot where we had run foul of another craft, and my father, with his pipe in his mouth, and his, "Take it coolly," which so exasperated the other parties, stood as alive before me. Here—yes, it was here—exactly here—where we anchored on that fatal night, when I was left an orphan; it was here that my father disappeared; and as I looked down at the water I almost thought I could perceive it again close over him, as it eddied by; and it was here that the black smoke— The whole scene came fresh to my memory, my eyes filled with tears, and for a little while I could not see to steer. But I soon recovered myself; the freshness of the air, the bright sky overhead, the busy scene before me, and the necessity of attending to my duty, chased away my painful remembrances; and when I had passed the spot, I was again cheerful and content.

In half-an-hour I had shot Putney Bridge, and was sweeping clear of the shallows on the reach below, when Marables and Fleming came up. "How!" exclaimed Marables; "have we passed the bridge? Why did you not call us?"

"I have shot it without help many and many a time," replied I, "when I was but ten years old. Why should I call you from your breakfast? But the tides are high now, and the stream rapid; you had better get a sweep out on the bow, or we may tail on the bank."

"Well!" replied Fleming, with astonishment; "I had no idea that he would have been any help to us; but so much the better." He then spoke in a low tone to Marables.

Marables shook his head. "Don't try it, Fleming, it will never do."

"So you said once about yourself," replied Fleming, with a laugh.

"I did—I did!" replied Marables, clenching both his hands, which at the time were crossed on his breast, with a look of painful emotion; "but I say again, don't try it; nay, I say more, you *shall* not."

"Shall not?" replied Fleming haughtily.

"Yes," replied Marables coolly; "I say shall not, and I'll stand by my words. Now, Jacob, give me the helm, and get your breakfast."

I gave up the helm to Marables, and was about to enter

the cabin, when Fleming caught me by the arm, and slewed me round. "I say, my joker, we may just as well begin as we leave off. Understand me, that into that cabin you never enter; and understand further, that if ever I find you in that cabin by day or night, I'll break every bone in your body. Your berth is forward; and as for your meals, you may either take them down there, or you may eat them on deck."

From what I had already witnessed, I knew that for some reason or another Fleming had the control over Marables; nevertheless I replied, "If Mr. Marables says it is to be so, well and good; but he has charge of this barge." Marables made no reply; he coloured up, seemed very much annoyed, and then looked up at the sky.

"You'll find," continued Fleming, addressing me in a low voice, "that I command here—so be wise. Perhaps the day may come when you may walk in and out of the cabin as you please, but that depends upon yourself. By-and-by, when we know more of each other——"

"Never, Fleming, never!" interrupted Marables, in a firm and loud tone. "It *shall* not be."

Fleming muttered what I could not hear, and going into the cabin brought me out my breakfast, which I despatched with good appetite; and soon afterwards I offered to take the helm, which offer was accepted by Marables, who retired to the cabin with Fleming, where I heard them converse for a long while in a low tone.

The tide was about three-quarters ebb, when the barge arrived abreast of Millbank. Marables came on deck, and taking the helm, desired me to go forward and see the anchor clear for letting go.

"Anchor clear!" said I. "Why, we have a good hour more before we meet the flood."

"I know that, Jacob, as well as you do; but we shall not go farther to-night. Be smart, and see all clear."

I went forward, and when the anchor and cable were ready, we let it go, and swung to the stream. I thought at the time that this was not making the best of our way, as in duty bound to our master; but as I was not aware what Marables' orders might be, I held my tongue. Whether Fleming thought that it was necessary to blind me, or whether it was true that they were only obeying their orders, he said to Marables in my hearing, "Will you go on shore and give the letters to Mr. Drummond's correspondent, or shall I go for you?"

"You had better go," replied Marables carelessly; and shortly after they went to dinner in the cabin, Fleming bringing me mine out on deck.

The flood tide now made, and we rode to the stream. Having nothing to do, and Marables as well as Fleming appearing to avoid me, I brought the Domine's Latin Testament, and amused myself with reading it. About a quarter of an hour before dusk, Fleming made his appearance to go on shore. He was genteelly, I may say fashionably, dressed in a suit of black, with a white neckcloth. At first I did not recognise him, so surprised was I at his alteration; and my thoughts, as soon as my surprise was over, naturally turned upon the singularity of a man who worked in a barge under another, now assuming the dress and appearance of a gentleman. Marables hauled up the little skiff which lay astern. Fleming jumped in and shoved off. I watched him till I perceived him land at the stairs, and then turned round to Marables: "I can't understand all this," observed I.

"I don't suppose you can," replied Marables; "but still I could explain it, if you will promise me faithfully not to say a word about it."

"I will make that promise, if you satisfy me that all is right," answered I.

"As to all being right, Jacob, that's as may be; but if I prove to you that there is no harm done to our master, I suppose you will keep the secret. However, I must not allow you to think worse of it than it really is; no, I'll trust to your good nature. You wouldn't harm me, Jacob?" Marables then told me that Fleming had once been well-to-do in the world, and during the long illness and subsequent death of Marables' wife, had lent him money; that Fleming had been very imprudent, and had run up a great many debts, and that the bailiffs were after him. On this emergency he had applied to Marables to help him, and that in consequence he had received him on board of the barge, where they never would think of looking for him; that Fleming had friends, and contrived to go on shore at night to see them, and get what assistance he could from them in money; in the meantime, his relations were trying what they could do to arrange with his creditors.

"Now," said Marables, after this narration, "how could I help assisting one who has been so kind to me? And what harm does it do Mr. Drummond? If Fleming can't do his work, or won't, when we unload, he pays another man himself; so Mr. Drummond is not hurt by it."

"That may be all true," replied I, "but I cannot imagine why I am not to enter the cabin, and why he orders about here as master."

"Why, you see, Jacob, I owe him money, and he allows me so much per week for the cabin, by which means I shall pay it off. Do you understand now?"

"Yes, I understand what you have said," replied I.

"Well then, Jacob, I hope you'll say nothing about it. It would only harm me, and do no good."

"That depends upon Fleming's behaviour towards me," replied I. "I will not be bullied and made uncomfortable by him, depend upon it; he has no business on board the barge, that's clear, and I'm bound 'prentice to her. I don't wish to hurt you, and as I suppose Fleming won't be long on board I shall say nothing, unless he treats me ill."

Marables then left me, and I reflected upon what he had said. It appeared all very probable, but still I was not satisfied. I resolved to watch narrowly, and if anything occurred which excited more suspicions, to inform Mr. Drummond upon our return. Shortly afterwards Marables came out again, and told me I might go to bed, and he would keep the deck till Fleming's return. I assented, and went down to the cuddy; but I did not much like this permission. It appeared to me as if he wanted to get rid of me, and I laid awake turning over in my mind all that I had heard and seen. About two o'clock in the morning I heard the sound of oars, and the skiff strike the side of the barge. I did not go up, but I put my head up the scuttle to see what was going on. It was broad moonlight, and almost as clear as day. Fleming threw up the painter of the skiff to Marables, and, as he held it, lifted out of the boat a blue bag, apparently well filled. The contents jingled as it was landed on the deck. He then put out a yellow silk handkerchief full of something else, and having gained the deck, Marables walked aft with the painter in his hand until the skiff had dropped astern, where he made it fast, and returned to Fleming, who stood close to the blue bag. I heard Fleming ask Marables, in a low voice, if I were in bed, and an answer given in the affirmative. I dropped my head immediately that I might not be discovered, and turned into my bed place. I was restless for a long while; thought upon thought, surmise upon surmise, conjecture upon conjecture, and doubt upon doubt, occupied my brain until at last I went fast asleep—so fast, that I did not wake until summoned by Fleming. I rose, and when I came on deck, found that the anchor had been weighed more than two hours, and that we were past all the bridges. "Why, Jacob, my man, you've had a famous nap," said Fleming, with apparent good-humour; "now go aft, and get your breakfast, it has been waiting for you this half-hour." By the manner of Fleming, I took it for granted that Marables had acquainted him with our conversation, and indeed, from that time, during our whole trip, Fleming treated me with kindness and familiarity. The veto had not, however, been taken off the cabin, which I never attempted to enter.

CHAPTER VII

The mystery becomes more and more interesting, and I determine to find it out—Prying after things locked up, I am locked up myself—Fleming proves to me that his advice was good when he recommended me to learn to swim.

ON our arrival off the Medway, I had just gone down to bed, and was undressing, when I heard Fleming come on deck and haul up the boat. I looked up the hatchway; it was very dark, but I could perceive Marables hand him the bag and handkerchief, with which he pulled on shore. He did not return until the next morning at daylight, when I met him as he came up the side. "Well, Jacob," said he, "you've caught me. I've been on shore to see my sweetheart; but you boys ought to know nothing about these things. Make the boat fast, there's a good lad."

When we were one night discharging our cargo, which was for government, I heard voices alongside. From habit, the least noise now awoke me; a boat striking the side was certain so to do. It was then about twelve o'clock. I looked up the

51

hatchway, perceived two men come on board and enter the cabin with packages. They remained there about ten minutes, and then, escorted to the side by Fleming, left the barge. When the barge was cleared, we hauled off to return, and in three days were again alongside of Mr. Drummond's wharf. The kindness both of Marables and of Fleming had been very great. They lived in a style very superior to what they could be expected to do, and I fared well in consequence.

On our arrival at the wharf, Marables came up to me, and said, "Now, Jacob, as I have honestly told you the secret, I hope you won't ruin me by saying a word to Mr. Drummond." I had before made up my mind to say nothing to my master until my suspicions were confirmed, and I therefore gave my promise; but I had also resolved to impart my suspicions, as well as what I had seen, to the old Domine. On the third day after our arrival I walked out to the school, and acquainted him with all that had passed, and asked him for his advice.

"Jacob," said he, "thou hast done well, but thou mightest have done better; hadst thou not given thy promise, which is sacred, I would have taken thee to Mr. Drummond, that thou mightest impart the whole, instanter. I like it not. Evil deeds are done in darkness. *Noctem peccatis et fraudibus objice nubem.* Still, as thou sayest, nought is yet proved. Watch, therefore, Jacob—watch carefully over thy master's interests, and the interests of society at large. It is thy duty, I may say, *Vigilare noctesque diesque.* It may be as Marables hath said, and all may be accounted for; still, I say, be careful, and be honest."

I followed the suggestions of the Domine. We were soon laden with another cargo of bricks, to be delivered at the same place, and proceeded on our voyage. Marables and Fleming, finding that I had not said a word to Mr. Drummond, treated me with every kindness. Fleming once offered me money, which I refused, saying that I had no use for it. I was on the best terms with them; at the same time I took notice of all that passed, without offering a remark to excite their suspicions. But, not to be too prolix, it will suffice to say that we made many trips during several months, and that during that time I made the following observations: that Fleming went on shore at night at certain places, taking with him bags and bundles; that he generally returned with others, which were taken into the cabin; that sometimes people came off at night, and remained some time in the cabin with him; and that all this took place when it was supposed that I was asleep. The cabin was invariably locked when the barge was lying at the wharfs, if Fleming was on shore, and at no time was I permitted to enter it. Marables was a complete cipher in Fleming's hands, who ordered everything as he pleased; and in the conversations which took place before me, with much less restraint than at first, there appeared to be no idea of Fleming's leaving us. As I felt convinced that there was no chance of discovery without further efforts on my part, and my suspicions increasing daily, I resolved upon running some hazard. My chief wish was to get into the cabin, and examine its contents; but this was not easy, and would in all probability be a dangerous attempt. One night I came on deck in my shirt. We were at anchor off Rotherhithe: it was a dark night, with a drizzling rain. I was hastening below, when I perceived a light still burning in the cabin, and heard the voices of Marables and Fleming. I thought this a good opportunity, and having no shoes walked softly on the wet deck to the cabin door, which opened forward, and peeped through the crevices. Marables and Fleming were sitting opposite each other at the little table. There were some papers before them, and they were dividing some money. Marables expostulated at his share not being sufficient, and Fleming laughed and told him he had earned no more. Fearful of being discovered, I made a silent retreat, and gained my bed. It was well that I had made the resolution, for just as I was putting my head below the hatch, and drawing it over the scuttle, the door was thrown open, and Fleming came out. I pondered over this circumstance, and the remark of Fleming, that Marables had not earned any more, and I felt convinced that the story told me by Marables relative to Fleming was all false. This conviction stimulated me more than ever to discover the secret, and many and many a night did I watch, with a hope of being able to examine the cabin; but it was to no purpose, either Fleming or Marables was always on board. I continued to report to the Domine all I had discovered, and he agreed at last that it was better that I should not say anything to Mr. Drummond until there was the fullest proof of the nature of their proceedings.

The cabin was now the sole object of my thoughts, and many

were the schemes resolved in my mind to obtain an entrance. Fatima never coveted admission to the dreadful chamber of Bluebeard, as I did to ascertain the secrets of this hidden receptacle. One night Fleming had quitted the barge, and I ascended from my dormitory. Marables was on deck, sitting upon the water-cask, with his elbow resting on the gunwale, his hand supporting his head, as if in deep thought. The cabin doors were closed, but the light still remained in it. I watched for some time, and perceiving that Marables did not move, walked gently up to him. He was fast asleep. I waited for some little time alongside of him. At last he snored. It was an opportunity not to be lost. I crept to the cabin door; it was not locked. Although I did not fear the wrath of Marables, in case of discovery, as I did that of Fleming, it was still with a beating heart and a tremulous hand that I gently opened the door, pausing before I entered, to ascertain if Marables were disturbed. He moved not, and I entered, closing the door after me. I caught up the light, and held it in my hand as I hung over the table. On each side were the two bed-places of Marables and Fleming, which I had before then had many a partial glimpse of. In front of the bed-places were two lockers, to sit down upon. I tried them—they were not fast—they contained their clothes. At the after part of the cabin were three cupboards. I opened the centre one, it contained crockery, glass, and knives and forks. I tried the one on the starboard side; it was locked, but the key was in it. I turned it gently, but being a good lock it snapped loud. I paused in fear, but Marables still slept. The cupboard had three shelves, and every shelf was loaded with silver spoons, forks, and every variety of plate, mixed with watches, bracelets, and ornaments of every description. There was, I perceived, a label on each, with a peculiar mark. Wishing to have an accurate survey, and encouraged by my discovery, I turned to the cupboard opposite, on the larboard side, and I opened it. It contained silk handkerchiefs in every variety, lace veils, and various other articles of value; on the lower shelf were laid three pairs of pistols. I was now satisfied, and closing the last cupboard, which had not been locked, was about to retreat, when I recollected that I had not relocked the first cupboard, and that they might not, by finding it open, suspect my visit, I turned the key. It made a louder snap than before. I heard Marables start from his slumber on deck ; in a moment I blew out the lamp, and remained quiet. Marables got up, took a turn or two, looked at the cabin doors, which were shut, and opened them a little. Perceiving that the lamp had, as he thought, gone out, he shut them again, and to my consternation turned the key. There I was, locked up until the arrival of Fleming—then to be left to his mercy. I hardly knew how to act. At last I resolved upon calling to Marables, as I dreaded his anger less than Fleming's. Then it occurred to me that Marables might come in, feel for the lamp to relight it, and that, as he came in on one side of the cabin, I might, in the dark, escape by the other. This all but forlorn hope prevented me for some time from applying to him. At last I made up my mind that I would, and ran from the locker to call through the door, when I heard the sound of oars. I paused again—loitered—the boat was alongside, and I heard Fleming jump upon the deck.

"Quick," said he to Marables, as he came to the cabin door, and tried to open it ; "we've no time to lose—we must get up the sacks and sink everything. Two of them have peached, and the fence will be discovered."

He took the key from Marables, and opened the door; I had replaced the lamp upon the table. Fleming entered, took a seat on the locker on the larboard side, and felt for the lamp. Marables followed him, and sat down on the starboard locker —escape was impossible. With a throbbing heart I sat in silence, watching my fate. In the meantime Fleming had taken out of his pocket his phosphorus match box. I heard the tin top pulled open—even the slight rustling of the one match selected was perceived. Another second it was withdrawn from the bottle, and a wild flame of light illumined the deck cabin, and discovered me to their view. Staggered at my appearance, the match fell from Fleming's hand, and all was dark as before; but there was no more to be gained by darkness—I had been discovered.

"Jacob!" cried Marables.

"Will not live to tell the tale," added Fleming, with a firm voice, as he put another match into the bottle, and then relighted the lamp. "Come," said Fleming fiercely ; "out of the cabin immediately."

I prepared to obey him. Fleming went out, and I was

following him round his side of the table, when Marables interposed.

"Stop, Fleming, what is that you mean to do?"

"Silence him!" retorted Fleming.

"But not murder him, surely?" cried Marables, trembling from head to foot. "You will not, dare not, do that."

"What is it that I dare not do, Marables? But it is useless to talk; it is now his life or mine. One must be sacrificed, and I will not die yet to please him."

"You shall not—by God, Fleming, you shall not!" cried Marables, seizing hold of my other arm, and holding me tight.

I added my resistance to that of Marables; when Fleming, perceiving that we should be masters, took a pistol from his pocket, and struck Marables a blow on the head, which rendered him senseless. Throwing away the pistol, he dragged me out of the cabin. I was strong, but he was very powerful; my resistance availed me nothing. By degrees he forced me to the side of the barge, and lifting me up in his arms, dashed me into the dark and rapidly flowing water. It was fortunate for me that the threat of Fleming, upon our first meeting, had induced me to practise swimming, and still more fortunate that I was not encumbered with any other clothes than my shirt, in which I had come on deck. As it was, I was carried away by the tide for some time before I could rise, and at such a distance that Fleming, who probably watched, did not perceive that I came up again. Still, I had but little hopes of saving myself in a dark night, and at nearly a quarter of a mile from shore. I struggled to keep myself afloat, when I heard the sound of oars; a second or two more, and I saw them over my head. I grasped at and seized the last, as the others passed me, crying, "Help!"

"What the devil! Oars, my men; here's somebody overboard," cried the man whose oar I had seized.

They stopped pulling; he dragged in his oar till he could lay hold of me, and then they hauled me into the boat. I was exhausted with cold, and my energetic struggles in the water; and it was not until they had wrapped me up in a greatcoat, and poured some spirits down my throat, that I could speak. They inquired to which of the craft I belonged.

"The *Polly* barge."

"The very one we are searching for. Where about is she, my lad?"

I directed them; the boat was a large wherry, pulling six oars, belonging to the river police. The officer in the stern-sheets, who steered her, then said, "How came you overboard?"

"I was thrown overboard," replied I, "by a man called Fleming."

"The name he goes by," cried the officer. "Give way, my lads. There's murder, it appears, as well as other charges."

In a quarter of an hour we were alongside; the officer and four men sprang out of the boat, leaving the other two, with directions for me to remain in the boat. Cold and miserable as I was, I was too much interested in the scene not to rise up from the stern-sheets, and pay attention to what passed. When the officer and his men gained the deck, they were met by Fleming in the advance, and Marables about a yard or two behind.

"What's all this?" cried Fleming boldly. "Are you river pirates, come to plunder us?"

"Not exactly," replied the officer; "but we are just come to overhaul you. Deliver up the key of your cabin," continued he, after trying the door, and finding it locked.

"With all my heart, if you prove yourselves authorised to search," replied Fleming; "but you'll find no smuggled spirits here, I can tell you. Marables, hand them the key; I see that they belong to the river guard."

Marables, who had never spoken, handed the key to the officer, who, opening a dark lanthorn, went down into the cabin and proceeded in his search, leaving two of the men to take charge of Fleming and Marables. But his search was in vain; he could find nothing, and he came out on the deck.

"Well," said Fleming sarcastically, "have you made a seizure?"

"Wait a little," said the officer; "how many men have you in this barge?"

"You see them," replied Fleming.

"Yes; but you have a boy—where is he?"

"We have no boy," replied Fleming; "two men are quite enough for this craft."

"Still I ask you, what has become of the boy? for a boy was on your decks this afternoon."

"If there was one, I presume he has gone on shore again."

"Answer me another question: which of you threw him overboard?"

At this query of the officer Fleming started, while Marables cried out, " It was not I; I would have saved him. Oh, that the boy were here to prove it ! "

" I am here, Marables," said I, coming on the deck, " and I am witness that yo⁊ tried to save me, until you were struck senseless by that ruffian Fleming, who threw me overboard, that I might not give evidence as to the silver and gold which I found in the cabin ; and which I overheard him tell you must be put into sacks and sunk, as two of the men had peached."

Fleming, when he saw me, turned round, as if not to look at me. His face I could not see ; but after remaining a few seconds in that position, he held out his hands in silence for the handcuffs, which the officer had already taken out of his pocket. Marables, on the contrary, sprang forward as soon as I had finished speaking, and caught me in his arms.

" My fine honest boy ! I thank God—I thank God ! All that he has said is true, sir. You will find the goods sunk astern, and the buoy-rope to them fastened to the lower pintle of the rudder. Jacob, thank God, you are safe ! I little thought to see you again. There, sir," continued he to the officer, holding out his hands, " I deserve it all. I had not strength of mind enough to be honest."

The handcuffs were put on Marables as well as on Fleming, and the officer, allowing me time to go down and put on my clothes, hauled up the sacks containing the valuables, and leaving two hands in charge of the barge, rowed ashore with us all in the boat. It was then about three o'clock in the morning, and I was very glad when we arrived at the receiving-house, and I was permitted to warm myself before the fire. As soon as I was comfortable I laid down on a bench and fell fast asleep.

CHAPTER VIII

One of the ups and downs of life—Up before the magistrates, then down the river again in the lighter—The Toms—A light heart upon two sticks—Receive my first lesson in singing— Our lighter well manned with two boys and a fraction.

I DID not awake the next morning till roused by the police, who brought us up before the magistrates. The crowd that followed appeared to make no distinction between the prisoners and the witness, and remarks not very complimentary, and to me very annoying, were liberally made. " He's a young hand for such work," cried one. " There's gallows marked in his face," observed another, to whom, when I turned round to look at him, I certainly could have returned the compliment. The station was not far from the magistrate's office, and we soon arrived. The principal officer went into the inner room, and communicated with the magistrates before they came out and took their seats on the bench.

"Where is Jacob Faithful? My lad, do you know the nature of an oath?"

I answered in the affirmative; the oath was administered, and my evidence taken down. It was then read over to the prisoners, who were asked if they had anything to say in their defence. Fleming, who had sent for his lawyer, was advised to make no answer. Marables quietly replied that all the boy had said was quite true.

" Recollect," said the magistrate, " we cannot accept you as king's evidence; that of the boy is considered sufficient."

" I did not intend that you should," replied Marables. "I only want to ease my conscience, not to try for my pardon."

They were then committed for trial, and led away to prison. I could not help going up to Marables and shaking his hand, before he was led away. He lifted up his two arms, for he was still handcuffed, and wiped his eyes, saying, " Let it be a warning to you, Jacob—not that I think you need it; but still I once was honest as yourself—and look at me now." And he cast his eyes down sorrowfully upon his fettered wrists. They quitted the room, Fleming giving me a look which was very significant of what my chance would be if ever I fell into his clutches.

" We must detain you, my lad," observed one of the magistrates, " without you can procure a sufficient bail for your appearance as witness on the trial."

I replied that I knew of no one, except my master, Mr. Drummond, and my schoolmaster, and had no means of letting them know of my situation.

The magistrate then directed the officer to go down by the first Brentford coach, acquaint Mr. Drummond with what had passed, and that the lighter would remain in charge of the river police until he could send hands on board of her; and I was allowed to sit down on a bench behind the bar. It was not until past noon that Mr. Drummond, accompanied by the Domine, made his appearance. To save time, the magistrates gave them my deposition to read ; they put in bail, and I was permitted to leave the court. We went down by the coach, but, as they went inside and I was out, I had not many questions asked until my arrival at Mr. Drummond's house, when I gave them a detailed account of all that had happened.

"*Proh! Deus!*" exclaimed the Domine, when I had finished my story. "What an escape! How narrowly, as Propertius hath it femininely, '*Eripitur nobis jampridem carus puer.*' Well was it that thou hadst learnt to swim—verily thou must have struggled lustily. '*Pugnat in adversas ire natator aquas,*' yea, lustily for thy life, child. Now, God be praised!"

But Mr. Drummond was anxious that the lighter should be brought back to the wharf; he therefore gave me my dinner, for I had eaten nothing that day, and then despatched me in a boat with two men to bring her up the river. The next morning we arrived ; and Mr. Drummond, not having yet selected any other person to take her in charge, I was again some days on shore, dividing my time between the Domine and Mr. Drummond's, where I was always kindly treated, not only by him, but also by his wife, and his little daughter Sarah.

A master for the lighter was soon found ; and as I passed a considerable time under his orders, I must describe him particularly. He had served the best part of his life on board a man-of-war, had been in many general and single actions, and, at the battle of Trafalgar, had wound up his servitude with the loss of both his legs and an out-pension from Greenwich Hospital, which he preferred to being received upon the establishment, as he had a wife and child. Since that time he had worked on the river. He was very active, and broad-shouldered, and had probably, before he lost his legs, been a man of at least five feet eleven, or six feet high; but as he found that he could keep his balance better upon short stumps than long ones, he had reduced his wooden legs to about eight inches in length, which, with his square body, gave him the appearance of a huge dwarf. He bore, and I will say most deservedly, an excellent character. His temper was always cheerful, and he was a little inclined to drink ; but the principal feature in him was lightness of heart; he was always singing. His voice was very fine and powerful. When in the service, he used to be summoned to sing to the captain and officers, and was the delight of the forecastle. His memory was retentive, and his stock of songs incredible; at the same time he seldom or never sang more than one or two stanzas of a song in the way of quotation, or if apt to what was going on, often altering the words to suit the occasion. He was accompanied by his son Tom, a lad of my own age, as merry as his father, and who had a good treble voice and a great deal of humour; he would often take the song up from his father, with words of his own putting in, with ready wit and good tune. We three composed the crew of the lighter, and as there had already been considerable loss from demurrage, were embarked as soon as they arrived. The name of the father was Tom Beazeley, but he was always known on the river as " Old Tom," or, as some more learned wag had christened him, *" the Merman on two sticks."* As soon as we had put our traps on board, as old Tom called them, he received his orders, and we cast off from the wharf. The wind was favourable. Young Tom was as active as a monkey, and as full of tricks. His father took the helm, while we two, assisted by a dog of the small Newfoundland breed, which Tom had taught to take a rope in his teeth, and be of no small service to two boys in bowsing on a tackle, made sail upon the lighter, and away we went, while old Tom's strain might be heard from either shore.

> " Loose, loose every sail to the breeze,
> The course of the vessel improve,
> I've done with the toil of the seas ;
> Ye sailors, I'm bound to my love."

"Tom, you beggar, is the bundle ready for your mother ? We must drop the skiff, Jacob, at Battersea Reach, and send the clothes on shore for the old woman to wash, or there'll be no clean shirts for Sunday. Shove in your shirts, Jacob, the old woman won't mind that. She used to wash for the mess. Clap on, both of you, and get another pull at those haulyards. That'll do, my bantams.

> ' Hoist, hoist every sail to the breeze,
> Come, shipmates, and join in the song,
> Let's drink while the barge cuts the seas,
> To the gale that may drive her along,'

"Tom, where's my pot of tea? Come, my boy, we must pipe to breakfast. Jacob, there's a rope towing overboard. Now, Tom, hand me my tea, and I'll steer with one hand, drink with the other, and as for the legs, the less we say about them the better.

> ' No glory I covet, no riches I want,
> Ambition is nothing to me,
> But one thing I beg of kind Heaven to grant——' "

Here Tom's treble chimed in, handing him the pot—

> " For *breakfast a good cup of tea*."

"Silence, you sea-cook! how dare you shove in your penny whistle? How's tide, Tom?"

"Three-quarters ebb."

"No, it an't, you thief; how is it, Jacob?"

"About half, I think."

"And you're right."

"What water have we down here on the side?"

"You must give the point a wide berth," replied I; "the shoal runs out."

"Thanky, boy, so I thought, but wasn't sure;" and then old Tom burst out in a beautiful air.

> " Trust not too much your own opinion,
> When your vessel's under weigh,
> Let good advice still bear dominion,
> That's a compass will not stray."

"Old Tom, is that you?" hallooed a man from another barge.

"Yes; what's left of me, my hearty."

"You'll not fetch the bridges this tide—there's a strong breeze right up the reaches below."

"Never mind, we'll do all we can.

> ' If unassailed by squall or shower,
> Wafted by the gentle gales,
> Let's not lose the favouring hour,
> While success attends our sails.' "

"Bravo, old Tom! why don't the boys get the lines out, for all the fishes are listening to you," cried the man, as the barges were parted by the wind and tide.

"I did once belong to a small craft, called the *Arion*,"

62

observed old Tom, "and they say as how the story was, that that chap could make the fish follow him just when he pleased. I know that when we were in the North Sea, the shoals of seals would follow the ship if you whistled; but those brutes have ears—now fish haven't got none.

> ' Oh well do I remember that cold dreary land,
>> .Where the northern light,
>> In the winter's night,
> Shone bright on its snowy strand.'

Jacob, have you finished your breakfast? Here, take the helm, while I and Tom put the craft a little into apple-pie order."

Old Tom then stumped forward, followed by his son and the Newfoundland dog, who appeared to consider himself as one of the most useful personages on board. After coiling down the ropes, and sweeping the decks, they went into the cabin to make their little arrangements.

" A good lock that, Tom," cried the father, turning the key of the cupboard. (I recollected it, and that its snapping so loud was the occasion of my being tossed overboard.) Old Tom continued : " I say, Tom, you won't be able to open that cupboard, so I'll put the sugar and the grog into it, you scamp. It goes too fast, when you're purser's steward.

> ' For grog is our larboard and starboard,
>> Our main-mast, our mizen, our log,
>> On shore, or at sea, or when harboured,
>> The mariner's compass is grog.' "

" But it arn't a compass to steer steady by, father," replied Tom.

" Then don't you have nothing to do with it, Tom."

" I only takes a little, father, because you mayn't take too much."

" Thanky for nothing ; when do I ever take too much, you scamp ? "

" Not too much for a man standing on his own pins, but too much for a man on two broomsticks."

" Stop your jaw, Mr. Tom, or I'll unscrew one of the broomsticks, and lay it over your shoulders."

"Before it's out of the socket, I'll give you *leg-bail.* What will you do then, father ?"

" Catch you when I can, Tom, as the spider takes the fly."

"What's the good o' that when you can't bear malice for ten minutes?"

"Very true, Tom; then thank your stars that you have two good legs, and that your poor father has none."

"I very often do thank my stars, and that's the truth of it; but what's the use of being angry about a drop of rum, or a handful of sugar?"

"Because you takes more than your allowance."

"Well, do you take less, then all will be right."

"And why should I take less, pray?"

"Because you're only half a man; you haven't any legs to provide for, as I have."

"Now I tell you, Tom, that's the very reason why I should have more, to comfort my old body for the loss of them."

"When you lost your legs you lost your ballast, father, and therefore you mustn't carry too much sail, or you'll topple overboard some dark night. If I drink the grog, it's all for your good, you see."

"You're a dutiful son in that way, at all events, and a sweet child, as far as sugar goes; but Jacob is to sleep in the cabin with me, and you'll shake your blanket forward."

"Now that I consider quite unnatural; why part father and son?"

"It's not that exactly, it's only parting son and the grog-bottle."

"That's just as cruel; why part two such good friends?"

"'Cause, Tom, he's too strong for you, and floors you sometimes."

"Well, but I forgives him; it's all done in good humour."

"Tom, you're a wag, but you wag your tongue to no purpose. Liquor arn't good for a boy like you, and it grows upon you."

"Well, don't I grow too? we grow together."

"You'll grow faster without it."

"I've no wish to be a tall man cut short, like you."

"If I hadn't been a tall man, my breath would have been cut short for ever; the ball which took my legs, would have cut you right in half."

"And the ball that would take your head off, would whistle over mine; so there we are equal again."

"And there's the grog, fast," replied old Tom, turning the key, and putting it into his pocket. "That's a stopper over all; so now we'll go on deck."

I have narrated this conversation, as it will give the reader a better idea of Tom, and his way of treating his father. Tom was fond of his father, and although mischievous, and too fond of drinking when he could obtain liquor, was not disobedient or vicious. We had nearly reached Battersea Fields when they returned on deck.

"Do you know, Jacob, how the parish of Battersea came into possession of those fields?"

"No, I do not."

"Well then, I'll tell you; it was because the Battersea people were more humane and charitable than their neighbours. There was a time when those fields were of no value; now they're worth a mint of money, they say. The body of a poor devil, who was drowned in the river, was washed on shore on those banks, and none of the parishes would be at the expense of burying it. The Battersea people, though they had least right to be called upon, would not allow the poor fellow's corpse to be lying on the mud, and they went to the expense. Now, when the fields became of value, the other parishes were ready enough to claim them; but the case was tried, and as it was proved that Battersea had buried the body the fields were decided to belong to that parish. So they were well paid for their humanity, and they deserved it. Mr. Drummond says you know the river well, Jacob."

"I was born on it."

"Yes, so I heard, and all about your father and mother's death. I was telling Tom of it, because he's too fond of *bowsing up his jib.*"

"Well, father, there's no occasion to remind Jacob; the tear is in his eye already," replied Tom, with consideration.

"I wish you never had any other *drop* in your *eye*—but never mind, Jacob, I didn't think of what I was saying. Look ye, d'ye see that little house with the two chimneys—that's mine, and there's my old woman. I wonder what she's about just now." Old Tom paused for a while, with his eyes fixed on the object, and then burst out—

> "I've crossed the wide waters, I've trod the lone strand,
> I've triumphed in battle, I've lighted the brand;
> I've borne the loud thunder of death o'er the foam;
> Fame, riches, ne'er found them,—yet still found a home.

Tom, boy, haul up the skiff and paddle on shore with the bundle; ask the old woman how she is, and tell her I'm hearty." Tom was in the boat in a moment, and pulling for the shore. "That makes me recollect when I returned to my mother, after the first three years of my sea service. I borrowed the skiff from the skipper—I was in a Greenland-man, my first ship, and pulled ashore to my mother's cottage under the cliff. I thought the old soul would have died with joy." Here old Tom was silent, brushed a tear from his eye, and as usual commenced a strain, *sotto voce*—

    " ' Why, what's that to you, if my eyes I'm a wiping ?
      A tear is a pleasure, d'ye see, in its way.'

How miserable," continued he, after another pause, "the poor thing was when I would go to sea—how she begged and prayed—boys have no feeling, that's sartin.

    ' O bairn, dinna leave me, to gang far away,
      O bairn, dinna leave me, ye're all that I hae,
      Think on a mither, the wind and the wave,
      A mither set on ye, her feet on the grave.'

However, she got used to it at last, as the woman said when she skinned the eels. Tom's a good boy, Jacob, but not steady, as they say you are. His mother spoils him, and I can't bear to be cross to him neither; for his heart's in the right place after all. There's the old woman shaking her dishclout at us as a signal. I wish I had gone on shore myself, but I can't step into these paper-built little boats, without my timber toes going through at the bottom."

CHAPTER IX

*The two Toms take to protocolling—Treaty of peace ratified
between the belligerent parties—Lots of songs and supper—
The largest mess of roast meat upon record.*

TOM then shoved off the skiff. When half-way between the lighter and the shore, while his mother stood watching us, he lay on his oars. "Tom, Tom!" cried his mother, shaking her fist at him, as he stooped down his head; "if you do, Tom!"

"Tom, Tom!" cried his father, shaking his fist also; "if you dare, Tom!"

But Tom was not within reach of either party, and he dragged a bottle out of the basket which his mother had entrusted to him, and putting it to his mouth, took a long swig.

"That's enough, Tom!" screamed his mother from the shore.

"That's too much, you rascal!" cried his father from the barge.

Neither admonition was, however, minded by Tom, who took what he considered his allowance, and then very coolly pulled alongside, and handed up the basket and bundle of clean clothes on deck. Tom then gave the boat's painter to his father, who, I perceived, intended to salute him with the end of it as soon as he came up; but Tom was too knowing—he surged the boat ahead, and was on deck and forward before his father could stump up to him. The main hatch was open, and Tom put that obstacle between his father and himself before he commenced his parley.

"What's the matter, father?" said Tom, smiling, and looking at me.

"Matter, you scamp! How dare you touch the bottle?"

"The bottle?—the bottle's there, as good as ever."

"The grog is what I mean—how dare you drink it?"

"I was half-way between my mother and you, and so I drank success and long life to you both. Arn't that being a very dutiful son?"

"I wish I had my legs back again, you rascal!"

"You wish you had the grog back again, you mean, father. You have to choose between—for if you had the grog, you'd keep your legs."

"For the matter of drinking the grog, you scamp, you seem determined to stand in my shoes."

"Well, shoes are of no use to you now, father—why shouldn't I? Why don't you trust me? If you hadn't locked the cupboard, I wouldn't have helped myself." And Tom, whose bootlace was loose, stooped down to make it fast.

Old Tom, who was still in wrath, thought this a good opportunity, as his son's head was turned the other way, to step over the bricks, with which, as I before said, the lighter had been laden level with the main hatchway, and take his son by surprise. Tom, who had no idea of this manœuvre, would

67

certainly have been captured, but fortunately for him one of
the upper bricks turned over, and let his father's wooden leg
down between two of the piles, where it was jammed fast.
Old Tom attempted to extricate himself, but could not. "Tom,
Tom, come here," cried he, "and pull me out."

"Not I," replied Tom coolly.

"Jacob, Jacob, come here. Tom, run and take the helm."

"Not I," replied Tom.

"Jacob, never mind the helm, she'll drift all right for a
minute," cried old Tom; "come and help me."

But I had been so amused with the scene, and having a
sort of feeling for young Tom, that I declared it impossible to
leave the helm without her going on the banks. I therefore
remained, wishing to see in what way the two Toms would
get out of their respective scrapes.

"Confound these——! Tom, you scoundrel, am I to stick
here all day?"

"No, father, I don't suppose you will. I shall help you
directly."

"Well then, why don't you do it?"

"Because I must come to terms. You don't think I'd help
myself to a thrashing, do you?"

"I won't thrash you, Tom. Shiver my timbers if I do."

"They're in a fair way of being shivered as it is, I think.
Now, father, we're both even."

"How's that?"

"Why, you clapped a stopper over all on me this morning,
and now you've got one on yourself."

"Well then, take off mine, and I'll take off yours."

"If I unlock your leg, you'll unlock the cupboard?"

"Yes."

"And you promise me a *stiff* one after dinner?"

"Yes, yes, as stiff as I stand here."

"No, that will be too much, for it would *set me fast*. I only
like it about half-and-half, as I took it just now."

Tom, who was aware that his father would adhere to his
agreement, immediately went to his assistance, and throwing
out some of the upper bricks released him from his confinement.
When old Tom was once more on the deck and on his legs, he
observed, "It's an ill wind that blows nobody good. The *loss*
of my legs has been the *saving* of you many a time, Mr. Tom."

It was now time to anchor, as we were meeting the flood. Tom, who officiated as cook, served up the dinner, which was ready, and we were all very pleasant; Tom treating his father with perfect confidence. As we had not to weigh again for some hours our repast was prolonged, and old Tom, having fulfilled his promise to his son of a *stiff one*, took one or two himself and became very garrulous.

"Come, spin us a good yarn, father; we've nothing to do, and Jacob will like to hear you."

"Well then, so I will," answered he; "what shall it be about?"

"Fire and water, of course," replied Tom.

"Well then, I'll tell you something about both, since you wish it; how I came into his Majesty's sarvice through *fire*, and how the officer who pressed me went out of it through *water*. I was still 'prentice, and wanted about three months to sarve my time, when of course I should no longer be protected from sarving the king, when the ship I was in sailed up the Baltic with a cargo of bullocks. We had at least two hundred on board, tied up on platforms on every deck, with their heads close to the sides, and all their sterns looking in board. They were fat enough when they were shipped, but soon dwindled away. The weather was very bad, and the poor creatures rolled against each other, and slipped about in a way that it pitied you to see them. However, they were stowed so thick that they held one another up, which proved of service to them in the heavy gales which tossed the ship about like a pea in a rattle. We had joined a large convoy, and were entering the Sound, when, as usual, it fell calm, and out came the Danish gunboats to attack us. The men-of-war who had charge of the convoy behaved nobly; but still they were becalmed, and many of us were a long way astern. Our ship was pretty well up, but she was too far in-shore; and the Danes made a dash at us with the hope of making a capture. The men-of-war, seeing what the enemy were about, sent boats to beat them off; but it was too late to prevent them boarding, which they did. Not wishing to peep through the bars of the gaol at Copenhagen, we left the ship in our boats on one side, just as the Danes boarded on the other, and pulled towards the men-of-war's armed boats coming to our assistance. The men-of-war's boats pulled right for the ship to retake her, which they did, certainly, but not before the enemy had set fire to the vessel, and had then pulled off towards another. Seeing this the men-of-war's boats again gave chase to the Danes, leaving us to extinguish the flames, which were now bursting out fore and aft, and climbing like fiery serpents up to the main catharpings. We soon found that it was impossible. We remained as long as the heat and smoke would permit us, and then we were obliged to be off; but I shall never forget the roaring and moaning of the poor animals who were then roasting alive. It was a cruel thing of the Danes to fire a vessel full of these poor creatures. Some had broken loose, and were darting up and down the decks goring others, and tumbling down the hatchways; others remained trembling, or trying to snuff up a mouthful of fresh air amongst the smoke, but the struggling and bellowing, as the fire caught the vessel fore and aft, and was grilling two hundred poor creatures at once, was at last shocking, and might have been heard for a mile. We did all we could. I cut the throats of a dozen, but they kicked and struggled so much, falling down upon, and treading you under their feet; and one lay upon me, and I expected to be burnt with them, for it was not until I was helped that I got clear of the poor animal. So we stayed as long as we could, and then left them to their fate ; and the smell of burnt meat as we shoved off was as horrible as the cries and wailings of the poor beasts themselves. The men-of-war's boats returned, having chased away the Danes, and very kindly offered us all a ship, as we had lost our own, so that you see that by *fire* I was forced into his Majesty's sarvice. Now the boat which took us belonged to one of the frigates who had charge of the convoy, and the lieutenant who commanded the boat was a swearing, tearing sort of a chap, who lived as if his life was to last for ever. After I was taken on board, the captain asked me if I would enter, and I thought that I might as well sarve the king handsomely, so I volunteered. It's always the best thing to do, when you're taken, and can't help yourself, for you are more trusted than a pressed man who is obstinate. I liked the sarvice from the first : the captain was not a particular man ; according to some people's idea of the sarvice, she wasn't in quite man-of-war fashion; but she was a happy ship, and the men would have followed and fought for the captain to the last drop of their blood. That's the sort of ship for me. I've seen cleaner decks, but I never saw merrier hearts. The only one of the officers disliked by the men was the lieutenant who pressed me; he had a foul mouth and no discretion; and as for swearing, it was really terrible to hear the words which came out of his mouth. I don't mind an oath rapped out in the heat of the moment, but he invented his oaths when he was cool, and let them out in his rage. We were returning home, after having seen the convoy safe, when we met with a gale of wind in our teeth, one of the very worst I ever fell in with. It had been blowing hard from the SW., and then shifted to the NW., and made a cross sea, which was tremendous. Now the frigate was a very old vessel, and although they had often had her into dock and repaired her below, they had taken no notice of her upper works, which were as rotten as a medlar. I think it was about three bells in the middle watch, when the wind was howling through the rigging, for we had no canvas on her 'cept a staysail and trysail, when the staysail sheet went, and she broached-to afore they could prevent her. The lieutenant I spoke of had the watch, and his voice was heard through the roaring of the wind, swearing at the men to haul down the staysail, that we might bend on the sheet, and set it right again; when she having, I said, broached-to, a wave—ay, a wave as high as the maintop almost, took the frigate right on her broadside, and the bulwarks of the quarter-deck being, as I said, quite rotten, cut them off clean level with the main chains, sweeping them, and guns, and men, all overboard together. The mizen-mast went, but the main-mast held on, and I was under its lee at the time, and was saved by clinging on like a nigger, while for a minute I was under the water, which carried almost all away with it to leeward. As soon as the water passed over me, I looked up and around me—it was quite awful; the quarter-deck was cut off as with a knife—not a soul left there, that I could see; no man at the wheel—mizen-mast gone—skylights washed away—waves making a clear breach, and no defence; boats washed away from the quarters—all silent on deck, but plenty of noise below and on the main-deck, for the ship was nearly full of water, and all below were hurrying up in their shirts, thinking that we were going down. At last the captain crawled up, and clung by the stanchions, followed by the first lieutenant and the officers, and by degrees all was quiet, the ship was cleared, and the hands were turned up to muster under the half-deck. There were forty-seven men who did not answer to their names—they

71

had been summoned to answer for their lives, poor fellows! and there was also the swearing lieutenant not to be found. Well, at last we got the hands on deck and put her before the wind, scudding under bare poles. As we went aft to the taffrail, the bulwark of which still remained, with about six feet of the quarter-deck bulwark on each side, we observed something clinging to the stern-ladder, dipping every now and then into the sea, as it rose under her counter, and assisted the wind in driving her before the gale. We soon made it out to be a man, and I went down, slipped a bowling knot over the poor fellow, and with some difficulty we were both hauled up again. It proved to be the lieutenant, who had been washed under the counter, and clung to the stern ladder, and had thus miraculously been preserved. It was a long while before he came to, and he never did any duty the whole week we were out, till we got into Yarmouth Roads; indeed, he hardly ever spoke a word to any one, but seemed to be always in serious thought. When we arrived, he gave his commission to the captain, and went on shore; went to school again, they say, and *bore up for a parson*, and for all I know, he'll preach somewhere next Sunday. So you see, *water* drove him out of the service, and *fire* forced me in. There's a yarn for you, Jacob."

"I like it very much," replied I.

"And now, father, give us a whole song, and none of your little bits." Old Tom broke out with the "Death of Nelson," in a style that made the tune and words ring in my ears for the whole evening.

The moon was up before the tide served, and we weighed our anchor; old Tom steering, while his son was preparing supper, and I remaining forward, keeping a sharp look-out that we did not run foul of anything. It was a beautiful night; and as we passed through the several bridges the city appeared as if it were illuminated, from the quantity of gas throwing a sort of halo of light over the tops of the buildings which occasionally marked out the main streets from the general dark mass—old Tom's voice was still occasionally heard, as the scene brought to his remembrance his variety of song.

> " For the murmur of thy lip, love,
> Comes sweetly unto me,
> As the sound of oars that dip, love,
> At moonlight in the sea,"

I never was more delighted than when I heard these snatches of different songs poured forth in such melody from old Tom's lips, the notes floating along the water during the silence of the night. I turned aft to look at him; his face was directed upwards, looking on the moon, which glided majestically through the heavens, silvering the whole of the landscape. The water was smooth as glass, and the rapid tide had swept us clear of the ranges of ships in the pool; both banks of the river were clear, when old Tom again commenced—

> " The moon is up, her silver beam
>> Shines bower, and grove, and mountain over ;
>> A flood of radiance heaven doth seem
>> To light thee, maiden, to thy lover.

Jacob, how does the bluff-nob bear? on the starboard bow ?"

"Yes—broad on the bow; you'd better keep up half a point, the tide sweeps us fast."

" Very true, Jacob; look out, and say when steady it is, boy.

> ' If o'er her orb a cloud should rest,
>> 'Tis but thy cheek's soft blush to cover.
>> He waits to clasp thee to his breast ;
>> The moon is up—go, meet thy lover.'

Tom, what have you got for supper, boy? What is that frizzing in your frying-pan? Smells good, anyhow."

"Yes; and I expect will taste good too. However, you look after the moon, father, and leave me and the frying-pan to play our parts."

"While I sing mine, I suppose, boy.

> ' The moon is up, round beauty's shrine,
>> Love's pilgrims bend at vesper hour,
>> Earth breathes to heaven, and looks divine,
>> And lovers' hearts confess her power.' "

Old Tom stopped, and the frying-pan frizzed on, sending forth an odour which, if not grateful to heaven, was peculiarly so to us mortals, hungry with the fresh air.

"How do we go now, Jacob ?"

"Steady, and all's right; but we shall be met with the wind next reach, and had better brail up the mainsail."

"Go, then, Tom, and help Jacob."

"I can't leave the *ingons,* father, not if the lighter tumbled
overboard; it would bring more tears in my eyes to spoil
them now that they are frying so merrily, than they did
when I was cutting them up. Besides, the liver would be as
black as the bends."

"Clap the frying-pan down on deck, Tom, and brail the
sail up with Jacob, there's a good boy. You can give it
another shake or two afterwards.

> ' Glide on, my bark; how sweet to rove,
>   With such a beaming eye above ! '

That's right, my boys, belay all that; now to our stations—
Jacob on the look-out, Tom to his frying-pan, and I to the
helm.

> ' No sound is heard to break the spell,
>   Except the water's gentle swell;
>   While midnight, like a mimic day,
>   Shines on to guide our moonlight way.'

Well, the moon's a beautiful creature—God bless her! How
often have we longed for her in the dark winter, channel-
cruising, when the waves were flying over the Eddystone, and
trying in their malice to put out the light. I don't wonder
at people making songs to the moon, nor at my singing them.
We'll anchor when we get down the next reach."

We swept the next reach with the tide, which was now
slacking fast. Our anchor was dropped, and we all went to
supper, and to bed. I have been particular in describing
the first day of my being on board with my new shipmates,
as it may be taken as a sample of our every-day life; Tom
and his father fighting and making friends, cooking, singing,
and spinning yarns. Still, I shall have more scenes to describe.
Our voyage was made, we took in a return cargo, and arrived
at the proprietor's wharf, when I found that I could not proceed with them the next voyage, as the trial of Fleming and
Marables was expected to come on in a few days. The lighter,
therefore, took in another cargo, and sailed without me; Mr.
Drummond, as usual, giving me the run of his house.

CHAPTER X

*I help to hang my late barge mate for his attempt to drown me—
One good turn deserves another—The subject suddenly dropped
at Newgate—A yarn in the law line—With due precautions
and preparations, the Domine makes his first voyage—To
Gravesend.*

IT was on the 7th of November, if I recollect rightly, that
Fleming and Marables were called up to trial at the Old
Bailey, and I was in the court with Mr. Drummond and the
Domine soon after ten o'clock. After the judge had taken
his seat, as their trial was first on the list, they were ushered
in. They were both clean and well dressed. In Fleming I
could perceive little difference—he was pale, but resolute ;
but when I looked at Marables, I was astonished. Mr.
Drummond did not at first recognise him ; he had fallen
away from seventeen stone to, at the most, thirteen—his
clothes hung loosely about him — his ruddy cheeks had
vanished—his nose was becoming sharp, and his full round
face had been changed to an oblong. Still there remained
that natural good-humoured expression in his countenance,
and the sweet smile played upon his lips. His eyes glánced
fearfully round the court—he felt his disgraceful situation—
the colour mounted to his temples and forehead, and he then
became again pale as a sheet, casting down his eyes, as if
desirous to see no more.

After the indictment had been read over, the prisoners
were asked by the clerk whether they pleaded guilty or not
guilty. "Not guilty," replied Fleming, in a bold voice.
"John Marables—guilty or not guilty ?" "Guilty," replied
Marables, "guilty, my lord ; " and he covered up his face
with his hands.

Fleming was indicted on three counts : an assault, with
intent to murder ; having stolen goods in his possession ;
and for a burglary in a dwelling-house, on such a date ;
but I understand that they had nearly twenty more charges
against him, had these failed. Marables was indicted for
having been an accessory to the last charge, as receiver of
stolen goods. The counsel for the crown, who opened the

trial, stated that Fleming, *alias* Barkett, *alias* Wenn, with many more *aliases*, had for a long while been at the head of the most notorious gang of thieves which had infested the metropolis for many years; that justice had long been in search of him, but that he had disappeared, and it had been supposed that he had quitted the kingdom to avoid the penalties of the law, to which he had subjected himself by his enormities. It appeared, however, that he had taken a step which not only blinded the officers of the police, but at the same time had enabled the gang to carry on their depredations with more impunity than ever. He had concealed himself in a lighter on the river, and appearing in her as one diligently performing his duty, and earning his livelihood as an honest man, had by such means been enabled to extend his influence, the number of his associates, and his audacious schemes. The principal means of detection in cases of burglary was by advertising the goods, and the great difficulty on the part of such miscreants was to obtain a ready sale for them — the receivers of stolen goods being aware that the thieves were at their mercy, and must accept what was offered. Now, to obviate these difficulties, Fleming had, as we before observed, concealed himself from justice on board of a river barge, which was made the receptacle for stolen goods ; those which had been nefariously obtained at one place, being by him and his associates carried up and down the river in the craft, and disposed of at a great distance, by which means the goods were never brought to light, so as to enable the police to recognise or trace them. This system had now been carried on with great success for upwards of twelve months, and would in all probability have not been discovered even now, had it not been that a quarrel as to profits had taken place, which had induced two of his associates to give information to the officers; and these two associates had also been permitted to turn king's evidence, in a case of burglary in which Fleming was a principal, provided that it was considered necessary. But there was a more serious charge against the prisoner—that of having attempted the life of a boy named Jacob Faithful, belonging to the lighter, and who it appeared had suspicions of what was going on, and in duty to his master had carefully watched the proceedings, and given notice to others of what he had discovered from time to time. The lad was the chief evidence, against the prisoner Fleming, and also against Marables, the other prisoner, of whom he could only observe, that circumstances would transpire during the trial in his favour, which he had no doubt would be well considered by his lordship. He would not detain the gentlemen of the jury any longer, but at once call on his witnesses.

I was then summoned, again asked the same questions as to the nature of an oath, and the judge being satisfied with my replies I gave my evidence as before ; the judge, as I perceived, carefully examining my previous deposition, to ascertain if anything I now said was at variance with my former assertions. I was then cross-examined by the counsel for Fleming, but he could not make me vary in my evidence. I did, however, take the opportunity, whenever I was able, of saying all I could in favour of Marables. At last the counsel said he would ask me no more questions. I was dismissed ; and the police-officer who had picked me up, and other parties who identified the various property as their own, and told the manner in which they had been robbed of it, were examined. The evidence was too clear to admit of doubt. The jury immediately returned a verdict of guilty against Fleming and Marables, but strongly recommended Marables to the mercy of the crown. The judge rose, put on his black cap, and addressed the prisoners as follows. The court was so still, that a pin falling might have been heard :—

"You, William Fleming, have been tried by a jury of your countrymen, upon the charge of receiving stolen goods, to which you have added the most atrocious crime of intended murder. You have had a fair and impartial trial, and have been found guilty ; and it appears that, even had you escaped in this instance, other charges, equally heavy, and which would equally consign you to condign punishment, were in readiness to be preferred against you. Your life has been one of guilt, not only in your own person, but also in abetting and stimulating others to crime ; and you have wound up your shameful career by attempting the life of a fellow-creature. To hold out to you any hope of mercy is impossible. Your life is justly forfeited to the offended laws of your country, and your sentence is that you be removed from this court to the place from whence you came, and from thence to the place of execution, there to be hanged by the neck till you are dead; and may God, in His infinite goodness, have mercy on your soul!

"You, John Marables, have pleaded guilty to the charges brought against you; and it has appeared, during the evidence brought out on the trial, that although you have been a party to these nefarious transactions, you are far from being hardened in your guilt." ["No, no!" exclaimed Marables.] "I believe sincerely that you are not, and much regret that one who, from the evidence brought forward, appears to have been, previously to this unfortunate connection, an honest man, should now appear in so disgraceful a situation. A severe punishment is, however, demanded by the voice of justice, and by that sentence of the law you must now be condemned; at the same time I trust that an appeal to the mercy of your sovereign will not be made in vain."

The judge then passed the sentence upon Marables, the prisoners were led out of court, and a new trial commenced; while Mr. Drummond and the Domine conducted me home. About a week after the trial, Fleming suffered the penalty of the law; while Marables was sentenced to transportation for life, which, however, previous to his sailing, was commuted to seven years.

In a few days the lighter returned. Her arrival was announced to me one fine sunny morning as I lay in bed, by a voice, whose well-known notes poured into my ear as I was half dozing on my pillow—

" Bright are the beams of the morning sky,
　　And sweet the dew the red blossoms sip,
　　But brighter the glances of dear woman's eye—

Tom, you monkey, belay the warp, and throw the fenders over the side. Be smart, or old Fuzzle will be growling about his red paint.

' And sweet is the dew on her lip.'"

I jumped out of my little crib, threw open the window, the panes of which were crystallised with the frost in the form of little trees, and beheld the lighter just made fast to the wharf, the sun shining brightly, old Tom's face as cheerful as the morn, and young Tom laughing, jumping about, and blowing his fingers. I was soon dressed, and shaking hands with my barge mates.

78

"Well, Jacob, how do you like the Old Bailey? Never was in it but once in my life, and never mean to go again, if I can help it; that was when Sam Bowles was tried for his life, but my evidence saved him. I'll tell you how it was. Tom, look a'ter the breakfast; a bowl of tea this cold morning will be worth having. Come, jump about."

"But I never heard the story of Sam Bowles," answered Tom.

"What's that to you? I'm telling it to Jacob."

"But I want to hear it—so go on, father. I'll start you. Well, d'ye see, Sam Bowles——"

"Master Tom, them as play with *bowls* may meet with *rubbers*. Take care I don't *rub* down your hide. Off, you thief, and get breakfast."

"No, I won't; if I don't have your *Bowles*, you shall have no *bowls* of tea. I've made my mind up to that."

"I tell you what, Tom, I shall never get any good out of you until I have both your legs ampitated. I've a great mind to send for the farrier."

"Thanky, father; but I find them very useful."

"Well," said I, "suppose we put off the story till breakfast time, and I'll go and help Tom to get it ready."

"Be it so, Jacob. I suppose Tom must have his way, as I spoiled him myself. I made him so fond of yarns, so I was a fool to be vexed.

' Oh life is a river, and man is the boat
That over its surface is destined to float ;
And joy is a cargo so easily stored,
That he is a fool who takes sorrow on board.'

Now I'll go on shore to master, and find out what's to be done next. Give me my stick, boy, and I shall crawl over the planks a little safer. A safe stool must have three legs, you know."

Old Tom then stumped away on shore. In about a quarter of an hour he returned, bringing half-a-dozen red herrings. "Here, Tom, grill these sodgers. Jacob, who is that tall old chap, with such a devil of a cutwater, that I met just now with master? We are bound for Sheerness this trip, and I'm to land him at Greenwich."

"What, the Domine?" replied I, from old Tom's description.

"His name did begin with a D, but that wasn't it."

"Dobbs?"

79

"Yes, that's nearer; he's to be a passenger on board of us, going down to see a friend who's very ill. Now, Tom, my hearty, bring out the crockery, for I want a little inside lining."

We all sat down to our breakfast, and as soon as old Tom had finished, his son called for the history of Sam Bowles.

"Well, now you shall have it. Sam Bowles was a shipmate of mine on board of the Greenlandman; he was one of our best harpooners, and a good, quiet, honest messmate as ever slung a hammock. He was spliced to as pretty a piece of flesh as ever was seen, but she wasn't as good as she was pretty. We were fitting out for another voyage, and his wife had been living on board with him some weeks, for Sam was devilish spoony on her and couldn't bear her to be out of his sight. As we 'spected to sail in a few days, we were filling up our complement of men, and fresh hands came on board every day.

"One morning, a fine tall fellow, with a tail as thick as a hawser, came on board and offered himself; he was taken by the skipper, and went on shore again to get his traps. While he was still on deck I went below, and seeing Sam with his little wife on his knee playing with his love-locks, I said that there was a famous stout and good-looking fellow that we should have as a shipmate. Sam's wife, who, like all women, was a little curious, put her head up the hatchway to look at him. She put it down again very quick, as I thought, and made some excuse to go forward in the eyes of her, where she remained some time, and then when she came aft told Sam that she would go on shore. Now, as it had been agreed that she should remain on board till we were clear of the river, Sam couldn't think what the matter was; but she was positive, and go away she did, very much to Sam's astonishment and anger. In the evening, Sam went on shore and found her out, and what d'ye think the little Jezebel told him?—why, that one of the men had been rude to her when she went forward, and that's why she wouldn't stay on board. Sam was in a devil of a passion at this, and wanted to know which was the man; but she fondled him, and wouldn't tell him, because she was afraid that he'd be hurt. At last she bamboozled him, and sent him on board again quite content. Well, we remained three days longer, and then dropped down the river to Greenwich, where the captain was to come on board, and we were to sail as soon as the wind was fair. Now this fine tall fellow was with us when we dropped down the river, and as Sam was sitting down on his chest eating a basin o' soup, the other man takes out a 'baccy pouch of sealskin—it was a very curious one, made out of the white and spotted part of a young seal's belly. ' I say, shipmate,' cries Sam, ' hand me over my 'baccy pouch. Where did you pick it up ? '

" ' Your pouch ! ' says he to him ; ' I killed the seal, and my fancy girl made the pouch for me.'

" ' Well, if that arn't cool ! you'd swear a man out of his life, mate. Tom,' says he to me, ' arn't that my pouch which my wife gave me when I came back last trip ? '

" I looked at it, and knew it again, and said it was. The tall fellow denied it, and there was a devil of a bobbery. Sam called him a thief, and he pitched Sam right down the main hatchway among the casks. After that there was a regular set-to, and Sam was knocked all to shivers, and obliged to give in. When the fight was over, I took up Sam's shirt for him to put on. ' That's my shirt,' cried the tall fellow.

" ' That's Sam's shirt,' replied I ; ' I know it's his.'

" ' I tell you it's mine,' replied the man ; ' my lass gave it to me to put on when I got up this morning. The other is his shirt.'

" We looked at the other, and they both were Sam's shirts. Now when Sam heard this, he put two and two together, and became very jealous and uneasy. He thought it odd that his wife was so anxious to leave the ship when this tall fellow came on board ; and what with the pouch and the shirt, he was puzzled. His wife had promised to come down to Greenwich and see him off. When we anchored, some of the men went on shore—among others the tall fellow. Sam, whose head was swelled up like a pumpkin, told one of his shipmates to say to his wife that he could not come on shore, and that she must come off to him. Well, it was about nine o'clock, dark, and all the stars were twinkling, when Sam says to me, ' Tom, let's go on shore ; my black eyes can't be seen in the dark.' As we hauled up the boat, the second mate told Sam to take his harpoon iron on shore for him, to have the hole for the becket punched larger. Away we went, and the first place, of course, that Sam went to, was the house where he knew that his wife put up at, as before. He went upstairs to her room, and I followed him. The door was not made fast, and

F

in we went. There was his little devil of a wife fast asleep in the arms of the tall fellow. Sam couldn't command his rage, and having the harpoon iron in his hand, he drove it right through the tall fellow's body before I could prevent him. It was a dreadful sight: the man groaned, and his head fell over the side of the bed. Sam's wife screamed, and made Sam more wroth by throwing herself on the man's body, and weeping over it. Sam would have pulled out the iron to run her through with, but that was impossible. The noise brought up the people of the house, and it was soon known that murder had been committed. The constables came, Sam was thrown into prison, and I went on board and told the whole story. Well, we were just about to heave up, for we had shipped two more men in place of Sam, who was to be tried for his life, and the poor fellow he had killed, when a lawyer chap came on board with what they call a *suppeny* for me ; all I know is, that the lawyer pressed me into his service, and I lost my voyage. I was taken on shore, and well fed till the trial came on. Poor Sam was at the bar for murder. The gentleman in his gown and wig began his yarn, stating that how the late fellow, whose name was Will Errol, was with his own wife when Sam harpooned him.

"'That's a lie !' cried Sam ; 'he was with my wife.'

" My lord," said the lawyer, " that is not the case; it was his own wife, and here are the marriage certificates."

"'False papers !' roared Sam. 'Here are mine ;' and he pulled out his tin case, and handed them to the court.

"The judge said that this was not the way to try people, and that Sam must hold his tongue ; so the trial went on, and at first they had it all their own way. Then our turn came, and I was called up to prove what had passed, and I stated how the man was with Sam's wife, and how he, having the harpoon iron in his hand, had run it through his body. Then they compared the certificates, and it was proved that the little Jezebel had married them both ; but she had married Sam first, so he had the most right to her ; but fancying the other man afterwards, she thought she might as well have two strings to her bow. So the judge declared that she was Sam's wife, and that any man, even without the harpoon in his hand, would be justified in killing a man whom he found in bed with his own wife. So Sam went scot-free ; but the judge wouldn't let off Sam's wife, as she had caused murder by her wicked conduct; he tried her a'terwards for *biggery*, as they call it, and sent her over the water for life. Sam never held up his head a'terwards; what with having killed an innocent man, and the 'haviour of his wife, he was always down. He went out to the fishery, and a whale cut the boat in two with her tail; Sam was stunned, and went down like a stone. So you see the mischief brought about by this little Jezebel, who must have two husbands, and be d—d to her."

"Well, that's a good yarn, father," said Tom, as soon as it was finished. "I was right in saying I would hear it. Wasn't I?"

"No," replied old Tom, putting out his large hand, and seizing his son by the collar; "and now you've put me in mind of it, I'll pay you off for old scores."

"Lord love you, father, you don't owe me anything," said Tom.

"Yes, I do; and now I'll give you a receipt in full."

"O Lord! they'll be drowned," screamed Tom, holding up both his hands with every symptom of terror.

Old Tom turned short round to look in the direction, letting go his hold. Tom made his escape, and burst out a-laughing. I laughed also, and so at last did his father.

I went on shore, and found that old Tom's report was correct—the Domine was at breakfast with Mr. Drummond. The new usher had charge of the boys, and the governors had allowed him a fortnight's holiday to visit an old friend at Greenwich. To save expense, as well as to indulge his curiosity, the old man had obtained a passage down in the lighter. "Never yet, Jacob, have I put my feet into that which floateth on the watery element," observed he to me; "nor would I now, but that it saveth money, which thou knowest well is with me not plentiful. Many dangers I expect, many perils shall I encounter; such have I read of in books, and well might Horace exclaim: '*Ille robur et æs triplex*,' with reference to the first man who ventured afloat. Still doth Mr. Drummond assure me that the lighter is of that strength as to be able to resist the force of the winds and waves; and, confiding in Providence, I intend to venture, Jacob, '*te duce.*'"

"Nay, sir," replied I, laughing at the idea which the Domine appeared to have formed of the dangers of river navigation, "old Tom is the *Dux*."

"Old Tom; where have I seen that name? Now I do

recall to mind that I have seen the name painted in large letters upon a cask at the tavern bar of the inn at Brentford; but what it did intend to signify, I did not inquire. What connection is there?"

"None," replied I; "but I rather think they are very good friends. The tide turns in half-an-hour, sir; are you ready to go on board?"

"Truly am I, and well prepared, having my habiliments in a bundle, my umbrella and my greatcoat, as well as my spencer for general wear. But where I am to sleep hath not yet been made known to me. Peradventure one sleepeth not—'*tanto in periculo.*'"

"Yes, sir, we do. You shall have my berth, and I'll turn in with young Tom."

"Hast thou, then, a young Tom as well as an old Tom on board?"

"Yes, sir; and a dog, also of the name of Tommy."

"Well, then, we will embark, and thou shalt make me known to this triad of Thomases. '*Inde* Tomos *dictus locus est.*' (Cluck, cluck.) Ovid, I thank thee."

CHAPTER XI

Much learning afloat—Young Tom is very lively upon the dead languages—The Domine, after experiencing the wonders of the mighty deep, prepares to revel upon lobscouse—Though the man of learning gets many songs and some yarns from old Tom, he loses the best part of a tale without knowing it.

THE old Domine's bundle and other paraphernalia being sent on board, he took farewell of Mr. Drummond and his family in so serious a manner, that I was convinced that he considered he was about to enter upon a dangerous adventure, and then I led him down to the wharf where the lighter lay alongside. It was with some trepidation that he crossed the plank and got on board, when he recovered himself and looked round.

"My sarvice to you, old gentleman," said a voice behind the Domine. It was that of old Tom, who had just come from the cabin. The Domine turned round and perceived old Tom.

"This is old Tom, sir," said I to the Domine, who stared with astonishment.

"Art thou, indeed? Jacob, thou didst not tell me that he had been curtailed of his fair proportions, and I was surprised. Art thou then Dux?" continued the Domine, addressing old Tom.

"Yes," interrupted young Tom, who had come from forward, "he is *ducks*, because he waddles on his short stumps; and I won't say who be goose. Eh, father?"

"Take care you don't *buy goose*, for your imperance, sir," cried old Tom.

"A forward boy," exclaimed the Domine.

"Yes," replied Tom; "I'm generally forward."

"Art thou forward in thy learning? Canst thou tell me Latin for goose?"

"To be sure," replied Tom. "Brandy."

"Brandy!" exclaimed the Domine. "Nay, child, it is *anser*.

"Then I was right," replied Tom. "You had your *answer!*"

"The boy is apt." (Cluck, cluck.)

"He is apt to be devilish saucy, old gentleman; but never mind that, there's no harm in him."

"This, then, is young Tom, I presume, Jacob?" said the Domine, referring to me.

"Yes, sir," replied I. "You have seen old Tom, and young Tom, and you have only to see Tommy."

"Want to see Tommy, sir?" cried Tom. "Here, Tommy, Tommy!"

But Tommy, who was rather busy with a bone forward, did not immediately answer to his call, and the Domine turned round to survey the river. The scene was busy, barges and boats passing in every direction, others lying on shore, with waggons taking out the coals and other cargoes, men at work, shouting or laughing with each other. "'*Populus in fluviis,*' as Virgil hath it. Grand indeed is the vast river, '*Labitur et labetur in omne volubilis œvum,*' as the generations of men are swept into eternity," said the Domine, musing aloud. But Tommy had now made his appearance, and Tom, in his mischief, had laid hold of the tail of the Domine's coat, and shown it to the dog. The dog, accustomed to seize a rope when it was shown to him, immediately seized the Domine's coat, making three desperate tugs at it. The Domine, who was in one of his reveries, and probably thought it was I who wished to direct his attention elsewhere, each time waved his hand without turning round, as much as to say, "I am busy now."

"Haul and hold," cried Tom to the dog, splitting his sides, and the tears running down his cheeks with laughing. Tommy made one more desperate tug, carrying away one tail of the Domine's coat; but the Domine perceived it not, he was still "*in nubibus*," while the dog galloped forward with the fragment, and Tom chased him to recover it. The Domine continued in his reverie, when old Tom burst out—

> " O England, dear England, bright gem of the ocean,
> Thy valleys and fields look fertile and gay,
> The heart clings to thee with a sacred devotion,
> And memory adores when in far lands away."

The song gradually called the Domine to his recollection; indeed, the strain was so beautiful that it would have vibrated in the ears of a dying man. The Domine gradually turned round, and when old Tom had finished, exclaimed, " Truly it did delight mine ear, and from such—and," continued the Domine, looking down upon old Tom—" without legs too ! "

" Why, old gentleman, I don't sing with my *legs*," answered old Tom.

" Nay, good Dux, I am not so deficient as not to be aware that a man singeth from the mouth ; yet is thy voice mellifluous, sweet as the honey of Hybla, strong——"

"As the Latin for goose," finished Tom. "Come, father, old *Dictionary* is in the doldrums; rouse him up with another stave."

" I'll rouse you up with the stave of a cask over your shoulders, Mr. Tom. What have you done with the old gentleman's swallow-tail ? "

" Leave me to settle that affair, father; I know how to get out of a scrape."

" So you ought, you scamp, considering how many you get into ; but the craft are swinging and heaving up. Forward there, Jacob, and sway up the mast ; there's Tom and Tommy to help you."

The mast was hoisted up, the sail set, and the lighter in the stream, before the Domine was out of his reverie.

" Are there whirlpools here ? " said the Domine, talking more to himself than to those about him.

" Whirlpools ! " replied young Tom, who was watching and mocking him ; " yes, that there are, under the bridges. I've watched a dozen *chips* go down one after the other."

"A dozen *ships !*" exclaimed the Domine, turning to Tom ; "and every soul lost ?"

"Never saw them afterwards," replied Tom, in a mournful voice.

"How little did I dream of the dangers of those so near me," said the Domine, turning away and communing with himself. "'Those who go down to the sea in ships, and occupy their business in great waters.'—'*Et vastas aperit Syrtes.*'—'These men see the works of the Lord, and His wonders in the deep.' '*Alternante vorans vasta Charybdis aqua.*' —'For at His word the stormy wind ariseth, which lifteth up. the waves thereof.'—'*Surgens a puppi ventus.—Ubi tempestas et cœli mobilis humor.*'—'They are carried up to the heavens, and down again to the deep.'—'*Gurgitibus miris et lactis vertice torrens.*'—'Their soul melteth away because of their trouble.' —'*Stant pavidi. Omnibus ignotœ mortis timor, omnibus hostem.*' —'They reel to and fro, and stagger like a drunken man.'"

"So they do, father, don't they, sometimes ?" observed Tom, leering his eye at his father. "That's all I've understood of his speech."

"They are at their wits' end," continued the Domine.

"Mind the end of your wit, master Tom," answered his father, wroth at the insinuation.

"'So when they call upon the Lord in their trouble'— '*Cujus jurare timent et fallere nomen*'—'He delivereth them out of their distress, for He maketh the storm to cease, so that the waves thereof are still;' yea, still and smooth as the peaceful water which now floweth rapidly by our anchored vessel—yet it appeareth to me that the scene hath changed. These fields met not mine eye before. '*Riparumque toros et prata recentia rivis.*' Surely we have moved from the wharf,' and the Domine turned round, and discovered, for the first time, that we were more than a mile from the place at which we had embarked.

"Pray, sir, what's the use of speech, sir ?" interrogated Tom, who had been listening to the whole of the Domine's long soliloquy.

"Thou asked a foolish question, boy. We are endowed with the power of speech to enable us to communicate our ideas."

"That's exactly what I thought, sir. Then, pray, what's the

use of your talking all that gibberish, that none of us could understand ?"

"I crave thy pardon, child; I spoke, I presume, in the dead languages."

"If they're dead, why not let them rest in their graves ?"

"Good; thou hast wit. (Cluck, cluck.) Yet, child, know that it is pleasant to commune with the dead."

"Is it? then we'll put you on shore at Battersea churchyard."

"Silence, Tom. He's full of his sauce, sir—you must forgive it."

"Nay, it pleaseth me to hear him talk; but it would please me more to hear thee sing."

"Then here goes, sir, to drown Tom's impudence—

    ' Glide on, my bark, the morning tide
    Is gently floating by thy side;
    Around thy prow the waters bright,
    In circling rounds of broken light,
    Are glittering, as if ocean gave
    Her countless gems unto the wave.'

That's a pretty air, and I first heard it sung by a pretty woman; but that's all I know of the song. She sang another—

    'I'd be a butterfly, born in a bower.' "

"You'd be a butterfly," said the Domine, taking old Tom literally, and looking at his person.

Young Tom roared, "Yes, sir, he'd be a butterfly, and I don't see why he shouldn't very soon. His legs are gone, and his wings aren't come, so he's a grub now; and that, you know, is the next thing to it. What a funny old beggar it is, father—aren't it ? "

"Tom, Tom, go forward, sir; we must shoot the bridge."

"Shoot !" exclaimed the Domine; "shoot what ?"

"You aren't afraid of firearms, are ye, sir ?" inquired Tom.

"Nay, I said not that I was afraid of firearms; but why should you shoot ?"

"We never could get on without it, sir; we shall have plenty of shooting by-and-by. You don't know this river."

"Indeed, I thought not of such doings; or that there were other dangers besides that of the deep waters."

"Go forward, Tom, and don't be playing with your betters,"

cried old Tom. "Never mind him, sir, he's only humbugging you."

"Explain, Jacob. The language of both old Tom and young Tom are to me as incomprehensible as would be that of the dog Tommy."

"Or as your Latin is to them, sir."

"True, Jacob, true. I have no right to complain; nay, I do not complain, for I am amused, although at times much puzzled."

We now shot Putney Bridge, and as a wherry passed us, old Tom carolled out—

> "Did you ever hear tell of a jolly young waterman?"

"No, I never did," said the Domine, observing old Tom's eyes directed towards him. Tom, amused by this *naïveté* on the part of the Domine, touched him by the sleeve on the other side, and commenced with his treble—

> " Did you ne'er hear a tale
> Of a maid in the vale?"

"Not that I can recollect, my child," replied the Domine.

"Then, where have you been all your life?"

"My life has been employed, my lad, in teaching the young idea how to shoot."

"So you're an old soldier, after all, and afraid of firearms. Why don't you hold yourself up? I suppose it's that enormous jib of yours that brings you down by the head."

"Tom, Tom, I'll cut you into pork pieces, if you go on that gait. Go and get dinner under weigh, you scamp, and leave the gentleman alone. Here's more wind coming.

> ' A wet sheet and a flowing sea,
> A wind that follows fast,
> And fills the white and rustling sail,
> And bends the gallant mast.
> And bends the gallant mast, my boys,
> While, like the eagle free,
> Away the good ship flies, and leaves
> Old England on the lee.'"

"Jacob," said the Domine, "I have heard by the mouth of Rumour, with her hundred tongues, how careless and indifferent are sailors unto danger; but I never could have believed that such lightness of heart could have been shown. Yon man, although certainly not in years, yet, what is he?— a remnant of a man resting upon unnatural and ill-proportioned support. Yon lad, who is yet but a child, appears as blythe and merry as if he were in possession of all this world can afford. I have an affection for that bold child, and would fain teach him the rudiments, at least, of the Latin tongue."

"I doubt if Tom would ever learn them, sir. He has a will of his own."

"It grieveth me to hear thee say so, for he lacketh not talent, but instruction ; and the Dux, he pleaseth me mightily —a second Palinurus. Yet how that a man could venture to embark upon an element, to struggle through the horrors of which must occasionally demand the utmost exertion of every limb, with the want of the two most necessary for his safety, is to me quite incomprehensible."

"He can keep his legs, sir."

"Nay, Jacob; how can he keep what are already gone? Even thou speakest strangely upon the water. I see the dangers that surround us, Jacob, yet I am calm ; I feel that I have not lived a wicked life—'*Integer vitæ, celerisque purus,*' as Horace truly saith, may venture, even as I have done, upon the broad expanse of water. What is it that the boy is providing for us? It hath an inviting smell."

"Lobscouse, master," replied old Tom ; "and not bad lining either."

"I recollect no such word—*unde derivatur*, friend?"

"What's that, master?" inquired old Tom.

"It's Latin for lobscouse, depend upon it, father," cried Tom, who was stirring up the savoury mess with a large wooden spoon. "He be a *deadly* lively old gentleman, with his dead language. Dinner's all ready. Are we to let go the anchor, or pipe to dinner first?"

"We may as well anchor, boys. We have not a quarter of an hour's more ebb, and the wind is heading us."

Tom and I went forward, brailed up the mainsail, cleared away, and let go the anchor. The lighter swung round rapidly to the stream. The Domine, who had been in a fit of musing, with his eyes cast upon the forests of masts which we had passed below London Bridge, and which were now some way astern of us, of a sudden exclaimed, in a loud voice, "*Parce precor ! Periculosum est !*"

The lighter swinging short round to her anchor, had surprised the Domine with the rapid motion of the panorama, and he thought we had fallen in with one of the whirlpools mentioned by Tom. "What has happened, good Dux? tell me," cried the Domine to old Tom, with alarm in his countenance.

"Why, master, I'll tell you after my own fashion," replied old Tom, smiling; and then singing, as he held the Domine by the button of his spencer—

> "'Now to her berth the craft draws nigh,
> With slackened sail, she feels the tide.
> "Stand clear the cable!" is the cry—
> The anchor's gone, we safely ride.'

And now, master, we'll bale out the lobscouse. We shan't weigh anchor again until to-morrow morning; the wind's right in our teeth, and it will blow fresh, I'm sartain. Look how the scud's flying; so now we'll have a jolly time of it, and you shall have your allowance of grog on board before you turn in."

"I have before heard of that potation," replied the Domine, sitting down on the coamings of the hatchway, "and fain would taste it."

CHAPTER XII

Is a chapter of tales in a double sense—The Domine, from the natural effects of his single-heartedness, begins to see double— A new definition of philosophy, with an episode on jealousy.

W E now took our seats on the deck round the saucepan, for we did not trouble ourselves with dishes, and the Domine appeared to enjoy the lobscouse very much. In the course of half-an-hour all was over: that is to say, we had eaten as much as we wished; and the Newfoundland dog, who, during our repast, lay close by young Tom, flapping the deck with his tail, and sniffing the savoury smell of the compound, had just licked all our plates quite clean, and was now finishing with his head in the saucepan; while Tom was busy carrying the crockery into the cabin, and bringing out the bottle and tin pannikins, ready for the promised carouse.

"There, now, master, there's a glass o' grog for you that would float a marlin-spike. See if that don't warm the *cockles* of your old heart."

"Ay," added Tom, "and set all your *muscles* as taut as weather backstays."

"Master Tom, with your leave, I'll mix your grog for you myself. Hand me back that bottle, you rascal."

"Just as you please, father," replied Tom, handing the bottle; "but recollect, none of your water bewitched. Only help me as you love me."

Old Tom mixed a pannikin of grog for Tom, and another for himself. I hardly need say which was the stiffer of the two.

"Well, father, I suppose you think the grog will run short. To be sure, one bottle aren't too much 'mong four of us."

"One bottle, you scamp; there's another in the cupboard."

"Then you must see double already, father."

Old Tom, who was startled at this news, and who imagined that Tom must have gained possession of the other bottle, jumped up and made for the cupboard, to ascertain whether what Tom asserted was correct. This was what Tom wished: he immediately changed pannikins of grog with his father, and remained quiet.

"There *is* another bottle, Tom," said his father, coming out and taking his seat again. "I knew there was. You young rascal, you don't know how you frightened me!" And old Tom put the pannikin to his lips. "Drowned the miller, by heavens!" said he. "What could I have been about?" ejaculated he, adding more spirit to his mixture.

"I suppose, upon the strength of another bottle in the locker, you are doubling the strength of your grog. Come, father," and Tom held out his pannikin, "do put a little drop of stuff in mine—it's seven-water grog, and I'm not on the black-list."

"No, no, Tom; your next shall be stronger. Well, master, how do you like your liquor?"

"Verily," replied the Domine, "it is a pleasant and seducing liquor. Lo and behold! I am at the bottom of my tin utensil."

"Stop till I fill it up again, old gentleman. I see you are one of the right sort. You know what the song says—

JACOB FAITHFUL

> ' A plague on those musty old lubbers,
>   Who tell us to fast and to think,
>   And patient fall in with life's rubbers,
>   With nothing but *water to drink !* '

Water, indeed ! The only use of water I know is to mix your grog with, and float vessels up and down the world. Why was the sea made salt but to prevent our drinking too much water. Water, indeed !

> ' A can of good grog, had they swigged it,
>   'Twould have set them for pleasure agog,
>   And in spite of the rules
>   Of the schools,
>   The old fools
>   Would have all of them swigged it,
>   And swore there was nothing like grog.' "

" I'm exactly of your opinion, father," said Tom, holding out his empty pannikin.

" Always ready for two things, Master Tom—grog and mischief; but, however, you shall have one more dose."

" It hath, then, medicinal virtues ? " inquired the Domine.

" Ay, that it has, master—more than all the quacking medicines in the world. It cures grief and melancholy, and prevents spirits from getting low."

" I doubt that, father," cried Tom, holding up the bottle; "for the more grog we drink, the more the *spirits become low*."

Cluck, cluck, came from the thorax of the Domine. "Verily, friend Tom, it appeareth, among other virtues, to sharpen the wits. Proceed, friend Dux, in the medicinal virtues of grog."

" Well, master, it cures love when it's not returned, and adds to it when it is. I've heard say it will cure jealousy; but that I've my doubts of. Now I think on it, I will tell you a yarn about a jealous match between a couple of fools. Jacob, aren't your pannikin empty, my boy ? "

" Yes," replied I, handing it up to be filled. It was empty, for, not being very fond of it myself, Tom, with my permission, had drunk it as well as his own.

" There, Jacob, is a good dose for you; you aren't always raving after it, like Tom."

" He isn't troubled with low spirits as I am, father."

" How long has that been your complaint, Tom ? ' inquired I

"Ever since I heard how to cure it. Come, father, give us the yarn."

"Well then, you must mind that an old shipmate o' mine, Ben Leader, had a wife named Poll—a pretty sort of craft in her way—neat in her rigging, swelling bows, taking sort of figure-head, and devilish well rounded in the counter; altogether she was a very fancy girl, and all the men were a'ter her. She'd a roguish eye, and liked to be stared at, as most pretty women do, because it flatters their vanities. Now, although she liked to be noticed so far by the other chaps, yet Ben was the only one she ever wished to be handled by; it was, 'Paws off, Pompey!' with all the rest. Ben Leader was a good-looking, active, smart chap, and could foot it in a reel or take a bout at single-stick with the very best o' them; and she was mortal fond of him, and mortal jealous if he talked to any other woman, for the women liked Ben as much as the men liked she. Well, as they returned love for love, so did they return jealousy for jealousy; and the lads and lasses, seeing that, had a pleasure in making them come to a misunderstanding. So every day it became worse and worse between them. Now, I always says that it's a stupid thing to be jealous, 'cause if there be *cause*, there be no *cause* for love; and if there be no *cause*, there be no *cause* for jealousy."

" You're like a row in a rookery, father—nothing but *caws*," interrupted Tom.

" Well, I suppose I am; but that's what I call chop logic—aren't it, master?"

" It was a syllogism," replied the Domine, taking the pannikin from his mouth.

" I don't know what that is, nor do I want to know," replied old Tom; "so I'll just go on with my story. Well, at last they came to downright fighting. Ben licks Poll 'cause she talked and laughed with other men, and Poll cries and whines all day 'cause he won't sit on her knee, instead of going on board and 'tending to his duty. Well, one night a'ter work was over, Ben goes on shore to the house where he and Poll used to sleep; and when he sees the girl in the bar, he says, 'Where is Poll?' Now, the girl at the bar was a fresh-comer, and answers, 'What girl?' So Ben describes her, and the bargirl answers, 'She be just gone to bed with her husband, I suppose;' for, you see, there was a woman like her who had gone up to her bed, sure enough. When Ben heard that, he gives his trousers one hitch, and calls for a quartern, drinks it off with a sigh, and leaves the house, believing it all to be true. A'ter Ben was gone, Poll makes her appearance, and when she finds Ben wasn't in the tap, says, ' Young woman, did a man go upstairs just now ? ' ' Yes,' replied the bar-girl, ' with his wife, I suppose ; they be turned in this quarter of an hour.' When Poll hears this, she almost turned mad with rage, and then as white as a sheet, and then she burst into tears and runs out of the house, crying out, ' Poor misfortunate creature that I am ! ' knocking everything down undersized, and running into the arms of every man who came athwart her hawse.''

" I understood him, but just now, that she was running on foot ; yet doth he talk about her *horse*. Expound, Jacob.''

" It was a nautical figure of speech, sir.''

" Exactly,'' rejoined Tom, " it meant her figure-head, old gentleman ; but my yarn won't cut a figure if I'm brought up all standing in this way. Suppose, master, you hear the story first and understand it a'terwards ? ''

" I will endeavour to comprehend by the context,'' replied the Domine.

" That is, I suppose, that you'll allow me to stick to my text. Well then, here's coil away again. Ben, you see, what with his jealousy and what with a whole quartern at a draught, became *somehow nohow ;* and he walked down to the jetty with the intention of getting rid of himself, and his wife, and all his troubles, by giving his soul back to his Creator, and his body to the fishes.''

" Bad philosophy,'' quoth the Domine.

" I agree with you, master,'' replied old Tom.

" Pray, what sort of a thing is philosophy ? '' inquired Tom.

" Philosophy,'' replied old Tom, " is either hanging, drowning, shooting yourself, or, in short, getting out of the world without help.''

" Nay,'' replied the Domine, " that is *felo de se.*''

" Well, I pronounce it quicker than you, master ; but it's one and the same thing—but to go on. While Ben was standing on the jetty, thinking whether he should take one more quid of 'baccy afore he dived, who should come down but Poll, with her hair all adrift, streaming and coach-whipping astern of her, with the same intention as Ben—to commit *philo-zoffy*. Ben, who was standing at the edge of the jetty, his eyes fixed upon the water as it eddied among the piles, looking as dismal as if he had swallowed a hearse and six, with the funeral feathers hanging out of his mouth——"

"A bold comparison," murmured the Domine.

"Never sees her; and she was so busy with herself that, although close to him, she never sees he—always remembering that the night was dark. So Poll turned her eyes up for all the world like a dying jackdaw."

"Tell me, friend Dux," interrupted the Domine, "doth a jackdaw die in any peculiar way?"

"Yes," replied young Tom; "he always dies black, master."

"Then doth he die as he liveth. (Cluck, cluck.) Proceed, good Dux."

"And don't you break the thread of my yarn any more, master, if you wish to hear the end on it. So Poll begins to blubber about Ben. 'O Ben, Ben,' cried she; 'cruel, cruel man; for to come—for to go; for to go—for to come!'

"'Who's there?' shouted Ben.

"'For to come—for to go,' cried Poll.

"'Ship ahoy!' hailed Ben, again.

"'For to go—for to come,' blubbered Poll; and then she couldn't bring out anything more for sobbing. With that, Ben, who thought he knew the voice, walks up to her and says, 'Be that you, Poll?'

"'Be that you, Ben?' replied Poll, taking her hands from her face and looking at him.

"'I thought you were in bed with—with—O Poll!' said Ben.

"'And I thought you were in bed with—O Ben!' replied Poll.

"'But I wasn't, Poll.'

"'No more warn't I, Ben.'

"'And what brought you here, Poll?'

"'I wanted for to die, Ben. And what brought you here, Ben?'

"'I didn't want for to live, Poll, when I thought you false.'

"Then Polly might have answered in the words of the old song, master; but her poor heart was too full, I suppose." And Tom sang—

"'Your Polly has never been false, she declares,
Since last time we parted at Wapping Old Stairs,'

Howsomever, in the next minute they were both hugging and kissing, sobbing, shivering and shaking in each other's arms; and as soon as they had settled themselves a little, back they went arm in arm to the house, had a good stiff glass to prevent their taking the rheumatism, went to bed, and were cured of the jealousy ever a'terwards—which, in my opinion, was a much better *philo-zoffy* than the one they had both been bound on. There, I've wound it all off at last, master, and now we'll fill up our pannikins."

"Before I consent, friend Dux, prythee inform me how much of this pleasant liquor may be taken without inebriating, *vulgo*, getting tipsy?"

"Father can drink enough to float a jolly-boat, master," replied Tom; "so you needn't fear. I'll drink pan for pan with you, all night long."

"Indeed you won't, mister Tom," replied the father.

"But I will, master."

I perceived that the liquor had already had some effect upon my worthy pedagogue, and was not willing that he should be persuaded into excess. I therefore pulled him by the coat as a hint, but he was again deep in thought, and he did not heed me. Tired of sitting so long I got up, and walked forward to look at the cable.

"Strange," muttered the Domine, "that Jacob should thus pull me by the garment. What could he mean?"

"Did he pull you, sir?" inquired Tom.

"Yea, many times; and then he walked away."

"It appears that you have been pulled too much, sir," replied Tom, dexterously appearing to pick up the tail of his coat, which had been torn off by the dog, and handing it to him.

"*Eheu! Jacobe—fili dilectissime—quid fecisti?*" cried the Domine, holding up the fragment of his coat with a look of despair.

"'A long pull, a strong pull, and a pull all together,'" sang out old Tom; and then looking at Tom, "Now, aren't you a pretty rascal, master Tom?"

"It is done," exclaimed the Domine, with a sigh, putting the fragment into the remaining pocket; "and it cannot be undone."

"Now, I think it is undone, and can be done, master," replied Tom. "A needle and thread will soon join the pieces

of your old coat again—in *holy* matrimony, I may safely
say——"

"True. (Cluck, cluck.) My housekeeper will restore it, yet
will she be wroth. '*Fœminæ curæque iræque ;*' but let us think
no more about it," cried the Domine, drinking deeply from
his pannikin, and each minute verging fast to intoxication.
"'*Nunc est bibendum, nunc pede libero pulsanda tellus.*' I feel as
if I were lifted up and could dance, yea, and could exalt my
voice and sing."

"Could you, my jolly old master? then we will both dance
and sing—

> ' Come, let us dance and sing,
> While all Barbadoes bells shall ring,
> Mars scrapes the fiddle string
> While Venus plays the lute.
> Hymen gay, trips away,
> Jocund at the wedding day.'

Now for chorus—

> ' Come, let us dance and sing.' "

CHAPTER XIII

*The "fun grows fast and furious"—The pedagogue does not scan
correctly, and his feet become very unequal—An allegorical
compliment almost worked up into a literal quarrel—At length
the mighty are laid low, and the Domine hurts his nose.*

I HEARD Tom's treble, and a creaking noise, which I recognised to proceed from the Domine, who had joined the
chorus, and I went aft, if possible to prevent further excess ;
but I found that the grog had mounted into the Domine's
head, and all my hints were disregarded. Tom was despatched for the other bottle, and the Domine's pannikin
was replenished, old Tom roaring out—

> " ' Come, sling the flowing bowl ;
> Fond hopes arise,
> The girls we prize
> Shall bless each jovial soul.
> The can, boys, bring,
> We'll dance and sing,
> While foaming billows roll.'

98

"Now for the chorus again—

    ' Come, sling the flowing bowl, &c.'

Jacob, why don't you join?" The chorus was given by
the whole of us. Domine's voice even louder, though not
quite so musical as old Tom's.

"*Evoé!*" cried the Domine; "*evoé! cantemus.*

    ' *Amo, amas*—I loved a lass,
        For she was tall and slender ;
    Amas, amat—she laid me flat,
        Though of the feminine gender.'

Truly do I not forget the songs of my youth, and of my
hilarious days; yet doth the potent spirit work upon me
like the god in the Cumean sibyl; and I shall soon prophesy
that which shall come to pass."

"So can I," said Tom, giving me a nudge, and laughing.

"Do thine office of Ganymede, and fill up the pannikin ;
put not in too much of the element. Once more exalt thy
voice, good Dux."

"Always ready, master," cried Tom, who sang out again in
praise of his favourite liquor—

    " Smiling grog is the sailor's best hope, his sheet anchor,
        His compass, his cable, his log,
    That gives him a heart which life's cares cannot canker ;
        Though dangers around him,
        Unite to confound him,
    He braves them, and tips off his grog.
      'Tis grog, only grog,
    Is his rudder, his compass, his cable, his log,
    The sailor's sheet anchor is grog."

"Verily, thou art an Apollo—or rather, referring to thy
want of legs, half an Apollo—that is, a *demi*-god. (Cluck,
cluck.) Sweet is thy lyre, friend Dux."

"Fair words, master; I'm no liar," cried Tom. " Clap a
stopper on your tongue, or you'll get into disgrace."

"*Ubi lapsus quid feci,*" exclaimed the Domine; "I spoke of thy
musical tongue, and furthermore, I spoke alle—gori—cal—ly."

"I know a man lies with his tongue as well as you do, old
chap; but as for telling a *hell of a* (something) *lie*, as you

states, I say I never did," rejoined old Tom, who was getting cross in his cups.

I now interfered, as there was every appearance of a fray; and in spite of young Tom, who wished, as he termed it, to *kick up a shindy*, prevailed upon them to make friends, which they did, shaking hands for nearly five minutes. When this was ended I again entreated the Domine not to drink any more, but go to bed.

"*Amice Jacobe*," replied the Domine, "the liquor hath mounted into thy brain, and thou wouldst rebuke thy master and thy preceptor. Betake thee to thy couch, and sleep off the effects of thy drink. Verily, Jacob, thou art *plenus Veteris Bacchi*; or, in plain English, thou art drunk. Canst thou conjugate, Jacob? I fear not. Canst thou decline, Jacob? I fear not. Canst thou scan, Jacob. I fear not. Nay, Jacob, methinks that thou art unsteady in thy gait, and not over clear in thy vision. Canst thou hear, Jacob? if so I will give thee an oration against inebriety, with which thou mayest down on thy pillow. Wilt thou have it in Latin or in Greek?"

"Oh, d—n your Greek and Latin!" cried old Tom; "keep that for to-morrow. Sing us a song, my old hearty; or shall I sing you one? Here goes—

> ' For while the grog goes round,
> All sense of danger's drowned,
> We despise it to a man;
> We sing a little——' '

"Sing a little," bawled the Domine.

> " And laugh a little——"

"Laugh a little," chorused young Tom.

> " And work a little——"

"Work a little," cried the Domine.

> " And swear a little——"

"Swear *not* a little," echoed Tom.

> " And fiddle a little——"

"Fiddle a little," hiccuped the Domine.

> " And foot it a little——"

"Foot it a little," repeated Tom.

> " And swig the flowing can,
> And fiddle a little,
> And foot it a little,
> And swig the flowing can——"

roared old Tom, emptying his pannikin.

> " And swig the flowing can——"

followed the Domine, tossing off his.

> " And swig the flowing can——"

cried young Tom, turning up his pannikin empty.

"Hurrah ! that's what I calls glorious. Let's have it over again, and then we'll have another dose. Come now, all together." Again was the song repeated, and when they came to "foot it a little" old Tom jumped on his stumps, seizing hold of the Domine, who immediately rose, and the three danced round and round for a minute or two singing the song and chorus, till old Tom, who was very far gone, tripped against the coamings of the hatchway, pitching his head into the Domine's stomach, who fell backwards clinging to young Tom's hand ; so that they all rolled on the deck together— my worthy preceptor underneath the other two.

"Foot it rather too much that time, father," said young Tom, getting up the first, and laughing. "Come, Jacob, let's put father on his pins again ; he can't right without a purchase." With some difficulty we succeeded. As soon as he was on his legs again, old Tom put a hand upon each of our shoulders, and commenced, with a drunken leer—

> " ' What though his timbers they are gone,
> And he's a slave to tipple,
> No better sailor ere was born
> Than Tom, the jovial cripple.'

Thanky, my boys, thanky ; now rouse up the old gentleman. I suspect we knocked the wind out of him. Hollo, there, are you hard and fast ? "

"The bricks are hard, and verily my senses are fast departing," quoth the Domine, rousing himself and sitting up, staring around him.

"Senses going, do you say, master?" cried old Tom. "Don't throw them overboard till we have made a finish. One more pannikin apiece, one more song, and then to bed. Tom, where's the bottle?"

"Drink no more, sir, I beg; you'll be ill to-morrow," said I to the Domine.

"*Deprome quadrimum,*" hiccuped the Domine. "*Carpe diem—quam minimum—creula postero*—Sing, friend Dux— *Quem virum—sumes celebrare—musis amicus*—Where's my patty-pan?—We are not Thracians—*Natis in usum—lœtiœ scyphis pugnare*—(hiccup)—*Thracumest*—therefore we—will not fight —but we will drink—*recepto dulce mihi furere est amico*—Jacob, thou art drunk—sing, friend Dux, or shall I sing?—

> '*Propria quœ maribus* had a little dog,
> *Quœ genus* was his name——'

My memory faileth me—what was the tune?"

"That tune was the one the old cow died of, I'm sure," replied Tom. "Come, old Nosey, strike up again."

"Nosey, from *nasus*—truly, it is a fair epithet; and it. remindeth me that my nose—suffered in the fall which I received just now. Yet I cannot sing—having no words——"

"Nor tune either, master," replied old Tom; "so here goes for you—

> ' Young Susan had lovers, so many, that she
>   Hardly knew upon which to decide;
> They all spoke sincerely, and promised to be
>   All worthy of such a sweet bride.
> In the morning she'd gossip with William, and then
>   The noon will be spent with young Harry;
> The evening with Tom; so, amongst all the men,
>   She never could tell which to marry.
>   Heigho! I am afraid
>   Too many lovers will puzzle a maid.' "

"It pleaseth me—it ringeth in mine ears—yea, most pleasantly. Proceed—the girl was as the Pyrrha of Horace—

> ' Quis multa gracillis—te puer in rosa—
> Perfusus liquidis urget odoribus.
> Grato, Pyrrha—sub antro?'"

'That's all high Dutch to me, master; but I'll go on if I can. My memory box be a little out of order. Let me see—oh!

> ' Now William grew jealous, and so went away ;
>   Harry got tired of wooing ;
> And Tom having teased her to fix on the day,
>   Received but a frown for so doing ;
> So, 'mongst all her lovers, quite left in the lurch,
>   She pined every night on her pillow ;
> And meeting one day a pair going to church,
>   Turned away, and died under a willow.
>   Heigho! I am afraid
>   Too many lovers will puzzle a maid.'

Now then, old gentleman, tip off your grog. You've got your allowance, as I promised you."

"Come, master, you're a cup too low," said Tom, who although in high spirits, was not at all intoxicated ; indeed, as I afterwards found, he could carry more than his father. "Come, shall I give you a song?"

"That's right, Tom ; a volunteer's worth two pressed men. Open your mouth wide, an' let your whistle fly away with the gale. You whistles in tune, at all events."

Tom then struck up, the Domine see-sawing as he sat, and getting very sleepy—

> " ' Luck in life, or good or bad,
>   Ne'er could make me melancholy ;
>   Seldom rich, yet never sad,
>   Sometimes poor, yet always jolly.
>   Fortune's in my scale, that's poz,
>   Of mischance put more than half in ;
>   Yet I don't know how it was,
>   I could never cry for laughing—
>   Ha! ha! ha! Ha! ha! ha!
>   I could never cry for laughing.'

Now for chorus, father—

> ' Ha! ha! ha! Ha! ha!
>   I could never cry for laughing.'

That's all I know ; and that's enough, for it won't wake up the old gentleman."

But it did. "Ha, ha, ha—ha, ha, ha! I could never die for laughing," bawled out the Domine, feeling for his pannikin ;

but this was his last effort. He stared round him. "Verily, verily, we are in a whirlpool—how everything turneth round and round! Who cares? Am I not an ancient mariner—'*Qui videt mare turgidum—et infames scopulos.*' Friend Dux, listen to me—*favet linguis.*"

"Well," hiccuped old Tom, "so I will—but speak—plain English—as I—do."

"That I'll be hanged if he does," said Tom to me. "In half-an-hour more I shall understand old Nosey's Latin just as well as his—plain English, as he calls it."

"I will discuss in any language—that is—in any tongue— be it in the Greek or the Latin—nay, even—(hiccups)—friend Dux—hast thou not partaken too freely—of—dear me! *Quò me, Bacche, rapis tui—plenum*—truly I shall be tipsy—and will but finish my pattypan—*dulce periculum est*—Jacob—can there be two Jacobs—and two old Toms—nay—*mirabile dictu* —there are two young Toms, and two dog Tommies—each with—two tails. *Bacche, parce—precor—precor—* Jacob, where art thou?—*Ego sum tu es*—thou art—*sumus*, we are—where am I? *Procumbit humi bos*—for Bos—read Dobbs—*amo, amas* —I loved a lass. *Tityre, tu patulæ sub teg—mine*—nay—I quote wrong—then must I be—I do believe that—I'm drunk."

"And I'm cock sure of it," cried Tom, laughing, as the Domine fell back in a state of insensibility.

"And I'm cock sure," said old Tom, rolling himself along the deck to the cabin hatch, "that I've as much—as I can stagger—under, at all events—so I'll sing myself to sleep— 'cause why—I'm happy. Jacob—mind you keep all the watches to-night—and Tom may keep the rest." Old Tom then sat up, leaning his back against the cabin hatch, and commenced one of those doleful ditties which are sometimes heard on the forecastle of a man-of-war; he had one or two of these songs that he always reserved for such occasions. While Tom and I dragged the Domine to bed, old Tom slowly drawled out his ditty—

> " ' Oh! we sailed to Virgi-ni-a, and thence to Fy-al,
> Where we watered our shipping, and so then weigh-ed all,
> Full in view, on the seas—boys—seven sail we did—es-py,
> Oh! we man-ned our capstern, and weighed spee-di-ly.'

That's right, my boys, haul and hold—stow the old Dictionary away—for he can't command the parts of speech.

' The very next morning—the engagement proved—hot,
And brave Admiral Benbow receiv-ed a chain—shot.
Oh, when he was wounded to his merry men—he—did—say,
Take me up in your arms, boys, and car-ry me a-way.'

Now, boys, come and help me—Tom—none of your foolery
—for your poor old father is—drunk."

We assisted old Tom into the other "bed-place" in the
cabin. "Thanky, lads—one little bit more, and then I'm
done—as the auctioneer says—going—going—

' Oh the guns they did rattle, and the bul-lets—did—fly,
When brave Benbow—for help loud—did cry,
Carry me down to the cock-pit—there is ease for my smarts,
If my merry men should see me—'twill sure—break—their—hearts.'

Going—old swan-hopper—as I am—going—gone."

Tom and I were left on the deck.

"Now, Jacob, if you have a mind to turn in, I'm not
sleepy—you shall keep the morning watch."

"No, Tom, you'd better sleep first. I'll call you at four
o'clock. We can't weigh till tide serves, and I shall have
plenty of sleep before that."

Tom went to bed, and I walked the deck till the morning,
thinking over the events of the day, and wondering what the
Domine would say when he came to his senses. At four
o'clock, as agreed, I roused Tom out and turned into his bed,
and was soon as fast asleep as old Tom and the Domine,
whose responsive snores had rung in my ears during the
whole time that I had walked the deck.

CHAPTER XIV

*Cold water and repentance—The two Toms almost moral, and
myself full of wise reflections—The chapter, being full of grave
saws, is luckily very short; and though a very sensible one, I
would not advise it to be skipped.*

ABOUT half-past eight the next morning, I was called up
by Tom to assist in getting the lighter under weigh. When
I came on deck I found old Tom as fresh as if he had not
drunk a drop the night before, very busily stumping about the

105

windlass, with which we hove up first the anchor and then the mast. "Well, Jacob, my boy, had sleep enough? Not too much, I daresay, but a bout like last night don't come often, Jacob—only once in a way; now and then I do believe it's good for my health. It's a great comfort to me, my lad, to have you on board with me, because, as you never drinks, I may now indulge a *little* oftener. As for Tom, can't trust him—too much like his father—had nobody to trust to for the look-out, except the dog Tommy, till you came with us. I can trust Tommy as far as keeping off the river sharks, he'll never let them take a rope-yarn off the deck, night or day; but a dog's but a dog after all. Now we're brought to, so clap on, my boy, and let's heave up with a will."

"How's the old gentleman, father?" said Tom, as we paused a moment from our labour at the windlass.

"Oh! he's got a good deal more to sleep off yet. There he lies, flat on his back, blowing as hard as a grampus. Better leave him as long as we can. We'll rouse him as soon as we turn the Greenwich reach. Tom, didn't you think his nose loomed devilish large yesterday?"

"Never seed such a devil of a cutwater in my life, father."

"Well then, you'll see a larger when he gets up, for it's swelled bigger than the brandy bottle. Heave and haul! Now bring to the fall, and up with the mast, boys, while I goes aft and takes the helm."

Old Tom went aft. During the night the wind had veered to the north, and the frost had set in sharp, the rime covered the deck of the barge, and here and there floating ice was to be seen coming down with the tide. The banks of the river and fields adjacent were white with hoar frost, and would have presented but a cheerless aspect, had not the sun shone out clear and bright. Tom went aft to light the fire, while I coiled away and made all snug forward. Old Tom as usual carolled forth—

> " Oh! for a soft and gentle wind,
>   I heard a fair one cry,
> But give to me the roaring breeze,
>   And white waves beating high,
> And white waves beating high, my boys,
>   The good ship tight and free,
> The world of waters is our own,
>   And merry men are we."

"A nice morning this for cooling a hot head, that's sartain. Tommy, you rascal, you're like a court lady, with her velvet *gownd*, covered all over with diamonds," continued old Tom, looking at the Newfoundland dog, whose glossy black hair was besprinkled with little icicles, which glittered in the sun. "You and Jacob were the only sensible ones of the party last night, for you both were sober."

"So was I, father. I was as sober as a judge," observed Tom, who was blowing up the fire.

"May be, Tom, as a judge a'ter dinner; but a judge on the bench be one thing, and a judge over a bottle be another, and not bad judges in that way either. At all events, if you warn't *served up*, it wasn't your fault."

"And I suppose," replied Tom, "it was only your misfortune that you were."

"No, I don't say that; but still, when I look at the dog, who's but a beast by nature, and thinks of myself who wasn't meant to be a beast, why, then I blushes, that's all."

"Jacob, look at father—now, does he blush?" cried Tom.

"I can't say that I perceive it," replied I, smiling.

"Well then, if I don't it's the fault of my having no legs. I'm sure, when they were knocked off I lost half the blood in my body, and that's the reason, I suppose. At all events, I meant to blush, so we'll take the will for the deed."

"But do you mean to keep sober in future, father?" said Tom.

"Never do you mind that—mind your own business, Mr. Tom. At all events, I shan't get tipsy till next time, and that's all I can say with safety, 'cause, d'ye see, I knows my failing. Jacob, did you ever see that old gentleman sail too close to the wind before?"

"I never did—I do not think that he was ever tipsy before last night."

"Then I pities him—his headache and his repentance. Moreover,.there be his nose and the swallow-tail of his coat to make him unhappy. We shall be down abreast of the hospital in half-an-hour. Suppose you go and give him a shake, Jacob. Not you, Tom, I won't trust you—you'll be doing him a mischief; you haven't got no fellow-feeling, not even for dumb brutes."

"I'll thank you not to take away my character that way,

107

father," replied Tom. "Didn't I put you to bed last night when you were speechless?"

"Suppose you did—what then?"

"Why then, I had a feeling for a dumb brute. I only say that, father, for the joke of it, you know," continued Tom, going up to his father and patting his rough cheek.

"I know that, my boy, you never were unkind, that's sartain; but you must have your joke—

> ' Merry thoughts are linked with laughter,
> Why should we bury them?
> Sighs and tears may come hereafter,
> No need to hurry them.
> They who through a spying-glass,
> View the minutes as they pass,
> Make the sun a gloomy mass,
> But the fault's their own, Tom.' "

In the meantime I was vainly attempting to rouse the Domine. After many fruitless attempts I put a large quantity of snuff on his upper lip, and then blew it up his nose. But, merciful powers! what a nose it had become—larger than the largest pear that I ever saw in my life. The whole weight of old Tom had fallen on it, and instead of being crushed by the blow, it appeared as if, on the contrary, it had swelled up, indignant at the injury and affront which it had received. The skin was as tight as the parchment of a drum, and shining as if it had been oiled, while the colour was a bright purple. Verily, it was the Domine's nose in a rage.

The snuff had the effect of partially awakening him from his lethargy. "Six o'clock—did you say, Mrs. Bately? Are the boys washed—and in the schoolroom? I will rise speedily —yet I am overcome with much heaviness. *Delapsus somnus ab——*" and the Domine snored again. I renewed my attempts, and gradually succeeded. The Domine opened his eyes, stared at the deck and carlines above him, then at the cupboard by his side; lastly, he looked at and recognised me. "*Eheu, Jacobe!*—where am I? And what is that which presses upon my brain? What is it so loadeth my cerebellum, even as if it were lead? My memory—where is it? Let me recall my scattered senses." Here the Domine was silent for some time. "Ah me! yea, and verily, I do recollect—

108

with pain of head and more pain of heart—that which I would fain forget, which is, that I did forget myself; and indeed have forgotten all that passed the latter portion of the night. Friend Dux hath proved no friend, but hath led me into the wrong path; and as for the potation called grog—*Eheu, Jacobe!* how have I fallen—fallen in my own opinion—fallen in thine—how can I look thee in the face! O Jacob! what must thou think of him who hath hitherto been thy preceptor and thy guide!" Here the Domine fell back on the pillow, and turned away his head.

"It is not your fault, sir," replied I, to comfort him; "you were not aware of what you were drinking—you did not know that the liquor was so strong. Old Tom deceived you."

"Nay, Jacob, I cannot lay that flattering unction to my wounded heart. I ought to have known, nay, now I recall to mind that thou wouldst have warned me—even to the pulling off of the tail of my coat—yet I heeded thee not, and I am humbled—even I, the master over seventy boys!"

"Nay, sir, it was not I who pulled off the tail of your coat, it was the dog."

"Jacob, I have heard of the wonderful sagacity of the canine species, yet could not I ever have believed that a dumb brute would have perceived my folly, and warned me from intoxication. *Mirabile dictu!* Tell me, Jacob, thou who hast profited by these lessons which thy master could give—although he could not follow up his precept by example—tell me, what did take place? Let me know the full extent of my backsliding."

"You fell asleep, sir, and we put you to bed."

"Who did me that office, Jacob?"

"Young Tom and I, sir; as for old Tom, he was not in a state to help anybody."

"I am humbled, Jacob——"

"Nonsense, old gentleman; why make a fuss about nothing?" said old Tom, who, overhearing our conversation, came into the cabin. "You had a drop too much, that's all, and what o' that? It's a poor heart that never rejoiceth. Rouse a bit, wash your face with cold Thames water, and in half-an-hour you'll be as fresh as a daisy."

"My head acheth!" exclaimed the Domine, "even as if there were a ball of lead rolling from one temple to the other; but my punishment is just."

"That is the punishment of making too free with the bottle, for sartain; but if it is an offence, then it carries its own punishment, and that's quite sufficient. Every man knows that when the heart's over light at night, that the head's over heavy in the morning. I have known and proved it a thousand times. Well, what then? I puts the good against the bad, and I takes my punishment like a man."

"Friend Dux, for so I will still call thee, thou lookest not at the offence in a moral point of vision."

"What's moral?" replied old Tom.

"I would point out that intoxication is sinful."

"Intoxication sinful! I suppose that means that it's a sin to get drunk. Now, master, it's my opinion that as God Almighty has given us good liquor, it was for no other purpose than to drink it; and therefore it would be ungrateful to Him, and a sin, not to get drunk—that is, with discretion."

"How canst thou reconcile getting drunk with discretion, good Dux?"

"I mean, master, when there's work to be done, the work should be done; but when there's plenty of time, and everything is safe, and all ready for a start the next morning, I can see no possible objection to a jollification. Come, master, rouse out; the lighter's abreast of the hospital almost by this time, and we must put you on shore."

The Domine, whose clothes were all on, turned out of his bed-place, and went with us on deck. Young Tom, who was at the helm, as soon as we made our appearance, wished him a good-morning very respectfully Indeed, I always observed that Tom, with all his impudence and waggery, had a great deal of consideration and kindness He had overheard the Domine's conversation with me, and would not further wound his feelings with a jest. Old Tom resumed his place at the helm, while his son prepared the breakfast, and I drew a bucket of water for the Domine to wash his face and hands. Of his nose not a word was said; and the Domine made no remarks to me on the subject, although I am persuaded it must have been very painful, from the comfort he appeared to derive in bathing it with the freezing water. A bowl of tea was a great solace to him, and he had hardly finished it when the lighter was abreast the hospital stairs. Tom jumped into the boat and hauled it alongside. I took the other oar, and the Domine, shaking hands with old Tom, said, "Thou didst mean kindly, and therefore I wish thee a kind farewell, good Dux."

"God be with you, master," replied old Tom; "shall we call for you as we come back?"

"Nay, nay," replied the Domine, "the travelling by land is more expensive, but less dangerous. I thank thee for thy songs, and—for all thy kindness, good Dux. Are my paraphernalia in the boat, Jacob?"

I replied in the affirmative. The Domine stepped in, and we pulled him on shore. He landed, took his bundle and umbrella under his arm, shook hands with Tom and then with me without speaking, and I perceived the tears start in his eyes as he turned and walked away.

"Well, now," said Tom, looking after the Domine, "I wish I had been drunk instead of he. He does so take it to heart, poor old gentleman!"

"He has lost his self-esteem, Tom," replied I. "It should be a warning to you. Come, get your oar to pass."

"Well, some people be fashioned one way and some another. I've been tipsy more than once, and I never lost anything but my reason, and that came back as soon as the grog left my head. I can't understand that fretting about having had a glass too much. I only frets when I can't get enough. Well, of all the noses I ever saw, his bests them by chalks; I did so want to laugh at it, but I knew it would pain him."

"It was very kind of you, Tom, to hold your tongue, and I thank you very much."

"And yet that old dad of mine swears I've got no fellow-feeling, which I consider a very undutiful thing for him to say. What's the reason, Jacob, that sons be always cleverer than their fathers?"

"I didn't know that was the case, Tom."

"But it is so *now*, if it wasn't in *olden time*. The proverb says, 'Young people *think* old people to be fools, but old people *know* young people to be fools.' We must alter that, for I says, 'Old people *think* young people to be fools, but young people *know* old people to be fools.'"

"Have it your own way, Tom, that will do, rewed of all."

We tossed in our oars, made the boat fast, and gained the deck, where old Tom still remained at the helm. "Well,"

111

said he, " Jacob, I never thought I should be glad to see the old gentleman clear of the lighter, but I was—devilish glad ; he was like a load on my conscience this morning ; he was trusted to my charge by Mr. Drummond, and I had no right to persuade him to make a fool of himself. But, however, what's done can't be helped, as you say sometimes, and it's no use crying ; still it was a pity, for he be for all the world like a child. There's a fancy kind of lass in that wherry, crossing our bows ; look at the streamers from her top-gallant.

> ' Come o'er the sea,
> Maiden, to me,
> Mine through sunshine, storm, and snows.
> Seasons may roll,
> But the true soul
> Burns the same wherever it goes.
> Then come o'er the sea,
> Maiden, with me.' "

"See you hanged first, you underpinned old hulk !" replied the female in the boat, which was then close under our bows. " Well, that be civil, for sartain," said old Tom, laughing.

CHAPTER XV

I am unshipped for a short time, in order to record shipments and engross invoices—Form a new acquaintance, what is called in the world "a warm man," though he passed the best part of his life among icebergs, and one whole night within the ribs of death—His wife works hard at gentility.

WE arrived at Sheerness the next morning, landed the bricks, which were for the Government buildings, and returned in ballast to the wharf. My first inquiry was for the Domine, but he had not yet returned ; and Mr. Drummond further informed me that he had been obliged to send away his under clerk, and wished me to supply his place until he could procure another. The lighter therefore took in her cargo, and sailed without me, which was of no consequence, as my apprenticeship still went on. I now lived with Mr. Drummond as one of his own family, and wanted for nothing. His continual kindness to me made me strive all I could to please him by diligence and attention, and I soon became very expert at accounts, and, as he said, very useful. The advantages to me, I hardly need observe, were considerable, and I gained information every day. Still, although I was glad to be of any use to Mr. Drummond, the confinement to the desk was irksome, and I anxiously looked for the arrival of the new clerk to take my place, and leave me free to join the lighter. Mr. Drummond did not appear to me to be in any hurry; indeed, I believe that he would have retained me altogether, had he not perceived that I still wished to be on the river.

"At all events, Jacob, I shall keep you here until you are master of your work; it will be useful to you hereafter," he said to me one day, "and you do not gain much by sailing up and down the river."

This was true; and I also derived much advantage from the evenings spent with Mrs. Drummond, who was a very sensible, good woman, and would make me read aloud to her and little Sarah as they sat at their needle. I had no idea, until I was employed posting up the books, that Mr. Drummond's concern was so extensive, or that there was so much capital employed in the business. The Domine returned a few days after my arrival. When we met his nose had resumed its former appearance, and he never brought up the subject of the evening on board of the lighter. I saw him frequently, mostly on Sundays after I had been to church with the family; and half-an-hour, at least, was certain to be dedicated to our reading together one of the classics.

As I was on shore several months I became acquainted with many families, one or two of which were worth noticing. Among the foremost was Captain Turnbull, at least such was his appellation until within the last two months previous to my making his acquaintance, when Mr. Turnbull sent out his cards, *George Turnbull, Esq.* The history of Captain Turnbull was as follows:—He had, with his twin-brother, been hung up at the knocker, and afterwards had been educated at the Foundling Hospital; they had both been apprenticed to the sea; grown up thoroughbred, capital seamen in the Greenland fishery; rose to be mates, then captains; had been very successful; owned part, then the whole of a ship, afterwards two or three ships; and had wound up with handsome fortunes. Captain Turnbull was a married man without a family; his wife, fine in person, vulgar in speech, a would-be fashionable lady, against which fashion Captain T. had for years pleaded poverty; but his brother who had remained a bachelor died, leaving him forty thousand pounds—a fact which could not be concealed. Captain Turnbull had not allowed his wife to be aware of the extent of his own fortune, more from a wish to live quietly and happily, than from any motive of parsimony, for he was liberal to excess; but now he had no further excuse to plead, and Mrs. Turnbull insisted upon fashion. The house they had lived in was given up, and a marine villa on the borders of the Thames, to a certain degree, met the views of both parties; Mrs. Turnbull anticipating dinners and *fêtes,* and the captain content to watch what was going on in the river, and amuse himself in a wherry. They had long been acquaintances of Mr. and Mrs. Drummond, and Captain Turnbull's character was such as always to command the respect of Mr. Drummond, as he was an honest friendly man. Mrs. Turnbull had now set up her carriage, and she was, in her own opinion, a very great personage. She would have cut all her former acquaintance, but on that point the captain was inflexible, particularly as regarded the Drummonds. As far as they were concerned, Mrs. Turnbull gave way, Mrs. Drummond being a ladylike woman, and Mr. Drummond universally respected as a man of talent and information. Captain, or rather Mr. Turnbull, was a constant visitor at our house, and very partial to me. He used to scold Mr. Drummond for keeping me so close to my desk, and would often persuade him to give me a couple of hours' run. When this was obtained, he would call a waterman, throw him a crown, and tell him to get out of his wherry as fast as he could. We then embarked, and amused ourselves pulling up and down the river, while Mrs. Turnbull, dressed in the extremity of the fashion, rode out in the carriage, and left her cards in every direction.

One day Mr. Turnbull called upon the Drummonds, and asked them to dine with him on the following Saturday; they accepted the invitation. "By-the-bye," said he, " I've got what my wife calls a *remind*. in my pocket;" and he pulled out of his coat-pocket a large card, "with Mr. and Mrs. Turnbull's compliments," &c., which card had been doubled in two by his sitting down upon it shortly after he came in. Mr. Turnbull straightened it again as well as he could, and laid it on the table. " And, Jacob," said he, " you'll come too. You don't want a remind ; but if you do, my wife will send you one."

I replied " that I wanted no remind for a good dinner."

" No, I dare say not, my boy ; but recollect that you come an hour or two before the dinner-hour to help me ; there's so much fuss with one thing or another that I'm left in the lurch. And as for trusting the keys of the spirit-room to that long-togged rascal of a butler, I'll see him harpooned first ; so do you come and help me, Jacob."

This having been promised, he asked Mr. Drummond to lend me for an hour or so, as he wished to take a row up the river. This was also consented to ; we embarked and pulled away for Kew Bridge. Mr. Turnbull was as good a hand at a yarn as old Tom, and many were the adventures he narrated to me of what had taken place during the vicissitudes of his life, more especially when he was employed in the Greenland fishery. He related an accident that morning, which particularly bore upon the marvellous, although I do not believe that he was at all guilty of indulging in a traveller's license.

" Jacob," said he, " I recollect once when I was very near eaten alive by foxes, and that in a very singular manner. I was then mate of a Greenland ship. We had been on the fishing ground for three months, and had twelve fish on board. Finding we were doing well, we fixed our ice-anchors upon a very large iceberg, drifting up and down with it, and taking fish as we fell in with them. One morning we had just cast loose the carcase of a fish which we had cut up, when the man in the crow's nest, on the look-out for another ' fall,' cried out that a large polar bear and her cub were swimming over to the iceberg, against the side of which, and about half a mile from us, the carcase of a whale was beating. As we had nothing to do seven of us immediately started in chase ; we had intended to have gone after the foxes, which had gathered there also in hundreds, to prey upon the dead whale. It was then quite calm. We soon came up with the bear, who at first was for making off ; but as the cub could not get on over the rough ice as well as the old one, she at last turned round at bay. We shot the cub to make sure of her, and it did make sure of the dam not leaving us till either she or we perished in the conflict. I never shall forget her moaning over the cub as it lay bleeding on the ice, while we fired bullet after bullet into her. At last she turned round, gave a roar and a gnashing snarl, which you might have heard a mile, and with her eyes flashing fire darted upon us. We received her in a body, all close together, with our lances to her breast; but she was so large and strong that she beat us all back, and two of us fell. Fortunately the others held their ground, and as she was then on end, three bullets were put into her chest, which brought her down. I never saw so large a beast in my life. I don't wish to make her out larger than she really was, but I have seen many a bullock at Smithfield which would not weigh two-thirds of her. Well, after that we had some trouble in despatching her; and while we were so employed, the wind blew up in gusts from the northward, and the snow fell heavy. The men were for returning to the ship immediately, which certainly was the wisest thing for us all to do; but I thought that the snowstorm would blow over in a short time, and not wishing to lose so fine a skin, resolved to remain and flay the beast; for I knew that if left there a few hours, as the foxes could not get hold of the carcase of the whale, which had not grounded, they would soon finish the bear and cub, and the skins be worth nothing. Well, the other men went back to the ship, and as it was, the snowstorm came on so thick that they lost their way, and would never have found her, if it was not that the bell was kept tolling for a guide to them. I soon found that I had done a very foolish thing; instead of the storm blowing over, the snow came down thicker and thicker; and before I had taken a quarter of the skin off I was becoming cold and numbed, and then I was unable to gain the ship, and with every prospect of being frozen to death before the storm was over. At last, I knew what was my only chance. I had flayed all the belly of the bear, but had not cut her open. I ripped her up, tore out all her inside, and then contrived to get into her body, where I lay, and having closed up the entrance hole, was warm and comfortable, for the animal heat had not yet been extinguished. This manœuvre, no doubt, saved my life; and I have heard that the French soldiers did the same in their unfortunate Russian campaign, killing their horses, and getting inside to protect themselves from the dreadful weather. Well, Jacob, I had not lain more than half-an-hour, when I knew by sundry jerks and tugs at my new-invented hurricane-house that the foxes were busy—and so they were, sure enough. There must have been hundreds of them, for they were at work in all directions, and some pushed their sharp noses into the opening where I had crept in; but I contrived to get out my knife and saw their noses across whenever they touched me, otherwise I should have been eaten up in a very short time. There were so many of them, and they were so ravenous, that they soon got through the bear's thick skin, and were tearing away at the flesh. Now I was not so much afraid of their eating me, as I thought that if I jumped up and discovered myself they would have all fled. No saying, though, two or three hundred ravenous devils take courage when together; but I was afraid that they would devour my covering from the weather, and then I should perish with the cold; and I also was afraid of having pieces nipped out of me, which would of course oblige me to quit my retreat. At last, daylight was made through the upper part of the carcase, and I was only protected by the ribs of the animal, between which every now and then their noses dived and nipped my sealskin jacket. I was just thinking of shouting to frighten them away, when I heard the report of half-a-dozen muskets, and some of the bullets struck the carcase, but fortunately did not hit me. I immediately hallooed as loud as I could, and the men hearing me, ceased firing. They had fired at the foxes, little thinking that I was inside of the bear. I crawled out; the storm was over, and the men of the ship had come back to look for me. My brother, who was also a mate on board of the vessel, who had not been with the first party, had joined them in the search, but with little hopes of finding me alive. He hugged me in his arms covered as I was with blood, as soon as he saw me. He's dead now, poor fellow! That's the story, Jacob."

"Thank you, sir," replied I; but perceiving that the memory of his brother affected him, I did not speak again for a few minutes. We then resumed our conversation, and pulling back with the tide, landed at the wharf.

On the day of the dinner-party, I went up to Mr. Turnbull's at three o'clock as he had proposed. I found the house in a bustle; Mr. and Mrs. Turnbull, with the butler and footman in the dining-room, debating as to the propriety of this and that being placed here and there, both servants giving their opinion, and arguing on a footing of equality, contradicting and insisting, Mr. Turnbull occasionally throwing in a word, and each time snubbed by his wife, although the servants dare not take any liberty with him. "Do, pray, Mr. Turnbull, leave *h*us to settle these matters. Get *h*up your wine; that is your department. Leave the room, Mr. Turnbull, *h*if you please. Mortimer and I know what we are about, without your *h*interference."

"Oh! by the Lord, I don't wish to interfere; but I wish you and your servants not to be squabbling, that's all. If they gave me half the cheek——"

"Do, pray, Mr. Turnbull, leave the room, and allow me to regulate my own 'ousehold."

"Come, Jacob, we'll go down into the cellar," said Mr. Turnbull; and accordingly we went.

I assisted Mr. Turnbull in his department as much as I could, but he grumbled very much. "I can't bear all this nonsense, all this finery and foolery. Everything comes up cold, everything is out of reach. The table's so long, and so covered with uneatables that my wife is hardly within hail; and, by jingo, with her the servants are masters. Not with me, at all events; for if they spoke to me as they do to Mrs. Turnbull, I would kick them out of the house. However, Jacob, there's no help for it. All one asks for is quiet; and I must put up with all this sometimes, or I should have no quiet from one year's end to another. When a woman will have her way, there's no stopping her; you know the old verse—

'A man's a fool who strives by force or skill
To stem the torrent of a woman's will;
For if she will, she will, you may depend on't,
And if she won't, she won't—and there's an end on't.'

Now let's go up into my room, and we will chat while I wash my hands."

As soon as Mr. Turnbull was dressed we went down into the drawing-room, which was crowded with tables, loaded with every variety of ornamental articles. "Now this is what my wife calls fashionable. One might as well be steering through an ice floe as try to come to an anchor here without running foul of something. It's *hard a port* or *hard a starboard* every minute; and if your coat-tail *jibes*, away goes something, and whatever it is that smashes, Mrs. T. always swears it was the most valuable thing in the room. I'm like a bull in a china-shop. One comfort is that I never come in here except when there's company. Indeed, I'm not allowed, thank God. Sit on a chair, Jacob, one of those spider-like French things, for my wife won't allow *blacks*, as she calls them, to come to an anchor upon her sky-blue silk sofas. How stupid to have furniture that one's not to make use of! Give me comfort; but it appears that's not to be bought for money."

CHAPTER XVI

High life above stairs, a little below the mark—Fashion, French, vertu, and all that.

SIX o'clock was now near at hand, and Mrs. Turnbull entered the drawing-room in full dress. She certainly was a very handsome woman, and had every appearance of being fashionable; but it was her language which exposed her. She was like the peacock. As long as she was silent you could but admire the plumage, but her voice spoilt all. "Now, Mr. Turnbull," said she, "I wish to *h*explain to you that there are certain *h*improprieties in your behaviour which I cannot put *h*up with, particularly that *h*of talking about when you were before the mast."

"Well, my dear, is that anything to be ashamed of?"

"Yes, Mr. Turnbull, that *h*is—one *h*always sinks them ere particulars in fashionable society. To *wirt*uperate in company an't pleasant, and Hi've thought of a plan which may *h*act as an *h*impediment to your vulgarity. Recollect, Mr. T., when-*h*ever I say that Hi've an 'eadache, it's to be a sign for you to 'old your tongue; and, Mr. T., *h*oblige me by wearing kid gloves all the evening."

"What, at dinner-time, my dear?"

"Yes, at dinner-time; your 'ands are not fit to be touched."

"Well, I recollect when you thought otherwise."

"When, Mr. T.? 'ave I not often told you so?"

"Yes, lately; but I referred to the time when one Poll Bacon of Wapping took my hand for better or for worse."

"Really, Mr. T., you quite shock me. My name was Mary, and the Bacons are a good old *H*inglish name. You 'ave their *h*arms quartered on the carriage in right o' me. That's something, I can tell you."

119

"Something I had to pay for pretty smartly, at all events."

"The payment, Mr. T., was on account of granting *h*arms to you, who never '*ad* any."

"And never wished for them. What do I care for such stuff?"

"And when you did choose, Mr. Turnbull, you might have consulted me, instead of making yourself the laughing-stock of Sir George Naylor and all the 'eralds. Who but a madman would have chosen three harpoons *saluims*, and three barrels *couchants*, with a spouting whale for a crest? Just to point out to everybody what should *h*ever be buried in *h*oblivion; and then your beastly motto—which I would have changed —'*Blubber for ever!*' Blubber indeed! *h*enough to make *h*any one *blubber* for ever."

"Well, the heralds told me they were just what I ought to have chosen, and very apposite, as they termed it."

"They took your money and laughed at you. Two pair of griffins, a lion, half-a-dozen leopards, and a hand with a dagger, wouldn't 'ave cost a farthing more. But what can you *h*expect from an '*og*?

"But if I was *cured*, I should be what you were—*Bacon.*"

"I won't demean myself, Mr. Turnbull."

"That's right, my dear, don't; there's no curing you. Recollect the motto you chose in preference to mine."

"Well, and a very proper one: '*Too much familiarity breeds contempt ;*' is it not so, Master Faithful?"

"Yes, madam, it was one of our copies at school."

"I beg your pardon, sir, it was my *h*own *h*invention."

Rap tap, rap tap tap, tap tap.

"Mr. and Mrs. Peters, of Petercumb Hall," announced the butler. Enter Mrs. Peters first, a very diminutive lady, and followed by Mr. Peters, six feet four inches without his shoes, deduct for stooping and curved shoulders seven inches. Mr. Peters had retired from the Stock Exchange with a competence, bought a place, named it Petercumb Hall, and set up his carriage. Another knock, and Mr. and Mrs. Drummond were announced. Compliments exchanged, and a pastile lighted by Mrs. Turnbull.

"Well, Drummond," said Mr. Turnbull, "what are coals worth now?"

"Mr. Turnbull, I've got such an 'eadache."

This was of course a matter of condolence from all present, and a stopper upon Mr. Turnbull's tongue.

Another sounding rap, and a pause, "Monsieur and Madame de Tagliabue coming up." Enter Monsieur and Madame de Tagliabue. The former, a dapper little Frenchman, with a neat pair of legs, and stomach as round as a pea. Madame sailing in like an outward-bound East Indiaman, with studding sails below and aloft; so large in her dimensions, that her husband might be compared to the pilot-boat plying about her stern.

"Charmée de vous voir, Madame Tom-bulle. Vous vous portez bien; n'est-ce pas?"

"*Ve*," replied Mrs. Turnbull, who thus exhausted her knowledge of the French language; while the monsieur tried in vain, first on one side and then on the other, to get from under the lee of his wife and make his bow. This was not accomplished until the lady had taken possession of a sofa, which she filled most comfortably.

Who these people were, and how they lived, I never could find out; they came in a fly from Brentford.

Another announcement. "My Lord Babbleton and Mr. Smith coming up."

"Mr. T., pray go down and receive his lordship. (There are two wax candles for you to light on the hall table, and you must walk up with them before his lordship," said the lady aside.)

"I'll be hanged if I do," replied Mr. Turnbull; "let the servants light him."

"Oh, Mr. T., I've such an 'eadache!"

"So you may have," replied Mr. T., sitting down doggedly.

In the meantime Mr. Smith entered, leading Lord Babbleton, a boy of twelve or thirteen years old, shy, awkward, red-haired, and ugly, to whom Mr. Smith was tutor. Mrs. T. had found out Mr. Smith, who was residing near Brentford with his charge, and made his acquaintance on purpose to have a lord on her visiting list, and to her delight the leader had not forgotten to bring his bear with him. Mrs. Turnbull sprang to the door to receive them, making a prepared courtesy to the aristocratical cub, and then shaking him respectfully by the hand. "Won't your lordship walk to the fire? Isn't your lordship cold? I hope your lordship's sty is better in your lordship's eye. Allow me to introduce to your lordship's notice, Mr. and Mrs. Peters—Madame and Mounsheer

Tagleebue—Mr. and Mrs. Drummond, the Right Honourable
Lord Viscount Babbleton." As for Mr. Turnbull and myself,
we were left out as unworthy of introduction. "We are ready
for dinner, Mr. Turnbull."

"Snobbs, get dinner dressed up," said Mr. T. to the butler.
"Oh, Mr. T., I've such an 'eadache."

This last headache was produced by Mr. T. forgetting himself and calling the butler by his real name, which was
Snobbs; but Mrs. Turnbull had resolved that it should be
changed to *Mortimer*—or rather, to *Mr.* Mortimer, as the
household were directed to call him, on pain of expulsion.

Dinner was announced. Madame Tagliabue, upon what
pretence I know not, was considered the first lady in the
room, and Lord Babbleton was requested by Mrs. Turnbull
to hand her down. Madame rose, took his lordship's hand,
and led him away. Before they were out of the room, his
lordship had disappeared among the ample folds of madame's
gown, and was seen no more until she pulled him out on their
arrival at the dinner-table. At last we were all arranged according to Mrs. Turnbull's wishes, although there were several chops
and changes about, until the order of precedence could be
correctly observed. A French cook had been sent for by Mrs.
Turnbull; and not being mistress of the language, she had a
card with the names of the dishes to refresh her memory, Mr.
Mortimer having informed her that such was always the custom
among great people, who, not ordering their own dinners, of
course they could not tell what there was to eat.

"Mrs. Turnbull, what soup have you there?"

"*Consummy* soup, my lord. Will your lordship *make use*
of that or of this here, which is *o'juss.*"

His lordship stared; made no answer; looked foolish; and
Mr. Mortimer placed some soup before him.

"Lord Babbleton takes soup," said Mr. Smith pompously;
and the little right honourable supped soup, much to Mrs.
Turnbull's satisfaction.

"Madame, do you soup? or do you fish?"

"Merci, no soup—*poisson.*"

"Don't be afraid, madame, we've a French cook; you won't
be *poisoned* here," replied Mrs. Turnbull, rather annoyed.

"Comment, my chère madame, I meant to say dat I prefer
de cod."

122

"Mr. T., some fish for madame. John, a clean plate for Lord Babbleton. What will your lordship condescend to make use of now?" (Mrs. Turnbull thought the phrase, *make use*, excessively refined and elegant.)

"Ah! madame, votre cuisine est superbe," exclaimed Monsieur Tagliabue, tucking the corner of his napkin into his buttonhole, and making preparations for well filling his little rotundity.

"*Ve*," replied Mrs. Turnbull. "Mrs. Peters, will you try the dish next Mr. Turnbull? What is it?" (looking at her card) "*Agno roty*. Will you, my lord? If your lordship has not yet got into your French—it means roast quarter of lamb."

"His lordship is very partial to lamb," said Mr. Smith, with emphasis.

"Mr. Turnbull, some lamb for Lord Babbleton, and for Mr. Peters."

"Directly, my dear. Well, Jacob, you see, when I was first mate——"

"Dear! Mr. Turnbull—I've such an 'eadache. Do, pray, cut the lamb. (*Aside.*) Mr. Mortimer, do go and whisper to Mr. Turnbull that I beg he will put on his gloves."

"Mrs. Peters, you're doing nothing. Mr. Mortimer, 'and round the side dishes, and let John serve out the champagne.

"Mrs. Peters, there's a *wolley went o' weaters*. Will you make use of some? Mrs. Drummond, will you try the dish coming round? It is—let me see—it is *chew farsy*. My Lord Babbleton, I 'ope the lamb's to your liking? Monshere Tagliabue—William, give monshere a clean plate. What will you take next?"

"Vraiment, madame, tout est excellent, superbe! Je voudrais embrasser votre cuisinier—c'est un artiste comme il n'y a pas?"

"*Ve*," replied Mrs. Turnbull.

The first course was removed, and the second, after some delay, made its appearance. In the interim, Mr. Mortimer handed round one or two varieties of wine.

"Drummond, will you take a glass of wine with me?" said Mr. Turnbull. "I hate your sour French wines. Will you take Madeira? I was on shore at Madeira once, for a few hours, when I was before the mast, in the——"

"Mr. Turnbull, I've such an 'eadache," cried his lady, in

an angry tone. "My lord, will you take some of this?—it is
—a *ding dong o' turf*—a turkey, my lord."

"His lordship is fond of turkey," said Mr. Smith dicta-
torially.

Monsieur Tagliabue, who sat on the other side of Mrs. T.,
found that the turkey was in request—it was some time before he could help himself.

"C'est superbe!" said monsieur, thrusting a truffle into
his mouth. "Apparemment, madame n'aime pas la cuisine
Anglaise?"

"*Ve*," replied Mrs. Turnbull. "Madame, what will you be
*h*assisted to?" continued Mrs. T.

"Tout de bon, madame."

"*Ve*; what are those by you, Mr. Peters?" inquired the
lady, in continuation.

"I really cannot exactly say, but they are fritters of some
sort."

"Let me see—hoh! bidet du poms. Madame, will you
eat some *bidet du poms?*"

"Comment, madame, je ne vous comprends pas——"

"*Ve.*"

"Monsieur Tagliabue, expliquez donc;" said the foreign
lady, red as a quarter of beef.

"Permettez," said monsieur, looking at the card. "Ah, c'est
impossible, ma chère," continued he, laughing. "Madame
Turnbull se trompait ; elle voudrait dire *Beignets de pommes.*"

"Vous trouvez notre langue fort difficile, n'est-ce pas?"
continued madame, who recovered her good-humour, and
smiled graciously at Mrs. T.

"*Ve*," replied Mrs. Turnbull, who perceived that she had
made some mistake, and was anxiously awaiting the issue of
the dialogue. It had, however, the effect of checking Mrs. T.,
who said little more during the dinner and dessert.

At last the ladies rose from the dessert, and left the gentlemen at the table ; but we were not permitted to remain long,
before coffee was announced, and we went upstairs. A
variety of French liqueurs were handed about, and praised
by most of the company. Mr. Turnbull, however, ordered a
glass of brandy, as a *settler.*

"Oh, Mr. Turnbull, I've such an 'eadache!"

After that the party became very dull. Lord Babbleton

fell asleep on the sofa. Mr. Peters walked round the room, admiring the pictures and asking the names of the masters.

"I really quite forget; but Mr. Drummond, you are a judge of paintings, I hear. Who do you think this is painted by?" said the lady, pointing to a very inferior performance. "I am not quite sure; but I think it is Van—Van *Daub*."

"I should think so too," replied Mr. Drummond drily; "we have a great many pictures in England, by the same hand."

The French gentleman proposed *écarté*, but no one knew how to play it except his wife; who sat down with him to pass away the time. The ladies sauntered about the room, looking at the contents of the tables, Mrs. Peters occasionally talking of Petercumb Hall; Mr. Smith played at patience in one corner; while Mr. Turnbull and Mr. Drummond sat in another in close conversation; and the lady of the house divided her attentions, running from one to the other, and requesting them not to talk so loud as to awake the Right Honourable Lord Viscount Babbleton. At last the vehicles were announced, and the fashionable party broke up, much to the satisfaction of everybody, and to none more than myself.

I ought to observe that all the peculiar absurdities I have narrated did not strike me so much at the time; but it was an event to me to dine out, and the scene was well impressed upon my memory. After what occurred to me in my after life, and when I became better able to judge of fashionable pretensions, the whole was vividly brought back to my recollection.

CHAPTER XVII

The Tomkinses' fête champêtre and fête dansante—Lights among the gooseberry-bushes—All went off well, excepting the lights, they went out—A winding up that had nearly proved a catastrophe—Old Tom proves that danger makes friends by a yarn, young Tom by a fact.

I REMAINED with Mr. Drummond about eight months, when at last the new clerk made his appearance—a little fat fellow, about twenty, with a face as round as a full moon, thick lips, and red cheeks. During this time I frequently had the pleasure of meeting with old and young Tom, who appeared very anxious that I should rejoin them; and I must say that I was equally willing to return to the lighter. Still Mr. Drummond put his veto on it, and Mrs. Drummond was also constantly pointing out the very desirable situation I might have on shore as a clerk in the office; but I could not bear it—seated nearly the whole day—perched up on a high stool —turning over Dr., contra Cr., and only occasionally interrupted by the head clerk, with his attempt to make rhymes. When the new clerk came, I expected my release, but I was disappointed. Mr. Drummond discovered him to be so awkward, and the head clerk declared that the time was so busy, that he could not spare me. This was true; Mr. Drummond had just come to a final arrangement, which had been some time pending, by which he purchased a wharf and large warehouses, with a house adjoining in Lower Thames Street—a very large concern, for which he had paid a considerable sum of money. What with the valuations, winding up of the Brentford concern on the old account, &c., there was much to do, and I toiled at the desk until the removal took place; and when the family were removed I was still detained, as there was no warehouseman to superintend the unloading and hoisting up of goods. Mr. Tomkins, the head clerk, who had been many years a faithful servant to Mr. Drummond, was admitted as a partner, and had charge of the Brentford wharf, a species of promotion which he and his wife resolved to celebrate with a party. After a long debate, it was resolved that they should give a ball, and Mrs. Tomkins exerted all her taste and ingenuity on the occasion. My friend Tomkins lived at a short distance from the premises, in a small house, surrounded with half an acre of garden, chiefly filled with gooseberry-bushes, and perambulated by means of four straight gravel walks. Mr. and Mrs. Drummond were invited, and accepted the invitation, which was considered by the Tomkinses as a great mark of condescension. As a specimen of Mr. Tomkins' poetical talents, I shall give his invitation to Mr. Drummond, written in the very best German text—

> " Mr. and Mrs. T—
> Sincerely hope to see
> Mr. and Mrs. Drum-
> Mond, to a very hum-
> Ble party that they in-
> Tend to ask their kin

JACOB FAITHFUL

> To, on the Saturday
> Of the week ensuing;
> When fiddles they will play,
> And other things be doing.

"*Belle Vue House.*"

To which *jeu d'esprit* Mr. Drummond answered with a pencil on a card—

> "Mr. and Mrs. Drum-
> Mond intend to come."

"Here, give Tomkins that, Jacob; it will please him better than any formal acceptation." Mr. and Mrs. Turnbull were also asked; the former accepted, but the latter indignantly refused.

When I arrived with Mr. and Mrs. Drummond many of the company were there; the garden was what they called illuminated, that is, every gooseberry-bush had one variegated lamp suspended about the centre; and, as Mr. Tomkins told me afterwards, the lamps were red and yellow according to the fruit they bore. It was a cold, frosty, clear night, and the lamps twinkled as brightly among the bare boughs of the gooseberry trees as the stars did in the heavens. The company in general were quite charmed with the novelty. "Quite a *minor Wauxhall*," cried one lady, whose exuberance of fat kept her warm enough to allow her to stare about in the open air. The entrance porch had a dozen little lamps, backed with laurel twigs, and looked very imposing. Mrs. Tomkins received her company upon the steps outside, that she might have the pleasure of hearing their praises of her external arrangements; still it was freezing, and she shivered not a little. The drawing-room, fourteen feet by ten, was fitted up as a ball-room, with two fiddlers and a fifer sitting in a corner, and a country dance was performing when we arrived. Over the mantelpiece was a square of laurel twigs, inclosing as a frame, this couplet, from the poetical brain of the master of the house, cut out in red paper, and bespangled with blue and yellow tinsel—

> "Here we are to dance so gay,
> While the fiddlers play away."

Other appropriate distiches, which I have now forgotten, were framed in the same way on each of the other compartments. But the dining-room was the *chef d'œuvre*. It was formed into

a bower, with evergreens, and on the evergreen boughs were
stuck real apples and oranges in all directions, so that you could
help yourself.

"Vell, I do declare, this is a paradise!" exclaimed the fat
lady, who entered with me.

"In all but one thing, ma'am," replied Mr. Turnbull, who,
with his coat off, was squeezing lemons for the punch, "there's
no *forbidden* fruit. You may help yourself."

This bon-mot was repeated by Mr. Tomkins to the end of
his existence, not only for its own sake, but because it gave
him an opportunity of entering into a detail of the whole *fête*—
the first he had ever given in his life. "Ah, Jacob, my boy,
glad to see you—come and help here—they'll soon be thirsty,
I'll warrant," said Mr. Turnbull, who was in his glory. The
company, although not so very select, were very happy; they
danced, drank punch, laughed, and danced again; and it was
not till a late hour, long after Mr. and Mrs. Drummond had
gone home, that I quitted the "festive scene;" Mr. Turnbull,
who walked away with me, declaring that it was worth a dozen
of his party, although they had not such grand people as Mrs.
Tagliabue, or the Right Honourable Lord Viscount Babbleton.
I thought so too, every one was happy, and every one at their
ease; and I do believe they would have stayed much longer,
but the musicians took so much punch that one fiddler broke
his fiddle, the other broke his head in going down the steps
into the garden, and the fifer swore he could blow no longer;
so, as there was an end to the music, clogs, pattens, and lanterns
were called for, the shawls were brought out of the kitchen,
and every one went away. Nothing could go off better. Mrs.
Tomkins had a cold and rheumatism the next day; but that
was not surprising, a *minor Wauxhall* not being seasonable in
the month of December.

A week after this party, we removed to Thames Street, and
I performed the duty of warehouseman. Our quantity of
lighters was now much increased, and employed in carrying
dry goods, &c. One morning old Tom came under the crane
to discharge his lighter, and wishing to see me, when the fall
had been overhauled down, to heave up the casks with which
the lighter was laden, instead of hooking on a cask, held on by
his hands, crying, "Hoist away," intending to be hoisted himself up to the door of the warehouse where I was presiding.

Now, there was nothing unusual in this whim of old Tom's, but still he ran a very narrow chance, in consequence of an extra whim of young Tom's, who, as soon as his father was suspended in the air, caught hold of his two wooden stumps, to be hoisted up also; and as he caught hold of them, standing on tiptoe, they both swung clear of the lighter, which could not approach to within five feet of the buildings. The crane was on the third story of the warehouse, and very high up. "Tom, Tom, you rascal, what the devil are you about?" cried the old man, when he felt the weight of his son's body hanging to him.

"Going up along with you, father—hope we shall go to heaven the same way."

"More likely to go to the devil together, you little fool; I never can bear your weight. Hoist away, there, quick."

Hearing the voices, I looked out of the door, and perceiving their situation ordered the men to hoist as fast as they could, before old Tom's strength should be exhausted; but it was a compound movement crane, and we could not hoist very fast, although we could hoist very great weights. At last, as they were wound up higher and higher, old Tom's strength was going fast. "O Tom, Tom, what must be done? I can't—I can't hold on but a little longer, and we shall be both dashed to pieces. My poor boy!"

"Well then, I'll let go, father; it was all my folly, and I'll be the sufferer."

"Let go!" cried old Tom; "no, no, Tom—don't let go, my boy; I'll try a little longer. Don't let go, my dear boy—don't let go!"

"Well, father, how much longer can you hold on?"

"A little—very little longer," replied the old man, struggling.

"Well, hold fast now," cried young Tom, who, raising his head above his arms, with a great exertion shifted one of his hands to his father's thigh, then the other; raising himself as before, he then caught at the seat of his father's trousers with his teeth; old Tom groaned, for his son had taken hold of more than the garments; he then shifted his hands round his father's body; from thence he gained the collar of his jacket; from the collar he climbed on his father's shoulders; from thence he seized hold of the fall above, and relieved his father of the weight. "Now, father, are you all right?" cried Tom, panting as he clung to the fall above him.

"I can't hold on ten seconds more, Tom—no longer—my clutch is going now."

"Hang on by your eyelids, father, if you love me," cried young Tom, in agony.

It was indeed an awful moment; they were now at least sixty feet above the lighter, suspended in the air. The men whirled round the wheel, and I had at last the pleasure of hauling them both in on the floor of the warehouse; the old man so exhausted that he could not speak for more than a minute. Young Tom, as soon as all was safe, laughed immoderately. Old Tom sat upright. "It might have been no laughing matter, Mr. Tom," said he, looking at his son.

"What's done can't be helped, father, as Jacob says. After all, you're more frightened than hurt."

"I don't know that, you young scamp," replied the old man, putting his hand behind him, and rubbing softly; "you've bit a piece clean out of my *starn*. Now, let this be a warning to you, Tom. Jacob, my boy, couldn't you say that I've met with an *accident*, and get a drop of something from Mr. Drummond?"

I thought, after his last observation, I might honestly say that he had met with an accident, and I soon returned with a glass of brandy, which old Tom was drinking off, when his son interrupted him for a share.

"You know, father, I shared the danger."

"Yes, Tom, I know you did," replied the father; "but this was sent to me on account of my *accident*, and as I had that all to myself, I shall have all this too."

"But, father, you ought to give me a drop, if it were only to *take the taste out of my mouth.*"

"Your own flesh and blood, Tom," replied his father, emptying his glass.

"Well, I always heard it was quite unnatural not to like your own flesh and blood," replied Tom; "but I see now that there may be reasons for it."

"Be content, Tom," replied his father, putting down the glass; "we're now just square. You've had your *raw nip*, and I've had mine."

Mr. Drummond now came up, and asked what had been the matter. "Nothing, sir—only an accident. Tom and I had a bit of a *hoist.*"

As this last word had a double meaning, Mr. Drummond
130

thought that a cask had surged, when coming out of the lighter, and struck them down. He desired old Tom to be more careful, and walked away, while we proceeded to unload the lighter. The new clerk was a very heavy, simple young man, plodding and attentive certainly, but he had no other merit; he was sent into the lighter to take the marks and numbers of the casks as they were hoisted up, and soon became a butt to young Tom, who gave him the wrong marks and numbers of all the casks to his interrogations.

"What's that, boy?" cried the pudding-faced fellow, with his pencil in one hand, and his book in the other.

"Pea soup, 13," replied Tom; "ladies' bonnets, 24. Now, then, master, chalk again, pipe-clay for sodgers, 3; red herrings, 26." All of which were carefully noted down by Mr. Gubbins, who, when the lighter was cleared, took the memoranda to Mr. Drummond.

Fortunately we had checked the number of the casks as they were received above—their contents were flour. Mr. Drummond sent for young Tom, and asked him how he dared play such a trick. Tom replied very boldly, "that it was meant as a good lesson to the young man, that in future he did his own work, and did not trust to others." To this Mr. Drummond agreed, and Master Tom was dismissed without punishment.

As the men had all gone to dinner, I went down into the lighter to have a little chat with my old shipmates. "Well, Jacob," said old Tom, "Tom's not a bit wiser than he was before—two scrapes to-day already."

"Well, father, if I prove my folly by getting into scrapes, I prove my wit by getting out of them."

"Yes, that may be true, Tom; but suppose we had both come down with a run, what would you have thought then?"

"I suspect, father, that I should have been past all thinking."

"I once did see a thing of that kind happen," said old Tom, calling to mind former scenes in his life; "and I'll tell you a yarn about it, boys, because they say danger makes friends." Tom and I sat down by old Tom, who narrated as follows:—

"When I was captain of the maintop in the *La Minerve*, forty-four gun frigate, we were the smartest ship up the Mediterranean; and many's the exercise we were the means of giving to other ships' companies, because they could not beat

us—no, not even hold a candle to us. In both fore and maintop
we had eight-and-twenty as smart chaps as ever put their foot
to a rattling, or slid down by an a'ter backstay. Now, the two
captains of the foretop were both prime young men, active as
monkeys, and bold as lions. One was named Tom Herbert,
from North Shields, a dark, good-looking chap, with teeth as
white as a nigger's, and a merry chap he was, always a showing
them. The other man was a cockney chap. Your Lunnuners
arn't often good seamen, but when they are seamen, there's no
better; they never allow any one to show them the way, that's
for sartain, being naturally spunky sort of chaps, and full of
tricks and fun. This fellow's name was Bill Wiggins, and
between him and Herbert there was always a jealousy who
should be the smartest man. I've seen both of them run out
on the yard in fine weather without holding on nothing, seize
the lift, and down to their station, haul up the earing, in no
time; up by the lift again, and down on deck, by the backstay,
before half the men had time to get clear of the top. In fact,
they often risked their lives in bad weather when there was no
occasion for it, that one might outdo the other. Now, this was
all very well, and a good example to the other men. The
captain and officers appeared to like these contests for superiority, but it ended in their hating each other, and not being
even on speaking terms, which, as the two captains of the top,
was bad. They had quarrelled often, and fought five times,
neither proving the better man; either both done up, or parted
by the master-at-arms, and reported to the first lieutenant, so
that at last they were not so much countenanced by the officers,
and were out of favour with the captain, who threatened to dis-
rate them both if ever they fought again. We were cruising off
the Gulf of Lions, where sometimes it blows hard enough to
blow the devil's horns off, though the gales never last very long.
We were under close-reefed fore and maintop sails, storm staysail and trysail, when there was a fresh hand at the bellows,
and the captain desired the officers of the watch, just before
dinner, to take in the foretop sail. Not to disturb the watch
below, the maintop men were ordered up forward to help the
foretop men of the watch, and I was of course aloft, ready to
lie out on the lee yard-arm, when Wiggins, who had the watch
below, came up in the top, not liking that Herbert should be at
work in such weather, without he being there too.

132

"'Tom,' says Wiggins to me, 'I'll take the yard-arm.'

"'Very well,' says I, 'with all my heart, then I'll look to the bunt.'

"Just at that time there came on a squall with rain, which almost blinded us; the sail was taken in very neatly, the clew-lines, chock-a-block, bunt-lines and leech-lines well up, reef-tackles overhauled, rolling tackles taut, and all as it should be. The men lied out on the yard, the squall wore worse and worse, but they were handing in the leech of the sail, when snap went one bunt-line, then the other; the sail flapped and flagged, till away went the leech-lines, and the men clung to the yards for their lives, for the sail mastered them, and they could do nothing. At last it split like thunder, buffeting the men on the yard-arms, till they were almost senseless, until to windward it wore away into long coach-whips, and the whole of the canvas left was at the lee yard-arm. The men laid in at last with great difficulty, quite worn-out by fatigue and clinging for their existence; all but Wiggins, who was barred by the sail to leeward from making his footing good on the horse; and there he was, poor fellow, completely in irons, and so beaten by the canvas that he could hardly be said to be sensible. It takes a long while to tell all this, but it wasn't the work of a minute. At last he made an attempt to get up by the lift, but was struck down, and would have been hurled overboard if it hadn't been that his leg fell over the horse, and there he was head downwards, hanging over a raging sea, ready to swallow him up as soon as he dropped into it. As every one expected he would be beat off before any assistance could be given, you may guess that it was an awful moment to those below who were looking up at him, watching for his fall and the roll of the ship, to see if he fell clear into the sea or was dashed to pieces in the fore-chains.

"I couldn't bear to see a fellow-creature, and good seaman in the bargain, in that state, and although the captain dare not *order* any one to help him, yet there were one or two midshipmen hastening up the fore-rigging, with the intent, I have no doubt, of trying to save him (for midshipmen don't value their lives at a quid of tobacco), so I seizes the studding sail halyards, and runs up the topmast rigging, intending to go down by the lift, and pass a bowling knot round him before he fell, when who should I meet at the cross-trees but Tom

Herbert, who snatched the rope out of my hand, bawling to me through the gale, 'This is my business, Tom.'

"Down he goes by the lift, the remainder of the canvas flapped over him, and I seed no more until I heard a cry from all below, and away went Herbert and Wiggins, both together, flying to leeward just as the ship was taking her recovery to windward. Fortunately they both fell clear of the ship about two feet, not more, and as their fall was expected they had prepared below. A master's mate, of the name of Simmonds, and the captain of the forecastle, both went overboard in bowling knots, with another in their hands, and in a minute or two they were all four on board again; but Herbert and Wiggins were both senseless, and a long while coming to again. Well, now, what do you think was the upshot of it? Why, they were the best friends in the world ever afterwards, and would have died for one another; and if one had a glass of grog from the officers for any little job, instead of touching his forelock and drinking it off to the officer's health, he always took it out of the gunroom, that he might give half of it to the other. So, d'ye see, my boys, as I said before I began my yarn, that danger makes friends.

> "'Tis said we vent'rous die hard,
>   When we leave the shore,
> Our friends may mourn, lest we return
>   To bless their sight no more.
> But this is all a notion
>   Bold Jack can't understand;
> Some die upon the ocean,
>   And some die upon dry land.'"

"And if we had tumbled, father, we should have just died betwixt and between, not water enough to float us. It would have been *woolez woos parlez woos*, plump in the mud, as you say sometimes."

"Why, yes, Tom. I've a notion that I should have been planted too deep ever to have struck," replied the old man, looking at his wooden stumps.

"Why, yes, father, *legs* are *legs*, when you tumble into six foot of mud. How you would have *dibbled* down, if your *daddles* hadn't held on."

"Well then, Tom, recollect that you never *sell* your father for a *lark* again."

Tom laughed, and catching at the word, although used in a different sense, sung—

"'Just like a *lark*, high poised in air.'

And so were you, father, only you didn't sing as he does, and you didn't leave your young one below in the nest."

"Ay, it is the young uns which prevent the old ones from rising in the world—that's very true, Tom. Holloa, who have we got here? My service to you, at all events."

CHAPTER XVIII

The art of hard lying made easy, though I am made very un-easy by hard lying—I send my ruler as a missive, to let the parties concerned know that I am a rebel to tyrannical rule —I am arraigned, tried, and condemned without a hearing —What I lose in speech is made up in feeling, the whole wound up with magnanimous resolves, and a little sobbing.

IT was the captain of the American schooner, from out of which we were then taking the casks of flour.

"We've no sarvice in our country, I've a notion, my old bobtail roarer," said he. "When do you come alongside of my schooner, for t'other lading, with this raft of yours? Not to-night, I guess."

"Well, you've guessed right this time," replied old Tom ; "we shall lie on the mud till to-morrow morning, with your permission."

"Yes, for all the world like a Louisiana alligator. You take things coolly, I've a notion, in the old country. I don't want to be hanging head and starn in this little bit of a river of your'n. I must be back to New York afore fever time."

"She be a pretty craft, that little thing of yours," observed old Tom ; "how long may she take to make the run?"

"How long? I expect in just no time ; and she'd go as fast again, only she won't wait for the breeze to come up with her."

"Why don't you heave-to for it?" said young Tom.

"Lose too much time, I guess. I've been chased by an

easterly wind all the way from your Land's End to our Narrows, and it never could overhaul me."

"And I presume the porpoises give it up in despair, don't they?" replied old Tom, with a leer; "and yet I've seen the creatures playing across the bows of an English frigate at her speed, and laughing at her."

"They never play their tricks with me, old snapper; if they do I cuts them in halves, and astarn they go, head part floating on one side, and tail part on the other."

"But don't they join together again when they meet in your wake?" inquired Tom.

"Shouldn't wonder," replied the American captain.

"Pray, captain, what may be that vessel they talk so much about at New York?" Old Tom referred to the first steam vessel, whose qualities at that time had been tried, and an exaggerated report of which had been copied from the American papers. "That ship, or whatever she may be, that sails without masts, yards or canvas; it is quite above my comprehension."

"Old country heads can't take it in. I'll tell you what— she goes slick through the water, ahead or astarn, broadside on, or up or down, or any way; and all you have to do is to poke the fire and warm your fingers; and the more you poke the faster she goes, 'gainst wind and tide."

"Well, I must see that to believe it though," replied old Tom.

"No fear of a capsize, I calculate. My little craft did upset with me one night, in a pretty considerable heavy *gal;* but she's smart, and came up again on the other side in a moment, all right as before. Never should have known any thing about it, if the man at the wheel had not found his jacket wet, and the men below had a round turn in all the clues of their hammocks."

"After that round turn, you may belay," cried young Tom, laughing.

"Yes, but don't let's have a stopper over all, Tom," replied his father. "I consider all this excessively divarting. Pray, captain, does everything else go fast in the new country."

"Everything with us clean slick, I guess."

"What sort of horses have you in America?" inquired I.

"Our Kentucky horses, I've a notion, would surprise you. They're almighty goers; at a trot, beat a NW. *gal* of wind,

I once took an Englishman with me in a gig up Allibama country, and he says, 'What's this great churchyard we are passing through?' 'And stranger,' says I, 'I calculate it's nothing but the milestones we are passing so slick.' But I once had a horse, who, I expect, was a deal quicker than that. I once seed a flash of lightning chase him for half-an-hour round the clearance, and I guess it couldn't catch him. But I can't wait no longer. I expect you'll come alongside to-morrow afore meridian.'

"Ay, ay, master," replied old Tom, tuning up—

> " '"Twas post meridian, half-past four,
> By signal I from Nancy parted,
> At five she lingered on the shore,
> With uplift eyes and broken-hearted.' "

"I calculate you are no fool of a screamer," said the American, shoving off his boat from the barge, and pulling to his vessel.

"And I calculate you're no fool of a liar," said young Tom, laughing.

"Well, so he is; but I do like a good lie, Jacob, there's some fun in it. But what the devil does the fellow mean by calling a gale of wind—*a gal?*"

"I don't know," replied Tom, "unless for the same reason that we call a girl *a blowing.*"

Our conversation was here interrupted by Mr. Hodgson, the new head-clerk, of whom I have hitherto said nothing. He came into the establishment in the place of Mr. Tomkins when we quitted the Battersea wharf, and had taken an evident dislike to me, which appeared to increase every day, as Mr. Drummond gave me fresh marks of his approbation. "You, Faithful, come out of that barge directly, and go to your desk. I will have no eye-servers under me. Come out, sir, directly."

"I say, Mr. Quilldriver," cried old Tom, "do you mean for to say that Jacob is an eye-sarver?"

"Yes, I do; and want none of your impertinence, or I'll unship you, you old blackguard."

"Well then, for the first part of your story, my sarvice to you, and you *lies;* and as for the second, that remains to be proved."

Mr. Hodgson's temper was not softened by this reply of

old Tom. My blood was also up, for I had borne much already; and young Tom was bursting with impatience to take my part. He walked carelessly by the head-clerk, saying to me as he passed by, "Why, I thought, Jacob, you were 'prentice to the river; but it seems that you're bound to the counting-house. How long do you mean to sarve?"

"I don't know," replied I, as I walked away sulkily; "but I wish I was out of my time."

"Very well, sir, I shall report your behaviour to Mr. Drummond. I'll make him know your tricks."

"Tricks! you won't let him know his tricks. His duty is to take his trick at the wheel," replied old Tom; "not to be brought up at your cheating tricks at the desk."

"Cheating tricks, you old scoundrel, what do you mean by that?" replied Mr. Hodgson, in a rage.

"My father means *ledger*demain, I suppose," replied young Tom.

This repartee, from a quarter so little expected, sent off the head-clerk more wroth than ever.

"You seemed to hit him hard there, Tom," said his father; "but I can't say that I understand how."

"You've had me taught to read and write, father," replied young Tom; "and a'ter that, a lad may teach himself everything. I pick up every day, here and there; and I never see a thing or a word that I don't understand but I find out the meaning when I can. I picked up that hard word at Bartlemy fair."

"And very hard you hit him with it."

"Who wouldn't to serve a friend? But mark my words, father, this won't last long. There's a squall blowing up, and Jacob, quiet as he seems to be, will show his teeth ere long."

Tom was correct in his surmise. I had not taken my seat at my desk more than a minute, when Mr. Hodgson entered, and commenced a tirade of abuse, which my pride could no longer allow me to submit to. An invoice, perfectly correct and well written, which I had nearly completed, he snatched from before me, tore into fragments, and ordered me to write it over again. Indignant at this treatment I refused, and throwing down my pen looked him determinedly in the face. Irritated at this defiance, he caught up a directory, and threw it at my head. No longer able to command myself, I seized a ruler and returned the salute. It was whizzing through the air as Mr. Drummond entered the room; and he was just in time to witness Mr. Hodgson struck on the forehead and felled to the ground, while I remained with my arm raised, standing upon the cross-bar of my high stool, my face glowing with passion.

Appearances were certainly against me. Assistance was summoned, and the head-clerk removed to his chamber, during all which time I remained seated on my stool before the desk, my breast heaving with tumultuous feelings. How long I remained there I cannot say, it might have been two hours; feelings long dormant had been aroused and whirled round and round in a continual cycle in my feverish brain. I should have remained probably much longer in this state of absorption, had I not been summoned to attend Mr. Drummond. It appeared that in the meantime Mr. Hodgson had come to his own senses, and had given his own version of the fracas, which had been, to an unjustifiable degree, corroborated by the stupid young clerk, who was no friend of mine, and who sought favour with his principal. I walked up to the drawing-room, where I found Mr. and Mrs. Drummond and little Sarah, whose eyes were red with crying. I entered without any feeling of alarm, my breast was too full of indignation. Mrs. Drummond looked grave and mournful; Mr. Drummond severe.

"Jacob Faithful, I have sent for you to tell you, that in consequence of your disgraceful conduct to my senior clerk, you can no longer remain under my roof. It appears that what I have been a witness to this day has been but a sequel to behaviour equally improper and impertinent; that so far from having, as I thought, done your duty, you have constantly neglected it; and that the association you have formed with that drunken old man and his insolent son, has led you into this folly. You may say that it was not your wish to remain on shore, and that you preferred being on the river. At your age, it is too often the case that young people consult their wishes rather than their interests; and it is well for them if they find those who are older, and wish them well, to decide for them. I had hoped to have been able to place you in a more respectable situation in society than was my original intention when you were thrown upon me a destitute orphan, but I now perceive my error. You have proved yourself not only deceitful but ungrateful."

"I have not," interrupted I calmly.

"You have. I have been a witness myself to your impropriety of conduct, which it appears has long been concealed from me ; but no more of that. I bound you apprentice to the river, and you must now follow up your apprenticeship ; but expect nothing farther from me. You must now work your own way up in the world, and I trust that you will reform and do well. You may return to the lighter until I can procure you a situation in another craft, for I consider it my duty to remove you from the influence of those who have led you astray, and with the old man and his son you shall not remain. I have one thing more to say. You have been in my counting-house for some months, and you are now about to be thrown upon the world. There are ten pounds for your services" (and Mr. Drummond laid the money on the table). "You may also recollect that I have some money belonging to you, which has been laid by until you shall be out of your apprenticeship. I consider it my duty still to retain that money for you ; as soon as your apprenticeship is expired, you may demand it, and it shall be made over to you. I trust, sincerely trust, Jacob, that the severe lesson you are now about to receive will bring you to a sense of what is right, and that you will forget the evil counsel you have received from your late companions. Do not attempt to justify yourself, it is useless." Mr. Drummond then rose, and left the room.

I should have replied, had it not been for this last sentence of Mr. Drummond's, which again roused the feelings of indignation, which in their presence had been gradually giving way to softer emotions. I therefore stood still, and firmly met the glance of Mr. Drummond as he passed me. My looks were construed into hardness of heart.

It appeared that Mr. Drummond had left the room by previous arrangement, that he might not be supposed to be moved from his purpose, and that Mrs. Drummond was then to have talked to me, and to have ascertained how far there was a chance of my pleading guilty, and begging for a mitigation of my sentence ; but the firm composure of innocence was mistaken for defiance, and the blood mounting to my forehead from a feeling of injustice—of injustice from those I loved and venerated—perhaps the most poignant feeling in existence to a sensitive and generous mind—was falsely estimated as proceeding from impetuous and disgraceful sources. Mrs. Drummond looked upon me with a mournful face, sighed, and said nothing; little Sarah watching me with her large black eyes, as if she would read my inmost soul.

"Have you nothing to say, Jacob," at last observed Mrs. Drummond, "that I can tell Mr. Drummond when his anger is not so great?"

"Nothing, madam," replied I, "except that I'll try to forgive him."

This reply was offensive even to the mild Mrs. Drummond. She rose from her chair. "Come, Sarah," said she; and she walked out of the room, wishing me, in a kind, soft voice, a "Good-bye, Jacob," as she passed me.

My eye swam with tears. I tried to return the salutation, but I was too much choked by my feelings; I could not speak, and my silence was again looked upon as contumacy and ingratitude. Little Sarah still remained—she had not obeyed her mother's injunctions to follow her. She was now nearly fourteen years old, and I had known her as a companion and a friend for five years. During the last six months that I had resided in the house, we had become more intimately acquainted. I joined her in the evening in all her pursuits, and Mr. and Mrs. Drummond appeared to take a pleasure in our intimacy. I loved her as a dear sister; my love was based on gratitude. I had never forgotten her kindness to me when I first came under her father's roof, and a long acquaintance with the sweetness of her disposition had rendered the attachment so firm, that I felt I could have died for her. But I never knew the full extent of the feeling until now that I was about to leave her, perhaps for ever. My heart sank when Mr. Drummond left the room; a bitter pang passed through it as the form of Mrs. Drummond vanished from my sight; but now was to be the bitterest of all. I felt it, and I remained with the handle of the door in my hand, gasping for breath—blinded with the tears that coursed each other rapidly down my cheeks. I remained a minute in this state, when I felt that Sarah touched my other listless hand.

"Jacob!" she would have said, but before half my name was out she burst into tears, and sobbed on my shoulder. My heart was too much surcharged not to take the infection —my grief found vent, and I mingled my sobs with those of

141

the affectionate girl. When we were more composed, I recounted to her all that had passed, and one, at least, in the world acknowledged that I had been treated unjustly. I had but just finished, when the servant interrupted us with a message to Sarah, that her mother desired her presence. She threw herself into my arms, and bade me farewell. When I released her, she hastened to obey her mother, but perceiving the money still upon the table, she pointed to it. "Your money, Jacob!"

"No, Sarah, I will not accept it. I would accept of anything from those who treat me kindly, and feel more and more grateful to them; but that I will not accept—I cannot, and you must not let it be left here. Say that I could not take it."

Sarah would have remonstrated, but perceiving that I was firm, and at the same time, perhaps, entering into my feelings, she again bade me farewell, and hastened away.

The reader may easily imagine that I did not put off my departure. I hastened to pack up my clothes, and in less than ten minutes after Sarah had quitted me I was on board the lighter, with old Tom and his son, who were then going to supper. They knew a part of what had happened, and I narrated the rest.

"Well," replied old Tom, after I had finished my story, "I don't know that I have done you any harm, Jacob, and I'm sorry that Mr. Drummond should suppose so. I'm fond of a drop, that's true; but I appeals to you, whether I ever force it on you—and whether I don't check that boy as much as I can; but then, d'ye see, although I preach, I don't practise, that's the worst of it. And I know I've to answer for making Tom so fond of grog; and though I never says anything about it, I often think to myself, that if Tom should chance to be pressed some of these days, and be punished for being in liquor, he'll think of his old father, and curse him in his heart, when he eyes the cat flourishing round before it strikes."

"I'll curse the cat, father, or the boatswain's mate, or the officer who complained of me, or the captain who flogs me, or my own folly, but I'll be hanged if ever I curse you, who have been so kind to me," replied Tom, taking his father's hand.

"Well, we must hope for the best, my dear boy," replied old Tom; "but, Jacob, you've not had fair play, that's sartain. It's very true that master did take you as an orphan, and help you to an education; but that's no reason why he should take away your free will, and after binding you 'prentice to the river, perch you up on a high stool, and grind your nose down to the desk. If so be he was so kind to you only to make you a slave, why, then, there was no kindness at all in my opinion; and as for punishment without hearing what a man has to say in his own defence—there's ne'er a Tartar in the sarvice, but would allow a man to speak before he orders him to strip. I recollect a story about that in the sarvice, but I'm in no humour to spin a yarn now. Now, you see, Jacob, Master Drummond has done a great deal for you, and now he has undone a great deal. I can't pretend to balance the account, but it does appear to me that you don't owe him much; for what thanks is there if you take a vessel in tow, and then cast her off half-way, when she most needs your assistance? But what hurts me most is his saying that you shan't stay in the lighter with us; if you had, you shouldn't have wanted, as long as pay and pension are forthcoming. Never mind—Tom, my boy, bring out the bottle—hang care; it killed the cat."

The grog did not, however, bring back old Tom's spirits. The evening passed heavily, and we retired to our beds at a seasonable hour, as we were to drop down to the schooner early the next morning. That night I did not close my eyes. I ran over in my mind all that had occurred, and indignation took full possession of my soul. My whole life passed in review before me. I travelled back to my former days—to the time which had been almost obliterated from my memory, when I had navigated the barge with my father. Again was the scene of his and my mother's death presented to my view; again I saw him disappear, and the column of black smoke ascend to the sky. The Domine, the matron, Marables, and Fleming, the scene in the cabin—all passed in rapid succession. I felt that I had done my duty, and that I had been unjustly treated; my head ached with tumultuous and long-suppressed feelings. Reader, I stated that when I was first taken in hand by Mr. Drummond I was a savage, although a docile one, to be reclaimed by kindness, and kindness only. You may have been surprised at the rapid change which took place in a few years; that change was produced by kindness. The conduct of Mr. Drummond, of his amiable wife and daughter, had been all kindness; the Domine and the worthy old matron had proved equally beneficent. Marables had been kind; and although now and then, as in the case of the usher at the school, and Fleming on board the lighter, I had received injuries, still these were but trifling checks to the uninterrupted series of kindness with which I had been treated by everybody. Thus was my nature rapidly formed by a system of kindness assisted by education; and had this been followed up, in a few years my new character would have been firmly established. But the blow was now struck, injustice roused up the latent feelings of my nature, and when I rose the next morning I was changed. I do not mean to say that all that precept and education had done for me was overthrown; but if not overthrown, it was so shaken to the base, so rent from the summit to the foundation, that at the slightest impulse in a wrong direction, it would have fallen in and left nothing but a mixed chaos of ruined prospects. If anything could hold it together, it was the kindness and affection of Sarah, to which I would again and again return in my revolving thoughts, as the only and bright star to be discovered in my clouded horizon.

How dangerous, how foolish, how presumptuous it is in adults to suppose that they can read the thoughts and the feelings of those of a tender age! How often has this presumption on their part been the ruin of a young mind, which, if truly estimated and duly fostered, would have blossomed and produced good fruit! The blush of honest indignation is as dark as the blush of guilt, and the paleness of concentrated courage as marked as that of fear; the firmness of conscious innocence is but too often mistaken as the effrontery of hardened vice, and the tears springing from a source of injury, the tongue tied from the oppression of a wounded heart, the trembling and agitation of the little frame convulsed with emotion, have often and often been ascribed by prejudging and self-opinionated witnesses to the very opposite passions to those which have produced them. Youth should never be judged harshly, and even when judged correctly, should it be in an evil course, may always be reclaimed;—those who decide otherwise, and leave it to drift about the world, have to answer for the castaway.

CHAPTER XIX

*The breach widened—I turn sportsman, poacher, and desperado
—Some excellent notions propounded of common law upon
common rights—The common-keeper uncommonly savage—I
warn him off—He prophesies that we shall both come to the
gallows—Some men are prophets in their own country—The
man right after all.*

HOLLO! in the lighter there—I say, you *lighter boy!*" were
the words I heard, as I was pacing the deck of the vessel in
deep cogitation. Tom and his father were both in the cabin;
there could be no doubt but that they were addressed to
me. I looked up and perceived the grinning, stupid, sneer-
ing face of the young clerk, Gubbins. "Why don't you
answer when you're called to, heh?" continued the numskull.
"You're wanted up here! come up directly."

"Who wants me?" replied I, reddening with anger.

"What's that to you? Do you mean to obey *my* order
or not?"

"No, I do not," replied I. "I'm not under the orders of such a
fool, thank God; and if you come within my reach, I'll try if I
can't break your head, thick as it is, as well as your master's."

The lout disappeared, and I continued to pace up and
down.

As I afterwards discovered, the message was from Mrs.
Drummond, who requested to speak to me. Sarah had communicated the real facts of my case, and Mrs. Drummond had
been convinced that what I had said was correct. She had
talked with her husband; she pointed out to him that my
conduct under Mr. Tomkins had been so exemplary that
there must have been some reason for so sudden a change.
Sarah had gone down into the counting-house, and obtained
the invoice which the senior clerk had torn up. The correctness of it established the fact of one part of my assertions, and
that nothing but malice could have warranted its having been
destroyed. Mr. Drummond felt more than he chose to acknowledge; he was now aware that he had been too precipitate; even my having refused the money assumed a different
appearance; he was puzzled and mortified. Few people like

to acknowledge that they have been in error. Mr. Drummond therefore left his wife to examine further into the matter, and gave her permission to send for me. The message given, and the results of it, have been stated. The answer returned was, that I would not come, and that I had threatened to break the clerk's head as well as that of Mr. Drummond; for although the scoundrel knew very well that in making use of the word "master" I referred to the senior clerk, he thought it proper to substitute that of Mr. Drummond. The effect of this reply may easily be imagined. Sarah was astonished, Mrs. Drummond shocked, and Mr. Drummond was almost pleased to find that he could not have been in the wrong. Thus was the breach made even wider than before, and all communication broken off. Much depends in this world upon messages being correctly given.

In half-an-hour we had hauled out of the tier and dropped down to the American schooner, to take out a cargo of flour, which old Tom had directions to land at the Battersea wharf; so that I was, for the time, removed from the site of my misfortune. I cannot say that I felt happy, but I certainly felt glad that I was away. I was reckless to a degree that was insupportable. I had a heavy load on my mind which I could not shake off—a prey upon my spirits—a disgust at almost everything. How well do I recollect with what different feelings I looked upon the few books which Mr. Drummond and the Domine had given me to amuse my leisure hours. I turned from them with contempt, and thought I would never open them again. I felt as if all ties on shore were now cut off, and that I was again wedded to the Thames; my ideas, my wishes, extended no farther, and I surveyed the river, and its busy scene, as I did before I had been taken away from it, as if all my energies, all my prospects, were in future to be bounded by its shores. In the course of four-and-twenty hours a revulsion had taken place, which again put me on the confines of barbarism.

My barge mates were equally dull as I was; they were too partial to me, and had too much kindness of heart, not to feel my situation, and anger at the injustice with which I had been treated. Employment, however, for a time relieved our melancholy thoughts. Our cargo was on board of the lighter, and we were again tiding it through the bridges.

We dropped our anchor above Putney Bridge a little after twelve o'clock, and young Tom, with the wish of amusing me, proposed that we should go on shore and walk. "Ah! do, my lads, do—it will do you good, Jacob; no use moping here a whole tide. I'll take care of the barkey. Mind you make the boat well fast, and take the sculls into the public-house there. I'll have the supper under weigh when you come back, and then we'll have a night on't. It's a poor heart that never rejoices; and Tom, take a bottle on shore, get it filled, and bring it off with you. Here's the money. But I say, Tom, honour bright."

"Honour bright, father;" and to do Tom justice, he always kept his promise, especially after the word had passed of "honour bright." Had there been gallons of spirits under his charge he would not have tasted a drop after that pledge.

"Haul up the boat, Jacob, quick," said Tom, as his father went into the cabin to fetch an empty bottle. Tom hastened down below forward, and brought up an old gun, which he put under the stern-sheets before his father came out on the deck. We then received the bottle from him, and Tom called out for the dog Tommy.

"Why, you're not going to take the dog. What's the use of that? I want him here to keep watch with me," said old Tom.

"Pooh! father; why can't you let the poor devil have a run on shore? He wants to eat grass, I'm sure, for I watched him this day or two. We shall be back before dark."

"Well, well, just as you please, Tom." Tommy jumped into the boat, and away we went.

"And now, Tom, what are you after?" said I, as soon as we were ten yards from the lighter.

"A'ter, Jacob? going to have a little shooting on Wimbledon Common; but father can't bear to see a gun in my hand, because I once shot my old mother. I did pepper her, sure enough; her old flannel petticoat was full of shot, but it was so thick that it saved her. Are you anything of a shot?"

"Never fired a gun in my life."

"Well then, we'll fire in turns, and toss up, if you like, for first shot."

We landed, carried the sculls up to the public-house, and left the bottle to be filled, and then, with Tommy bounding before us, and throwing about his bushy tail with delight, ascended

147

Putney Hill, and arrived at the Green Man public-house, at the corner of Wimbledon Common. " I wonder where green men are to be found ? " observed Tom, laughing ; " I suppose they live in the same country with the blue dogs my father speaks about sometimes. Now then, it's time to load."

The bowl of a tobacco-pipe full of powder was then inserted, with an equal dose of shot, and all being ready we were soon among the furze. A halfpenny decided it was my first shot, and fate further decided that a water-wagtail should be the mark. I took good aim, as I thought, at least I took sufficient time, for I followed him with the muzzle of the gun for three or four minutes at least, as he ran to and fro ; at last I fired. Tommy barked with delight, and the bird flew away. " I think I must have hit it," said I ; " I saw it wag its tail."

" More proof of a miss than a hit," replied Tom. " Had you hit it, he'd never have wagged his tail again."

" Never mind," said I, " better luck next time."

Tom then knocked a blackbird off a furze bush, and loading the gun handed it to me. I was more successful than before ; a cock-sparrow three yards distant yielded to the prowess of my arm, and I never felt more happy in my life than in this first successful attempt at murder.

Gaily did we trudge over the common, sometimes falling in with gravel-pits half full of water, at others bogs and swampy plains, which obliged us to make a circuit. The gun was fired again and again ; but our game-bag did not fill very fast. However, if we were not quite so well pleased when we missed as when we hit, Tommy was, every shot being followed up with a dozen bounds, and half a minute's barking. At last we began to feel tired, and agreed to repose a while in a cluster of furze bushes. We sat down, pulled out our game, and spread it in a row before us. It consisted of two sparrows, one greenfinch, one blackbird, and three tomtits. All of a sudden we heard a rustling in the furze, and then a loud squeal. It was the dog, who, scenting something, had forced his way into the bush, and had caught a hare, which having been wounded in the loins by some other sportsman, had dragged itself there to die. In a minute we had taken possession of it, much to the annoyance of Tommy, who seemed to consider that there was no co-partnership in the concern, and would not surrender his prize until after sundry admonitory kicks. When we had fairly

beaten him off we were in an esctasy of delight. We laid the
animal out between us, and were admiring it from the ear to
the tip of his tail, when we were suddenly saluted with a
voice close to us. "Oh, you blamed young poachers, so I've
caught you, have I?" We looked up and beheld the common-
keeper. "Come—come along with me; we've a nice clink at
Wandsworth to lock you up in. I've been looking arter you
some time. Hand your gun here."

"I should rather think not," replied I. "The gun belongs
to us and not to you," and I caught up the gun and presented
the muzzle at him.

"What! do you mean to commit murder? Why, you young
villains!"

"Do you want to commit a robbery?" retorted I fiercely;
"because if you do, I mean to commit murder. Then I shoot
him, Tom."

"No, Jacob, no; you mustn't shoot men," replied Tom,
who perceived that I was in a humour to keep my word with
the common-keeper. "Indeed you can't," continued he,
whispering to me; "the gun's not loaded."

"Do you mean to refuse to give me up your gun?" repeated
the man.

"Yes, I do," replied I, cocking the lock; "so keep off."

"Oh! you young reprobates—you'll come to the gallows
before long, that's certain. Then, do you refuse to come
with me?"

"I should rather think we do," replied I.

"You refuse, do you? Recollect I've caught you in the
fact, poaching, with a dead hare in your possession."

"Well, it's no use crying about it. What's done can't be
helped," replied I.

"Don't you know that all the game, and all the turf, and
all the bog, and all the gravel, and all the furze on this
common belong to the Right Honourable Earl Spencer?"

"And all the blackbirds, and all the greenfinches, and all
the sparrows, and all the tomtits too, I suppose?" replied I

"To be sure they do—and I'm common-keeper. Now you'll
give me up that hare immediately."

"Look you," replied Tom, "we didn't kill that hare, the
dog caught it, and it is his property. We shan't interfere in the
matter. If Tommy chooses to let you have it, well and good.

149

Here, Tommy, this here gentleman says" (and Tom pointed to the keeper) "that this hare" (and Tom pointed to the hare) "is not yours; now will you 'watch it,' or let him have it?"

At the word "watch it," Tommy laid down with his forepaws over the hare, and showing a formidable set of ivories, looked fiercely at the man, and growled.

"You see what he says; now you may do as you please," continued Tom, addressing the man.

"Yes—very well—you'll come to the gallows, I see that; but I'll just go and fetch a half-dozen men to help me, and then we'll have you both in gaol."

"Then be smart," replied I, jumping up and levelling the gun. Tommy jumped up also to fly at the man, but Tom caught him by the neck and restrained him. The common-keeper took to his heels, and as soon as he was out of gun-shot turned round, shook his fist, and then hastened away to obtain the reinforcement he desired.

"I wish the gun had been loaded," said I.

"Why, Jacob, what's come over you? Would you have fired at him? The man is only doing his duty—we have no business here."

"I think otherwise," replied I. "A hare on a common is as much mine as Lord Spencer's. A common belongs to everybody."

"That's my opinion too; but nevertheless if he gets hold of us he'll have us in gaol; and therefore I propose we make off as fast as we can in the opposite way to which he is gone."

We started accordingly, and as the keeper proceeded in the direction of Wandsworth, we took the other direction; but it so happened, that on turning round after a quarter of an hour's walk, we perceived the man coming back with three or four others. "We must run for it," cried Tom, "and then hide ourselves." After ten minutes' hard run we descended into a hollow and swampy place; looking round to see if they could perceive us, and finding that they were not in sight, we plunged into a thick cluster of furze bushes, which completely concealed us. Tommy followed us, and there we lay. "Now they never will find us," said Tom, "if I can only keep the dog quiet. Lie down, Tommy. Watch, and lie down." The dog appeared to understand what was required; he lay between us perfectly still.

We had remained there about half-an-hour when we heard voices. I motioned to Tom to give me the powder to load the gun, but he refused. The voices came nearer; Tommy gave a low growl. Tom held his mouth with his hands. At last they were close to the bushes, and we heard the common-keeper say, "They never went over the hill, that's for certain, the little wagrants; they can't be far off—they must be down in the hollow. Come along."

"But I'm blessed if I'm not up to my knees in the bog," cried one of the men; "I'll not go further down, dang me if I do."

"Well then, let's try the side of the bog," replied the keeper, "I'll show you the way." And the voices retreated, fortunately for us, for there had been a continual struggle between us and the dog for the last minute, I holding his forepaws, and Tom jamming up his mouth. We were now all quiet again, but dare not leave our hiding-place.

We remained there for half-an-hour, when it became nearly dark, and the sky, which had been quite clear when we set out, clouded over. Tom put up his head, looked all round, and perceiving nobody proposed that we should return as fast as we could; to which I agreed. But we were scarcely clear of the furze in which we had been concealed, when a heavy fall of snow commenced, which, with the darkness, prevented us from distinguishing our way. Every minute the snowstorm increased, the wind rose, and hurled the flakes into our faces until we were blinded. Still we made good way against it, and expected every minute to be on the road, after which our task would be easy. On we walked in silence, I carrying the gun, Tom with the hare over his shoulder, and Tommy at our heels. For upwards of an hour did we tread our way through the furze, but could find no road. Above us all was dark as pitch; the wind howled; our clothes were loaded with snow; and we began to feel no inconsiderable degree of fatigue.

At last, quite tired out, we stopped. "Tom," said I, "I'm sure we've not kept a straight course. The wind was on our starboard side, and our clothes were flaked with snow on that side, and now you see we've got it in our quarter. What the devil shall we do?"

"We must go on till we fall in with something, at all events," replied Tom.

"And I expect that will be a gravel-pit," replied I; "but

never mind, 'better luck next time.' I only wish I had that rascal of a common-keeper here. Suppose we turn back again, and keep the wind on the starboard side of us as before; we must pitch upon something at last."

We did so, but our difficulties increased every moment; we floundered in the bogs, we tumbled over the stumps of the cut furze, and had I not caught hold of Tom as he was sliding down, he would have been at the bottom of a gravel-pit. This obliged us to alter our course, and we proceeded for a quarter of an hour in another direction, until, worn-out with cold and fatigue, we began to despair.

"This will never do, Tom," said I, as the wind rose and roared with double fury. "I think we had better get into the furze, and wait till the storm is over."

Tom's teeth chattered with the cold; but before he could reply, they chattered with fear. We heard a loud scream over-head. "What was that?" cried he. I confess that I was as much alarmed as Tom. The scream was repeated, and it had an unearthly sound. It was no human voice—it was between a scream and a creak. Again it was repeated, and carried along with the gale. I mustered up courage sufficient to look up to where the sound proceeded from, but the darkness was so intense, and the snow blinded me so completely, that I could see nothing. Again and again did the dreadful sound ring in our ears, and we remained fixed and motionless with horror; even the dog crouched at our feet trembling. We spoke not a word—neither of us moved; the gun had fallen from my hand; the hare lay at Tom's feet; we held each other's hand in silence, and there we remained for more than a quarter of an hour, every moment more and more sinking under the effects of cold, fatigue, and horror. Fortunately for us, the storm, in which, had it continued much longer, we should in all probability have perished, was by that time over; the snow ceased to fall; the clouds were rolled away to leeward; and a clear sky, bespangled with a thousand twinkling lights, roused us from our state of bodily and mental suffering. The first object which caught my eye was a post within two yards of us. I looked at it, followed it up with my eyes, and to my horror be-held a body suspended and swinging in chains over our heads.

As soon as I recovered from the shock which the first view occasioned, I pointed it out to Tom, who had not yet moved

152

He looked up, started back, and fell over the dog; jumped up again, and burst out into as loud a laugh as his frozen jaws would permit. "It's old Jerry Abershaw," said he, "I know him well, and now I know where we are." This was the case. Abershaw had, about three years before, been hung in chains on Wimbledon Common; and the unearthly sound we had heard was the creaking of the rusty iron as the body was swung to and fro by the gale. "All's right, Jacob," said Tom, looking up at the brilliant sky, and then taking up the hare, "we'll be on the road in five minutes." I shouldered the gun, and off we set. "By the Lord, that rascally common-keeper was right," continued Tom, as we renewed our steps; "he prophesied we should come to the gallows before long, and so we have. Well, this has been a pretty turn-out. Father will be in a precious stew."

"Better luck next time, Tom," replied I, "it's all owing to that turf-and-bog rascal. I wish we had him here."

"Why, what would you do with him?"

"Take down old Abershaw, and hang him up in his place, as sure as my name's Jacob."

CHAPTER XX

Our last adventure not fatal—Take to my grog kindly—Grog makes me a very unkind return—Old Tom at his yarns again —How to put your foot in a mischief, without having a hand in it—Candidates for the cat-o'-nine-tails.

WE soon recovered the road, and in half-an-hour were at Putney Bridge; cold, wet, and tired, but not so bad as when we were stationary under the gallows; the quick walking restored the circulation. Tom went in for the bottle of spirits, while I went for the sculls and carried them down to the boat, which was high and dry, and nearly up to the thwarts with snow. When Tom joined me, he appeared with two bottles under his arms. "I have taken another upon tick, Jacob," said he, "for I'm sure we want it, and so will father say when he hears our story." We launched our boat, and in a couple of minutes were close to the lighter, on the deck of which stood old Tom.

"Boat ahoy! is that you, lads?" cried he.

"Yes, father, all's right," replied Tom, as we laid in our oars.

"Thank God!" replied the old man. "Boys, boys, how

153

you frightened me! where have you been? I thought you had met with some disaster. How have I been peeping through the snowstorm these last two hours, watching for the boat, and I'm as wet as a shag, and as cold as charity. What has been the matter? Did you bring the bottle, Tom?"

"Yes, father, brought two, for we shall want them to-night, if we go without for a week; but we must all get on dry rigging as fast as possible, and then you shall have the story of our cruise."

In a few minutes we had changed our wet clothes and were seated at the cabin table, eating our supper, and narrating our adventures to the old man. Tommy, poor fellow, had his share, and now lay snoring at our feet, as the bottles and pannikins were placed upon the little table.

"Come, Jacob, a drop will do you good," said old Tom, filling me one of the pannikins. "A'ter all, it's much better being snug here in this little cabin, than shivering with fear and cold under old Abershaw's gallows; and Tom, you scamp, if ever you go gunning again, I'll disinherit you."

"What have you got to leave, father, except your wooden leg?" replied Tom. "Yours would be but a *wooden-leg*-acy."

"How do you know but what I can '*post the coal?*'"

"So you will, if I boil a pot o' 'tatoes with your legacy; but it will only be char-coal."

"Well, I believe you are about right, Tom; still, somehow or other, the old woman always picks out a piece or two of gold when I'm rather puzzled how to raise the wind. I never keeps no 'count with her. If I follow my legs before she, I hope the old soul will have saved something; for you know when a man goes to kingdom come his pension goes with him. However, let me only hold on another five years, and then you'll not see her want; will you, Tom?"

"No, father; I'll sell myself to the king, and stand to be shot at, at a shilling a day, and give the old woman half."

"Well, Tom, 'tis but natural for a man to wish to serve his country; so here's to you, my lad, and may you never do worse! Jacob, do you think of going on board of a man-of-war?"

"I'd like to serve my apprenticeship first, and then I don't care how soon."

"Well, my boy, you'll meet more fair play on board of a king's ship, than you have from those on shore."

"I should hope so," replied I bitterly.

"And I hope to see you a man before I die yet, Jacob. I shall very soon be laid up in ordinary—my toes pain me a good deal lately!"

"Your toes!" cried Tom and I, both at once.

"Yes, boys; you may think it odd, but sometimes I feel them just as plain as if they were now on, instead of being long ago in some shark's maw. At nights I has the cramp in them, till it almost makes me halloo out with pain. It's a hard thing when one has lost the sarvice of his legs, that all the feelings should remain. The doctor says as how it's narvous. Come, Jacob, shove in your pannikin. You seem to take it more kindly than you did."

"Yes," replied I, "I begin to like grog now." The *now*, however, might be comprehended within the space of the last twenty-four hours. My depressed spirits were raised with the stimulus, and, for the time, I got rid of the eternal current of thought which pressed upon my brain.

"I wonder what your old gentleman, the Domine, as you call him, thought, after he got on shore again," said old Tom. "He seemed to be mighty cut up. I suppose you'll give him a hail, Jacob?"

"No," replied I, "I shall not go near him, nor any one else, if I can help it; Mr. Drummond may think I wish to make it up again. I've done with the shore. I only wish I knew what is to become of me; for you know I am not to serve in the lighter with you."

"Suppose Tom and I look out for another craft, Jacob? I care nothing for Mr. Drummond. He said t'other day I was a drunken old swab—for which, with my sarvice to him, he lies. A drunken fellow is one who can't, for the soul of him, keep from liquor when he can get it, and who's over-taken before he is aware of it. Now that's not the case with me. I keep sober when there's work to be done; and when I know that everything is safe under hatches, and no fear of nothing, why then I gets drunk like a rational being, with my eyes open—'cause why—'cause I chooses."

"That's exactly my notion of the thing," observed Tom, draining his pannikin, and handing it over to his father for a fresh supply.

"Mind you keep to that notion, Tom, when you gets in the

king's sarvice, that's all; or you'll be sure to have your back
scratched, which I understand is no joke a'ter all. Yet I do
remember once, in a ship I was in, when half-a-dozen fellows
were all fighting who should be flogged."

"Pray give us that yarn, father; but before you begin just
fill my pannikin. I shoved it over half-an-hour ago, just by
way of a hint."

"Well then," said old Tom, pouring out some spirits into
Tom's pannikin, "it was just as follows. It was when the ship
was laying at anchor in Bermuda harbour, that the purser sent
a breaker of spirits on shore, to be taken up to some lady's
house, whom he was very anxious to splice, and I suppose that
he found a glass of grog helped the matter. Now, there were
about twenty of the men who had liberty to go on shore to
stretch their limbs—little else could they do, poor fellows, for
the first lieutenant looked sharp after their kits, to see that they
did not sell any of their rigging; and as for money, we had been
five years without touching a farthing of pay, and I don't suppose there was a matter of threepence among the men before
the mast. However, liberty's liberty a'ter all; and if they
couldn't go ashore and get glorious, rather than not go on shore
at all, they went ashore and kept sober perforce. I do think,
myself, it's a very bad thing to keep the seamen without a farthing
for so long; for you see a man who will be very honest with a
few shillings in his pocket is often tempted to help himself,
just for the sake of getting a glass or two of grog, and the
temptation's very great, that's sartain, 'ticularly in a hot climate,
when the sun scorches you, and the very ground itself is so
heated that you can hardly bear the naked foot to it.[1] But to
go on. The yawl was ordered on shore for the liberty men,
and the purser gives this breaker, which was at least half full,
and I dare say there might be three gallons in it, under my
charge as coxswain, to deliver to madam at the house. Well,
as soon as we landed, I shoulders the breaker, and starts with
it up the hill.

"'What have you there, Tom?' said Bill Short.

"'What I wish I could share with you, Bill,' says I; 'it's

---

[1] This has been corrected; the men have for some time received a
portion of their pay on foreign stations, and this portion has been
greatly increased during Sir James Graham's administration.

some of old Nipcheese's *eights*, that he has sent on shore to bowse his jib up with, with his sweetheart.'

" 'I've seen the madam,' said Holmes to me—for you see all the liberty men were walking up the hill at the same time—'and I'd rather make love to the breaker than to her. She's as fat as an ox, as broad as she's long, built like a Dutch schuyt, and as yellow as a nabob.'

" 'But old Tummings knows what he's about,' said a Scotch lad, of the name of M'Alpine; 'they say she has lots of gold dust, more ducks and ingons, and more inches of water in her tank than any one on the island.'

"You see, boys, Bermuda be a queer sort of place, and water very scarce—all they get there is a godsend, as it comes from heaven; and they look sharp out for the rain, which is collected in large tanks, and an inch or two more of water in the tank is considered a great catch. I've often heard the ladies there talking after a shower—

"'Good-morning, marm. How do you do this fine morning?'

" 'Pretty well, I tank you, marm. Charming shower hab last night.'

"'Yes, so all say; but me not very lucky. Cloud not come over my tank. How many inches of water you get last night, marm?'

" 'I get good seven inches, and I tink a little bit more, which make me very happy.'

" 'Me no so lucky, marm; so help me God, me only get four inches of water in my tank, and dat nothing.'

" 'Well, but I've been yawning again, so now to keep my course. As soon as I came to the house I knocked at the door, and a little black girl opens the jalousies, and put her finger to her thick lips.

" 'No make noise; missy sleep.'

" 'Where am I to put this?'

"'Put down there; by-and-by I come fetch it;' and then she closed the jalousies, for fear her mistress should be woke up, and she get a hiding, poor devil. So I puts the breaker down at the door, and walks back to the boat again. Now, you see these liberty men were all by when I spoke to the girl, and seeing the liquor left with no one to guard it, the temptation was too strong for them. So they looked all about them, and then at one another, and caught one another's meaning by the eye; but they said nothing. 'I'll have no hand in it,' at last

says one, and walked away. ' Nor I,' said another, and walked
away too. At last all of them walked away except eight, and
then Bill Short walks up to the breaker and says—

"'I won't have no *hand* in it either;' but he gave the breaker
a kick, which rolls it away two or three yards from the door.

"' No more will I,' said Holmes, giving the breaker another
kick, which rolled it out in the road. So they all went on,
without having a *hand* in it, sure enough, till they had kicked
the breaker down the hill to the beach. Then they were at
a dead stand, as no one would spile the breaker. At last a
black carpenter came by, and they offered him a glass, if he
would bore a hole with his gimlet, for they were determined
to be able to swear, every one of them, that they had *no hand
in it*. Well, as soon as the hole was bored, one of them
borrowed a couple of little mugs from a black woman who
sold beer, and then they let it run, the black carpenter shoving
one mug under as soon as the other was full, and they drinking
as fast as they could. Before they had half finished, more of
the liberty men came down. I suppose they scented the good
stuff from above as a shark does anything in the water, and
they soon made a finish of it; and when it was all finished,
they were all drunk, and made sail for a cruise, that they
might not be found too near the empty breaker. Well, a
little before sunset I was sent on shore with the boat to fetch
off the liberty men, and the purser takes this opportunity of
going ashore to see his madam, and the first thing he falls
athwart of is his own empty breaker.

"' How's this?' says he; 'didn't you take this breaker up
as I ordered you?'

"' Yes, sir,' replied I, 'I did, and gave it in charge to the
little black thing; but madam was asleep, and the girl did
not allow me to put it inside the door.' At that he began to
storm, and swore that he'd find out the malefactors, as he
termed the liberty men, who had emptied his breaker; and
away he went to the house. As soon as he was gone, we got
hold of the breaker, and made a *bull* of it."

"How did you manage that?" inquired I.

"Why, Jacob, a *bull* means putting a quart or two of water
into a cask which has had spirits in it; and what with the
little that may be left, and what has soaked in the wood, if
you roll it and shake it well, it generally turns out pretty fair

grog. At all events it's always better than nothing. Well, to go on—but suppose we fill up again and take a fresh departure, as this is a tolerable long yarn, and I must wet the threads, or they may chance to break."

Our pannikins, which had been empty, were all replenished, and then old Tom proceeded.

"It was a long while before we could pick up the liberty men, who were reeling about every corner of the town, and quite dark before I came on board. The first lieutenant was on deck, and had no occasion to ask me why I waited so long, when he found they were all lying in the stern-sheets. 'Where the devil could they have picked up the liquor?' said he, and then he ordered the master-at-arms to keep them under the half-deck till they were sober. The next morning the purser comes off, and makes his complaint on the quarter-deck, as how somebody had stolen his liquor. The first lieutenant reports to the captain, and the captain orders up all the men who came off tipsy.

"'Which of you took the liquor?' said he. They all swore that they had no hand in it. 'Then how did you get tipsy? Come now, Mr. Short, answer me; you came off beastly drunk—who gave you the liquor?'

"'A black fellow, sir,' replied Short; which was true enough, as the mugs were filled by the black carpenter, and handed by him.

"Well, they all swore the same, and then the captain got into a rage, and ordered them all to be put down on the report. The next day the hands were turned up for punishment, and the captain said, 'Now, my lads, if you won't tell who stole the purser's grog, I will flog you all round. I only want to flog those who committed the theft, for it is too much to expect of seamen, that they would refuse a glass of grog when offered to them.'

"Now Short and the others had a parley together, and they had agreed how to act. They knew that the captain could not bear flogging, and was a very kind-hearted man. So Bill Short steps out, and says, touching his forelock to the captain, 'If you please, sir, if all must be flogged, if nobody will peach, I think it better to tell the truth at once. It was I who took the liquor.'

"'Very well, then,' said the captain; 'strip, sir.' So Bill

159

Short pulls off his shirt, and is seized up. 'Boatswain's mate,' said the captain, 'give him a dozen.'

"'Beg your honour's pardon,' said Jack Holmes, stepping out of the row of men brought out for punishment; 'but I can't bear to see an innocent man punished, and since one must be flogged, it must be the right one. It warn't Bill Short that took the liquor; it was I.'

"'Why, how's this?' said the captain; 'didn't you own that you took the liquor, Mr. Short?'

"'Why, yes, I did say so, 'cause I didn't wish to see *everybody* flogged; but the truth's the truth, and I had no hand in it.'

"'Cast him loose—Holmes, you'll strip, sir.' Holmes stripped and was tied up. 'Give him a dozen,' said the captain; when out steps M'Alpine, and swore it was him, and not Holmes; and axed leave to be flogged in his stead. At which the captain bit his lips to prevent laughing, and then they knew all was right. So another came forward, and says it was him, and not M'Alpine; and another contradicts him again, and so on. At last the captain says, 'One would think flogging was a very pleasant affair, you are all so eager to be tied up; but, however, I shan't flog to please you. I shall find out who the real culprit is, and then punish him severely. In the meantime, you keep them all on the report, Mr. P——,' speaking to the first lieutenant. 'Depend upon it, I'll not let you off, although I do not choose to flog innocent men.' So they piped down, and the first lieutenant, who knew that the captain never meant to take any more notice of it, never made no inquiries, and the thing blew over. One day, a month or two after, I told the officers how it was managed, and they laughed heartily."

We continued our carouse till a late hour, old Tom constantly amusing us with his long yarns; and that night, for the first time, I went to bed intoxicated. Old Tom and his son assisted me into my bed-place, old Tom observing, "Poor Jacob, it will do him good; his heart was heavy, and now he'll forget it all, for a little time, at all events."

"Well but, father, I don't like to see Jacob drunk," replied young Tom. "It's not like him—it's not worthy of him; as for you or me, it's nothing at all, but I feel Jacob was never meant to be a toper. I never saw a lad so altered in a short time, and I expect bad will come of it when he leaves us."

I awoke, as might be supposed, after my first debauch, with a violent headache, but I had also a fever, brought on by my previous anxiety of mind. I rose, dressed, and went on deck, where the snow was nearly a foot deep. It now froze hard, and the river was covered with small pieces of floating ice. I rubbed my burning forehead with the snow, and felt relief. For some time I assisted Tom to heave it overboard, but the fever pressed upon me, and in less than half-an-hour I could no longer stand the exertion. I sat down on the water-cask, and pressed my hands to my throbbing temples.

"You are not well, Jacob?" inquired Tom, coming up to me with the shovel in his hand, and glowing with health and exercise.

"I am not, indeed, Tom," replied I; "feel how hot I am."

Tom went to his father, who was in the cabin, padding with extra flannel his stumps to defend them from the cold, which always made him suffer much, and then led me into the cabin. It was with much difficulty I could walk; my knees trembled, and my eyesight was defective. Old Tom took my hand as I sank on the locker.

"Do you think that it was taking too much last night?" inquired Tom of his father.

"There's more here than a gallon of liquor would have brought about," replied old Tom. "No, no—I see it all. Go to bed again, Jacob."

They put me into bed, and I was soon in a state of stupor, in which I remained until the lighter had arrived at the Brentford Wharf, and for many days afterwards.

CHAPTER XXI

On a sick bed—Fever, firmness, and folly—"Bound 'prentice to a waterman"—I take my first lesson in love, and give my first lesson in Latin—The love lesson makes an impression on my auricular organ—Verily, none are so deaf as those who won't hear.

WHEN I recovered my senses I found myself in bed, and Captain Turnbull sitting by my side. I had been removed to his house when the lighter had arrived at the wharf.

Captain Turnbull was then talking with Mr. Tomkins, the former head clerk, now in charge. Old Tom came on shore and stated the condition I was in, and Mr. Tomkins having no spare bed in his house, Captain Turnbull immediately ordered me to be taken to his residence, and sent for medical advice. During the time I had remained in this state, old Tom had informed Captain Turnbull, the Domine, and Mr. Tomkins of the circumstances which had occurred, and how much I had been misrepresented to Mr. Drummond ; and not saying a word about the affair of Wimbledon Common, or my subsequent intemperance, had given it as his opinion that ill-treatment had produced the fever. In this, I believe, he was nearly correct, although my disease might certainly have been aggravated and hastened by those two unmentioned causes. They all of them took my part, and Mr. Turnbull went to London to state my condition to Mr. Drummond, and also to remonstrate at his injustice. Circumstances had since occurred which induced Mr. Drummond to lend a ready ear to my justification ; but the message I had sent was still an obstacle. This, however, was partly removed by the equivocating testimony of the young clerk, when he was interrogated by Captain Turnbull and Mr. Drummond ; and wholly so by the evidence of young and old Tom, who, although in the cabin, had overheard the whole of the conversation ; and Mr. Drummond desired Captain Turnbull to inform me, as soon as I recovered, that all was forgotten and forgiven. It might have been on his part, but not on mine ; and when Captain Turnbull told me so, with the view of raising my spirits, I shook my head as I lay on the pillow. As the reader will have observed, the feeling roused in me by the ill-usage I had received was a vindictive one—one that must have been deeply implanted in my heart, although till then it had never been roused into action, and now, once roused, was not to be suppressed. That it was based on pride was evident, and with it my pride was raised in proportion. To the intimation of Captain Turnbull I therefore give a decided dissent. "No, sir, I cannot return to Mr. Drummond. That he was kind to me, and that I owe much to his kindness, I readily admit; and now that he has acknowledged his error in supposing me capable of such ingratitude, I heartily forgive him ; but I cannot and will not receive any more favours from him. I cannot put myself in a situation to be again mortified as I have been. I feel I should no longer have the same pleasure in doing my duty as I once had, and I never could live under the same roof with those who at present serve him. Tell him all this, and pray tell little Sarah how grateful I feel to her for all her kindness to me, and that I shall always think of her with regret, at being obliged to leave her." And at the remembrance of little Sarah I burst into tears, and sobbed on my pillow. Captain Turnbull, whether he rightly estimated my character, or felt convinced that I had made up my mind, did not renew the subject.

"Well, Jacob," replied he, "we'll not talk of that any more. I'll give your messages just in your own words. Now, take your draught, and try to get a little sleep."

I complied with this request, and nothing but weakness now remaining, I rapidly regained my strength; and with my strength my feelings of resentment increased in proportion. Nothing but the very weak state that I was in when Captain Turnbull spoke to me, would have softened me down to give the kind message that I did; but my vindictive mind was subdued by disease, and better feelings predominated. The only effect this had was to increase my animosity against the other parties who were the cause of my ill-treatment, and I vowed that they, at least, should one day repent their conduct.

The Domine called upon me the following Sunday. I was dressed and looking through the window when he arrived. The frost was now intense, and the river was covered with large masses of ice, and my greatest pleasure was to watch them as they floated down with the tide "Thou hast had a second narrow escape, my Jacob," said he, after some preliminary observations. "Once again did death (*pallida mors*) hover over thy couch; but thou hast arisen, and thy fair fame is again established. When wilt thou be able to visit Mr. Drummond, and be able to thank him for his kindness?"

"Never, sir," replied I. "I will never again enter Mr. Drummond's house."

"Nay, Jacob, this savoureth of enmity. Are not we all likely to be deceived—all likely to do wrong? Did not I, even I, in thy presence, backslide into intemperance and folly? Did not I disgrace myself before my pupil—and shalt thou, in thy tender years, harbour ill-will against one who hath cherished thee when thou wert destitute, and who was deceived with regard to thee by the base and evil-speaking ? "

"I am obliged to Mr. Drummond for all his kindness, sir," replied I, " but I never wish to enter his house. I was turned out of it, and never will again go into it."

" *Eheu! Jacobe*, thou art in error ; it is our duty to forgive, as we hope to be forgiven."

" I do forgive, sir, if that is what is requested ; but I cannot, and will not, accept of further favours."

The Domine urged in vain, and left me. Mr. Tomkins also came, and argued the point without success. I was resolved. I was determined to be independent ; and I looked to the river as my father, mother, home, and everything. As soon as my health was reinstated, Captain Turnbull one day came to me. "Jacob," said he, " the lighter has returned ; and I wish to know if you intend to go on board again, and afterwards go into the vessel into which Mr. Drummond proposes to send you."

" I will go into no vessel through Mr. Drummond's means or interest," replied I.

" What will you do then ? " replied he.

" I can always enter on board a man-of-war," replied I, " if the worst comes to the worst ; but if I can serve out my apprenticeship on the river, I should prefer it."

" I rather expected this answer, Jacob, from what you have said to me already ; and I have been trying if I cannot help you to something which may suit you You don't mind being obliged to me ? "

" Oh no ; but promise you will never doubt me—never accuse me." My voice faltered, and I could say no more.

" No, my lad, that I will not ; I know you, as I think, pretty well ; and the heart that feels a false accusation as yours does is sure to guard against committing what you are so angry at being accused of. Now, Jacob, listen to me. You know old deaf Stapleton, whose wherry we have so often pulled up and down the river ? I have spoken to him to take you as his help, and he has consented. Will you like to go ? He has served his time, and has a right to take a 'prentice."

" Yes," replied I, " with pleasure ; and with more pleasure, from expecting to see you often."

" Oh, I promise you all my custom, Jacob," replied he,

laughing. "We'll often turn old Stapleton out, and have a row together. Is it agreed?"

"It is," replied I; "and many thanks to you."

"Well then, consider it settled. Stapleton has a very good room, and all that's requisite on shore, at Fulham. I have seen his place, and I think you will be comfortable."

I did not know at the time how much Captain Turnbull had been my friend—that he had made Stapleton take better lodgings, and had made up the difference to him, besides allowing him a trifle per week, and promising him a gratuity occasionally, if I were content with my situation. In a few days I had removed all my clothes to Stapleton's, had taken my leave of Mr. Turnbull, and was established as an apprentice to a waterman on the Thames. The lighter was still at the wharf when I left, and my parting with old Tom and his son was equally and sincerely felt on both sides.

"Jacob," said old Tom, "I likes your pride after all, 'cause why, I think you have some right to be proud; and the man who only asks fair play, and no favour, always will rise in this world. But look you, Jacob, there's sometimes a current 'gainst a man, that no one can make head against; and if so be that should be your case for a time, recollect the old house, the old woman, and old Tom, and there you'll always find a hearty welcome, and a hearty old couple, who'll share with you what they have, be it good, bad, or indifferent. Here's luck to you, my boy; and recollect, I means to go to the expense of painting the sides of my craft blue, and then you'll always know her as she creeps up and down the river."

"And, Jacob," said young Tom, "I may be a wild one, but I'm a true one; if ever you want me, in fair weather and in foul—good or bad—for fun or for mischief—for a help, or for a friend in need, through thick or thin, I'm yours, even to the gallows; and here's my hand upon it."

"Just like you, Tom," observed his father; "but I know what you mean, and all's right."

I shook hands with them both, and we parted.

Thus did I remove from the lighter, and at once take up the profession of a waterman. I walked down to the Fulham side, where I found Stapleton at the door of the public-house, standing with two or three others, smoking his pipe. "Well, lad, so you're chained to my wherry for two or three years; and I'm to 'nitiate you into all the rules and regulations of the company. Now I'll tell you one thing, which is, d'ye see, when the river's covered with ice, as it is just now, haul your wherry up high and dry, and smoke your pipe till the river is clear, as I do now."

"I might have guessed that," replied I, bawling in his ear, "without your telling me."

"Very true, my lad; but don't bawl in my ear quite so loud, I hears none the better for it; my ears require coaxing, that's all."

"Why, I thought you were as deaf as a post."

"Yes, so I be with strangers, 'cause I don't know the pitch of their voice; but with those about me I hear better when they speak quietly—that's human natur. Come, let's go home, my pipe is finished, and as there's nothing to be done on the river, we may just as well make all tidy there."

Stapleton had lost his wife; but he had a daughter, fifteen years old, who kept his lodgings and *did for him,* as he termed it. He lived in part of some buildings leased by a boat-builder; his windows looked out on the river; and on the first floor a bay-window was thrown out, so that at high water the river ran under it. As for the rooms, consisting of five, I can only say that they could not be spoken of as large and small, but as small and smaller. The sitting-room was eight feet square, the two bedrooms at the back, for himself and his daughter, just held a small bed each, and the kitchen, and my room below, were to match; neither were the tenements in the very best repair, the parlour especially, hanging over the river, being lopsided, and giving you the uncomfortable idea that it would every minute fall into the stream below. Still, the builder declared that it would last many years without sinking further, and that was sufficient. At all events, they were very respectable accommodations for a waterman, and Stapleton paid for them £10 per annum. Stapleton's daughter was certainly a very well-favoured girl. She had rather a large mouth; but her teeth were very fine, and beautifully white. Her hair was auburn—her complexion very fair, her eyes were large, and of a deep blue, and from her figure, which was very good, I should have supposed her to have been eighteen, although she was not past fifteen, as I found out afterwards. There was a frankness and honesty of countenance about her, and an intellectual smile, which was very agreeable.

166

"Well, Mary, how do you get on?" said Stapleton, as we ascended to the sitting-room. "Here's young Faithful come to take up with us."

"Well, father, his bed's all ready; and I have taken so much dirt from the room that I expect we shall be indicted for filling up the river. I wonder what nasty people lived in this house before us."

"Very nice rooms, nevertheless; ain't they, boy?"

"Oh yes, very nice for idle people; you may amuse yourself looking out on the river, or watching what floats by, or fishing with a pin at high water," replied Mary, looking at me.

"I like the river," replied I gravely; "I was born on it, and hope to get my bread on it."

"And I like this sitting-room," rejoined Stapleton; "how mighty comfortable it will be to sit at the open window, and smoke in the summer-time, with one's jacket off!"

"At all events you'll have no excuse for dirtying the room, father; and as for the lad, I suppose his smoking days have not come yet."

"No," replied I; "but my days for taking off my jacket are, I suspect."

"Oh yes," replied she, "never fear that; father will let you do all the work you please, and look on—won't you, father?"

"Don't let your tongue run quite so fast, Mary; you're not over fond of work yourself."

"No; there's only one thing I dislike more," replied she, "and that's holding my tongue."

"Well, I shall leave you and Jacob to make it out together; I am going back to the Feathers." And old Stapleton walked downstairs, and went back to the inn, saying, as he went out, that he should be back to his dinner.

Mary continued her employment of wiping the furniture of the room with a duster for some minutes, during which I did not speak, but watched the floating ice on the river. "Well," said Mary, "do you always talk as you do now? if so, you'll be a very nice companion. Mr. Turnbull, who came to my father, told me that you was a sharp fellow, could read, write, and do everything, and that I should like you very much; but if you mean to keep it all to yourself, you might as well not have had it.'

"I am ready to talk when I have anything to talk about," replied I.

167

"That's not enough. I'm ready to talk about nothing, and you must do the same."

"Very well," replied I. 'How old are you?"

"How old am I? Oh, then you consider me nothing. I'll try hard but you shall alter your opinion, my fine fellow. However, to answer your question, I believe I'm about fifteen."

"Not more! well, there's an old proverb, which I will not repeat."

"I know it, so you may save yourself the trouble, you saucy boy; but now for your age?"

"Mine! let me see; well, I believe that I am nearly seventeen."

"Are you really so old? Well, now, I should have thought you no more than fourteen."

This answer at first surprised me, as I was very stout and tall for my age; but a moment's reflection told me that it was given to annoy me. A lad is as much vexed at being supposed younger than he really is, as a man of a certain age is annoyed at being taken for so much older. "Pooh!" replied I; "that shows how little you know about men."

"I wasn't talking about men, that I know of; but still I do know something about them. I've had two sweethearts already."

"Indeed! and what have you done with them?"

"Done with them! I jilted the first for the second, because the second was better looking; and when Mr. Turnbull told me so much about you, I jilted the second to make room for you; but now I mean to try if I can't get him back again."

"With all my heart," replied I, laughing. "I shall prove but a sorry sweetheart, for I never made love in my life."

"Have you ever had anybody to make love to?"

"No."

"That's the reason, Mr. Jacob, depend upon it. All you have to do is to swear that I'm the prettiest girl in the world, that you like me better than anybody else in the world; do anything in the world that I wish you to do—spend all the money you have in the world in buying me ribbons and fairings, and then——"

"And then, what?"

"Why, then I shall hear all you have to say, take all you have to give, and laugh at you in the bargain."

"I went close up to Mary, and repeated a few words of Latin."

"But I shouldn't stand that long."

"Oh yes, you would. I'd put you out of humour, and coax you in again. The fact is, Jacob Faithful, I made my mind up, before I saw you, that you should be my sweetheart, and when I will have a thing, I will, so you may as well submit to it at once; if you don't, as I keep the key of the cupboard, I'll half starve you; that's the way to tame any brute, they say. And I tell you why, Jacob, I mean that you shall be my sweetheart; it's because Mr. Turnbull told me that you knew Latin. Now tell me, what is Latin?"

"Latin is a language which people spoke in former times, but now they do not."

"Well then, you shall make love to me in Latin, that's agreed."

"And how do you mean to answer me?"

"Oh, in plain English, to be sure."

"But how are you to understand me?" replied I, much amused with the conversation.

"Oh, if you make love properly I shall soon understand you; I shall read the English of it in your eyes."

"Very well, I have no objection; when am I to begin?"

"Why, directly, you stupid fellow, to be sure. What a question!"

I went close up to Mary, and repeated a few words of Latin "Now," says I, "look into my eyes, and see if you can translate them."

"Something impudent, I'm sure," replied she, fixing her blue eyes on mine.

"Not at all," replied I, "I only asked for this," and I snatched a kiss, in return for which I received a box on the ear, which made it tingle for five minutes. "Nay," replied I, "that's not fair; I did as you desired—I made love in Latin."

"And I answered you, as I said I would, in plain English," replied Mary, reddening up to the forehead, but directly after bursting out into a loud laugh. "Now, Mr. Jacob, I plainly see that you know nothing about making love. Why, bless me, a year's dangling, and a year's pocket-money, should not have given you what you have had the impudence to take in so many minutes. But it was my own fault, that's certain, and I have no one to thank but myself. I hope I didn't hurt you—I'm very sorry if I did; but no more making love in Latin, I've had quite enough of that."

169

"Well then, suppose we make friends," replied I, holding out my hand.

"That's what I really wished to do, although I've been talking so much nonsense," replied Mary. "I know we shall like one another, and be very good friends. You can't help feeling kind towards a girl you've kissed; and I shall try by kindness to make up to you for the box on the ear; so now sit down and let's have a long talk. Mr. Turnbull told us that he wished you to serve out your apprenticeship on the river with my father, so that if you agree, we shall be a long while together. I take Mr. Turnbull's word, not that I can find it out yet, that you are a very good-tempered, good-looking, clever, modest lad; and as an apprentice who remains with my father must live with us, of course I had rather it should be one of that sort than some ugly, awkward brute who——"

"Is not fit to make love to you," replied I.

"Who is not fit company for me," replied Mary. "I want no more love from you at present. The fact is that father spends all the time he can spare from the wherry at the alehouse, smoking; and it's very dull for me, and having nothing to do, I look out of the window, and make faces at the young men as they pass by, just to amuse myself. Now, there was no great harm in that a year or two ago; but now, you know, Jacob——"

"Well, now, what then?"

"Oh, I'm bigger, that's all; and what might be called sauciness in a girl may be thought something more of in a young woman. So I've been obliged to leave it off; but being obliged to remain at home, with nobody to talk to, I never was so glad as when I heard that you were to come; so you see, Jacob, we must be friends. I daren't quarrel with you long, although I shall sometimes, just for variety, and to have the pleasure of making it up again. Do you hear me—or what are you thinking of?"

"I'm thinking that you're a very odd girl."

"I dare say that I am, but how can I help that? Mother died when I was five years old, and father couldn't afford to put me out, so he used to lock me in all day, till he came home from the river; and it was not till I was seven years old, and of some use, that the door was left open. I never shall forget the day when he told me that in future he should trust me, and leave the door open. I thought I was quite a woman, and have thought so ever since. I recollect that I often peeped out, and longed to run about the world; but I went two or three yards from the door, and felt so frightened that I ran back as fast as I could. Since that I have seldom quitted the house for an hour, and never have been out of Fulham."

"Then you have never been at school?"

"Oh no—never. I often wish that I had. I used to see the little girls coming home, as they passed our door so merrily, with their bags from the school-house; and I'm sure if it were only to have the pleasure of going there and back again for the sake of the run, I would have worked hard, if for nothing else."

"Would you like to learn to read and write?"

"Will you teach me?" replied Mary, taking me by the arm, and looking me earnestly in the face.

"Yes, I will, with pleasure," replied I, laughing. "We will pass the evening better than making love, after all, especially if you hit so hard. How came you so knowing in those matters?"

"I don't know," replied Mary, smiling. "I suppose, as father says, its human nature, for I never learnt anything; but you will teach me to read and write?"

"I will teach you all I know myself, Mary, if you wish to learn. Everything but Latin—we've had enough of that."

"Oh! I shall be so much obliged to you. I shall love you so!"

"There you are again."

"No, no, I didn't mean that," replied Mary earnestly. "I meant that—after all, I don't know what else to say. I mean I shall love you for your kindness, without your loving me again, that's it."

"I understand you; but now, Mary, as we are to be such good friends, it is necessary that your father and I should be good friends; so I must ask you what sort of a person he is, for I know little of him, and of course wish to oblige him."

"Well then, to prove to you that I am sincere, I will tell you something. My father, in the first place, is a very good-tempered sort of man. He works pretty well, but might gain more, but he likes to smoke at the public-house. All he requires of me is his dinner ready, his linen clean, and the house

171

tidy. He never drinks too much, and is always civil spoken; but he leaves me too much alone, and talks too much about human nature, that's all."

" But he's so deaf—he can't talk to you."

"Give me your hand—now promise—for I'm going to do a very foolish thing, which is to trust a man—promise you'll never tell it again."

"Well, I promise," replied I, supposing her secret of no consequence.

"Well then—mind—you've promised. Father is no more deaf than you or I."

"Indeed!" replied I; "why, he goes by the name of Deaf Stapleton?"

"I know he does, and makes everybody believe that he is so; but it is to make money."

"How can he make money by that?"

"There's many people in business who go down the river, and they wish to talk of their affairs without being overheard as they go down. They always call for Deaf Stapleton; and there's many a gentleman and lady, who have much to say to each other without wishing people to listen—you understand me?"

" Oh yes, I understand—Latin!"

" Exactly—and they call for Deaf Stapleton; and by this means he gets more good fares than any other waterman, and does less work."

" But how will he manage now that I am with him?"

" Oh, I suppose it will depend upon his customers; if a single person wants to go down, you will take the sculls; if they call for oars, you will both go; if he considers Deaf Stapleton only is wanted, you will remain on shore; or perhaps he will insist upon your being deaf too."

" But I do not like deceit."

" No, it's not right; although it appears to me that there is a great deal of it. Still I should like you to sham deaf, and then tell me all that people say. It would be so funny. Father never will tell a word."

" So far, your father, to a certain degree, excuses himself."

" Well, I think he will soon tell you what I have now told you, but till then you must keep your promise; and now you must do as you please, as I must go down into the kitchen, and get dinner on the fire."

172

" I have nothing to do," replied I ; " can I help you ? "

" To be sure you can, and talk to me, which is better still. Come down and wash the potatoes for me, and then I'll find you some more work. Well, I do think we shall be very happy."

I followed Mary Stapleton down into the kitchen, and we were soon very busy, and very noisy, laughing, talking, blowing the fire, and preparing the dinner. By the time that her father came home, we were sworn friends.

CHAPTER XXII

Is very didactic, and treats learnedly on the various senses, and "human nature;" is also diffuse on the best training to produce a moral philosopher—Indeed, it contains materials with which to build up one system, and half-a-dozen theories, as these things are now made.

I WAS rather curious, after the secret confided to me by Mary Stapleton, to see how her father would behave ; but when we had sat and talked some time, as he appeared to have no difficulty in answering to any observation in a common pitch of the voice, I observed to him that he was not so deaf as I thought he was.

" No, no," replied he, " in the house I hear very well, but in the open air I can't hear at all, if a person speaks to me two yards off. Always speak to me close to my ear in the open air, but not loud, and then I shall hear you very well." I caught a bright glance from Mary's blue eye, and made no answer. "This frost will hold, I'm afraid," continued Stapleton, " and we shall have nothing to do for some days but to blow our fingers and spend our earnings ; but there's never much doing at this time of the year. The winter cuts us watermen up terribly. As for me, I smokes my pipe and thinks on human natur ; but what you are to do, Jacob, I can't tell."

" Oh, he will teach me to read and write," replied Mary.

" I don't know that he shall," replied Stapleton. " What's the use of reading and writing to you ? We've too many senses already in my opinion, and if so be we have learning to boot, why, then, all the worse for us."

" How many senses are there, father ? "

"How many?   I'm sure I can't tell, but more than enough to puzzle us."

"There are only five, I believe," said I; "first, there's *hearing*."

"Well," replied Stapleton, "hearing may be useful at times, but not hearing at times is much more convenient.   I make twice as much money since I lost the better part of my hearing."

"Well then, there's *seeing*," continued I.

"Seeing is useful at times, I acknowledge; but I knows this, that if a man could pull a young couple about the river, and not be able to see now and then, it would be many a half-crown in his pocket."

"Well then, now we come to *tasting*."

"No use at all--only a vexation.   If there was no tasting, we should not care whether we ate brown bread or roast beef, drank water or XX ale; and in these hard times, that would be no small saving."

"Well then, let me see, there's *smelling*."

"Smelling's no use whatever.   For one good smell by the river's side, there be ten nasty ones; and there is everywhere, to my conviction."

"Which is the next, Jacob?" said Mary, smiling archly.

"*Feeling*."

"Feeling! that's the worst of the whole.   Always feel too cold in winter, too hot in summer—feel a blow too; feeling only gives pain; that's a very bad sense."

"Well then, I suppose you think we should get on better without our senses."

"No, not without all of them.   A little hearing and a little seeing be all very well; but there are other senses which you have forgot, Jacob.   Now, one I takes to be the very best of the bunch is *smoking*."

"I never heard that was a sense," replied I, laughing.

"Then you haven't half finished your education, Jacob."

"Are reading and writing *senses*, father?" inquired Mary.

"To be sure they be, girl; for without sense you can't read and write; and *rowing* be a sense just as well; and there be many other senses; but, in my opinion, most of the senses be nonsense, and only lead to mischief."

"Jacob," said Mary, whispering to my ear, "isn't *loving* a sense?"

174

" No, that's nonsense," replied I.

" Well then," replied she, " I agree with my father, that nonsense is better than sense; but still I don't see why I should not learn to read and write, father."

" I've lived all my life without it, and never felt the want of it—why can't you ? "

" Because I do feel the want of it."

" So you may, but they leads to no good. Look at those fellows at the Feathers; all were happy enough before Jim Holder, who is a scholar, came among them, and now since he reads to them, they do nothing but grumble, and growl, and talk about I don't know what—corn laws and taxes, and liberty, and all other nonsense. Now, what could you do more than you do now, if you larnt to read and write ? "

" I could amuse myself when I've nothing to do, father, when you and Jacob are away. I often sit down, after I've done all my work, and think what I shall do next, and at last I look out of the window and make faces at people, because I've nothing better to do. Now, father, you must let him learn me to read and write."

" Well, Mary, if you will, you will; but recollect, don't blame me for it—it must be all on your own head, and not on my conscience. I've lived some forty or fifty years in this world, and all my bad luck has been owing to having too much senses, and all my good luck to getting rid of them."

" I wish you would tell me how that came to pass," said I ; " I should like to hear it very much, and it will be a lesson to Mary."

" Well, I don't care if I do, Jacob, only I must light my pipe first ; and, Mary, do you go for a pot o' beer."

" Let Jacob go, father. I mean him to run on all my errands now."

" You mustn't order Jacob, Mary."

" No, no—I wouldn't think of ordering him, but I know he will do it—won't you, Jacob ? "

" Yes, with pleasure," replied I.

" Well, with all my heart, provided it be all for love," said Stapleton.

" Of course all for love," replied Mary, looking at me, " or Latin—which, Jacob ? "

" What's Latin ? " said her father.

"Oh! that's a new sense Jacob has been showing me some-thing of, which, like many others, proved to be nonsense."

I went for the beer, and when I returned found the fire burning brightly, and a strong *sense* of smoking from old Stapleton's pipe. He puffed once or twice more, and then commenced his history as follows :—

"I can't exactly say when I were born, nor where," said old Stapleton, taking his pipe out of his mouth, "because I never axed either father or mother, and they never told me, because why, I never did ax, and that be all agreeable to human natur." Here Stapleton paused and took three whiffs of his pipe. "I recollects when I was a little brat about two foot nothing, mother used to whack me all day long, and I used to cry in proportion. Father used to cry shame, and then mother would fly at him; he would whack she; she would up with her apron in one corner and cry, while I did the same with my pinbefore in another — all that was nothing but human natur." [A pause, and six or seven whiffs of the pipe.]

"I was sent to school at a penny a week, to keep me out of the way, and out of mischief. I larnt nothing but to sit still on the form and hold my tongue, and so I used to amuse myself twiddling my thumbs, and looking at the flies as they buzzed about the room in the summer-time; and in the winter, 'cause there was no flies of no sort, I used to watch the old missus a knitting of stockings, and think how soon the time would come when I should go home and have my supper, which in a child was nothing but human natur. [Puff, puff, puff.] Father and mother lived in a cellar; mother sold coals and 'tatoes, and father used to go out to work in the barges on the river. As soon as I was old enough, the school-missus sent word that I ought to larn to read and write, and that she must be paid threepence a week; so father took me away from school, because he thought I had had education enough; and mother perched me on a basket upside down, and made me watch that nobody took the goods while she was busy down below. And then I used to sit all day long watching the coals and 'tatoes, and never hardly speaking to nobody; so having nothing better to do, I used to think about this, and that, and everything, and when dinner would be ready, and when I might get off the basket; for you see *thinking* be another of the senses, and when one has nothing to do, and nothing to say, to think be nothing more than human natur. [Puff, puff, and a pause for a drink out of the pot.] At last I grew a big stout boy, and mother said that I ate too much, and must earn my livelihood somehow or other, and father for once agreed with her; but there was a little difficulty how that was to be done, so until that was got over, I did nothing at all but watch the coals and 'tatoes as before. One day mother wouldn't give me wituals enough, so I helped myself; so she whacked me, so I, being strong, whacked she; so father, coming home, whacked me, so I takes to my heels and runs away a good mile before I thought at all about how I was to live; and there I was, very sore, very unhappy, and very hungry. [Puff, puff, puff, and a spit.] I walks on, and on, and then I gets behind a coach, and then the fellow whips me, and I gets down again in a great hurry, and tumbles into the road, and before I could get up again, a gemman in a gig drives right over me, and breaks my leg. I screams with the pain, which if I hadn't had the sense of *feeling*, of course I shouldn't have minded. He pulls up and gets out, and tells me he's very sorry. I tells him so am I. His servant calls some people, and they takes me into a public-house, and lays me on the table all among the pots of beer, sends for a doctor who puts me into bed, and puts my leg right again; and then I was provided for, for at least six weeks, during which the gemman calls and axes how I feel myself, and I says, 'Pretty well, I thanky.' [Puff, puff—knock the ashes out, pipe refilled, relighted, a drink of beer, and go on.] So when I was well, and on my pins again, the gentleman says, 'What can I do for you?' and the landlord cuts him short by saying that he wanted a pot-boy, if I liked the profession. Now, if I didn't like the pots I did the porter, which I had no share of at home, so I agrees. The gemman pays the score, gives me half a guinea, and tells me not to be lying in the middle of the road another time. I tells him I won't, so he jumps into his gig, and I've never cast eyes upon him since. I stayed three years with my master, taking out beer to his customers, and always taking a little out of each pot for myself, for that's nothing but human natur, when you likes a thing; but I never got into no trouble until one day I sees my missus a kissing in the back parlour with a fellow who travels for orders. I never said nothing at first; but at last I sees too much, and then I

M

tells master, who gets into a rage, and goes in to his wife, stays with her half-an-hour, and then comes out and kicks me out of the door, calling me a liar, and telling me never to show my face again. I shies a pot at his head, and showed him any- thing but my face, for I took to my heels, and ran for it as fast as I could. So much for *seeing*; if I hadn't seen, that wouldn't have happened. So there I was adrift, and good-bye to porter. [Puff, puff; 'Mary, where's my 'baccy stopper?' poke down, puff, puff, spit, and proceed.] Well, I walks towards Lunnen, thinking on husbands and wives, porter, and human natur, until I finds myself there, and then I looks at all the lighted lamps, and recollects that I haven't no lodging for the night, and then all of a sudden I thinks of my father and mother, and wonders how they be going on. So I thought I'd go and see, and away I went; comes to the cellar, and goes down. There is my mother with a quartern of gin before her, walking to and fro, and whimpering to herself; so says I, 'Mother, what's the matter now?' at which she jumps up and hugs me, and tells me I'm her only comfort left. I looks at the quartern and thinks otherwise; so down I sits by her side, and then she pours me out a glass, and pours out all her grief, telling me how my father had left her for another woman, who kept another cellar in another street, and how she was very unhappy, and how she had taken to gin—which was nothing but human natur, you see, and how she meant to make away with herself; and then she sent for more quarterns, and we finished them. What with the joy of finding me, and the grief at losing my father, and the quarterns of gin, she went to bed crying drunk, and fell fast asleep. So did I, and thought home was home after all. Next morning I takes up the business, and finds trade not so bad after all; so I takes the command of all, keeps all the money, and keeps mother in order, and don't allow drinking nor disorderly conduct in the house, but goes to the public-house every night for a pipe and a pot.

"Well, everything goes on very well for a month, when who should come home but father, which I didn't approve of, be- cause I liked being master. So, I being a strong chap, then says, 'If you be come to ill-treat my mother, I'll put you in the kennel, father. Be off to your new woman. Arn't you ashamed of yourself?' says I. So father looks me in the face, and tells me to stand out of his way, or he'll make cat's meat of me; and then he goes to my mother, and after a quarter of an hour of sobbing on her part, and coaxing on his, they kiss and make friends; and then they both turns to me, and orders me to leave the cellar, and never to show my face again. I refuses: father flies at me, and mother helps him; and between the two I was hustled out to find my bread how and where I could. I've never taken a woman's part since. [Puff, puff, puff, and a deep sigh.] I walks down to the water-side, and having one or two shillings in my pocket, goes into a public-house to get a drop of drink and a bed. And when I comes in, I sees a man hand a note for change to the landlady, and she gives him change. 'That won't do,' says he, and he was half tipsy. 'I gave you a ten-pound note, and this here lad be witness.' 'It was only a one,' says the woman. 'You're a d—d old cheat,' says he, 'and if you don't give me the change, I'll set your house on fire, and burn you alive.' With that there was a great row, and he goes out for the constable, and gives her in charge, and gives me in charge as a witness, and then she gives him in charge, and so we all went to the watch-house together, and slept on the benches. The next morning we all appeared before the magistrate, and the man tells his story, and calls me as a witness; but recollecting how much I had suffered from *seeing*, I wouldn't see anything this time. It might have been a ten-pound note, for it certainly didn't look like a one; but my evidence went rather for than against the woman, for I only proved the man to be drunk, and she was let off, and I walked home with her. So says she, 'You're a fine boy, and I'll do you a good turn for what you have done for me. My husband is a waterman, and I'll make you free of the river; for he hasn't no 'prentice, and you can come on shore and stay at the public-house, when you arn't wanted.' I jumped at the offer, and so, by *not seeing*, I gets into a regular livelihood. Well, Jacob, how do you like it?"

"Very much," replied I.

"And you, Mary?"

"Oh! I like it very much; but I want father to go on, and to know how he fell in love, and married my mother."

"Well, you shall have it all by-and-by; but now I must take a spell."

CHAPTER XXIII

*A very sensible chapter, having reference to the senses—Staple-
ton, by keeping his under control, keeps his head above water
in his wherry—Forced to fight for his wife, and when he had
won her, to fight on to keep her—No great prize, yet it made
him a prize-fighter.*

OLD Stapleton finished his pipe, took another swig at the
porter, filled, relighted, puffed to try it, cleared his mouth, and
then proceeded :—

"Now, you see, Bartley, her husband, was the greatest rogue
on the river ; he was up to everything, and stood at nothing.
He fleeced as much on the water as she did on the land ; for
I often seed her give wrong change afterwards when people
were tipsy, but I made a rule always to walk away. As for
Bartley, his was always night work, and many's the coil of rope
I have brought on shore, that, although he might have paid
for, he didn't buy it of the lawful owner, but I never *seed* or
heard, that was my maxim ; and I fared well till I served my
time, and then they gave me their old wherry, and built a new
one for themselves. So I set up on my own account, and then
I seed, and heard, and had all my senses, just as they were
before—more's the pity, for no good came of it. [Puff, puff,
puff, puff.] The Bartleys wanted me to join them, but that
wouldn't do; for though I never meddled with other people's
concerns, yet I didn't choose to go wrong myself. I've seed
all the world cheating each other for fifty years or more, but
that's no concern of mine, I can't make the world better ; so
all I thinks about it is to keep honest myself, and if every one
was to look after his own soul, and not trouble themselves
about their neighbours, why then it would be all the better for
human natur. I plied at the Swan Stairs, gained my livelihood,
and spent it as I got it ; for I was then too young to look out
a'ter a rainy day.

"One night a young woman in a cloak comes down to the
stairs with a bundle in her arms, and seems in a very great
taking, and asks me for a boat. I hauls out of the row alongside of the hard, and hands her in. She trips as she steps in,
and I catches to save her from falling, and in catching her I

puts my hand upon the bundle in her arms, and feels the warm face of a baby. 'Where am I to go, ma'am?' says I. 'Oh! pull across, and land me on the other side,' says she; and then I hears her sobbing to herself, as if her heart would break. When we were in the middle o' the stream, she lifts up her head, and then first she looks at the bundle and kisses it, and then she looks up at the stars which were glittering above in the sky. She kisses the child once more, jumps up, and afore I could be aware of what she was about, she tosses me her purse, throws her child into the water, and leaps in herself. I pulls sharp round immediately, and seeing her again, I made one or two good strokes, comes alongside of her, and gets hold of her clothes. A'ter much ado I gets her into the wherry, and as soon as I seed she was come to again, I pulls her back to the stairs where she had taken me from. As soon as I lands I hears a noise and talking, and several people standing about. It seems it were her relatives, who had missed her, and were axing whether she had taken a boat; and while they were describing her, and the other watermen were telling them how I had taken a fare of that description, I brings her back. Well, they takes charge of her, and leads her home; and then for the first time I thinks of the purse at the bottom of the boat, which I picks up, and sure enough there were four golden guineas in it, besides some silver. Well, the men who plied at the stairs axed me all about it; but I keeps my counsel, and only tells them how the poor girl threw herself into the water, and how I pulled her out again; and in a week I had almost forgot all about it, when up comes an officer, and says to me, 'You be Stapleton, the waterman?' and I says, 'Yes, I be.' 'Then you must come along with me;' and he takes me to the police-office, where I finds the poor young woman in custody for being accused of having murdered her infant. So they begins to tax me upon my Bible oath, and I was forced to tell the whole story; for though you may lose all your senses when convenient, yet somehow or another, an oath on the Bible brings them all back again. 'Did you see the child?' said the magistrate. 'I seed a bundle,' said I. 'Did you hear the child cry?' said he. 'No,' says I, 'I didn't;' and then I thought I had got the young woman off, but the magistrate was an old fox, and had all the senses at his fingers' ends. So says he, 'When the young woman stepped into the boat, did she give you the bundle?' 'No,' says I again. 'Then you never touched it?' 'Yes, I did, when her foot slipped.' 'And what did it feel like?' 'It felt like a piece of human natur,' says I, 'and quite warm like.' 'How do you mean?' says he. 'Why, I took it by the feel for a baby.' 'And it was quite warm, was it?' 'Yes,' replied I, 'it was.' 'Well then, what else took place?' 'Why, when we were in the middle of the stream, she and her child went overboard; I pulled her in again, but couldn't see the child.' Fortunately for the poor girl, they didn't ask me which went overboard first, and that saved her from hanging. She was confined six months in prison, and then let out again; but you see, if it hadn't been for my unfortunately *feeling* the child, and feeling it was warm, what proved its being alive, the poor young woman would have got off altogether, perhaps. So much for the sense of feeling, which I say is of no use to nobody, but only a vexation." [Puff—the pipe out, relighted—puff, puff.]

"But, father," said Mary, "did you ever hear the history of the poor girl?"

"Yes, I heard as how it was a hard case, how she had been seduced by some fellow, who had left her and her baby, upon which she determined to drown herself, poor thing! and her baby too. Had she only tried to drown her baby, I should have said it was quite unnatural; but as she wished to drown herself at the same time, I considers that drowning the baby to take it to heaven with her was quite natural, and all agreeable to human natur. Love's a sense which young women should keep down as much as possible, Mary; no good comes of *that* sense."

"And yet, father, it appears to me to be human nature," replied Mary.

"So it is, but there's mischief in it, girl; so do you never have anything to do with it."

"Was there mischief when you fell in love with my mother and married her?"

"You shall hear, Mary," replied old Stapleton, who recommenced.

"It was 'bout two months after the poor girl threw herself into the river, that I first seed your mother. She was then mayhap two years older than you may be, and much such a same sort of person in her looks. There was a young man who plied from our stairs, named Ben Jones; he and I were great friends, and used for to help each other, and when a fare called for oars, used to ply together. One night he says to me, 'Will, come up, and I'll show you a devilish fine piece of stuff.' So I walks with him, and he takes me to a shop where they dealed in marine stores, and we goes and finds your mother in the back parlour. Ben sends out for pipes and beer, and we sat down and made ourselves comfortable. Now, Mary, your mother was a very jilting kind of girl, who would put one fellow off to take another, just as her whim and fancy took her. [I looked at Mary, who cast down her eyes.] Now these women do a mint of mischief among men, and it seldom ends well; and I'd sooner see you in your coffin to-morrow, Mary, than think you should be one of this flaunting sort. Ben Jones was quite in for it, and wanted for to marry her, and she had turned off a fine young chap for him, and he used to come there every night, and it was supposed that they would be spliced in the course of a month; but when I goes there she cuts him almost altogether, and takes to me, making such eyes at me, and drinking beer out of my pot, and refusing his'n, till poor Jones was quite mad and beside himself. Well, it wasn't in human natur to stand those large blue eyes (just like yours, Mary), darting fire at a poor fellow; and when Jones got up in a surly humour, and said it was time to go away, instead of walking home arm-in-arm, we went side by side, like two big dogs, with their tails as stiff up as a crowbar, and ready for a fight, neither he nor I saying a word, and we parted without saying good-night. Well, I dreamed of your mother all that night, and the next day went to see her, and felt worser and worser each time, and she snubbed Jones, and at last told him to go about his business. This was 'bout a month after I had first seen her; and then one day Jones, who was a prime fighter, says to me, 'Be you a man?' and slaps me on the ear. So, I knowing what he'd be a'ter, pulls off my duds, and we sets to. We fights for ten minutes or so, and then I hits him a round blow on the ear, and he falls down on the *hard*, and couldn't come to time. No wonder, poor fellow! for he had gone to eternity. [Here old Stapleton paused for half a minute, and passed his hand across his eyes.] I was tried for manslaughter; but it being proved that he came up and struck me first, I was acquitted, after lying two months in gaol, for

I couldn't get no bail; but it was because I had been two months in gaol that I was let off. At first, when I came out, I determined never to see your mother again; but she came to me, and wound round me, and I loved her so much that I couldn't shake her off. As soon as she found that I was fairly hooked, she began to play with others; but I wouldn't stand that, and every fellow that came near her was certain to have a turn-out with me, and so I became a great fighter; and she, seeing that I was the best man, and that no one else would come to her, one fine morning agreed to marry me. Well, we were spliced, and the very first night I thought I saw poor Ben Jones standing by my bedside, and for a week or so I was not comfortable; but howsomever it wore off. I plied at the stairs, and gained my money. But my pipe's out, and I'm dry with talking. Suppose I take a spell for a few minutes."

Stapleton relighted his pipe, and for nearly half-an-hour smoked in silence. What Mary's thoughts were I cannot positively assert; but I imagined that, like myself, she was thinking about her mother's conduct and her own. I certainly was making the comparison, and we neither of us spoke a word.

"Well," continued Stapleton, at last, "I married your mother, Mary, and I only hope that any man who may take a fancy to you, will not have so much trouble with his wife as I had. I thought that a'ter she were settled she would give up all her nonsense, and behave herself; but I suppose it was in her natur and she couldn't help it. She made eyes and gave encouragement to the men, until they became saucy, and I became jealous, and I had to fight one, and then the other, until I became a noted pugilist. I will say that your mother seemed always very happy when I beat my man, which latterly I always did; but still she liked to be *fit* for, and I had hardly time to earn my bread. At last, some one backed me against another man in the ring for fifty pound a side, and I was to have half if I won. I was very short of blunt at the time, and I agreed; so, a'ter a little training, the battle was fought, and I won easy; and the knowing ones liked my way of hitting so much that they made up another match with a better man, for two hundred pounds; and a lord and other great people came to me, and I was introduced to them at the public-house, and all was settled. So I became a regular prize-fighter, all through your mother, Mary. Nay, don't

184

cry, child, I don't mean to say that your mother, with all her love of being stared at and talked to, would have gone wrong; but still it was almost as bad in my opinion. Well, I was put into training, and after five weeks we met at Mousley Hurst, and a hard fight it was—but I've got the whole of it somewhere, Mary; look in the drawer there, and you'll see a newspaper."

Mary brought out the newspaper, which was rolled up and tied with a bit of string, and Stapleton handed it over to me, telling me to read it aloud. I did so, but I shall not enter into the details.

"Yes, that's all right enough," said Stapleton, who had taken advantage of my reading to smoke furiously to make up for lost time, "but no good came of it, for one of the gemmen took a fancy to your mother, Mary, and tried to win her away from me. I found him attempting to kiss her, and she refusing him—but laughing, and, as I thought, more than half-willing; so I floored him, and put him out of the house, and after that I never would have anything more to say with lords and gemmen, nor with fighting either. I built a new wherry and stuck to the river, and I shifted my lodgings, that I mightn't mix any more with those who knew me as a boxer. Your mother was then brought to bed with you, and I hoped for a good deal of happiness, as I thought she would only think of her husband and child; and so she did until you were weaned, and then she went on just as afore. There was a captain of a vessel lying in the river who used now and then to stop and talk with her; but I thought little about that, seeing how every one talked with her and she with everybody; and besides she knew the captain's wife, who was a very pretty woman, and used very often to ask Mary to go and see her, which I permitted. But one morning, when I was going off to the boat—for he had come down to me to take him to his vessel—just as I was walking away with the sculls over my shoulder, I recollects my 'baccy box, which I had left, and I goes back and hears him say before I came into the door, 'Recollect, I shall be here again by two o'clock, and then you promised to come on board my ship, and see——' I didn't hear the rest, but she laughed, and said yes, she would. I didn't show myself, but walked away and went to the boat. He followed me, and I rowed him up the river and took my fare; and then I determined to watch them, for I felt mighty jealous. So, I lays off on my oars in the middle of the stream, and sure enough I see the captain and your mother get into a small skiff belonging to his ship, and pull away ; the captain had one oar, and one of his men another.   I pulled a'ter them as fast as I could, and at last they seed me ; and not wishing me to find her out, she begged them to pull away as fast as they could, for she knew how savage I would be.   Still I gained upon them, every now and then looking round and vowing vengeance in my heart, when all of a sudden I heard a scream, and perceived their boat to capsize, and all hands in the water. They had not seen a warp of a vessel getting into the row, and had run over it, and, as it tautened, they capsized.   Your mother went down like a stone, Mary, and was not found for three days a'terward ; and when I seed her sink I fell down in a fit."   Here old Stapleton stopped, laid down his pipe, and rested his face in his hands.   Mary burst into tears.   After a few minutes he resumed : "When I came to, I found myself on board of the ship in the captain's cabin, with the captain and his wife watching over me ; and then I came to understand that it was she who had sent for your mother, and that she was living on board, and that your mother had at first refused, because she knew that I did not like her to be on the river, but wishing to see a ship, had consented.   So it was not so bad a'ter all, only that a woman shouldn't act without her husband.   But you see, Mary, all this would not have happened if it hadn't been that I overheard part of what was said ; and you might now have had a mother, and I a wife to comfort us, if it had not been for my unfortunate *hearing*—so, as I said before, there's more harm than good that comes from these senses—at least so it has proved to me.   And now you have heard my story, and how your mother died, Mary ; so take care you don't fall into the same fault, and be too fond of being looked at, which it does some-how or another appear to me you have a bit of a hankering a'ter —but like mother, like child, they say, and that's human natur."

When Stapleton had concluded his narrative, he smoked his pipe in silence.   Mary sat at the table, with her hands pressed to her temples, apparently in deep thought ; and I felt any-thing but communicative.   In half-an-hour the pot of beer was finished, and Stapleton rose.

"Come, Mary, don't be thinking so much ; let's all go to bed.   Show Jacob his room, and then come up."

"Jacob can find his own room, father," replied Mary, "without my showing him ; he knows the kitchen, and there is but one other below."

I took my candle, wished them good-night, and went to my bed, which, although very homely, was at all events comfortable.

CHAPTER XXIV

The warmth of my gratitude proved by a very cold test—The road to fortune may sometimes lead over a bridge of ice— Mine lay under it—Amor Vincit everything but my obstinacy, which young Tom and the old Domine in the sequel will prove to their cost.

FOR many days the frost continued, until at last the river was frozen over, and all communication by it was stopped. Stapleton's money ran short, our fare became very indifferent, and Mary declared that we must all go begging with the market gardeners if it lasted much longer.

"I must go and call upon Mr. Turnbull, and ax him to help us," said Stapleton one day, pulling his last shilling out and laying it on the table. "I'm cleaned out ; but he's a good gentleman, and will lend me a trifle." In the afternoon Stapleton returned, and I saw by his looks that he had been successful. "Jacob," said he, "Mr. Turnbull desires that you will breakfast with him to-morrow morning, as he wishes to see you."

I set off accordingly at daylight the next morning, and was in good time for breakfast. Mr. Turnbull was as kind as ever, and began telling me long stories about the ice in the northern regions.

"By-the-bye, I hear there is an ox to be roasted whole, Jacob, a little above London Bridge ; suppose we go and see the fun."

I consented, and we took the Brentford coach, and were put down at the corner of Queen Street, from whence we walked to the river. The scene was very amusing and exciting. Booths were erected on the ice in every direction, with flags flying, people walking, and some skating, although the ice was too rough for that pastime. The whole river was crowded with people, who now walked in security over where they a month before would have met with death. Here and there smoke ascended from various fires, on which sausages and other eatables were cooking; but the great attraction was the ox roasting whole, close to the centre pier of the bridge. Although the ice appeared to have fallen at the spot where so many hundreds were assembled, yet as it was now four or five feet thick, there was no danger. Here and there, indeed, were what were called rotten places, where the ice was not sound; but these were intimated by placards, warning people not to approach too near, and close to them were ropes and poles for succour, if required. We amused ourselves for some time with the gaiety of the scene, for the sun shone out brightly, and the sky was clear. The wind was fresh from the north-ward, and piercing cold in the shade, the thermometer being then, it was said, twenty-eight degrees below the freezing point. We had been on the ice about three hours, amusing ourselves, when Mr. Turnbull proposed our going home, and we walked up the river towards Blackfriars Bridge, where we proposed to land, and take the coach at Charing Cross.

"I wonder how the tide is now," observed Mr. Turnbull to me; "it would be rather puzzling to find out."

· "Not if I can find a hole," replied I, looking for one. "Stop, here is one." I threw in a piece of ice, and found that it was strong ebb. We continued our walk over the ice, which was now very rough, when Mr. Turnbull's hat fell off, and the wind catching it, it blew away, skimming across the ice at a rapid rate. Mr. Turnbull and I gave chase, but could scarcely keep up with it, and, at all events, could not overtake it. Many people on the river laughed as we passed, and watched us in our chase. Mr. Turnbull was the foremost, and, heedless in the pursuit, did not observe a large surface of rotten ice before him; neither did I, until all at once I heard it break and saw Mr. Turnbull fall in and disappear. Many people were close to us, and a rope was laid across the spot to designate the danger. I did not hesitate—I loved Mr. Turnbull, and my love and my feelings of resentment were equally potent. I seized the bight of the rope, twisted it round my arm, and plunged in, after recollecting it was ebb-tide; fortunate for Mr. Turnbull it was that he had accidentally put the question. I sank under the ice, and pushed down the stream, and in a few seconds f It myself grappled by him I sought, and at almost the same time the rope hauling in from above. As soon as they found there was resistance, they knew that I, at least, was attached to it, and they hauled in quicker, not, however, until I had lost my recollection. Still I clung to the rope with the force of a drowning man, and Mr. Turnbull did the same to me, and we shortly made our appearance at the hole in which we had been plunged. A ladder was thrown across, and two of the men of the Humane Society came to our assistance, pulled us out, and laid us upon it. They then drew back and hauled us on the ladder to a more secure situation. We were both still senseless; but having been taken to a public-house on the river-side, were put to bed, and medical advice having been procured, were soon restored. The next morning we were able to return in a chaise to Brentford, where our absence had created the greatest alarm. Mr. Turnbull spoke but little the whole time; but he often pressed my hand, and when I requested him to drop me at Fulham, that I might let Stapleton and his daughter know that I was safe, he consented, saying, " God bless you, my fine boy; I will see you soon."

When I went up the stairs of Stapleton's lodgings, I found Mary by herself; she started up as soon as she saw me.

" Where *have* you been, you naughty boy ? " said she, half crying, half smiling.

" Under the ice," I replied, " and only thawed again this morning."

" Are you in earnest, Jacob ? " said she ; " now don't plague and frighten me, I've been too frightened already. I never slept a wink last night." I then told her the circumstances which had occurred. " I was sure something had happened," she replied. " I told my father so, but he wouldn't believe it. You promised to be at home to give me my lesson, and I know you never break your word ; but my father smoked away, and said that when boys are amused, they forget their promises, and that it was nothing but human natur. Oh, Jacob, I'm so glad you're back again, and after what has happened, I don't mind your kissing me for once." And Mary held her face towards me, and returned my kiss.

" There, that must last you a long while, recollect," said she, laughing ; " you must not think of another, until you're under the ice again."

" Then I trust it will be the last," replied I, laughing.

"You are not in love with me, Jacob, that's clear, or you would not have made that answer," replied Mary.

I had seen a great deal of Mary, and though she certainly was a great flirt, yet she had many excellent and amiable qualities. For the first week after her father had given us the history of his life, his remarks upon her mother appeared to have made a decided impression upon her, and her conduct was much more staid and demure ; but as the remembrance wore off, so did her conduct become coquettish and flirting as before. Still it was impossible not to be fond of her, and even with all her caprice there was such a fund of real good feeling and amiableness, which when called forth was certain to appear, that I often thought how dangerous and captivating a girl she would be when she grew up. I had again produced the books, which I had thrown aside with disgust, to teach her to read and write. Her improvement was rapid, and would have been still more so if she had not been just as busy in trying to make me fond of her as she was in surmounting the difficulties of her lessons. But she was very young; and although, as her father declared, it was her *natur* to run after the men, there was every reason to hope that a year or two would render her less volatile, and add to those sterling good qualities which she really possessed. In heart and feeling she was a modest girl, although the buoyancy of her spirits often carried her beyond the bounds prescribed by decorum, and often called forth a blush upon her own animated countenance, when her good sense, or the remarks of others, reminded her of her having committed herself. It was impossible to know Mary and not like her, although, at a casual meeting, a rigid person might go away with an impression by no means favourable. As for myself, I must say that the more I was in her company, the more I was attached to her, and the more I respected her.

Old Stapleton came home in the evening. He had, as usual, been smoking, and thinking of human natur, at the Feathers public-house. I told him what had happened, and upon the strength of it he sent for an extra pot of beer for Mary and me, which he insisted upon our drinking between us—a greater proof of goodwill on his part could not have been given. Although Captain Turnbull appeared to have recovered from the effects of the accident, yet it seemed that such was not the case, as the morning after his arrival he was taken ill

with shivering and pains in his loins, which ended in ague
and fever, and he did not quit his bed for three or four weeks.
I, on the contrary, felt no ill effects; but the constitution of
a youth is better able to meet such violent shocks than that of a
man of sixty years old, already sapped by exposure and fatigue.
As the frost still continued, I complied with Captain Turnbull's
request to come up and stay with him, and for many days,
until he was able to leave his bed, I was his constant nurse.
The general theme of his conversation was on my future prospects, and a wish that I would embark in some pursuit or
profession more likely to raise me in the world; but on this
head I was positive, and also another point, which was, that
I would in future put myself under an obligation to no one.
I could not erase from my memory the injuries I had received,
and my vindictive spirit continually brooded over them. I was
resolved to be independent and free. I felt that in the company
I was in I was with my equals, or, if there were any superiority,
it was on my part, arising from education, and I never would
submit to be again in the society of those above me, in which
I was admitted as a favour, and by the major part looked down
upon, and at the same time liable, as I had once been, to be
turned out with contumely on the first moment of caprice.
Still I was very fond of Captain Turnbull. He had always
been kind to me, spoke to me on terms of equality, and had
behaved with consistency, and my feelings towards him, since
the accident, had consequently strengthened; but we always
feel an increased regard towards those to whom we have been
of service, and my pride was softened by the reflection that,
whatever might be Mr. Turnbull's good-will towards me, he
never could, even if I would permit it, repay me for the life
which I had preserved. Towards him I felt unbounded regard
—towards those who had ill-treated me unlimited hatred; towards the world in general a mixture of feeling which I could
hardly analyse; and, as far as regarded myself, a love of liberty
and independence which nothing would ever have induced me
to compromise. As I did not wish to hurt Captain Turnbull's
feelings by a direct refusal to all his proffers of service, and
remarks upon the advantages which might arise, I generally
made an evasive answer; but when on the day proposed for
my departure he at once came to the point, offering me everything, and observing that he was childless, and therefore my

acceptance of his offer would be injurious to nobody, when he took me by the hand, and drawing me near to him, passed his arm round me, and spoke to me in the kind accents of a father—almost entreating me to consent—the tears of gratitude coursed each other rapidly down my cheeks. But my resolution was no less firm, although it was with a faltering voice that I replied—"You have been very kind to me, sir—very kind—and I shall never forget it; and I hope I shall deserve it—but—Mr. Drummond, and Mrs. Drummond, and Sarah, were also kind to me—very kind to me—you know the rest. I will remain as I am, if you please; and if you wish to do me a kindness, if you wish me to love you, as I really do, let me be as I am—free and independent. I beg it of you as the greatest favour that you can possibly confer on me—the only favour which I can accept, or shall be truly thankful for."

Captain Turnbull was some minutes before he could reply. He then said, "I see it is useless, and I will not tease you any more; but, Jacob, do not let the fire of injustice which you have received from your fellow-creatures prey so much upon your mind, or induce you to form the mistaken idea that the world is bad. As you live on, you will find much good; and recollect, that those who have injured you, from the misrepresentation of others, have been willing, and have offered, to repair their fault. They can do no more, and I wish you could get over this vindictive feeling. Recollect, we must forgive, as we hope to be forgiven."

"I do forgive—at least, I do sometimes," replied I, "for Sarah's sake—but I can't always."

"But you ought to forgive, for other reasons, Jacob."

"I know I ought—but if I cannot, I cannot."

"Nay, my boy, I never heard you talk so—I was going to say—wickedly. Do you not perceive that you are now in error? You will not abandon a feeling which your own good sense and religion tell you to be wrong—you cling to it—and yet you will admit of no excuse for the errors of others."

"I feel what you say—and the truth of it, sir," replied I; "but I cannot combat the feeling. I will, therefore, admit every excuse you please, for the faults of others; but at the same time, I am surely not to be blamed if I refuse to put myself in a situation where I am again liable to meet with mortification. Surely I am not to be censured if I prefer to work for my bread after my own fashion, and prefer the river to dry land?"

"No, that I acknowledge; but what I dislike in the choice is that it is dictated by feelings of resentment."

"What's done can't be helped," replied I quickly, wishing to break off the conversation.

"Very true, Jacob; but I follow that up with another of your remarks, which is, 'Better luck next time.' God bless you, my boy; take care of yourself, and don't get under the ice again!"

"For you I would to-morrow," replied I, taking the proffered hand; "but if I could only see that Hodgson near a hole——"

"You'd not push him in?"

"Indeed I would," replied I bitterly.

"Jacob, you would not, I tell you—you think so now, but if you saw him in distress, you would assist him as you did me. I know you, my boy, better than you know yourself."

Whether Captain Turnbull or I were right remains to be proved in the sequel. We then shook hands, and I hastened away to see Mary, whom I had often thought of during my absence.

"Who do you think has been here?" said Mary, after our first greeting.

"I cannot guess," replied I. "Not old Tom and his son?"

"No; I don't think it was old Tom, but it was such an old quiz—with such a nose—O heavens! I thought I should have died with laughing as soon as he went downstairs. Do you know, Jacob, that I made love to him, just to see how he'd take it. You know who it is now?"

"Oh yes! you mean the Domine, my schoolmaster."

"Yes, he told me so; and I talked so much about you, and about your teaching me to read and write, and how fond I was of learning, and how I should like to be married to an elderly man who was a great scholar, who would teach me Latin and Greek, that the old gentleman became quite chatty, and sat for two hours talking to me. He desired me to say that he should call here to-morrow afternoon, and I begged him to stay the evening, as you are to have two more of your friends here. Now, who do you think are those?"

"I have no others, except old Tom Beazeley and his son."

"Well, it is your old Tom after all, and a nice old fellow he is, although I would not like him for a husband; but as for his son—he's a lad after my own heart—I'm quite in love with him."

"Your love will do you no harm, Mary; but recollect, what may be a joke to you may not be so to other people. As for the Domine meeting old Beazeley and his son, I don't exactly know how that will suit, for I doubt if he will like to see them."

"Why not?" inquired Mary.

Upon a promise never to hint at them, I briefly stated the circumstances attending the worthy man's voyage on board of the lighter. Mary paused, and then said, "Jacob, did we not read the last time that the most dangerous rocks to men were *wine* and *women?*"

"Yes, we did, if I recollect right."

"Humph," said she; "the old gentleman has given plenty of lessons in his time, and it appears that he has received *one.*"

"We may do so to the last day of our existence, Mary."

"Well, he is a very clever, learned man, I've no doubt, and looks down upon all of us (not you, Jacob) as silly people. I'll try if *I* can't give him a lesson."

"You, Mary, what can you teach him?"

"Never mind, we shall see;" and Mary turned the discourse on her father. "You know, I suppose, that father is gone up to Mr. Turnbull's."

"No, I did not."

"Yes, he has; he was desired to go there this morning, and hasn't been back since. Jacob, I hope you won't be so foolish again, for I don't want to lose my master."

"Oh, never fear; I shall teach you all you want to know before I die," I replied.

"Don't be too sure of that," replied Mary, fixing her large blue eyes upon me; "how do you know how much I may wish to have of your company?"

"Well, if I walk off in a hurry, I'll make you over to young Tom Beazeley. You're half in love with him already, you know," replied I, laughing.

"Well, he is a nice fellow," replied she; "he laughs more than you do, Jacob."

"He has suffered less," replied I gloomily, calling to mind had what occurred; "but, Mary, he is a fine young man, and

194

a good-hearted clever fellow to boot; and when you do know him, you will like him very much." As I said this, I heard her father coming upstairs; he came in high good-humour with his interview with Captain Turnbull, called for his pipe and pot, and was excessively fluent upon "human natur."

CHAPTER XXV

"The feast of reason and the flow of soul"—Stapleton, on human nature, proves the former; the Domine, in his melting mood, the latter—Sall's shoe particularly noted, and the true "reading made easy" of a mind at ease, by old Tom.

THE afternoon of the next day I heard a well-known voice, which carolled forth, as Mary huddled up her books, and put them out of the way; for at that time I was, as usual, giving her a lesson :—

> " And many strange sights I've seen,
>   And long I've been a rover,
> And everywhere I've been,
>   But now the wars are over.
> I've been across the line,
>   Where the sun will burn your nose off ;
> And I've been in northern climes,
>   Where the frost would bite your toes off.
> Fal de ral, fal de ral, fal de ral de liddy."

" Heave ahead, Tom, and let me stump up at my leisure. It's like warping 'gainst wind and tide with me—and I gets up about as fast as lawyers go to heaven."

I thought when Tom came up first, that he had been at unusual trouble in setting off his person, and certainly a better-looking, frank, open, merry countenance was seldom to be seen. In person he was about an inch taller than I, athletic, and well-formed. He made up to Mary, who, perceiving his impatience, and either to check him before me, or else from her usual feeling of coquetry, received him rather distantly, and went up to old Tom, with whom she shook hands warmly.

" Whew ! what's in the wind now; Jacob ? Why, we parted the best friends in the world," said Tom, looking at Mary.

"Sheer off yourself, Tom," replied I, laughing, "and you'll see that she'll come to again."

"Oh, oh! so the wind's in that quarter, is it?" replied Tom. "With all my heart—I can show false colours as well as she can. But I say, Jacob, before I begin my manœuvres, tell me if you wish me to hoist the neutral flag; for I won't interfere with you."

"Here's my hand upon it, Tom, that the coast is clear as far as I'm concerned; but take care—she's a clipper, and not unlikely to slip through your fingers, even when you have her under your lee, within hail."

"Let me alone, Jacob, for that."

"And more, Tom, when you're in possession of her, she will require a good man at the helm."

"Then she's just the craft after my fancy. I hate your steady, slow-sailing craft, that will steer themselves almost; give me one that requires to be managed by a man and a seaman."

"If well manned, she will do anything, depend upon it, Tom, for she's as sound below as possible; and although she is down to her bearings on the puff of the moment, yet she'd not careen further."

"Well then, Jacob, all's right; and now you've told me what tack she's on, see if I don't shape a course to cut her off."

"Well, Jacob, my good boy, so you've been under the water again. I thought you had enough of it when Fleming gave you such a twist; but, however, this time you went to sarve a friend, which was all right. My sarvice to you, Mr. Stapleton," continued old Tom, as Stapleton made his appearance. "I was talking to Jacob about his last dive."

"Nothing but human natur," replied Stapleton.

"Well, now," replied old Tom, "I consider that going plump into the river, when covered with ice, to be quite contrary to human natur."

"But not to save a friend, father?"

"No—because that be Jacob's nature; so you see one nature conquered the other, and that's the whole long and short of it."

"Well now, suppose we sit down and make ourselves comfortable," observed Stapleton; "but here be somebody else coming up—who can it be?"

"I say, old codger, considering you be as deaf as a post, you hears pretty well," said old Tom.

"Yes, I hear very well in the house, provided people don't speak loud."

"Well, that's a queer sort of deafness; I think we are all troubled with the same complaint," cried Tom, laughing.

During this remark the Domine made his appearance. "*Salve Domine*," said I upon his entering, taking my worthy pedagogue by the hand.

"*Et tu quoque, fili mi, Jacobe!* But whom have we here? the deaf man, the maiden, and—ehu!—the old man called old Tom, and likewise the young Tom;" and the Domine looked very grave.

"Nay, sir," said young Tom, going up to the Domine, "I know you are angry with us, because we both drank too much when we were last in your company; but we promise—don't we, father?—not to do so again."

This judicious reply of young Tom's put the Domine more at his ease; what he most feared was raillery and exposure on their parts.

"Very true, old gentleman; Tom and I did bowse our jibs up a little too taut when we last met—but what then?—there was the grog, and there was nothing to do."

"All human natur," observed Stapleton.

"Come, sir, you have not said one word to me," said Mary, going up to the Domine. "Now, you must sit down by me, and take care of me, and see that they all behave themselves and keep sober."

The Domine cast a look at Mary, which was intended for her alone, but which was not unperceived by young Tom or me. "We shall have some fun, Jacob," said he aside, as we all sat down to the table, which just admitted six, with close stowage. The Domine on one side of Mary, Tom on the other, Stapleton next to Tom, then I and old Tom, who closed in on the other side of the Domine, putting one of his timber toes on the old gentleman's corns, which induced him to lift up his leg in a hurry, and draw his chair still closer to Mary, to avoid a repetition of the accident; while old Tom was axing pardon, and Stapleton demonstrating that on the part of old Tom, not to *feel* with a wooden leg, and on the part of the Domine, to *feel* with a bad corn was all nothing but "human natur." At last we were all seated, and Mary, who had provided for the evening, produced two or three pots of beer, a bottle of spirits, pipes, and tobacco.

"Liberty Hall—I smokes," said Stapleton, lighting his pipe, and falling back on his chair.

"I'll put a bit of clay in my mouth too," followed up old Tom; "it makes one thirsty, and enjoy one's liquor."

"Well, I malts," said Tom, reaching a pot of porter, and taking a long pull, till he was out of breath. "What do you do, Jacob?"

"I shall wait a little, Tom."

"And what do you do, sir?" said Mary to the Domine. The Domine shook his head. "Nay, but you must—or I shall think you do not like my company. Come, let me fill a pipe for you." Mary filled a pipe, and handed it to the Domine, who hesitated, looked at her, and was overcome. He lighted it and smoked furiously.

"The ice is breaking up—we shall have a change of weather —the moon quarters to-morrow," observed old Tom, puffing between every observation; "and then honest men may earn their bread again. Bad times for you, old codger, heh!" continued he, addressing Stapleton. Stapleton nodded an assent through the smoke, which was first perceived by old Tom. "Well, he arn't deaf, a'ter all; I thought he was only shamming a bit. I say, Jacob, this is the weather to blow your fingers, and make your eyes bright."

"Rather to blow a cloud, and make your eyes water," replied Tom, taking up the pot. "I'm just as thirsty with swallowing smoke, as if I had a pipe myself—at all events I pipe my eye. Jacob," continued Tom to me, apart, "do look how the old gentleman is *funking* Mary, and casting sheep's eyes at her through the smoke."

"He appears as if he were inclined to board her in the smoke," replied I.

"Yes, and she to make no fight of it, but surrender immediately," said Tom.

"Don't you believe it, Tom, I know her better; she wants to laugh at him, nothing more. She winked her eye at me just now, but I would not laugh, as I do not choose that the old gentleman should be trifled with. I will tax her severely to-morrow."

During all this time old Tom and Stapleton smoked in silence. The Domine made use of his eyes in dumb parlance to Mary, who answered him with her own bright glances, and Tom and I began to find it rather dull; when at last old Tom's pipe was exhausted, and he laid it down. "There, I'll smoke no more; the worst of a pipe is that one can't smoke and talk at the same time. Mary, my girl, take your eyes off the Domine's nose, and hand me that bottle of stuff. What, glass to mix it in! that's more genteel than we are on board, Tom."

Tom filled a rummer of grog, took half off at a huge sip, and put it down on the table. "Will you do as we do, sir?" said he, addressing the Domine.

"Nay, friend Dux, nay, pr'ythee persuade me not—avaunt!" and the Domine, with an appearance of horror, turned away from the bottle handed towards him by old Tom.

"Not drink anything?" said Mary to the Domine, looking at him with surprise; "but indeed you must, or I shall think you despise us, and do not think us fit to be in your company."

"Nay, maiden, entreat me not. Ask anything of me but this," replied the Domine.

"Ask anything but this—that's just the way people have of refusing," replied Mary; "were I to ask anything else, it would be the same answer, 'ask anything but this.' Now, if you will not drink to please me, I shall quarrel with you. You shall drink a glass, and I'll mix it for you." The Domine shook his head. Mary made a glass of grog, and then put it to her lips. "Now, if you refuse to drink it, after I have tasted it, I'll never speak to you again." So saying, she handed the glass to the Domine.

"Verily, maiden, I must needs refuse, for I did make a mental vow."

"What vow was that? Was it sworn on the Bible?"

"Nay, not on the sacred book, but in my thoughts most solemnly."

"Oh! I make those vows every day, and never keep one of them; so that won't do. Now, observe, I give you one more chance. I shall drink a little more, and if you do not immediately put your lips to the same part of the tumbler, I'll never drink to you again." Mary put the tumbler again to her lips, drank a little, with her eyes fixed upon the Domine, who watched her with distended nostrils and muscular agitation of

199

countenance. With her sweetest smile she handed him the tumbler; the Domine half held out his hand, withdrew it, put it down again, and by degrees took the tumbler. Mary conquered, and I watched the malice of her look as the liquor trickled down the Domine's throat. Tom and I exchanged glances. The Domine put down the tumbler, and then, looking round like a guilty person, coloured up to the eyes; but Mary, who perceived that her victory was but half achieved, put her hand upon his shoulder, and asked him to let her taste the grog again. I also, to make him feel more at ease, helped myself to a glass. Tom did the same, and old Tom, with more regard to the feelings of the Domine than in his own bluntness of character I would have given him credit for, said in a quiet tone, "The old gentleman is afraid of grog, because he seed me take a drop too much, but that's no reason why grog arn't a good thing, and wholesome in moderation. A glass or two is very well, and better still when sweetened by the lips of a pretty girl; and even if the Domine does not like it, he's too much of a gentleman not to give up his dislikes to please a lady. More's the merit; for if he did like it, it would be no sacrifice, that's sartain. Don't you think so, my old boozer?" continued he, addressing Stapleton, who smoked in silence.

"Human natur," replied Stapleton, taking the pipe out of his mouth, and spitting under the table.

"Very true, master; and so here's to your health, Mr. Domine, and may you never want a pretty girl to talk to, or a glass of grog to drink her health with."

"Oh, but the Domine don't care about pretty girls, father," replied Tom; "he's too learned and clever; he thinks about nothing but the moon, and Latin, and Greek, and philosophy, and all that."

"Who can say what's under the skin, Tom? There's no knowing what is, and what isn't—Sall's shoe for that."

"Never heard of Sall's shoe, father; that's new to me."

"Didn't I ever tell you that, Tom? Well then, you shall have it now—that is, if all the company be agreeable."

"Oh yes," cried Mary; "pray tell us."

"Would you like to hear it, sir?"

"I never heard of Sall Sue in my life, and would fain hear her history," replied the Domine; "proceed, friend Dux."

"Well then, you must know when I was aboard of the

Terp-sy-chore, there was a foretop-man, of the name of Bill Harness, a good sort of chap enough, but rather soft in the upper works. Now we'd been on the Jamaica station for some years, and had come home, and merry enough, and happy enough we were (those that were left of us), and we were spending our money like the devil. Bill Harness had a wife, who was very fond of he, and he were very fond of she; but she was a slatternly sort of a body, never tidy in her rigging, all adrift at all times, and what's more, she never had a shoe up at heel, so she went by the name of Slatternly Sall, and the first lieutenant, who was a 'ticular sort of a chap, never liked to see her on deck, for you see she put her hair in paper on New Year's day, and never changed it or took it out till the year came round again. However, be it as it may be, she loved Bill, and Bill loved she, and they were very happy together. A'ter all, it arn't whether a woman's tidy without that makes a man's happiness; it depends upon whether she be right within; that is, if she be good-tempered, and obliging, and civil, and 'commodating, and so forth. A'ter the first day or two, person's nothing—eyes get palled, like the capstern when the anchor's up to the bows; but what a man likes is, not to be disturbed by vagaries, or gusts of temper. Well, Bill was happy; but one day he was devilish unhappy, because Sall had lost one of her shoes, which wasn't to be wondered at, considering as how she was always slipshod. 'Who has seen my wife's shoe?' says he. 'Hang your wife's shoe,' said one, 'it warn't worth casting an eye upon.' Still he cried out, 'Who has seen my wife's shoe?'—'I seed it,' says another. 'Where?' says Bill. 'I seed it down at heel,' says the fellow. But Bill still hallooed out about his wife's shoe, which it appeared she had dropped off her foot as she was going up the forecastle ladder to take the air a bit, just as it was dark. At last Bill made so much fuss about it that the ship's company laughed, and all called out to each other, 'Who has seen Sall's shoe?'—'Have you got Sall's shoe?' and they passed the word fore and aft the whole evening, till they went to their hammocks. Notwithstanding, as Sall's shoe was not forthcoming, the next morning Bill goes on the quarter-deck, and complains to the first lieutenant as how he had lost Sall's shoe. 'D—n Sall's shoe,' said he, 'haven't I enough to look after without your wife's confounded shoes, which can't be worth twopence?' Well, Bill argues that his wife has only one shoe left, and that won't keep two feet dry, and begs the first lieutenant to order a search for it; but the first lieutenant turns away, and tells him to go to the devil, and all the men grin at Bill's making such a fuss about nothing. So Bill at last goes up to the first lieutenant, and whispers something, and the first lieutenant booms him off with his speaking trumpet, as if he was making too free, in whispering to his commanding officer, and then sends for the master-at-arms. 'Collier,' says he, 'this man has lost his wife's shoe, let a search be made for it immediately. Take all the ship's boys, and look everywhere for it; if you find it bring it up to me.' So away goes the master-at-arms with his cane, and collects all the boys to look for Sall's shoe; and they go peeping about the main-deck, under the guns, and under the hencoops, and in the sheep-pen, and everywhere, now and then getting a smart slap with the cane behind, upon the taut part of their trousers, to make them look sharp, until they all wished Sall's shoe at Old Nick and her too, and Bill in the bargain. At last one of the boys picks it out of the manger, where it had lain all the night, poked up and down by the noses of the pigs, who didn't think it eatable, although it might have smelt human-like; the fact was, it was the same boy who had picked up Sall's shoe when she dropped it, and had shied it forward. It sartainly did not seem to be worth all the trouble, but howsomever it was taken aft by the master-at-arms, and laid on the capstern head. Then Bill steps out, and takes the shoe before the first lieutenant, and cuts it open, and from between the lining pulls out four ten-pound notes, which Sall had sewn up there by way of security; and the first lieutenant tells Bill he was a great fool to trust his money in the shoe of a woman who always went slipshod, and tells him to go about his business, and stow his money away in a safer place next time. A'ter, if anything was better than it looked to be, the ship's company used always to say it was like Sall's shoe. There you have it all."

"Well," says Stapleton, taking the pipe out of his mouth, "I know a fact, much of a muchness with that, which happened to me when I was below the river, tending a ship at Sheerness—for at one time, d'ye see, I used to ply there. She was an old fifty-gun ship, called the *Adamant*, if I recollect right

One day the first lieutenant, who, like yourn, was a mighty particular sort of chap, was going round the main-deck, and he sees an old pair of canvas trousers stowed in under the trunnion of one of the guns. So says he, 'Whose be these?' Now, no man would answer, because they knowed very well that it would be as good as a fortnight in the black list. With that, the first lieutenant bundles them out of the port, and away they floats astern with the tide. It was about half-an-hour after that that I comes off with the milk for the wardroom mess, and a man named Will Heaviside says to me, 'Stapleton,' says he, 'the first lieutenant has thrown my canvas trousers overboard, and be d—d to him; now I must have them back.'—'But where be they?' says I; 'I suppose down at the bottom by this time, and the flat-fish dubbing their noses into them.'—'No, no,' says he, 'they won't never sink, but float till eternity; they be gone down with the tide, and they will come back again. Only you keep a sharp look-out for them, and I'll give you five shillings, if you bring them.' Well, I seed little chance of ever seeing them again, or of my seeing five shillings; but as it so happened next tide, the very 'dentical pair of trousers comes up staring me in the face. I pulls them in, and takes them to Will Heaviside, who appears to be mightily pleased, and gives me the money. 'I wouldn't have lost them for ten, no, not for twenty pounds,' says he. 'At all events you've paid me more than they are worth,' says I. 'Have I?' says he; 'stop a bit;' and he outs with his knife and rips open the waistband, and pulls out a piece of linen, and out of the piece of linen he pulls out a *child's caul*. 'There,' says he, 'now you knows why the trousers wouldn't sink, and I'll leave you to judge whether they arn't worth five shillings.' That's my story."

"Well, I can't understand how it is, that a caul should keep people up," observed old Tom.

"At all events, a *call* makes people come up fast enough on board a man-of-war, father."

"That's true enough, but I'm talking of a child's caul, not of a boatswain's, Tom."

"I'll just tell you how it is," replied Stapleton, who had recommenced smoking; "it's human natur."

"What is your opinion, sir?" said Mary to the Domine.

"Maiden," replied the Domine, taking his pipe out of his

mouth, " I opine that it's a vulgar error. Sir Thomas Browne,
I think it is, hath the same idea ; many and strange were the
superstitions which have been handed down by our less enlightened ancestors, all of which mists have been cleared
away by the powerful rays of truth."

" Well, but, master, if a vulgar error saves a man from Davy
Jones's locker, arn't it just as well to sew it up in the waistband of your trousers ? "

" Granted, good Dux, if it would save a man ; but how is
it possible ? It is contrary to the first elements of science."

" What matter does that make, provided it holds a
man up ? "

" Friend Dux, thou art obtuse."

" Well, perhaps I am, as I don't know what that is."

" But, father, don't you recollect," interrupted Tom, "what
the parson said last Sunday, that faith saved men ? Now,
Master Domine, may it not be the faith that a man has in
the caul which may save him ? "

" Young Tom, thou art astute."

" Well, perhaps I am, as father said, for I don't know what
that is. You knock us all down with your dictionary."

" Well, I do love to hear people make use of such hard
words," said Mary, looking at the Domine. " How very
clever you must be, sir ! . I wonder whether I shall ever
understand them ? "

" Nay, if thou wilt, I will initiate — sweet maiden, wilt
steal an hour or so to impregnate thy mind with the seeds
of learning, which in so fair a soil must needs bring forth
good fruit.'

" That's a fine word that *impregnate*—will you give us the
English of it, sir ? " said young Tom to the Domine.

" It is English, Tom, only the old gentleman *razeed* it a
little. The third ship in the lee line of the Channel fleet
was a eighty, called the *Impregnable*, but the old gentleman
knows more about books than sea matters."

"A marvellous misconception," quoth the Domine.

" There's another," cried Tom, laughing ; " that must be
a three-decker. Come, father, here's the bottle, you must
take another glass to wash that down."

" Pray, what was the meaning of that last long word, sir," said
Mary, taking the Domine by the arm ; " mis—something."

"The word," replied the Domine, "is a compound from conception, borrowed from the Latin tongue, implying conceiving, and the *mis* prefixed, which negatives or reverses the meaning; misconception therefore implies not to conceive. I can make you acquainted with many others of a similar tendency as *mis*-conception; *videlicet, mis*-apprehension, *mis*-understanding, *mis*-contriving, *mis*-applying, *mis*——"

"Dear me, what a many *misses*," cried Mary, "and do you know them all?"

"Indeed do I," replied the Domine, "and many, many more are treasured in my memory, *quod nunc describere longum est.*"

"Well, I'd no idea that the old gentleman was given to running after the girls in that way," said old Tom to Stapleton.

"Human natur," replied the other.

"No more did I," continued Mary; "I shall have nothing to say to him;" and she drew off her chair a few inches from that of the Domine.

"Maiden," quoth the Domine, "thou art under a *mis*-take."

"Another miss, I declare," cried Tom, laughing.

"What an old Turk!" continued Mary, getting further off.

"Nay, then, I will not reply," said the Domine indignantly, putting down his pipe, leaning back on his chair, and pulling out his great red handkerchief, which he applied to his nose, and produced a sound that made the windows of the little parlour vibrate for some seconds.

"I say, master Tom, don't you make too free with your betters," said old Tom, when he perceived the Domine affronted.

"Nay," replied the Domine, "there's an old adage which saith, 'As the old cock crows, so doth the young.' Wherefore didst thou set him the example?"

"Very true, old gentleman, and I axes your pardon, and here's my hand upon it."

"And so do I, sir, and here's my hand upon it," said young Tom, extending his on the Domine's other side.

"Friend Dux, and thou, young Tom, I do willingly accept thy proffered reconciliation; knowing, as I well do, that there may be much mischief in thy composition, but naught of malice." The Domine extended his hands, and shook both those offered to him warmly.

"There," said old Tom, "now my mind's at ease, as old Pigtown said."

"I know not the author whom thou quotest from, good Dux."

"Author !—I never said he was an author; he was only captain of a schooner, trading between the islands, that I sailed with a few weeks in the West Indies."

"Perhaps, then, you will relate to the company present, the circumstances which took place to put old Pegtop's (I may not be correct in the name), but whoever it may be——"

"Pigtown, master."

"Well then, that put old Pigtown's mind at ease; for I am marvellously amused with thy narrations, which do pass away the time most agreeably, good Dux."

"With all my heart, old gentleman; but first let us fill up our tumblers. I don't know how it is, but it does appear to me that grog drinks better out of a glass than out of metal, and if it wasn't that Tom is so careless—and the dog has no respect for crockery any more than persons, I would have one or two on board for particular service; but I'll think about that, and hear what the old woman has to say on the subject. Now to my yarn. D'ye see, old Pigtown commanded a little schooner which plied between the isles, and he had been in her for a matter of forty years, and was as well known as Port Royal Tom."

"Who might Port Royal Tom be ?" inquired the Domine; "a relation of yours ?"

"I hope not, master, for I wanted none of his acquaintance. He was a shark about twenty feet long, who rode guard in the harbour, to prevent the men-of-war's men from deserting, and was pensioned by government."

"Pensioned by government! nay, but that soundeth strangely. I have heard that pensions have been most lavishly bestowed, but not that it extended so far. Truly it must have been a sinecure."

"I don't know what that last may be," replied old Tom; "but I heard our boatswain, in the *Minerve*, who talked politics a bit, say 'as how half the pensions were held by a pack of d—d sharks;' but in this here shark's case, it wasn't in money, master; but he'd regular rations of bullocks' liver to persuade him to remain in the harbour, and no one dare swim on shore when he was crushing round and round the ships. Well, old Pigtown, with his white trousers and straw hat, red nose and big belly, was as well known as could be, and was a capital old fellow for remembering and executing commissions, provided you gave him the money first; if not, he always took care to forget them. Old Pigtown had a son, a little dark or so, which proved that his mother wasn't quite as fair as a lily; and this son was employed in a drogher, that is, a small craft which goes round to the bays of the island, and takes off the sugars to the West India traders. One fine day the drogher was driven out to sea, and never heard of a'terwards. Now, old Pigtown was very anxious about what had come of his son, and day after day expected he would come back again, but he never did, for very good reasons, as you shall hear by-and-by; and every one knowing old Pigtown, and he knowing everybody, it was at least fifty times a day that the question was put to him, 'Well, Pigtown, have you heard anything of your son?' And fifty times a day he would reply, 'No; and *my mind's but ill at ease.*' Well, it was two or three months afterwards, that when I was in the schooner with him, as we lay becalmed between the islands, with the sun frizzing our wigs, and the planks so hot that you couldn't walk without your shoes, that we hooked a large shark which came bowling under our counter. We got him on board and cut him up. When we opened his inside, what should I see but something shining. I took it out, and sure enough it was a silver watch. So I hands it to old Pigtown. He looks at it very 'tentively, opens the outside case, reads the maker's name, and then shuts it up again. 'This here watch,' says he, 'belonged to my son Jack. I bought it of a chap in a south whaler for three dollars and a roll of pigtail, and a very good watch it was, though I perceive it to be stopped now. Now, d'ye see, it's all clear; the drogher must have gone down in a squall; the shark must have picked up my son Jack, and must have *disgested* his body, but has not been able to *disgest* his watch. Now I knows what's become of him, and so—*my mind's at ease.*"

"Well," observed old Stapleton, "I agrees with old Poptown, or whatever his name might be, that it were better to know the worst at once, than to be kept on the worry all your days. I consider it's nothing but human natur. Why, if one has a bad tooth, which is the best plan, to have it out

207

with one good wrench at once, or to be tormented night and day the whole year round?"

"Thou speakest wisely, friend Stapleton, and like a man of resolve—the anticipation is often, if not always, more painful than the reality. Thou knowest, Jacob, how often I have allowed a boy to remain unbuttoned in the centre of the room for an hour previous to the application of the birch; and it was with the consideration that the impression would be greater upon his mind than even upon his nether parts. Of all the feelings in the human breast, that of suspense is——"

"Worse than hanging," interrupted young Tom.

"Even so, boy [cluck, cluck], an apt comparison, seeing that in suspense you are hanging, as it were, in the very region of doubt, without being able to obtain a footing even upon conjecture. Nay, we may further add another simile, although not so well borne out, which is, that the agony of suspense doth stop the breath of a man for the time, as hanging doth stop it altogether, so that it may be truly said, that suspense is put an end to by suspending." [Cluck, cluck.]

"And now that you've got rid of all that, master, suppose you fill up your pipe," observed old Tom.

"And I will fill up your tumbler, sir," said Mary; "for you must be dry with talking such hard words."

The Domine this time made no objection, and again enveloped Mary and himself in a cloud of smoke, through which his nose loomed like an Indiaman in a Channel fog.

CHAPTER XXVI

The Domine's bosom grows too warm ; so the party and the frost break up—I go with the stream and against it ; make money both ways—Coolness between Mary and me—No chance of a Thames' edition of Abelard and Eloise—Love, learning, and Latin all lost in a fit of the sulks.

I SAY, master Stapleton, suppose we were to knock out half a port," observed old Tom, after a silence of two minutes; "for the old gentleman blows a devil of a cloud—that is, if no one has an objection." Stapleton gave a nod of assent, and I rose and put the upper window down a few inches. "Ay, that's right, Jacob; now we shall see what Miss Mary and he are about. You've been enjoying the lady all to yourself, master," continued Tom, addressing the Domine.

"Verily and truly," replied the Domine, "even as a second Jupiter."

"Never heard of him."

"I presume not; still, Jacob will tell thee that the history is to be found in Ovid's Metamorphoses."

"Never heard of the country, master."

"Nay, friend Dux, it is a book, not a country, in which thou mayst read how Jupiter at first descended unto Semele in a cloud."

"And pray, where did he come from, master?"

"He came from heaven."

"The devil he did. Well, if ever I gets there, I mean to stay."

"It was love, all-powerful love, which induced him, maiden," replied the Domine, turning with a smiling eye to Mary.

"'Bove my comprehension altogether," replied old Tom.

"Human natur," muttered Stapleton, with the pipe still between his lips.

"Not the first vessels that have run foul in a fog," observed young Tom.

"No, boy; but generally there arn't much love between them at those times. But, come, now that we can breathe again, suppose I give you a song. What shall it be, young woman, a sea ditty, or something spooney?"

"Oh! something about love, if you've no objection, sir," said Mary, appealing to the Domine.

"Nay, it pleaseth me, maiden, and I am of thy mind. Friend Dux, let it be Anacreontic."

"What the devil's that?" cried old Tom, lifting up his eyes, and taking the pipe out of his mouth.

"Nothing of your own, father, that's clear; but something to borrow, for it's to be on tick," replied Tom.

"Nay, boy, I would have been understood that the song should refer to woman or wine."

"Both of which are to his fancy," observed young Tom to me, aside.

"Human natur," quaintly observed Stapleton.

"Well then, you shall have your wish. I'll give you one

209   o

that might be warbled in a lady's chamber, without stirring
the silk curtains—

> ' Oh ! the days are gone when beauty bright
>   My heart's chain wove,
> When my dream of life, from morn to night
>   Was Love—still Love.
>   New hope may bloom,
>   And days may come,
>   Of milder, calmer beam ;
> But there's nothing half so sweet in life,
>   As Love's young dream ;
> Oh ! there's nothing half so sweet in life,
>   As Love's young dream.' "

The melody of the song, added to the spirits he had drunk,
and Mary's eyes beaming on him, had a great effect upon the
Domine. As old Tom warbled out, so did the pedagogue
gradually approach the chair of Mary ; and as gradually
entwine her waist with his own arm, his eyes twinkling
brightly on her. Old Tom, who perceived it, had given
Tom and me a wink, as he repeated the two last lines ; and
when we saw what was going on, we burst into an uncon-
trollable fit of laughter. "Boys ! boys !" said the Domine,
starting up, "thou hast awakened me, by thy boisterous
mirth, from a sweet musing created by the harmony of friend
Dux's voice. Neither do I discover the source of thy cachin-
nation, seeing that the song is amatory and not comic. Still
it may not be supposed, at thy early age, that thou canst be
affected with what thou art too young to feel. Prythee
continue, friend Dux—and, boys, restrain thy mirth."

> " Though the bard to purer fame may soar
>   When wild youth's past ;
> Though he find the wise, who frowned before,
>   To smile at last.
>   He'll never meet
>   A joy so sweet
>   In all his noon of fame,
> As when he sung to woman's ear,
>   The soul-felt flame ;
> And at every close, she blushed to hear
>   The once-loved name."

At the commencement of this verse, the Domine appeared to be on his guard; but gradually moved by the power of song, he dropped his elbow on the table, and his pipe underneath it; his forehead sank into his broad palm, and he remained motionless. The verse ended, and the Domine forgetting all around him, softly ejaculated, without looking up, "Eheu! Mary."

"Did you speak to me, sir?" said Mary, who, perceiving us tittering, addressed the Domine with a half-serious, half-mocking air.

"Speak, maiden? nay, I spoke not; yet thou mayest give me my pipe, which apparently hath been abducted while I was listening to the song."

"Abducted! that's a new word; but it means smashed into twenty pieces, I suppose," observed young Tom. "At all events, your pipe is, for you let it fall between your legs."

"Never mind," said Mary, rising from her chair and going to the cupboard, "here's another, sir."

"Well, master, am I to finish, or have you had enough of it?"

"Proceed, friend Dux, proceed; and believe that I am all attention."

> "Oh that hallowed form is ne'er forgot
>   Which first love traced,
> Still it lingering haunts the greenest spot
>   On memory's waste.
>   'Twas odour fled
>   As soon as shed,
> 'Twas memory's wingèd dream;
> 'Twas a light that ne'er can shine again
>   On life's dull stream;
> Oh! 'twas a light that ne'er can shine again
>   On life's dull stream."

"Nay," said the Domine, again abstracted, "the metaphor is not just. 'Life's dull stream.' '*Lethe tacitus amnis*,' as Lucan hath it; but the stream of life flows—ay, flows rapidly —even in my veins. Doth not the heart throb and beat— yea, strongly—peradventure too forcibly against my better judgment? '*Confiteor misere molle cor esse mihi*,' as Ovid saith. Yet must it not prevail! Shall one girl be victorious over seventy boys? Shall I, Domine Dobbs, desert my post?——

Again succumb to—— I will even depart, that I may be at my desk at matutinal hours."

"You don't mean to leave us, sir?" said Mary, taking the Domine's arm.

"Even so, fair maiden, for it waxeth late, and I have my duties to perform," said the Domine, rising from his chair.

"Then you will promise to come again."

"Peradventure I may."

"If you do not promise me that you will, I will not let you go now."

"Verily, maiden——"

"Promise," interrupted Mary.

"Truly, maiden——"

"Promise," cried Mary.

"In good sooth, maiden——"

"Promise," reiterated Mary, pulling the Domine towards her chair.

"Nay, then, I do promise, since thou wilt have it so," replied the Domine.

"And when will you come?"

"I will not tarry," replied the Domine; "and now good night to all."

The Domine shook hands with us, and Mary lighted him downstairs. I was much pleased with the resolution and sense of his danger thus shown by my worthy preceptor, and hoped that he would have avoided Mary in future, who evidently wished to make a conquest of him for her own amusement and love of admiration; but still I felt that the promise exacted would be fulfilled, and I was afraid that a second meeting, and that perhaps not before witnesses, would prove mischievous. I made up my mind to speak to Mary on the subject as soon as I had an opportunity, and insist upon her not making a fool of the worthy old man. Mary remained below a much longer time than was necessary, and when she reappeared and looked at me, as if for a smile of approval, I turned from her with a contemptuous air. She sat down and looked confused. Tom was also silent, and paid her no attention. A quarter of an hour passed, when he proposed to his father that they should be off, and the party broke up. Leaving Mary silent and thoughtful, and old Stapleton finishing his pipe, I took my candle and went to bed.

The next day the moon changed, the weather changed, and a rapid thaw took place. "It's an ill wind that blows nobody good," observed old Stapleton; "we watermen will have the river to ourselves again, and the hucksters must carry their gingerbread-nuts to another market." It was, however, three or four days before the river was clear of the ice, so as to permit the navigation to proceed; and during that time, I may as well observe, that there was dissension between Mary and me. I showed her that I resented her conduct, and at first she tried to pacify me; but finding that I held out longer than she expected, she turned round and was affronted in return. Short words and no lessons were the order of the day; and as each party appeared determined to hold out, there was little prospect of a reconciliation. In this she was the greatest sufferer, as I quitted the house after breakfast, and did not return until dinner-time. At first old Stapleton plied very regularly, and took all the fares; but about a fortnight after we had worked together, he used to leave me to look after employment, and remain at the public-house. The weather was now fine, and after the severe frost it changed so rapidly that most of the trees were in leaf, and the horse-chestnuts in full blossom. The wherry was in constant demand, and every evening I handed from four to six shillings over to old Stapleton. I was delighted with my life, and should have been perfectly happy if it had not been for my quarrel with Mary still continuing, she as resolutely refraining from making advances as I. How much may life be embittered by dissension with those you live with, even where there is no very warm attachment; the constant grating together worries and annoys, and although you may despise the atoms, the aggregate becomes insupportable. I had no pleasure in the house; and the evenings, which formerly passed so agreeably, were now a source of vexation, from being forced to sit in company with one with whom I was not on good terms. Old Stapleton was seldom at home till late, and this made it still worse. I was communing with myself one night, as I had my eyes fixed on my book, whether I should not make the first advances, when Mary, who had been quietly at work, broke the silence by asking me what I was reading. I replied in a quiet, grave tone.

"Jacob," said she, in continuation, "I think you have used

me very ill to humble me in this manner. It was your business to make it up first."

"I am not aware that I have been in the wrong," replied I.

"I do not say that you have; but what matter does that make? You ought to give way to a woman."

"Why so?"

"Why so! don't the whole world do so? Do you not offer everything first to a woman? Is it not her right?"

"Not when she is in the wrong, Mary."

"Yes, when she is in the wrong, Jacob; there's no merit in doing it when she's in the right."

"I think otherwise; at all events, it depends on how much she has been in the wrong, and I consider you have shown a bad heart, Mary."

"A bad heart! in what way, Jacob?"

"In realising the fable of the boys and the frogs with the poor old Domine, forgetting that what may be sport to you is death to him."

"You don't mean to say that he'll die of love," replied Mary, laughing.

"I should hope not; but you may contrive, and you have tried, all in your power to make him very wretched."

"And, pray, how do you know that I do not like the old gentleman, Jacob? You appear to think that a girl is to fall in love with nobody but yourself. Why should I not love an old man with so much learning? I have been told that old husbands are much prouder of their wives than young ones, and pay them more attention, and don't run after other women. How do you know that I am not serious?"

"Because I know your character, Mary, and am not to be deceived. If you mean to defend yourself in that way, we had better not talk any more."

"Lord, how savage you are! Well then, suppose I did pay the old gentleman any attention. Did the young ones pay me any? Did either you, or your precious friend, Mr. Tom, even speak to me?"

"No; we saw how you were employed, and we both hate a jilt."

"Oh! you do. Very well, sir; just as you please. I may make both of your hearts ache for this, some day or another."

"Forewarned, forearmed, Mary; and I shall take care that

214

they are both forewarned as well as myself. As I perceive that you are so decided, I shall say no more. Only for your own sake, and your own happiness, I caution you. Recollect your mother, Mary, and recollect your mother's death."

Mary covered her face, and burst into tears. She sobbed for a few minutes, and then came to me. "You are right, Jacob, and I am a foolish—perhaps wicked—girl; but forgive me, and indeed I will try to behave better. But, as father says, it is human nature in me, and it's hard to conquer our natures, Jacob."

"Will you promise me not to continue your advances to the Domine, Mary?"

"I will not, if I can help it, Jacob. I may forget for the moment, but I'll do all I can. It's not very easy to look grave when one is merry, or sour when one is pleased."

"But what can induce you, Mary, to practise upon an old man like him? If it were young Tom I could understand it. There might be some credit, and your pride might be flattered by the victory; but an old man——"

"Still, Jacob, old or young, it's much the same. I would like to have them all at my feet, and that's the truth. I can't help it. And I thought it a great victory to bring there a wise old man, who was so full of Latin and learning, and who ought to know better. Tell me, Jacob, if old men allow themselves to be caught, as well as young, where is the crime of catching them? Isn't there as much vanity in an old man, in his supposing that I really could love him, as there is in me, who am but a young foolish girl, in trying to make him fond of me?"

"That may be; but still recollect that he is in earnest, and you are only joking, which makes a great difference; and recollect further, that in trying at all, we very often lose all."

"That I would take my chance of, Jacob," replied Mary, proudly throwing her curly ringlets back with her hand from her white forehead; "but what I now want is to make friends with you. Come, Jacob, you have my promise to do my best."

"Yes, Mary, and I believe you, so there's my hand."

"You don't know how miserable I have been, Jacob, since we quarrelled," said Mary, wiping the tears away, which again commenced flowing; "and yet I don't know why, for I'm sure I have almost hated you this last week—that I have; but the fact is, I like quarrelling very well for the pleasure of making it up again, but not for the quarrel to last so long as this has done."

"It has annoyed me too, Mary, for I like you very much in general."

"Well then, now it's all over; but, Jacob, are you sure you are friends with me?"

"Yes, Mary."

Mary looked archly at m   "You know the old saw, and I feel the truth of it."

"What, 'kiss and make friends'?" replied I; "with all my heart," and I kissed her, without any resistance on her part.

"No, I didn't mean that, Jacob."

"What then?"

"Oh! 'twas another."

"Well then, what was the other?"

"Never mind, I forget it now," said she, laughing and rising from the chair. "Now I must go to my work again, and you must tell me what you've been doing this last fortnight."

Mary and I entered into a long and amicable conversation, till her father came home, when we retired to bed. "I think," said old Stapleton, the next morning, "that I've had work enough; and I've belonged to two benefit clubs for so long as to 'title me to an allowance. I think, Jacob, I shall give up the wherry to you, and you shall in future give me one third of your earnings, and keep the rest to yourself. I don't see why you're to work hard all day for nothing." I remonstrated against this excess of liberality; but old Stapleton was positive, and the arrangement was made. I afterwards discovered, what may probably occur to the reader, that Captain Turnbull was at the bottom of all this. He had pensioned old Stapleton that I might become independent by my own exertions before I had served my apprenticeship; and after breakfast, old Stapleton walked down with me to the beach, and we launched the boat. "Recollect, Jacob," said he, "one third, and honour bright;" so saying, he adjourned to his old quarters, the public-house, to smoke his pipe and think of human natur. I do not recollect any day of my life on which I felt more happy than on this—I was working for myself, and independent. I jumped into my wherry, and without waiting for a fare I pushed off, and gaining the stream, cleaved through the water with delight as my reward; but after a quarter of an hour I sobered down, with the recollection that although I might pull about for nothing for my own amusement, that as Stapleton was entitled to one third, I had no right to neglect his interest; and I shot my wherry into the row, and stood with my hand and forefinger raised watching the eye of every one who came towards the hard. I was fortunate that day, and when I returned, was proceeding to give Stapleton his share, when he stopped me. "Jacob, it's no use dividing now; once a week will be better. I likes things to come in a lump; 'cause d'ye see—it's—it's—human natur."

CHAPTER XXVII

A good fare—Eat your pudding and hold your tongue—The Domine crossed in love—The crosser also crossed—I find that "all the world's a stage," not excepting the stern-sheets of my wherry—Cleopatra's barge apostrophised on the river Thames.

I CONSIDER that the present was the period from which I might date my first launching into human life. I was now nearly eighteen years old, strong, active, and well-made, full of spirits, and overjoyed at the independence which I had so much sighed for. Since the period of my dismissal from Mr. Drummond's, my character had much altered. I had become grave and silent, brooding over my wrongs, harbouring feelings of resentment against the parties, and viewing the world in general through a medium by no means favourable. I had become in some degree restored from this unwholesome state of mind, from having rendered an important service to Captain Turnbull, for we love the world better as we feel that we are more useful in it; but the independence now given to me was the acme of my hopes and wishes. I felt so happy, so buoyant in mind, that I could even think of the two clerks in Mr. Drummond's employ without feelings of revenge. Let it, however, be remembered, that the world was all before me in anticipation only.

"Boat, sir?"

"No, thanky, my lad, I want old Stapleton—is he here?"

"No, sir, but this is his boat."

"Humph, can't he take me down?"

"No, sir; but I can, if you please."

"Well then, be quick."

A sedate-looking gentleman, about forty-five years of age, stepped into the boat, and in a few seconds I was in the stream, shooting the bridge with the ebbing tide.

"What's the matter with deaf Stapleton?"

"Nothing, sir; but he's getting old, and has made the boat over to me."

"Are you his son?"

"No, sir, his 'prentice."

"Humph! sorry deaf Stapleton's gone."

"I can be as deaf as he, sir, if you wish it."

"Humph!"

The gentleman said no more at the time, and I pulled down the river in silence; but in a few minutes he began to move his hands up and down, and his lips, as if he was in conversation. Gradually his action increased, and words were uttered. At last he broke out: "It is with this conviction, I may say important conviction, Mr. Speaker, that I now deliver my sentiments to the Commons' House of Parliament, trusting that no honourable member will decide until he has fully weighed the importance of the arguments which I have submitted to his judgment." He then stopped, as if aware that I was present, and looked at me; but, prepared as I was, there was nothing in my countenance which exhibited the least sign of merriment, or indeed of having paid any attention to what he had been saying, for I looked carelessly to the right and left at the banks of the river. He again entered into conversation.

"Have you been long on the river?"

"Born on it, sir."

"How do you like the profession of a waterman?"

"Very well, sir; the great point is to have regular customers."

"And how do you gain them?"

"By holding my tongue; keeping their counsel and my own."

"Very good answer, my boy. People who have much to do cannot afford to lose even their time on the water. Just now I was preparing and thinking over my speech in the House of Commons."

"So I supposed, sir, and I think the river is a very good place for it, as no one can overhear you except the person whose services you have hired—and you need not mind him."

"Very true, my lad; but that's why I liked deaf Stapleton
—he could not hear a word."

"But, sir, if you've no objection, I like to hear it very
much; and you may be sure that I should never say anything
about it, if you will trust me."

"Do you, my lad? well, then, I'll just try it over again.
You shall be the Speaker—mind you hold your tongue, and
don't interrupt me."

The gentleman then began: "Mr. Speaker, I should not
have ventured to address the House at this late hour, did I not
consider that the importance of the question now before it is—
so important—no, that won't do—did I not consider that the
question now before it is of that, I may say, paramount importance as to call forth the best energies of every man who is a
well-wisher to his country. With this conviction, Mr. Speaker,
humble individual as I am, I feel it my duty, I may say, my
bounden duty, to deliver my sentiments upon the subject.
The papers which I now hold in my hand, Mr. Speaker, and
to which I shall soon have to call the attention of the House,
will, I trust, fully establish——"

"I say, waterman, be you taking that chap to Bedlam?"
cried a shrill female voice close to us. The speech was
stopped; we looked up, and perceived a wherry with two
females passing close to us. A shout of laughter followed the
observation, and my fare looked very much confused and
annoyed.

I had often read the papers in the public-house, and remembering what was usual in the House in case of interruption,
called out, "Order, order!" This made the gentleman laugh,
and as the other wherry was now far off, he recommenced his
oration, with which I shall not trouble my readers. It was a very
fair speech, I have no doubt, but I forget what it was about.

I landed him at Westminster Bridge, and received treble my
fare. "Recollect," said he, on paying me, "that I shall look
out for you when I come again, which I do every Monday
morning, and sometimes oftener. What's your name?"

"Jacob, sir."

"Very well; good-morning, my lad."

This gentleman became a very regular and excellent
customer, and we used to have a great deal of conversation, independent of debating, in the wherry; and I must

acknowledge that I received from him not only plenty of money, but a great deal of valuable information.

A few days after this I had an opportunity of ascertaining how far Mary would keep her promise. I was plying at the river-side as usual, when old Stapleton came up to me, with his pipe in his mouth, and said, "Jacob, there be that old gentleman up at our house with Mary. Now, I sees a great deal, but I says nothing. Mary will be her mother over again, that's sartain. Suppose you go and see your old teacher, and leave me to look a'ter a customer. I begin to feel as if handling the sculls a little would be of sarvice to me. We all think idleness be a very pleasant thing when we're obliged to work, but when we are idle, then we feel that a little work be just as agreeable—that's human natur."

I thought that Mary was very likely to forget all her good resolutions, from her ardent love of admiration, and I was determined to go and break up the conference. I therefore left the boat to Stapleton, and hastened to the house. I did not like to play the part of an eavesdropper, and was quite undecided how I should act, whether to go in at once or not; when, as I passed under the window, which was open, I heard very plainly the conversation which was going on. I stopped in the street, and listened to the Domine in continuation. "But, fair maiden, *omnia vincit amor*—here am I, Domine Dobbs, who have long passed the grand climacteric, and can already muster three score years; who have authority over seventy boys—being Magister Princeps et Dux of Brentford Grammar School; who have affectioned only the sciences, and communed only with the classics; who have ever turned a deaf ear to the allurements of thy sex, and even hardened my heart to thy fascination—here am I, even I, Domine Dobbs, suing at the feet of a maiden who has barely ripened into womanhood, who knoweth not to read or write, and whose father earns his bread by manual labour. I feel it all—I feel that I am too old—that thou art too young—that I am departing from the ways of wisdom, and am regardless of my worldly prospects. Still, *omnia vincit amor*, and I bow to the all-powerful god, doing him homage through thee, Mary. Vainly have I resisted—vainly have I, as I have lain in bed, tried to drive thee from my thoughts, and tear thine image from my heart. Have I not felt thy presence everywhere? Do not I astonish my worthy coadjutor, Mistress Bately, the matron, by calling her by the name of Mary, when I had always before addressed her by her baptismal name of Deborah? Nay, have not the boys in the classes discovered my weakness, and do they not shout out **Mary** in the hours of play? *Mare periculosum et turbidum* hast thou been to me. I sleep not—I eat not—and every sign of love which hath been adduced by Ovidius Naso, whom I have diligently collated, do I find in mine own person. Speak, then, maiden. I have given vent to my feelings, do thou the same, that I may return, and leave not my flock without their shepherd. Speak, maiden."

"I will, sir, if you will get up," replied Mary, who paused, and then continued. "I think, sir, that I am young and foolish, and you are old and—and——"

"Foolish, thou wouldst say."

"I had rather you said it, sir, than I; it is not for me to use such an expression towards one so learned as you are. I think, sir, that I am too young to marry; and that perhaps you are —too old. I think, sir, that you are too clever—and that I am very ignorant; that it would not suit you in your situation to marry; and that it would not suit me to marry you—equally obliged to you all the same."

"Perhaps thou hast in thy reply proved the wiser of the two," answered the Domine; "but why, maiden, didst thou raise those feelings, those hopes in my breast, only to cause me pain, and make me drink deep of the cup of disappointment? Why didst thou appear to cling to me in fondness, if thou felt not a yearning towards me?"

"But are there no other sorts of love besides the one you would require, sir? May I not love you because you are so clever, and so learned in Latin? May I not love you as I do my father?"

"True, true, child; it is all my own folly, and I must retrace my steps in sorrow. I have been deceived; but I have been deceived only by myself. My wishes have clouded my understanding, and have obscured my reason; have made me forgetful of my advanced years, and of the little favour I was likely to find in the eyes of a young maiden. I have fallen into a pit through blindness, and I must extricate myself, sore as will be the task. Bless thee, maiden, bless thee! May another be happy in thy love, and never feel the barb of disappointment.

I will pray for thee, Mary—that Heaven may bless thee." And the Domine turned away and wept.

Mary appeared to be moved by the good old man's affliction, and her heart probably smote her for her coquettish behaviour. She attempted to console the Domine, and appeared to be more than half crying herself. "No, sir, do not take on so, you make me feel very uncomfortable. I have been wrong—I feel I have—though you have not blamed me. I am a very foolish girl."

"Bless thee, child—bless thee!" replied the Domine, in a subdued voice.

"Indeed, sir, I don't deserve it—I feel I do not; but pray do not grieve, sir; things will go cross in love. Now, sir, I'll tell you a secret, to prove it to you. I love Jacob—love him very much, and he does not care for me—I am sure he does not; so, you see, sir, you are not the only one—who is—very unhappy;" and Mary commenced sobbing with the Domine.

"Poor thing!" said the Domine; "and thou lovest Jacob? truly is he worthy of thy love. And, at thy early age, thou knowest what it is to have thy love unrequited. Truly is this a vale of tears—yet let us be thankful. Guard well thy heart, child, for Jacob may not be for thee; nay, I feel that he will not be."

"And why so, sir?" replied Mary despondingly.

"Because, maiden—but nay, I must not tell thee; only take my warning, which is meant in kindness and in love. Fare thee well, Mary—fare thee well! I come not here again."

"Good-bye, sir, and pray forgive me; this will be a warning to me."

"Verily, maiden, it will be a warning to us both. God bless thee!"

I discovered by the sound, that Mary had vouchsafed to the Domine a kiss, and heard soon afterwards his steps, as he descended the stairs. Not wishing to meet him, I turned round the corner and went down to the river, thinking over what had passed. I felt pleased with Mary, but I was not in love with her.

The spring was now far advanced, and the weather was delightful. The river was beautiful, and parties of pleasure were constantly to be seen floating up and down with the tide. The Westminster boys, the Funny Club, and other amateurs in their fancy dresses, enlivened the scene; while the races for prize wherries, which occasionally took place, rendered the water one mass of life and motion. How I longed for my apprentice‑ ship to be over, that I might try for a prize ! One of my best customers was a young man, who was an actor at one of the theatres, and who, like the M.P., used to rehearse the whole time he was in the boat ; but he was a lively, noisy personage, full of humour, and perfectly indifferent as to appearances. He had a quiz and a quirk for everybody that passed in another boat, and would stand up and rant at them until they con‑ sidered him insane. We were on very intimate terms, and I never was more pleased than when he made his appearance, as it was invariably the signal for mirth. The first time I certainly considered him to be a lunatic, for playhouse phraseology was quite new to me. " Boat, sir ? " cried I to him, as he came to the hard.

" My affairs do even drag me homeward. Go on ; I'll follow thee," replied he, leaping into the boat. " Our fortune lies upon this jump."

I shoved off the wherry : " Down, sir ? "

" Down," replied he, pointing downwards with his finger, as if pushing at something—

> " Down, down to h—ll, and say I sent you there."

" Thanky, sir, I'd rather not, if it's all the same to you."

" Our tongue is rough, coz—and my condition is not smooth." We shot the bridge, and went rapidly down with the tide, when he again commenced—

> " Thus with imagined wing our soft scene flies,
> In motion of no less celerity
> Than that of thought."

Then his attention was drawn by a collier's boat, pulled by two men as black as chimney-sweeps, with three women in the stern-sheets. They made for the centre of the river, to get into the strength of the tide, and were soon abreast and close to the wherry, pulling with us down the stream.

" There's a dandy young man," said one of the women, with an old straw bonnet and very dirty ribbons, laughing, and pointing to my man.

> " Plead you to me, fair dame ? I know you not ;
> At Ephesus I am but two hours old,
> As strange unto your town as to your talk."

"Well, he be a reg'lar rum cove, I've a notion," said another of the women, when she witnessed the theatrical airs of the speaker, who immediately recommenced—

> "The barge she sat in, like a burnished throne,
> Burned on the water—the poop was beaten gold,
> Purple the sails, and so perfumèd that
> The winds were love-sick with them ; the oars were silver,
> Which to the tune of flutes kept stroke, and made
> The water, which they beat, to follow faster,
> As amorous of their strokes. For her own person,
> It beggared all description."

"Come, I'll be blowed but we've had enough of that, so just shut your pan," said one of the women angrily.

> " Her gentlewomen, like the Naiades,
> So many mermaids tend her."

"Mind what you're arter, or your mouth will tend to your mischief, young fellow."

> " From the barge
> A strange, invisible perfume hits the sense
> Of the adjacent wharfs."

"Jem, just run him alongside, and break his head with your oar."
"I think as how I will, if he don't mend his manners."

> " I saw her once
> Hop forty paces through the public streets."

"You lie, you liver-faced rascal. I never walked the streets in my life; I'm a lawful married woman. Jem, do you call yourself a man, and stand this here ?"
"Well now, Sal, but he's a nice young man. Now, an't he?" observed one of the other women.

> " Away,
> Away, you trifler. Love ! I know thee not,
> I care not for thee, Kate : this is no world
> To play with mammets, and to tilt with lips ;
> We must have bloody noses and cracked crowns."

"I've a notion you will too, my hearty," interrupted one of the colliers. "That 'ere long tongue of yours will bring you into disgrace. Bill, give her a jerk towards the wherry, and we'll duck him."

"My friend," said the actor, addressing me—

> "'Let not his unwholesome corpse come between the wind
>   And my nobility.'

Let us exeunt, O.P."

Although I could not understand his phrases, I knew very well what he meant, and pulling smartly, I shoved towards the shore, and ahead. Perceiving this, the men in the boat, at the intimation of the women, who stood up waving their bonnets, gave chase to us, and my companion appeared not a little alarmed. However, by great exertion on my part, we gained considerably, and they abandoned the pursuit.

"Now, by two-headed Janus," said my companion, as he looked back upon the colliers—

> "'Nature hath framed strange fellows in her time,
>   Some that will evermore peep through their eyes,
>   And laugh like parrots at a bagpiper,
>   And others of such a vinegar aspect
>   That they'll not show their teeth by way of smile,
>   Though Nestor swear the jest be laughable.'

And now," continued he, addressing me, "what's your name, sir? Of what condition are you—and of what place, I pray?"

Amused with what had passed, I replied, "That my name was Jacob; that I was a waterman, and born on the river."

"I find thee apt; but tell me, art thou perfect that our ship hath touched upon the deserts of Bohemia?"

"Do you land at Westminster, sir?"

> "'No; at Blackfriars—there attend my coming.'

"Base is the slave who pays; nevertheless, what is your fare, my lad?

> 'What money's in my purse? Seven groats and twopence.'
> > "'By Jove, I am not covetous of gold,
> >   Nor care I who doth feed upon my cost.'

But,

> 'I can get no remedy for this consumption of the purse.'

Here, my lad, is that enough?"

"Yes, sir, I thank you."

"Remember poor Jack, sir," said the usual attendant at the landing-place, catching his arm as he careened the wherry on getting out.

"'If he fall in, good-night—or sink or swim.'

Jack, there is a penny for you. Jacob, farewell—we meet again;'' and away he went, taking three of the stone steps at each spring. This gentleman's name was, as I afterwards found out, Tinfoil, an actor of second-rate merit on the London boards. The Haymarket Theatre was where he principally performed, and as we became better acquainted he offered to procure me orders to see the play when I should wish to go there.

CHAPTER XXVIII

The picnic party—Sufferings by oil, ice, fire, and water—Upon the whole the "divarting vagabonds," as the Thespian heroes and heroines are classically termed, are very happy, excepting Mr. Winterbottom, whose feelings are by sitting down, down to zero.

ONE morning he came down to the hard, and as usual I expected that he would go down the river. I ran to my boat, and hauled in close.

"No, Jacob, no; this day you will not carry Cæsar and his fortunes, but I have an order for you."

"Thank you, sir; what is the play?"

"The play—pooh! no play; but I hope it will prove a farce, nevertheless, before it's over. We are to have a picnic party upon one of those little islands up the river by Kew. All sock and buskin, all theatricals; if the wherries upset, the Haymarket may shut up, for it will be '*exeunt omnes*' with all its best performers. Look you, Jacob, we shall want three wherries, and I leave you to pick out the other two—oars in each, of course. You must be at Whitehall steps exactly at nine o'clock, and I dare say the ladies won't make you wait more than an hour or two, which, for them, is tolerably punctual."

Mr. Tinfoil then entered into the arrangement for remuneration, and walked away; and I was conning over in my mind whom I should select from my brother watermen, and whether

I should ask old Stapleton to take the other oar in my boat, when I heard a voice, never to be mistaken by me—

> " ' Life is like a summer day,
> Warmed by a sunny ray.'

"Lower away yet, Tom. That'll do, my trump.

> ' Sometimes a dreary cloud,
> Chill blast, or tempest loud.'

"Look out for Jacob, Tom," cried the old man, as the head of the lighter, with her mast lowered down, made its appearance through the arch of Putney Bridge, with bright blue streaks on her sides.

"Here he is, father," replied Tom, who was standing forward by the windlass, with the fall in his hand.

I had shoved off, on hearing old Tom's voice, and was alongside almost as soon as the lighter had passed under the bridge, and discovered old Tom at the helm. I sprang on the deck, with the chain-painter of the wherry in my hand, made it fast, and went aft to old Tom, who seized my hand.

"This is as it should be, my boy, both on the look-out for each other. The heart warms when we know the feeling is on both sides. You're seldom out of our thoughts, boy, and always in our hearts. Now, jump forward, for Tom's fretting to greet you, I see, and you may just as well help him to sway up the mast when you are there."

I went forward, shook hands with Tom, and then clapped on the fall, and assisted him to hoist the mast. We then went aft to his father, and communicated everything of interest which had passed since our last meeting at old Stapleton's.

"And how's Mary?" inquired Tom; "she's a very fine lass, and I've thought of her more than once; but I saw that all you said about her was true. How she did flam that poor old Domine!"

"I have had a few words with her about it, and she has promised to be wiser," replied I; "but, as her father says, ' in her, it's human natur.'"

"She's a fine craft," observed old Tom, "and they always be a little ticklish. But, Jacob, you've had some inquiries made after you, and by the women too."

"Indeed!" replied I.

"Yes; and I have had the honour of being sent for into the parlour. Do you guess now?"

227

"Yes," said I, a gloom coming over my countenance. "I presume it is Mrs. Drummond and Sarah whom you refer to?"

"Exactly."

Tom then informed me that Mrs. Drummond had sent for him, and asked a great many questions about me, and desired him to say that they were very glad to hear that I was well and comfortable, and hoped that I would call and see her and Sarah when I came that way. Mrs. Drummond then left the room, and Tom was alone with Sarah, who desired him to say that her father had found out that I had not been wrong; that he had dismissed both the clerks; and that he was very sorry he had been so deceived. "And then," said Tom, " Miss Sarah told me to say from herself that she had been very unhappy since you had left them, but that she hoped that you would forgive and forget some day or another, and come back to them; and that I was to give you her love, and call next time we went up the river for something that she wanted to send to you. So you perceive, Jacob, that you are not forgotten, and justice has been done to you."

"Yes," replied I, " but it has been done too late; so let us say no more about it. I am quite happy as I am."

I then told them of the picnic party of the next day, upon which Tom volunteered to take the other oar in my boat, as he would not be wanted while the barge was at the wharf. Old Tom gave his consent, and it was agreed he should meet me next morning at daylight.

"I've a notion there'll be some fun, Jacob," said he, "from what you say."

"I think so too; but you've towed me two miles, and I must be off again, or I shall lose my dinner; so good-bye." I selected two other wherries in the course of the afternoon, and then returned home.

It was a lovely morning when Tom and I washed out the boat, and, having dressed ourselves in our neatest clothes, we shoved off in company with the two other wherries, and dropped leisurely down the river with the last of the ebb. When we pulled in to the stairs at Whitehall, we found two men waiting for us, with three or four hampers, some baskets, an iron saucepan, a frying-pan, and a large tin pail with a cover, full of rough ice to cool the wines. We were directed to put all these articles into one boat, the others to be reserved for the company.

"Jacob," said Tom, "don't let us be kitchen; I'm togged out for the parlour."

This point had just been arranged, and the articles put into the wherry, when the party made their appearance, Mr. Tinfoil acting as master of the ceremonies.

"Fair Titania," said he, to the lady who appeared to demand, and therefore received the most attention, "allow me to hand you to your throne."

"Many thanks, good Puck," replied the lady, "we are well placed; but dear me, we haven't brought, or we have lost our vinaigrette—we positively cannot go without it. What can our women have been about?"

"Pease-blossom and Mustard-seed are much to blame," replied Tinfoil; "but shall I run back for it?"

"Yes," replied the lady, "and be here again ere the leviathan can swim a league."

"I'll put a girdle round the earth in forty minutes," replied the gentleman, stepping out of the boat.

"Won't you be a little out of breath before you come back, sir?" said Tom, joining the conversation.

This remark, far from giving offence, was followed by a general laugh. Before Mr. Tinfoil was out of sight, the lost vinaigrette was dropped out of the lady's handkerchief; he was therefore recalled, and the whole of the party being arranged in the two boats, we shoved off. The third boat, in which the provender had been stowed, followed us, and was occupied by the two attendants, a call-boy and scene-shifter, who were addressed by Tinfoil as Caliban and Stephano.

"Is all our company here?" said a pert-looking, little pug-nosed man, who had taken upon himself the part of Quince, the carpenter, in the Midsummer Night's Dream. "You, Nick Bottom," continued he, addressing another, "are set down for Pyramus."

The party addressed did not, however, appear to enter into the humour. He was a heavy-made, rather corpulent, white-faced personage, dressed in white jean trousers, white waist-coat, brown coat, and white hat. Whether anything had put him out of humour, I know not, but it is evident that he was the butt of the ladies and of most of the party.

"I'll just thank you," replied this personage, whose real
229

name was Winterbottom, "to be quiet, Mr. Western, for I shan't stand any of your nonsense."

"Oh, Mr. Winterbottom, surely you are not about to sow the seeds of discord so early. Look at the scene before you; hear how the birds are singing, how merrily the sun shines, and how beautifully the water sparkles! Who can be cross on such a morning as this?"

"No, miss," replied Mr. Winterbottom, "not at all, not at all; only my name's Winterbottom, and not Bottom. I don't wear an ass's head to please anybody—that's all. I won't be *bottom*—that's *flat*."

"That depends upon circumstances, sir," observed Tom.

"What business have you to shove your oar in, Mr. Waterman?"

"I was hired for the purpose," replied Tom, dipping his oar in the water, and giving a hearty stroke.

"Stick to your own element then—shove your oar into the water, but not into our discourse."

"Well, sir, I won't say another word, if you don't like it."

"But you may to me," said Titania, laughing, "whenever you please."

"And to me too," said Tinfoil, who was amused with Tom's replies.

Mr. Winterbottom became very wroth, and demanded to be put on shore directly, but the Fairy Queen ordered us to obey him at our peril, and Mr. Winterbottom was carried up the river very much against his inclination.

"Our friend is not himself," said Mr. Tinfoil, producing a key bugle; "but—

'Music hath charms to soothe the savage breast,
To soften rocks, and rend the knotted oak;'

and therefore will we try the effect of it upon his senses." Mr. Tinfoil then played the air in "Midas"—

"Pray, Goody, please to moderate," &c.,

during which Mr. Winterbottom looked more sulky than ever. As soon as the air was finished, another of the party responded with his flute, from the other boat; while Mr. Quince played what he called base, by snapping his fingers. The sounds of the instruments floated along the flowing and smooth water, reaching the ears and attracting the attention of many who for a time rested from their labour, or hung listlessly over the gunnels of the vessels, watching the boats and listening to the harmony. All was mirth and gaiety. The wherries kept close to each other, and between the airs the parties kept up a lively and witty conversation, occasionally venting their admiration upon the verdure of the sloping lawns and feathering trees, with which the banks of the noble river are so beautifully adorned ; even Mr. Winterbottom had partially recovered his serenity, when he was again irritated by a remark of Quince, who addressed him.

"You can play no part but Pyramus, for Pyramus is a sweet-faced man—a proper man as one shall see on a summer's day, a most lovely gentlemanlike man ; therefore, you must needs play Pyramus."

"Take care I don't play the devil with your physiognomy, Mr. Western," retorted Winterbottom.

Here Caliban, in the third boat, began playing the fiddle and singing to it—

> "Gaffer, Gaffer's son, and his little jackass,
> Were trotting along the road ; "

the chorus of which ditty was "Ec-aw, Ec-aw !" like the braying of a jackass.

"Bless thee, Bottom, bless thee ; thou art translated," cried Quince, looking at Winterbottom.

"Very well—very well, Mr. Western. I don't want to upset the wherry, and therefore you're safe at present, but the reckoning will come—so I give you warning."

"Slaves of my lamp, do my bidding. I will have no quarrelling here. You, Quince, shut your mouth; you, Winterbottom, draw in your lips, and I, your queen, will charm you with a song," said Titania, waving her little hand. The fiddler ceased playing, and the voice of the fair actress riveted all our attention.

> "Wilt thou waken, bride of May,
> While flowers are fresh, and sweet bells chime,
> Listen and learn from my roundelay,
> How all life's pilot-boats sailed one day
> A match with Time !
>
> Love sat on a lotus-leaf aloft,
> And saw old Time in his loaded boat,
> Slowly he crossed Life's narrow tide,
> While Love sat clapping his wings, and cried,
> 'Who will pass Time ?'

Patience came first, but soon was gone,
With helm and sail to help Time on ;
Care and Grief could not lend an oar,
And Prudence said (while he stayed on shore),
    'I wait for Time.'

Hope filled with flowers her cork-tree bark,
And lighted its helm with a glow-worm's spark ;
Then Love, when he saw his bark fly past,
Said, 'Lingering Time will soon be passed,'
    'Hope outspeeds Time.'

Wit went nearest old Time to pass,
With his diamond oar and boat of glass,
A feathery dart from his store he drew,
And shouted, while far and swift it flew,
    'Oh, Mirth kills Time.'

But Time sent the feathery arrow back,
Hope's boat of Amaranthus missed its track :
Then Love bade its butterfly-pilots move,
And laughing, said, 'They shall see how Love
    Can conquer Time.'"

I need hardly say that the song was rapturously applauded, and most deservedly so. Several others were demanded from the ladies and gentlemen of the party, and given without hesitation ; but I cannot now recall them to my memory. The bugle and flute played between whiles, and all was laughter and merriment.

"There's a sweet place," said Tinfoil, pointing to a villa on the Thames. "Now, with the fair Titania and ten thousand a year, one could there live happy."

"I'm afraid the fair Titania must go to market without the latter encumbrance," replied the lady. "The gentleman must find the ten thousand a year, and I must bring as my dowry——"

"Ten thousand charms," interrupted Tinfoil ; "that's most true, and pity 'tis 'tis true. Did your fairyship ever hear my epigram on the subject?

    ' Let the lads of the East love the maids of *Cash-mere*,
      Nor affection with interests clash ;
    Far other idolatry pleases us here,
      We adore but the maids of *Mere Cash*.'"

232

"Excellent, good Puck! Have you any more?"

"Not of my own, but you have heard what Winterbottom wrote under the bust of Shakspeare last Jubilee?"

"I knew not that Apollo had ever visited him."

"You shall hear—

> ' In *this here* place the bones of Shakspeare lie,
> But *that ere* form of his shall never die;
> A *speedy end and soon* this world may have,
> But Shakspeare's name shall *bloom* beyond the grave.' "

"I'll trouble you, Mr. Tinfoil, not to be so very witty at my expense," growled out Winterbottom. "I never wrote a line of poetry in my life."

"No one said you did, Winterbottom; but you won't deny that you wrote those lines."

Mr. Winterbottom disdained a reply. Gaily did we pass the variegated banks of the river, swept up with a strong flood-tide, and at last arrived at a little island agreed upon as the site of the picnic. The company disembarked, and were busy looking for a convenient spot for their entertainment, Quince making a rapid escape from Winterbottom, the latter remaining on the bank. "Jenkins," said he to the man christened Caliban, "you did not forget the salad?"

"No, sir; I brought it myself. It's on the top of the little hamper."

Mr. Winterbottom, who it appears was extremely partial to salad, was satisfied with the reply, and walked slowly away.

"Well," said Tom to me, wiping the perspiration from his brow with his handkerchief, "I wouldn't have missed this for anything. I only wish father had been here. I hope that young lady will sing again before we part."

"I think it very likely, and that the fun is only begun," replied I. "But come, let's lend a hand to get the prog out of the boat."

"Pat! Pat! and here's a marvellous convenient place for our rehearsal. This green plot shall be our stage," cried Quince, addressing the others of the party.

The locality was approved of, and now all were busy in preparation. The hampers were unpacked, and cold meats, poultry, pies of various kinds, pastry, &c., appeared in abundance.

"This is no manager's feast," said Tinfoil; "the fowls are

not made of wood, nor is small beer substituted for wine. Don Juan's banquet to the Commendador is a farce to it."

"All the manager's stage banquets are farces, and very sorry jokes into the bargain," replied another.

"I wish old Morris had to eat his own suppers."

"He must get a new set of teeth, or they'll prove a *deal* too tough."

"Hiss! turn him out! he's made a pun."

The hampers were now emptied; some laid the cloth upon the grass, and arranged the plates, and knives and forks. The ladies were as busy as the gentlemen—some were wiping the glasses, others putting salt into the salt-cellars. Titania was preparing the salad. Mr. Winterbottom, who was doing nothing, accosted her: "May I beg as a favour that you do not cut the salad too small? it loses much of its crispness."

"Why, what a Nebuchadnezzar you are! However, sir, you shall be obeyed."

"Who can fry fish?" cried Tinfoil. "Here are two pairs of soles and some eels. Where's Caliban?"

"Here I am, sir," replied the man, on his knees, blowing up a fire which he had kindled. "I have got the soup to mind."

"Where's Stephano?"

"Cooling the wine, sir."

"Who, then, can fry fish, I ask?"

"I can, sir," replied Tom; "but not without butter."

"Butter shalt thou have, thou disturber of the element. Have we not *Hiren* here?"

"I wasn't *hired* as a cook, at all events," replied Tom; "but I'm rather a *dab* at it."

"Then shalt thou have the *place*," replied the actor.

"With all my heart and *soul*," cried Tom, taking out his knife, and commencing the necessary operation of skinning the fish.

In half-an-hour all was ready. The fair Titania did me the honour to seat herself upon my jacket, to ward off any damp from the ground. The other ladies had also taken their respective seats, as allotted by the mistress of the revels; the tables were covered by many of the good things of this life; the soup was ready in a tureen at one end, and Tom had just placed the fish on the table, while Mr. Quince and Winterbottom, by the commands of Titania, were despatched for the wine and other varieties of potations. When they returned,

"'Oh, Lord! oh! oh!' shrieked Mr. Quince."

eyeing one another askance, Winterbottom looking daggers at his opponent, and Quince not quite easy, even under the protection of Titania, Tom had just removed the frying-pan from the fire, with its residuary grease still bubbling. Quince having deposited his load, was about to sit down, when a freak came into Tom's head, which, however, he dared not put into execution himself; but "a nod is as good as a wink to a blind horse," says the proverb. Winterbottom stood before Tom, and Quince with his back to them. Tom looked at Winterbottom, pointing slily to the frying-pan, and then to the hinder parts of Quince. Winterbottom snatched the hint and the frying-pan at the same moment. Quince squatted himself down with a surge, as they say at sea, quoting at the time : " Marry, our play is the most lamentable comedy," but putting his hands behind him to soften his fall, they were received into the hot frying-pan, inserted behind him by Winterbottom.

"Oh, Lord ! oh ! oh !" shrieked Mr. Quince, springing up like lightning, bounding in the air with the pain, his hands behind him still adhering to the frying-pan.

At the first scream of Mr. Quince the whole party had been terrified, the idea was that a snake had bitten him, and the greatest alarm prevailed ; but when they perceived the cause of the disaster, even his expressions of pain could not prevent their mirth. It was too ludicrous. Still the gentlemen and ladies condoled with him, but Mr. Quince was not to be reasoned with. He walked away to the river-side, Mr. Winterbottom slily enjoying his revenge, for no one but Tom had an idea that it was anything but an accident. Mr. Quince's party of pleasure was spoiled, but the others did not think it necessary that theirs should be also. A " really very sorry for poor Western," and a half-dozen " poor fellows !" intermingled with tittering, was all that his misfortunes called forth after his departure ; and then they set-to like French falconers. The soup was swallowed, the fish disappeared, joints were cut up, pies delivered up their hidden treasures, fowls were dismembered like rotten boroughs, corks were drawn, others flew without the trouble, and they did eat and were filled. Mr. Winterbottom kept his eye upon the salad, his favourite condiment, mixed it himself, offered it to all, and was glad to find that no one would spare time to eat it; but Mr. Winterbottom could eat for everybody, and he did eat. The fragments were cleared away, and handed over to us. We were very busy, doing as ample justice to them as the party had done before us, when Mr. Winterbottom was observed to turn very pale, and appeared very uneasy.

"What's the matter?" inquired Mr. Tinfoil.

"I'm—I'm not very well—I—I'm afraid something has disagreed with me. I—I'm very ill," exclaimed Mr. Winterbottom, turning as white as a sheet, and screwing up his mouth.

"It must be the salad," said one of the ladies; "no one has eaten it but yourself, and we are all well."

"I—rather think—it must be—oh—I do recollect that I thought the oil had a queer taste."

"Why, there was no oil in the castors," replied Tinfoil. "I desired Jenkins to get some."

"So did I, particularly," replied Winterbottom. "Oh!— oh, dear—oh, dear!"

"Jenkins," cried Tinfoil, "where did you get the oil for the castors? What oil did you get? Are you sure it was right?"

"Yes, sir, quite sure," replied Jenkins. "I brought it here in a bottle, and put it into the castors before dinner."

"Where did you buy it?"

"At the chemist's, sir. Here's the bottle;" and Jenkins produced a bottle with *castor* oil in large letters labelled on the side.

The murder was out. Mr. Winterbottom groaned, rose from his seat, for he felt very sick indeed. The misfortunes of individuals generally add to the general quota of mirth, and Mr. Winterbottom's misfortune had the same effect as that of Mr. Quince. But where was poor Mr. Quince all this time? He had sent for the iron kettle in which the soup had been warmed up, and filling it full of Thames water, had immersed the afflicted parts in the cooling element. There he sat with his hands plunged deep, when Mr. Winterbottom made his appearance at the same spot, and Mr. Quince was comforted by witnessing the state of his enemy. Indeed, the sight of Winterbottom's distress did more to soothe Mr. Quince's pain than all the Thames water in the world. He rose, and leaving Winterbottom, with his two hands to his head, leaning against a tree, joined the party, and pledged the ladies in succession, till he was more than half tipsy.

In the space of half-an-hour Mr. Winterbottom returned,

trembling and shivering as if he had been suffering under an ague. A bumper or two of brandy restored him, and before the day closed in, both Winterbottom and Quince, one applying stimulants to his stomach, and the other drowning his sense of pain in repeated libations, were in a state (to say the least of it) of incipient intoxication. But there is a time for all things, and it was time to return. The evening had passed freely ; song had followed song. Tinfoil had tried his bugle, and played not a little out of tune ; the flute also neglected the flats and sharps as of no consequence ; the ladies thought the gentlemen rather too forward ; and, in short, it was time to break up the party. The hampers were repacked, and handed, half empty, into the boat. Of wine there was little left ; and by the direction of Titania, the plates, dishes, &c., only were to be returned, and the fragments divided among the boatmen. The company re-embarked in high spirit, and we had the ebb-tide to return with. Just as we were shoving off, it was remembered that the ice-pail had been left under the tree, besides a basket with sundries. The other wherries had shoved off, and they were in consequence brought into our boat, in which we had the same company as before, with the exception of Mr. Western, *alias* Quince, who preferred the boat which carried the hampers, that he might loll over the side, with his hands in the water. Mr. Winterbottom soon showed the effects of the remedy he had taken against the effects of the castor oil. He was uproarious, and it was with difficulty that he could be persuaded to sit still in the boat, much to the alarm of Titania and the other ladies. He would make violent love to the Fairy Queen ; and as he constantly shifted his position to address her and throw himself at her feet, there was some danger of the boat being upset. At last Tom proposed to him to sit on the pail before her, as then he could address her with safety ; and Winterbottom staggered up to take the seat. As he was seating himself, Tom took off the cover, so that he was plunged into the half-liquid ice ; but Mr. Winterbottom was too drunk to perceive it. He continued to rant and to rave, and protest and vow, and even spout for some time, when suddenly the quantity of caloric extracted from him produced its effect.

"I—I—really believe that the night is damp—the dew falls —the seat is damp, fair Titania."

"It's only fancy, Mr. Winterbottom," replied Titania, who was delighted with his situation. "Jean trousers are cool in the evening; it's only an excuse to get away from me, and I never will speak again to you if you quit your seat."

"The fair Titania, the mistress of my soul—and body too, it she pleases—has—but to command—and her slave obeys."

"I rather think it is a little damp," said Tinfoil, "allow me to throw a little sand upon your seat;" and Tinfoil pulled out a large paper bag full of salt, which he strewed over the ice.

Winterbottom was satisfied, and remained; but by the time we had reached Vauxhall Bridge, the refrigeration had become so complete that he was fixed on the ice, which the application of the salt had made solid. He complained of cold, shivered, attempted to rise, but could not extricate himself. At last his teeth chattered, and he became almost sober; but he was helpless from the effects of the castor oil, his intermediate intoxication, and his present state of numbness. He spoke less and less; at last he was silent, and when we arrived at Whitehall stairs, he was firmly fixed in the ice. When released he could not walk, and he was sent home in a hackney coach.

"It was cruel to punish him so, Mr. Tinfoil," said Titania.

"Cruel punishment. Why, yes; a sort of *impailment*," replied Mr. Tinfoil, offering his arm.

The remainder of the party landed and walked home, followed by the two assistants, who took charge of the crockery; and thus ended the picnic party, which, as Tom said, was the very funniest day he had ever spent in his life.

CHAPTER XXIX

Mr. Turnbull "sets his house in order"—Mrs. T. thinks such conduct very disorderly—The captain at his old tricks with his harpoon—He pays his lady's debts of honour, and gives the applicant a quittance under his own foot—Monsieur and Madame Tagliabue withdraw from the society of "ces barbares les Anglais."

IT was on the Sunday after the picnic party, when feeling I had neglected Captain Turnbull, and that he would think it unkind of me not to go near him, after having accompanied

Mary to church, I set off on foot to his villa near Brentford. I rang at the porter's lodge, and asked whether he was at home.

"Yes, sir," replied the old woman at the lodge, who was very communicative, and very friendly with me; "and missus be at home too."

I walked up the carriage-drive of one hundred yards, which led to the entrance door; and when I rang, it was opened by a servant I had not seen before as belonging to the establishment. "Where is Mr. Turnbull?" inquired I.

"He is in his own room, sir," replied the man; "but you must send up your name, if you please, as every one is not admitted."

I must observe to the reader that I was not dressed in jacket and trousers. The money I earned was more than sufficient to supply all my expenses, and I had fitted on what are called at sea, and on the river, *long togs;* i.e., I was dressed as most people are on shore. The servant evidently took me for a gentleman; and perhaps, as far as dress went, I was entitled to that distinction. Many people are received as such in this world with less claims than I had. I gave my name; the man left me at the door, and soon returned, requesting that I would follow him. I must say that I was rather astonished. Where were *Mr.* Mortimer, and the two men in flaunting liveries, and long cotton epaulettes with things like little marline-spikes hanging to the ends of them? Even the livery was changed, being a plain brown coat, with light blue collar and cuffs. I was, however, soon made acquainted with what had taken place, on my entering the apartment of Mr. Turnbull—his study, as Mrs. T. called it, although Mr. Turnbull insisted upon calling it his cabin, a name certainly more appropriate, as it contained but two small shelves of books, the remainder of the space being filled up with favourite harpoons, porpoises' skulls, sharks' jaws, corals, several bears' skins, brown and white, and one or two models of the vessels which had belonged to his brother and himself, and which had been employed in the Greenland fishery. It was, in fact, a sort of museum of all he had collected during his voyages. Esquimaux implements, ornaments, and dresses, were lying about in corners; and skins of rare animals, killed by himself, such as black foxes, &c., were scattered about the carpet. His sea-chest, full of various articles, was also one of the ornaments of the room, much to the annoyance of Mrs. T., who had frequently exerted her influence to get rid of it, but in vain. The only articles of furniture were two sofas, a large table in the centre, and three or four heavy chairs. The only attempt at adornment consisted in a dozen coloured engravings, framed and glazed, of walrus shooting, &c., taken from the folio works of Captains Cook and Mulgrave; and a sketch or two by his brother, such as the state of the *William* pressed by an iceberg on the morning of the 25th of January, lat.—, long. —.

Captain T. was in his morning-gown, evidently not very well, at least he appeared harassed and pale. "My dear Jacob, this is very kind of you. I did mean to scold you for not coming before; but I'm too glad to see you to find the heart now. But why have you kept away so long?"

"I have really been very well employed, sir. Stapleton has given me up the wherry, and I could not neglect his interests, even if I did my own."

"Always right, boy; and how are you getting on?"

"I am very happy, sir, very happy, indeed."

"I'm glad to hear it, Jacob; may you always be so. Now, take the other sofa, and let us have a long palaver, as the Indians say. I have something to tell you. I suppose you observed a change—heh?"

"Yes, sir; I observed that *Mr.* Mortimer was not visible."

"Exactly. Well, *Mr.* Mortimer, or John Snobbs, the rascal, is at present in Newgate for trial; and I mean to send him out on a voyage for the good of his health. I caught the scoundrel at last, and I'll show him no more mercy than I would to a shark that has taken the bait. But that's not all. We have had a regular mutiny, and attempt to take the ship from me; but I have them all in irons, and ordered for punishment. Jacob, money is but too often a curse, depend upon it."

"You'll not find many of your opinion, sir," replied I, laughing.

"Perhaps not; because those who have it are content with the importance which it gives to them, and won't allow the damnable fact; and because those who have it not are always sighing after it, as if it were the only thing worth looking after in this world. But now I will just tell you what has happened since I last saw you, and then you shall judge."

As, however, Captain T.'s narrative ran to a length of nearly three hours, I shall condense the matter for the information of the reader. It appeared that Mrs. T. had continued to increase the lengths of her drives in her carriage, the number of her acquaintances, and her manifold expenses, until **Mr.** T. had remonstrated in very strong terms. His remonstrances did not, however, meet with the attention which he had expected; and he found out by accident, moreover, that the money with which he had constantly supplied Mrs. T. to defray her weekly bills, had been otherwise appropriated, and that the bills for the two last quarters had none of them been paid. This produced an altercation, and a desire on his part to know in what manner these sums had been disbursed. At first the only reply from Mrs. T., who considered it advisable to brazen it out, and if possible gain the ascendancy which was necessary, was a contemptuous toss of her head, which undulated the three yellow ostrich feathers in her bonnet, as she walked out of the room and entered her carriage. This, to Mr. T., who was a matter-of-fact man, was not very satisfactory; he waited per force until the carriage returned, and then demanded an explicit answer. Mrs. T. assumed the highest ground, talked about fashionable expenses, her knowledge of what was due to his character, &c. Mr. T. rejoined about necessary expenses, and that it was due to his character to pay his tradesmen's bills. Mrs. T. then talked of good breeding, best society, and her *many plaisers,* as she termed them. Mr. T. did not know what *many pleasures* meant in French; but he thought she had been indulged in as many as most women, since they had come down to this establishment. But to the question: why were not the bills paid, and what had she done with the money? Spent it in *pin money. Pin* money! thirty pounds a week in *pins!* it would have bought harpoons enough for a three years' voyage. She must tell the truth. She wouldn't tell anything, but called for her salts, and called him a *brute.* At all events, he wouldn't be called a *fool.* He gave her till the next morning to consider of it. The next morning the bills were all sent in as requested, and amounted to six hundred pounds. They were paid and receipted. " Now, Mrs. T., will you oblige me by letting me know what you have done with this six hundred pounds ? " Mrs. T. would not—she was not to be treated in that manner. **Mr.** T. was not on board a whaler now, to bully and frighten

as he pleased. She would have justice done her. Have
a separation, *h*alimony, and a divorce. She might have them
all if she pleased, but she should have no more money; that
was certain. Then she would have a fit of hysterics. So she
did, and lay the whole of the day on the sofa, expecting Mr. T
would pick her up. But the idea never came into Mr. T.'s head.
He went to bed; and, feeling restless, he rose very early, and
saw from his window a cart drive up to the wall, and the parties
who came with it leap over and enter the house, and return
carrying to it two large hampers. He snatched up one of his
harpoons, walked out the other way, and arrived at the cart
just as the hampers had been put in, and they were about to
drive off; challenged them, and instead of being answered, the
horse was flogged, and he nearly run over. He then let fly his
harpoon into the horse, which dropped, and pitched out the
two men on their heads insensible; secured them, called to
the lodge for assistance, sent for constables, and gave them in
charge. They proved to be hampers, forwarded by Mr. Mortimer, who had been in the habit of so doing for some time.
These hampers contained his best wine, and various other
articles, which also proved that Mr. Mortimer must have had
false keys. Leaving the culprits and property in charge of two
constables, Mr. T. returned to the house in company with the
third constable. The door was opened by Mr. Mortimer, who
followed him into his study, told him he should leave the house
directly, had always lived with *gentlemen* before, and requested
that he might have what was due to him. Mr. T. thought
the request but reasonable, and therefore gave him in charge
of the constable. Mr. Snobbs, rather confounded at such un-
gentlemanly behaviour, was with the others marched off to
Bow Street. Mr. T. sends for the other two servants in livery,
and assures them that he has no longer any occasion for their
services, having the excessive vulgar idea that this peculation
must have been known to them. Pays them their wages, requests they will take off their liveries, and leave the house.
Both willing. *They* also had always lived with *gentlemen* before.
Mr. T. takes the key of the butler's pantry, that the plate may
not consider him too vulgar to remain in the house, and then
walks to the stables. Horses neigh, as if to say they are all
ready for their breakfasts; but the door locked. Hails the
coachman; no answer. Returning from the stables, perceives

coachee, rather dusty, coming in at the lodge gate ; requests to
know why he did not sleep at home and take care of his horses.
He was missus's coachman, not master's, and could satisfy her ;
but could not satisfy Mr. T., who paid him his wages, and,
deducting his liveries, sent him after the others. Coachee also
was very glad to go—had always lived with *gentlemen* before.
Meets the lady's maid, who tells him Mrs. T. is much too ill to
come down to breakfast. Rather fortunate, as there was no
breakfast to be had. Dresses himself, gets into a pair-horse
coach, arrives at the White Horse Cellar, swallows his breakfast, goes to Bow Street, commits Mr. Mortimer *alias* Snobbs
and his confederates for trial. Hires a job-man to bring the
horses up for sale, and leaves his carriage at the coachmaker's.
Obtains a temporary footman, and then Mr. T. returns to his
villa. A very good morning's work. Finds Mrs. T. up in the
parlour, very much surprised and shocked at his conduct—at
no Mr. Mortimer—at no servants, and indebted to her own
maid for a cup of tea. More recriminations—more violence—
another threat of *h*alimony, and the carriage ordered, that she
may seek counsel. No coachman—no carriage—no horses—
no nothing, as her maid declares. Mrs. T. locks herself up in
her room, and another day is passed with as little matrimonial
comfort as can be expected.

In the meantime the news flies in every direction. Brentford is full of it. Mr. T. had been living too fast—is done up—
had been had up at Bow Street—creditors had poured in with
bills—servants discharged—carriage and horses seized. Mrs.
T., poor creature, in hysterics, and—nobody surprised at it ;
indeed, everybody expected it. The Peters of Petercumb
Hall heard it, and shook their heads at the many upstarts there
were in the world. Mr. Smith requested the Right Honourable Lord Viscount Babbleton never to mention to his father,
the Right Honourable Marquis of Spring-guns, that he had
ever been taken to see the Turnbulls, or that he, Mr. Smith,
would infallibly lose his situation in *esse,* and his living in
posse ; and Monsieur and Madame Tagliabue were even more
astounded ; but they felt deeply, and resolved to pay a visit
the next morning, at least Monsieur Tagliabue did, and
madame acknowledged the propriety of it.

The next morning some little order had been restored ; the
footman hired had been given in charge of a sufficient quantity

of plate, the rest had been locked up. The cook was to stay her month; the housemaid had no wish to leave; and as for the lady's maid, she would remain as long as she could, to console her poor mistress, and accept what she was inclined to give her in return, in the way of clothes, dresses, &c., although, of course, she could not hurt her character by remaining too long in a family where there was no carriage, or gentlemen out of livery. Still Mr. T. did obtain some breakfast, and had just finished it, when Monsieur Tagliabue was announced, and was received.

"Ah! Monsieur T., I hope madame is better. Madame Tagliabue did nothing but cry all last night when she heard the very bad news about de debt, and all dat."

"Very much obliged to madame," replied Turnbull gruffly; "and now, pray, sir, what may be your pleasure?"

"Ah! Monsieur Turnbull, I feel very much for you; but suppose a gentleman no lose his *honour*, what matter de money?" (Mr. Turnbull stared.) "You see, Monsieur Turnbull, honour be everything to a gentleman. If a gentleman owe money to one rascally tradesfellow, and not pay him, dat no great matter; but he always pay de debt of honour. Every gentleman pay dat. Here, Monsieur Turnbull" (and the little Frenchman pulled out a piece of paper from his pocket) "be a leetle note of Madame Turnbull, which she gave to Madame Tagliabue, in which she acknowledged she owe two hundred pounds for money lost at *écarté*. Dat you see, Monsieur Turnbull, be what gentlemen call debt of honour, which every gentleman pay, or else he lose de character, and be called one blackguard by all de world. Madame Tagliabue and I too much fond of you and Madame Turnbull not to save your character, and so I come by her wish to beg you to settle this leetle note—this *leetle* debt of *honour;*" and Monsieur Tagliabue laid the note on the table, with a very polite bow.

Mr. Turnbull examined the note; it was as described by Monsieur Tagliabue. So, thought he, now the whole story's out; she has been swindled out of her money by this rascally French couple. "Now, Monsieur Tagliabue," said he, "allow me to put a question or two, before I pay this money; and if you answer me sincerely, I shall raise no objection. I think Mrs. T. has already lost about six hundred pounds at *écarté* before?" (Monsieur T., who presumed that Mrs. Turnbull had made him acquainted with the fact, answered in the affirmative.) "And I think that two months ago she never knew what *écarté* was."

"Dat is true; but the ladies are very quick to learn."

"Well, but now do you think that, as she knew nothing about the game, and you and your wife are well acquainted with it, it was honourable on your part to allow her to lose so much money?"

"Ah! monsieur, when a lady say she will play, *comment faire*, what can you do?"

"But why did you never play at this house, Monsieur Tagliabue?"

"Ah! Monsieur Turnbull, it is for de lady of de house to propose de game."

"Very true," replied Mr. Turnbull, writing a cheque for the two hundred pounds; "there is your money, Mr. Tagliabue; and now that you are paid, allow me to observe that I consider you and your wife a couple of swindlers, and beg that you will never enter my doors again."

"Vat you say, sar? *Swind-lare!* God dam! Sar, I will have satisfaction."

"You've got your money—is that sufficient, or do you want anything else?" replied Mr. T., rising from his chair.

"Yes, sar, I do want more—I will have more."

"So you shall, then," replied Mr. Turnbull, kicking him out of the room, along the passage and out of the front door. Monsieur Tagliabue turned round every now and then, and threatened, and then tried to escape, as he perceived the upraised boot of Mr. Turnbull. When fairly out of the house, he turned round, "Monsieur Turnbull, I will have de satisfaction, de terrible satisfaction, for this. You shall pay. By God, sar, you shall pay—de money for this."

That evening Mr. Turnbull was summoned to appear at Bow Street on the following morning for the assault. He met Monsieur Tagliabue with his lawyer, and acknowledged that he had kicked him out of his house for swindling his wife, refused all accommodation, and was prepared with his bail. Monsieur Tagliabue stormed and blustered, talked about his acquaintance with the nobility; but the magistrate had seen too much of foreigners to place much reliance on their asseverations. "Who are you, monsieur?"

"Sar, I am a gentleman."

" What profession are you of, sir ? "

" Sar, a gentleman has no profession."

" But how do you live, Monsieur Tagliabue ? "

" As a gentleman always does, sar."

" You mentioned Lord Scrope just now as your particular friend, I think ? "

" Yes, sar, me very intimate with Lord Scrope ; me spend three months at Scrope Castle with mi Lady Scrope ; mi Lady Scrope very fond of Madame Tagliabue."

" Very well, Monsieur Tagliabue ; we must proceed with another case until Mr. Turnbull's bail arrives. Sit down for a little while, if you please."

Another case was then heard, which lasted about half-an-hour ; but previous to hearing it, the magistrate, who knew that Lord Scrope was in town, had despatched a runner with a note to his lordship, and the answer was now brought back. The magistrate read it, and smiled ; went on with the other case, and when it was finished, said, " Now, M. Tagliabue, you have said that you were intimate with Lord Scrope."

" Yes, sar, very intimate."

" Well, Lord Scrope I have the pleasure of knowing ; and as he is in town I wrote a note to him, and here is his answer. I will read it."

M. Tagliabue turned pale as the magistrate read the following :—

" DEAR SIR,—A fellow of the name you mention came from Russia with me, as my valet. I discharged him for dishonesty. After he left, Lady Scrope's attendant, who it appeared was, unknown to us, married to him, left also, and then I discovered their peculations to have been so extensive that had we known where to have laid hold of him, I should certainly have brought them before you. Now the affair is forgotten ; but a greater scoundrel never existed.—Yours, SCROPE."

" Now, sir, what have you to say for yourself ? " continued the magistrate, in a severe tone. M. Tagliabue fell on his knees and begged for mercy from the magistrate, from Lord Scrope, and lastly from Mr. Turnbull, to whom he proffered the draft for £200. The magistrate, seeing that Mr. Turnbull did not take it, said to him, " Make no ceremony of taking your money back again, Mr. Turnbull ; the very offer of it proves that he has gained it dishonestly; and £600 arc quite enough to have lost." Mr. Turnbull then took the cheque and tore it in pieces, and the magistrate ordered M. Tagliabue to be taken to the Alien Office, and he was sent to the other side of the Channel, in company with his wife, to play *écarté* with whomsoever he pleased. Thus ended this episode of Monsieur Tagliabue.

CHAPTER XXX

Mr. Turnbull finds out that money, though a necessary evil, is not a source of happiness—The Domine finds out that a little calumny is more effectual than Ovid's remedy for love; and I find out that walking gives one a good appetite for fillet of veal and bacon—I set an example to the clergy in refusing to take money for a seat in church.

AND now you see, Jacob, what a revolution has taken place; not very pleasant, I grant, but still it was very necessary. I have since been paying all my bills, for the report of my being in difficulty has brought them in fast enough; and I find that in these last five months my wife has spent a whole year's income; so it was quite time to stop."

"I agree with you, sir; but what does Mrs. Turnbull say now—has she come to her senses?"

"Pretty well, I expect, although she does not quite choose to acknowledge it. I have told her that she must dispense with a carriage in future; and so she shall, till I think she deserves it. She knows that she must either have *my company* in the house, or none at all. She knows that the Peters of Petercumb Hall have cut her, for they did not answer a note of hers, sent by the gardener; and Mr. Smith has written a very violent answer to another of her notes, wondering at her attempting to push herself into the company of the aristocracy. But what has brought her to her senses more than all, is the affair of Monsieur Tagliabue. The magistrate, at my request, gave me the note of Lord Scrope, and I have taken good care that she should read the police report as well; but the fact is, she is so much mortified that I say nothing to her. She has been following the advice of these French swindlers, who have led her wrong, to be able to cheat her of her money.

I expect she will ask me to sell this place, and go elsewhere; but at present we hardly exchange a word during the whole day."

" I feel very sorry for her, sir; for I really believe her to be a very good, kind-hearted person."

" That's like you, Jacob—and so she is. At present she is in a state to be pitied. She would throw a share of the blame upon other people, and cannot—she feels it is all herself. All her bubbles of grandeur have burst, and she finds herself not half so respectable as she was before her vanity induced her to cut her former acquaintance, and try to get into the society of those who laughed at her, and at the same time were not half so creditable. But it's that cursed money which has proved her unhappiness—and, I may add, mine."

" Well, sir, I see no chance of its ever adding to my misfortunes, at all events."

" Perhaps not, Jacob, even if you ever should get any; but, at all events, you may take a little to-morrow, if you please. I cannot ask you to dine here, it would not be pleasant to you, and show a want of feeling to my wife; but I should like you to come up with the wherry to-morrow, and we'll take a cruise."

" Very well, I shall be at your orders—at what time ? "

" Say ten o'clock, if the weather is fine; if not, the next day."

" Then, sir, I'll now wish you good-bye, as I must go and see the Domine."

Mr. Turnbull shook my hand, and we parted. I was soon at Brentford, and was continuing my course through the long main street, when I met Mr. and Mrs. Tomkins, the former head clerk who had charge of the Brentford Wharf. " I was intending to call upon you, sir, after I had paid a visit to my old master."

" Very well, Jacob; and recollect we dine at half-past three —fillet of veal and bacon—don't be too late for dinner."

I promised that I would not, and in a few minutes more arrived at the grammar-school. I looked at its peaked, antiquated front, and called to mind my feelings when, years back, I had first entered its porch. What a difference between the little uncouth, ignorant savage, tricked out like a harlequin, and now the tall, athletic, well-dressed youth, happy in his independence, and conscious, although not vain, of his acquirements ! and I mentally blessed the founders. But I had to talk to the Domine, and to keep my appointment with the veal and bacon at half-past three, so I could not spare any time for meditation. I therefore unfolded my arms, and, making use of my legs, entered the wicket, and proceeded to the Domine's room. The door was ajar, and I entered without being perceived. I have often been reminded, by Flemish paintings which I have seen since, of the picture which then presented itself. The room was not large, but lofty. It had but one window, fitted with small diamond-shaped panes, in heavy wood-work, through which poured a broad, but subdued stream of light. On one side of the window was an ancient armoire, containing the Domine's library, not gilt and lettered, but well thumbed and worn. On the other his huge chest of drawers, on which lay, alas! for the benefit of the rising generation, a new birch rod of large dimensions. The table was in the centre of the room, and the Domine sat at it, with his back to the window, in a dressing-gown, once black, having been a cassock, but now brown with age. He was on his high and narrow-backed chair, leaning forwards, with both elbows on the table, his spectacles on his luxuriant nose, and his hands nearly meeting on the top of his bald crown, earnestly poring over the contents of a book. A large Bible, which he constantly made use of, was also on the table, and had apparently been shoved from him to give place to the present object of his meditations. His pipe lay on the floor, in two pieces, having been thrown off without his perceiving it. On one side of him was a sheet of paper, on which he evidently had been writing extracts. I passed by him without his perceiving me, and, gaining the back of his chair, looked over his shoulder. The work he was so intent upon was "Ovid's Remedy of Love."

It appeared that he had nearly finished reading through the whole, for in less than a minute he closed the book, and laying his spectacles down, threw himself back in his chair. "Strange," soliloquised the Domine. "Yet, verily, is some of his advice important, and I should imagine commendable, yet I do not find my remedy therein. *'Avoid idleness.'*—Yes, that is sage counsel—and employment to one that hath not employed himself may drive away thought; but I have never been idle, and mine hath not been love in idleness. *'Avoid her presence.'*—That I must do; yet doth she still present herself to mine imagination, and I doubt whether the tangible reality could be more clearly perceptible. Even now doth she stand before me in all her beauty. '*Read not Propertius and Tibullus.*'—That is easily refrained from; but read what I will, in a minute the type passeth from my eyes, and I see but her face beaming from the page. Nay, cast my eyes in what direction I may wist, it is the same. If I look at the stained wall, the indistinct lines gradually form themselves into her profile; if I look at the clouds, they will assume some of the redundant outlines of her form; if I cast mine eyes upon the fire in the kitchen grate, the coals will glow and cool until I see her face; nay, but yesterday, the shoulder of mutton upon the spit gyrated until it at last assumed the decapitated head of Mary. '*Think of her faults and magnify them.*'— Nay, that were unjust and unchristian. Let me rather correct mine own. I fear me, that when Ovid wrote his picture, he intended it for the use of young men, and not for an old fool like me. Behold! I have again broken my pipe—the fourth pipe that I have destroyed this week. What will the dame say? Already hath she declared me demented, and God knows she is not very far from the truth;" and the Domine covered up his face in his hands. I took this opportunity to step to the door and appear to enter it, dropping the latch, and rousing the Domine by the noise, who extended to me his hand. "Welcome, my son—welcome to thine old preceptor, and to the walls which first received thee, when thou wert cast on shore as a tangle weed from the river. Sit, Jacob; I was thinking of thee and thine."

"What, sir! of old Stapleton and his daughter, I suppose."

"Even so; ye were all in my thoughts at the moment that thou madest thy appearance. They are well?"

"Yes, sir," replied I. "I see but little of them; the old man is always smoking, and as for the girl—why, the less one sees of her the better, I should say."

"Nay, Jacob, this is new to me; yet is she most pleasant."

I knew the Domine's character, and that if anything could cure his unfortunate passion, it would be a supposition on his part that the girl was not correct. I determined at all events to depreciate her, as I knew that what I said would never be mentioned by him, and would therefore do her no harm. Still, I felt that I had to play a difficult game, as I was deter- mined not to state what was not the fact. "Pleasant, sir;

yes, pleasant to everybody; the fact is, I don't like such girls as she is."

"Indeed, Jacob; what, is she light?" I smiled, and made no answer. "Yet I perceived it not," replied the Domine.

"She is just like her mother," observed I.

"And what was her mother?"

I gave a brief account of her mother, and how she met her death in trying to escape from her husband. The Domine mused. "Little skilled am I in women, Jacob, yet what thou sayest not only surpriseth but grieveth me. She is fair to look upon."

"Handsome is that handsome does, sir. She'll make many a man's heart ache yet, I expect."

"Indeed, Jacob, I am full of marvel at what thou hast already told me."

"I have seen more of her, sir."

"I pray thee tell me more."

"No, sir, I had rather not. You may imagine all you please."

"Still she is young, Jacob; when she becometh a wife she might alter."

"Sir, it is my firm opinion (and so it was), that if you were to marry her to-morrow, she would run away from you in a week."

"Is that thy candid opinion, Jacob?"

"I will stake my life upon her so doing, although not as to the exact time."

"Jacob, I thank thee—thank thee much; thou hast opened mine eyes—thou hast done me more good than Ovid. Yes, boy; even the ancients, whom I have venerated, have not done me so kind an act as thou, a stripling, whom I have fostered. Thou hast repaid me, Jacob; thou hast rewarded me, Jacob; thou hast protected me, Jacob; thou hast saved me, Jacob—hast saved me, both from myself and from her; for know, Jacob—know—that mine heart did yearn towards that maiden; and I thought her even to be perfection. Jacob, I thank thee! Now leave me, Jacob, that I may commune with myself, and search out my own heart, for I am awakened —awakened as from a dream, and I would fain be quite alone."

I was not sorry to leave the Domine, for I also felt that I would fain be in company with the fillet of veal and bacon, so I shook hands, and thus ended my second morning call. I was in good time at Mr. Tomkins's, who received me with great kindness. He was well pleased with his new situation, which was one of respectability and consequence, independently of profit; and I met at his table one or two people, who, to my knowledge, would have considered it degrading to have visited him when only head clerk to Mr. Drummond. We talked over old affairs, not forgetting the ball, and the illuminations, and Mr. Turnbull's *bon-mot* about Paradise; and after a very pleasant evening, I took my leave with the intention of walking back to Fulham, but I found old Tom waiting outside, on the look-out for me.

"Jacob, my boy, I want you to come down to my old shop one of these days. What day will you be able to come? The lighter will be here for a fortnight, at least, I find from Mr. Tomkins, as she waits for a cargo coming by canal, and there is no other craft expected above bridge, so tell me what day will you come and see the old woman, and spend the whole day with us. I wants to talk a bit with you, and ax your opinion about a good many little things."

"Indeed!" replied I, smiling. "What, are you going to build a new house?"

"No, no—not that; but you see, Jacob, as I told you last winter, it was time for me to give up night work up and down the river. I'm not so young as I was about fifty years ago, and there's a time for all things. I do mean to give up the craft in the autumn, and go on shore for a *full due;* but at the same time I must see how I can make matters out, so tell me what day you will come."

"Well, then, shall we say Wednesday?"

"Wednesday's as good a day as any other day; come to breakfast, and you shall go away after supper, if you like; if not, the old woman shall sling a hammock for you."

"Agreed, then; but where's Tom?"

"Tom? I don't know; but I think he's gone after that daughter of Stapleton's. He begins to think of the girls now, Jacob; but as the old buffer her father says, 'It's all human natur.' Howsomever, I never interferes in these matters; they seem to be pretty well matched, I think."

"How do you mean?"

"Why, as for good looks, they be well enough matched, that's sure; but I don't mean that, I mean he is quite as knowing as she is, and will shift his helm as she shifts hers. 'Twill be a long running fight, and when one strikes, t'other won't have much to boast of. Perhaps they may sheer off after all, perhaps they may sail as consorts — God only knows; but this I knows, that Tom's sweetheart may be as tricky as she pleases, but Tom's wife won't be—'cause why? He'll keep her in order. Well, good-night; I have a long walk."

When I returned home, I found Mary alone. "Has Tom been here?" inquired I.

"What makes you ask that question?" replied Mary.

"To have it answered—if you have no objection."

"Oh no! Well then, Mr. Jacob, Tom has been here, and very amusing he has been."

"So he always is," replied I.

"And where may you have been?" I told her. "So you saw old Domine. Now, tell me, what did he say about me?"

"That I shall not tell," replied I; "but I will tell you this, that he will never think about you any more; and you must not expect ever to see him again."

"But recollect that he promised."

"He kept his promise, Mary."

"Oh, he told you so, did he? Did he tell you all that passed?"

"No, Mary, he never told me that he had been here, neither did he tell me what had passed; but I happen to know all."

"I cannot understand that."

"Still, it is true; and I think, on the whole, you behaved pretty well, although I cannot understand why you gave him a kiss at parting."

"Good heaven! where were you? You must have been in the room. And you heard every word that passed?"

"Every word," replied I.

"Well," said Mary, "I could not have believed that you could have done so mean a thing."

"Mary, rather accuse your own imprudence; what I heard was to be heard by every one in the street as well as by me. If you choose to have love scenes in a room not eight feet from the ground with the window wide open, you must not be surprised at every passer-by hearing what you say."

"Well, that's true, I never thought of the window being

open; not that I would have cared if all the world had heard me, if *you* had not."

It never occurred to me till then why Mary was annoyed at my having overheard her, but at once I recollected what she had said about me. I made no answer. Mary sat down, leaned her forehead against her hands, and was also silent; I therefore took my candle and retired. It appeared that Mary's pride was much mortified at my having heard her confession of being partial to me—a confession which certainly made very little impression on me, as I considered that she might, a month afterwards, confess the same relative to Tom, or any other individual who took her fancy; but in this I did not do her justice. Her manners were afterwards much changed towards me; she always appeared to avoid, rather than to seek further intimacy. As for myself, I continued, as before, very good friends, kind towards her, but nothing more. The next morning I was up at Mr. Turnbull's by the time agreed upon; but before I set off, rather a singular occurrence took place. I had just finished cleaning my boat, and had resumed my jacket, when a dark man, from some foreign country, came to the hard with a bundle under his arm.

"How much for to go to the other side of the river—how much pence?"

"Twopence," replied I; but not caring to take him, I continued, "but you only pay one penny to cross the bridge."

"I know very well, but suppose you take me?"

He was a well-looking, not very dark man; his turban was of coloured cloth; his trousers not very wide; and I could not comprehend whether he was a Turk or not. I afterwards found out he was a Parsee, from the East Indies. He spoke very plain English. As he decided upon crossing, I received him, and shoved off; when we were in the middle of the stream, he requested me to pull a little way up. "That will do," said he, opening his bundle and spreading a carpet on the stern flooring of the wherry. He then rose, looking at the sun, which was then rising in all its majesty, bowed to it with his hands raised, three times, then knelt on the carpet, and touched it several times with his forehead, again rose on his feet, took some common field flowers from his vest, and cast them into the stream, bowed again, folded up his carpet, and begged me to pull on shore.

254

"I say my prayers," said the man, looking at me with his dark, piercing eye.

"Very proper; whom did you say them to?"

"To my God."

"But why don't you say them on shore?"

"Can't see sun in the house; suppose I go out, little boys laugh and throw mud. Where no am seen, river very proper place."

We landed, and he took out threepence, and offered it to me. "No, no," said I, "I don't want you to pay for saying your prayers."

"No take money?"

"Yes, take money to cross the river, but not take money for saying prayers. If you want to say them any other morning come down, and if I am here, I'll always pull you into the stream."

"You very good man; I thank you."

The Parsee made me a low salaam, and walked away. I may here observe, that the man generally came down at sunrise two or three days in the week, and I invariably gave him a pull off into the stream, that he might pursue his religious ceremony. We often conversed, and at last became intimate.

Mr. Turnbull was at the bottom of the lawn, which extended from his house to the banks of the river, looking out for me when I pulled up. The basket with our dinner, &c., was lying by him on the gravel walk.

"This is a lovely morning, Jacob; but it will be rather a warm day, I expect," said he. "Come, let us be off at once; lay in your sculls, and let us get the oars to pass."

"How is Mrs. Turnbull, sir?"

"Pretty well, Jacob; more like the Molly Bacon that I married than she has been for some years. Perhaps, after all, this affair may turn out one of the best things that ever happened. It may bring her to her senses—bring happiness back to our hearth; if so, Jacob, the money is well spent."

CHAPTER XXXI

Mr. Turnbull and I go on a party of pleasure—It turns out to be an adventure, and winds up with a blunderbuss, a tin box, and a lady's cloak.

WE pulled leisurely up the stream, talking, and every now and then resting on our oars, to take breath ; for, as the old captain said, "Why should we make a toil of pleasure ? I like the upper part of the river best, Jacob, because the water is clear, and I love clear water. How many hours have I, when a boy on board ship, hung over the gunwale of a boat, lowered down in a calm, and watched the little floating objects in the dark blue unfathomable water beneath me ; objects of all sizes, of all colours, and of all shapes —all of them beautiful and to be admired ; yet of them, perhaps, not one in a hundred millions ever meets the eye of man. You know, Jacob, that the North Seas are full of these animals—you cannot imagine the quantity of them ; the sailors call them blubbers, because they are composed of a sort of transparent jelly, but the real name I am told is Medusæ, that is the learned name. The whale feeds on them, and that is the reason why the whale is found where they are."

"I should like very much to go a voyage to the whale fishery," replied I ; "I've heard so much about it from you."

"It is a stirring life, and a hard life, Jacob, still it is an exciting one. Some voyages will turn out very pleasant, but others are dreadful, from their anxiety. If the weather continues fine, it is all very well ; but sometimes when there is a continuance of bad weather, it is dreadful. I recollect one voyage which made me show more grey hairs than all the others, and I think I have been twenty-two in all. We were in the drift ice, forcing our way to the northward, when it came on to blow ; the sea rose, and after a week's gale it was tremendous. We had little daylight, and when it was daylight, the fog was so thick that we could see but little ; there we were, tossing among the large drift ice, meeting immense icebergs which bore down with all the force of the gale, and each time we narrowly escaped perishing. The rigging was loaded with ice ; the bows of the ship were cased with it ; the men

256

were more than half frozen, and we could not move a rope through a block, without pouring boiling water through it first, to clear it out. But then the long, dreary, dreadful nights, when we were rising on the mountain wave, and then pitching down into the trough, not knowing but that at each send we might strike upon the ice below, and go to the bottom immediately afterwards. All pitchy dark—the wind howling, and as it struck you, cutting you to the backbone with its cold, searching power, the waves dancing all black around you, and every now and then perceiving by its white colour and the foam encircling it, a huge mass of ice borne upon you, and hurled against you as if there were a demon who was using it as an engine for your destruction. I never shall forget the *turning* of an iceberg, during the dreadful gale, which lasted for a month and three days."

" I don't know what that means, sir."

" Why, you must know, Jacob, that the icebergs are all fresh water, and are supposed to have been detached from the land by the force of the weather and other causes. Now although ice floats, yet it floats deep; that is, if an iceberg is five hundred feet high above the water, it is generally six times as deep below the water—do you understand ? "

" Perfectly, sir."

" Now, Jacob, the water is much warmer than the air, and in consequence the ice under the water melts away much faster; so that if an iceberg has been some time afloat, at last the part that is below is not so heavy as that which is above; then it turns, that is, it upsets, and floats in another position."

" I understand you, sir."

" Well, we were close to an iceberg, which was to windward of us, a very tall one, indeed, and we reckoned that we should get clear of it, for we were carrying a press of sail to effect it. Still all hands were eagerly watching the iceberg, as it came down very fast before the storm. All of a sudden it blew twice as hard as before, and then one of the men shouted out, 'Turning, turning !' and sure enough it was. There was its towering summit gradually bowing towards us, until it almost appeared as if the peak was over our heads. Our fate appeared inevitable, as the whole mountain of ice was descending on the vessel, and would, of course, have crushed us into atoms. We all fell on our knees, praying mentally, and watching its awful descent; even the man at the helm did the same, although he did not let go the spokes of the wheel. It had nearly half turned over, right for us, when the ice below, being heavier on one side than on the other, gave it a more slanting impetus, and shifting the direction of its fall, it plunged into the sea about a cable's length astern of us, throwing up the water to the heavens in foam, and blinding us all with the violence with which it dashed into our faces. For a minute the run of the waves was checked, and the sea appeared to boil and dance, throwing up peaked, pointed masses of water in all directions, one sinking, another rising; the ship rocked and reeled as if she were drunk; even the current of the gale was checked for a moment, and the heavy sails flapped and cleared themselves of their icy varnishing—then all was over. There was an iceberg of another shape astern of us, the gale recommenced, the waves pressed each other on as before, and we felt the return of the gale, awful as it was, as a reprieve. That was a dreadful voyage, Jacob, and turned one-third of my hair grey; and what made it worse was, that we had only three fish on board on our return. However, we had reason to be thankful, for eighteen of our vessels were lost altogether, and it was the mercy of God that we were not among the number."

"Well, I suppose you told me that story to prevent my going a voyage?"

"Not a bit, Jacob; if it should chance that you find it your interest to go to the North Pole, or anywhere else, I would say go, by all means, let neither difficulty nor danger deter you; but do not go merely from curiosity—that I consider foolish. It's all very well for those who come back to have the satisfaction to talk of such things, and it is but fair that they should have it; but when you consider how many there are who never come back at all, why, then, it's very foolish to push yourself into needless danger and privation. You are amused with my recollections of Arctic voyages; but just call to mind how many years of hardship, of danger, cold, and starvation I have undergone to collect all these anecdotes, and then judge whether it be worth any man's while to go for the sake of mere curiosity."

I then amused Mr. Turnbull with the description of the picnic party, which lasted until we had pulled far beyond Kew Bridge. We thrust the bow of the wherry into a bunch of sedges, and then we sat down to our meal, surrounded by hundreds of blue dragon-flies, that flitted about as if to inquire what we meant by intruding upon their domiciles. We continued there chatting and amusing ourselves till it was late, and then shoved off and pulled down with the stream. The sun had set, and we had yet six or seven miles to return to Mr. Turnbull's house, when we perceived a slight, handsome young man, in a small skiff, who pulled towards us.

"I say, my lads," said he, taking us both for watermen, "have you a mind to earn a couple of guineas, with very little trouble?"

"Oh yes," replied Mr. Turnbull, "if you can show us how. A fine chance for you, Jacob," continued he, aside.

"Well, then, I shall want your services, perhaps, for not more than an hour; it may be a little longer, as there is a lady in question, and we may have to wait. All I ask is that you pull well and do your best. Are you agreed?"

We consented; and he requested us to follow him, and then pulled for the shore.

"This is to be an adventure, sir," said I.

"So it seems," replied Mr. Turnbull; "all the better. I'm old now, but I'm fond of a spree."

The gentleman pulled into a little boat-house by the river's side, belonging to one of the villas on the bank, made fast his boat, and then stepped into ours.

"Now, we've plenty of time; just pull quietly for the present." We continued down the river, and after we had passed Kew Bridge, he directed us in-shore, on the right side, till we came to a garden sweeping down to the river from a cottage *ornée*, of large dimensions, about fifty yards from the bank. The water was up to the brick wall, which rose from the river about four or five feet. "That will do, st—, st—, not a word," said he, rising in the stern-sheets, and looking over. After a minute or two reconnoitring, he climbed from the boat on to the parapet of the wall, and whistled two bars of an air which I had till then never heard. All was silent. He crouched behind a lilac bush, and in a minute he repeated the same air in a whistle as before; still there was no appearance of movement at the cottage. He continued at intervals to whistle the portion of the air, and at last a light appeared at an upper window. It was removed, and reappeared three times. "Be

ready now, my lads," said he. In about two minutes afterwards a female in a cloak appeared, coming down the lawn,
with a box in her hand, panting with excitement.

"O William, I heard your first signal, but I could not
get into my uncle's room for the box; at last he went out,
and here it is."

The gentleman seized the box from her, and handed it to
us in the boat.

"Take great care of that, my lads," said he; "and now,
Cecilia, we have no time to lose; the sooner you are in the
boat the better."

"How am I to get down there, William?" replied she.

"Oh, nothing more easy. Stop, throw your cloak into the
boat, and then all you have to do is, first to get upon the top
of the wall, and then trust to the watermen below, and to me
above for helping you."

It was not, however, quite so easy a matter; the wall was
four feet high above the boat, and, moreover, there was a
trellised work of iron, above a foot high, which ran along the
wall. Still she made every effort on her own part, and we
considered that we had arranged so as to conquer the difficulty, when the young lady gave a scream. We looked up
and beheld a third party on the wall. It was a stout, tall,
elderly man, as far as we could perceive in the dark, who
immediately seized hold of the lady by the arm, and was
dragging her away. This was resisted by the young gentleman, and the lady was relinquished by the other, to defend
himself; at the same time that he called out—

"Help, help! Thieves, thieves!"

"Shall I go to his assistance?" said I to Mr. Turnbull.
"One must stay in the boat."

"Jump up, then, Jacob, for I never could get up that wall."

I was up in a moment, and gaining my feet, was about to
spring to the help of the young man, when four servants, with
lights and with arms in their hands, made their appearance,
hastening down the lawn. The lady had fainted on the grass;
the elderly gentleman and his antagonist were down together,
but the elderly gentleman had the mastery, for he was upper-
most. Perceiving the assistance coming, he called out, "Look
to the watermen, secure them." I perceived that not a moment
was to be lost. I could be of no service, and Mr. Turnbull

might be in an awkward scrape. I sprang into the boat, shoved off, and we were in the stream and at thirty yards' distance before they looked over the wall to see where we were.

"Stop in that boat! stop!" they cried.

"Fire, if they don't," cried their master.

We pulled as hard as we could. A musquetoon was discharged, but the shot dropped short; the only person who fell was the man who fired it. To see us he had stood upon the coping bricks of the wall, and the recoil tumbled him over into the river. We saw him fall, and heard the splash; but we pulled on as hard as we could, and in a few minutes the scene of action was far behind us. We then struck across to the other side of the river, and when we had gained close to the shore, we took breath.

"Well," said Mr. Turnbull, "this is a spree I little looked for; to have a blunderbuss full of shot sent after me."

"No," replied I, laughing, "that's carrying the joke rather too far on the river Thames."

"Well, but what a pretty mess we are in; here we have property belonging to God knows whom, and what are we to do with it?"

"I think, sir, the best thing we can do is for you to land at your own house with the property, and take care of it until we find out what all this is about; and I will continue on with the sculls to the hard. We shall hear or find out something about it in a day or two; they may still follow up the pursuit and trace us."

"The advice is good," replied Mr. Turnbull, "and the sooner we cut over again the better, for we are nearly abreast of my place."

We did so; Mr. Turnbull landed in his garden, taking with him the tin box (it was what they call a deed-box), and the lady's cloak. I did not wait, but boating the oars, took my sculls and pulled down to Fulham as fast as I could. I had arrived, and was pulling gently in, not to injure the other boats, when a man with a lantern come into the wherry.

"Have you anything in your boat, my man?" said he.

"Nothing, sir," replied I. The man examined the boat, and was satisfied.

"Tell me, did you see a boat with two men in it as you came along?"

"No, sir," replied I, "nothing has passed me."

"Where do you come from now?"

"From a gentleman's place near Brentford."

"Brentford? Oh, then you were far below them. They are not down yet."

"Have you a job for me, sir?" said I, not wishing to appear anxious to go away.

"No, my man, no; nothing to-night. We are on the look-out, but we have two boats in the stream, and a man at each landing-place."

I made fast my boat, shouldered my oars and sculls, and departed, not at all sorry to get away. It appeared that as soon as it was ascertained that we were not to be stopped by being fired at, they saddled horses, and the distance by the road being so much shorter, had, by galloping as hard as they could, arrived at Fulham some ten minutes before me. It was, therefore, most fortunate that the box had been landed, or I should have been discovered. That the contents were of value was evident, from the anxiety to secure them; but the mystery was still to be solved. I was quite tired with exertion and excitement when I arrived at Stapleton's. Mary was there to give me my supper, which I ate in silence, complained of a headache, and went to bed.

CHAPTER XXXII

The waterman turns water-knight—I become chivalrous, see a beautiful face, and go with the stream—The adventure seems to promise more law than love, there being papers in the case, that is, in a tin box.

THAT night I dreamed of nothing but the scene, over and over again, and the two bars of music were constantly ringing in my ears. As soon as I had breakfasted the next morning, I set off to Mr. Turnbull's, and told him what had occurred.

"It was indeed fortunate that the box was landed," said he, "or you might have now been in prison. I wish I had had nothing to do with it; but, as you say, 'what's done can't be helped.' I will not give up the box, at all events, until I know which party is entitled to it, and I cannot help thinking that the lady is. But, Jacob, you will have to reconnoitre, and find out what this story is. Tell me, do you think you could remember the tune which he whistled so often?"

"It has been running in my head the whole night, and I have been trying it all the way as I pulled here. I think I have it exact. Hear, sir." I whistled the two bars.

"Quite correct, Jacob, quite correct; well, take care not to forget them. Where are you going to-day?"

"Nowhere, sir."

"Suppose, then, you pull up the river, and find out the place where we landed, and when you have ascertained that, you can go on and see whether the young man is with the skiff; at all events, you may find out something—but pray be cautious."

I promised to be very careful, and departed on my errand, which I undertook with much pleasure, for I was delighted with anything like adventure. I pulled up the river, and in about an hour and a quarter came abreast of the spot. I recognised the cottage *ornée*, the parapet wall, even the spot where we lay, and perceived that several bricks were detached and had fallen into the river. There appeared to be no one stirring in the house, yet I continued to pull up and down, looking at the windows. At last one opened, and a young lady looked out, who, I was persuaded, was the same that we had seen the night before. There was no wind, and all was quiet around. She sat at the window, leaning her head on her hand. I whistled the two bars of the air. At the first bar she started up, and looked earnestly at me as I completed the second. I looked up; she waved her handkerchief once, and then shut the window. In a few seconds she made her appearance on the lawn, walking down towards the river. I immediately pulled in under the wall. I laid in my sculls, and held on, standing up in the boat.

"Who are you, and who sent you?" said she, looking down on me, and discovering one of the most beautiful faces I had ever beheld.

"No one sent me, ma'am," replied I, "but I was in the boat last night. I am sorry you were so unfortunate, but your box and cloak are quite safe."

"You were one of the men in the boat. I trust no one was hurt when they fired at you?"

"No, ma'am."

"And where is the box?"

"In the house of the person who was with me."

"Can he be trusted? For they will offer large rewards for it."

"I should think so, ma'am," replied I, smiling; "the person who was with me is a gentleman of large fortune, who was amusing himself on the river. He desires me to say that he will not give up the box until he knows to whom the contents legally belong."

"Good heavens, how fortunate! Am I to believe you?"

"I should hope so, ma'am."

"And what are you, then? You are not a waterman?"

"Yes, ma'am, I am."

She paused, looked earnestly at me for a little while, and then continued, "How did you learn the air you whistled?"

"The young gentleman whistled it six or seven times last night before you came. I tried it this morning coming up, as I thought it would be the means of attracting your attention. Can I be of any service to you, ma'am?"

"Service—yes, if I could be sure you were to be trusted— of the greatest service. I am confined here—cannot send a letter—watched as I move—only allowed the garden, and even watched while I walk here. They are most of them in quest of the tin box to-day, or I should not be able to talk to you so long." She looked round at the house anxiously, and then said, "Stop here a minute, while I walk a little." She then retreated, and paced up and down the garden walk. I still remained under the wall, so as not to be perceived from the house. In about three or four minutes she returned, and said, "It would be very cruel—it would be more than cruel—it would be very wicked of you to deceive me, for I am very unfortunate and very unhappy." The tears started in her eyes. "You do not look as if you would. What is your name?"

"Jacob Faithful, ma'am, and I will be true to my name, if you will put your trust in me. I never deceived any one that I can recollect; and I'm sure I would not you—now that I've seen you."

"Yes, but money will seduce everybody."

"Not me, ma'am; I've as much as I wish for."

"Well then, I will trust you, and think you sent from heaven to my aid; but how am I to see you? To-morrow my uncle will be back, and then I shall not be able to speak

264

to you one moment, and if seen to speak to you, you will be laid in wait for, and perhaps shot."

"Well, madam," replied I, after a pause, "if you cannot speak, you can write. You see that the bricks on the parapet are loose here. Put your letter under this brick—I can take it away even in day-time, without being noticed, and can put the answer in the same place, so that you can secure it when you come out."

"How very clever! Good heavens, what an excellent idea!"

"Was the young gentleman hurt, ma'am, in the scuffle last night?" inquired I.

"No, I believe not much, but I wish to know where he is, to write to him; could you find out?" I told her where we had met him, and what had passed. "That was Lady Auburn's," replied she; "he is often there—she is our cousin; but I don't know where he lives, and how to find him I know not. His name is William Wharncliffe. Do you think you could find him out?"

"Yes, ma'am, with a little trouble it might be done. They ought to know where he is at Lady Auburn's."

"Yes, some of the servants might—but how will you get to them?"

"That, ma'am, I must find out. It may not be done in one day, or two days, but if you will look every morning under this brick, if there is anything to communicate you will find it there."

"You can write and read, then?"

"I should hope so, ma'am," replied I, laughing.

"I don't know what to make of you. Are you really a waterman?"

"Really, and——" She turned her head round at the noise of a window opening.

"You must go—don't forget the brick;" and she disappeared.

I shoved my wherry along by the side of the wall, so as to remain unperceived until I was clear of the frontage attached to the cottage, and then taking my sculls pulled into the stream; and as I was resolved to see if I could obtain any information at Lady Auburn's, I had to pass the garden again, having shoved my boat down the river instead of up, when I was under the wall. I perceived the young lady walking with a tall man by her side; he speaking very energetically, and using much gesticulation, she holding down her head. In another minute they were shut out from my sight. I was so much stricken with the beauty and sweetness of expression in the young lady's countenance, that I was resolved to use my best exertions to be of service to her. In about an hour and a half I had arrived at the villa, abreast of which we had met the young gentleman, and which the young lady had told me belonged to Lady Auburn. I could see no one in the grounds, nor indeed in the house. After watching a few minutes, I landed as near to the villa as I could, made fast the wherry, and walked round to the entrance. There was no lodge, but a servant's door at one side. I pulled the bell, having made up my mind how to proceed as I was walking up. The bell was answered by an old woman, who, in a snarling tone, asked me "What did I want?"

"I am waiting below, with my boat, for Mr. Wharncliffe; has he come yet?"

"Mr. Wharncliffe! No, he's not come, nor did he say that he would come; when did you see him?"

"Yesterday. Is Lady Auburn at home?"

"Lady Auburn—no, she went to town this morning; everybody goes to London now, that they may not see the flowers and green trees, I suppose."

"But I suppose Mr. Wharncliffe will come," continued I, "so I must wait for him."

"You can do just as you like," replied the old woman, about to shut the gate in my face.

"May I request a favour of you, ma'am, before you shut the gate—which is, to bring me a little water to drink, for the sun is hot, and I have had a long pull up here;" and I took out my handkerchief and wiped my face.

"Yes, I'll fetch you some," replied she, shutting the gate and going away.

"This don't seem to answer very well," thought I to myself. The old woman returned, opened the gate, and handed me a mug of water. I drank some, thanked her, and returned the mug.

"I am very tired," said I; "I should like to sit down and wait for the gentleman."

"Don't you sit down when you pull?" inquired the old woman.

" Yes," replied I.

" Then you must be tired of sitting, I should think, not of standing ; at all events, if you want to sit you can sit in your boat, and mind it at the same time." With this observation she shut the door upon me, and left me without any more comment.

After this decided repulse on the part of the old woman, I had nothing to do but to take her advice, viz., to go and look after my boat. I pulled down to Mr. Turnbull's, and told him my good and bad fortune. It being late, he ordered me some dinner in his study, and we sat there canvassing over the affair. " Well," said he, as we finished, " you must allow me to consider this as my affair, Jacob, as I was the occasion of our getting mixed up in it. You must do all that you can to find this young man, and I shall hire Stapleton's boat by the day until we succeed ; you need not tell him so, or he may be anxious to know why. To-morrow you go down to old Beazeley's ? "

" Yes, sir ; you cannot hire me to-morrow."

" Still I shall, as I want to see you to-morrow morning before you go. Here's Stapleton's money for yesterday and to-day, and now good-night."

I was at Mr. Turnbull's early the next morning, and found him with the newspaper before him. " I expected this, Jacob," said he ; " read that advertisement." I read as follows : " Whereas, on Friday night last, between the hours of nine and ten, a tin box, containing deeds and papers, was handed into a wherry, from the grounds of a villa between Brentford and Kew, and the parties who owned it were prevented from accompanying the same. This is to give notice, that a reward of twenty pounds will be paid to the watermen, upon their delivering up the same to Messrs. James and John White, of No. 14 Lincoln's Inn Fields. As no other parties are authorised to receive the said tin box of papers, all other applications for it must be disregarded. An early attention to this advertisement will oblige."

" There must be papers of no little consequence in that box, Jacob, depend upon it," said Mr. Turnbull ; " however, here they are, and here they shall remain until I know more about it, that's certain. I intend to try what I can do myself with the old woman, for I perceive the villa is to be let for three months—here is the advertisement in the last column. I shall go to town to-day, and obtain a ticket from the agent, and it is hard but I'll ferret out something.   I shall see you to-morrow. Now you may go, Jacob."

I hastened away, as I had promised to be down to old Tom's to breakfast.   An hour's smart pulling brought me to the landing-place, opposite to his house.

CHAPTER XXXIII

A ten-pound householder occupied with affairs of State—The advantage of the word " implication "—An unexpected meeting and a reconciliation—Resolution versus bright black eyes— Verdict for the defendant, with heavy damages.

THE house of old Tom Beazeley was situated on the verge of Battersea Fields, about a mile and a half from the bridge bearing the same name; the river about twenty yards before it, the green grass behind it, and not a tree within half a mile of it. There was nothing picturesque in it but its utter loneliness; it was not only lonely but isolated, for it was fixed upon a delta of about half an acre, between two creeks, which joined at about forty yards from the river, and ran up through the fields, so that the house was at high water upon an island, and at low water was defended by an impassable barrier of mud, so that the advances to it could be made only from the river, where a small *hard*, edged with posts worn down to the conformation of decayed double teeth, offered the only means of access.   The house itself was one story high ; dark red bricks, and darker tiles upon the roof; windows very scarce and very small, although built long before the damnable tax upon light, for it was probably built in the time of Elizabeth, to judge by the peculiarity of the style of architecture observable in the chimneys ; but it matters very little at what epoch was built a tenement which was rented at only ten pounds per annum.   The major part of the said island was stocked with cabbage plants ; but on one side there was half a boat set upright, with a patch of green before it.   At the time that old Beazeley hired it, there was a bridge, rudely constructed of old ship plank, by which you could gain a path which led across the Battersea Fields ; but as all the communications of old Tom were by water, and

Mrs. Beazeley never ventured over the bridge, it was gradually knocked away for firewood, and when it was low-water, one old post, redolent of mud, marked the spot where the bridge had been. The interior was far more inviting. Mrs. Beazeley was a clean person and frugal housewife, and every article in the kitchen, which was the first room you entered, was as clean and as bright as industry could make it. There was a parlour also, seldom used ; both of the inmates, when they did meet, which was not above a day or two in three weeks, during the time that old Beazeley was in charge of the lighter, preferring comfort to grandeur. In this isolated house, upon this isolated spot, did Mrs. Beazeley pass a life of almost isolation.

And yet, perhaps, there never was a more lively or a more happy woman than Mrs. Beazeley, for she was strong and in good health, and always employed. She knew that her husband was following up his avocation on the river, and laying by a provision for their old age, while she herself was adding considerably to it by her own exertions. She had married old Tom long before he had lost his legs, at a time when he was a prime active sailor, and the best man of the ship. She was a net-maker's daughter, and had been brought up to the business, at which she was very expert. The most difficult part of the art is that of making large *seines* for taking sea-fish ; and when she had no order for those to complete, the making of casting-nets beguiled away her time as soon as her household cares had been disposed of. She made money and husbanded it, not only for herself and her partner, but for her son, young Tom, upon whom she doted. So accustomed was she to work hard and be alone, that it was difficult to say whether she was most pleased or most annoyed when her husband and son made their appearance for a day or two, and the latter was alternately fondled and scolded during the whole of his sojourn ; Tom, as the reader may suppose from a knowledge of his character, caring about as much for the one as the other.

I pulled into the hard, and made fast my boat. There was no one outside the door when I landed ; on entering, I found them all seated at the table, and a grand display of fragments, in the shape of herring-bones, &c. " Well, Jacob—come at last —thought you had forgot us ; piped to breakfast at eight bells —always do, you know," said old Tom, on my making my appearance.

"Have you had your breakfast, Jacob?" said Mrs. Beazeley.

"No," replied I; "I was obliged to go up to Mr. Turnbull's, and that detained me."

"No more sodgers, Jacob," said Tom; "father and I ate them all."

"Have you?" replied Mrs. Beazeley, taking two more red herrings out of the cupboard, and putting them on the fire to grill; "no, no, master Tom, there's some for Jacob yet."

"Well, mother, you make nets to some purpose, for you've always a fish when it's wanted."

I despatched my breakfast, and as soon as all had been cleared away by his wife, old Tom, crossing his two timber legs, commenced business; for it appeared, what I was not aware of, that we had met on a sort of council of war.

"Jacob, sit down by me; old woman, bring yourself to an anchor in the high chair; Tom, sit anywhere, so you sit still."— "And leave my net alone, Tom," cried his mother, in parenthesis. —"You see, Jacob, the whole long and short of it is this, I feel my toes more and more, and flannel's no longer warm. I can't tide it any longer, and I think it high time to lie up in ordinary and moor abreast of the old woman. Now, there's Tom, in the first place, what's to do with he? I think that I'll build him a wherry, and as I'm free of the river, he can finish his apprenticeship with my name on the boat; but to build him a wherry would be rather a heavy pull for me."

"If you mean to build it yourself, I think it will prove a *heavy pull* for me," replied Tom.

"Silence, Tom; I built you, and God knows you're light enough."

"And, Tom, leave my net alone," cried his mother.

"Father made me light-fingered, mother."

"Ay, and light-hearted too, boy," rejoined the dame, looking fondly at her son.

"Well," continued old Tom, "supposing that Tom be provided for in that way; then now I comes to myself. I've an idea that I can do a good bit of work in patching up boats; for you see I always was a bit of a carpenter, and I know how the builders extortionate the poor watermen when there's a trifle amiss. Now, if they knew I could do it, they'd all come to me fast enough; but then there's a puzzle. I've been thinking this week how I can make them know it. I can't put out a board and say, Beazeley, *Boat-builder,* because I'm no boat-builder, but still I want a sign."

"Lord, father, haven't you got one already?" interrupted young Tom; "you've half a boat stuck up there, and that means that you're half a boat-builder."

"Silence, Tom, with your frippery; what do you think, Jacob?"

"Could you not say, 'Boats repaired here'?"

"Yes, but that won't exactly do; they like to employ a builder—and there's the puzzle."

"Not half so puzzling as this net," observed Tom, who had taken up the needle unobserved by his mother, and begun to work; "I've made only ten stitches, and six of them are long ones."

"Tom, Tom, you good-for-nothing; why don't you let my net alone?" cried Mrs. Beazeley; "now 'twill take me as much time to undo ten stitches as to have made fifty."

"All right, mother."

"No, Tom, all's wrong; look at these meshes?"

"Well, then, all's fair, mother."

"No, all's foul, boy; look how it's tangled."

"Still, I say, all's fair, mother, for it is but **fair to give the** fish one or two chances to get away, and that's just what I've done; and now, father, I'll settle your affair to your own satisfaction, as I have mother's."

"That will be queer satisfaction, Tom, I guess; but let's hear what you have to say."

"Why, then, father, it seems that you're no boat-builder, but you want people to fancy that you are—an't that the question?"

"Why, 'tis something like it, Tom, but I do nobody no harm."

"Certainly not; it's only the boats which will suffer. Now, get a large board, with 'Boats *built to order,* and boats repaired, by Tom Beazeley.' You know if any man is fool enough to order a boat, that's his concern; you didn't say you're a boat-builder, although you have no objection to try your hand."

"What do you say, Jacob?" said old Tom, appealing to me.

"I think that Tom has given very good advice, and I would follow it."

"Ah! Tom has a head," said Mrs. Beazeley fondly. "Tom, let go my net again, will you? What a boy you are!

Now touch it again if you dare!" and Mrs. Beazeley took up a little poker from the fireplace and shook it at him.

"Tom has a head, indeed," said young Tom, "but as he has no wish to have it broken, Jacob, lend me your wherry for half-an-hour, and I'll be off."

I assented, and Tom, first tossing the cat upon his mother's back, made his escape, crying—

"Lord, Molly, what a fish,"

as the animal fixed in its claws to save herself from falling, making Mrs. Beazeley roar out and vow vengeance, while old Tom and I could not refrain from laughter.

After Tom's departure, the conversation was renewed, and everything was finally arranged between old Tom and his wife, except the building of the wherry, at which the old woman shook her head. The debate would be too long, and not sufficiently interesting to detail; one part, however, I must make the reader acquainted with. After entering into all the arrangements of the house, Mrs. Beazeley took me upstairs to show me the rooms, which were very neat and clean. I came down with her, and old Tom said, "Did the old woman show you the room with the white curtains, Jacob?"

"Yes," replied I, "and a very nice one it is."

"Well, Jacob, there's nothing sure in this world. You're well off at present, and 'leave well alone' is a good motto; but recollect this, that room is for you when you want it, and everything else we can share with you. It's offered freely, and you will accept it the same. Is it not, old lady?"

"Yes, that it is, Jacob; but may you do better—if not, I'll be your mother for want of a better."

I was moved with the kindness of the old couple; the more so as I did not know what I had done to deserve it. Old Tom gave me a hearty squeeze of the hand, and then continued: "But about this wherry—what do you say, old woman?"

"What will it cost?" replied she gravely.

"Cost? let me see—a good wherry, with sculls and oars, will be a matter of thirty pounds."

The old woman screwed up her mouth, shook her head, and then walked away to prepare for dinner.

"I think she could muster the blunt, Jacob, but she don't

272

like to part with it. Tom must coax her. I wish he hadn't shied the cat at her. He's too full of fun."

As old Beazeley finished, I perceived a wherry pulling in with some ladies. I looked attentively, and recognised my own boat, and Tom pulling. In a minute more they were at the *hard*, and who, to my astonishment, were there seated, but Mrs. Drummond and Sarah. As Tom got out of the boat and held it steady against the *hard*, he called to me. I could not do otherwise than go and assist them out, and once more did I touch the hands of those whom I never thought to meet again. Mrs. Drummond retained my hand a short time after she landed, saying, "We are friends, Jacob, are we not?"

"Oh yes, madam," replied I, much moved, in a faltering voice.

"I shall not ask that question," said Sarah gaily, "for we parted friends."

And as I recalled to mind her affectionate behaviour, I pressed her hand, and the tears glistened in my eyes as I looked into her sweet face. As I afterwards discovered, this was an arranged plan with old and young Tom, to bring about a meeting without my knowledge. Mrs. Beazeley courtesied and stroked her apron; smiled at the ladies, looked very *cat*-tish at Tom, showed the ladies into the house, where old Tom assisted to do the honours after his own fashion, by asking Mrs. Drummond if she would like *to whet her whistle* after her *pull*. Mrs. Drummond looked round to me for explanation, but young Tom thought proper to be interpreter. "Father wants to know, if you please, ma'am, whether, after your *pull* in the boat, you wouldn't like to have a *pull* at the brandy bottle?"

"No," replied Mrs. Drummond, smiling; "but I should be obliged for a glass of water. Will you get me one, Jacob?"

I hastened to comply, and Mrs. Drummond entered into conversation with Mrs. Beazeley. Sarah looked at me, and went to the door, turning back as inviting me to follow. I did so, and we soon found ourselves seated on the bench in the old boat.

"Jacob," said she, looking earnestly at me, "you surely will be friends with *my* father?"

I think I should have shaken my head, but she laid an emphasis on *my*, which the little gipsy knew would have its

s

effect. All my resolutions, all my pride, all my sense of
injury vanished before the mild, beautiful eyes of Sarah, and
I replied hastily, "Yes, Miss Sarah, I can refuse *you* nothing."

"Why *Miss*, Jacob?"

"I am a waterman, and you are much above me."

"That is your own fault; but say no more about it."

"I must say something more, which is this: do not attempt
to make me leave my present employment. I am happy, because I am independent; and that I will, if possible, be for
the future."

"Any one can pull an oar, Jacob."

"Very true, Miss Sarah, and is under no obligation to any
one by so earning his livelihood. He works for all, and is
paid for all."

"Will you come and see us, Jacob? Come to-morrow—now
do—promise me. Will you refuse your old playmate, Jacob?"

"I wish you would not ask that."

"How then can you say that you are friends with my father?
I will not believe you unless you promise to come."

"Sarah," replied I earnestly, "I will come; and to prove
to you that we are friends, I will ask a favour of him."

"O Jacob, this is kind, indeed," cried Sarah, with her
eyes swimming with tears. "You have made me so—so very
happy!"

The meeting with Sarah humanised me, and every feeling
of revenge was chased from my memory. Mrs. Drummond
joined us soon after, and proposed to return. "And Jacob
will pull us back," cried Sarah. "Come, sir, look after your
fare, in both senses. Since you will be a waterman, you shall
work." I laughed, and handed them to the boat. Tom took
the other oar, and we were soon at the steps close to Mr.
Drummond's house.

"Mamma, we ought to give these poor fellows something
to drink; they've worked very hard," said Sarah, mocking.
"Come up, my good men." I hesitated. "Nay, Jacob, if to-
morrow, why not to-day? The sooner these things are over
the better."

I felt the truth of this observation, and followed her. In a
few minutes I was again in that parlour in which I had been
dismissed, and in which the affectionate girl burst into tears
on my shoulder, as I held the handle of the door. I looked

at it, and looked at Sarah. Mrs. Drummond had gone out of the room to let Mr. Drummond know that I had come. "How kind you were, Sarah!" said I.

"Yes, but kind people are cross sometimes, and so am I—and so was——"

Mr. Drummond came in, and stopped her. "Jacob, I am glad to see you again in my house; I was deceived by appearances, and did you injustice." How true is the observation of the wise man, that a soft word turneth away wrath; that Mr. Drummond should personally acknowledge that he was wrong to me—that he should confess it—every feeling of resentment was gone, and others crowded in their place. I recollected how he had protected the orphan; how he had provided him with instruction; how he had made *his* house a home to me; how he had tried to bring me forward under his own protection. I recollected—which, alas! I never should have forgotten—that he had treated me for years with kindness and affection, all of which had been obliterated from my memory by one single act of injustice. I felt that I was a culprit, and burst into tears; and Sarah, as before, cried in sympathy.

"I beg your pardon, Mr. Drummond," said I, as soon as I could speak; "I have been very wrong in being so revengeful after so much kindness from you."

"We both have been wrong—but say no more on the subject, Jacob. I have an order to give, and then I will come up to you again;" and Mr. Drummond quitted the room.

"You dear, good boy," said Sarah, coming up to me. "Now I really do love you."

What I might have replied was put a stop to by Mrs. Drummond entering the room. She made a few inquiries about where I at present resided, and Sarah was catechising me rather inquisitively about Mary Stapleton, when Mr. Drummond re-entered the room, and shook me by the hand with a warmth which made me more ashamed of my conduct towards him. The conversation became general, but still rather embarrassed, when Sarah whispered to' me, "What is the favour you would ask of my father?" I had forgotten it at the moment, but I immediately told him that I would be obliged if he would allow me to have a part of the money belonging to me which he held in his possession.

"That I will, with pleasure, and without asking what

275

you intend to do with it, Jacob. How much do you require ?"

"Thirty pounds, if there is so much."

Mr. Drummond went down, and in a few minutes returned with the sum in notes and guineas. I thanked him, and shortly afterwards took my leave.

"Did not young Beazeley tell you I had something for you, Jacob ?" said Sarah, as I wished her good-bye.

"Yes; what is it ?"

"You must come and see," replied Sarah, laughing. Thus was a finale to all my revenge brought about by a little girl of fifteen years old, with large dark eyes.

Tom had taken his glass of grog below, and was waiting for me at the steps. We shoved off, and returned to his father's house, where dinner was just ready. After dinner old Tom recommenced the argument. "The only hitch," says he, "is about the wherry. What do you say, old woman ?" The old woman shook her head.

"As that is the only hitch," said I, "I can remove it, for here is the money for the wherry, which I make a present to Tom," and I put the money into young Tom's hand. Tom counted it out before his father and mother, much to their astonishment.

"You are a good fellow, Jacob," said Tom ; "but, I say, do you recollect Wimbledon Common ?"

"What then ?" replied I.

"Only Jerry Abershaw, that's all."

"Do not be afraid, Tom, it is honestly mine."

"But how did you get it, Jacob ?" said old Tom.

It may appear strange, but impelled by a wish to serve my friends I had asked for the money which I knew belonged to me, but never thought of the manner in which it had been obtained. The question of old Tom recalled everything to my memory, and I shuddered when I recollected the circumstances attending it. I was confused, and did not like to reply. "Be satisfied, the money is mine," replied I.

"Yes, Jacob, but how ?" replied Mrs. Beazeley; "surely you ought to be able to tell how you got so large a sum."

"Jacob has some reason for not telling, missus, depend upon it ; mayhap Mr. Turnbull, or whoever gave it to him, told him to hold his tongue." But this answer would not satisfy Mrs.

Beazeley, who declared she would not allow a farthing to be taken, unless she knew how it was obtained.

"Tom, give back the money directly," said she, looking at me suspiciously.

Tom laid it on the table before me, without saying a word. "Take it, Tom," said I, colouring up. "I had it from my mother."

"From your mother, Jacob!" said old Tom. "Nay, that could not well be, if my memory sarves me right. Still, it may be."

"Deary me, I don't like this at all," cried Mrs. Beazeley, getting up, and wiping her apron with a quick motion. "O Jacob, that must be—not the truth."

I coloured up to the tips of my ears, at being suspected of falsehood. I looked round, and saw that even Tom and his father had a melancholy doubt in their countenances; and certainly my confused appearance would have caused suspicion in anybody. "I little thought," said I at last, "when I hoped to have so much pleasure in giving, and to find that I had made you happy in receiving the money, that it would have proved a source of so much annoyance. I perceive that I am suspected of having obtained it improperly, and of not having told the truth. That Mrs. Beazeley may think so, who does not know me, is not to be wondered at; but that you," continued I, turning to old Tom, "or you," looking at his son, "should suspect me, is very mortifying, and I did not expect it. I tell you that the money is mine, honestly mine, and obtained from my mother. I ask you, do you believe me?

"I, for one, do believe you, Jacob," said young Tom, striking his fist on the table. "I can't understand it, but I know you never told a lie, or did a dishonourable act since I've known you."

"Thank you, Tom," said I, taking his proffered hand.

"And I would swear the same, Jacob," said old Tom; "although I have been longer in the world than my boy has, and have, therefore, seen more; and sorry am I to say, many a good man turned bad, from temptation being too great. But when I looked in your face, and saw the blood up to your forehead, I did feel a little suspicious, I must own; but I beg your pardon, Jacob, no one can look in your face now, and not see that you are innocent. I believe all you say, in spite of the old woman and—the devil to boot—and there's my hand upon it."

"Why not tell—why not tell?" muttered Mrs. Beazeley, shaking her head, and working at her net faster than ever.

But I had resolved to tell, and did so, narrating distinctly the circumstances by which the money had been obtained. I did it, however, with feelings of mortification which I cannot express. I felt humiliation—I felt that, for my own wants, that money I never could touch. Still, my explanation had the effect of removing the doubts even of Mrs. Beazeley, and harmony was restored. The money was accepted by the old couple, and promised to be applied for the purpose intended.

"As for me, Jacob," said Tom, "when I say I thank you, you know I mean it. Had I had the money, and you had wanted it, you will believe me when I say that I would have given it to you."

"That I'm sure of, Tom."

"Still, Jacob, it is a great deal of money; and I shall tie by my earnings as fast as I can, that you may have it in case you want it; but it will take many a heavy pull and many a shirt wet with labour, before I can make up a sum like that."

I did not stay much longer after this little fracas; I was hurt—my pride was wounded by suspicion, and fortunate it was that the occurrence had not taken place previous to my meeting with Mrs. Drummond and Sarah, otherwise no reconciliation would have taken place in that quarter. How much are we the sport of circumstances, and how insensibly they mark out our career in this world! With the best intentions we go wrong; instigated by unworthy motives, we fall upon our feet, and the chapter of accidents has more power over the best regulated mind than all the chapters in the Bible.

CHAPTER XXXIV

How I was revenged upon my enemies—We try the bars of music but find that we are barred out—Being no go, we go back.

I SHOOK hands with Tom, who, perceiving that I was vexed, had accompanied me down to the boat with his usual sympathy, and had offered to pull with me to Fulham, and walk

278

back; which offer I declined, as I wished to be alone. It was a fine moonlight night, and the broad light and shadow, with the stillness of all around, were peculiarly adapted to my feelings. I continued my way up the river, revolving in my mind the scenes of the day; the reconciliation with one whom I never intended to have spoken to again; the little quarrel with those whom I never expected to have been at variance with, and that at the time when I was only exerting myself to serve them; and then I thought of Sarah, as an oasis of real happiness in this contemplated desert, and dwelt upon the thought of her as the most pleasant and calming to my still agitated mind. Thus did I ruminate till I had passed Putney Bridge, forgetting that I was close to my landing-place, and continuing in my reverie to pull up the river, when my cogitations were disturbed by a noise of men laughing and talking, apparently in a state of intoxication. They were in a four-oared wherry, coming down the river, after a party of pleasure, as it is termed, generally one ending in intoxication. I listened.

"I tell you I can spin an oar with any man in the king's service," said the man in the bow. "Now look."

He threw his oar out of the rowlocks, spun it in the air, but unfortunately did not catch it when it fell, and consequently it went through the bottom, starting two of the planks of the fragile-built boat, which immediately filled with water.

"Hilloa! waterman!" cried another, perceiving me, "quick, or we shall sink." But the boat was nearly up to the thwarts in water before I could reach her, and just as I was nearly alongside, she filled and turned over.

"Help, waterman, help me first; I'm senior clerk," cried a voice which I well knew. I put out my oar to him as he struggled in the water, and soon had him clinging to the wherry. I then tried to catch hold of the man who had sunk the boat by his attempt to toss the oar, but he very quietly said, "No, d—n it, there's too many, we shall swamp the wherry; I'll swim on shore," and suiting the action to the word, he made for the shore with perfect self-possession, swimming in his clothes with great ease and dexterity.

I picked up two more, and thought that all were saved, when turning round and looking towards the bridge, I saw resplendent in the bright beams of the moon, and "round as its orb," the well-remembered face of the stupid young clerk who had been so inimical to me, struggling with all his might. I pulled to him, and putting out my oar over the bow, he seized it, after rising from his first sink, and was, with the other three, soon clinging to the side of the wherry.

"Pull me in—pull me in, waterman!" cried the head clerk, whose voice I had recognised.

"No; you will swamp the boat."

"Well, but pull me in, if not the others. I'm the senior clerk."

"Can't help that, you must hold on," replied I, "while I pull you on shore; we shall soon be there." I must say that I felt a pleasure in allowing him thus to hang in the water. I might have taken them all in, certainly, although at some risk, from their want of presence of mind and hurry, arising from the feeling of self-preservation; but I desired them to hold on, and pulled for the landing-place, which we soon gained. The person who had preferred swimming had arrived before us, and was waiting on the beach.

"Have you got them all, waterman?" said he

"Yes, sir, I believe so; I have four."

"The tally is right," replied he, "and four greater galloots were never picked up; but never mind that. It was my non-sense that nearly drowned them; and therefore I'm very glad you've managed so well. My jacket went down in the boat, and I must reward you another time."

"Thank you, sir, no occasion for that, it's not a regular fare."

"Nevertheless, give us your name."

"Oh, you may ask Mr. Hodgson, the senior clerk, or that full-moon-faced fellow—they know my name."

"Waterman, what do you mean?" replied Mr. Hodgson, shivering with cold.

"Very impudent fellow," said the junior of the round face.

"If they know your name they won't tell it," replied the other. "Now, I'll first tell you mine, which is Lieutenant Wilson, of the navy; and now let's have yours, that I may ask for it, and tell me what stairs you ply from."

"My name is Jacob Faithful, sir," replied I; "and you may ask your friends whether they know it or not when their teeth don't chatter quite so much."

At the mention of my name the senior and junior clerk walked off, and the lieutenant, telling me that I should hear from him again, was about to leave. "If you mean to give me money, sir, I tell you candidly I shall not take it. I hate these two men for the injuries they have heaped on me; but I don't know how it is, I feel a degree of pleasure in having saved them, that I wish for no better revenge. So farewell, sir."

"Spoken as you ought, my lad—that's glorious revenge. Well then, I will not come; but if ever we meet again, I shall never forget this night and Jacob Faithful." He held out his hand, shook mine warmly, and walked away.

When they were gone, I remained for some little time quite stupefied at the events of the day. The reconciliation—the quarrel—the revenge. I was still in thought when I heard the sound of a horse's hoofs. This recalled me, and I was hauling up my boat, intending to go home to Stapleton's, but with no great eagerness. I felt a sort of dislike to Mary Stapleton which I could not account for; but the fact was, I had been in company with Sarah Drummond. The horse stopped at the foot of the bridge, and the rider giving it to his servant, who was mounted on another, to hold, came down to where I was hauling up my boat. "My lad, is it too late for you to launch your boat? I will pay you well."

"Where do you wish to go to, sir? It is now past ten o'clock."

"I know it is, and I hardly expected to find a waterman here; but I took the chance. Will you take me about two miles up the river?"

I looked at the person who addressed me, and was delighted to recognise in him the young man who had hired Mr. Turnbull and me to take him to the garden, and who had been captured when we escaped with the tin box; but I did not make myself known. "Well, sir, if you wish it, I've no objection," replied I, putting my shoulder to the bow of my wherry, and launching her again into the water. At all events, this has been a day of adventure, thought I, as I threw my sculls again into the water, and commenced pulling up the stream. I was some little while in meditation whether I should make myself known to the young man; but I decided that I would not. Let me see, thought I, what sort of a person this is—whether he is as deserving as the young lady appeared to consider. "Which side, sir?" inquired I.

"The left," was the reply.

I knew that well enough, and I pulled in silence until nearly up to the wall of the garden which ran down to the bank of the river. "Now pull in to that wall, and make no noise," was the injunction, which I obeyed, securing the boat to the very part where the coping bricks had been displaced. He stood up, and whistled the two bars of the tune as before, waited five minutes, repeated it, and watched the windows of the house; but there was no reply, or signs of anybody being up or stirring. "It is too late; she is gone to rest."

"I thought there was a lady in the case, sir," observed I. "If you wish to communicate with her, I think I could manage it."

"Could you?" replied he. "Stop a moment; I'll speak to you by-and-by." He whistled the tune once more, and after waiting another ten minutes dropped himself down on the stern-sheets, and told me to pull back again. After a minute's silence he said to me, "You think you could communicate with her, you say. Pray, how do you propose?"

"If you will write a letter, sir, I'll try to let it come to her hand."

"How?"

"That, sir, you must leave me to find out, and trust to opportunity; but you must tell me what sort of person she is, that I may not give it to another; and also who there is in the house that I must be careful does not see me."

"Very true," replied he. "I can only say, that if you do succeed I will reward you handsomely; but she is so strictly watched that I am afraid it will be impossible. However, a despairing, like a drowning, man will catch at a straw; and I will see whether you will be able to assist me."

He then informed me that there was no one in the house except her uncle and his servants, all of whom were spies upon her; that my only chance was watching if she were permitted to walk in the garden alone, which might be the case; and perhaps, by concealing myself from eight o'clock in the morning till the evening under the parapet wall, I might find an opportunity. He directed me to be at the foot of the bridge next morning at seven o'clock, when he would come with a letter written for me to deliver, if possible. We had then arrived at Fulham. He landed, and, putting a guinea in my hand, mounted his horse, which his servant walked up and down waiting for him, and rode off. I hauled up my boat and went home, tired with the manifold events of the day. Mary Stapleton, who had sat up for me, was very inquisitive to know what had occasioned my coming home so late ; but I evaded her questions, and she left me in anything but good-humour, but about that I never felt so indifferent.

The next morning the servant made his appearance with the letter, telling me that he had orders to wait till the evening ; and I pulled up the river. I placed it under the loose brick, as agreed upon with the young lady, and then shoved off to the other side of the river, where I had a full view of the garden, and could notice all that passed. In half-an-hour the young lady came out, accompanied by another female, and sauntered up and down the gravel-walk. After a while she stopped, and looked on the river, her companion continuing her promenade. As if without hoping to find anything there, she moved the brick aside with her foot ; perceiving the letter, she snatched it up eagerly, and concealed it in her dress, and then cast her eyes on the river. It was calm, and I whistled the bar of music. She heard it, and turning away hastened into the house. In about half-an-hour she returned, and, watching her opportunity, stooped down to the brick. I waited a few minutes, when both she and her companion went into the house. I then pulled in under the wall, lifted up the brick, took the letter, and hastened back to Fulham ; when I delivered the letter to the servant, who rode off with it as fast as he could, and I returned home quite pleased at the successful issue of my attempt, and not a little curious to learn the real facts of this extraordinary affair.

CHAPTER XXXV

The Domine reads me a sermon out of the largest book I ever fell in with, covering nearly two acres of ground—The pages not very easy to turn over, but the type very convenient to read without spectacles—He leaves off without shutting his book, as parsons usually do at the end of their sermons.

THE next day being Sunday, as usual I went to see the Domine and Mr. Turnbull. I arrived at the school just as all the boys were filing off, two and two, for church, the advance led by the usher, and the rear brought up by the Domine in person; and I accompanied them. The Domine appeared melancholy and out of spirits—hardly exchanging a word with me during our walk. When the service was over, he ordered the usher to take the boys home, and remained with me in the churchyard, surveying the tombstones, and occasionally muttering to himself. At last the congregation dispersed, and we were alone.

"Little did I think, Jacob," said he at last, "that when I bestowed such care upon thee in thy childhood I should be rewarded as I have been! Little did I think that it would be to the boy who was left destitute that I should pour out my soul when afflicted, and find in him that sympathy which I have long lost, by the removal of those who were once my friends! Yes, Jacob, those who were known to me in my youth—those few in whom I confided and leant upon—are now lying here in crumbling dust, and the generation hath passed away; and I now rest upon thee, my son, whom I have directed in the right path, and who hast, by the blessing of God, continued to walk straight in it. Verily, thou art a solace to me, Jacob; and though young in years, I feel that in thee I have received a friend, and one that I may confide in. Bless thee, Jacob! bless thee, my boy! and before I am laid with those who have gone before me, may I see thee prosperous and happy! Then I will sing the *Nunc dimittis*; then will I say, 'Now, Lord, let Thy servant depart in peace.'"

"I am happy, sir," replied I, "to hear you say that I am of any comfort to you, for I feel truly grateful for all your kindness to me; but I wish that you did not require comfort."

"Jacob, in what part of a man's life does he not require comfort and consolation; yea, even from the time when, as a child, he buries his weeping face in his mother's lap till the hour that summons him to his account? Not that I consider this world to be, as many have described it, a 'vale of tears.' No, Jacob; it is a beautiful world, a glorious world, and would be a happy world, if we would only restrain those senses and those passions with which we have been endowed, that we may fully enjoy the beauty, the variety, the inexhaustible bounty of a gracious Heaven. All was made for enjoyment and for happiness; but it is we ourselves who, by excess, defile that which otherwise were pure. Thus, the fainting traveller may drink wholesome and refreshing draughts from the bounteous, overflowing spring; but should he rush heedlessly into it, he muddies the source, and the waters are those of bitterness. Thus, Jacob, was wine given to cheer the heart of man; yet didst not thou witness me, thy preceptor, debased by intemperance? Thus, Jacob, were the affections implanted in us as a source of sweetest happiness, such as those which now yearn in my breast towards thee; yet hast thou seen me, thy preceptor, by yielding to the infatuation and imbecility of threescore years, dote, in my folly, upon a maiden, and turn the sweet affections into a source of misery and anguish." I answered not, for the words of the Domine made a strong impression upon me, and I was weighing them in my mind. "Jacob," continued the Domine after a pause, "next to the book of life, there is no subject of contemplation more salutary than the book of death, of which each stone now around us may be considered as a page, and each page contains a lesson. Read that which is now before us. It would appear hard that an only child should have been torn away from its doting parents, who have thus imperfectly expressed their anguish on the tomb; it would appear hard that their delight, their solace, the object of their daily care, of their waking thoughts, of their last imperfect recollections as they sank into sleep, of their only dreams, should thus have been taken from them; yet did I know them, and Heaven was just and merciful. The child had weaned them from their God; they lived but in him; they were without God in the world. The child alone had their affections, and they had been lost, had not He in His mercy removed it. Come this way, Jacob." I followed the Domine till he stood before another tombstone in a corner of the churchyard. "This stone, Jacob, marks the spot where lie the remains of one who was my earliest and dearest friend—for in my youth I had friends, because I had anticipations, and little thought that it would have pleased God that I should do my duty in that station to which I have been called. He had one fault, which proved a source of misery through life, and was the cause of an untimely death. He was of a revengeful disposition. He never forgave an injury, forgetting, poor sinful mortal, for how much he had need to be forgiven. He quarrelled with his relations; he was shot in a duel with his friend! I mention this, Jacob, as a lesson to thee; not that I feel myself worthy to be thy preceptor, for I am humbled, but out of kindness and love towards thee, that I might persuade thee to correct that fault in thy disposition."

"I have already made friends with Mr. Drummond, sir," answered I; "but still your admonition shall not be thrown away."

"Hast thou, Jacob? then is my mind much relieved. I trust thou wilt no longer stand in thine own light, but accept the offers which, in the fulness of his heart to make redress, he may make unto thee."

"Nay, sir, I cannot promise that I wish to be independent and earn my own livelihood."

"Then hear me, Jacob, for the spirit of prophecy is on me; the time will come when thou shalt bitterly repent. Thou hast received an education by my unworthy endeavours, and hast been blessed by Providence with talents far above the situation in life to which thou wouldst so tenaciously adhere; the time will come when thou wilt repent, yea, bitterly repent. Look at that marble monument with the arms so lavishly emblazoned upon it. That, Jacob, is the tomb of a proud man, whose career is well known to me. He was in straitened circumstances, yet of gentle race; but, like the steward in the Scripture, 'work he could not, to beg he was ashamed.' He might have prospered in the world, but his pride forbade him. He might have made friends, but his pride forbade him. He might have wedded himself to wealth and beauty, but there was no escutcheon, and his pride forbade him. He did marry, and entail upon his children poverty. He died, and the little he possessed was taken from his children's necessities to build this record to his dust. Do not suppose that I would check that honest pride which will prove a safeguard from unworthy actions. I only wish to check that undue pride which will mar thy future prospects. Jacob, that which thou termest *independence* is naught but pride."

I could not acknowledge that I agreed with the Domine, although something in my breast told me that he was not wrong. I made no answer. The Domine continued to muse —at last he again spoke.

"Yes, it is a beautiful world; for the Spirit of God is on it. At the separation of chaos it came over the water, and hath since remained with us, everywhere, but invisible. We see

His hand in the variety and the beauty of creation, but His Spirit we see not; yet do we feel it in the still small voice of conscience, which would lead us into the right path. Now, Jacob, we must return, for I have the catechism and collects to attend to."

I took leave of the Domine, and went to Mr. Turnbull's, to whom I gave an account of what had passed since I last saw him. He was much pleased with my reconciliation with the Drummonds, and interested about the young lady to whom appertained the tin box in his possession. "I presume, Jacob, we shall now have that mystery cleared up."

"I have not told the gentleman that we have possession of the box," replied I.

"No; but you told the young lady, you silly fellow; and do you think she will keep it a secret from him?"

"Very true; I had forgotten that."

"Jacob, I wish you to go to Mr. Drummond's and see his family again; you ought to do so." I hesitated. "Nay, I shall give you a fair opportunity without wounding that pride of yours, sir," replied Mr. Turnbull. "I owe him some money for some wine he purchased for me, and I shall send the cheque by you."

To this I assented, as I was not sorry of an opportunity of seeing Sarah. I dined with Mr. Turnbull, who was alone, his wife being on a visit to a relation in the country. He again offered me his advice as to giving up the profession of a waterman; but if I did not hear him with so much impatience as before, nor use so many arguments against it, I did not accede to his wishes, and the subject was dropped. Mr. Turnbull was satisfied that my resistance was weakened, and hoped in time to have the effect which he desired. When I went home, Mary told me that Tom Beazeley had been there, that his wherry was building, that his father had given up the lighter, and was now on shore very busy in getting up his board to attract customers, and obtain work in his new occupation.

I had not launched my wherry the next morning, when down came the young gentleman to whom I had despatched the letter. "Faithful," said he, "come to the tavern with me; I must have some conversation with you." I followed him; and as soon as we were in a room, he said, "First let me pay my debt, for I owe you much," and he laid five guineas on the table. " I find from Cecilia that you have possession of the tin case of deeds which has been so eagerly sought after by both parties. Why did you not say so? And why did you not tell me that it was you whom I hired on the night when I was so unfortunate?"

"I considered the secret as belonging to the young lady, and having told her, I left it to her discretion to make you acquainted or not, as she pleased."

"It was thoughtful and prudent of you, at all events, although there was no occasion for it. Nevertheless I am pleased that you did so, as it proves you to be trustworthy. Now, tell me, who is the gentleman who was with you in the boat, and who has charge of the box? Observe, Faithful, I do not intend to demand it. I shall tell him the facts of the case in your presence, and then leave him to decide whether he will surrender up the papers to the other party, or to me. Can you take me there now?"

"Yes, sir," replied I, "I can, if you please; I will pull you up in half-an-hour. The house is at the river's side."

The young gentleman leaped into my wherry, and we were, in less than the time I had mentioned, in the parlour of Mr. Turnbull. I will not repeat the conversation in detail, but give the outline of the young man's story.

CHAPTER XXXVI

A long story, which ends in the opening of the tin box, which proves to contain deeds much more satisfactory to Mr. Wharncliffe than the deeds of his uncle—Begin to feel the blessings of independence, and suspect that I have acted like a fool— After two years' consideration, I become quite sure of it, and, as Tom says, "No mistake."

THE gentleman who prevented my taking off the young lady is uncle to both of us. We are, therefore, first cousins. Our family name is Wharncliffe. My father was a major in the army. He died when I was young, and my mother is still alive, and is sister to Lady Auburn. The father and mother of Cecilia are both dead. He went out to India to join his brother, another uncle, of whom I shall speak directly. He has now been dead three years, and out of the four brothers there is only one left, my uncle, with whom Cecilia is living, and whose Christian name is Henry. He was a lawyer by profession, but he purchased a patent place, which he still enjoys. My father, whose name was William, died in very moderate circumstances; but still he left enough for my mother to live upon, and to educate me properly. I was brought up to the law under my uncle Henry, with whom, for some years, I resided. Cecilia's father, whose name was Edward, left nothing; he had ruined himself in England, and had gone out to India at the request of my uncle there, whose name was James, and who had amassed a large fortune. Soon after the death of Cecilia's father, my uncle James came home on furlough, for he held a very high and lucrative situation under the Company. A bachelor from choice, he was still fond of young people; and having but one nephew and one niece to leave his money to, as soon as he arrived with Cecilia, whom he brought with him, he was most anxious to see me. He therefore took up his quarters with my uncle Henry, and remained with him during his sojourn in England; but my uncle James was of a very cold and capricious temper. He liked me best because I was a boy, and one day declared I should be his heir. The next day he would alter his intention, and declare that Cecilia, of whom he was very fond, should inherit everything. If we affronted him, for at the age of sixteen as a boy, and fourteen as a girl, worldly prospects were little regarded, he would then declare that we should not be a shilling the better for his money. With him, money was everything: it was his daily theme of conversation, his only passion; and he valued and respected people in proportion to what they were supposed to possess. With these feelings he demanded for himself the greatest deference from Cecilia and me, as his expectant heirs. This he did not receive; but on the whole he was pleased with us, and after remaining three years in England, he returned to the East Indies. I had heard him mention to my uncle Henry his intention of making his will, and leaving it with him before he sailed; but I was not certain whether it had been done or not. At all events, my uncle Henry took care that I should not be in the way; for at that time my uncle carried on his profession as a lawyer, and I was working in his office. It was not until after my uncle James

T

returned to India that he gave up business, and purchased the patent place which I mentioned. Cecilia was left with my uncle Henry, and as we lived in the same house, our affections as we grew up ripened into love. We often used to laugh at the threats of my uncle James, and agreed that whoever might be the fortunate one to whom he left his property, we would go halves, and share it equally.

"In the meantime I still followed up my profession in another house, in which I at present am a partner. Four years after the return of my uncle James to India, news came home of his death; but it was also stated that no will could be found, and it was supposed that he died intestate. Of course, my uncle Henry succeeded as heir-at-law to the whole property, and thus were the expectations and hopes of Cecilia and of myself dashed to the ground. But this was not the worst of it. My uncle, who had witnessed our feelings for each other, and had made no comment, as soon as he was in possession of the property, intimated to Cecilia that she should be his heiress, provided that she married according to his wishes, and pointed out to her that a fortune such as she might expect would warrant the alliance of the first nobleman in the kingdom; and he very plainly told me that he thought it advisable that I should find lodgings for myself, and not be any longer an inmate in the same house as was my cousin, as no good would result from it. Thus, sir, were we not only disappointed in our hopes, but thwarted in our affections, which had for some time been exchanged. Maddened at this intimation, I quitted the house; and at the same time the idea of my uncle James having made a will still pressed upon me, as I called to mind what I had heard him say to my uncle Henry previous to his sailing for India. There was a box of deeds and papers, the very box now in your possession, which my uncle invariably kept in his bed-room. I felt convinced that the will, if not destroyed (and I did not believe my uncle would dare to commit an act of felony), was in that box. Had I remained in the house, I would have found some means to have opened it; but this was no longer possible. I communicated my suspicions to Cecilia, and begged her to make the attempt, which would be more easy, as my uncle would not suspect her of being bold enough to venture it, even if he had the suspicion. Cecilia promised, and one day my uncle fortunately left his keys upon his dressing-table when he came down to breakfast, and went out without missing them.   Cecilia discovered them, and opened the box, and amongst other parchments found a document labelled outside as the will of our uncle James; but women understand little about these things, and she was in such trepidation for fear that my uncle should return, that she could not examine very minutely.   As it was, my uncle did return for his keys, just as she had locked the box and placed the keys upon the table.   He asked her what she was doing there, and she made some excuse.   He saw the keys on the table, and whether suspecting her, for she coloured up very much, or afraid that the attempt might be made at my suggestion, he removed the box and locked it up in a closet, the key of which, I believe, he left with his banker in town.   When Cecilia wrote to me an account of what had passed, I desired her to find the means of opening the closet, that we might gain possession of the box; and this was easily effected, for the key of another closet fitted the lock exactly.   I then persuaded her to put herself under my protection, with the determination that we would marry immediately; and we had so arranged that the tin box was to have accompanied us.   You are aware, sir, how unfortunately our plan turned out—at least so far unfortunately, that I lost, as I thought, not only Cecilia but the tin box, containing, as I expect, the will of my uncle, of which I am more than ever convinced from the great anxiety shown by my uncle Henry to recover it.   Since the loss, he has been in a state of agitation which has worn him to a shadow.   He feels that his only chance is that the watermen employed might have broken open the box, expecting to find money in it, and being disappointed, have destroyed the papers to avoid detection.   If such had been the case, and it might have been, had it not fallen into such good hands, he then would have obtained his only wish, that of the destruction of the will, although not by his own hands.   Now, sir, I have given you a full and honest account of the affair, and leave you to decide how to act."

"If you leave me to decide, I shall do it very quickly," replied Mr. Turnbull.   "A box has fallen into my hands, and I do not know who is the owner.   I shall open it, and take a list of the deeds it contains, and advertise them in the *Times* and other newspapers.   If your dead uncle's will is in it, it will,

of course, be advertised with the others, and after such publicity
your uncle Henry will not venture, I presume, to say a word,
but be too glad not to be exposed."

Mr. Turnbull ordered a locksmith to be summoned, and the
tin box was opened.   It contained the document of the uncle's
purchase of the patent place in the courts, and some other
papers, but it also contained the parchment so much looked
after—the last will and testament of James Wharncliffe, Esq.,
dated two months previous to his quitting England.   "I think,"
observed Mr. Turnbull, "that in case of accident it may be as
well that this will should be read before witnesses.   You
observe, it is witnessed by Henry Wharncliffe, with two others.
Let us take down their names."

The will was read by young Wharncliffe, at the request of
Mr. Turnbull.   Strange to say, the deceased bequeathed the
whole of his property to his nephew, William Wharncliffe, and
his niece, Cecilia, provided they married ; if they did not, they
were left £20,000 each, and the remainder of the fortune to go
to the first male child born after the marriage of either niece or.
nephew.   To his brother, the sum of £10,000 was bequeathed,
with a liberal arrangement, to be paid out of the estate, so long
as his niece lived with him.   The will was read, and returned
to Mr. Turnbull, who shook hands with Mr. Wharncliffe and
congratulated him.

"I am so much indebted to you, sir, that I can hardly
express my gratitude, but I am still more indebted to this intelligent lad, Faithful.   You must no longer be a waterman,
Faithful," and Mr. Wharncliffe shook my hand.   I made no
answer to the latter observation, for Mr. Turnbull had fixed his
eye upon me.   I merely said that I was very happy to have
been of use to him.

"You may truly say, Mr. Wharncliffe," observed Mr. Turnbull, "that your future prosperity will be through his means;
and as it appears by the will that you have £9000 per annum
safe in the Funds, I think you ought to give a prize wherry, to
be rowed for every year."

"And I will take that," replied I, "for a receipt in full for
my share in the transaction."

"And now," said Mr. Turnbull, interrupting Mr. Wharncliffe,
who was about to answer me, "it appears to me that it may be
as well to avoid any exposure—the case is too clear.   Call

upon your uncle; state in whose hands the documents are; tell him that he must submit to your terms, which are, that he proves the will, and permits the marriage to take place immediately, and that no more will be said on the subject. He, as a lawyer, knows how severely and disgracefully he might be punished for what he has done, and will be too happy now to accede to your terms. In the meantime I keep possession of the papers, for the will shall never leave my hands, until it is lodged in Doctors' Commons."

Mr. Wharncliffe could not but approve of this judicious arrangement, and we separated; and, not to interfere with my narrative, I may as well tell the reader at once that Mr. Wharncliffe's uncle bowed to circumstances, pretended to rejoice at the discovery of the will, never mentioned the loss of his tin box, put the hand of Cecilia into that of William, and they were married one month after the meeting at Mr. Turnbull's, which I have now related.

The evening was so far advanced before this council of war was over, that I was obliged to defer the delivery of the cheque to Mr. Drummond until the next day. I left about eleven o'clock, and arrived at noon; when I knocked at the door the servant did not know me.

"What did you want?"

"I wanted to speak with Mrs. or Miss Drummond, and my name is Faithful."

He desired me to sit down in the hall, while he went up: "And wipe your shoes, my lad." I cannot say that I was pleased at this command, as I may call it, but he returned, desiring me to walk up, and I followed him.

I found Sarah alone in the drawing-room.

"Jacob, I'm so glad to see you, and I'm sorry that you were made to wait below, but—if people who can be otherwise, will be watermen, it is not our fault. The servants only judge by appearances."

I felt annoyed for a moment, but it was soon over. I sat down by Sarah, and talked with her for some time.

"The present I had to make you was a purse of my own knitting, to put your—earnings in," said she, laughing; and then she held up her finger in mockery, crying, "Boat, sir; boat, sir. Well, Jacob, there's nothing like independence, after all, and you must not mind my laughing at you."

" I do not heed it, Sarah," replied I ; (but I did mind it very much), " there is no disgrace."

" None whatever, I grant ; but a want of ambition, which I cannot understand. However, let us say no more about it."

Mrs. Drummond came into the room, and greeted me kindly. " When can you come and dine with us, Jacob? Will you come on Wednesday?"

" O mamma ! he can't come on Wednesday ; we have company on that day."

" So we have, my dear, I had forgotten it ; but on Thursday we are quite alone. Will you come on Thursday, Jacob?"

I hesitated, for I felt that it was because I was a waterman that I was not admitted to the table where I had been accustomed to dine at one time, whoever might be invited.

" Yes, Jacob," said Sarah, coming to me, " it must be Thursday, and you must not deny us ; for although we have greater people on Wednesday, the party that day will not be so agreeable to me as your company on Thursday."

The last compliment from Sarah decided me, and I accepted the invitation. Mr. Drummond came in, and I delivered to him Mr. Turnbull's cheque. He was very kind, but said little further than that he was glad that I had promised to dine with them on Thursday. The footman came in and announced the carriage at the door, and this was a signal for me to take my leave. Sarah, as she shook hands with me, laughing, asserted that it was not considerate in them to detain me any longer, as I must have lost half-a-dozen good fares already. " So go down to your boat, pull off your jacket, and make up for lost time," continued she ; " one of these days, mamma and I intend to go on the water, just to patronise you." I laughed, and went away, but I was cruelly mortified. I could not be equal to them, because I was a waterman. The sarcasm of Sarah was not lost upon me ; still there was so much kindness mixed with it that I could not be angry with her. On the Thursday I went there, as agreed ; they were quite alone ; friendly and attentive ; but still there was a degree of constraint which communicated itself to me. After dinner, Mr. Drummond said very little ; there was no renewal of offers to take me into his employ, nor any inquiry as to how I got on in the profession which I had chosen. On the whole, I found myself uncomfortable, and was glad to leave early ; nor did I

feel at all inclined to renew my visit. I ought to remark that
Mr. Drummond was now moving in a very different sphere
than when I first knew him. He was consignee of several
large establishments abroad, and was making a rapid fortune.
His establishment was also on a very different scale, every department being appointed with elegance and conducive to
luxury. As I pulled up the river, something within my breast
told me that the Domine's prophecy would turn out correct,
and that I should one day repent of my having refused the
advances of Mr. Drummond—nay, I did not exactly know
whether I did not, even at that moment, very much doubt the
wisdom of my asserting my independence.

And now, reader, that I may not surfeit you with an un-
interesting detail, you must allow nearly two years to pass
away before I recommence my narrative. The events of that
time I shall sum up in one or two pages. The Domine continued
the even tenor of his way—blew his nose, and handled his
rod with as much effect as ever. I seldom passed a Sunday
without paying him a visit, and benefiting by his counsel.
Mr. Turnbull was always kind and considerate, but gradually
declining in health, having never recovered from the effects of
his submersion under the ice. Of the Drummonds I saw but
little ; when we did meet, I was kindly received, but I never
volunteered a call, and it was usually from a message through
Tom that I went to pay my respects. Sarah had grown a
very beautiful girl, and the well-known fact of Mr. Drummond's wealth, and her being an only daughter, was an introduction to a circle much higher than they had been formerly
accustomed to. Every day, therefore, the disparity increased,
and I felt less inclined to make my appearance at their house.

Stapleton, as usual, continued to smoke his pipe and descant
upon *human natur.* Mary had grown into a splendid woman,
but coquettish as ever. Poor Tom Beazeley was fairly entrapped by her charms, and was a constant attendant upon
her; but she played him fast and loose—one time encouraging
and smiling on him, at another rejecting and flouting him.
Still Tom persevered, for he was fascinated, and having returned me the money advanced for his wherry, he expended
all his earnings on dressing himself smartly, and making presents to her. She had completely grown out of any control
from me, and appeared to have a pleasure in doing every-

thing she knew I disapproved; still, we were on fair friendly terms as inmates of the same house.

Old Tom Beazeley's board was up, and he had met with great success; and all day he might be seen hammering at the bottoms of boats of every description, and heard, at the same time, lightening his labour with his variety of song. I often called there on my way up and down the river, and occasionally passed a few hours listening to his yarns, which, like his songs, appeared to be inexhaustible.

With respect to myself, it would be more a narrative of feelings than of action. My life glided on as did my wherry—silently and rapidly. One day was but the forerunner of another, with slight variety of incident and customers. My acquaintance, as the reader knows, were but few, and my visits occasional. I again turned to my books during the long summer evenings, in which Mary would walk out, accompanied by Tom and other admirers; Mr. Turnbull's library was at my service, and I profited much. After a time, reading became almost a passion, and I was seldom without a book in my hand. But although I improved my mind, I did not render myself happier. On the contrary, I felt more and more that I had committed an act of egregious folly in thus asserting my independence. I felt that I was superior to my station in life, and that I lived with those who were not companions; that I had thrown away, by foolish pride, those prospects of advancement which had offered themselves, and that I was passing my youth unprofitably. All this crowded upon me more and more every day, and I bitterly repented, as the Domine told me that I should, my spirit of independence—now that it was too late. The offers of Mr. Drummond were never renewed, and Mr. Turnbull, who had formed the idea that I was still of the same opinion, and who, at the same time, in his afflicted state—for he was a martyr to the rheumatism—naturally thought more of himself and less of others, never again proposed that I should quit my employment. I was still too proud to mention my wishes, and thus did I continue plying on the river, apathetic almost as to gain, and only happy when, in the pages of history or among the flowers of poetry, I could dwell upon times that were past, or revel in imagination. Thus did reading, like the snake which is said to contain in its body a remedy for the poison of its fangs, become, as it enlarged my mind, a source of discontent at my humble situation ; but, at the same time, the only solace in my unhappiness, by diverting my thoughts from the present. Pass, then, nearly two years, reader, taking the above remarks as an outline, and filling up the picture from the colours of your imagination, with incidents of no peculiar value, and I again resume my narrative.

CHAPTER XXXVII

A chapter of losses to all but the reader, though at first Tom works with his wit, and receives the full value of his exertions—We make the very worst bargain we ever made in our lives—We LOSE our fare, we LOSE our boat, and we LOSE our liberty—All loss and no profit—Fare very unfair—Two guineas' worth of argument, not worth twopence, except on the quarter-deck of a man-of-war.

J ACOB," said Tom to me, pulling his wherry into the *hard* alongside of mine, in which I was sitting with one of Mr. Turnbull's books in my hand, "Jacob, do you recollect that my time is up to-morrow ? I shall have run off my seven years, and when the sun rises, I shall be free of the river. How much more have you to serve ? "

" About fifteen months, as near as I can recollect, Tom, Boat; sir ? "

" Yes ; oars, my lad ; be smart, for I'm in a hurry. How's tide ? "

" Down, sir, very soon ; but it's now slack water. Tom, see if you can find Stapleton."

" Pooh ! never mind him, Jacob, I'll go with you. I say, Jones, tell old ' human natur' to look after my boat," continued Tom, addressing a waterman of our acquaintance.

" I thought you had come up to see *her*," said I to Tom, as we shoved off.

" See *her* at Jericho first," replied Tom ; " she's worse than a dog vane."

" What, are you *two* again ? "

" Two indeed—it's all two—we are two fools. She is too fanciful ; I am too fond ; she behaves too ill, and I put up with too much. However, it's all *one*."

"I thought it was all *two* just now, Tom."

"But two may be made one, Jacob, you know."

"Yes, by the parson; but you are no parson."

"Anyhow, I am something like one just now," replied Tom, who was pulling the foremost oar; "for you are a good clerk, and I am sitting behind you."

"That's not so bad," observed the gentleman in the stern-sheets, whom we had forgotten in the colloquy.

"A waterman would make but a bad parson, sir," replied Tom.

"Why so?"

"He's not likely to practise as he preaches."

"Again, why so?"

"Because all his life he looks one way and pulls another."

"Very good—very good, indeed."

"Nay, sir, good in practice, but still not good *in deed*—there's a puzzle."

"A puzzle, indeed, to find such a regular chain of repartee in a wherry."

"Well, sir, if I'm a regular chain to-day, I shall be like an irregular watch to-morrow."

"Why so, my lad?"

"Because I shall be *out of my time.*"

"Take that, my lad," said the gentleman, tossing half-a-crown to Tom.

"Thanky, sir; when we meet again may you have no more wit than you have now."

"How do you mean?"

"Not wit enough to keep your money, sir—that's all?"

"I presume you think that I have not got much."

"Which, sir; wit or money?"

"Wit, my lad."

"Nay, sir, I think you have both; the first you purchased just now, and you would hardly have bought it if you had not money to spare."

"But I mean wit of my own."

"No man has wit of his own; if he borrows it, it's not his own; if he has it in himself, it's *mother* wit, so it's not his."

We pulled into the stairs near London Bridge, and the gentleman paid me his fare. "Good-bye, my lad," said he to Tom.

"Fare you well, for well you've paid your fare," replied Tom, holding out his arm to assist him out of the boat. "Well,

Jacob, I've made more by my head than by my hands this morning. I wonder, in the long run, which gains most in the world."

"Head, Tom, depend upon it; but they work best together."

Here we were interrupted : "I say, you watermen, have you a mind for a good fare?" cried a dark-looking, not over clean, square-built, short young man, standing on the top of the flight of steps.

"Where to, sir?"

"Gravesend, my jokers, if you arn't afraid of salt water."

"That's a long way, sir," replied Tom ; "and for salt water, we must have salt to our porridge."

"So you shall, my lads, and a glass of grog into the bargain."

"Yes; but the bargain an't made yet, sir. Jacob, will you go?"

"Yes, but not under a guinea."

"Not under two guineas," replied Tom, aside. "Are you in a great hurry, sir?" continued he, addressing the young man.

"Yes, in a devil of a hurry ; I shall lose my ship. What will you take me for?"

"Two guineas, sir."

"Very well. Just come up to the public-house here, and put in my traps."

We brought down his luggage, put it into the wherry, and started down the river with the tide. Our fare was very communicative, and we found out that he was the master's mate of the *Immortalité*, forty-gun frigate, lying off Gravesend, which was to drop down next morning and wait for sailing orders at the Downs. We carried the tide with us, and in the afternoon were close to the frigate, whose blue ensign waved proudly over the taffrail. There was a considerable sea arising from the wind meeting the tide, and before we arrived close to her we had shipped a great deal of water ; and when we were alongside, the wherry, with the chest in her bows, pitched so heavily that we were afraid of being swamped. Just as a rope had been made fast to the chest, and they were weighing it out of the wherry, the ship's launch with water came alongside, and, whether from accident or wilfully I know not, although I suspect the latter, the midshipman who steered her shot her against the wherry, which was crushed in, and immediately filled, leaving Tom and me in the water, and in danger

299

of being jammed to death between the launch and the side of the frigate. The seamen in the boat, however, forced her off with their oars, and hauled us in, while our wherry sank with her gunwale even with the water's edge, and floated away astern.

As soon as we had shaken ourselves a little, we went up the side, and asked one of the officers to send a boat to pick up our wherry.

"Speak to the first lieutenant—there he is," was the reply.

I went up to the person pointed out to me: "If you please, sir——"

"What the devil do you want?"

"A boat, sir, to——"

"A boat! the devil you do!"

"To pick up our wherry, sir," interrupted Tom.

"Pick it up yourself," said the first lieutenant, passing us, and hailing the men aloft. "Maintop, there, hook on your stays. Be smart. Lower away the yards. Marines and after-guard, clear launch. Boatswain's mate."

"Here, sir."

"Pipe marines and after-guard to clear launch."

"Ay, ay, sir."

"But we shall lose our boat, Jacob," said Tom to me. "They stove it in, and they ought to pick it up." Tom then went up to the master's mate, whom he had brought on board, and explained our difficulty.

"Upon my soul, I daren't say a word. I'm in a scrape for breaking my leave. Why the devil didn't you take care of your wherry, and haul ahead when you saw the launch coming?"

"How could we, when the chest was hoisting out?"

"Very true. Well, I am sorry for you, but I must look after my chest." So saying he disappeared down the gang-way ladder.

"I'll try it again anyhow," said Tom, going up to the first lieutenant. "Hard case to lose our boat and our bread, sir," said Tom, touching his hat.

The first lieutenant, now that the marines and after-guard were at a regular stamp and go, had, unfortunately, more leisure to attend to us. He looked at us earnestly, and walked aft to see if the wherry was yet in sight. At that moment up came the master's mate, who had not yet reported himself to the first lieutenant.

"'Tom," said I, "there is a wherry close to, let us get into it, and go after our boat ourselves."

"Wait one moment to see if they will help us—and get our money, at all events," replied Tom; and we both walked aft.

"Come on board, sir," said the master's mate, touching his hat with humility.

"You've broke your leave, sir," replied the first lieutenant, "and now I've to send a boat to pick up the wherry through your carelessness."

"If you please, they are two very fine young men," observed the mate. "Make capital foretopmen. Boat's not worth sending for, sir."

This hint, given by the mate to the first lieutenant to regain his favour, was not lost. "Who are you, my lads?" said the first lieutenant to us.

"Watermen, sir."

"Watermen, heh! was that your own boat?"

"No, sir," replied I; "it belonged to the man that I serve with."

"Oh! not your own boat? Are you an apprentice, then?"

"Yes, sir, both apprentices."

"Show me your indentures."

"We don't carry them about with us."

"Then how am I to know that you are apprentices?"

"We can prove it, sir, if you wish it."

"I do wish it; at all events, the captain will wish it."

"Will you please to send for the boat, sir? she's almost out of sight."

"No, my lads, I can't find king's boats for such service."

"Then we had better go ourselves, Tom," said I, and we went forward to call the waterman, who was lying on his oars close to the frigate.

"Stop—stop—not so fast. Where are you going, my lads?"

"To pick up our boat, sir."

"Without my leave, heh?"

"We don't belong to the frigate, sir."

"No; but I think it very likely that you will, for you have no protections."

"We can send for them, and have them down by to-morrow morning."

"Well, you may do so, if you please, my lads; but you

cannot expect me to believe everything that is told me. Now, for instance, how long have you to serve, my lad?" said he, addressing Tom.

"My time is up to-morrow, sir."

"Up to-morrow. Why, then, I shall detain you until to-morrow, and then I shall press you."

"If you detain me now, sir, I am pressed to-day."

"Oh no! you are only detained until you prove your apprenticeship, that's all."

"Nay, sir, I certainly am pressed during my apprenticeship."

"Not at all, and I'll prove it to you. You don't belong to the ship until you are victualled on her books. Now I shan't *victual* you to-day, therefore you won't be *pressed*."

"I shall be pressed with hunger, at all events," replied Tom, who never could lose a joke.

"No, you shan't; for I'll send you both a good dinner out of the gunroom. So you won't be pressed at all," replied the lieutenant, laughing at Tom's reply.

"You will allow me to go, sir, at all events," replied I; for I knew that the only chance of getting Tom and myself clear was my hastening to Mr. Drummond for assistance.

"Pooh! nonsense; you must both row in the same boat as you have done. The fact is, my lads, I've taken a great fancy to you both, and I can't make up my mind to part with you."

"It's hard to lose our bread, this way," replied I.

"We will find you bread, and hard enough you will find it," replied the lieutenant, laughing; "it's like a flint."

"So we ask for bread, and you give us a stone," said Tom, "that's 'gainst Scripture."

"Very true, my lad; but the fact is, all the Scriptures in the world won't man the frigate. Men we must have, and get them how we can, and where we can, and when we can. Necessity has no law; at least it obliges us to break through all laws. After all, there's no great hardship in serving the king for a year or two, and filling your pockets with prize-money. Suppose you volunteer?"

"Will you allow us to go on shore for half-an-hour to think about it?" replied I.

"No; I'm afraid of the crimps dissuading you. But I'll give you till to-morrow morning, and then I shall be sure of one, at all events."

"Thanky for me," replied Tom.

"You're very welcome," replied the first lieutenant, as, laughing at us, he went down the companion-ladder to his dinner.

"Well, Jacob, we are in for it," said Tom, as soon as we were alone. "Depend upon it there's no mistake this time."

"I am afraid not," replied I, "unless we can get a letter to your father or Mr. Drummond, who, I am sure, would help us. But that dirty fellow who gave the lieutenant the hint, said the frigate sailed to-morrow morning; there he is, let us speak to him."

"When does the frigate sail?" said Tom to the master's mate, who was walking the deck.

"My good fellow, it's not the custom on board of a man-of-war for men to ask officers to answer such impertinent questions. It's quite sufficient for you to know that when the frigate sails, you will have the honour of sailing in her."

"Well, sir," replied I, nettled at his answer, "at all events you will have the goodness to pay us our fare. We have lost our wherry, and our liberty perhaps, through you; we may as well have our two guineas."

"Two guineas! It's two guineas you want, heh?"

"Yes, sir, that was the fare agreed upon."

"Why, you must observe, my men," said the master's mate, hooking a thumb into each armhole of his waistcoat, "there must be a little explanation as to that affair. I promised you two guineas as watermen; but now that you belong to a man-of-war, you are no longer watermen. I always pay my debts honourably when I can find the lawful creditors, but where are the watermen?"

"Here we are, sir."

"No, my lads, you are men-of-war's men now, and that quite alters the case."

"But we are not so yet, sir; even if it did alter the case, we are not pressed yet."

"Well then, you'll be to-morrow, perhaps; at all events we shall see. If you are allowed to go on shore again, I owe you two guineas as watermen; and if you are detained as men-of-war's men, why, then, you will only have done your duty in pulling down one of your officers. You see, my lads, I say nothing but what's fair."

"Well, sir, but when you hired us we were watermen," replied Tom.

"Very true, so you were; but recollect the two guineas were not due until you had completed your task, which was not until you came on board. When you came on board you were pressed, and became men-of-war's men. You should have asked for your fare before the first lieutenant got hold of you. Don't you perceive the justice of my remarks?"

"Can't say I do, sir; but I perceive there's very little chance of our being paid," said Tom.

"You are a lad of discrimination," replied the master's mate. "And now I advise you to drop the subject, or you may induce me to pay you 'man-of-war fashion.'"

"How's that, sir?"

"Over the face and eyes, as the cat paid the monkey," replied the master's mate, walking leisurely away.

"No go, Tom," said I, smiling at the absurdity of the arguments.

"I'm afraid it's *no go* in every way, Jacob. However, I don't care much about it. I have had a little hankering after seeing the world, and perhaps now's as well as any other time; but I'm sorry for you, Jacob."

"It's all my own fault," replied I; and I fell into one of those reveries so often indulged in of late, as to the folly of my conduct in asserting my independence, which had now ended in my losing my liberty. But we were cold from the ducking we had received, and moreover very hungry. The first lieutenant did not forget his promise; he sent us up a good dinner and a glass of grog each, which we discussed under the half-deck, between two of the guns. We had some money in our pockets, and we purchased some sheets of paper from the bumboat people, who were on the main-deck supplying the seamen; and I wrote to Mr. Drummond and Mr. Turnbull, as well as to Mary and old Tom, requesting the two latter to forward our clothes to Deal, in case of our being detained. Tom also wrote to comfort his mother, and the greatest comfort which he could give was, as he said, to promise to keep sober. Having entrusted these letters to the bumboat woman, who promised faithfully to put them into the post-office, we had then nothing else to do but to look out for some place to sleep. Our clothes had dried on us, and we were walking under the half-deck; but not a soul spoke to, or even took the least notice of us. In a newly-manned ship just ready to sail, there is a universal feeling of selfishness prevailing among the ship's company. Some, if not most, had like us been pressed, and their thoughts were occupied with their situation, and the change in their prospects. Others were busy making their little arrangements with their wives or relations; while the mass of the seamen, not yet organised by discipline, or known to each other, were in a state of disunion and individuality, which naturally induced every man to look after himself without caring for his neighbour. We therefore could not expect, nor did we receive, any sympathy; we were in a scene of bustle and noise, yet alone. A spare topsail, which had been stowed for the present between two of the guns, was the best accommodation which offered itself. We took possession of it, and, tired with exertion of mind and body, were soon fast asleep.

CHAPTER XXXVIII

There are many ups and downs in this world—We find ourselves in the Downs—Our captain comes on board, and gives us a short sermon upon antipathies, which most of us never heard the like of—He sets us all upon the go, with his stop watch, and never calls the watch, until the watch is satisfied with all hands.

At daylight the next morning we were awakened with a start by the shrill whistles of the boatswain and his mates piping all hands to unmoor. The pilot was on board, and the wind was fair. As the frigate had no anchor down, but was hanging to the moorings in the river, we had nothing to do but to cast off, sheet home, and in less than half-an-hour we were under all sail, stemming the last quarter of the flood-tide. Tom and I had remained on the gangway, watching the proceedings, but not assisting, when the ship being fairly under sail, the order was given by the first lieutenant to coil down the ropes.

"I think, Jacob, we may as well help," said Tom, laying hold of the main tack, which was passed aft, and hauling it forward.

"With all my heart," replied I, and I hauled it forward, while he coiled it away.

While we were thus employed the first lieutenant walked forward and recognised us. "That's what I like, my lads," said he; "you don't sulk, I see, and I shan't forget it."

"I hope you won't forget that we are apprentices, sir, and allow us to go on shore," replied I.

"I've a shocking bad memory in some things," was his reply, as he continued forward to the forecastle. He did not, however, forget to victual us that day, and insert our names in pencil upon the ship's books; but we were not put into any mess, or stationed.

We anchored in the Downs on the following morning. It came on to blow hard in the afternoon, and there was no communication with the shore, except by signals, until the third day, when it moderated, and the signal was made, "Prepare to weigh, and send boat for captain." In the meantime, several boats came off, and one had a postman on board. I had letters from Mr. Drummond and Mr. Turnbull, telling me that they would immediately apply to the Admiralty for our being liberated, and one from Mary, half of which was for me, and the rest to Tom. Stapleton had taken Tom's wherry and pulled down to old Tom Beazeley, with my clothes, which, with young Tom's, had been despatched to Deal. Tom had a letter from his mother, half indited by his father, and the rest from herself; but I shall not trouble the reader with the contents, as he may imagine what was likely to be said upon such an occasion.

Shortly afterwards our clothes, which had been sent to the care of an old shipmate of Tom's father, were brought on board, and we hardly had received them, when the signalman reported that the captain was coming off. There were so many of the men in the frigate who had never seen the captain, that no little anxiety was shown by the ship's company to ascertain how far, by the "cut of his jib," that is, his outward appearance, they might draw conclusions as to what they might expect from one who had such unlimited power to make them happy or miserable. I was looking out of the main-deck port with Tom, when the gig pulled alongside, and was about to scrutinise the outward and visible signs of the captain, when I was attracted by the face of a lieutenant sitting by his side, whom I immediately recognised. It was Mr. Wilson, the officer who had spun the oar and sunk the wherry, from which, as the reader may remember, I rescued my friends, the senior and junior clerk. I was overjoyed at this, as I hoped that he would interest himself in our favour. The pipe of the boatswain re-echoed as the captain ascended the side. He appeared on the quarter-deck—every hat descending to do him honour; the marines presented arms, and the marine officer at their head lowered the point of his sword. In return, the omnipotent personage, taking his cocked hat with two fingers and a thumb, by the highest peak, lifted it one inch off his head, and replaced it, desiring the marine officer to dismiss the guard. I had now an opportunity, as he paced to and fro with the first lieutenant, to examine his appearance. He was a tall, very large-boned, gaunt man, with an enormous breadth of shoulders, displaying herculean strength (and this we found he eminently possessed). His face was of a size corresponding to his large frame; his features were harsh, his eye piercing, but his nose, although bold, was handsome, and his capacious mouth was furnished with the most splendid row of large teeth that I ever beheld. The character of his countenance was determination rather than severity. When he smiled, the expression was agreeable. His gestures and his language were emphatic, and the planks trembled with his elephantine walk.

He had been on board about ten minutes, when he desired the first lieutenant to turn the hands up, and all the men were ordered on the larboard side of the quarter-deck. As soon as they were all gathered together, looking with as much awe on the captain as a flock of sheep at a strange, mischief-meaning dog, he thus addressed them: "My lads, as it so happens that we are all to trust to the same planks, it may be just as well that we should understand one another. I *like* to see my officers attentive to their duty, and behave themselves as gentlemen. I *like* to see my men well disciplined, active, and sober. What I *like* I *will* have—you understand me. Now," continued he, putting on a stern look, "now just look in my face, and see if you think you can play with me." The men looked in his face, and saw that there was no chance of playing with him; and so they expressed by their countenances. The captain appeared satisfied by their mute

307

acknowledgments, and to encourage them, smiled, and showed his white teeth, as he desired the first lieutenant to pipe down.

As soon as the scene was over, I walked up to Mr. Wilson, the lieutenant, who was standing aft, and accosted him. "Perhaps, sir, you do not recollect me; but we met one night when you were sinking in a wherry, and you asked my name."

"And I recollect it, my lad; it was Faithful, was it not?"

"Yes, sir," and I then entered into an explanation of our circumstances, and requested his advice and assistance.

He shook his head. "Our captain," said he, "is a very strange person. He has commanding interest, and will do more in defiance of the rules of the Admiralty than any one in the service. If an Admiralty order came down to discharge you, he would obey it; but as for regulations, he cares very little for them. Besides, we sail in an hour. However, I will speak to him, although I shall probably get a rap on the knuckles, as it is the business of the first lieutenant and not mine."

"But, sir, if you requested the first lieutenant to speak?"

"If I did, he would not, in all probability; men are too valuable, and the first lieutenant knows that the captain would not like to discharge you. He will, therefore, say nothing until it is too late, and then throw all the blame upon himself for forgetting it. Our captain has such interest that his recommendation would give a commander's rank to-morrow, and we must all take care of ourselves. However, I will try, although I can give you very little hopes."

Mr. Wilson went up to the captain, who was still walking with the first lieutenant, and touching his hat introduced the subject, stating, as an apology, that he was acquainted with me.

"Oh, if the man is an acquaintance of yours, Mr. Wilson, we certainly must decide," replied the captain, with mock politeness. "Where is he?" I advanced, and Tom followed me. We stated our case. "I always like to put people out of suspense," said the captain, "because it unsettles a man— so now hear me; if I happened to press one of the blood royal, and the king, and the queen, and all the little princesses were to go down on their knees, I'd keep him, without an Admiralty order for his discharge. Now, my lads, do you perceive your chance?" Then turning away to Mr. Wilson, he said, "You will oblige me by stating upon what grounds you ventured to interfere in behalf of these men, and I trust your explanation will be satisfactory. Mr. Knight," continued he, to the first lieutenant, " send these men down below, watch, and station them."

We went below by the gangway ladder, and watched the conference between the captain and Mr. Wilson, who we were afraid had done himself no good by trying to assist us. But when it was over, the captain appeared pleased, and Mr. Wilson walked away with a satisfied air. As I afterwards dis-covered, it did me no little good. The hands were piped to dinner, and after dinner we weighed and made sail, and thus were Tom and I fairly, or rather unfairly, embarked in his Majesty's service.

" Well, Tom," said I, " it's no use crying. What's done can't be helped ; here we are, now let us do all we can to make friends."

" That's just my opinion, Jacob. Hang care, it killed the cat ; I shall make the best of it, and I don't see why we may not be as happy here as anywhere else. Father says we may, if we do our duty, and I don't mean to shirk mine. The more the merrier, they say, and I'll be hanged but there's not enough of us here."

I hardly need say, that for the first three or four days we were not very comfortable. We had been put into the seventh mess, and were stationed in the foretop ; for although we had not been regularly bred up as seamen, the first lieutenant so decided, saying that he was sure that in a few weeks there would be no smarter men in the ship.

We were soon clear of the Channel, and all hands were anxious to know our destination, which, in this almost solitary instance, had been really kept a secret, although surmises were correct. There is one point, which by the present arrangements invariably makes known whether a ship is "fitting foreign," or for home service, which is, by the stores and provisions ordered on board ; and these stores are so arranged, according to the station to which the vessel is bound, that it is generally pretty well known what her destination is to be. This is bad, and at the same time easily remedied ; for if every ship, whether for home service or foreign, was ordered to fit foreign, no one would be able to ascertain where she was about to proceed. With a very little trouble strict secrecy might be preserved, now that the Navy Board is abolished ; but during its existence that was impossible. The *Immortalité* was a very fast-sailing vessel, and when the captain (whose name I have forgotten to mention, it was Hector Maclean) opened his sealed orders, we found that we were to cruise for two months between the Western Isles and Madeira, in quest of some privateers, which had captured many of our outward-bound West Indiamen, notwithstanding that they were well protected by convoy, and after that period to join the admiral at Halifax, and relieve a frigate which had been many years on that station. In a week we were on our station, the weather was fine, and the whole of the day was passed in training the men to the guns, small arms, making and shortening sail, reefing topsails, and manœuvring the ship. The captain would never give up his point, and sometimes we were obliged to make or shorten sail twenty times running until he was satisfied.

"My lads," he would say to the ship's company, sending for them aft, "you have done this pretty well, you have only been two minutes; not bad for a new ship's company, but I *like* it done in a minute and a half. We'll try again." And sure enough it was try again, until in the minute and a half it was accomplished. Then the captain would say, "I knew you could do it, and having once done it, my lads, of course you can do it again."

Tom and I adhered to our good resolutions. We were as active and as forward as we could be; and Mr. Knight, the first lieutenant, pointed us out to the captain. As soon as the merits of the different men were ascertained several alterations were made in the watch and station bills, as well as in the ratings on the ship's books, and Tom and I were made *second* captains, larboard and starboard, of the foretop. This was great promotion for so young hands, especially as we were not bred as regular sailors; but it was for the activity and zeal which we displayed. Tom was a great favourite among the men, always joking, and ready for any lark or nonsense; moreover, he used to mimic the captain, which few others dared do. He certainly seldom ventured to do it below; it was generally in the foretop, where he used to explain to the men what he *liked*. One day we both ventured it, but it was on an occasion which excused it. Tom and I were aft, sitting in the jolly-boat astern, fitting some of her gear, for we belonged to the boat at that time, although we were afterwards shifted into the cutter. The frigate was going about four knots through the water, and the sea was pretty smooth. One of the marines fell overboard, out of the forechains. "Man overboard!" was cried out immediately, and the men were busy clearing away the starboard cutter, with all the expedition requisite on such an occasion. The captain was standing aft on the signal chest, when the marine passed astern; the poor fellow could not swim, and Tom, turning to me, said, "Jacob, I should *like* to save that jolly," and immediately dashed overboard.

"And I should *like* to help you, Tom," cried I, and followed him.

The captain was close to us, and heard us both. Between us, we easily held up the marine, and the boat had us all on board in less than a minute. When we came up the side, the captain was at the gangway. He showed his white teeth, and shook the telescope in his hand at us. "I heard you both; and I should *like* to have a good many more impudent fellows like you."

We continued our cruise, looking sharp out for the privateers, but without success; we then touched at Madeira for intelligence, and were informed that they had been seen more to the southward. The frigate's head was turned in that direction until we were abreast of the Canary Isles, and then we traversed east and west, north or south, just as the wind and weather or the captain's *like* thought proper We had now cruised seven weeks out of our time without success, and the captain promised five guineas to the man who should discover the objects of our search. Often did Tom and I climb to the mast-head and scan the horizon, and so did many others; but those who were stationed at the look-out were equally on the alert. The ship's company were now in a very fair state of discipline, owing to the incessant practice; and every evening the hands were turned up to skylark, that is, to play and amuse themselves. There was one amusement which was the occasion of a great deal of mirth, and it was a favourite one of the captain's, as it made the men smart. It is called, "Follow my leader." One of the men leads, and all who choose, follow him; sometimes forty or fifty will join. Whatever the leader does, the rest must do also; wherever he goes they must follow. Tom, who was always the foremost for fun, was one day the leader, and after having scampered up the rigging, laid out on the yards, climbed in by the lifts, crossed from mast to mast by the

311

stays, slid down by the backstays, blacked his face in the
funnel, in all which motions he was followed by about thirty
others, hallooing and laughing. While the officers and other
men were looking on and admiring their agility, a novel idea
came into Tom's head. It was then about seven o'clock in the
evening, the ship was lying becalmed. Tom again sprang up
the rigging, laid out to the main yard-arm, followed by me and
the rest, and as soon as he was at the boom iron, he sprang up,
holding by the lift, and crying out, " Follow my leader," leaped
from the yard-arm into the sea. I was second, and crying out,
" Follow my leader " to the rest, I followed him, and the others,
whether they could swim or not, did the same, it being a point
of honour not to refuse.

The captain was just coming up the ladder, when he saw, as
he imagined, a man tumble overboard, which was Tom in his
descent; but how much more was he astonished at seeing
twenty or thirty more tumbling off by twos or threes, until it
appeared that half the ship's company were overboard. He
thought that they were possessed with devils, like the herd of
swine in the Scriptures. Some of the men who could not swim,
but were too proud to refuse to follow, were nearly drowned.
As it was, the first lieutenant was obliged to lower the cutter to
pick them up, and they were all brought on board.

" Confound that fellow," said the captain to the first lieutenant; " he is always at the head of all mischief. Follow my
leader, indeed! Send Tom Beazeley here." We all thought
that Tom was about to catch it. " Hark ye, my lad," said the
captain, " a joke's a joke, but everybody can't swim as well as
you. I can't afford to lose any of my men by your pranks, so
don't try that again—I don't *like* it."

Every one thought that Tom got off very cheaply; but he
was a favourite with the captain, although that never appeared
but indirectly. " Beg pardon, sir," replied Tom, with great
apparent humility, " but they were all so dirty—they'd blacked
themselves at the funnel, and I thought a little washing would
not do them any harm."

" Be off, sir, and recollect what I have said," replied the
captain, turning away, and showing his white teeth.

I heard the first lieutenant say to the captain, " He's worth
any ten men in the ship, sir. He keeps them all alive and
merry, and sets such a good example."

312

CHAPTER XXXIX

" To be, or not to be," that is the question—Splinters on board
of a man-of-war, very different from splinters in the finger on
shore—Tom prevents this narrative from being wound up by
my going down—I receive a lawyer's letter, and instead of
being annoyed, am delighted with it.

IN the meantime Tom had gone up to the fore-royal yard, and
was looking round for the five guineas, and just as the conversation was going on, cried out, " Sail ho !"

" Strange sail reported."

" Where ? " cried the first lieutenant, going forward.

" Right under the sun."

" Mast-head there—do you make her out ? "

" Yes, sir ; I think she's a schooner ; but I can only see
down to her main-yard."

" That's one of them, depend upon it," said the captain.

" Up there, Mr. Wilson, and see what you make of her. Who
is the man who reported it ? "

" Tom Beazeley, sir."

" Confound the fellow, he makes all my ship's company jump
overboard, and now I must give him five guineas. What do
you make of her, Mr. Wilson ? "

" A low schooner, sir, very rakish indeed, black sides. I
cannot make out her ports ; but I should think she can show a
very pretty set of teeth. She is becalmed as well as we."

" Well then, we must whistle for a breeze. In the meantime, Mr. Knight, we will have the boats all ready."

If you whistle long enough the wind is certain to come. In
about an hour the breeze did come, and we took it down with
us ; but it was too dark to distinguish the schooner, which we
had lost sight of as soon as the sun had set. About midnight
the breeze failed us, and it was again calm. The captain and
most of the officers were up all night, and the watch were
employed preparing the boats for service. It was my morning
watch, and at break of day I saw the schooner from the fore-
sail-yard, about four miles to the NW. I ran down on deck,
and reported her.

" Very good, my lad. I have her, Mr. Knight," said the

captain, who had directed his glass to where I pointed; "and I will have her too, one way or the other. No signs of wind. Lower down the cutters. Get the yards and stays hooked all ready. We'll wait a little, and see a little more of her when it's broad daylight."

At broad daylight the schooner, with her appointments, was distinctly to be made out. She was pierced for sixteen guns, and was a formidable vessel to encounter with the boats. The calm still continuing, the launch, yawl, and pinnace were hoisted out, manned, and armed. The schooner got out her sweeps, and was evidently preparing for their reception. Still the captain appeared unwilling to risk the lives of his men in such a dangerous conflict, and there we all lay alongside, each man sitting in his place with his oar raised on end. Cat's-paws of wind, as they call them, flew across the water here and there, ruffling its smooth surface, portending that a breeze would soon spring up, and the hopes of this chance rendered the captain undecided. Thus did we remain alongside, for Tom and I were stationed in the first and second cutters, until twelve o'clock, when we were ordered out to take a hasty dinner, and the allowance of spirits was served out. At one it was still calm. Had we started when the boats were first hoisted out, the affair would have been long before decided. At last the captain, perceiving that the chance of a breeze was still smaller then than in the forenoon, ordered the boats to shove off. We were still about the same distance from the privateer, from three and a half to four miles. In less than half-an-hour we were within gunshot; the privateer swept her broadside to us, and commenced firing guns with single round shot, and with great precision. They ricochetted over the boats, and at every shot we made sure of our being struck. At this time a slight breeze swept along the water. It reached the schooner, filled her sails, and she increased her distance. Again it died away, and we neared her fast. She swept round again, and recommenced firing, and one of her shot passed through the second cutter, in which I was stationed, ripping open three of her planks, and wounding two men besides me. The boat, heavy with the gun, ammunition chests, &c., immediately filled and turned over with us, and it was with difficulty that we could escape from the weighty hamper that was poured out of her. One of the poor fellows, who had not been wounded, remained entangled under the boat, and never rose again. The remainder of the crew rose to the surface and clung to the side of the boat. The first cutter hauled to our assistance, for we had separated to render the shot less effectual; but it was three or four minutes before she was able to render us any assistance, during which time the other two wounded men, who had been apparently injured in the legs or body, exhausted with loss of blood, gradually unloosed their holds and disappeared under the calm blue water. I had received a splinter in my left arm, and held on longer than the others who had been maimed; but I could not hold on till the cutter came. I lost my recollection, and sank. Tom, who was in the bow of the cutter, perceiving me go down dived after me, brought me up again to the surface, and we were both hauled in. The other five men were also saved. As soon as we were picked up, the cutter followed the other boats, which continued to advance towards the privateer. I recovered my senses, and found that a piece of one of the thwarts of the boat, broken off by the shot, had been forced through the fleshy part of my arm below the elbow, where it still remained. It was a very dangerous as well as a painful wound. The officer of the boat, without asking me, laid hold of the splinter and tore it out; but the pain was so great, from its jagged form, and the effusion of blood so excessive after this operation, that I again fainted. Fortunately no artery was wounded, or I must have lost my arm. They bound it up, and laid me at the bottom of the boat. The firing from the schooner was now very warm; and we were within a quarter of a mile of her, when the breeze sprang up, and she increased her distance a mile. There was a prospect of wind from the appearance of the sky, although for a time it again died away. We were within less than half-a-mile of the privateer, when we perceived that the frigate was bringing up a smart breeze, and rapidly approached the scene of conflict.

The breeze swept along the water and caught the sails of the privateer, and she was again, in spite of all the exertions of our wearied men, out of gunshot; and the first lieutenant very properly decided upon making for the frigate, which was now within a mile of us. In less than ten minutes the boats were hoisted in, and the wind now rising fast, we were under all sail, going at the rate of seven miles an hour; the privateer having also gained the breeze, and gallantly holding her own,

I was taken down into the cockpit, the only wounded man brought on board. The surgeon examined my arm, and at first shook his head, and I expected immediate amputation; but on re-examination he gave his opinion that the limb might be saved. My wound was dressed, and I was put into my hammock, in a screened bulk under the half-deck, where the cooling breeze from the ports fanned my feverish cheeks. But I must return to the chase.

In less than an hour the wind had increased, so that we could with difficulty carry our royals; the privateer was holding her own about three miles right ahead, keeping our three masts in one. At sunset they were forced to take in the royals, and the sky gave every prospect of a rough gale. Still we carried on every stitch of canvas which the frigate could bear; keeping the chase in sight with our night-glasses, and watching all her motions.

The breeze increased; before morning there was a heavy sea, and the frigate could only carry top-gallant sails over double-reefed topsails. At daylight we had neared the schooner, by the sextants, about a quarter of a mile, and the captain and officers went down to take some repose and refreshment, not having quitted the deck for twenty-four hours. All that day did we chase the privateer, without gaining more than a mile upon her, and it now blew up a furious gale. The top-gallant sails had been before taken in, the topsails were close reefed, and we were running at the speed of nearly twelve miles an hour; still so well did the privateer sail, that she was barely within gunshot when the sun went down below the horizon, angry and fiery red. There was now great fear that she would escape, from the difficulty of keeping the glasses upon her during the night, in a heavy sea, and the expectation that she would furl all and allow us to pass her. It appeared, however, that this manœuvre did not enter into the head of the captain of the privateer; he stood on under a press of sail, which even in daytime would have been considered alarming; and at daylight, owing to the steerage during the night never being so correct as during the day, she had recovered her distance, and was about four miles from us. The gale, if anything, had increased, and Captain Maclean determined, notwithstanding, to shake a reef out of the topsails.

In the morning, as usual, Tom came to my cot, and asked

me how I was? I told him I was better and in less pain, and that the surgeon had promised to dress my wound after breakfast, for the bandages had not been removed since I had first come on board. "And the privateer, Tom, I hope we shall take her; it will be some comfort to me that she is captured."

"I think we shall, if the masts stand, Jacob; but we have an enormous press of sail, as you may guess by the way in which the frigate jumps; there is no standing on the fore-'castle, and there is a regular waterfall down in the waist from forward. We are nearing her now. It is beautiful to see how she behaves; when she heels over, we can perceive that all her men are lashed on deck, and she takes whole seas into her fore and aft mainsail, and pours them out again as she rises from the lurch. She deserves to escape, at all events."

She did not, however, obtain her deserts, for about twelve o'clock in the day we were within a mile of her. At two, the marines were firing small arms at her, for we would not yaw to fire at her a gun, although she was right under our bows. When within a cable's length we shortened sail, so as to keep at that distance astern, and the chase, after having lost several men by musketry, the captain of her waved his hat in token of surrender. We immediately shortened sail to keep the weather gage, pelting her until every sail was lowered down; we then rounded to, keeping her under our lee, and firing at every man who made his appearance on deck. Taking possession of her was a difficult task, a boat could hardly live in such a sea; and when the captain called aloud for volunteers, and I heard Tom's voice in the cutter as it was lowering down, my heart misgave me lest he should meet with some accident. At last I knew, from the conversation on deck, that the cutter had got safe on board, and my mind was relieved. The surgeon came up and dressed my arm, and I then received comparative bodily as well as mental relief.

It was not until the next day, when we lay to, with the schooner close to us, that the weather became sufficiently moderate to enable us to receive the prisoners and put our own men and officers on board. The prize proved to be an American-built schooner, fitted out as a French privateer. She was called the *Cerf Agile*, mounting fourteen guns, of nearly three hundred tons measurement, and with a crew of one hundred and seventy men, of which forty-eight were away in prizes. It was, perhaps, fortunate that the boats were not able to attack her, as they would have received a very warm reception. Thus did we succeed in capturing this mischievous vessel, after a chase of two hundred and seventy miles. As soon as all the arrangements were made, we shaped our course, with the privateer in company, for Halifax, where we arrived in about five weeks. My wound was now nearly healed; but my arm had wasted away, and I was unable to return to my duty. It was well known that I wrote a good hand, and I volunteered, as I could do nothing else, to assist the purser and the clerk with the ship's books, &c.

The admiral was at Bermuda, and the frigate which we were to relieve had, from the exigence of the service, been despatched down to the Honduras, and was not expected back for some months. We sailed from Halifax to Bermuda, and joined the admiral, and after three weeks we were ordered on a cruise. My arm was now perfectly recovered, but I had become so useful in the clerk's office that I was retained, much against my own wishes; but the captain *liked* it, as Tom said, and after that there was no more said about the matter.

America was not the seat of war at that period, and with the exception of chasing French runners there was nothing to be done on the North American station. I have, therefore, little to narrate during the remainder of the time that I was on board the frigate. Tom did his duty in the foretop, and never was in any disgrace; on the contrary, he was a great favourite both with officers and men, and took more liberties with the captain than any one else dared to have done; but Captain Maclean knew that Tom was one of his foremost and best men, always active, zealous, and indifferent as to danger, and Tom knew exactly how far he could venture to play with him. I remained in the clerk's office, and as it was soon discovered that I had received an excellent education, and always behaved myself respectfully to my superiors, I was kindly treated, and had no reason to complain of a man-of-war.

Such was the state of affairs, when the other frigate arrived from the Honduras, and we, who had been cruising for the last four months in Boston Bay, were ordered in by a cutter, to join the admiral at Halifax. We had now been nearly a year from England without receiving any letters. The reader may therefore judge of my impatience when, after

318

the anchor had been let go and the sails furled, the admiral's boat came on board with several bags of letters for the officers and ship's company. They were handed down into the gun-room, and I waited with impatience for the sorting and distribution.

"Faithful," said the purser, "here are two letters for you."

I thanked him, and hastened into the clerk's office that I might read them without interruption. The first was addressed in a formal hand quite unknown to me. I opened it with some degree of wonderment as to who could possibly write to so humble an individual. It was from a lawyer, and the contents were as follows :—

"Sir,—We hasten to advise you of the death of your good friend Mr. Alexander Turnbull. By his will, which has been opened and read, and of which you are the executor, he has made you his sole heir, bequeathing you, at the present, the sum of £30,000, with the remainder of his fortune at the demise of his wife. With the exception of £5000 left to Mrs. Turnbull for her own disposal, the legacies do not amount to more than £800. The jointure, arising from the interest of the money secured to Mrs. Turnbull during her life, is £1080 per annum, upon the 3 per cent. Consols, so that at her demise you will come into £36,000 Consols, which at 76, will be equal to £27,360 sterling. I beg to congratulate you upon your good fortune, and, with Mr. Drummond, have made application to the Admiralty for your discharge. This application, I am happy to say, has been immediately attended to, and by the same mail that conveys this letter is forwarded an order for your discharge and a passage home. Should you think proper to treat our firm as your legal advisers, we shall be most happy to enrol you among our clients.—I am, Sir, yours very respectfully,   John Fletcher."

I must leave the reader to judge of this unexpected and welcome communication. At first I was so stunned that I appeared as a statue with the letter in my hand, and in this condition I remained until roused by the first lieutenant, who had come to the office to desire me to pass the word for "letters for England," and to desire the sail-maker to make a bag.

"Faithful—why, what's the matter? Are you ill, or —— ?"

I could not reply, but I put the letter into his hand. He read the contents, expressing his astonishment by occasional exclamations. "I wish you joy, my lad, and may it be my turn next time. No wonder you looked like a stuck pig. Had I received such news, the captain might have hallooed till he was hoarse, and the ship might have tumbled overboard, before I should have roused myself. Well, I suppose we shall get no more work out of you——"

"The captain wants you, Mr. Knight," said one of the midshipmen, touching his hat.

Mr. Knight went into the cabin, and in a few minutes returned, holding the order for my discharge in his hand.

"It's all right, Faithful, here is your discharge, and an order for your passage home."

He laid it on the table and then went away, for a first lieutenant in harbour has no time to lose. The next person who came was Tom, holding in his hand a letter from Mary, with a postscript from his mother.

"Well, Jacob," said he, "I have news to tell you. Mary says that Mr. Turnbull is dead, and has left her father £200, and that she has been told that he has left you something handsome."

"He has, indeed, Tom," replied I; "read this letter."

While Tom was reading, I perceived the letter from Mr. Drummond, which I had forgotten. I opened it. It communicated the same intelligence as that of the lawyer, in fewer words; recommended my immediate return, and enclosed a bill upon his house for £100 to enable me to appear in a manner corresponding to my present condition.

"Well," said Tom, "this is indeed good news, Jacob. You are a gentleman at last, as you deserve to be. It has made me so happy; what do you mean to do?"

"I have my discharge here," replied I, "and am ordered a passage home."

"Better still. I am so happy, Jacob; so happy. But what *is* to become of me?" and Tom passed the back of his hand across his eyes to brush away a tear.

"You shall soon follow me, Tom, if I can manage it either by money or by influence."

"I will manage it if you don't, Jacob. I won't stay here without you, that I am determined."

"Do nothing rashly, Tom. I am sure I can buy your discharge, and on my arrival in England I will not think of anything else until it is done."

"You must be quick, then, Jacob, for I'm sure I can't stay here long."

"Trust to me, Tom; you'll still find me Jacob Faithful," said I, extending my hand. Tom squeezed it earnestly, and with moistened eyes turned away and walked forward.

The news had spread through the ship, and many of the officers as well as the men came to congratulate me. What would I have given to have been allowed only one half-hour to myself—one half-hour in which I might be permitted to compose my excited feelings—to have returned thanks for such unexpected happiness, and paid a tribute to the memory of so sincere a friend. But in a ship this is almost impossible, unless, as an officer, you can retreat to your own cabin; and those gushings from the heart, arising from grief or pleasure, the tears so sweet in solitude, must be prostituted before the crowd, or altogether repressed. At last the wished-for opportunity did come. Mr. Wilson, who had been away on service, came to congratulate me as soon as he heard the news, and with an instinctive perception of what might be my feelings, asked me whether I would not like to write my letters in his cabin, which, for a few hours, was at my service. I thankfully accepted the offer, and when summoned by the captain had relieved my overcharged heart, and had composed my excited feelings.

"Jacob Faithful, you are aware there is an order for your discharge," said he kindly. "You will be discharged this afternoon into the *Astrea;* she is ordered home, and will sail with despatches in a few days. You have conducted yourself well since you have been under my command; and although you are now in a situation not to require a good certificate, still you will have the satisfaction of feeling that you have done your duty in the station of life to which you have, for a certain portion of it, been called—I wish you well."

Although Captain Maclean, in what he said, never lost sight of the relative situations in which we had been placed, there was a kindness of manner, especially in the last words, "I wish you well," which went to my heart. I replied that I had been very happy during the time I had been under his command,

and thanked him for his good wishes. I then bowed and left the cabin. But the captain did not send me on board the *Astrea*, although I was discharged into her. He told the first lieutenant that I had better go on shore and equip myself in a proper manner, and, as I afterwards found out, spoke of me in very favourable terms to the captain of the *Astrea*, acknowledging that I had received the education of a gentleman, and had been illegally impressed; so that when I made my appearance on board the *Astrea*, the officers of the gunroom requested that I would mess with them during the passage home.

I went on shore, obtained the money for my bill, hastened to a tailor, and with his exertions, and other fitting-out people, procured all that was requisite for the outward appearance of a gentleman. I then returned to the *Immortalité*, and bade farewell to the officers and seamen with whom I had been most intimate. My parting with Tom was painful. Even the few days which I had been away, I perceived, had made an alteration in his appearance.

"Jacob," said he, "don't think I envy you; on the contrary, I am as grateful, even more grateful than if such good fortune had fallen to my own lot; but I cannot help fretting at the thought of being left here without you, and I shall fret until I am with you again."

I renewed my promises to procure his discharge, and forcing upon him all the money I thought that I could spare, I went over the side as much affected as poor Tom. Our passage home was rapid. We had a continuance of NW. winds, and we flew before them, and in less than three weeks we dropped our anchor at Spithead. Happy in the change of my situation, and happier still in anticipation, I shall only say that I never was in better spirits, or in company with more agreeable young men than were the officers of the *Astrea*; and although we were so short a time together, we separated with mutual regret.

CHAPTER XL

*I interrupt a matrimonial duet and capsize the boat—Being on
dry land, no one is drowned—Tom leaves a man-of-war
because he don't like it—I find the profession of a gentleman
preferable to that of a waterman.*

MY first object on my return was to call upon old Tom,
and assure him of his son's welfare. My wishes certainly
would have led me to Mr. Drummond's, but I felt that
my duty required that I should delay that pleasure. I
arrived at the hotel late in the evening, and early next
morning I went down to the steps at Westminster Bridge,
and was saluted with the usual cry of " Boat, sir ? " A
crowd of recollections poured into my mind at the well-
known sound ; my life appeared to have passed in review
in a few seconds, as I took my seat in the stern of a wherry,
and directed the waterman to pull up the river. It was
a beautiful morning, and even at that early hour almost too
warm—the sun was so powerful. I watched every object
that we passed with an interest I cannot describe ; every tree,
every building, every point of land—they were all old friends,
who appeared, as the sun shone brightly on them, to rejoice in
my good fortune. I remained in a reverie too delightful to be
wished to be disturbed from it, although occasionally there
were reminiscences which were painful ; but they were but as
light clouds, obscuring for a moment, as they flew past, the
glorious sun of my happiness. At last the well-known tenement
of old Tom, his large board with " Boats built to order," and
the half of the boat stuck up on end, caught my sight, and I
remembered the object of my embarkation. I directed the
waterman to pull to the *hard,* and, paying him well, dismissed
him ; for I had perceived that old Tom was at work, stumping
round a wherry, bottom up, and his wife was sitting on a bench
in the boat-arbour, basking in the warm sun, and working away
at her nets. I had landed so quietly, and they both were so
occupied with their respective employments, that they had not
perceived me, and I crept round by the house to surprise them.
I had gained a station behind the old boat, where I overheard
the conversation.

" It's my opinion," said old Tom, who left off hammering for a time, "that all the nails in Birmingham won't make this boat water-tight. The timbers are as rotten as a pear, and the nails fall through them. I have put in one piece more than agreed for, and if I don't put in another here she'll never swim."

"Well, then, put another piece in," replied Mrs. Beazeley.

"Yes, so I will; but I've a notion I shall be out of pocket by this job. Seven-and-sixpence won't pay for labour and all. However, never mind," and Tom carolled forth—

> " Is not the sea
> Made for the free—
> Land for courts and chains alone ?
> There we are slaves,
> But on the waves
> Love and liberty's all our own."

"Now, if you do sing, sing truth, Beazeley," said tne old woman. "An't our boy pressed into the service ? And how can you talk of liberty ?"

Old Tom answered by continuing his song—

> " No eye to watch, and no tongue to wound us ;
> All earth forgot, and all heaven around us."

"Yes, yes," replied the old woman; "no eye to watch, indeed. He may be in sickness, and in sorrow; he may be wounded, or dying of a fever; and there's no mother's eye to watch over him. As to all on earth being forgot, I won't believe that Tom has forgotten his mother."

Old Tom replied—

> " Seasons may roll,
> But the true soul
> Burns the same wherever it goes."

"So it does, Tom—so it does; and he's thinking this moment of his father and mother, I do verily believe, and he loves us more than ever."

"So I believe," replied old Tom; "that is, if he hasn't anything better to do. But there's a time for all things, and when a man is doing his duty as a seaman, he mustn't let his thoughts wander. Never fear, old woman, he'll be back again.

> ' There's a sweet little cherub that sits up aloft,
> To take care of the life of poor Jack.' "

"God grant it! God grant it!" replied the old woman, wiping her eyes with her apron, and then resuming her netting.

"He seems," continued she, "by his letters to be over fond of that girl Mary Stapleton, and I sometimes think that she cares not a little for him; but she's never of one mind long. I didn't like to see her flaunting and flirting so with the soldiers, and at the same time Tom says that she writes that she cares for nobody but him."

"Women are—women! that's sartain," replied old Tom, musing for a time, and then showing that his thoughts were running on his son by bursting out—

> "Mary, when yonder boundless sea
> Shall part us, and perchance for ever,
> Think not my heart can stray from thee,
> Or cease to mourn thine absence—never!
> And when in distant climes I roam,
> Forlorn, unfriended, broken-hearted——"

"Don't say so, Tom—don't say so," interrupted the old woman.

Tom continued—

> "Oft shall I sigh for thee and home,
> And all those joys for which I parted."

"Ay, so he does, poor fellow, I'll be bound to say. What would I give to see his dear smiling face!" said Mrs. Beazeley.

"And I'd give no little, missus, myself. But still it's the duty for every man to serve his country; and so ought Tom, as his father did before him. I shall be glad to see him back, but I'm not sorry that he's gone. Our ships must be manned, old woman; and if they take men by force it's only because they won't volunteer—that's all. When they're once on board they don't mind it. You women require pressing just as much as the men, and it's all much of a muchness."

"How's that, Tom?"

"Why, when we make love and ask you to marry, don't you always pout, and say, 'No'? You like being kissed, but we must take it by force. So it is with manning a ship. The men all say, 'No;' but when they are once there, they like the service very much—only, you see, like you, they want pressing. Don't Tom write and say that he's quite happy, and don't care where he is so long as he's with Jacob?"

"Yes, that's true; but they say Jacob is to be discharged and come home, now that he's come to a fortune, and what will Tom say then?"

"Why, that *is* the worst of it. I believe that Jacob's heart is in the right place; but still, riches spoil a man. But we shall see. If Jacob don't prove 'true blue,' I'll never put faith in man again. But there be changes in this world, that's sartain.

'We all have our taste of the ups and the downs,
    As Fortune dispenses her smiles and her frowns;
    But may we not hope, if she's frowning to-day,
    That to-morrow she'll lend us the light of her ray?'

I only wish Jacob was here—that's all."

"Then you have your wish, my good old friend," cried I, running up to Tom and seizing his hand. But old Tom was so taken by surprise that he started back and lost his equilibrium, dragging me after him, and we rolled on the turf together. Nor was this the only accident, for old Mrs. Beazeley was so alarmed that she also sprang from the bench fixed in the half of the old boat stuck on end, and threw herself back against it. The boat, rotten when first put up, and with the disadvantage of exposure to the elements for many years, could no longer stand such pressure. It gave way to the sudden force applied by the old woman, and she and the boat went down together, she. screaming and scuffling among the rotten planks, which now, after so many years' close intimacy, were induced to part company. I was first on my legs, and ran to the assistance of Mrs. Beazeley, who was half smothered with dust and flakes of dry pitch; and old Tom coming to my assistance, we put the old woman on her legs again.

"O deary me!" cried the old woman; "O deary me! I do believe my hip is out! Lord, Mr. Jacob, how you frightened me!"

"Yes," said old Tom, shaking me warmly by the hand, "we were all taken aback, old boat and all. What a shindy you have made, bowling us all down like ninepins! Well, my boy, I'm glad to see you, and notwithstanding your gear, you're Jacob Faithful still."

"I hope so," replied I; and we then adjourned to the house, where I made them acquainted with all that had passed, and what I intended to do relative to obtaining Tom's discharge. I then left them, promising to return soon, and, hailing a wherry going up the river, proceeded to my old friend the Domine, of whose welfare, as well as Stapleton's and Mary's, I had been already assured.

But as I passed through Putney Bridge, I thought I might as well call first upon old Stapleton; and I desired the waterman to pull in. I hastened to Stapleton's lodgings, and went upstairs, where I found Mary in earnest conversation with a very good-looking young man, in a sergeant's uniform of the 93rd Regiment. Mary, who was even handsomer than when I had left her, starting up, at first did not appear to recognise me, then coloured up to the forehead, as she welcomed me with a constraint I had never witnessed before. The sergeant appeared inclined to keep his ground, but on my taking her hand, and telling her that I brought a message from a person whom I trusted she had not forgotten, he gave her a nod and walked downstairs. Perhaps there was a severity in my countenance as I said, "Mary, I do not know whether, after what I have seen, I ought to give the message; and the pleasure I anticipated in meeting you again is destroyed by what I have now witnessed. How disgraceful is it thus to play with a man's feelings—to write to him, assuring him of your regard and constancy, and at the same time encouraging another."

Mary hung down her head. "If I have done wrong, Mr. Faithful," said she after a pause, "I have not wronged Tom; what I have written I felt."

"If that is the case why do you wrong another person? why encourage another young man only to make him unhappy?"

"I have promised him nothing; but why does not Tom come back and look after me? I can't mope here by myself. I have no one to keep company with; my father is always away at the alehouse, and I must have somebody to talk to. Besides, Tom is away, and may be away a long while, and absence cures love in men, although it does not in women."

"It appears then, Mary, that you wish to have two strings to your bow in case of accident."

"Should the first string break a second would be very acceptable," replied Mary. "But it is always this way," continued she, with increasing warmth, "I never can be in a situation which is not right—whenever I do anything which may appear improper, so certain do *you* make your appearance when least

expected and least wished for—as if you were born to be my
constant accuser."

"Does not your own conscience accuse you, Mary?"

"Mr. Faithful," repeated she, very warmly, "you are not my
father confessor; but do as you please—write to Tom if you
please, and tell him all you have seen, and anything you may
think—make him and make me miserable and unhappy—do it,
I pray. It will be a friendly act; and as you are now a great
man, you may persuade Tom that I am a jilt and a good-for-
nothing."

Here Mary laid her hands on the table, and buried her face
in them.

"I did not come here to be your censor, Mary, you are certainly at liberty to act as you please, without my having any
right to interfere; but as Tom is my earliest and best friend, so
far as his interests and happiness are concerned, I shall carefully watch over them. We have been so long together, and I
am so well acquainted with all his feelings, that I really believe
that if ever there was a young man sincerely and devotedly
attached to a woman, he is so to you; and I will add, that if
ever there was a young man who deserved love in return, it is
Tom. When I left, not a month back, he desired me to call
upon you as soon as I could, and assure you of his unalterable
attachment; and I am now about to procure his discharge, that
he may be able to return. All his thoughts are upon this point,
and he is now waiting with the utmost impatience the arrival of
it, that he may again be in your company; you can best judge
whether his return will or will not be a source of happiness."

Mary raised her head—her face was wet with her tears.

"Then he will soon be back again, and I shall see him.
Indeed, his return shall be no source of unhappiness, if I can
make him happy—indeed, it shall not, Mr. Faithful; but pray
don't tell him of my foolish conduct, pray don't—why make
him unhappy?—I entreat you not to do it. I will not do so
again. Promise me, Jacob, will you?" continued Mary, taking
me by the arm, and looking beseechingly in my face.

"Mary, I never will be a mischief-maker; but recollect, I
exact the performance of your promise."

"Oh, and I will keep it, now that I know he will soon be
home. I can, I think I can—I'm sure I can wait a month or
two without flirting. But I do wish that I was not left so

much alone. I wish Tom was at home to take care of me, for there is no one else. I can't take care of myself."

I saw by Mary's countenance that she was in earnest, and I therefore made friends with her, and we conversed for two hours, chiefly about Tom. When I left her, she had recovered her usual spirits, and said at parting, looking archly at me, "Now you will see how wise and how prudent I shall be."

I shook my head, and left her that I might find out old friend Stapleton, who, as usual, was at the door of the public-house smoking his pipe. At first he did not recognise me, for when I accosted him, he put his open hand to his ear as usual, and desired me to speak a little louder, but I answered, " Nonsense, Stapleton, that won't do with me." He then took his pipe out of his mouth, and looked me full in the face.

"Jacob, as I'm alive ! Didn't know you in your long togs— thought you was a gentleman wanting a boat. Well, I hardly need say how glad I am to see you after so long; that's no more than human natur. And how's Tom ? Have you seen Mary?"

These two questions enabled me to introduce the subject that I wished. I told him of the attachment and troth pledged between the two, and how wrong it was for him to leave her so much alone. The old man agreed with me and said, that as to talking to the men, that was on Mary's part nothing but "human natur," and that as for Tom wishing to be at home and seeing her again, that also was nothing but " human natur ; " but that he would smoke his pipe at home in future, and keep the soldiers out of the house. Satisfied with this assurance I left him, and taking another wherry, went up to Brentford to see the Domine.

CHAPTER XLI

All the little boys are let loose, and the Domine is caught— Anxious to supply my teeth, he falls in with other teeth, and Mrs. Bately also shows her teeth—Gin outside, gin in, and gin out again, and old woman out also—Domine in for it again —More like a Whig Ministry than a novel.

I FOUND the worthy old Domine in the schoolroom, seated at his elevated desk, the usher not present, and the boys making a din enough to have awaked a person from a trance, That he was in one of his deep reveries, and that the boys had taken advantage of it, was evident. "Mr. Dobbs," said I, walking close up to the desk, but the Domine answered not. I repeated his name in a louder voice.

"Cosine of $x + a\ b - z - \frac{1}{2}$; such must be the result," said the Domine, talking to himself. "Yet it doth not prove correct. I may be in error. Let me revise my work," and the Domine lifted up his desk to take out another piece of paper. When the desk lid was raised, I removed his work and held it behind me.

"But how is this?" exclaimed the Domine, and he looked everywhere for his previous calculations. "Nay," continued he, "it must have been the wind;" and then he cast his eyes about until they fixed upon me laughing at him. "Eheu! what do my eyes perceive? It is—yet it is not—yes, most truly it is, my son Jacob. Welcome, most welcome," cried the old man, descending from his desk and clasping me in his arms. "Long is it since I have seen thee, my son, *Interea magnum sol circumvolvitur annum.* Long, yes long, have I yearned for thy return, fearful lest, *nudus in ignota arena,* thou mightest, like another Palinurus, have been cast away. Thou art returned, and all is well; as the father said in the Scripture, I have found my son which I had lost, but no prodigal thou, though I use the quotation as apt. Now all is well; thou hast escaped the danger of the battle, the fire and the wreck, and now thou mayest hang up thy wet garment as a votive offering; as Horace hath it, *Uvida suspendisse potenti vestimenta maris Deo.*"

During the apostrophe of the Domine, the boys perceiving that he was no longer wrapped up in his algebra, had partly settled to their desks, and in their apparent attention to their lessons, reminded me of the humming of bees before a hive on a summer's day.

"Boys," cried the Domine, "*nunc est ludendum;* verily ye shall have a holiday; put up your books, and depart in peace."

The books were hastily put up, in obedience to the command; the depart in peace was not so rigidly adhered to—they gave a loud shout, and in a few seconds the Domine and I stood alone in the schoolroom.

"Come, Jacob, let us adjourn to my sanctum; there may we commune without interruption. Thou shalt tell me thine adventures, and I will communicate to thee what hath been made known to me relative to those with whom thou wert acquainted."

"First let me beg you to give me something to eat, for I am not a little hungry," interrupted I, as we gained the kitchen.

"Verily shalt thou have all that we possess, Jacob; yet now, I think, that will not be much, seeing that I and our worthy matron did pick the bones of a shoulder of mutton, this having been our fourth day of repast upon it. She is out, yet I will venture to intrude into the privacy of her cupboard for thy sake. Peradventure, she may be wroth, yet will I risk her displeasure." So saying, the old Domine opened the cupboard, and, one by one, handed to me the dishes with their contents. "Here, Jacob, are two hard dumplings from yesterday. Canst thou relish cold, hard dumplings?—but stop, here is something more savoury—half of a cold cabbage, which was left this day. We will look again. Here is meat—yes, it is meat; but now do I perceive it is a piece of lights reserved for the dinner of the cat to-morrow. I am fearful that we must not venture upon that, for the dame will be wroth."

"Pray, put it back, sir; I would not interfere with puss on any account."

"Nay, then, Jacob, I see naught else, unless there may be viands on the upper shelf. Sir, here is bread, the staff of life, and also a fragment of cheese; and now methinks I discern something dark at the back of the shelf." The Domine extended his hand, and immediately withdrew it, jumping from his chair with a loud cry. He had put his fingers into a rat gin, set by the old woman for those intruders, and he held up his arm and stamped as he shouted out with the pain. I hastened to him, and pressing down the spring released his fingers from the teeth, which, however, had drawn blood as well as bruised him; fortunately, like most of the articles of their ménage, the trap was a very old one, and he was not much hurt. The Domine thrust his fingers into his capacious mouth, and held them there some time without speaking. He began to feel a little ease, when in came the matron.

"Why, what's all this?" said she, in a querulous tone. "Jacob here, and all my cupboard on the table. Jacob, how dare you go to my cupboard?"

"It was the Domine, Mrs. Bately, who looked there for something for me to eat, and he has been caught in a rat-trap."

"Serve him right; I have forbade him that cupboard. Have I not, Mr. Dobbs?"

"Yea, and verily," quoth the Domine, "and I do repent me that I took not thine advice, for look at my fingers;" and the Domine extended his lacerated digits.

"Dear me! well, I'd no idea that a rat-trap pinched so hard," replied the old woman, whose wrath was appeased. "How it must hurt the poor things. I won't set it again, but leave them all to the cat; he'll kill them, if he only can get at them." The old lady went to a drawer, unlocked it, brought out some fragments of rags, and a bottle of friar's balsam, which she applied to the Domine's hand, and then bound it up, scolding him the whole time. "How stupid of you, Mr. Dobbs; you know that I was only out for a few minutes. Why didn't you wait—and why did you go to the cupboard? Haven't I always told you not to look into it? and now you see the consequences."

"Verily my hand burneth," replied the Domine.

"I will go for cold water, and it will ease you. What a deal of trouble you do give, Mr. Dobbs; you're worse than a charity boy;" and the old lady departed to the pump.

"Vinegar is a better thing, sir," said I, "and there is a bottle in the cupboard, which I dare say is vinegar." I went to the cupboard, and brought out the bottle, took out the cork and smelt it. "This is not vinegar, sir, it is Hollands or gin."

"Then would I like a glass, Jacob, for I feel a sickening faintness upon me; yet be quick, peradventure the old woman may return."

"Drink out of the bottle, sir," said I, perceiving that the Domine looked very pale, "and I will give you notice of her approach." The Domine put the bottle to his mouth, and was taking a sufficient draught, when the old woman returned by another door which was behind us; she had gone that way for a wash-basin. Before we could perceive her, she came behind the Domine, snatched the bottle from his mouth with a jerk that threw a portion of the spirits in his eyes and blinded him.

"That's why you went to my cupboard, is it, Mr. Dobbs?" cried she, in a passion. "That's it, is it? I thought my bottle went very fast; seeing that I don't take more than a teaspoonful every night, for the wind which vexes me so much. I'll set the rat-trap again, you may depend upon it; and now you may get somebody else to bind your fingers."

"It was I who took it out, Mrs. Bately; the Domine would have fainted with pain. It was very lucky that he has a housekeeper who is careful to have something of the kind in the house, or he might have been dead. You surely don't begrudge a little of your medicine to recover Mr. Dobbs?"

"Peace, woman, peace," said the Domine, who had gained courage by his potation. "Peace, I say. I knew not that thou hadst in thy cupboard either a gin for my hand, or gin for thy mouth; since I have been taken in the one, it is but fair that I should take in the other. In future both thy gins will not be interfered with by me. Bring me the basin that I may appease my angry wounds, and then hasten to procure some viands to appease the hunger of my son Jacob; lastly, appease thine own wrath. *Pax.* Peace, I say;" and the old woman, who perceived that the Domine had asserted his right of dominion, went to obey his orders, grumbling till she was out of hearing. The application of the cold pump-water soon relieved the pain of the good old Domine, and, with his hand remaining in the basin, we commenced a long conversation.

At first I narrated to him the events which had occurred during my service on board of the frigate. When I told him of my parting with Tom, he observed, "Verily do I remember that young Tom, a jocund, pleasant, yet intrusive lad. Yet do I wish him well, and am grieved that he should be so taken by that maiden Mary. Well may we say of her, as Horace hath of Pyrrha—'*Quis multâ gracilis te puer in rosâ, perfusis liquidis urgit odoribus, grate, Pyrrha, sub antro. Cui flavam religas comam, simplex munditiis.*' I grieve at it, yea, grieve much. *Heu, quoties fidem mutatosque Deos flebit!* Verily, Jacob, I do prophesy that she will lead him into error, yea, perhaps into perdition."

"I trust not, sir," replied I; but the Domine made no answer. For half-an-hour he was in deep and serious thought, during which Mrs. Bately entered, and spreading a cloth, brought in from the other room some rashers of bacon and eggs, upon which I made a hasty and hearty meal. The old matron's temper was now smoothed, and she welcomed me kindly, and shortly after went out for a fresh basin of cold water for the Domine to bathe his hand. This roused him, and he recommenced the conversation.

"Jacob, I have not yet congratulated thee upon thy accession to wealth; not that I do not sincerely rejoice in it, but because the pleasure of thy presence has made me unmindful of it. Still, was it fortunate for thee that thou hadst raised up such a friend as Mr. Turnbull; otherwise what would have been the result of thy boasted independence? Thou wouldst probably have remained many years on board of a man-of-war, and have been killed, or have returned mutilated, to die unknown."

"You were right, sir," replied I; "my independence was nothing but pride; and I did bitterly repent, as you said I should do, even before I was pressed into the king's service—but Mr. Drummond never repeated his offers."

"He never did, Jacob; but as I have since been informed by him, although he was taken by surprise at thy being forced away to serve thy country, still he was not sure that you would accept them; and he, moreover, wished you fully to feel thine own folly. Long before you had made friends with him, he had attested the will of Mr. Turnbull, and was acquainted with the contents. Yet did he watch over thee, and had he thought that thy way of life had led thee into that which was wrong, he would have interfered to save thee; but he considered with Shakspeare, that 'sweet were the uses of adversity,' and that thou wouldst be more schooled by remaining some time under her unprepossessing frowns. He hath ever been thy friend."

"I can believe it. I trust he is well, and his family."

"They were well and prosperous but a little while ago, Jacob; yet I have seen but little of them since the death of Mr. Turnbull. It will pain thee to hear that affliction at thy absence hastened his dissolution. I was at his death-bed, Jacob, and I verily believe he was a good man, and will meet the reward of one; yet did he talk most strangely, and reminded me of that remnant of a man you call old Tom. 'It's no use, old gentleman,' said he, as he lay in his bed supported by pillows, for he had wasted away till he was but a skeleton, having broken a blood-vessel with his violent coughing, 'It's no use pouring that doctor's stuff down my throat; my anchor's short stay a-peak, and in a few minutes I shall trip it, I trust for heaven, where I hope there are moorings laid down for me.' 'I would fain comprehend thee,' replied I, 'but thou speakest in parables.' 'I mean to say that Death has driven his harpoon in up to the shank, and that I struggle in vain. I have run out all my line. I shall turn up in a few minutes—so give my love and blessing to Jacob—he saved my life once—but now I'm gone.' With these last words his spirit took its flight; and thus, Jacob, did your benefactor breathe his last, invoking a blessing on your head."

I remained silent for a few minutes, for I was much affected by the Domine's description; he at length resumed the conversation.

"Thou hast not yet seen the Drummonds, Jacob?"

"I have not," I replied, "but I will call upon them to-morrow; but it is time that I should go, for I have to return to London."

"Thou needest not, Jacob. Thine own house is at hand."

"My own house!"

"Yes; by the will of Mr. Turnbull, his wife has been left a handsome jointure, but, for reasons which he did not explain, the house and furniture are not left to her, but, as residuary legatee, belong to thee."

"Indeed!—then where is Mrs. Turnbull?"

"At Bath, where she hath taken up her residence. Mr. Drummond, who hath acted in thy behalf, permitted her to take away such articles as she might wish, but they were but few, chiefly those little objects which filled up rather than adorned the drawing-room. The house is all ready for thy reception, and thou mayest take possession this evening."

"But why did not Mr. Turnbull leave it to his widow?"

"I cannot exactly say, but I think he did not wish her to remain in this place. He therefore left her £5000 at her own disposal, to enable her to purchase and furnish another."

I then took my leave of the Domine, and it being rather late, I resolved to walk to the house and sleep there.

CHAPTER XLII

In which I take possession of my own house, and think that it looks very ill-furnished without a wife—Tom's discharge is sent out, but by accident it never reaches him—I take my new station in society.

ON my arrival the front gates were opened by the gardener's wife, who made me a profound courtesy. The gardener soon afterwards made his appearance, hat in hand. Everything was neat, and in good order. I entered the house, and as soon as possible rid myself of their obsequious attentions. I wished to be alone. Powerful feelings crowded on my mind. I hastened to Mr. Turnbull's study, and sat down in the chair so lately occupied by him. The proud feeling of possession, softened into gratitude to Heaven, and sorrow at his death, came over me, and I remained for a long while in a deep reverie. "And all this, and more, much more, are mine," I mentally exclaimed; "the sailor before the mast, the waterman on the river, the charity-boy, the orphan sits down in quiet possession of luxury and wealth. What have I done to deserve all this?" My heart told me nothing, or if anything, it was almost valueless, and I poured forth my soul in thanks to Heaven. I felt more composed after I had performed this duty, and my thoughts then dwelt upon my benefactor. I surveyed the room—the drawings, the furs and skins, the harpoons and other instruments, all remaining in their respective places, as when I last had an interview with Mr. Turnbull. I remembered his kindness, his singleness of heart, his honesty, his good sense, and his real worth; and I shed many tears for his loss. My thoughts then passed to Sarah Drummond, and I felt much uneasiness on that score. Would she receive me, or would she still remember what I had been? I recollected her kindness and goodwill towards me. I weighed these, and my present condition, against my origin and my former occupation; and could not ascertain how the scale might turn. I shall soon see, thought I. To-morrow, even, may decide the question. The gardener's wife knocked at the door, and announced that my bed was prepared. I went to sleep, dreaming of Sarah, young Tom, the Domine, and Mary Stapleton,

336

I was up early the next morning, and hastened to the hotel; when having arranged my person to the best of my power (but at the same time never so little to my satisfaction), I proceeded to the house of Mr. Drummond. I knocked; and this time I was not desired to wait in the hall, but was immediately ushered up into the drawing-room. Sarah Drummond was sitting alone at her drawing. My name was announced as I entered. She started from her chair, and blushed deeply as she moved towards me. We joined hands in silence. I was breathless with emotion. Never had she appeared so beautiful. Neither party appeared willing to break silence. At last I faltered out, " Miss Drummond," and then I stopped.

" Mr. Faithful," replied she; and then, after a break, " How very silly this is; I ought to have congratulated you upon your safe return, and upon your good fortune, and indeed, *Mr.* Faithful, no one can do so more sincerely."

" Miss Drummond," replied I, confused, " when I was an orphan, a charity-boy, and a waterman you called me Jacob; if the alteration in my prospects induces you to address me in so formal a manner—if we are in future to be on such different terms—I can only say, that I wish that I were again—Jacob Faithful, the waterman."

" Nay," replied she, " recollect that it was your own choice to be a waterman. You might have been different—very different. You might at this time have been partner with my father, for he said so but last night, when we were talking about you. But you refused all; you threw away your education, your talents, your good qualities, from a foolish pride which you considered independence. My father almost humbled himself to you—not that it is ever humiliating to acknowledge and attempt to repair a fault, but still he did more than could be expected from most people. Your friends persuaded you, but you rejected their advice; and what was still more unpardonable, even I had no influence over you. As long as you punished yourself I did not upbraid you, but now that you have been so fortunate, I tell you plainly——"

" What ? "

" That it is more than you deserve, that's all."

" You have said but the truth, Miss Drummond. I was very proud and very foolish, but I had repented of my folly long before I was pressed; and I candidly acknowledge that I do not merit the good fortune I have met with. Can I say more ? "

" No; I am satisfied with your repentance and acknowledgment. So now you may sit down and make yourself agreeable."

" Before I do that, allow me to ask, as you address me as Mr. Faithful, how am I to address you ? I should not wish to be considered impertinent ? "

" My name is Miss Drummond, but those who feel intimate with me call me Sarah."

" I may reply that my name is Faithful, but those who feel intimate with me call me Jacob."

" Very true; but allow me to observe that you show very little tact. You should never force a lady into a corner. If I appear affronted when you call me Sarah, then you will do wise to fall back upon Miss Drummond. But why do you fix your eyes upon me so earnestly ? "

" I cannot help it, and must beg your pardon; but you are so improved in appearance since I last saw you. I thought no one could be more perfect, but——"

" Well, that's not a bad beginning, Jacob. I like to hear of my perfections. Now follow up your *but.*"

" I hardly know what I was going to say, but I think it was, that I do not feel as if I ought or can address you otherwise than as Miss Drummond."

" Oh ! you've thought better of it, have you ? Well, I begin to think myself that you look so well in your present dress, and have become so very different a person, that I ought not to address you by any other name than Mr. Faithful. So now we are agreed."

" That's not what I meant to say."

" Well, then, let me know what you did mean to say."

This puzzling question fortunately did not require an answer, for Mr. Drummond came into the room and extended his hand.

" My dear Jacob," said he, in the most friendly manner, " I'm delighted to see you back again, and to have the pleasure of congratulating you on your good fortune. But you have business to transact which will not admit of any delay. You must prove the will, and arrange with the lawyers as soon as possible. Will you come now ? All the papers are below, and I have the whole morning to spare. We will be back to dinner, Sarah, if Jacob has no other engagement."

"I have none," replied I; "and shall be most happy to avail myself of your kindness. Miss Drummond, I wish you a good morning."

"*Au revoir,* Mr. Faithful," replied Sarah, courtesying formally, with a mocking smile.

The behaviour of Mr. Drummond towards me was most kind and parental, and my eyes were often suffused with tears during the occupation of the morning. The most urgent business was got through, and an interview with Mr. Turnbull's solicitor put the remainder in progress; still it was so late when we had accomplished it, that I had no time to dress. On my return, Mrs. Drummond received me with her usual kindness. I narrated during the evening my adventures since we parted, and took that opportunity to acknowledge to Mr. Drummond how bitterly I had repented my folly, and I may add ingratitude, towards him.

"Jacob," said he, as we were sitting at the tea-table with Mrs. Drummond and Sarah, "I knew at the time that you were toiling on the river for shillings that you were the inheritor of thousands, for I not only witnessed but read the will of Mr. Turnbull; but I thought it best that you should have a lesson which you would never forget in after life. There is no such thing in this world as independence, unless in a savage state. In society we are all mutually dependent upon each other. Independence of mind we may have, but no more. As a waterman you were dependent upon your customers, as every poor man must be upon those who have more means; and in refusing my offers, you were obliged to apply for employment to others. The rich are as entirely dependent upon others as the poor; they depend upon them for their food, their clothes, their necessities, and their luxuries. Such ever will be the case in society, and the more refined the society may be—the more civilised its parts—the greater is the mutual dependence. Still it is an error originating in itself from high feelings, and therefore must be considered as an error on the right side; but recollect how much you might have thrown away, had not you, in the first place, secured such a friend as Mr. Turnbull, and secondly, if the death of that friend had not so soon put you in possession."

I was but too ready to acknowledge the truth of these remarks. The evening passed away so rapidly that it was midnight before I rose to take my leave, and I returned to the hotel as happy in my mind, and as grateful as ever any mortal could possibly be. The next day I removed to the house left me by Mr. Turnbull, and the first order I gave was for a wherry. Such was the force of habit, I could not do without one; and half my time was spent upon the river, pulling every day down to Mr. Drummond's, and returning in the evening, or late at night. Thus passed away two months, during which I occasionally saw the Domine, the Stapletons, and old Tom Beazeley. I had exerted myself to procure Tom's discharge, and at last had the pleasure of telling the old people that it was to go out by the next packet. By the Drummonds I was received as a member of the family —there was no hindrance to my being alone with Sarah for hours; and although I had not ventured to declare my sentiments, they appeared to be well understood, as well by the parents as by Sarah herself.

Two days after I had communicated this welcome intelligence to the old couple, as I was sitting at breakfast, attended by the gardener and his wife (for I had made no addition to my establishment), what was my surprise at the appearance of young Tom, who entered the room as usual, laughing as he held out his hand.

"Tom!" exclaimed I, "why, how did you come here?"

"By water, Jacob, as you may suppose."

"But how have you received your discharge? Is the ship come home?"

"I hope not; the fact is, I discharged myself, Jacob."

"What! did you desert?"

"Even so. I had three reasons for so doing. In the first place, I could not remain without you; in the second, my mother wrote to say Mary was taking up with a sodger; and the third was, I was put into the report for punishment, and should have been flogged, as sure as the captain had a pair of epaulettes."

"Well, but sit down and tell me all about it. You know your discharge is obtained."

"Yes, thanks to you, Jacob; all the better, for now they won't look after me. All's well that ends well. After you went away, I presume I was not in the very best of humours; and that rascal of a master's mate who had us pressed, thought proper to bully me beyond all bearing. One day he called me a lying scoundrel; upon which I forgot that I was on board of a man-of-war, and replied that he was a confounded cheat, and that he had better pay me his debt of two guineas for bringing him down the river. He reported me on the quarter-deck for calling him a cheat, and Captain Maclean, who, you know, won't stand any nonsense, heard the arguments on both sides; upon which he declared that the conduct of the master's mate was not that of an officer or a gentleman, and therefore *he* should leave the ship, and that my language to my superior officer was subversive to the discipline of the service, and therefore he should give me a good flogging. Now, Jacob, you know that if the officers don't pay their debts, Captain Maclean always does, and with interest into the bargain; so finding that I was in for it, and no mistake, I swam ashore the night before Black Monday, and made my way to Miramichi without any adventure, except a tussle with a sergeant of marines, whom I left for dead about three miles out of the town. At Miramichi I got on board of a timber ship, and here I am."

"I am sorry that you deserted, nevertheless," replied I; "it may come to mischief."

"Never fear; the people on the river know that I have my discharge, and I'm safe enough."

"Have you seen Mary?"

"Yes, and all's right in that quarter. I shall build another wherry, wear my badge and dress, and stick above bridge. When I'm all settled I'll splice, and live along with the old couple."

"But will Mary consent to live there? It is so quiet and retired that she won't like it."

"Mary Stapleton has given herself airs enough, in all conscience, and has had her own way quite enough. Mary Beazeley will do as her husband wishes, or I will know the reason why."

"We shall see, Tom. Bachelors' wives are always best managed, they say. But now you want money to buy your boat."

"Yes, if you'll lend it to me; I don't like to take it away from the old people, and I'll pay you when I can, Jacob."

"No, you must accept this, Tom; and when you marry you must accept something more," replied I, handing the notes to him.

"With all my heart, Jacob. I never can repay you for what you have done for me, and so I may just as well increase the debt."

"That's good logic, Tom."

"Quite as good as independence; is it not, Jacob?"

"Better, much better, as I know to my cost," replied I, laughing.

Tom finished his breakfast, and then took his leave. After breakfast, as usual, I went to the boat-house, and unchaining my wherry pulled up the river, which I had not hitherto done; my attendance upon Sarah having invariably turned the bow of my wherry in the opposite direction. I swept by the various residences on the banks of the river, until I arrived opposite to that of Mr. Wharncliffe, and perceived a lady and gentleman in the garden. I knew them immediately, and, as they were standing close to the wall, I pulled in and saluted them.

"Do you recollect me?" said I to them, smiling.

"Yes," replied the lady, "I do recollect your face—surely —it is Faithful, the waterman!"

"No, I am not a waterman; I am only amusing myself in my own boat."

"Come up," replied Mr. Wharncliffe; "we can't shake hands with you at that distance."

I made fast my wherry and joined them. They received me most cordially.

"I thought you were not a waterman, Mr. Faithful, although you said that you were," said Mrs. Wharncliffe. "Why did you deceive us in that way?"

"Indeed, at that time I was, from my own choice and my own folly, a waterman; now I am so no longer."

We were soon on the most intimate terms, and I narrated part of my adventures. They expressed their obligations to me, and requested that I would accept their friendship.

"Would you like to have a row on the water? It is a beautiful day, and if Mrs. Wharncliffe will trust herself——"

"Oh! I should like it above all things. Will you go, William? I will run for a shawl."

In a few minutes we were all three embarked, and I rowed them to my villa. They had been admiring the beauty of the various residences on the banks of the Thames.

"How do you like that one?" inquired I of Mrs. Wharncliffe.

"It is very handsome, and I think one of the very best."

"That is mine," replied I. "Will you allow me to show it to you."

"Yours!"

"Yes, mine; but I have a very small establishment, for I am a bachelor."

We landed, and after walking about the grounds, went into the house.

"Do you recollect this room?" said I to Mr. Wharncliffe.

"Yes, indeed I do; it was here that the box was opened, and my uncle's—— But we must not say anything about that—he is dead."

"Dead!"

"Yes; he never held his head up after his dishonesty was discovered. He pined and died within three months, sincerely repenting what he had attempted."

I accepted their invitation to dinner, as I rowed them back to their own residence; and afterwards had the pleasure of enrolling them among my sincerest friends. Through them I was introduced to Lady Auburn and many others, and I shall not forget the old housekeeper recognising me one day, when I was invited to Lady Auburn's villa.

"Bless me! what tricks you young gentlemen do play. Only to think how you asked me for water, and how I pushed the door in your face, and wouldn't let you rest yourself. But if you young gentlemen will disguise yourselves, it's your own faults, and you must take the consequences."

My acquaintances now increased rapidly, and I had the advantage of the best society. I hardly need observe that it was a great advantage; for, although I was not considered awkward, still I wanted that polish which can only be obtained by an admixture with good company. The reports concerning me were various, but it was generally believed that I was a young man who had received an excellent education, and might have been brought forward, but that I had taken a passion for the river, and had chosen to be a waterman in preference to any other employment; that I had since come into a large fortune, and had resumed my station in society. How far the false was blended with the true, those who have read my adventures will readily perceive. For my part, I cared little what they said, and I gave myself no trouble to refute the various assertions. I was not ashamed of my birth, because it had no effect upon the Drummonds; still I knew the world too well to think it necessary to blazon it. On the whole, the balance was in my favour; there was a degree of romance in my history, with all its variations, which interested, and, joined to the knowledge of my actual wealth, made me to be well received, and gained me attention wherever I went. One thing was much to my advantage—my extensive reading, added to the good classical education which I had received. It is not often in society that an opportunity occurs when any one can prove his acquisitions, but when it does come, they always make an impression; and thus did education turn the scale in my favour, and every one was much more inclined to believe the false rather than the true versions of my history.

CHAPTER XLIII

The Domine proves Stapleton's "human natur" to be correct— The red-coat proves too much of a match for the blue—Mary sells Tom, and Tom sells what is left of him, for a shilling— We never know the value of anything till we have lost it.

I HAD often ruminated in what manner I could render the Domine more comfortable. I felt that to him I was as much indebted as to any living being, and one day I ventured to open the subject; but his reply was decided.

"I see, Jacob, my son, what thou wouldst wish; but it must not be. Man is but a creature of habit; habit becomes to him not only necessity but luxury. For five-and-forty years have I toiled, instilling precepts and forcing knowledge into the brains of those who have never proved so apt as thou. Truly, it hath been a painful task, yet can I not relinquish it. I might at one time, that is, during the first ten years, have met the offer with gratitude; for I felt the humiliation and annoyance of wearying myself with the rudiments, when I would fain have commented upon the various peculiarities of style in the ancient Greek and Latin authors; but now, all that has passed away. The eternal round of concord, prosody, and syntax has charms for me from habit; the rule of three is preferable to the problems of Euclid, and even the Latin grammar has its delights. In short, I have a *hujus* pleasure in *hic, hæc, hoc;* [cluck, cluck;] and even the flourishing of the twigs of that tree of knowledge, the birch, hath become a pleasurable occupation to me, if not to those upon whom it is inflicted. I am like an old horse, who hath so long gone round and round in a mill that he cannot walk straight forward; and if it pleases the Almighty, I will die in harness. Still I thank thee, Jacob; and thank God that thou hast again proved the goodness of thy heart, and given me one more reason to rejoice in thee and in thy love; but thine offer, if accepted, would not add to my happiness; for what feeling can be more consolatory to an old man near into his grave than the reflection that his life, if not distinguished, has at least been useful?"

I had not for some time received a visit from Tom, and surprised at this, I went down to his father's to make inquiry about him. I found the old couple sitting indoors; the weather was fine, but old Tom was not at his work; even the old woman's netting was thrown aside.

"Where is Tom?" inquired I, after wishing them good-morning.

"Oh! deary me," cried the old woman, putting her apron up to her eyes; "that wicked, good-for-nothing girl!"

"Good heavens! what is the matter?" inquired I of old Tom.

"The matter, Jacob," replied old Tom, stretching out his two wooden legs, and placing his hands upon his knees, "is, that Tom has 'listed for a sodger."

"Listed for a soldier!"

"Yes, that's as sartain as it's true; and what's worse, I'm told the regiment is ordered to the West Indies. So, what with fever o' mind and yellow fever, he's food for the land crabs, that's sartain. I think now," continued the old man, brushing a tear from his eye with his forefinger, "that I see his bones bleaching under the palisades; for I know the place well."

"Don't say so, Tom; don't say so!"

"O Jacob! beg pardon if I'm too free now; but can't you help us?"

"I will if I can, depend upon it; but tell me how this happened."

"Why, the long and the short of it is this: that girl Mary

Stapleton has been his ruin. When he first came home he was well received, and looked forward to being spliced and living with us; but it didn't last long. She couldn't leave off her old tricks; and so, that Tom might not get the upper hand, she plays him off with the sergeant of a recruiting party, and flies off from one to the other, just like the ticker of the old clock there does from one side to the other. One day the sergeant was the fancy man, and the next day it was Tom. At last Tom gets out of patience, and wishes to come to a fair understanding. So he axes her whether she chooses to have the sergeant or to have him; she might take her choice, but he had no notion of being played with in that way, after all her letters and all her promises. Upon this she huffs outright, and tells Tom he may go about his business, for she didn't care if she never sees him no more. So Tom's blood was up, and he calls her a d——d jilt, and, in my opinion, he was near to the truth; so then they had a regular breeze, and part company. Well, this made Tom very miserable, and the next day he would have begged her pardon and come to her terms, for, you see, Jacob, a man in love has no discretion; but she being still angry, tells him to go about his business, as she means to marry the sergeant in a week. Tom turns away again quite mad, and it so happens that he goes into the public-house where the sergeant hangs out, hoping to be revenged on him, and meaning to have a regular set-to, and see who is the best man; but the sergeant wasn't there, and Tom takes pot after pot to drive away care, and when the sergeant returned Tom was not a little in liquor. Now, the sergeant was a knowing chap, and when he comes in and perceives Tom with his face flushed, he guesses what was to come, so instead of saying a word, he goes to another table and dashes his fist upon it, as if in a passion. Tom goes up to him, and says, 'Sergeant, I've known that girl long before you, and if you are a man you'll stand up for her.' 'Stand up for her, yes,' replied the sergeant; 'and so I would have done yesterday, but the blasted jilt has turned me to the right-about and sent me away. I won't fight now, for she won't have me—any more than she' will you.' Now when Tom hears this, he becomes more pacified with the sergeant, and they set down like two people under the same misfortune, and take a pot together, instead of fighting; and then, you see, the sergeant plies Tom with liquor, swearing that he will go back to the regiment and leave Mary altogether, and advises Tom to do the same. At last, what with the sergeant's persuasions, and Tom's desire to vex Mary, he succeeds in 'listing him, and giving him the shilling before witnesses; that was all the rascal wanted. The next day Tom was sent down to the depot, as they call it, under a guard; and the sergeant remains here to follow up Mary without interruption. This only happened three days ago, and we only were told of it yesterday by old Stapleton, who threatens to turn his daughter out of doors."

"Can't you help us, Jacob?" said the old woman, whimpering.

"I hope I can, and if money can procure his discharge it shall be obtained. But did you not say that he was ordered to the West Indies?"

"The regiment is in the West Indies, but they are recruiting for it, so many have been carried off by the yellow fever last sickly season. A transport, they say, will sail next week, and the recruits are to march for embarkation in three or four days."

"And what is the regiment, and where is the depot?"

"It is the 47th Fusiliers, and the depot is at Maidstone."

"I will lose no time, my good friends," replied I; "to-morrow I will go to Mr. Drummond, and consult with him." I returned the grateful squeeze of old Tom's hand, and, followed by the blessings of the old woman, I hastened away.

As I pulled up the river, for that day I was engaged to dine with the Wharncliffes, I resolved to call upon Mary Stapleton, and ascertain by her deportment whether she had become that heartless jilt which she was represented, and if so, to persuade Tom, if I succeeded in obtaining his discharge, to think no more about her. I felt so vexed and angry with her, that after I landed I walked about a few minutes before I went to the house, that I might recover my temper. When I walked up the stairs I found Mary sitting over a sheet of paper, on which she had been writing. She looked up as I came in, and I perceived that she had been crying. "Mary," said I, "how well you have kept the promise you made to me when last we met! See what trouble and sorrow you have brought upon all parties except yourself."

"Except myself; no, Mr. Faithful, don't except myself, I

347

am almost mad—I believe that I am mad—for surely such folly as mine is madness," and Mary wept bitterly.

"There is no excuse for your behaviour, Mary—it is unpardonably wicked. Tom sacrificed all for your sake—he even deserted, and desertion is death by the law. Now what have you done?—taken advantage of his strong affection to drive him to intemperance, and induce him, in despair, to enlist for a soldier. He sails for the West Indies to fill up the ranks of a regiment thinned by the yellow fever, and will perhaps never return again—you will then have been the occasion of his death. Mary, I have come to tell you that I despise you."

"I despise and hate myself," replied Mary mournfully, "I wish I were in my grave. Oh, Mr. Faithful, do, for God's sake—do get him back. You can, I know you can—you have money and everything."

"If I do, it will not be for your benefit, Mary, for you shall trifle with him no more. I will not try for his discharge unless he faithfully promises never to speak to you again."

"You don't say that—you don't mean that!" cried Mary, sweeping the hair with her hand back from her forehead, and her hand still remaining on her head. "O God! O God! what a wretch I am! Hear me, Jacob, hear me," cried she, dropping on her knees and seizing my hands; "only get him his discharge—only let me once see him again, and I swear by all that's sacred, that I will beg his pardon on my knees as I now do yours. I will do everything—anything—if he will but forgive me, for I cannot, I will not live without him."

"If this is true, Mary, what madness could have induced you to have acted as you have?"

"Yes," replied Mary, rising from her knees, "madness, indeed, more than madness to treat so cruelly one for whom I only care to live. You say Tom loves me; I know he does, but he does not love me as I do him. Oh, my God! my heart will break!" After a pause, Mary resumed. "Read what I have written to him—I have already written as much in another letter. You will see that if he cannot get away, I have offered to go out with him as his wife, that is, if he will have such a foolish, wicked girl as I am."

I read the letter; it was as she said, praying forgiveness, offering to accompany him, and humiliating herself as much as it was possible. I was much affected. I returned the letter.

"You can't despise me so much as I despise myself," continued Mary; "I hate, I detest myself for my folly. I recollect now how you used to caution me when a girl. O mother, mother, it was a cruel legacy you left to your child, when you gave her your disposition. Yet why should I blame her? I must blame myself."

"Well, Mary, I will do all I can, and that as soon as possible. To-morrow I will go down to the depot."

"God bless you, Jacob; and may you never have the misfortune to be in love with such a one as myself."

CHAPTER XLIV

I am made very happy—In other respects a very melancholy chapter, which, we are sorry to inform the reader, will be followed up by one still more so.

I LEFT Mary, and hastened home to dress for dinner. I mentioned the subject of wishing to obtain Tom's discharge to Mr. Wharncliffe, who recommended my immediately applying to the Horse Guards; and, as he was acquainted with those in office, offered to accompany me. I gladly accepted his offer; and the next morning he called for me in his carriage, and we went there. Mr. Wharncliffe sent up his card to one of the secretaries, and we were immediately ushered up, when I stated my wishes. The reply was: "If you had time to procure a substitute it would be easily arranged; but the regiment is so weak, and the aversion to the West Indies so prevalent after this last very sickly season, that I doubt if His Royal Highness would permit any man to purchase his discharge. However, we will see. The duke is one of the kindest-hearted of men, and I will lay the case before him. But let us see if he is still at the depot; I rather think not." The secretary rang the bell.

"The detachment of the 47th Fusiliers from the depot—has it marched? And when does it embark?"

The clerk went out, and in a few minutes returned with some papers in his hand. "It marched the day before yesterday, and was to embark this morning, and sail as soon as the wind was fair."

349

My heart sank at this intelligence.

"How is the wind, Mr. G——? Go down and look at the tell-tale."

The clerk returned. "ENE., sir, and has been steadily so these two days."

"Then," replied the secretary, "I am afraid you are too late to obtain your wish. The orders to the port-admiral are most peremptory to expedite the sailing of the transports, and a frigate has been now three weeks waiting to convoy them. Depend upon it, they have sailed to-day."

"What can be done?" replied I mournfully.

"You must apply for his discharge, and procure a substitute. He can then have an order sent out, and be permitted to return home. I am very sorry, as I perceive you are much interested; but I'm afraid it is too late now. However, you may call to-morrow. The weather is clear with this wind, and the port-admiral will telegraph to the Admiralty the sailing of the vessels. Should anything detain them, I will take care that His Royal Highness shall be acquainted with the circumstances this afternoon, if possible, and will give you his reply."

We thanked the secretary for his politeness, and took our leave. Vexed as I was with the communications I had already received, I was much more so when one of the porters ran to the carriage to show me, by the secretary's order, a telegraphic communication from the Admiralty, containing the certain and unpleasant information, "Convoy to West Indies sailed this morning."

"Then it is all over for the present," said I, throwing myself back in the carriage; and I continued in a melancholy humour until Mr. Wharncliffe, who had business in the city, put me down as near as the carriage went to the house of Mr. Drummond. I found Sarah, who was the depositary of all my thoughts, pains, and pleasures, and I communicated to her this episode in the history of young Tom. As most ladies are severe judges of their own sex, she was very strong in her expressions against the conduct of Mary, which she would not allow to admit of any palliation. Even her penitence had no weight with her.

"And yet, how often is it the case, Sarah, not perhaps to the extent carried on by this mistaken girl; but still, the disappointment is as great, although the consequences are

350

not so calamitous. Among the higher classes, how often do young men receive encouragement, and yield themselves up to a passion to end only in disappointment! It is not necessary to plight troth; a young woman may not have virtually committed herself, and yet, by merely appearing pleased with the conversation and company of a young man, induce him to venture his affections in a treacherous sea, and eventually find them wrecked."

"You are very nautically poetical, Jacob," replied Sarah. "Such things do happen; but I think that women's affections are, to use your phrase, oftener wrecked than those of men. That, however, does not exculpate either party. A woman must be blind, indeed, if she cannot perceive, in a very short time, whether she is trifling with a man's feelings, and base, indeed, if she continues to practise upon them."

"Sarah!" replied I, and I stopped.

"Well?"

"I was," replied I, stammering a little, "I was going to ask you if you were blind?"

"As to what, Jacob?" said Sarah, colouring up.

"As to my feelings towards you."

"No; I believe you like me very well," replied she, smiling.

"Do you think that that is all?"

"Where do you dine to-day, Jacob?" replied Sarah.

"That must depend upon you and your answer. If I dine here to-day, I trust to dine here often. If I do not dine here to-day, probably I never may again. I wish to know, Sarah, whether you have been blind to my feelings towards you; for, with the case of Mary and Tom before me, I feel that I must no longer trust to my own hopes, which may end in disappointment. Will you have the kindness to put me out of my misery?"

"If I have been blind to your feelings, I have not been blind to your merit, Jacob. Perhaps I have not been blind to your feelings, and I am not of the same disposition as Mary Stapleton. I think you may venture to dine here to-day," continued she, colouring and smiling as she turned away to the window.

"I can hardly believe that I'm to be so happy, Sarah," replied I, agitated. "I have been fortunate, very fortunate; but the hopes you have now raised are so much beyond my

351

expectations—so much beyond my deserts—that I dare not indulge in them. Have pity on me, and be more explicit."

"What do you wish me to say?" replied Sarah, looking down upon her work, as she turned round to me.

"That you will not reject the orphan who was fostered by your father; and who reminds you of what he was, that you may not forget at this moment what I trust is the greatest bar to his presumption—his humble origin."

"Jacob, that was said like yourself—it was nobly said; and if you were not born noble, you have true nobility of mind. I will imitate your example. Have I not often, during our long friendship, told you that I loved you?"

"Yes, as a child you did, Sarah."

"Then as a woman I repeat it. And now are you satisfied?"

I took Sarah by the hand. She did not withdraw it, but allowed me to kiss it over and over again.

"But your father and mother, Sarah?"

"Would never have allowed our intimacy if they had not approved of it, Jacob, depend upon it. However, you may make yourself easy on that score, by letting them know what has passed; and then, I presume, you will be out of your misery."

Before the day was over I had spoken to Mrs. Drummond, and requested her to open the business to her husband, as I really felt it more than I could dare to do. She smiled as her daughter hung upon her neck; and when I met Mr. Drummond at dinner-time I was "out of my misery," for he shook me by the hand, and said, "You have made us all very happy, Jacob; for that girl appears determined either to marry you or not to marry at all. Come; dinner is ready."

I will leave the reader to imagine how happy I was, what passed between Sarah and me in our *tête-à-tête* of that evening, how unwilling I was to quit the house, and how I ordered a postchaise to carry me home, because I was afraid to trust myself on that water on which the major part of my life had been safely passed, lest any accident should happen to me and rob me of my anticipated bliss. From that day I was as one of the family, and finding the distance too great took up my abode at apartments contiguous to the house of Mr. Drummond. But the course of other people's love did not run so smooth, and I must now return to Mary Stapleton and Tom Beazeley.

I had breakfasted, and was just about to take my wherry and go down to acquaint the old couple with the bad success of my application. I had been reflecting with gratitude upon my own happiness in prospect, indulging in fond anticipations, and then, reverting to the state in which I had left Mary Stapleton and Tom's father and mother, contrasting their misery with my joy, arising from the same source, when who should rush into the dining-room but young Tom, dressed in nothing but a shirt, and a pair of white trousers, covered with dust, and wan with fatigue and excitement.

"Good heavens! Tom, are you back? then you must have deserted."

"Very true," replied Tom, sinking on a chair, "I swam on shore last night, and have made from Portsmouth to here since eight o'clock. I hardly need say that I am done up. Let me have something to drink, Jacob, pray."

I went to the cellaret and brought him some wine, of which he drank off a tumbler eagerly. During this, I was revolving in my mind the consequences which might arise from this hasty and imprudent step. "Tom," said I, "do you know the consequences of desertion?"

"Yes," replied he gloomily, "but I could not help it. Mary told me in her letter that she would do all I wished, would accompany me abroad. She made all the amends she could, poor girl; and, by heavens! I could not leave her; and when I found myself fairly under weigh, and there was no chance, I was almost mad. The wind baffled us at the Needles, and we anchored for the night; I slipped down the cable and swam on shore, and there's the whole story."

"But, Tom, you will certainly be recognised and taken up for a deserter."

"I must think of that," replied Tom. "I know the risk that I run; but perhaps if you obtain my discharge, they may let me off."

I thought this was the best plan to proceed upon, and requesting Tom to keep quiet, I went to consult with Mr. Wharncliffe. He agreed with me that it was Tom's only chance, and I pulled to his father's to let them know what had occurred, and then went on to the Drummonds. When I returned home late in the evening, the gardener told me that Tom had gone out, and had not returned. My heart misgave

me that he had gone to see Mary, and that some misfortune
had occurred, and I went to bed with most anxious feelings.
My forebodings were proved to be correct, for the next morning I was informed that old Stapleton wished to see me. He
was ushered in, and as soon as he entered, he exclaimed,
"All's up, Master Jacob—Tom's nabbed—Mary fit after fit—
human natur."

"Why, what *is* the matter, Stapleton?"

"Why, it's just this—Tom desarts to come to Mary. Cause
why?—he loves her—human natur. That soldier chap comes
in and sees Tom, clutches hold, and tries to take possession
of him. Tom fights, knocks out sergeant's starboard eye, and
tries to escape—human natur. Soldiers come in, pick up
sergeant, seize Tom, and carry him off. Mary cries, and
screams, and faints—human natur—poor girl can't keep her
head up—two women with burnt feathers all night. Sad job,
Mister Jacob. Of all the senses love's the worst, that's sartain
—quite upset me, can't smoke my pipe this morning—Mary's
tears quite put my pipe out," and old Stapleton looked as if
he was ready to cry himself.

"This is a sad business, Stapleton," replied I. "Tom will
be tried for desertion, and God knows how it will end. I will
try all I can, but they have been very strict lately."

"Hope you will, Mister Jacob. Mary will die, that's sartain.
I'm more afraid that Tom will. If one does, t'other will. I
know the girl—just like her mother, never could carry her
helm amidships, hard a-port or hard a-starboard. She's mad
now to follow him—will go to Maidstone. I take her as soon
as I go back to her. Just come up to tell you all about it."

"This is a gloomy affair, Stapleton."

"Yes, for sartain—wish there never was such a thing as
human natur."

After a little conversation, and a supply of money, which I
knew would be acceptable, Stapleton went away, leaving me
in no very happy state of mind. My regard for Tom was
excessive, and his situation one of peculiar danger. Again
I repaired to Mr. Wharncliffe for advice, and he readily interested himself most warmly.

"This is, indeed, an awkward business," said he, "and will
require more interest than I am afraid that I command. If
not condemned to death, he will be sentenced to such a flog-

ging as will break him down in spirit as well as in body, and sink him into an early grave. Death were preferable of the two. Lose no time, Mr. Faithful, in going down to Maidstone, and seeing the colonel commanding the depot. I will go to the Horse Guards, and see what is to be done."

I wrote a hurried note to Sarah to account for my absence, and sent for post horses. Early in the afternoon I arrived at Maidstone, and finding out the residence of the officer commanding the depot, sent up my card. In few words I stated to him the reason of my calling upon him.

" It will rest altogether with the Horse Guards, Mr. Faithful, and I am afraid I can give you but little hope. His Royal Highness has expressed his determination to punish the next deserter with the utmost severity of the law. His leniency on that point has been very injurious to the service, and he *must do it*. Besides, there is an aggravation of the offence in his attack upon the sergeant, who has irrecoverably lost his eye."

" The sergeant first made him drunk, and then persuaded him to enlist." I then stated the rivalship that subsisted between them, and continued, " Is it not disgraceful to enlist men in that way—can that be called voluntary service ? "

" All very true," replied the officer, " but still expediency winks at even more. I do not attempt to defend the system, but we must have soldiers. The seamen are impressed by force, the soldiers are entrapped by other means, even more discreditable ; the only excuse is expediency, or, if you like it better, necessity. All I can promise you, sir, is, what I would have done even if you had not appealed to me, to allow the prisoner every comfort which his situation will permit, and every advantage at his court-martial which mercy, tempered by justice, will warrant."

" I thank you, sir ; will you allow me and his betrothed to see him ? "

" Most certainly ; the order shall be given forthwith."

I thanked the officer for his kindness, and took my leave.

CHAPTER XLV

Read it.

I HASTENED to the black hole where Tom was confined, and the order for my admission having arrived before me, I was permitted by the sergeant of the guard to pass the sentry. I found Tom sitting on a bench notching a stick with his knife, whistling a slow tune.

"This is kind, Jacob, but not more than I expected of you—I made sure that I should see you to-night or to-morrow morning. How's poor Mary? I care only for her now—I am satisfied—she loves me and—I knocked out the sergeant's eye—spoilt his wooing, at all events."

"But, Tom, are you aware of the danger in which you are?"

"Yes, Jacob, perfectly; I shall be tried by a court-martial and shot. I've made up my mind to it—at all events, it's better than being hung like a dog, or being flogged to death like a nigger. I shall die like a gentleman, if I have never been one before, that's some comfort. Nay, I shall go out of the world with as much noise as if a battle had been fought, or a great man had died."

"How do you mean?"

"Why, there'll be more than one *bullet-in.*"

"This is no time for jesting, Tom."

"Not for you, Jacob, as a sincere friend, I grant; not for poor Mary, as a devoted girl; not for my poor father and mother—no, no," continued Tom. "I feel for them; but for myself I neither fear nor care. I have not done wrong—I was pressed against the law and Act of Parliament, and I deserted. I was enlisted when I was drunk and mad, and I deserted. There is no disgrace to me; the disgrace is to the government which suffers such acts. If I am to be a victim, well and good—we can only die once."

"Very true, Tom; but you are young to die, and we must hope for the best."

"I have given up all hope, Jacob. I know the law will be put in force. I shall die and go to another and a better world, as the parson says, where, at all events, there will be no

356

muskets to clean, no drill, and none of your confounded pipe-clay, which has almost driven me mad. I should like to die in a blue jacket—in a red coat I will not, so I presume I shall go out of the world in my shirt, and that's more than I had when I came in."

"Mary and her father are coming down to you, Tom."

"I'm sorry for that, Jacob; it would be cruel not to see her—but she blames herself so much that I cannot bear to read her letters. But, Jacob, I will see her, to try if I can comfort her; but she must not stay; she must go back again till after the court-martial, and the sentence, and then—if she wishes to take her farewell, I suppose I must not refuse." A few tears dropped from his eyes as he said this. "Jacob, will you wait and take her back to town?—she must not stay here—and I will not see my father and mother until the last. Let us make one job of it, and then all will be over."

As Tom said this the door of the cell again opened, and Stapleton supported in his daughter. Mary tottered to where Tom stood, and fell into his arms in a fit of convulsions. It was necessary to remove her, and she was carried out. "Let her not come in again, I beseech you, Jacob; take her back, and I will bless you for your kindness. Wish me farewell now, and see that she does not come again." Tom wrung me by the hand, and turned away to conceal his distress. I nodded my head in assent, for I could not speak for emotion, and followed Stapleton and the soldiers who had taken Mary out. As soon as she was recovered sufficiently to require no further medical aid, I lifted her into the post-chaise, and ordered the boys to drive back to Brentford. Mary continued in a state of stupor during the journey; and when I arrived at my own house, I gave her into the charge of the gardener's wife, and despatched her husband for medical assistance. The application of Mr. Wharncliffe was of little avail, and he returned to me with disappointment in his countenance. The whole of the next week was the most distressing that I ever passed; arising from my anxiety for Tom, my daily exertions to reason Mary into some degree of submission to the will of Providence; her accusations of herself and her own folly; her incoherent ravings, calling herself Tom's murderer, which alarmed me for her reason; the distress of old Tom and his wife, who, unable to remain in their solitude, came all to me for intelligence, for comfort, and for what, alas! I dared not give them—hope. All this, added to my separation from Sarah, during my attendance to what I considered my duty, reduced me to a debility, arising from mental exertion, which changed me to almost a skeleton.

At last the court-martial was held, and Tom was condemned to death. The sentence was approved of, and we were told that all appeals would be unavailing. We received the news on the Saturday evening, and Tom was to suffer on the Tuesday morning. I could no longer refuse the appeals of Mary; indeed, I received a letter from Tom, requesting that all of us, the Domine included, would come down and bid him farewell. I hired a carriage for old Tom, his wife, Stapleton, and Mary, and putting the Domine and myself in my own chariot, we set off early on the Sunday morning for Maidstone. We arrived about eleven o'clock, and put up at an inn close to the barracks. It was arranged that the Domine and I should see Tom first, then his father and mother, and lastly Mary Stapleton.

"Verily," said the Domine, "my heart is heavy, exceeding heavy; my soul yearneth after the poor lad, who is thus to lose his life for a woman—a woman from whose toils I did myself escape. Yet is she exceeding fair and comely, and now that it is unavailing, appeareth to be penitent."

I made no reply; we had arrived at the gate of the barracks. I requested to be admitted to the prisoner, and the doors were unbarred. Tom was dressed with great care and cleanliness— in white trousers and shirt and waistcoat, but his coat lay on the table; he would not put it on. He extended his hand towards me with a faint smile.

"It's all over now, Jacob; and there is no hope, that I am aware of, and have made up my mind to die; but I wish these last farewells were over, for they unman me. I hope you are well, sir," continued Tom to the Domine.

"Nay, my poor boy, I am as well as age and infirmity will permit, and why should I complain when I see youth, health, and strength about to be sacrificed, and many made miserable, when many might be made so happy?" And the Domine blew his nose, the trumpet sound of which re-echoed through the cell, so as to induce the sentry to look through the bars.

"They are all here, Tom," said I. "Would you like to see them now?"

"Yes; the sooner it is over, the better."

"Will you see your father and mother first?"

"Yes," replied Tom, in a faltering tone.

I went out, and returned with the old woman on my arm, followed by old Tom, who stumped after me with the assistance of his stick. Poor old Mrs. Beazeley fell on her son's neck, sobbing convulsively.

"My boy—my boy—my dear, dear boy!" said she at last, and she looked up steadfastly in his face. "My God! he'll be dead to-morrow!"

Her head again sank on his shoulder, and her sobs were choking her. Tom kissed his mother's forehead as the tears coursed down his cheeks, and motioned me to take her away. I placed her down on the floor, where she remained silent, moving her head up and down with a slow motion, her face buried in her shawl. It was but now and then that you heard a convulsive drawing of her breath. Old Tom had remained a silent but agitated spectator of the scene. Every muscle in his weather-beaten countenance twitched convulsively, and the tears at last forced their way through the deep furrows on his cheeks. Tom, as soon as his mother was removed, took his father by the hand, and they sat down together.

"You are not angry with me, father, for deserting?"

"No, my boy, no. I was angry with you for 'listing, but not for deserting. What business had you with the pipe-clay? But I do think I have reason to be angry elsewhere, when I reflect that after having lost my two legs in defending her, my country is now to take from me my boy in his prime. It's but a poor reward for long and hard service—poor encouragement to do your duty; but what do they care? they have had my sarvices, and they have left me a hulk. Well, they may take the rest of me, if they please, now that they—— Well, it's no use crying; what's done can't be helped," continued old Tom, as the tears ran down in torrents. "They may shoot you, Tom; but this I know well, you'll die game, and shame them by proving to them they have deprived themselves of the sarvices of a good man when good men are needed. I would not have so much cared," continued old Tom, after a pause—("look to the old woman, Jacob, she's tumbling over to port)—if you had fallen on board a king's ship, in a good frigate action—some must be killed when there's hard fighting; but to be drilled through by your own countrymen, to die by their hands, and worst of all, to die in a red coat instead of a true blue——"

"Father, I will not die in a red coat—I won't put it on."

"That's some comfort, Tom, anyhow, and comfort's wanted."

"And I'll die like a man, father."

"That you will, Tom, and that's some comfort."

"We shall meet again, father."

"Hope so, Tom, in heaven—that's some comfort."

"And now, father, bless me, and take care of my poor mother."

"Bless you, Tom, bless you!" cried the old man, in a suffocating voice, extending both his hands towards Tom, as they rose up; but the equilibrium was no longer to be maintained, and he reeled back in the arms of me and Tom. We lowered him gently down by the side of his wife; the old couple turned to each other, and embracing, remained sobbing in each other's arms.

"Jacob," said Tom, squeezing me by the hand, with a quivering lip, "by your regard for me, let now the last scene be got over—let me see Mary, and let this tortured heart once more be permitted a respite." I sent out the Domine. Tom leant against the wall with his arms folded, in appearance summoning up all his energy for the painful meeting. Mary was led in by her father. I expected she would have swooned away as before; but, on the contrary, although she was pale as death, and gasping for breath, from intensity of feeling, she walked up to Tom where he was standing, and sat down on the form close to him. She looked anxiously round upon the group, and then said, "I know that all I now say is useless, Tom; but still I must say it—it is I who, by my folly, have occasioned all this distress and misery—it is I who have caused you to suffer a—dreadful death—yes, Tom, I am your murderer."

"Not so, Mary, the folly was my own," replied Tom, taking her hand.

"You cannot disguise or palliate to me, dearest Tom," replied Mary; "my eyes have been opened, too late it is true, but they have been opened; and although it is kind of you to say so, I feel the horrid conviction of my own guilt.

See what misery I have brought about. There is a father who has sacrificed his youth and his limbs to his country, sobbing in the arms of a mother whose life is bound up with that of her only son. To them," continued Mary, falling down upon her knees, " to them I must kneel for pardon, and I ask it as they hope to be forgiven. Answer me—oh ! answer me ! can you forgive a wretch like me ? "

A pause ensued. I went up to old Tom, and kneeling by his side, begged him to answer.

" Forgive her, poor thing—yes ; who could refuse it, as she kneels there ? Come," continued he, speaking to his wife, " you must forgive her. Look up, dame, at her, and think that our poor boy may be asking the same of Heaven tomorrow at noon."

The old woman looked up, and her dimmed eyes caught a sight of Mary's imploring and beautiful attitude ; it was not to be withstood.

" As I hope for mercy to my poor boy, whom you have killed, so do I forgive you, unhappy young woman."

" May God reward you, when you are summoned before Him," replied Mary. " It was the hardest task of all. Of you, Jacob, I have to ask forgiveness for depriving you of your early and truest friend—yes, and for much more. Of you, sir," addressing the Domine, " for my conduct towards you, which was cruel and indefensible—will you forgive me ? "

" Yes, Mary, from my heart, I do forgive you," replied I.

" Bless thee, maiden, bless thee ! " sobbed the Domine.

" Father, I must ask of you the same—I have been a wilful child—forgive me ! "

" Yes, Mary ; you could not help it," replied old Stapleton, blubbering, " it was all human natur."

" And now," said Mary, turning round on her knees to Tom, with a look expressive of anguish and love, " to you, Tom, must be my last appeal. I know *you* will forgive me—I know you have—and this knowledge of your fervent love makes the thought more bitter that I have caused your death. But hear me, Tom, and all of you hear me. I never loved but you. I have liked others much, I liked Jacob, but you only ever did make me feel I had a heart ; and, alas ! you only have I sacrificed. When led away by my folly to give you pain, I suffered more than you—for you have had my only, you shall have my eternal and unceasing love. To your memory I am hereafter wedded, to join you will be my only wish; and if there could be a boon granted me from heaven, it would be to die with you, Tom—yes, in those dear arms."

Mary held out her arms to Tom, who, falling down on his knees, embraced her, and thus they remained with their faces buried in each other's shoulders. The whole scene was now at its climax; it was too oppressive, and I felt faint, when I was aroused by the voice of the Domine, who, lifting up both his arms, and extending them forth, solemnly prayed, " O Lord, look down upon these Thy servants in affliction; grant to those who are to continue in their pilgrimage strength to bear Thy chastening—grant to him who is to be summoned to Thee, that happiness which the world cannot give; and, O God most mighty, God most powerful, lay not upon us burdens greater than we can bear. My children, let us pray."

The Domine knelt down, and repeated the Lord's Prayer; all followed his example, and then there was a pause.

"Stapleton," said I, pointing to Mary. I beckoned to the Domine. We assisted up old Tom, and then his wife, and led them away; the poor old womam was in a state of stupefaction, and until she was out in the air was not aware that she had quitted her son. Stapleton had attempted to detach Mary from Tom, but in vain; they were locked together as if in death. At last Tom, roused by me, suffered his hold to be loosened, and Mary was taken out in a happy state of insensibility, and carried to the inn by her father and the Domine.

" Are they all gone ? " whispered Tom to. me, as his head reclined on my shoulder.

" All, Tom."

" Then the bitterness of death is past. God have mercy on them, and assuage their anguish'; they want His help more than I do."

A passionate flood of tears, which lasted some minutes, relieved the poor fellow; he raised himself, and drying his eyes, became more composed.

" Jacob, I hardly need tell my dying request, to watch over my poor father and mother, to comfort poor Mary. God bless

362

you, Jacob! you have indeed been a faithful friend, and may God reward you. And now, Jacob, leave me; I must commune with my God, and pray for forgiveness. The space between me and eternity is but short."

Tom threw himself into my arms, where he remained for some minutes; he then broke gently away, and pointed to the door. I once more took his hand, and we parted.

CHAPTER XLVI

In which, as usual in the last chapter of a work, everything is wound up much to the reader's satisfaction, and not a little to the author's, who lays down his pen, exclaiming, "Thank God!"

I WENT back to the inn, and ordering the horses to be put to, I explained to all but Mary the propriety of their now returning home. Mary was lifted in, and it was a relief to my mind to see them all depart. As for myself, I resolved to remain until the last; but I was in a state of feverish agitation, which made me restless. As I paced up and down the room, the newspaper caught my eye. I laid hold of it mechanically, and looked at it. A paragraph riveted my attention. "His Majesty's ship *Immortalité*, Chatham, to be paid off." Then our ship has come home. But what was that now? Yet something whispered to me that I ought to go and see Captain Maclean, and try if anything could be done. I knew his commanding interest, and although it was now too late, still I had an impulse to go and see him, which I could not resist. "After all," said I to myself, "I'm of no use here, and I may as well go." This feeling, added to my restlessness, induced me to order horses, and I went to Chatham, found out that Captain Maclean was still on board, and took boat off to the frigate. I was recognised by the officers, who were glad to see me, and I sent a message to the captain, who was below, requesting to see him. I was asked into the cabin, and stated to him what had occurred, requesting his assistance if possible.

"Faithful," replied he, "it appears that Tom Beazeley has deserted twice; still there is much extenuation. At all events, the punishment of death is too severe, and I don't *like* it.—I

363

can save him, and I will. By the rule of the services, a deserter from one service can be claimed from the other, and must be tried by his officers. His sentence is, therefore, not legal. I shall send a party of marines, and claim him as a deserter from the navy, and they must and shall give him up—make yourself easy, Faithful, his life is as safe as yours."

I could have fallen on my knees and thanked him, though I could hardly believe that such good news was true.

"There is no time to lose, sir," replied I respectfully; "he is to be shot to-morrow at nine o'clock."

"He will be on board here to-morrow at nine o'clock, or I am not Captain Maclean. But, as you say, there is no time to lose. It is now nearly dark, and the party must be off immediately. I must write a letter on service to the commanding officer of the depot. Call my clerk."

I ran out and called the clerk. In a few minutes the letter was written, and a party of marines, with the second lieutenant, despatched with me on shore. I ordered post-chaises for the whole party, and before eleven we were at Maidstone. The lieutenant and I sat up all night, and at daylight we summoned the marines and went to the barracks, where we found the awful note of preparation going forward, and the commanding officer up and attending to the arrangements. I introduced the lieutenant, who presented the letter on service.

"Good heavens; how fortunate! You can establish his identity, I presume."

"Every man here can swear to him."

"'Tis sufficient, Mr. Faithful. I wish you and your friend joy of this reprieve. The rules of the service must be obeyed, and you will sign a receipt for the prisoner."

This was done by the lieutenant, and the provost-marshal was ordered to deliver up the prisoner. I hastened with the marines into the cell, the door was unlocked. Tom, who was reading his Bible, started up, and perceiving the red jackets, thought that he was to be led out to execution.

"My lads," exclaimed he, "I am ready; the sooner this is over the better."

"No, Tom," said I, advancing, "I trust for better fortune. You are claimed as a deserter from the *Immortalité*."

364

Tom stared, lifted the hair from his forehead, and threw himself into my arms; but we had no time for a display of feelings. We hurried Tom away from the barracks; again I put the whole party into chaises, and we soon arrived at Chatham, where we embarked on board of the frigate. Tom was given into the charge of the master-at-arms as a deserter, and a letter was written by Captain Maclean, demanding a court-martial on him.

"What will be the result?" inquired I of the first lieutenant.

"The captain says little or nothing, as he was pressed as an apprentice, which is contrary to Act of Parliament."

I went down to cheer Tom with this intelligence, and taking my leave, set off for London with a light heart. Still I thought it better not to communicate this good news until assurance was made doubly sure. I hastened to Mr. Drummond's, and detailed to them all which had passed. The next day Mr. Wharncliffe went with me to the Admiralty, where I had the happiness to find that all was legal, and that Tom could only be tried for his desertion from a man-of-war; and that, if he could prove that he was an apprentice, he would in all probability be acquitted. The court-martial was summoned three days after the letter had been received by the Admiralty. I hastened down to Chatham to be present. It was very short; the desertion was proved, and Tom was called upon for his defence. He produced his papers, and proved that he was pressed before his time had expired. The court was cleared for a few minutes, and then reopened. Tom was acquitted on the ground of illegal detention, contrary to Act of Parliament, and he was free. I returned my thanks to Captain Maclean and the officers for their kindness, and left the ship with Tom in the cutter, ordered for me by the first lieutenant. My heart swelled with gratitude at the happy result. Tom was silent, but his feelings I could well analyse. I gave to the men of the boat five guineas to drink Tom's health, and, hastening to the inn, ordered the carriage, and with Tom, who was a precious deposit, for upon his welfare depended the happiness of so many, I hurried to London as fast as I could, stopped at the Drummonds' to communicate the happy intelligence, and then proceeded to my own house, where we slept. The next morning I dressed Tom in some of my clothes, and we embarked in the wherry.

"Now, Tom," said I, "you must keep in the background at first, while I prepare them. Where shall we go first?"

"Oh! to my mother," replied Tom.

We passed through Putney Bridge, and Tom's bosom heaved as he looked towards the residence of Mary. His heart was there, poor fellow! and he longed to have flown to the poor girl, and have dried her tears; but his first duty was to his parents.

We soon arrived abreast of the residence of the old couple, and I desired Tom to pull in, but not turn his head round, lest they should see him before I had prepared them; for too much joy will kill as well as grief. Old Tom was not at his work, and all was quiet. I landed and went to the house, opened the door, and found them both sitting by the kitchen fire in silence, apparently occupied in watching the smoke as it ascended up the spacious chimney.

"Good morning to you both," said I; "how do you find yourself, Mrs. Beazeley?"

"Ah! deary me!" replied the old woman, putting her apron up to her eyes.

"Sit down, Jacob, sit down," said old Tom; "we *can* talk of him now."

"Yes, now that he's in heaven, poor fellow!" interposed the old woman.

"Tell me, Jacob," said old Tom, with a quivering lip, "did you see the last of him? Tell me all about it. How did he look? How did he behave? Was he soon out of his pain? And—Jacob—where is he buried?"

"Yes, yes," sobbed Mrs. Beazeley; "tell me where is the body of my poor child."

"Can you bear to talk about him?" said I.

"Yes, yes, we can't talk too much; it does us good," replied she. "We have done nothing but talk about him since we left him."

"And shall, till we sink down into our own graves," said old Tom, "which won't be long. I've nothing to wish for now, and I'll never sing again, that's sartain. We shan't last long, either of us. As for me," continued the old man, with a melancholy smile, looking down at his stumps, "I may well say that I've *two* feet in the grave already. But come, Jacob, tell us all about him."

"I will," replied I; "and my dear Mrs. Beazeley, you must prepare yourself for different tidings than what you expect. Tom is not yet shot."

"Not dead!" shrieked the old woman.

"Not yet, Jacob," cried old Tom, seizing me by the arm, and squeezing it with the force of a vice, as he looked me earnestly in the face.

"He lives; and I am in hopes he will be pardoned."

Mrs. Beazeley sprang from her chair, and seized me by the other arm.

"I see—I see by your face. Yes, Jacob, he is pardoned, and we shall have our Tom again."

"You are right, Mrs. Beazeley; he is pardoned, and will soon be here."

The old couple sank down on their knees beside me. I left them, and beckoned from the door to Tom, who flew up, and in a moment was in their arms. I assisted him to put his mother into her chair, and then went out to recover myself from the agitating scene. I remained about an hour outside, and then returned. The old couple seized me by the hands, and invoked blessings on my head.

"You must now part with Tom a little while," said I; "there are others to make happy besides yourselves."

"Very true," replied old Tom; "go, my lad, and comfort her. Come, missus, we mustn't forget others."

"Oh no. Go, Tom; go and tell her that I don't care how soon she is my daughter."

Tom embraced his mother, and followed me to the boat; we pulled up against the tide, and were soon at Putney.

"Tom, you had better stay in the boat. I will either come or send for you."

It was very unwillingly that Tom consented, but I overruled his entreaties, and he remained. I walked to Mary's house and entered. She was up in the little parlour, dressed in deep mourning. When I entered she was looking out upon the river; she turned her head, and perceiving me, rose to meet me.

"You do not come to upbraid me, Jacob, I am sure," said she, in a melancholy voice; "you are too kind-hearted for that."

"No, no, Mary; I am come to comfort you, if possible."

"That is not possible. Look at me, Jacob. Is there not a worm—a canker—that gnaws within?"

The hollow cheek and wild flaring eye, once so beautiful, but too plainly told the truth.

"Mary," said I, "sit down; you know what the Bible says, 'It is good for us to be afflicted.'"

"Yes, yes," sobbed Mary, "I deserve all I suffer; and I bow in humility. But am I not too much punished, Jacob? Not that I would repine; but is it not too much for me to bear, when I think that I am the destroyer of one who loved me so?"

"You have not been the destroyer, Mary."

"Yes, yes; my heart tells me that I have."

"But I tell you that you have not. Say, Mary, dreadful as the punishment has been, would you not kiss the rod with thankfulness, if it cured you of your unfortunate disposition, and prepared you to make a good wife?"

"That it has cured me, Jacob, I can safely assert; but it has also killed me as well as him. But I wish not to live; and I trust, in a few short months, to repose by his side."

"I hope you will have your wish, Mary, very soon, but not in death."

"Merciful heavens! what do you mean, Jacob?"

"I said you were not the destroyer of poor Tom—you have not been, he has not *yet* suffered; there was an informality, which has induced them to revise the sentence."

"Jacob," replied Mary, "it is cruelty to raise my hopes only to crush them again. If not yet dead, he is still to die. I wish you had not told me so," continued she, bursting into tears; "what a state of agony and suspense must he have been in all this time, and I—I have caused his sufferings! I trusted he had long been released from this cruel, heartless world."

The flood of tears which followed, assured me that I could safely impart the glad intelligence. "Mary, Mary, listen to me."

"Leave me, leave me," sobbed Mary, waving her hand.

"No, Mary, not until I tell you that Tom is not only alive, but—pardoned."

"Pardoned!" shrieked Mary.

"Yes, pardoned, Mary—free, Mary—and in a few minutes will be in your arms."

Mary dropped on her knees, raised her hands and eyes to heaven, and then fell into a state of insensibility. Tom, who had followed me and remained near the house, had heard the shriek, and could no longer retain himself; he flew into the room as Mary fell, and I put her into his arms. At the first signs of returning sensibility I left them together, and went to find old Stapleton, to whom I was more brief in my communication. Stapleton continued to smoke his pipe during my narrative.

" Glad of it, glad of it," said he, when I finished. " I were just thinking how all these senses brought us into trouble, more than all, that sense of love. Got me into trouble, and made me kill a man; got my poor wife into trouble, and drowned her; and now almost shot Tom, and killed Mary. Had too much of HUMAN NATUR lately—nothing but moist eyes and empty pipes. Met that sergeant yesterday, had a turn up. Tom settled one eye, and, old as I am, I've settled the other for a time. He's in bed for a fortnight—couldn't help it—human natur."

I took leave of Stapleton, and calling in upon Tom and Mary, shaking hands with the one and kissing the other, I despatched a letter to the Domine, acquainting him with what had passed, and then hastened to the Drummonds and imparted the happy results of my morning's work to Sarah and her mother.

" And now, Sarah, having so successfully arranged the affairs of other people, I should like to plead in my own behalf. I think that after having been deprived almost wholly of your dear company for a month, I deserve to be rewarded."

" You do indeed, Jacob," said Mrs. Drummond, " and I am sure that Sarah thinks so too, if she will but acknowledge it."

" I do acknowledge it, mamma; but what is this reward to be ? "

" That you will allow your father and mother to arrange an early day for our nuptials, and also allow Tom and Mary to be united at the same altar."

" Mamma, have I not always been a dutiful daughter ? "

" Yes, my love, you have."

" Then I shall do as I am bidden by my parents, Jacob, it

will be probably the last command I receive from them, and I shall obey it; will that please you, dear Jacob?"

That evening the day was fixed, and now I must not weary the reader with a description of my feelings, or of my happiness in the preparations for the ceremony. Sarah and I, Mary and Tom, were united on the same day, and there was nothing to cloud our happiness. Tom took up his abode with his father and mother; and Mary, radiant with happiness, even more beautiful than ever, has settled down into an excellent, doting wife. For Sarah, I hardly need say the same; she was my friend from childhood, she is now all that a man could hope and wish for. We have been married several years, and are blessed with a numerous family.

I am now almost at a conclusion. I have only to acquaint the reader with a few particulars relative to my early friends. Stapleton is still alive, and is wedded to his pipe, which with him, although the taste for tobacco has been considered as an acquired one, may truly be asserted to be human nature. He has two wherries with apprentices, and from them gains a good livelihood, without working himself. He says that the boys are not so honest as I was, and cheat him not a little; but he consoles himself by asserting that it is nothing but human natur. Old Tom is also strong and hearty, and says that he don't intend to follow his legs for some time yet. His dame, he says, is peaking, but Mary requires no assistance. Old Tom has left off mending boats, his sign is taken down, for he is now comfortable. When Tom married, I asked him what he wished to do; he requested me to lend him money to purchase a lighter. I made him a present of a new one, just launched by Mr. Drummond's firm. But old Stapleton made over to him the £200 left to him by Mr. Turnbull, and his mother brought out an equal sum from her hoards. This enabled Tom to purchase another lighter, and now he has six or seven, I forget which; at all events he is well off, and adding to his wealth every year. They talked of removing to a better house, but the old couple wish to remain. Old Tom, especially, has built an arbour where the old boat stood, and sits there carolling his songs, and watching the craft as they go up and down the river.

Mr. and Mrs. Wharncliffe still continue my neighbours and dearest friends. Mrs. Turnbull died a few months back, and

I am now in possession of the whole property. My father and mother-in-law are well and happy. Mr. Drummond will retire from business as soon as he can wind up his multifarious concerns. I have but one more to speak of—the old Domine. It is now two years since I closed the eyes of this worthy man. As he increased in years so did he in his abstraction of mind, and the governors of the charity thought it necessary to superannuate him with a pension. It was a heavy blow to the old man, who asserted his capabilities to continue to instruct; but people thought otherwise, and he accepted my offer to take up his future residence with us, upon the understanding that it was necessary that our children, the eldest of whom at that time was but four years old, should be instructed in Latin and Greek. He removed to us with all his books, &c., not forgetting the formidable birch; but as the children would not take to the Latin of their own accord, and Mrs. Faithful would not allow the rod to be made use of, the Domine's occupation was gone. Still, such was the force of habit, that he never went without the Latin grammar in his pocket, and I have often watched him sitting down in the poultry-yard, fancying, I presume, that he was in his school. There would he decline, construe, and conjugate aloud, his only witnesses being the poultry, who would now and then raise a gobble, gobble, gobble, while the ducks with their quack, quack, quack, were still more impertinent in their replies. A sketch of him in this position has been taken by Sarah, and now hangs over the mantelpiece of my study, between two of Mr. Turnbull's drawings, one of an iceberg on the 17th of August '78, and the other showing the dangerous position of the *Camel* whaler, jammed between the floes of ice, in latitude ——, and longitude ——.

Reader, I have now finished my narrative. There are two morals, I trust, to be drawn from the events of my life, one of which is, that in society we naturally depend upon each other for support, and that he who would assert his independence throws himself out of the current which bears to advancement; the other is, that with the advantages of good education, and good principle, although it cannot be expected that every one will be so fortunate as I have been, still there is every reasonable hope, and every right to expect, that we shall do well in this world. Thrown up, as the Domine expressed himself, as a tangled weed from the river, you have seen the orphan and charity-boy rise to wealth and consideration; you have seen how he who was friendless secured to himself the warmest friends; he who required everything from others became in a situation to protect and assist in return; he who could not call one individual his relation, united to the object of his attachment, and blessed with a numerous family; and to amass all these advantages and this sum of happiness, the only capital with which he embarked was a good education and good principles.

Reader, farewell!

THE END

THE MISSION

OR

SCENES IN AFRICA

CONTENTS

CHAPTER I

CHAPTER II

CHAPTER III

▼

CONTENTS

CHAPTER IV

CHAPTER V

CHAPTER VI

CHAPTER VII

CHAPTER VIII

CHAPTER IX

CONTENTS

CHAPTER X

CHAPTER XI

CHAPTER XII

CHAPTER XIII

CHAPTER XIV

CHAPTER XV

CONTENTS

CHAPTER XVI

CHAPTER XVII

CHAPTER XVIII

CHAPTER XIX

CHAPTER XX

CHAPTER XXI

CONTENTS

CHAPTER XXII

CHAPTER XXIII

CHAPTER XXIV

CHAPTER XXV

CHAPTER XXVI

CHAPTER XXVII

CONTENTS

CHAPTER XXVIII

CHAPTER XXIX

THE MISSION;

OR, SCENES IN AFRICA

CHAPTER I

THE EXPEDITION

Account of Sir Charles Wilmot—Loss of the Grosvenor*—Sir Charles's doubts respecting the survival of his wife and children—Alexander Wilmot—His character—The newspaper paragraph—Details of the wreck of the* Grosvenor*—Surmises as to the fate of the passengers.*

IT was in the autumn of the year 1828, that an elderly and infirm gentleman was slowly pacing up and down in a large dining-room. He had apparently finished his dinner, although it was not yet five o'clock, and the descending sun shone bright and warm through the windows, which were level with the ground, and from which there was a view of a spacious park, highly ornamented with old timber. He held a newspaper in one hand, and had the other behind his back, as if for support, for he was bent forward, and looked very feeble and emaciated.

After pacing for some time, he sat down in an easy-chair, and remained in deep thought, holding the newspaper in both his hands.

This old gentleman's name was Sir Charles Wilmot. He had in early life gone out to India as a writer, and after remaining there for a few years, during which he had amassed a handsome fortune, was advised to leave the country for a time on account of his health. He returned to England on furlough, and had not been there more than six months when the death, without issue, of his eldest brother, Sir Henry Wilmot, put him in possession of the entailed estates and of the baronetcy.

This decided him not to return to India for his wife and three daughters, whom he had left out there, but to write, desiring them to return home by the first ship. The reply which he received was most painful; his wife and two of his daughters had been carried off by the cholera, which had been very fatal during the previous rainy season. His remaining daughter was about to sail, in obedience to his wishes, in the *Grosvenor* East-Indiaman, under the care of Colonel and Mrs. James, who were near connections.

This was a heavy blow with which it pleased God to visit him in his prosperity, and was almost a total wreck of all his hopes and anticipations. But he was a good man and a religious one, and he bowed in humility to the dispensation, submitting with resignation to his loss, and still thankful to Heaven that it had graciously spared one of the objects of his affections to console him, and to watch his declining years.

Sir Charles Wilmot took possession of the family mansion and estate in Berkshire, in which he was still residing at the time our history commences. By degrees he became more resigned, and waited with anxiety for the return of his only daughter, who now seemed more dear to him than ever. He employed himself in making preparations for her reception, fitting up her apartments in the Oriental style which she had been accustomed to, and devising every little improvement and invention which he thought would give pleasure to a child of ten years old.

But it pleased Heaven that Sir Charles should be more severely chastised; the *Grosvenor's* time of arrival had elapsed, and still she was not reported in the Channel; week after week of anxiety and suspense passed slowly away, and the East India ship did not make her appearance. It was supposed that she had been captured by the enemy, but still no tidings of her capture were received. At length, however, this state of anxiety and doubt was put an end to by the dreadful intelligence that the ship had been wrecked on the east coast of Africa, and that nearly the whole of the crew and passengers had perished. Two men belonging to

2

her had been brought home by a Danish East-Indiaman, and shortly after the first intelligence, these men arrived in London, and gave a more particular detail of what had occurred.

Sir Charles, in a state of feverish anxiety, as soon as he heard of their arrival, hastened up to town to question these men; and the result of his interrogatories fully convinced him that he was now quite bereaved and childless. This was the last blow and the most severe; it was long before he could resign himself to the unsearchable dispensations of Providence; but time and religion had at last overcome all his repining feelings,—all disposition to question the goodness or wisdom of his Heavenly Father, and he was enabled to say, with sincerity, " Not my will, but Thine be done."

But although Sir Charles was thus left childless, as years passed away, he at last found that he had those near to him for whom he felt an interest, and one in particular who promised to deserve all his regard. This was his grand-nephew, Alexander Wilmot, who was the legal heir to the title and entailed property,—the son of a deceased nephew, who had fallen during the Peninsular war.

On this boy Sir Charles had lavished those affections which it pleased Heaven that he should not bestow upon his own issue, and Alexander Wilmot had gradually become as dear to him as if he had been his own child. Still the loss of his wife and children was ever in his memory, and as time passed on, painful feelings of hope and doubt were occasionally raised in Sir Charles's mind, from the occasional assertions of travellers, that all those did not perish who were supposed so to do when the *Grosvenor* was wrecked, and that, from the reports of the natives, some of them and of their descendants were still alive. It was a paragraph in the newspaper, containing a renewal of these assertions, which had attracted the attention of Sir Charles, and which had put him in the state of agitation and uneasiness in which we have described him at the opening of this chapter.

We left him in deep and painful thought, with the newspaper in his hands. His reveries were interrupted by the entrance of Alexander Wilmot, who resided with him, being now twenty-two years of age, and having just finished his college education. Alexander Wilmot was a tall, handsome young man, very powerful in frame, and very partial to all

3

athletic exercises; he was the best rower and the best cricketer at Oxford, very fond of horses and hunting, and an excellent shot; in character and disposition he was generous and amiable, frank in his manner, and obliging to his inferiors. Every one liked Alexander Wilmot, and he certainly deserved to be liked, for he never injured or spoke ill of anybody. Perhap his most prominent fault was obstinacy; but this was more shown in an obstinate courage and perseverance to conquer what appeared almost impossible, and at the greatest risk to himself; he was of that disposition that he would hardly get out of the way of a mad bull if it crossed his path, but risk his life probably, and to no purpose; but there is no perfection in this world, and it was still less to be expected in a young man of only twenty-two years of age.

"Well, uncle, I've conquered him," said Alexander, as he came into the room, very much heated with exercise.

"Conquered whom, my boy?" replied Sir Charles.

"The colt; I've backed him, and he is now as gentle as a lamb; but he fought hard for two hours at least."

"Why should you run such risk, Alexander, when the horsebreaker would have broke him just as well?"

"But not so soon, uncle."

"I did not know that you were in such want of a horse as to require such hurry; I thought you had plenty in the stable."

"So I have, uncle, thanks to you, more than I can use; but I like the pleasure—the excitement."

"There you state the truth, my dear Alexander; when you have lived as long as I have, you will find more pleasure in quiet and repose," replied Sir Charles, with a heavy sigh.

"Something has disturbed you, my dear uncle," said Alexander, going up to Sir Charles and taking his hand; "what is it, sir?"

"You are right, Alexander; something has unsettled me, has called up painful feelings and reminiscences; it is that paragraph in the newspaper."

Alexander was now as subdued almost as his uncle; he took a chair and quietly read the paragraph.

"Do you think there is any foundation for this, my dear sir?" said he, after he had read it.

4

"It is impossible to say, my dear boy; it may be so, it has often been asserted before. The French traveller Le Vaillant states that he received the same information, but was prevented from ascertaining the truth; other travellers have subsequently given similar accounts. You may easily credit the painful anxiety which is raised in my mind when I read such a statement as this. I think I see my poor Elizabeth the wife or slave to some wild savage; her children, merciful Heaven! my grandchildren, growing up as the brutes of the field, in ignorance and idolatry. It is torture, my dear Alexander—absolute torture, and requires long prayer and meditation to restore my mind to its usual tone, and to enable me to bow to the dispensations of the Divine will."

"Although I have long been acquainted with the general statement, my dear uncle, respecting the loss of the ship, I have never yet heard any such details as would warrant this apprehension of yours. It is generally supposed that all perished, perished indeed most miserably, except the few men who made their way to the Cape, and returned to England."

"Such was the supposition, my dear boy, but subsequent reports have to a certain degree contradicted it, and there is reason to believe that all did not perish who were accounted as dead. If you have nothing particularly to engage you at this moment, I will enter into a detail of what did occur, and of the proofs that the fate of a large portion, among which that of your aunt Elizabeth, was never ascertained."

"If it will not be too painful to you, my dear uncle, I will most gladly hear it."

"I will not dwell longer upon it than is necessary, Alexander; believe me, the subject is distressing, but I wish you to know it also, and then to give me your opinion. You are of course aware that it was on the coast of Caffraria, to the southward of Port Natal, that the *Grosvenor* was wrecked. She soon divided and went to pieces, but by a sudden—I know not that I can say a *fortunate*—change of wind, yet such was the will of Heaven,—the whole of the crew and passengers (with the exception of sixteen who had previously attempted to gain the shore by a hawser, and one man who was left on board in a state of intoxication) were all safely

5

landed, even to the little children who were coming home in
the vessel; among whom was my poor Elizabeth."

Alexander made no observation when Sir Charles paused
for a while: the latter then continued:—

"By the time that they had all gained the shore, the day
was far spent; the natives, who were of the Caffre race, and
who had been busy in obtaining all the iron that they could
from the mainmast, which had drifted on shore, left the
beach at dark. The wretched sufferers lighted fires, and
having collected some casks of beef and flour, and some live
stock, they remained on the rocks during that night. The
next morning the captain proposed that they should make
their way to Cape Town, the Dutch settlement, to which
they all unanimously consented; certainly a most wild propo-
sition, and showing very little judgment."

"Could they have done otherwise, my dear uncle?"

"Most certainly; they knew that they were in a country
of lawless savages, who had already come down and taken by
force everything that they could lay their hands upon. The
captain calculated that they would reach Cape Town in
sixteen or seventeen days. How far his calculation was
correct, is proved by the fact that those who did reach it at
last were one hundred and seventeen days on their journey.
But even admitting that the distance could have been performed in the time stated by the captain, the very idea of
attempting to force their way through a country inhabited
by savage people, with such a number of helpless women and
children, and without any arms for their defence, was indeed
an act of folly and madness, as it eventually proved."

"What then should have been their plan?"

"Observe, Alexander, the ship was wrecked not a cable's
length from the shore, firmly fixed upon a reef of rocks upon
which she had been thrown; the water was smooth, and
there was no difficulty in their communication. The savages,
content with plundering whatever was washed on shore, had
to the time of their quitting the rocks left them uninjured.
They might have gone on board again, have procured arms
to defend themselves and the means of fortifying their
position against any attempt of the savages, who had no
other weapons but assagais or spears, and then might have
obtained the provisions and other articles necessary for their

6

support. Armed as they might have been, and numerous as they were, for there were one hundred and fifty souls on board at the time of the wreck, they might have protected themselves until they had built boats or small vessels out of the timber of the wreck; for all their carpenters and black-smiths were safely landed on shore with them. By taking this course they might have coasted along shore, and have arrived without difficulty at the Cape."

" Most certainly, sir, it would have been the most judicious plan."

" The captain must have been very deficient in judgment to have acted as he did. He had everything to his hand— the means—the men to build the boats, provisions, arms, sails and cordage, and yet he threw all these chances away, and attempted to do what was impossible."

" He was not one of those who were saved, I believe, sir ? "

" No, he is one of those who have not been heard of; but to proceed: The first day of their march from the site of the wreck ought to have been a warning to them to turn back. The savages robbed them of everything and threw stones at them. A Dutchman of the name of Trout, who had fled to the Caffre country for some murder he had com-mitted in the colony, fell in with them and told them the attempt was impracticable, from the number of savage nations, the width of the rivers, the desert countries without water, and the number of wild beasts which they would encounter; but still they were not persuaded, and went on to their de-struction. They were not five miles from the wreck at the time, and might have returned to it before night."

" May it not fairly be supposed that after such a dreadful shipwreck anything was considered preferable by the major portion of them, especially the passengers, to re-embarking?"

" It may be so; but still it was a feeling that was to be surmounted, and would have been, had they been counselled by a judicious leader; for he might fairly have pointed out to them,—without re-embarkation, how are you to arrive in England ?"

" Very true, uncle. Pray continue."

" From the accounts given by the seamen who returned, before they had travelled a week they were attacked by a large party of natives, to whose blows and ill-treatment as they passed along they had hitherto submitted; but as in this instance the natives appeared determined to massacre them, they resisted as well as they could, and, being nearly one hundred men in force, succeeded in driving them off, not without receiving many severe wounds. After a few days more travelling, their provisions were all expended, and the seamen began to murmur, and resolved to take care of themselves, and not to be encumbered with women and children. The consequence was, that forty-three of the number separated from the rest, leaving the captain and all the male and female passengers and children (my dear Elizabeth among them), to get on as they could."

" How cruel!"

" Yes! but self-preservation is the first law of nature, and I fear it is in vain to expect that persons not under the influence of religious principles will risk their lives, or submit to much self-denial, for the sake of alleviating the miseries of others. The reason given for this separation was, that it was impossible to procure food for so large a number, and that they would be more likely to obtain sustenance when divided. The party who thus proceeded in advance encountered the most terrible difficulties; they coasted along the seashore because they had no other food than the shellfish found on the rocks; they had continually to cross rivers from a mile to two miles wide; they were kept from their slumbers by the wild beasts which prowled around them, and at length they endured so much from want of water, that their sufferings were extreme. They again subdivided and separated, wandering they hardly knew where, exposed to a burning sun, without clothing and without food. One by one they sat down and were left behind to die, or to be devoured by the wild beasts before they were dead. At last they were reduced to such extremity, that they proposed to cast lots for one to be killed to support the others; they turned back on their route, that they might find the dead bodies of their companions for food. Finally, out of the whole crew, three or four, purblind and staggering from exhaustion, craving for death, arrived at the borders of the colony, where they were kindly received and gradually recovered."

"You now speak of the first party who separated from the captain and the passengers, do you not, uncle?"

"Yes."

"And what became of the captain's party?"

"No tidings were heard of them; their fate was unknown; it was long supposed that they had all perished; for if the sufferings of the seamen, inured to toil and danger, had been so great, what chance was there for helpless women and children? But after some years, there was a report that they had been saved, and were living with the savages. Le Vaillant first mentioned it, and then it died away and was not credited; but since that, the reports of various travellers appear to give confirmation to what Le Vaillant asserted. The paragraph you have now read in the newspaper has again renewed the assertion, and the parties from whom it proceeds are by all accounts worthy of credence. You may imagine, my dear boy, what a pang it gives me when I read these reports,—when I reflect that my poor girl, who was with that party, may at this moment be alive, may have returned to a state of barbarism,—the seeds of faith long dead in her bosom,—now changed to a wild, untutored savage, knowing no God."

"But, my dear uncle, allowing that my aunt is alive, she was not so young at the time of the wreck as to forget entirely what she had been taught."

"That is possible; but then her condition must be still more painful, or rather I should say must have been, for probably she is dead long before this, or if not dead, she must be a woman advanced in life; indeed, as you may observe in the account given by the traveller in the paragraph you have read, it speaks only of the *descendants* of those who were lost in the *Grosvenor*. The idea of my grandchildren having returned to a state of barbarism is painful enough; I wish it were possible that I could discover the truth, for it is the uncertainty which so much distresses me. I have but a few years to live, Alexander; I am a very old man, as you know, and may be summoned to-morrow or to-night, for we know not what a day may bring forth. If I were only certain that my child had died, miserable as her death must have been, it would be happiness, to the idea that she was one of those whose descendants they

9

speak of. If you knew how for the last thirty years this has preyed upon my mind, you would comprehend my anxiety on this account; but God's will be done. Do not let me detain you longer, Alexander; 1 should prefer being alone."

Alexander, at this intimation, took the proffered hand of his grand-uncle in a reverential and feeling manner, and, without saying any more, quitted the room.

CHAPTER II

Alexander's reflections—His plan—Sir Charles opposes it—His unwilling consent—Alexander's departure.

THE conversation which he had had with his grand-uncle made a very forcible impression upon Alexander Wilmot; it occasioned him to pass a very sleepless night, and he remained till nearly four o'clock turning it over in his mind. The loss of the *Grosvenor* Indiaman had occurred long before he was born; he was acquainted with the outline of what had taken place, and had been told, when a child, that a relation of his family had perished; but although the narrative had, at the time, made some impression upon his young mind, he had seldom, if ever, heard it spoken of since, and may have been said to have almost forgotten it. He was therefore not a little surprised when he found how great an influence it had upon his grand-uncle, who had never mentioned it to him before; indeed it had escaped Alexander's memory that it was his grand-uncle's only surviving daughter who had been lost in the vessel.

Alexander Wilmot was warmly attached to the old gentleman; indeed he would have been very ungrateful if he had not been, for it was impossible that any one could have been treated with more kindness and liberality than he was by Sir Charles. It was but the week before, that he had expressed a wish to travel on the continent, and Sir Charles had immediately given his consent that he should remain abroad, if he pleased, for two years. When he approved, however, of Alexander's plans, he had made a

10

remark as to his own age and infirmity, an' the probable chance that they might not meet again in .nis world ; and this remark of his grand-uncle left such an impression upon Alexander, that he almost repented having made the request, and had been ever since in a state of indecision as to whether he should avail himself of his grand-uncle's . kindness and disregard of self shown toward him in thus having granted his permission.

The conversation with Sir Charles had brought up a new idea in his mind ; he had witnessed the anxiety and longing which his good old relation had shown about the fate of his daughter ; he had heard from his own lips how long the ignorance of her fate had preyed upon his mind, and that to be satisfied on this point was the one thing wanting to enable the old man to die happy,—to permit him to say with sincerity, " Lord, now lettest Thou Thy servant depart in peace." Why, then, should he not go to discover the truth ? It would not, perhaps, occupy him so long as the two years of travelling on the continent, which had been consented to by his grand-uncle, and, instead of travelling for his own pleasure, he might be the means of satisfying the mind and quieting the anxiety of one who had been so kind to him. Indeed, he should actually prefer a journey into the interior of Africa to a mere sojourn of some time on the continent ; the very peril and danger, the anticipation of distress and hardship, were pleasing to his high and courageous mind, and before he fell asleep Alexander had made up his mind that he would propose the expedition, and if he could obtain his uncle's permission would proceed upon it forthwith. Having come to this resolution, he fell fast asleep and dreamed away, till eight o'clock in the morning, that he was hunting elephants and having hand-to-hand conflicts with every variety of beast with which he had peopled Africa in his fancy. When he was called up in the morning, he found his determination of the night before rather strengthened than otherwise, and accordingly, after breakfast was over, he opened the subject.

" My dear sir," said he to Sir Charles, " you were kind enough to give me your permission to travel on the continent for two years."

" I did do so, Alexander ; it is natural at your age that

11

you should wish to see the world, and you have my full permission. When do you think of starting?"

"That depends upon circumstances, sir, and I must be altogether guided by you; to tell you the truth, I do not think that one sees much of the world by following in the beaten track made by so many of our countrymen."

"There I agree with you; in the present high state of civilisation there will be found little or no difference in the manners and customs of people; in the courts, none; very little in the best society, in which you will of course mix; and not so very much as people may imagine among the mass of population; but the scenery of the countries and the remains of ancient times are still interesting, and will afford pleasure; it must be your own reflections and comments upon what you see which must make it profitable; most people, however, travel from the love of change added to the love of excitement."

"I grant it, sir, and I do not mean to say but that I should receive much pleasure from a continental tour; perhaps I may add that I should derive more profit if I were to delay it till I am a little older and a little wiser; do you not think so?"

"I certainly do, Alexander. What then? do you propose remaining in England for the present?—if so, I am sure it is on my account, and I am very grateful to you for your sacrifice."

"If you wish it, sir, I will undoubtedly remain in England; at all events, if I do not go elsewhere. I have abandoned my continental tour for the present; but I have another proposal to make, which I hope will meet with your approbation."

"Why, my dear Alexander, on what expedition would you now proceed? Do you wish to visit the United States or South America?"

"No, sir; I wish to make a voyage of still more interest— I wish to go to Africa,—that is, to embark for the Cape of Good Hope, and from thence proceed to the northward, to ascertain, if possible, what now is a source of sad disquiet to you, the actual fate of those who were wrecked in the *Grosvenor*, and have not since been heard of with any degree of certainty."

Sir Charles was for a time silent. He pressed his hands

to his forehead; at last he removed them, and said,—"I cannot, much as I wish it, no,—I cannot consent, my dear boy; the danger will be too great. You must not risk your life. It is very kind of you—very kind; but no, it must not be."

"Indeed, sir, I think, on reflection you will alter your mind. As for danger—what danger can there be when missionaries are permitted to form their stations, and reside uninjured among the very savages who were so hostile when the *Grosvenor* was lost? The country, which was then a desert, is now inhabited by Europeans, within 200 miles of the very spot where the *Grosvenor* was wrecked. The continual emigration since the Cape has fallen under British government, and the zeal of those who have braved all dangers to make known the Word of God to the heathen and idolater, have in forty years made such an alteration, that I see no more danger in the mission which I propose than I do in a visit to Naples; and as for time, I have every reason to expect that I shall be back sooner than in the two years which you have proposed for my stay on the continent."

"But if some accident were to happen to you, I should never forgive myself for having given my consent, and the few days that are left to me would be rendered miserable."

"My dear sir, we are in the hands of God; and (shortsighted as we are) in running away from danger, as often run into it. What we call an accident, the fall of a brick or a stone, the upsetting of a vehicle, anything trivial or seemingly improbable, may summon us away when we least expect it: 'In the midst of life we are in death, and that death I may meet by staying in this country, which I might have avoided by going on this expedition. Difficulties may arise, and some danger there may be, I admit; but when prepared to encounter both, we are more safe than when, in fancied security, we are taken unawares. Do not, I entreat you, sir, refuse me this favour; I have considered well, and shall be most unhappy if I am not permitted to obtain the information for you which you have so much at heart. Let my travels be of some advantage to you as well as to myself. Do not refuse, I entreat you."

"You are a good boy, Alexander, and your kindness makes me still more unwilling to part with you. I hardly know what to say. Let us drop the subject for the present; we will talk of it to-morrow or next day. I must have time for reflection."

Alexander Wilmot did not fail to renew his entreaties on the following day, but could not gain Sir Charles's consent. He was not, however, discouraged. He had taken from the library all the works he could find relative to Southern Africa, and continually enforcing his arguments by quotations from various authors, all tending to prove that he might travel through the country without much risk, if he took proper precautions, his grand-uncle's objections grew daily more feeble, and at last Sir Charles gave his unwilling consent. In the meantime, the books which Alexander had read had produced a great effect upon him. When he first proposed the mission, it was more from a feeling of gratitude toward his old relative than any other, but now he was most anxious to go on his own account. The narratives of combats with wild beasts, the quantity and variety of game to be found, and the continual excitement which would be kept up, inflamed his imagination and his love of field sports, and he earnestly requested to be permitted to depart immediately, pointing out to Sir Charles that the sooner he went away, the sooner he would be back again. This last argument was not without its weight, and Alexander was allowed to make every preparation for his journey. Inquiries were made, and a passage secured on board of a free-trader which was to touch at the Cape, and in six weeks from the time that the subject had been brought up, Alexander Wilmot took leave of his grand-uncle.

"May God bless you, sir, and keep you well till my return," said Alexander, pressing his hand.

"May the Lord protect you, my dear boy, and allow you to return and close my eyes," replied Sir Charles, with much emotion.

Before night Alexander Wilmot was in London, from thence he hastened down to Portsmouth to embark. The next day, the *Surprise* weighed anchor and ran through the Needles, and before the night closed in was well down the Channel, standing before the wind, with studding sails below and aloft.

CHAPTER III

*Alexander's melancholy—Finds a friend—Sea-sickness— Mr.
Fairburn—The passengers—Conversations—The Cape—Mr.
Fairburn's account of the treatment of the Hottentots by the
Dutch.*

A MELANCHOLY feeling clouded the features of Alexander Wilmot as, on the following morning, the vessel, under a heavy press of sail, was fast leaving the shores of his native country. He remained on the poop of the vessel with his eyes fixed upon the land, which every moment became more indistinct. His thoughts may easily be imagined. Shall I ever see that land again? Shall I ever return, or shall my bones remain in Africa, perhaps not even buried, but bleaching in the desert? And if I do return, shall I find my old relation still alive, or called away, loaded as he is with years, to the silent tomb? We are in the hands of a gracious God. His will be done.

Alexander turned away, as the land had at last become no longer visible, and found a young man of about his own age standing close to him, and apparently as much lost in reverie as he had been. As in turning round Alexander brushed against him, he thought it right to apologise for the unintentional act, and this occasioned a conversation.

"I believe, sir," said the other party, who was a tall, spare, slight-built man, with a dark complexion, "that we were both indulging in similar thoughts as we took leave of our native shores. Every Englishman does the same, and indeed every true lover of his country, let the country be what it will. We find the feeling as strong in the savage as in the enlightened; it is universal. Indeed, we may fairly say that it extends lower—down to the brute species, from their love of localities."

"Very true, sir," replied Alexander; "but with brutes, as you say, it is merely the love of locality; with men, I trust, the feeling is more generous and noble."

"So it ought to be, or else why are we so much more nobly

15

endowed? This is not your first voyage, I presume?" continued the stranger.

"Indeed, it is," said Alexander; "I never was out of England, or on board of a vessel, before yesterday."

"I should have imagined otherwise," remarked his companion; "the other passengers are all suffering from sea-sickness, while you and I only are on the deck. I presumed, therefore, that you had been afloat before."

"I did feel very giddy yesterday evening," observed Alexander, "but this morning I have no unpleasant sensation whatever. I believe that some people do not suffer at sea."

"A very few; but it appears that you are one of those most fortunate, for by experience I know how painful and distressing the sickness is for some time. Breakfast will soon be ready; do you think that you can eat any?"

"Yes, a little—not much; a cup of tea or coffee," replied Alexander; "but I cannot say that I have my usual appetite. What bird is that which skims along the water?"

"It is the *procellarius*, as we naturalists call it, but in English, the stormy petrel; its presence denotes rough weather coming on."

"Then I wish it had not made its appearance," said Alexander, laughing; "for with rough weather, there will of course be more motion in the vessel, and I feel the motion too much already."

"I think if you eat your breakfast (although without appetite), and keep on deck, you may get over any further indisposition," replied the stranger.

"Have we many passengers on board?"

"No; nine or ten, which is considered a small number, at least by the captain, who was complaining of his ill-luck. They are mostly females and children. There is a Cape gentleman who has long resided in the colony, and is now returning there. I have had some conversation with him, and he appears a very intelligent person. But here is the steward coming aft, to let us know that breakfast is ready."

The person who had thus conversed with Alexander Wilmot was a Mr. Swinton, who, as he had accidentally observed, was a naturalist; he was a person of some independent property, whose ardour for science had induced him

16

to engage in no profession, being perfectly satisfied with his income, which was sufficient for his wants and to enable him to follow up his favourite study. He was now on his passage to the Cape of Good Hope, with no other object than to examine the natural productions of that country, and to prosecute his researches in science there, to a greater extent than had hitherto been practicable.

Before they had arrived at Madeira, at which island the ship remained three days to take in wine and fresh provisions, a great intimacy had been established between Alexander and Mr. Swinton, although as yet neither knew the cause of the other's voyage to the Cape; they were both too delicate to make the inquiry, and waited till the other should of his own accord impart his reasons.

We have mentioned that there were other passengers, one of whom was a gentleman who resided in Cape Town, and who held a lucrative situation under the government. He was an elderly gentleman, of about sixty years of age, of a very benign and prepossessing appearance; and it so happened that Alexander found out, on looking over his letters of introduction when at anchor at Madeira, that he possessed one to this gentleman. This of course he presented at once, although they were already on intimate terms; and this introduction made Mr. Fairburn (for such was his name) take an immediate interest in his welfare, and also warranted his putting the question, as to what were Alexander's views and intentions in visiting the Cape: for Mr. Fairburn knew from the letter that he was heir to Sir Charles Wilmot, and therefore that he was not likely to be going out as a speculator or emigrant.

It hardly need be said that Alexander made no hesitation in confiding to one who could so materially assist him in the object of his voyage.

The other passengers were three young ladies bound to their friends in India, and a lady returning with her two marriageable daughters to rejoin her husband, who was a colonel in the Bengal army. They were all pleasant people, the young ladies very lively, and on the whole the cabin of the *Surprise* contained a very agreeable party; and soon after they left Madeira, they had fine weather, smooth water, and everything that could make a voyage endurable.

The awnings were spread, chairs brought up, and the major portion of the day was spent upon the quarter-deck and poop of the vessel, which for many days had been running down before the trade-winds, intending to make Rio, and there lay in a supply of fresh provisions for the remainder of her voyage.

One morning, as Alexander and Mr. Fairburn were sitting together, Alexander observed—

"You have passed many years at the Cape, Mr. Fairburn, have you not?"

"Yes; I was taken prisoner when returning from India, and remained a year in Cape Town during the time that it was in the hands of the Dutch; I was about to be sent home as a prisoner to Holland, and was embarked on board one of the vessels in Saldanha Bay, when they were attacked by the English. Afterwards, when the English captured the Cape, from my long residence in, and knowledge of the country, I was offered a situation, which I accepted: the colony was restored to the Dutch, and I came home. On its second capture I was again appointed, and have been there almost ever since."

"Then you are well acquainted with the history of the colony?"

"I am, certainly, and if you wish it, shall be happy to give you a short account of it."

"It will give me the greatest pleasure, for I must acknowledge that I know but little, and *that* I have gleaned from the travels which I have run through very hastily."

"I think it was in the year 1652 that the Dutch decided upon making a settlement at the Cape. The aborigines, or natives, who inhabited that part of the country about Cape Town, were the Hottentots, a mild, inoffensive people, living wholly upon the produce of their cattle; they were not agriculturists, but possessed large herds of cattle, sheep and goats, which ranged the extensive pastures of the country. The history of the founding of one colony is, I fear, the history of most, if not all—commencing in doing all that is possible to obtain the goodwill of the people until a firm footing has been obtained in the land, and then treating them with barbarity and injustice.

"The Hottentots, won over by kindness and presents,

thought it of little consequence that strangers should possess a small portion of their extensive territory, and willingly consented that the settlement should be made. They, for the first time in their lives, tasted what proved the cause of their ruin and subsequent slavery—tobacco and strong liquors. These two poisons, offered gratuitously till the poor Hottentots had acquired a passion for them, then became an object of barter—a pipe of tobacco or a glass of brandy was the price of an ox; and thus daily were the colonists becoming enriched, and the Hottentots poor.

"The colony rapidly increased, until it was so strong, that the governor made no ceremony of seizing upon such land as the government wished to retain or to give away; and the Hottentots soon discovered that not only their cattle, but the means of feeding them, were taken from them. Eventually, they were stripped of everything except their passion for tobacco and spirits, which they could not get rid of. Unwilling to leave the land of their forefathers, and seeing no other way of procuring the means of intoxication which they coveted, they sold themselves and their services to the white colonists, content to take care of those herds which had once been their own, and to lead them out to pasture on the very lands which had once been their birthright."

"Did they then become slaves?" inquired Alexander.

"No; although much worse treated, they never were slaves, and I wish to point that out; but they became a sort of feudal property of the Dutch, compelled to hire themselves out, and to work for them upon nominal wages, which they seldom or never received, and liable to every species of harsh treatment and cruelty, for which they could obtain no redress. Yet still they were not bought and sold as were the slaves which were subsequently introduced into the colony from the east coast of Africa and Madagascar. The position of the slave was, in my opinion, infinitely superior, merely from the self-interest of the owner, who would not kill or risk the life of a creature for whom he had paid two or three hundred rix-dollars; whereas, the Dutch boors, or planters, thought little of the life of a Hottentot. If the cattle were to be watched where lions were plentiful, it was not a slave who had charge of them, but a Hottentot, as he

19

had cost nothing, and the planter could procure another. In short, the life of a Hottentot was considered as of no value, and there is no denying that they were shot by their masters or employers upon the most trifling offence."

" How dreadful! but did the Dutch government suffer this ? "

" They could not well help it, and therefore were compelled to wink at it; the criminals were beyond its reach. But now I will proceed to give you some further insight, by describing the Dutch boors, or planters, who usurped and stood in the shoes of the poor Hottentots.

" The Dutch government seized upon all the land belonging to the Hottentots, and gave it away in grants to their own countrymen, who now became herdsmen, and possessed of a large quantity of cattle ; they also cultivated the ground to a certain extent round about their habitations. As the colony increased, so did the demand for land, until the whole of the country that was worth having was disposed of as far as to the country of the Caffres, a fine, warlike race, of whom we will speak hereafter. It must not, however, be supposed that the whole of the Hottentot tribes became serfs to the soil. Some few drove away their cattle to the northward, out of reach of the Dutch, to the borders of the Caffre land ; others, deprived of their property, left the plains, and took to the mountains, living by the chase and by plunder. This portion were termed boshmen, or bushmen, and have still retained that appellation: living in extreme destitution, sleeping in caves, constantly in a state of starvation, they soon dwindled down to a very diminutive race, and have continued so ever since.

" The Dutch boors, or planters, who lived in the interior and far away from Cape Town, had many enemies to contend with : they had the various beasts of the forest, from the lion to the jackal, which devastated their flocks and herds, and also these bushmen, who lived upon plunder. Continually in danger, they were never without their muskets in their hands, and they and their descendants became an athletic, powerful, and bulky race, courageous, and skilled in the use of firearms, but at the same time cruel and avaricious to the highest degree. The absolute power they possessed over the slaves and Hottentots demoralised them, and made them tyrannical and bloodthirsty. At too great a distance from the seat of government for its power to reach them, they defied it and knew no law but their own imperious wills, acknowledging no authority,—guilty of every crime openly, and careless of detection."

" I certainly have read of great cruelty on the part of these Dutch boors, but I had no idea of the extent to which it was carried."

"The origin was in that greatest of all curses, slavery; nothing demoralises so much. These boors had been brought up with the idea that a Hottentot, a bushman, or a Caffre were but as the mere brutes of the field, and they have treated them as such. They would be startled at the idea of murdering a white man, but they will execute wholesale slaughter among these poor natives, and think they have committed no crime. But the ladies are coming up, and we shall be interrupted, so I will not task your patience any more to-day. I shall therefore conclude what I may term part the first of my little history of the Cape colony."

CHAPTER IV

Natural history discussed—Mr. Swinton's enthusiasm—Further history of the Cape—Dutch barbarity—Alexander's indignation.

ALEXANDER WILMOT was too much pleased with Mr. Swinton not to cultivate his acquaintance, and they soon became very intimate. The conversation often turned upon Mr. Swinton's favourite study, that of natural history.

" I confess myself wholly ignorant of the subject," observed Alexander one day, "though I feel that it must be interesting to those who study it; indeed, when I have walked through the museums, I have often wished that I had some one near who could explain to me what I wished to know and was puzzled about. But it appears to me that the study of natural history is such an immense undertaking if you comprehend all its branches. Let me see,—there is botany, mineralogy, and geology—these are included, are they not?"

"Most certainly," replied Mr. Swinton, laughing; "and perhaps the three most interesting branches. Then you have zoology, or the study of animals, ornithology for birds, entomology for insects, conchology for shells, ichthyology for fishes; all very hard names, and enough to frighten a young beginner. But I can assure you, a knowledge of these subjects, to an extent sufficient to create interest and afford continual amusement, is very easily acquired."

"'The proper study of mankind is man,' says the poet," observed Alexander, smiling.

"Poets deal in fiction, Mr. Wilmot," replied Mr. Swinton; "to study man is only to study his inconsistencies and his aberrations from the right path, which the freewill permitted to him induces him to follow; but in the study of nature, you witness the directing power of the Almighty, who guides with an unerring hand, and who has so wonderfully apportioned out to all animals the means of their providing for themselves. Not only the external, but the inward structure of animals, shows such variety and ingenuity to surmount all difficulties, and to afford them all the enjoyment their nature is capable of, that after every examination you rise with increased astonishment and admiration at the condescension and goodness of the Master Hand, thus to calculate and provide for the necessities of the smallest insect; and you are compelled to exclaim with the Psalmist, 'O God, how manifold are Thy works; in wisdom hast Thou made them all!'"

"You certainly do put the study in a new and most pleasurable light," replied Alexander.

"The more you search into nature, the more wonderful do you find her secrets, and, by the aid of chemistry, we are continually making new discoveries. Observe, Mr. Wilmot," said Swinton, picking up a straw which had been blown by the wind on the quarter-deck, "do you consider that there is any analogy between this straw and the flint in the lock of that gun?"

"Certainly, I should imagine them as opposite particles of nature as well might be."

"Such is not the case. This piece of wheat-straw contains more than sixty per cent. of silica or flint in its composition; so that, although a vegetable, it is nearly two-thirds composed

22

of the hardest mineral substance we know of. You would scarcely believe that the fibres of the root of this plant were capable of dissolving, feeding upon, and digesting such a hard substance; but so it is."

"It is very wonderful."

"It is, but it is not a solitary instance; the phosphate of lime, which is the chief component part of the bones of animals, is equally sought by plants, dissolved in the same manner, and taken into their bodies; barley and oats have about thirty per cent. of it in their composition, and most woods and plants have more or less."

"I am less surprised at that than I am with the flint, which appears almost incomprehensible."

"Nothing is impossible with God; there is a rush in Holland which contains much more silex than the wheat-straw, and it is employed by the Dutch to polish wood and brass, on that very account. We know but little yet, but we do know that mineral substances are found in the composition of most living animals, if not all; indeed, the colouring-matter of the blood is an oxide and phosphate of iron."

"I can now understand why you are so enthusiastic in the science, Mr. Swinton, and I regret much that the short time which will be occupied in the remainder of our voyage will not enable me to profit as I should wish by your conversation; for when we arrive at the Cape, I fear our pursuits will lead us different ways."

"I presume they will, for I am about to penetrate as far as possible into the interior of the country," replied Mr. Swinton, "which of course is not your intention."

"Indeed, but it is," replied Alexander; "I am about to do the same, although perhaps not in the same direction. May I ask your intended route, if not too inquisitive?"

"Not at all; I can hardly say myself. I shall be guided by the protection may fall in with. Africa is a wide field for science, and I can hardly go anywhere without being well rewarded for my journey; and I will say, that should it meet both our views, I should very glad if we were to travel in company."

Mr. Fairburn, who had come on deck, had been standing close to them at the latter portion of the conversation, and made the observation—

"I think it would be a very good plan if Mr. Swinton would venture to go where you are bound, Mr. Wilmot, but you can talk of that another day, when you have been longer together. There is nothing that requires more deliberation than the choice of a travelling companion; any serious imperfection of temper may make a journey very miserable. Now, Wilmot, if you are tired of natural history, and wish to change it for the painful history of human nature, I am ready to continue my observations."

"With great pleasure, sir."

"I hope you have no objection to my reaping the benefit also?" said Mr. Swinton.

"Oh, most certainly not," replied Mr. Fairburn, "although I fear you will not gain much information, as you have been at the Cape before. In a former conversation with Mr. Wilmot I have pointed out the manner in which the Cape was first settled, and how the settlers had gradually reduced the original possessors of the land to a state of serfdom; I will now continue.

"The Dutch boors, as they increased their wealth in cattle, required more pasture, and were now occupying the whole of the land south of the Caffre country: the Caffres are wild, courageous savages, whose wealth consists chiefly in cattle, but in some points they may be considered superior to the Hottentots.

"The weapon of the Hottentot may be said to be the bow and arrow, but the Caffre scorns this warfare, or indeed any treachery; his weapons are his assegai, or spear, and his shield; he fights openly and bravely. The Caffres also cultivate their land to a certain extent, and are more cleanly and civilised. The boors on the Caffre frontier were often plundered by the bushmen, and perhaps occasionally by some few of the Caffres who were in a lawless state on the frontier; but if any complaint was made to the Caffre chiefs, every redress in their power was given: this, however, did not suit the Dutch boors.

"They had entered the Caffre country, and had perceived that the Caffres possessed large herds of cattle, and their avarice pointed out to them how much easier it would be to grow rich by taking the cattle of the Caffres than by rearing them themselves. If the bushmen stole a few head of cattle,

24

complaints were immediately forwarded to Cape Town, and permission asked to raise a force, and recover them from the Caffres.

"The force raised was termed a *Commando,* and was composed of all the Dutch boors and their servants, well armed and mounted ; these would make an incursion into the Caffre territory, and because a few head of cattle had been stolen by parties unknown, they would pour down upon the Caffres, who had but their assegais to oppose to destructive firearms, set the kraals or villages in flames, murder indiscriminately man, woman, and child, and carry off, by way of indemnification for some trifling loss, perhaps some twenty thousand head of cattle belonging to the Caffres.

"The Caffres, naturally indignant at such outrage and robbery, made attacks upon the boors to recover the cattle, but with this difference between the Christian boor and the untutored savage : the boors murdered women and children wantonly, the Caffres never harmed them, and did not even kill men, if they could obtain possession of their property without bloodshed."

"But how could the Dutch government permit such atrocities ? "

"The representations made to the government were believed, and the order was given in consequence. It is true that afterwards the government attempted to put a stop to these horrors, but the boors were beyond their control ; and in one instance in which the home government had insisted that punishment should be inflicted for some more than common outrage on the part of the boors, the Cape governor returned for answer, that he could not venture to do as they wished, as the system was so extensive and so common, that all the principal people in the colony were implicated, and would have to be punished.

"Such was therefore the condition of the colony at the time that it fell into the possession of the English—the Hottentots serfs to the land, and treated as the beasts of the field ; the slave-trader supplying slaves ; and continual war carried on between the boors and the Caffres."

"I trust that our government soon put an end to such barbarous iniquities."

"That was not so easy ; the frontier boors rose in arms

against the English government, and the Hottentots, **who**
had been so long patient, now fled and joined the Caffres.
These people made a combined attack upon the frontier boors,
burned their houses to the ground, carried off the cattle, and
possessed themselves of their arms and ammunition. The
boors rallied in great force; another combat took place, in
which the Hottentots and Caffres were victorious, killing the
leader of the boors, and pursuing them with great slaughter,
till they were stopped by the advance of the English troops.
But I cannot dwell long upon this period of the Cape history;
these wars continued until the natives, throwing themselves
upon the protection of the English, were induced to lay down
their arms, and the Hottentots to return to their former masters.
The colony was then given up to the Dutch, and remained
with them until the year 1806, when it was finally annexed
to the British empire. The Dutch had not learned wisdom
from what had occurred; they treated the Hottentots worse
than before, maiming them and even murdering them in
their resentment, and appeared to defy the British government; but a change was soon to take place."

"Not before it was necessary, at all events," said
Alexander.

"It was by the missionaries chiefly that this change was
brought about; they had penetrated into the interior, and
saw with their own eyes the system of cruelty and rapine
that was carried on; they wrote home accounts, which were
credited, and which produced a great alteration. To the
astonishment and indignation of the boors, law was introduced
where it had always been set at defiance; they were told
that the life of a Hottentot was as important in the eye of
God, and in the eye of the law, as that of a Dutch boor, and
that the government would hold it as such. Thus was the
first blow struck; but another and a heavier was soon to
fall upon those who had so long sported with the lives of
their fellow-creatures. The press was called to the aid of
the Hottentot, and a work published by a missionary roused
the attention of the public at home to their situation. Their
cause was pleaded in the House of Commons, and the Hottentot was emancipated for ever."

"Thank God!" exclaimed Alexander; "my blood has
been boiling at the description which you have been giving.

Now, when I hear that the poor Hottentot is a free man, it will cool down again."

"Perhaps it will be as well to leave off just now, Mr. Wilmot," said Mr. Fairburn; "we will renew our conversation to-morrow, if wind and weather permit, as the seamen say."

CHAPTER V

Aquatic birds—Guano—Mr. Fairburn's narrative continued—Stuurman—Mokanna—The attack—Failure of the Caffres.

THE next day the ship was off Rio, and immediately sent her boats for provisions and supplies; the passengers did not land, as the captain stated that he would not stay an hour longer than was necessary, and on the second evening after their arrival they again made sail for the Cape.

The gulls were flying in numbers astern of the ship, darting down and seizing everything edible which was thrown overboard, and the conversation turned upon aquatic birds.

"What difference is there in the feathers of aquatic birds and others?" inquired Alexander; "a hen, or any land bird, if it falls into the water, is drowned as soon as its feathers are saturated with the water."

"There is, I believe, no difference in the feathers of the birds," replied Mr. Swinton; "but all aquatic birds are provided with a small reservoir, containing oil, with which they anoint their feathers, which renders them waterproof. If you will watch a duck pluming and dressing itself, you will find it continually turns its bill round to the end of its back, just above the insertion of the tail; it is to procure this oil, which, as it dresses its feathers that they may carefully overlap each other, it smears upon them so as to render them impenetrable to the water; but this requires frequent renewal, or the duck would be drowned as well as the hen."

"How long can a sea-bird remain at sea?"

"I should think not very long, although it has been supposed otherwise; but we do not know so much of the habits of these birds as of others."

"Can they remain long under water?"

"The greater portion of them cannot; ducks and that class, for instance. Divers can remain some time; but the birds that remain the longest under water are the semi-aquatic, whose feet are only half-webbed. I have watched the common English water-hen for many minutes walking along at the bottom of a stream, apparently as much in its element as if on shore, pecking and feeding as it walked."

"You say that aquatic birds cannot remain long at sea,—where do they go to?"

"They resort to the uninhabited islands over the globe, rocks that always remain above water, and the unfrequented shores of Africa and elsewhere; there they congregate to breed and bring up their young. I have seen twenty or thirty acres of land completely covered with these birds or their nests, wedged together as close as they could sit. Every year they resort to the same spot, which has probably been their domicile for centuries,—I might say since the creation. They make no nests, but merely scrape so as to form a shallow hole to deposit their eggs. The consequence of their always resorting to the same spot is that, from the voidings of the birds and the remains of fish brought to feed the young, a deposit is made over the whole surface, a fraction of an inch every year, which by degrees increases until it is sometimes twenty or thirty feet deep, if not more, and the lower portion becomes almost as hard as rock. The deposit is termed guano, and has, from time immemorial, been used by the Peruvians and Chilians as manure for the land; it is very powerful, as it contains most of the essential salts, such as ammonia, phosphates, &c., which are required for agriculture. Within these last few years samples have been brought to England, and as the quantities must be inexhaustible, when they are sought for and found, no doubt it may one day become a valuable article of our carrying trade. Here comes Mr. Fairburn; I hope he intends to continue his notices of the Cape settlement."

"They have interested me very much, I must confess; he appears well acquainted with the colony."

"He has had the advantage of a long residence, and during that time an insight into all the public documents: this you may be certain of, that he knows more than he will tell."

SCENES IN AFRICA

As soon as Mr. Fairburn joined them, Alexander requested him to continue his narrative, which he did as follows.

"You must not suppose, Mr. Wilmot, that because the English had now possession of the colony, everything went right; governors who are appointed to the control of a colony require to be there some time before they can see with their own eyes; they must, from their want of information, fall into the hands of some interested party or another, who will sway their councils. Thus it was at the Cape.

"It is true that much good had already been done by the abolition of slavery and the emancipation of the Hottentot; but this was effected, not by the colonial government, but by the representations of the missionaries and an influential and benevolent party at home. The prejudices against the Hottentots, and particularly the Caffres, still existed, and were imbibed by the colonial authorities. Commandoes, or, as they should be more properly termed, marauding parties, were still sent out, and the Caffre was continually oppressed, and, in defiance of the government orders, little justice could be obtained for the Hottentot, although his situation was somewhat improved.

"I will give one instance to show how the rights of the Hottentots were respected by the Cape authorities in 1810, —previous to the emancipation, it is true, but still at a time when the position of the Hottentots and their sufferings had been strenuously pressed upon the colonial authorities by the government at home.

"When the conduct of the Dutch boors had roused the Caffres and Hottentots to war, there were three brothers by the name of Stuurman, Hottentots, who were the leaders. Peace was at length restored, which was chiefly effected by the exertions of these men, who retired peaceably with their own kraal to Algoa Bay; and the government, being then Dutch, appointed Stuurman as captain of the kraal. This independent horde of Hottentots gave great offence to the Dutch boors,—the more so as the three brothers had been the leaders of the Hottentots in the former insurrection. For seven years they could find no complaint to make against them, until at last two of his Hottentots, who had engaged to serve a boor for a certain time, went back to the kraal at the expiration of the term, against the wish

of the boor, who would have detained them; the boor
went and demanded them back, but Stuurman refused to
give them up; upon which, although justice was clearly on
the side of the Hottentots, an armed force was despatched
to the kraal. Stuurman still refused to surrender the men,
and the armed men retired, for they knew the courage of
the Hottentots, and were afraid to attack them.

"By treachery they gained possession of Stuurman and
one of his brothers (the other having been killed hunting
the buffalo), and sent them to Cape Town, from whence,
against all justice, they were sent as prisoners to Robben
Island, where malefactors are confined. They made their
escape and returned to Caffreland. Three years afterwards,
Stuurman, anxious to see his family, returned to the colony
without permission. He was discovered and apprehended,
and sent as a convict to New South Wales; for the government was at that time English.

"Such was the fate of the first Hottentot who stood up
for the rights of his countrymen, and such was the conduct
of the English colonial government; so you will observe, Mr.
Wilmot, that although the strides of cruelty and oppression
are most rapid, the return to even-handed justice is equally
slow. Eventually the gross injustice to this man was acknowledged, for an order from the home government was procured
for his liberation and return; but it was too late,—Stuurman
had died a convict.

"I have mentioned this circumstance, as it will prepare
you for a similar act of injustice to the Caffres. When the
colony was in possession of the Dutch there was a space of
about thirty thousand square miles between the colonial
boundary (that is, the land formerly possessed by the Hottentots) and the Great Fish River. This extent of thirty
thousand square miles belonged to the Caffres, and was the
site of continual skirmishing and marauding between the
Dutch boors and the Caffres.

"In 1811 it was resolved by the colonial government that
the Caffres should be driven from this territory, and confined
to the other side of the Great Fish River. This was an act
of injustice and great hardship, and was proceeded in with
extreme cruelty, the Caffres being obliged to leave all their
crops, and turned out with great and unnecessary slaughter.

"It may be proper, however, to state the causes which led to this Caffre war with the English. At this time the colonial governor had entered into negotiations with a Caffre chief of the name of Gaika. He was a chief of a portion of the Caffres, but not the principal chief, and although the English treated with him as such, the Caffres would not acknowledge his authority. This is a very frequent error committed in our intercourse with savage nations, who are as pertinacious of their rights as the monarchs of Europe. The error on our part was soon discovered, but the government was too proud to acknowledge it.

"It so happened that the other Caffre chiefs formed a powerful confederacy against Gaika, who, trusting to the support of the English, had treated them with great arrogance. They fought and conquered him, carrying off, as usual, his cattle. As this was a war between the Caffres, and confined to their own land, we certainly had no business to interfere ; but the colonial government thought otherwise, and an expedition was prepared.

"The Caffres sent forward messengers declaring their wish to remain at peace with the English, but refusing to submit to Gaika, who was only a secondary chief, and whom they had conquered. No regard was paid to this remonstrance ; the English troops were sent forward, the Caffres attacked in their hamlets, slaughtered or driven into the woods, 23,000 head of cattle taken from them, of which 9000 were given to Gaika, and the rest distributed to the Dutch boors, or sold to defray part of the expenses of the expedition.

"Deprived of their means of subsistence by the capture of their cattle, the Caffres were rendered furious and reckless, and no sooner had the expedition returned, than they commenced hostilities. They poured into the frontier districts, captured several detached military forts, drove the Dutch boors from the Zurweld, or neutral territory, and killed a great many of our soldiers and of the Dutch boors. All the country was overrun as far as the vicinity of Algoa Bay, and nothing could at first check their progress."

"Why, it really does not appear that the colonial government, when in our hands, was more considerate than when it was held by the Dutch," replied Alexander.

"Not much, I fear," said Mr. Fairburn.

31

"The councils of the Caffre chiefs were at that time much influenced by a most remarkable personage of the name of Mokanna. In the colony he was usually known by the sobriquet of 'Links,' or the left-handed. He was not a chief, but had by his superior intellect obtained great power. He gave himself out to be a prophet, and certainly showed quite as much skill as ever did Mahommed or any other false prophet. He had often visited Cape Town, and had made himself master of all that he could acquire of European knowledge.

"This man, by his influence, his superior eloquence, and his pretended revelations from heaven, was now looked up to by the whole Caffre nation; and he promised the chiefs, if they would implicitly obey his orders, he would lead them to victory, and that he would drive the English into the ocean. He resolved upon the bold measure of making an attack upon Graham's Town, and marched an army of between nine and ten thousand men to the forest bordering on the Great Fish River.

"According to the custom of the Caffres, who never use surprise or ambush on great occasions, they sent a message to the commandant of Graham's Town, stating that they would breakfast with him the next morning. The commandant, who had supposed the message to be a mere bravado, was very ill prepared when on the following morning he perceived, to his great astonishment, the whole force of the Caffres on the heights above the town.

"Had the Caffres advanced in the night, there is no doubt but that they would have had possession of the place, and that with the greatest ease. There were about 350 regular troops and a small force of Hottentots in Graham's Town, and fortunately a few field-pieces. The Caffres rushed to the assault, and for some time were not to be checked; they went up to the very muzzles of the field-pieces, and broke their spears off short, to decide the battle by a hand-to-hand conflict.

"At this critical moment, the field-pieces opened their fire of grape and canister, and the front ranks of the Caffres were mowed down like grass. After several rallyings under Mokanna, the Caffres gave way and fled. About 1400 of the bravest remained on the field of battle, and as many more perished from their wounds before they could regain their country. Mokanna, after using every exertion, accompanied the Caffre army in their flight."

"It certainly was a bold attempt on the part of the Caffres, and showed Mokanna to be a great man even in the failure."

"It was so unprecedented an attempt, that the colonial government were dreadfully alarmed, and turned out their whole force of militia as well as of regular troops. The Caffre country was again overrun, the inhabitants destroyed, without distinction of age or sex, their hamlets fired, cattle driven away, and when they fled to the thickets, they were bombarded with shells and Congreve rockets. Mokanna and the principal chiefs were denounced as outlaws, and the inhabitants threatened with utter extermination if they did not deliver them up dead or alive. Although driven to despair, and perishing from want, not a single Caffre was to be found who would earn the high reward offered for the surrender of the chiefs."

"The more I hear of them, the more I admire the Caffres," observed Alexander Wilmot; "and I may add— but never mind, pray go on."

"I think I could supply the words which you have checked, Mr. Wilmot, but I will proceed, or dinner will be announced before I have finished this portion of my history."

"The course adopted by Mokanna under these circumstances was such as will raise him much higher in your estimation. As he found that his countrymen were to be massacred until he and the other chiefs were delivered up, dead or alive, he resolved to surrender himself as a hostage for his country. He sent a message to say that he would do so, and the next day, with a calm magnanimity that would have done honour to a Roman patriot, he came, unattended, to the English camp. His words were 'People say that I have occasioned this war: let me see if my delivering myself up will restore peace to my country.' The commanding officer, to whom he surrendered himself, immediately forwarded him as a prisoner to the colony."

"What became of him?"

"Of that hereafter; but I wish here to give you the

33 c

substance of a speech made by one of Mokanna's head men, who came after Mokanna's surrender into the English camp. I am told that the imperfect notes taken of it afford but a very faint idea of its eloquence; at all events, the speech gives a very correct view of the treatment which the Caffres received from our hands.

"'This war,' said he, 'British chiefs, is an unjust one, for you are trying to extirpate a people whom you have forced to take up arms. When our fathers and the fathers of the boors first settled on the Zurweld, they dwelt together in peace. Their flocks grazed the same hills, their herdsmen smoked out of the same pipe; they were brothers until the herds of the Amakosa (Caffres) increased so much as to make the hearts of the Dutch boors sore. What those covetous men could not get from our fathers for old buttons, they took by force. Our fathers were men; they loved their cattle; their wives and children lived upon milk; they fought for their property; they began to hate the colonists, who coveted their all, and aimed at their destruction.

"'Now their kraals and our fathers' kraals were separate. The boors made commandoes for our fathers; our fathers drove them out of the Zurweld, and we dwelt there because we had conquered it; there we married wives; there our children were born; the white men hated us, but could not drive us away; when there was war, we plundered you; when there was peace, some of our bad people stole; but our chiefs forbade it.

"'We lived in peace; some bad people stole, perhaps; but the nation was quiet; Gaika stole; his chiefs stole; you sent him copper; you sent him beads; you sent him horses, on which he rode to steal more; to *us* you only sent *commandoes*. We quarrelled with Gaika about grass;—no business of yours; you send a commando; you take our last cow; you leave only a few calves, which die for want, and so do our children; you give half the spoil to Gaika; half you kept yourselves.

"'Without milk; our corn destroyed; we saw our wives and children perish; we followed, therefore, the tracks of our cattle into the colony; we plundered, and we fought for our lives; we found you weak, and we destroyed your soldiers; we saw that we were strong, and we attacked your

34

headquarters, and if we had succeeded, our right was good, for you began the war; we failed, and you are here.

"'We wish for peace; we wish to rest in our huts; we wish to get milk for our children; our wives wish to till the land; but your troops cover the plains, and swarm in the thickets, where they cannot distinguish the men from the women, and shoot *all*. You wish us to submit to Gaika; that man's face is fair to you, but his heart is false; leave him to himself; make peace with us: let him fight for himself; and we shall not call upon you for help; set Mokanna at liberty, and all our chiefs will make peace with you at any time you fix; but if you still make war, you may indeed kill the last man of us, but Gaika shall not rule over the followers of those who think him a woman.'

"If eloquence consists (as it does not in the English House of Commons) in saying much in few words, I know no speech more comprehensive of the facts and arguments of a case than the above. I am sorry to say it had no effect in altering the destination of Mokanna, or of obtaining any relief for his countrymen, who were still called upon to deliver up the other chiefs *outlawed* by the government."

"I before remarked the absurdity of that expression," said Mr. Swinton; "we outlaw a member of our own society and belonging to our own country; but to *outlaw* the chiefs of another country is something too absurd; I fear the English language is not much studied at the Cape."

"At all events, every attempt made to obtain possession of these *outlawed* chiefs was unavailing. After plundering the country of all that could be found in it, leaving devastation and misery behind, the expedition returned without obtaining their object, but with the satisfaction of knowing that by taking away 30,000 more cattle, they left thousands of women and children to die of starvation. But I must leave off now. The results of the war, and the fate of Mokanna, shall be the subject of another meeting."

"We are much obliged to you, Mr. Fairburn, for the interesting narrative you have given us. It is, however, to be hoped that you will have no more such painful errors and injustice to dwell upon."

"As I before observed, Mr. Wilmot, it requires time for prejudice and falsehood to be overthrown; and until they are mastered, it cannot be expected that justice can be administered. The colonial government had to contend with the whole white population of the colony who rose up in arms against them, considering, from long habit, that any interference with their assumed despotism over the natives was an infringement of their rights.

"You must also recollect how weak was the power of the colonial government for a long time, and how impossible it was to exert that power over such an extensive country; and to give you some idea of this, I will state what was the reply of some of the Dutch boors to the traveller La Vaillant, when the latter expressed his opinion that the government should interfere with an armed force to put an end to their cruelty and oppression.

"'Are you aware,' said they, 'what would be the result of such an attempt?—Assembling all in an instant, we would massacre half of the soldiers, salt their flesh, and send it back by those we might spare, with threats to do the same thing to those who should be bold enough to appear among us afterwards.' It is not an easy task for any government to deal with such a set of people, Mr. Wilmot."

"I grant it," replied Alexander; "and the conviction makes me more anxious to know what has been since done."

CHAPTER VI

Sharks—Their cowardice—Attack on one by Neptune—Divers' Dangers—Mr. Fairburn continues his story—Mokanna's fate—Disturbances among the Caffre tribes.

THE following morning the wind was very slight, and before noon it fell calm. Two sharks of a large size came under the stern of the vessel, and the sailors were soon very busy trying to hook one of them; but they refused the bait, which was a piece of salt pork, and after an hour they quitted the vessel and disappeared, much to the disappointment of both passengers and ship's company, the former wishing very much to see the sharks caught, and the latter very anxious to cut them up and fry them for their suppers.

"I thought that sharks always took the bait," observed Alexander.

"Not always, as you have now seen," replied Mr. Swinton; "all depends upon whether they are hungry or not. In some harbours where there are plenty of fish, I have seen sharks in hundreds, which not only refused any bait, but would not attempt to seize a man if he was in the water; but I am surprised at these Atlantic sharks refusing the bait, I must confess, for they are generally very ravenous, as are, indeed, all the sharks which are found in the ocean."

"I can tell you, sir, why they refused the bait," said the boatswain of the vessel, who was standing by; "it's because we are now on the track of the Brazilian slavers, and they have been well fed lately, depend upon it."

"I should not be surprised if you were correct in your idea," replied Mr. Swinton.

"There are many varieties of sharks, are there not?" inquired Wilmot.

"Yes, a great many; the fiercest, however, and the largest kind is the one which has just left us, and is termed the white shark; it ranges the whole Atlantic Ocean, but is seldom found far to the northward, as it prefers the tropics: it is, however, to be seen in the Mediterranean, in the Gulf of Lyons, and is there remarkably fierce. In the English Channel you find the blue shark, which is seldom dangerous; there is also a very large-sized but harmless shark found in the north seas, which the whalers frequent. Then there is the spotted or tiger-shark, which is very savage, although it does not grow to a large size; the hammer-headed shark, so called from the peculiar formation of its head; and the ground shark, perhaps the most dangerous of all, as it lies at the bottom and rises under you without giving you notice of its approach. I believe I have now mentioned the principal varieties."

"If a man was to fall overboard and a shark was nigh, what would be the best plan to act upon—that is, if there would be any chance of escape from such a brute?"

"The best plan, and I have seen it acted upon with success, is, if you can swim well, to throw yourself on your back and splash as much as you can with your feet, and halloo as loud as you can. A shark is a cowardly animal, and noise will drive it away.

"When I went out two or three years ago, I had a New-foundland dog, which was accustomed to leap into the water from almost any height. I was very partial to him, and you may imagine my annoyance when, one day, as we were becalmed along the Western Islands, and a large shark came up alongside, the dog, at once perceiving it, plunged off the taffrail to seize it, swimming towards the shark, and barking as loud as he could. I fully expected that the monster would have despatched him in a moment; but to my surprise the shark was frightened and swam away, followed by the dog, until the boat that was lowered down picked him up."

"I don't think the shark could have been very hungry."

"Probably not; at all events, I should not have liked to have been in Neptune's place. I think the most peculiar plan of escaping from sharks is that pursued by the Cingalese divers, and often with success."

"Tell me, if you please."

"The divers who go down for the pearl oysters off Ceylon generally drop from a boat, and descend in ten or twelve fathoms of water before they come to the bed of pearl oysters, which is upon a bank of mud: it often happens that when they are down, the sharks make for them, and I hardly need say that these poor fellows are constantly on the watch, looking in every direction while they are filling their baskets. If they perceive a shark making for them, their only chance is to stir up the mud on the bank as fast as they can, which prevents the animal from distinguishing them, and under the cover of the clouded water they regain the surface; nevertheless, it does not always answer, and many are taken off every year."

"A lady, proud of her pearl necklace, little thinks how many poor fellows may have been torn to pieces to obtain for her such an ornament."

"Very true; and when we consider how many pearl-fisheries may have taken place, and how many divers may have been destroyed, before a string of fine pearls can be obtained, we might almost say that every pearl on the neck-lace has cost the life of a human creature."

"How are the pearls disposed of, and who are the proprietors?"

"The government are the proprietors of the fishery, I believe; but whether they farm it out yearly, or not, I cannot tell; but this I know, that as the pearl oysters are taken, they are landed unopened and packed upon the beach in squares of a certain dimension. When the fishing is over for the season, these square lots of pearl oysters are put up to auction, and sold to the highest bidder, of course 'contents unknown;' so that it becomes a species of lottery; the purchaser may not find a single pearl in his lot, or he may find two or three, which will realise twenty times the price which he has paid for his lot."

"It is, then, a lottery from beginning to end; the poor divers' lottery is shark or no shark; the purchasers', pearls or no pearls. But Mr. Fairburn is coming up the ladder, and I am anxious to know what was the fate of Mokanna."

Mr. Fairburn, who had come on deck on purpose to continue the narrative, took his seat by his two fellow-passengers and went on as follows:—

"I stated that Mokanna had been forwarded to the Cape. You must have perceived that his only crime was that of fighting for his native land against civilised invaders; but this was a deep crime in the eyes of the colonial government; he was immediately thrown into the common gaol, and finally was condemned to be imprisoned for life on Robben Island, a place appropriated for the detention of convicted felons and other malefactors, who there work in irons at the slate-quarries."

"May I ask, where is Robben Island?"

"It is an island a few miles from the mainland, close to Table Bay, upon which the Cape Town is built.

"Mokanna remained there about a year, when, having made his intentions known to some Caffres who were confined there with him, he contrived out of the iron hoops of the casks to make some weapons like cutlasses, with which he armed his followers, rose upon the guard and overpowered them; he then seized the boat, and with his Caffres made for the mainland. Unfortunately, in attempting to disembark upon the rocks of the mainland, the boat was upset in the surf, which was very violent; Mokanna clung some time to a rock, but at last was washed off, and thus perished the unfortunate leader of the Caffres."

"Poor fellow," said Alexander; "he deserved a better fate and a more generous enemy; but did the war continue?"

"No; it ended in a manner every way worthy of that in which it was begun. You recollect that the war was commenced to support Gaika, our selected chief of the Caffres, against the real chiefs. The Caffres had before been compelled to give up their territories on our side of the Fish River; the colonial government now insisted upon their retiring still further, that is, beyond the Keisi and Chumi rivers, by which 3000 more square miles were added to the colonial territory. This was exacted, in order that there might be a neutral ground to separate the Caffres and the Dutch boors, and put an end to further robberies on either side. The strangest part of the story is, that this territory was not taken away from the Caffre chiefs, against whom we had made war, but from Gaika, our ally, to support whom we had entered into the war."

"Well, it was even-handed—not justice, but injustice, at all events."

"Exactly so; and so thought Gaika, for when speaking of the protection he received from the colonial government, he said, ' But when I look upon the large extent of fine country which has been taken from me, I am compelled to say, that, although protected, I am *rather oppressed* by my *protectors.*'"

"Unjust as was the mode of obtaining the neutral ground, I must say that it appears to me to have been a good policy to put one between the parties."

"I grant it; but what was the conduct of the colonial government? This neutral ground was afterwards given away in large tracts to the Dutch boors, so as again to bring them into contact with the Caffres."

"Is it possible?"

"Yes; to men who had always been opposed to the English government, who had twice risen in rebellion against them, and who had tried to bring in the Caffres to destroy the colony. Neither were the commandoes, or excursions against the Caffres, put an end to: Makomo, the son of

Gaika, our late ally, has, I hear, been the party now attacked. I trust, however, that we may soon have affairs going on in a more favourable and reputable manner; indeed, I am sure that, now the government at home have been put in possession of the facts, such will be the case.

"I have now given you a very brief insight into the history of the Cape up to the present time. There are many points which I have passed over, not wishing to diverge from a straightforward narrative; but upon any questions you may wish to ask, I shall be most happy to give you all the information in my power. I cannot, however, dismiss the subject without making one remark, which is, that it is principally, if not wholly, to the missionaries, to their exertions and to their representations, that what good has been done is to be attributed. They are entitled to the greatest credit and the warmest praise; and great as has been the misrule of this colony for many years, it would have been much greater and much more disgraceful, if it had not been for their efforts. Another very important alteration has been taking place in the colony, which will eventually be productive of much good. I refer to the British immigration, which every year becomes more extensive; and as soon as the British population exceeds and masters that of the old Dutch planters and boors, we shall have better feeling in the colony. Do not suppose that all the Dutch boors are such as those whose conduct I have been obliged to point out. There are many worthy men, although but few educated or enlightened.

"I know from my own observation that the failings and prejudices against the natives are fast fading away, and that lately the law has been able to hold its ground, and has been supported by the people inhabiting the districts. The Dutch, with all their prejudices and all their vices, will soon be swallowed up by the inundation of English settlers, and will gradually be so incorporated and intermingled by marriage that no distinction will be known. Time, however, is required for such consolidation and cementation; that time is arriving fast, and the future prospects of the Cape are as cheering, as you may think, from my narrative, they have been disheartening and gloomy."

"I trust in God that such will be the case," replied Alexander. "If this wind continues, in a few days we shall be at the Cape, and I shall be most anxious to hear how affairs are going on."

"I had a letter just before I set out from England, stating that the Zulu tribes, to the northward of the Caffres, are in an unquiet state; and as you must pass near to these tribes on your journey, I am anxious to know the truth. At all events, Chaka is dead; he was murdered about two years back by his own relations."

"Who was Chaka?" inquired Alexander.

"That I have yet to tell you; at present we have only got as far as the Caffres, who are immediately on our frontiers."

CHAPTER VII

Mr. Swinton agrees to accompany Alexander—Land, ho!—Cape Town—Major Henderson—He joins the party—Begum—Chaka's history.

THE wind continued fair, and the vessel rapidly approached the Cape. Alexander, who had contracted a great friendship for Mr. Swinton, had made known to him the cause of his intended journey into the interior, and the latter volunteered, if his company would not be displeasing, to accompany Alexander on his tedious and somewhat perilous expedition.

Alexander gladly accepted the offer, and requested Mr. Swinton would put himself to no expense, as he had unlimited command of money from his grand-uncle, and Mr. Swinton's joining the caravan would make no difference in his arrangements.

After it had been agreed that they should travel together, the continued subject of discourse and discussion was the nature of the outfit, the number of waggons, their equipment, the stores, the number of horses and oxen which should be provided; and they were busy every day adding to their memoranda as to what it would be advisable to procure for their journey.

Mr. Fairburn often joined in the discussion, and gave

42

his advice, but told them that, when they arrived at Cape Town, he might be more useful to them. Alexander, who, as we have before observed, was a keen hunter, and very partial to horses and dogs, promised himself much pleasure in the chase of the wild animals on their journey, and congratulated himself upon being so well provided with guns and rifles, which he had brought with him, more with the idea that they might be required for self-defence than for sport.

At last, "Land, ho!" was cried out by the man who was at the mast-head in the morning watch, and soon afterwards the flat top of Table Mountain was distinctly visible from the deck. The *Surprise*, running before a fresh breeze, soon neared the land, so that the objects on it might be perceived with a glass. At noon they were well in for the bay, and before three o'clock the *Surprise* was brought to an anchor between two other merchant vessels, which were filling up their home cargoes.

After a three months' voyage passengers are rather anxious to get on shore; and therefore before night all were landed, and Alexander found himself comfortably domiciled in one of the best houses in Cape Town; for Mr. Fairburn had, during the passage, requested Alexander to take up his abode with him.

Tired with the excitement of the day, he was not sorry to go to bed early, and he did not forget to return his thanks to Him who had preserved him through the perils of the voyage.

The next morning Mr. Fairburn said to Alexander—

"Mr. Wilmot, I should recommend you for the first ten days to think nothing about your journey. Amuse yourself with seeing the public gardens, and other things worthy of inspection; or, if it pleases you, you can make the ascent of Table Mountain with your friend Swinton. At all events, do just as you please; you will find my people attentive, and ready to obey your orders. You know the hours of meals; consider yourself at home, and as much master here as I am. As you may well imagine, after so long an absence, I have much to attend to in my official capacity, and I think it will be a week or ten days before I shall be comfortably reseated in my office, and have things going on smoothly, as they

43

ought to do. You must therefore excuse me, if I am not quite so attentive a host at first as I should wish to be. One thing only I recommend you to do at present, which is, to accompany me this afternoon to Government House, that I may introduce you to the governor. It is just as well to get over that mark of respect which is due to him, and then you will be your own master."

Alexander replied with many thanks. He was graciously received by the governor, who promised him every assistance in his power in the prosecution of his journey. Having received an invitation for dinner on the following day, Alexander bowed and took his leave in company with Mr. Fairburn.

On the following day Alexander was visited by Mr. Swinton. Mr. Swinton was accompanied by a major in the Bengal Cavalry, whom he introduced as Major Henderson. He had arrived a few days before from Calcutta, having obtained leave of absence for the recovery of his health, after a smart jungle-fever, which had nearly proved fatal. The voyage, however, had completely reinstated him, and he appeared full of life and spirits. They walked together to the Company's gardens, in which were a few lions, and some other Cape animals, and the discourse naturally turned upon them. Major Henderson described the hunting in India, especially the tiger-hunting on elephants, to which he was very partial; and Alexander soon discovered that he was talking to one who was passionately fond of the sport. After a long conversation they parted, mutually pleased with each other. A day or two afterwards Mr. Swinton, who had been talking about their intended journey with Alexander, said to him —

"You must not be surprised at the off-hand and unceremonious way we have in the colonies. People meeting abroad, even Englishmen occasionally, throw aside much ceremony. I mention this, because Major Henderson intends to call this afternoon, and propose joining our party into the interior. I do not know much of him, but I have heard much said in his favour, and it is easy to see by his manners and address that he is a gentleman. Of course, when he stated his intention, I could do nothing but refer him to you, which I did. What do you think, Wilmot?"

44

"I think very well of Major Henderson, and I consider that, as the journey must be one of some peril, the more Europeans the better, especially when we can find one who is used to danger from his profession, and also to dangerous hunting, which we must also expect. So far from not wishing him to join us, I consider him a most valuable acquisition, and am delighted at the idea."

"Well, I am glad to hear you say so, for I agree with you. He is hunting mad, that is certain, and I hear, a most remarkable shot. I think with you he will be an acquisition. It appears that it was his intention to have gone into the interior, even if he went by himself; and he has two Arab horses which he brought with him from India with that view."

"If you see him before he comes, you may say that you have stated his wishes to me, and that I am quite delighted at his joining our party,—it being perfectly understood that he is at no expense for anything connected with the outfit."

"I will tell him so," replied Swinton; "and I think the sooner we begin to collect what is necessary the better. We must have Major Henderson in our councils. Depend upon it, he will be very useful and very active; so, for the present, farewell."

Mr. Swinton and Major Henderson called together that afternoon, and the latter, as soon as he was admitted into the party, began to talk over the plans and preparations.

"My suite is not very large," said he; "I have two horses and two dogs, a Parsee servant, and a Cape baboon. I should like to take the latter with us as well as my servant. My servant, because he is a good cook; and my monkey, because, if we are hard put to it, she will show us what we may eat and what we may not; there is no taster like a monkey. Besides, she is young and full of tricks, and I like something to amuse me."

"The baboons have another good quality: they give notice of danger sooner than a dog," observed Swinton. "I think, Wilmot, we must admit the monkey into the party."

"I shall be most happy," replied Alexander, laughing; "pray give her my compliments, Major Henderson, and say how happy I shall be."

45

"I call her Begum," said Major Henderson; "because she is so like the old Begum princess whom I was once attending, when in India with my troop, as guard of honour. You must look out for some good horses, Mr. Wilmot; you will want a great many, and if you do not wish them to have sore backs, don't let the Hottentots ride them."

"We have been discussing the point, Major Henderson, as to whether it will not be better to go round in a vessel to Algoa Bay, complete our equipment there, and make that our starting place."

"If you do, you will save a long journey by land, and find yourself not very far from what I understand are the best of hunting-grounds, near to the country of the Vaal River."

The topics then dwelt upon were what articles they should procure in Cape Town, and what they should defer providing themselves with until their arrival at Algoa Bay. They agreed to provide all their stores at Cape Town, and as many good horses as they could select; but the waggons and oxen, and the hiring of Hottentots, they put off until they arrived at Algoa Bay.

Mr. Fairburn was now more at leisure, and Alexander had more of his society. One evening after dinner Mr. Fairburn had opened a map of the country, to give Alexander some information relative to his projected journey. He pointed out to him the track which appeared most advisable through the Caffre country, and then observed that it was difficult to give any advice as to his proceedings after he had passed this country, governed by Hinza, as everything would depend upon circumstances.

"Do you know anything of the country beyond?"

"Not much; we know that it was overrun by the Zulus, the tribe of which Chaka was the chief; and last year our troops went to the assistance of the Caffres, who were attacked by another tribe from the northward, called the Mantatees. These were dispersed by our troops with immense slaughter. The Zulu country, you perceive, is on the east side of the great chain of mountains, and to the northward of Port Natal. The Mantatees came from the west side of the mountains, in about the same parallel of latitude. It is impossible to say what may be going on at present, or what may take place before you arrive at your destination, as these northern irruptions are continual."

"You promised me the history of that person, Chaka."

"You shall have it now: he was the king of the Zulu nation—I hardly know what to call him. He was the Nero and the Napoleon of Africa; a monster in cruelty and crime, yet a great warrior and conqueror. He commenced his career by murdering his relatives to obtain the sovereignty. As soon as he had succeeded, he murdered all those whom he thought inimical to him, and who had been friends to his relatives."

"But are the Zulus Caffres?"

"No; but there are many races to the northward which we consider as Caffre races. You may have observed, in the history of the world, that the migrations of the human race are generally from the north to the south: so it appears to have been in Africa. Some convulsion among the northern tribes, probably a pressure from excessive population, had driven the Zulus to the southward, and they came down like an inundation, sweeping before them all the tribes that fell in their path. Chaka's force consisted of nearly 100,000 warriors, of whom 15,000 were always in attendance to execute his orders. In every country which he overran he spared neither age nor sex; it was one indiscriminate slaughter."

"What a monster!"

"He ruled by terror, and it is incredible that his orders met with such implicit obedience. To make his army invincible, he remodelled it, divided it into companies, distinguished by the colour of their shields, and forbade them to use any other weapon but a short stabbing-spear, so that they always fought at close quarters. He weeded his army by picking out 1000 of his veteran warriors, who had gained his victories, and putting them to death. Any regiment sent out to battle, if they were defeated, were instantly destroyed on their return; it was, therefore, victory or death with them; and the death was most cruel, being that of impalement. Well he was surnamed 'the Bloody.'"

"Yes, indeed."

"His tyranny over his own people was dreadful. On one occasion a child annoyed him; he ordered it to be killed; but the child ran among seventy or eighty other children, and could not be distinguished, so he ordered the whole to be put to death. He murdered two or three hundred of his wives in one day. At the slightest suspicion he would order out his chiefs to execution, and no one knew when his turn might come. His will was law: every one trembled and obeyed. To enter into a detail of all his cruelties would fill volumes; it will be sufficient to mention the last act of his life. His mother died, and he declared that she had perished by witchcraft. Hundreds and hundreds were impaled, and, at last, tired of these slow proceedings, he ordered out his army to an indiscriminate slaughter over the whole country, which lasted for fourteen days."

"How horrible!"

"He was a demon who revelled in blood; but his own turn came at last. He was murdered by his brother Dingaam, who knew that he was about to be sacrificed; and thus perished the bloody Chaka. His brother Dingaam is now on the Zulu throne, and appears inclined to be quiet. There is another great warrior chief named Moselekatsee, who revolted from Chaka, and who is much such another character; but our accounts of these people are vague at present, and require time to corroborate their correctness. You will have to act and decide when you arrive there, and must be guided by circumstances. With the caravan you propose to travel with, I think there will not be much danger; and if there is, you must retreat. The favour of these despots is easily to be obtained by judicious presents, which of course you will not be unprovided with. I have ordered your letters to the authorities to be made out, and you will have the governor's signature to them. When do you propose to start?"

"We shall be ready in a few days, and have only to find a vessel going to Algoa Bay."

"You will be asked to take charge of several articles which are to be sent to the missionary station which you will pass on your way. I presume you have no objection?"

"Certainly not; they deserve every encouragement, and any kindness and attention I can show them will give me great pleasure."

Alexander received many proposals from different parties who wished to join the expedition, but they were all civilly declined. In a few days a vessel arrived, which was about to go round to the settlement at Algoa Bay. Their stores, horses, and dogs, not forgetting Begum the baboon, were all embarked, and, taking leave of Mr. Fairburn and the governor, Alexander, Major Henderson, and Mr. Swinton embarked, and on the evening of the fourth day found themselves safe at anchor in company with ten or twelve vessels which were lying in Algoa Bay.

CHAPTER VIII

Night in Algoa Bay—The Major meets Maxwell—Preparations to start—The caravan—Description of it—The departure.

THE vessels which lay at anchor in Algoa Bay had just arrived from England, with a numerous collection of emigrants, who, to improve their fortunes, had left their native land to settle in this country. Many had landed, but the greater proportion were still on board of the vessels. The debarkation was rapidly going on, and the whole bay was covered with boats landing with people and stores, or returning for more. The wind blowing from the westward, there was no surf on the beach; the sun was bright and warm, and the scene was busy and interesting; but night came on, and the panorama was closed in.

Alexander and his companions remained on the deck of their vessel till an undisturbed silence reigned where but an hour or two before all was noise and bustle. The stars, so beautiful in the southern climes, shone out in cloudless brilliancy; the waters of the bay were smooth as glass, and reflected them so clearly that they might have fancied that there was a heaven beneath as well as above them. The land presented a dark opaque mass, the mountains in the distance appearing as if they were close to them, and rising precipitately from the shore. All was of one sombre hue, except where the lights in the houses in the town twinkled here and there, announcing that some had not yet dismissed their worldly cares, and sought repose from the labours of the day. Yet all was silent, except occasionally the barking

49   D

of a dog, or the voice of the sentry in Fort Frederick, announcing that "all was well."

"What a gathering in a small space of so many people with so many different histories, so many causes for leaving their native land, and with so many different fortunes in store for them, must there be on board of an emigrant ship," observed Mr. Swinton.

"Yet all united in one feeling, and instigated by the same desire,—that of independence, and, if possible, of wealth," rejoined Major Henderson.

"Of that there can be no doubt," said Alexander; "but it must be almost like beginning a new life; so many ties broken by the vast ocean which has separated them; new interests usurping the place of old ones; all novelty and adventure to look forward to; new scenes added to new hopes and new fears; but we must not remain too long even to watch these beautiful heavens, for we must rise at daylight, so I shall set the example, and wish you both good-night."

At daylight on the following morning the long-boat was hoisted out, and the horses safely conveyed on shore. After a hasty breakfast, Alexander and his two companions landed, to see if it were possible to obtain any roof under which they could shelter themselves; but the number of emigrants who had arrived put that out of the question, every house and every bed being engaged. This was a great disappointment, as they had no wish to return on board and re-occupy the confined space which had been allotted to them.

Having found accommodation for their horses, they proceeded to examine the town and resume their search for lodgings. The streets presented a bustling and animated scene; waggons with goods, or returning empty with their long teams of oxen; horses, sheep, and other animals, just landed; loud talking; busy inquirers; running to and fro of men; Hottentots busy with the gods, or smoking their pipes in idle survey; crates and boxes, and packages of all descriptions, mixed up with agricultural implements and ironware, lining each side of the road, upon which were seated wives and daughters watching the property, and children looking round with astonishment, or playing or crying.

50

Further out of the town were to be seen tents pitched by the emigrants, who had provided themselves with such necessaries before they had quitted England, and who were bivouacking like so many gipsies, independent of lodgings and their attendant expenses, and cooking their own provisions in kettles or frying-pans. As Alexander perceived the latter, he said, "At all events, we have found lodgings now; I never thought of that."

"How do you mean?"

"I have two tents in the luggage I brought from Cape Town; we must get them on shore, and do as these people have done."

"Bravo! I am glad to hear that," replied Major Henderson; "anything better than remaining on board to be nibbled by the cockroaches. Shall we return at once?"

"By all means," said Mr. Swinton; "we have but to get our mattresses and a few other articles."

"Leave my man to do all that," said the Major; "he is used to it. In India we almost live in tents when up the country. But here comes one that I should know;—Maxwell, I believe?"

"Even so, my dear Henderson," replied the military officer who had been thus addressed; "why, what brought you here?—surely you are not a settler?"

"No; I am here because I am not a settler," replied Henderson, laughing; "I am always on the move; I am merely on my own way with my two friends here to shoot a hippopotamus. Allow me to introduce Mr. Wilmot and Mr. Swinton. But I see you are on duty; are you in the fort?"

"Yes; I came from Somerset about a month back. Can I be of any use to you?"

"That depends upon circumstances; we are now going on board for our tents, to pitch them on the hill there, as we can get no lodgings."

"Well, I cannot offer you beds in the fort, but I think if you were to pitch your tents outside the fort, on the glacis, you would be better than on the hill; your baggage would be safer, and I should be more able to render you any attention or assistance you may require."

"An excellent idea; if it were only on account of the

51

baggage," replied Henderson; "we accept your offer with pleasure."

"Well then, get them on shore as quick as you can; my men will soon have them out for you and assist in transporting your luggage; and don't distress yourself about your dinner, I will contrive to have something cooked for you."

"A friend in need is a friend indeed, my good fellow. We will accept your offers as freely as they are made: so farewell for an hour or so."

As they parted with Captain Maxwell, Henderson observed, "That was a lucky meeting, for we shall now get on well. Maxwell is an excellent fellow, and he will be very useful to us in making our purchases, as he knows the people and the country: and our luggage will be safe from all pilferers."

"It is indeed very fortunate," replied Mr. Swinton. "Where did you know Captain Maxwell?"

"In India. We have often been out hunting tigers together. How he would like to be of our party; but that is of course impossible."

"But how shall we manage about our living, Major Henderson?" observed Wilmot; "it will never do to quarter ourselves on your friend."

"Of course not; we should soon eat up his pay and allowance. No, no; we will find dinners, and he will help us to cook them first and eat them afterwards."

"Upon such terms, I shall gladly take up my quarters in the fort," replied Alexander. "But which is our boat out of all these?"

"Here, sir," cried out one of the sailors; "come along, my lads," continued he to the other men, who were lounging about, and who all jumped into the boat, which pushed off, and they were soon on board of the ship.

As the master of the vessel was equally glad to get rid of his passengers and their luggage as they were to leave, the utmost expedition was used by all parties, and in a few hours everything was landed, Begum, the baboon, being perched upon the stores conveyed in the last boat. A party of soldiers sent down by Captain Maxwell assisted the seamen to carry the various packages up to the fort, and before the evening closed in, the tents were pitched, their beds made up, and their baggage safely housed, while they were amusing themselves after dining with Captain Maxwell, leaning on the parapet and watching the passing and repassing of the boats which were unlading the vessels.

As there was little chance of rain in the present season, they lay down on their mattresses in perfect security and comfort, and did not wake up the next morning until breakfast was ready. After breakfast they sallied out with Captain Maxwell to look after waggons and oxen, and as, on the arrival of the emigrants, a number of waggons had been sent down to take them to their destinations, Captain Maxwell soon fell in with some of the Dutch boors of the interior with whom he had been acquainted, and who had come down with their waggons; but previous to making any bargains, Alexander went with Captain Maxwell to the landroost, for whom he had brought a letter from the governor.

This gentleman immediately joined the party, and through his intervention, before night, four excellent waggons with their tilts and canvas coverings, and four span of oxen of fourteen each, were bought and promised to be brought down and delivered up in good order, as soon as they had carried up the freights with which they were charged.

As these waggons could not return under four days, the next object that they had in view was to procure some more horses, and here they met with difficulty; for Major Henderson, who, as an excellent judge of horses, was requested to select them, would not accept of many that were offered. Still they had plenty of time, as the waggons would require fitting out previous to their departure, and this would be a work of some days; and many articles which they had decided to procure at Algoa Bay, instead of the Cape, were now to be sought for and selected.

At the time appointed, the waggons and teams were delivered over and paid for. Carpenters were then engaged, and the waggons were fitted out with lockers all round them, divided off to contain the luggage separate, so that they might be able to obtain in a minute anything that they might require. While this work was proceeding, with the assistance of the landroost, they were engaging Hottentots and other people to join the expedition, some as drivers to the waggons, others as huntsmen, and to perform such duties as might be required of them. Some very steady brave men were selected, but it was impossible to make up the whole force which they wished to take of people of known character; many of them were engaged rather from their appearance, their promises, and the characters they obtained from others or gave themselves, than from any positive knowledge of them. This could not be avoided; and as they had it in their power to dismiss them for bad conduct, it was to be presumed that they could procure others.

It was more than three weeks before everything was ready for their departure, and then the caravan was composed as follows:—

The persons who belonged to it were our three gentlemen; the servant of Major Henderson; eight drivers of the teams of oxen; twelve Hottentot and other hunters (for some of them were of a mixed race); two Hottentots who had charge of the horses, and two others who had charge of a flock of Cape sheep, which were to follow the caravan, and serve as food until they could procure oxen by purchase, or game with their guns: so that the whole force of the party amounted to twenty men: two Hottentot women, wives of the principal men, also accompanied the caravan to wash and assist in cooking.

The animals belonging to the caravan consisted of fifty-six fine oxen, which composed the teams; twelve horses, as Major Henderson could only procure six at Algoa Bay, or they would have purchased more; thirteen dogs of various sizes, and Begum, the baboon, belonging to Major Henderson; to these were to be added the flock of sheep.

The waggons were fitted out as follows, chiefly under the direction of Major Henderson and Mr. Swinton.

The first waggon, which was called Mr. Wilmot's waggon, was fitted up with boxes or lockers all round, and contained all the stores for their own use, such as tea, sugar, coffee, cheeses, hams, tongues, biscuits, soap, and wax candles, wine and spirits in bottles, besides large rolls of tobacco for the Hottentots or presents, and Alexander's clothes; his mattress lay at the bottom of the waggons, between the lockers. The waggon was covered with a double sail-cloth tilt, and with curtains before and behind; the carpenter's tools were also in one of the lockers of this waggon.

The second waggon was called Mr. Swinton's waggon; it was fitted up with lockers in the same way as the other, but it had also a large chest with a great quantity of drawers for insects, bottles of spirits for animals, and everything necessary for preserving them; a ream or two of paper for drying plants, and several other articles, more particularly a medicine-chest well filled, for Mr. Swinton was not unacquainted with surgery and physic. The other lockers were filled with a large quantity of glass beads and cutlery for presents, several hundred pounds of bullets, ready cast, and all the kitchen ware and crockery. It had the same covering as the first, and Mr. Swinton's mattress was at night spread in the middle between the lockers.

The third waggon was called the armoury, or the Major's waggon; it was not fitted up like the two first. The whole bottom of it was occupied with movable chests, and four large casks of spirits, and the Major made up his bed on the top of the chests. In the chests were gunpowder in bottles and a quantity of small shot for present use; tobacco in large rolls; 1 cwt. of snuff; all the heavy tools, spades, shovels, and axes, and a variety of other useful articles.

The tilt frame was much stouter than that of the two other waggons, for the hoops met each other so as to make it solid. It was covered with a tarred sail-cloth so as to be quite waterproof, and under the tilt-frame were suspended all the guns, except the two which Alexander and Mr. Swinton retained in their own waggons in case of emergency. The back and front of this waggon were closed with boards, which were let down and pulled up on hinges, so that it was a little fortress in case of need; and as it could be locked up at any time, the Hottentots were not able to get at the casks of spirits without committing a sort of burglary. Begum was tied up in this waggon at night.

The fourth waggon was called the store waggon, and contained several articles which were not immediately wanted ; such as casks of flour and bags of rice : it also held most of the ammunition, having six casks of gunpowder, a quantity of lead, two coils of rope, iron bars, bags of nails of various sizes, rolls of brass wire, and the two tents, with three chairs and a small table. Like the waggon of Major Henderson, it was covered with waterproof cloth.

Such was the fit-out which was considered necessary for this adventurous expedition, and the crowds who came to see the preparations for the great hunting-party, as it was called, were so great and so annoying that the utmost haste was made to quit the town. At last the waggons were all loaded, the Hottentots collected together from the liquor-shops, their agreements read to them by the landroost, and any departure from their agreements, or any misconduct, threatened with severe punishment.

The horses and oxen were brought in, and the next morning was fixed for their departure. Having taken leave of the landroost and other gentlemen of the town, who had loaded them with civilities, they retired to the fort, and passed the major part of the night with Captain Maxwell; but to avoid the crowd which would have accompanied them, and have impeded their progress, they had resolved to set off before daylight. At two o'clock in the morning the Hottentots were roused up, the oxen yoked, and an hour before daybreak the whole train had quitted the town, and were travelling at a slow pace, lighted only by the brilliant stars of the southern sky.

CHAPTER IX

The plans of the adventurers—Big Adam's bravery—Milius—His refreshments—What his house contained—Speech to the Hottentots—The Bushman boy, Prince Omrah.

THE plans of our travellers had been well digested. They had decided that they would first prosecute the object of their journey by proceeding straight through the Caffre country to the borders of the Undata River, near or whereabout it was reported that the descendants of the whites

56

would be found located; and as soon as Alexander had accomplished his mission, that they would cross the chain of mountains, and return through the Bushmen and the Koranna country. Their reason for making this arrangement was, that throughout the whole of the Caffre country, with the exception of lions and elephants in the forest, and hippopotami in the rivers, there was little or no game to be found, the Caffres having almost wholly destroyed it.

This plan had been suggested by Major Henderson, and had been approved by Alexander and Mr. Swinton,—Alexander being equally desirous as the Major to have plenty of field-sport, and Mr. Swinton anxious to increase his stock and knowledge of the animal kingdom. There was little to be feared in their advance through the Caffre country, as the missionaries had already planted two missions, one at Butterworth and the other at Chumie; and the first of these Alexander had decided upon visiting, and had, in consequence, several packages in his waggon, which had been entrusted to his care.

It was on the 7th of May 1829, that the caravan quitted Algoa Bay for Graham's Town. The weather had been for some weeks fine, the heavy rains having ceased, and the pasturage was now luxuriant; the waggons proceeded at a noiseless pace over the herbage, the sleepy Hottentots not being at all inclined to exert themselves unnecessarily. Alexander, Swinton, and Henderson were on horseback, a little ahead of the first waggon.

"I don't know how you feel," said the Major; "but I feel as if I were a prisoner just released from his chains. I breathe the air of independence and liberty now. After the bustle, and noise, and crowding together of the town, to find ourselves here so quiet and solitary is freedom."

"I had the same feeling," replied Alexander; "this wide-extended plain, of which we cannot yet discern the horizontal edge; these brilliant stars scattered over the heavens, and shining down upon us; no sound to meet our ears but the creaking of the waggon-wheels in the slow and measured pace, is to me delightful. They say man is formed for society, and so he is; but it is very delightful occasionally to be alone."

"Yes; alone as we are," replied Swinton, laughing; "that

is, with a party of thirty people, well armed, in search of adventure. To be clear of the bustle of the town, and no longer cooped up in the fort, is pleasant enough; but, I suspect, to be quite alone in these African wilds would be anything but agreeable."

"Perhaps so."

"Neither would you feel so much at ease if you knew that your chance of to-morrow's dinner was to depend wholly upon what you might procure with your gun. There is a satisfaction in knowing that you have four well-filled waggons behind you."

"I grant that also," replied the Major; "but still there is solitude even with this company, and I feel it."

"A solitary caravan—but grant that there is some difference between that and a solitary individual," rejoined Swinton; "however, we have not come to solitude yet, for we shall find Dutch boors enough between this and Graham's Town."

"I think, Wilmot," observed Henderson, "that I should, if I were you, proceed by slow stages at first, that we may get our men into some kind of order and discipline, and also that we may find out whether there are any who will not suit us; we can discharge them at Graham's Town, and procure others in their place, at the same time that we engage our interpreters and guides."

"I think your plan very good," replied Alexander; "besides, we shall not have our waggons properly laden and arranged until we have been out three or four days."

"One thing is absolutely necessary, which is, to have a guard kept every night," said Swinton; "and there ought to be two men on guard at a time; for one of them is certain to fall asleep, if not both. I know the Hottentots well."

"They will be excellent guards, by your account," said Alexander; "however, the dogs will serve us more faithfully."

"I do not mean my remark to include all Hottentots; some are very faithful, and do their duty; but it comprehends the majority."

"Are they courageous?" inquired Alexander.

"Yes, certainly, they may be considered as a brave race of

58

men; but occasionally there is a poltroon, and, like all cowards, he brags more than the rest."

"I've a strong suspicion that we have one of that kind among our hunters," replied Henderson; "however, it is not fair to prejudge; I may be mistaken."

"I think I know which you refer to, nevertheless," said Alexander; "it is the great fellow that they call Big Adam."

"You have hit upon the man, and to a certain degree corroborated my opinion of him. But the day is dawning, the sun will soon be above those hills."

"When we stop, I will have some grease put to those waggon-wheels," said Alexander.

"I fear it will be of little use," replied the Major; "creak they will. I don't know whether the oxen here are like those in India; but this I know, that the creaking of the carts and hackeries there is fifty times worse than this. The natives never grease the wheels; they say the oxen would not go on if they did not hear the music behind them."

"Besides, the creaking of the wheels will by-and-by be of service; when we are travelling through grass higher than our heads, we shall not be able to stop behind a minute, if we have not the creaking of the wheels to direct us how to follow."

"Well, then, I suppose we must save our grease," said Alexander.

"In a very few days you will be so accustomed to it," said the Major, "that if it were to cease, you would feel the loss of it."

"Well, it may be so; use is second nature; but at present I feel as if the loss would be gain. There is the sun just showing himself above the hill. Shall we halt or go on?"

"Go on for another hour, and the men can thus examine the traces and the waggons by daylight, and then, when we stop, we can remedy any defects."

"Be it so; there is a house, is there not, on the rising ground, as far as you can see?"

"Yes, I think so," replied the Major.

"I know it very well," said Swinton; "it is the farm of

a Dutch boor, Milius, whom we saw at Algoa Bay. I did
not think that we had got on so fast. It is about three
miles off, so it will just be convenient for our breakfast. It
will take us a good hour to arrive there, and then we will
unyoke the oxen. How many have we yoked?"

"Ten to each waggon. The other sixteen are following
with the sheep and horses; they are as relays."

"Let us gallop on," said the Major.

"Agreed," replied the others; and putting spurs to their
horses, they soon arrived at the farmhouse of the Dutch
planter.

They were saluted with the barking and clamour of about
twenty dogs, which brought out one of the young boors, who
drove away the dogs by pelting them with bullock-horns,
and other bones of animals which were strewed about. He
then requested them to dismount. The old boor soon
appeared, and gave them a hearty welcome, handing down
from the shelf a large brandy-bottle, and recommending a
dram, of which he partook himself, stating that it was good
brandy, and made from his own peaches.

Shortly afterwards the wife of the boor made her appearance, and having saluted them, took up her station
at a small table, with the tea apparatus before her.
That refreshing beverage she now poured out for the
visitors, handing a box, with some sugar-candy in it, for
them to put a bit into their mouths, and keep there as
they drank their tea, by way of sweetening it. The old
boor told them he had expected them, as he had been
informed that they were to set out that day; but he had
concluded that they would arrive in the afternoon, and not
so early.

We may as well here give a description of a Dutch
farmer's house at the Cape settlement.

It was a large square building, the wall built up of clay,
and then plastered with a composition made by the boors,
which becomes excessively hard in time; after which it is
whitewashed. The roof was thatched with a hard sort of
rushes, more durable and less likely to catch fire than straw.
There was no ceiling under the roof, but the rafters over-
head were hung with a motley assemblage of the produce of
the chase and farm, as large whips made of rhinoceros-hide,

60

leopard and lion skins, ostrich eggs and feathers, strings of onions, rolls of tobacco, bamboos, &c.

The house contained one large eating-room, a small private room, and two bedrooms. The windows were not glazed, but closed with skins every night. There was no chimney or stove in the house, all the cooking being carried on in a small outhouse.

The furniture was not very considerable : a large table, a few chairs and stools, some iron pots and kettles, a set of Dutch teacups, a teapot, and a brass kettle, with a heater. The large, brass-clasped, family Dutch Bible occupied a small table, at which the mistress of the house presided, and behind her chair were the carcasses of two sheep, suspended from a beam.

Inquiries about the news at the Cape, and details of all the information which our travellers could give, had occupied the time till breakfast was put on the table. It consisted of mutton boiled and stewed, butter, milk, fruits, and good white bread. Before breakfast was over the caravan arrived, and the oxen were unyoked. Our travellers passed away two hours in going over the garden and orchards, and visiting the cattlefolds, and seeing the cows milked. They then yoked the teams, and wishing the old boor a farewell, and thanking him for his hospitality, they resumed their journey.

"Is it always the custom here to receive travellers in this friendly way?" observed Alexander, as they rode away.

"Always," replied Swinton; "there are no inns on the road, and every traveller finds a welcome. It is considered a matter of course."

"Do they never take payment?"

"Never, and it must not be offered; but they will take the value of the corn supplied to your horses, as that is quite another thing. One peculiarity you will observe as you go along, which is, that the Dutch wife is a fixture at the little tea-table all day long. She never leaves it, and the tea is always ready for every traveller who claims their hospitality; it is an odd custom."

"And I presume that occasions the good woman to become so very lusty."

61

"No doubt of it; the whole exercise of the day is from the bedroom to the teapot, and back again," replied Swinton, laughing.

"One would hardly suppose that this apparently good-natured and hospitable people could have been guilty of such cruelty to the natives as Mr. Fairburn represented."

"Many of our virtues and vices are brought prominently forward by circumstances," replied Swinton. "Hospitality in a thinly-inhabited country is universal, and a Dutch boor is hospitable to an excess. Their cruelty to the Hottentots and other natives arises from the prejudices of education: they have from their childhood beheld them treated as slaves, and do not consider them as fellow-creatures. As Mr. Fairburn truly said, nothing demoralises so much, or so hardens the heart of man, as slavery existing and sanctioned by law."

"But are not the Dutch renowned for cruelty and love of money?"

"They have obtained that reputation, and I fear there is some reason for it. They took the lead, it must be remembered, as a commercial nation, more commercial than the Portuguese, whose steps they followed so closely: that this eager pursuit of wealth should create a love of money is but too natural, and to obtain money, men, under the influence of that passion, will stop at nothing. Their cruelties in the East are on record; but the question is, whether the English, who followed the path of the Dutch, would not, had they gone before them, have been guilty of the same crimes to obtain the same ends? The Spaniards were just as cruel in South America, and the Portuguese have not fallen short of them; nay, I doubt if our own countrymen can be acquitted in many instances. The only difference is, that the other nations who preceded them in discoveries had greater temptation, because there were more riches and wealth to be obtained."

"Your remarks are just; well may we say in the Lord's Prayer, 'Lead us not into temptation,' for we are all too frail to withstand it."

At noon they again unyoked, and allowed the cattle to graze for an interval; after which they proceeded till an hour before dark, when they mustered the men, and gave them their several charges and directions. At Alexander's request the Major took this upon himself, and he made a long speech to the Hottentots, stating that it was their intention to reward those who did their duty, and to punish severely those who did not. They then collected wood for the fires, and had their supper,—the first meal which they had taken out of doors. Mahomed, the Parsee servant of Major Henderson, cooked very much to their satisfaction ; and having tied the oxen to the waggons, to accustom them to the practice, more than from any danger to be apprehended, the watch was set to keep up the fires : they then all retired to bed, the gentlemen sleeping in their waggons, and the Hottentots underneath them, or by the sides of the fires which had been lighted.

It will be unnecessary to enter into a detail of the journey to Graham's Town, which was performed without difficulty. They did not arrive there until eight days after their departure from Algoa Bay, as they purposely lost time on the road, that things might find their places. At Graham's Town they received every kindness and attention from the few military who were there and the landroost. Here they dismissed three of the men, who had remained drunk in the liquor-houses during their stay, and hired nine more, who were well recommended ; among these were two perfectly well acquainted with the Caffre language and country ; so that they were serviceable both as interpreters and guides. The day after their arrival, when they were out in the skirts of the town, Mr. Swinton perceived something moving in the bushes. He advanced cautiously, and discovered that it was a poor little Bushman boy, about twelve years old, quite naked, and evidently in a state of starvation, having been left there in a high fever by his people. He was so weak that he could not stand, and Mr. Swinton desired the Hottentot who was with him to lift him up, and carry him to the waggons. Some medicine and good food soon brought the little fellow round again, and he was able to walk about. He showed no disposition to leave them ; indeed he would watch for Mr. Swinton, and follow him as far as he could. The child evidently appeared to feel attachment and gratitude, and when they were about to depart, Mr. Swinton, through the medium of one of the Hottentots who could speak the language, asked him if he would like to stay with them. The answer was in the affirmative, and it was decided that he should accompany them, the Major observing that he would be a very good companion for Begum.

"What name shall we give him?" said Swinton.

"Why, as my baboon is by title a princess, I think we cannot create him less than a prince. Let us call him Omrah."

"Omrah be it then," replied Mr. Swinton, "until we can name him in a more serious way."

So Omrah was put into the waggon, with Begum to amuse him, and our travellers took their departure from Graham's Town.

CHAPTER X

Wild beasts—Insubordination of the Hottentots—Danger from elephants—Their hideous shrieks—Big Adam's terror—Lieutenant Moodie's wonderful escape—Sagacity of the elephant—Intentions of the party.

IT was in the afternoon that they moved from Graham's Town. They had intended to have started earlier, but they found it impossible to collect the Hottentots, who were taking their farewells of their wives and their liquor-shops. As it was, most of them were in a state of intoxication, and it was considered advisable to get them out of the town as soon as possible. Late in the evening they arrived at Hermann's Kraal, a small military fort, where they remained for the night to give the Hottentots an opportunity of recovering from the effects of the liquor. The next morning they again started, and the landscape now changed its aspect, being covered with thick bushes, infested with wild beasts.

A barren and sterile country was soon spread before them, the sun was oppressively hot, and not a sign of water was to be observed in any direction. At last they arrived at a muddy pool, in which elephants had evidently been enjoying themselves, and the oxen and horses were but too glad to do the same. At night they halted as before, having lighted fires to keep off the wild beasts and the elephants.

The following morning they renewed their journey at daylight, and the scene again changed ; they now plunged into the dense forests bordering on the great Fish River, which they forded in safety. The prospects all around were very beautiful, the river smoothly gliding through stupendous mountains and precipices, with verdant valleys on each side of its banks. In the afternoon they arrived at Fort Wiltshire, the outermost defence of the colony, situated on the banks of the Keiskamma. English troops were stationed there, to prevent any marauding parties from passing the river, or to intercept them on their return with their booty.

As this was the last spot where they could expect to see any of their countrymen, and they were kindly received by the officers, they agreed to remain two days, that they might obtain all the information which they could, and rearrange the stowing of the waggons before they started. The original plan had been to direct their course to Chumie, the first missionary station, which was about twenty-five miles distant ; but as it was out of their way, they now resolved to proceed direct to Butterworth, which was forty miles further in the Caffre country, and the more distant of the two missions. Our party took leave of their kind entertainers, and, having crossed without difficulty at the ford the Keiskamma river, had passed the neutral ground, and were in the land of the Caffres.

Up to the present they had very little trouble with the Hottentots whom they had hired. As long as they were within reach of the law they behaved well; but now that they had passed the confines of the Cape territory, some of them began to show symptoms of insubordination. The dismissal of one, however, with an order to go back immediately, and threatening to shoot him if he was ever seen in the caravan, had the desired effect of restoring order. The country was now a series of hills and dales, occasionally of deep ravines, and their route lay through the paths made by the elephants, which were numerous. A Hottentot of the name of Bromen, who was considered as their best man and most practised hunter, begged Alexander and his companions to be careful how they went along, if they preceded the rest on horseback; as the elephants always return by the same path at evening or after nightfall, in whatever direction they may have been feeding, and it is very dangerous to intercept them.

For two days they continued their course in nearly a straight line for the missionary establishment. On the second evening, just about dusk, as they were crossing a woody hill, by the elephants' path, being then about two hundred yards in advance of the waggons, they were saluted with one of the most hideous shrieks that could be conceived. Their horses started back; they could see nothing, although the sound echoed through the hills for some seconds.

"What was that?" exclaimed Alexander.

"Shout as loud as you can," cried the Major; "and turn your horses to the waggons."

Alexander and Swinton joined the Major in the shout, and were soon accompanied by the whole mass of Hottentots, shouting and yelling as loud as they could.

"Silence, now," cried the Major; every one was hushed, and they listened for a few seconds.

"It was only one, sir, and he is gone," said Bremen. "We may go on."

"Only one what?" inquired Alexander.

"An elephant, sir," replied the Hottentot; "it's well that he did not charge you; he would have tumbled you down the precipice, horse and all. There must be a herd here, and we had better stop as soon as we are down the other side of the hill."

"I think so too," replied the Major.

"I shall not get that shriek out of my ears for a month," said Alexander; "why, the roar of a lion cannot be so bad."

"Wait till you hear it," replied Swinton.

They had now arrived at the bottom of the hill which they had been passing, and by the light of the stars they selected a spot for their encampment. Whether they were near to any Caffre kraals or not it was impossible to say; but they heard no barking of dogs or lowing of oxen. Having collected all the cattle, they formed a square of the four waggons, and passed ropes from the one to the other; the horses and sheep were driven within the square, and the oxen were, as usual, tied up to the sides of the waggons.

It should here be observed, that the oxen were turned out to graze early in the morning, yoked in the afternoon, and they travelled then as far as they could after nightfall, to avoid the extreme heat of the day, the continual visits of the Caffres, and the risk of losing the cattle if they were allowed to be loose and fed during the night.

On the night we have been referring to, a more than usual number of fires were lighted, to keep off the elephants and other wild animals. The hyenas and wolves were very numerous, and prowled the whole night in hopes of getting hold of some of the sheep; but as yet there had not been seen or heard a lion, although an occasional track had been pointed out by the Hottentots.

When the Hottentots had finished their labour, our travellers had to wait till the fires were lighted and a sheep killed before they could have their suppers cooked by Mahomed. Begum, the baboon, had been released from her confinement since their crossing the Fish River, and as usual, when they sat down, came and made one of the party, generally creeping in close to her master until supper was served, when she would have her finger in every dish, and steal all she could, sometimes rather to their annoyance.

Our little Bushman had now quite recovered not only his strength but his gaiety, and was one of the most amusing little fellows that could be met with.

He could not make himself understood except to one or two of the Hottentots; but he was all pantomime, trying, by gestures and signs, to talk to Mr. Swinton and his companions. He endeavoured to assist Mahomed as much as he could, and appeared to have attached himself to him, for he kept no company with the Hottentots.

He was not more than three feet and a half high, and with limbs remarkably delicate, although well made. His face was very much like a monkey's, and his gestures and manners completely so; he was quite as active and full of fun. The watch had been set as soon as the fires were lighted; and close to where Alexander and the others were seated, Big Adam, the Hottentot we have mentioned as having raised doubts in the mind of the Major as to his courage, had just mounted guard, with his gun in his hand. Omrah came up to where they were sitting, and they nodded and smiled at him, and said, "How do you do?" in English.

The boy, who had already picked up a few sentences, answered in the same words, "How do you do?" and then pointing to Big Adam, whose back was turned, he began making a number of signs, and nodding his head; at last he bent down, putting his arm in front of him, and raising it like an elephant's trunk, walking with the measured steps of that animal, so as fully to make them understand that he intended to portray an elephant. Having so done, he went up behind Big Adam, and gave a shriek so exactly like that which the elephant had given an hour before, that the Hottentot started up, dropped his musket, and threw himself flat on the ground, in order that the supposed animal might pass by him unperceived.

The other Hottentots had been equally startled, and had seized their muskets, looking in every direction for the approach of the animal; but the convulsions of laughter which proceeded from the party soon told them that there was nothing to apprehend, and that little Omrah had been playing his tricks. Big Adam rose up, looking very foolish; he had just before been telling his companions how many elephants he had killed, and had been expressing his hopes that they soon should have an elephant-hunt.

"Well," observed Swinton, after the laugh was over, "it proves that Adam is an elephant-hunter, and knows what to do in time of danger."

"Yes," replied the Major; "and it also proves that our opinion of him was just, and that with him the best part of valour is discretion."

"The most wonderful escape from an elephant which we have on record here," observed Swinton, "is that of Lieutenant Moodie; did you ever hear of it? I had it from his own lips."

"I never did, at all events," said Alexander; "and if the Major has, he will listen very patiently, to oblige me."

"I have never heard the precise particulars, and shall therefore be as glad to be a listener as Wilmot."

"Well, then, I will begin. Lieutenant Moodie was out elephant-hunting with a party of officers and soldiers, when one day he was told that a large troop of elephants was close at hand, and that several of the men were out, and in pursuit of them. Lieutenant Moodie immediately seized his gun, and went off in the direction where he heard the firing.

"He had forced his way through a jungle, and had just come to a cleared spot, when he heard some of his people calling out, in English and Dutch, 'Take care, Mr. Moodie, take care.' As they called out, he heard the crackling of branches broken by the elephants as they were bursting through the wood, and then tremendous screams, such as we heard this night. Immediately afterwards four elephants burst out from the jungle, not two hundred yards from where he stood. Being alone on the open ground, he knew that if he fired and did not kill, he could have no chance; so he hastily retreated, hoping that the animals would not see him. On looking back, however, he perceived, to his dismay, that they were all in chase of him, and rapidly gaining on him; he therefore resolved to reserve his fire till the last moment, and, turning towards some precipitous rocks, hoped to gain them before the elephants could come up with him. But he was still at least fifty paces from the rocks, when he found that the elephants were within half that distance of him,—one very large animal, and three smaller,—all in a row, as if determined that he should not escape, snorting so tremendously that he was quite stunned with the noise."

"That's what I call a very pretty position," observed the Major. "Go on, Swinton; the affair is becoming a little nervous."

"As his only chance, Lieutenant Moodie turned round, and levelled his gun at the largest elephant; but unfortunately the powder was damp, and the gun hung fire, till he was in the act of taking it from his shoulder, when it went off, and the ball merely grazed the side of the elephant's head. The animal halted for an instant, and then made a furious charge upon him. He fell; whether struck down by the elephant's trunk he cannot say. The elephant then thrust at him as he lay, with his tusk; fortunately it had but one, and more fortunately it missed its mark, ploughing up the ground within an inch of Mr. Moodie's body.

"The animal then caught him up with its trunk by his middle, and dashed him down between his fore-feet to tread him to death. Once it pressed so heavily on his chest, that all his bones bent under the weight, but somehow or other, whether from the animal being in a state of alarm, it never contrived to have its whole weight upon him; for Mr. Moodie had never lost his recollection, and kept twisting his body and his limbs, so as to prevent it from obtaining a direct tread upon him. While he was in this state of distress, another officer and a Hottentot hunter came up to his assistance, and fired several shots at the animal, which was severely wounded, and the other three took to their heels. At last the one which had possession of Mr. Moodie turned round, and giving him a cuff with its fore-feet followed the rest. Mr. Moodie got up, picked up his gun, and staggered away as fast as his aching bones would permit him. He met his brother, who had just been informed by one of the Hottentots, who had seen him under the elephant, that he was killed."

"Well, that was an escape," observed Wilmot.

"What made it more remarkable was, that he had hardly time to explain to his brother his miraculous preservation, before he witnessed the death of one of the hunters, a soldier, who had attracted the notice of a large male elephant which had been driven out of the jungle. The fierce animal gave chase to him, and caught him immediately under the height where Mr. Moodie and his brother were standing, carried the poor fellow for some distance on his trunk, then threw him down, and stamping upon him until he was quite dead, left the body for a short time. The elephant then returned, as if to make sure of its destruction; for it kneeled down on the body, and kneaded it with his fore-legs; then, rising, it seized it again with its trunk, carried it to the edge of the jungle, and hurled it into the bushes."

"Dreadful! I had no idea that there was such danger in an elephant-hunt; yet I must say," continued Alexander, "that, although it may appear foolishness, it only makes me more anxious to have one."

"Well, as we advance, you will have no want of opportunity; but it will be better to get the Caffres to join us, which they will with great delight."

"Why, they have no weapons, except their spears."

"None; but they will attack him with great success, as you will see; they watch their opportunity as he passes, get behind, and drive their spears into his body until the animal is exhausted from loss of blood, and they are so quick that the elephant seldom is able to destroy one of them. They consider the elephant of as high rank as one of their kings, and it is very laughable to hear them, as they wound him, beg pardon of him, and cry out, 'Great man, don't be angry; great captain, don't kill us.'"

"But how is it that they can approach so terrible an animal without destruction?"

"It is because they do approach quite close to him. An elephant sees but badly, except straight before him, and he turns with difficulty. The Caffres are within three feet of his tail or flank when they attack, and they attack him in the elephant-paths, which are too narrow for the animal to turn without difficulty; the great risk that they run is from another elephant breaking out to the assistance of the one attacked."

"The animals do assist each other, then?"

"Yes; there was a remarkable instance of it in the affair of Lieutenant Moodie. I mentioned that it was a large male elephant which killed the soldier just after Mr. Moodie's escape. Shortly afterward a shot from one of the hunters broke the fore-leg of this animal, and prevented him from running, and there it stood to be fired at. The female elephant, which was in the jungle, witnessing the distress of its mate, regardless of her own danger, immediately rushed out to his assistance, chasing away the hunters, and walked round and round her mate, constantly returning to his side, and caressing him. When the male attempted to walk, she had the sagacity to place her flank against the wounded side, so as to support him, and help him along. At last the female received a severe wound, and staggered into the bush, where she fell; and the male was soon after laid prostrate by the side of the poor soldier whom he had killed."

"There is something very touching in the last portion of your story, Swinton," observed Alexander; "it really makes one feel a sort of respect for such intelligent and reasoning animals."

"I think the first portion of the story ought to teach you to respect them also," said the Major. "Seriously, however, I quite agree with you; their sagacity, as my Indian experience has taught me, is wonderful;—but here comes supper, and I am not sorry for it."

"Nor I," replied Alexander. "To-morrow we shall be at the missionary station, if the guides are correct. I am very anxious to get there, I must say. Does not the chief of the Amakosa tribe live close to the Mission-house,—Hinza, as they call him?"

"Yes," replied Swinton, "he does, and we must have a present ready for him, for I think it would be advisable to ask an escort of his warriors to go with us after we leave the Mission."

"Yes, it will be quite as well," replied the Major, "and then we shall have some elephant-hunting: but Bremen tells me that there are plenty of hippopotami in the river there, close to the Mission."

"Water-elephants," replied Swinton; "I suppose you will not leave them alone?"

"Certainly not if our commander-in-chief will allow us to stop."

"I think your commander-in-chief," replied Wilmot, "is just as anxious to have a day's sport with them as you are, Major; so you will certainly have his permission."

"I think we ought to put Omrah on a horse. He is a nice light-weight for a spare horse, if required."

"Not a bad idea," replied Alexander. "What a tiger he would make for a cab in the park!"

"More like a monkey," replied the Major; "but it is time to go to bed; so, good night."

CHAPTER XI

Arrival at Mr. S.'s station—The quarrel between Hinza and Voosani—An escort proposed—The Caffre character—The Sabbath—Painful position of a missionary's wife.

THE caravan proceeded on the following morning, and by noon they arrived at the Mission station of Butterworth, which was about one hundred and forty miles from the colonial boundaries. This station had only been settled about three years, but even in that short time it wore an air of civilisation strongly contrasted with the savage country around it. The Mission-house was little better than a large cottage, it is true, and the church a sort of barn; but it was surrounded by neat Caffre huts and gardens full of produce.

On the arrival of the caravan, Mr. S., the missionary, came out to meet the travellers, and to welcome them. He had been informed that they would call at the station, and bring some articles which had been sent for. It hardly need be said that, meeting at such a place, and in such a country, the parties soon became on intimate terms. Mr. S. offered them beds and accommodation in his house, but our travellers refused; they were well satisfied with their own; and having unyoked their oxen, and turned them out to graze with those belonging to the station, they accepted the missionary's invitation to join his repast.

Alexander having stated the object of his expedition, requested the advice of Mr. S. as to his further proceedings, and asked him whether it would not be advisable to see the Caffre king, and make him a present. This

Mr. S. strongly advised them to do; and to ask for a party of Caffres to accompany the caravan, which would not only insure them safety, but would prove in many respects very useful. All that would be necessary would be to find them in food and to promise them a present, if they conducted themselves well. "You are aware," continued he, "that Hinza's domain only extends as far as the Bashee or St. John's River, and you will have to proceed beyond that; but with some of the Caffre warriors you will have no difficulty, as the tribes further will not only fear your strength, but also the anger of Hinza, should they commit any depredation. But things, I regret to say, do not look very peaceable just now."

"Indeed! what is the quarrel, and with whom?"

"Hinza has quarrelled with a powerful neighbouring chief of the name of Voosani, who reigns over the Tambookie tribes, about some cattle, which are the grand cause of quarrels in these countries, and both parties are preparing for war. But whether it will take place is doubtful, as they are both threatened with a more powerful enemy, and may probably be compelled to unite, in order to defend themselves."

"And who may that be?"

"Quetoo, the chief of the Amaquabi, is in arms with a large force, and threatens the other tribes to the northward of us; if he conquers them, he will certainly come down here. He was formerly one of Chaka's generals, and is, like him, renowned for slaughter. At present he is too far to the northward to interfere with you, but I should advise you to lose no time in effecting your mission; for should he advance, you will be compelled to retreat immediately. I had better send to Hinza to-morrow to let him know that strangers have come and wish to see him, that they may make him a present. That notice will bring him fast enough; not but that he well knows you are here, and has known that you have been in his country long ago."

"It will be as well, after the information you have given us," said Mr. Swinton.

"What is your opinion of the Caffres, Mr. S., now that you have resided so long with them?"

"They are, for heathens, a fine nation, — bold, frank, and, if anything is confided to them, scrupulously honest; but cattle-stealing is certainly not considered a crime among them, although it is punished as one. Speaking as a minister of the Gospel, I should say they are the most difficult nation to have anything to do with that it ever has been my lot to visit. They have no religion whatever; they have no idols; and no idea of the existence of a God. When I have talked to them about God, their reply is, 'Where is He? show Him to me.'"

"But have they no superstitions?"

"They believe in necromancy, and have their conjurers, who do much harm, and are our chief opponents, as we weaken their influence, and consequently their profits. If cattle are stolen, they are referred to. If a chief is sick, they are sent for to know who has bewitched him; they must of course mention some innocent person, who is sacrificed immediately. If the country is parched from want of rain, which it so frequently is, then the conjurers are in great demand: they are sent for to produce rain. If, after all their pretended mysteries, the rain does not fall so as to save their reputation, they give some plausible reason, generally ending, however, in the sacrifice of some innocent individual; and thus they go on, making excuses after excuses until the rain does fall, and they obtain all the credit of it. I need hardly say that these people are our greatest enemies."

"Are you satisfied with the success which you have had?"

"Yes, I am, when I consider the difficulty to be surmounted. Nothing but the Divine assistance could have produced such effects as have already taken place. The chiefs are to a man opposed to us."

"Why so?"

"Because Christianity strikes at the root of their sensuality; it was the same when it was first preached by our Divine Master. The riches of a Caffre consist not only in his cattle, but in the number of his wives, who are all his slaves. To tell them that polygamy is unlawful and wrong, is therefore almost as much as to tell them that it is not right to hold a large herd of cattle; and as the

75

chiefs are of course the opulent of the nation, they oppose us. You observe in Caffreland, as elsewhere, it is 'hard for a rich man to enter into the kingdom of heaven.' I have asked the chiefs why they will not come to church, and their reply has been, 'The great Word is calculated to lessen our pleasures and diminish the number of our wives; to this we can never consent.'"

"But still you say you have made some progress."

"If I have, let it be ascribed to the Lord, and not to me and my otherwise useless endeavours; it must be His doing; and without His aid and assistance, the difficulties would have been insurmountable. It is for me only to bear in mind the scriptural injunction, 'In the morning sow thy seed, and in the evening withhold not thy hand; for thou knowest not whether shall prosper, either this or that, or whether they both shall be alike good.'"

"But have they no idea whatever of a Supreme Being, either bad or good? have they no idea, as some of the African tribes have, of the devil?"

"None; and in their language they have no word to express the idea of the Deity; they swear by their kings of former days as great chiefs, but no more. Now if they had any religion whatever, you might, by pointing out to them the falsity and absurdity of that religion, and putting it in juxtaposition with revealed Truth, have some hold upon their minds; but we have not even that advantage."

"But cannot you make an impression upon their minds by referring to the wonders of nature,—by asking them who made the sun and stars? Surely they might be induced to reflect by such a method."

"I have tried it a hundred times, and they have laughed at me for my fables, as they have termed them. One of the chiefs told me to hold my tongue, that his people might not think me mad. The Scriptures, indeed, teach us that, without the aid of direct revelation, men are also without excuse if they fail to attain to a certain know-ledge of the Deity,—'even His eternal power and God-head,'—by a devout contemplation of the visible world, which with all its wonders is spread out before them as an open volume. But beyond this, all knowledge of the origin or manner of creation is derived, not from the deductions of human reasoning, but from the Divine testimony'; for it is expressly. said, 'Through faith we understand that the worlds were made by the word of God.'"

"Nevertheless you must admit that, among the civilised nations of Europe, many who deny revelation, and treat the Bible as a fable, acknowledge that the world must have been made by a Supreme Power."

"My dear sir, many affect to deny the truth of revelation out of pride and folly, who still in their consciences cannot but believe it. Here, there being no belief in a Deity, they will not be persuaded that the world was made by one. Indeed, we have much to contend with, and perhaps one of the greatest difficulties is in· the translation of the Scriptures. I sit down with an interpreter who cannot read a single word, and with perhaps a most erroneous and imperfect knowledge of divine things. We open the sacred volume, and it is first translated into barbarous Dutch to the Caffre interpreter, who then has to tell us how that Dutch is to be put into the Caffre language. Now you may imagine what mistakes may arise. I have found out lately that I have been stating the very contrary to what I would have said. With this translation, I stand up to read a portion of the Word of God, for my interpreter cannot read, and hence any slight defect or change in a syllable may give altogether a different sense from what I desire to inculcate."

"That must indeed be a great difficulty, and require a long residence and full acquaintance with the language to overcome."

"And even then not overcome, for the language has no words to express abstract ideas; but the Lord works after His own way, and at His own season."

"You do not then despair of success?"

"God forbid; I should be indeed a most unworthy servant of our Divine Master, if I so far distrusted His power. No; much good has been already done, as you will perceive when we meet to-morrow to perform Divine service; but there is much more to do, and, with His blessing, will in His own good time be perfected; but I

77

have duties to attend to which call me away for the present; I shall therefore wish you good night. At all events, the Mission has had one good effect: you are perfectly safe from Caffre violence and Caffre robbery. This homage is paid to it even by their kings and chiefs."

"I will say, that if we are only to judge by the little we have seen, the Mission appears to have done good," observed the Major. "In the first place, we are no longer persecuted, as we have been during our journey, for presents; and, as you may observe, many of the Caffres about are clothed in European fashions, and those who have nothing but their national undress, I may call it, wear it as decently as they can."

"I made the same observation," said Alexander. "I am most anxious for to-morrow, as I wish to see how the Caffres behave; and really, when you consider all the difficulties which Mr. S. has mentioned, it is wonderful that he and those who have embraced the same calling should persevere as they do."

"My dear Wilmot," replied Mr. Swinton, "a missionary, even of the most humble class, is a person of no ordinary mind; he does not rely upon himself or upon his own exertions,—he relies not upon others, or upon the assistance of this world; if he did, he would, as you say, soon abandon his task in despair. No; he is supported, he is encouraged, he is pressed on by faith—faith in Him who never deserts those who trust and believe in Him; he knows that, if it is His pleasure, the task will be easy, but at the same time that it must be at His own good time. Convinced of this, supported by this, encouraged by this, and venturing his life for this, he toils on, in full assurance that if he fails another is to succeed, —that if he becomes a martyr, his blood will moisten the arid soil from which the future seed will spring. A missionary may be low in birth, low in education, as many are; but he must be a man of exalted mind, —what in any other pursuit we might term an enthusiast; and in this spreading of the Divine Word, he merits respect for his fervour, his courage, and self-devotion; his willingness, if the Lord should so think fit, to accept the crown of martyrdom."

78

"You are right, Swinton; nothing but what you have described could impel a man to pass a life of privation and danger among a savage race—leaving all, and following his Master in the true apostolic sense. Well, they will have their reward."

"Yes, in heaven, Wilmot; not on earth," replied Swinton.

The next day, being the Sabbath, with the assistance of Mahomed, who was valet as well as cook to the whole party, they divested themselves of their beards, which had not been touched for many days, and dressed themselves in more suitable apparel than their usual hunting costume,—a respect paid to the Sabbath by even the most worldly and most indifferent on religious points. The bell of the Mission church was tolled, and the natives were seen coming from all directions. Our party went in, and found Mr. S. already there, and that seats had been provided for them. The numbers of natives who were assembled in the church were about two hundred, but many more were at the windows, and sitting by the open door. Many of them were clothed in some sort of European apparel; those who were not, drew their krosses close round them, so as to appear more covered. A hymn in the Caffre language was first sung, and then prayers, after which the Litany and responses; the Commandments were repeated in the same language. Mr. S. then read a chapter in the Bible, and explained it to the assembly. Profound silence and quiet attention generally prevailed, although in some few instances there was mockery from those outside. Mr. S. gave the blessing, and the service was ended.

"You have already done much," observed Mr. Swinton. "I could hardly have believed that a concourse of savages could have been so attentive, and have behaved with such decorum."

"It certainly is the most difficult point gained,—to command their attention, I mean," replied Mr. S. ; "after that, time and patience, with the assistance of God, will effect the rest."

"Do you think that there are many who, if I may use the term, feel their religion ? "

"Yes, many; and prove it by travelling about and sowing the seed. There are many who not only are qualified so to do, but are incessantly labouring to bring their countrymen to God."

"That must be very satisfactory to you."

"It is; but what am I, and the few who labour with me, to the thousands and thousands who are here in darkness and require our aid? There are now but three missions in all Caffreland; and there is full employment for two hundred, if they could be established. But you must excuse me, I have to catechise the children, who are my most promising pupils. We will meet again in the evening, for I have to preach at a neighbouring village. Strange to say, many who doubt and waver will listen to me there; but they appear to think that there is some witchcraft in the Mission church, or else are afraid to acknowledge to their companions that they have been inside of it."

The missionary then left them, and Alexander observed—

"I don't know how you feel, but I assure you it has been a great pleasure to me to have found myself in this humble church, and hearing Divine service in this wild country."

Both Swinton and Major Henderson expressed the same opinion.

"I am not afraid of being laughed at," continued Alexander, "when I tell you that I think it most important, wherever we may be during our travels, to keep the Sabbath holy, by rest and reading the service."

"With pleasure, as far as I am concerned, and I thank you for the proposal," replied Swinton.

"And I am equally pleased that you have proposed it, Wilmot," said Major Henderson; "even we may be of service to the good cause, if, as we pass through the land, the natives perceive that we respect the Sabbath as the missionary has requested them to do. We are white men, and considered by them as superior; our example, therefore, may do good."

The evening was passed away very agreeably with Mr. S., who was inexhaustible in his anecdotes of the Caffres.

He informed them that Hinza intended to call the next morning to receive his presents, and that he would be interpreter for them if they wished it.

Alexander, having thanked the missionary, said, " I think you mentioned, sir, that some of your brother missionaries have their wives with them. Since you have told me so much of the precarious tenure by which you hold your ground here, and I may add your lives, I think that the wives of the missionaries must have even more to encounter than their husbands."

"You are right, sir," replied the missionary; "there is no situation so trying, so perilous, and I may say, so weary to the mind and body, as that of a female missionary. She has to encounter the same perils and the same hardships as her husband, without having the strength of our sex to support them; and what is more painful than all, she is often left alone in the Mission-house while her husband, who has left her, is proceeding on his duty, at the hourly peril of his life. There she is alone, and compelled to listen to all the reports and falsehoods which are circulated : at one moment she is told that her husband has been murdered ; at another, that he is still alive. She has no means of hearing from him, as there is no communication throughout the country ; thus is she left in this horrible state of suspense and anxiety, perhaps for many weeks. I have a letter from a brother missionary which is in my writing desk, wherein the case in point is well portrayed ; I will get it and read that portion to you." Mr. S. went to the other end of the room, and came back with a letter, from which he read as follows :—

"Having been detained among those distant tribes for nearly two months, report upon report had been circulated that the interpreters and guides, as well as myself, had all been murdered. On my arrival within forty miles of the station, I was informed that all doubt upon the subject had been removed by a party of natives who had passed the Mission station, and who pretended an acquaintance with all the particulars of the massacre. We had been travelling the whole day, and night had come on ; I was most anxious to proceed, that I might relieve the mind of my dear wife, but the earnest remonstrances of my little party, who re-

81   F

presented it as certain death to all of us to cross the plains, which were infested with lions and other savage beasts who were prowling in every direction, at length induced me to wait till the next day. But scarcely had day begun to dawn when I sallied forth, without either arms or guide, except a pocket compass, leaving my fellow-travellers to bring on the waggon as soon as they should arouse from their slumbers. This impatience had, however, well-nigh cost me my life; for having to wade through many miles of deep sand with a vertical sun over my head, I had not accomplished half the journey before my strength began to fail, and an indescribable thirst was induced. Nevertheless, I reached the Mission in safety, and with truly grateful feelings to the Preserver of men. A few minutes prior to my arrival, the wife of one of my brother missionaries, little imagining that I was at hand and alive, had entered our dwelling, to apprise my wife of the latest intelligence, confirming all that had been said before respecting my fate, and to comfort her under the distressing dispensation. At this affecting crisis, while both were standing in the centre of the room, the one relating, the other weeping, I opened the door, bathed in perspiration, covered with dust, and in a state of complete exhaustion. 'Oh, dear!' cried our friend; 'is it he—or is it his spirit?' I must, my dear sir, leave to your imagination the scene that followed."

"Yes, sir," said Mr. S., folding up the letter, "a missionary's wife, who follows him into such scenes and such perils and privations, does, indeed, 'cleave to her husband.'"

"Indeed she does," replied Mr. Swinton; "but we will tax you no longer, my dear sir. Good night."

CHAPTER XII

*The royal visit—Mutual civilities—The band of warriors—
Hippopotami—Their carcasses—Omrah's cunning—The trick
—Big Adam sulky—A narrow escape—Preparations for the
hunt.*

ON the following day, a little before noon, loud shouts
and men dancing and calling out the titles of the king
of the Caffres announced his approach. These men were
a sort of heralds, who invariably preceded him on a visit of
ceremony. A band of warriors armed with their assegais
and shields next made their appearance, and then Hinza,
accompanied by fifty of his chief councillors: with the exception of their long krosses of beast-skins thrown over
their shoulders, they were all naked, and each daubed with
grease and red ochre. As soon as they arrived in front
of the Mission-house, they sat down in a circle on each
side of the Caffre king, who was treated with marked respect by all, and by the common people in particular,
who assembled on his presence. Every one who happened
to pass by gave what was termed a 'salute' of honour to
the king, who did not appear to consider that it required
any acknowledgment on his part.

Our travellers, accompanied by the missionary, advanced
into the circle, and saluted his majesty. Mr. S. then explained the object of their journey, and their wish that
a small party of the king's warriors should accompany them
on their expedition. As soon as the speech was ended,
a few pounds of coloured beads, a roll of tobacco, two pounds
of snuff, and some yards of scarlet cloth, were laid before
his majesty as a present. Hinza nodded his head with
approval when the articles were spread before him, and
then turned to his councillors, with whom he whispered
some time, and then he replied "that the strange white
men should pass through his country without fear, that
his warriors should accompany them as far as they wished
to go; but," he added, "do the strangers know that there
is disorder in the country beyond?"

Mr. S. replied that they did, and were anxious to go and return as soon as possible, on that account.

Hinza replied, "It is well; if there is danger, my warriors will let them know—if it is necessary, they will fight for them—if the enemy is too strong, the white men must return."

Hinza then ordered some of his councillors to take charge of the presents, and inquired of Mr. S. how many warriors they wished to have, and when they wished to go.

The reply was, that fifty warriors would be sufficient, and that they wished to depart on the following morning. "It is well," replied Hinza; "fifty warriors are enough, for my men eat a great deal—they shall be ready."

The council then broke up, and the king, having shaken hands with our travellers, departed with his train: toward the evening an old cow was sent to them as a present from his majesty. The Hottentots soon cut it up and devoured it. Everything was now arranged for their immediate departure.

The next morning, at break of day, the band of Caffre warriors were all in readiness, each with his shield and three assegais in his hand. They were all fine, tall young men, from twenty to thirty years of age. Alexander desired Mr. S. to tell them that, if they behaved well and were faithful, they should every one receive a present when they were dismissed; a notification which appeared to give general satisfaction. The oxen had already been yoked, and taking leave of the worthy missionary, our travellers mounted their horses and resumed their journey. For the whole day they proceeded along the banks of the Kae River, which ran its course through alternate glens and hills clothed with fine timber; and as they were on an eminence, looking down upon the river, the head Caffre warrior, who had, with the others, hung up his shield at the side of the waggon, and now walked by our travellers, with his assegai in his hand, pointed out to them, as the sun was setting behind a hill, two or three large black masses on the further bank of the river.

"What are they, and what does he say?"

"Sea-cows," replied the interpreter.

"*Hippopotami!* We must have a shot at them, Wilmot," cried the Major.

"To be sure; tell them we will stop and kill one if we can," said Wilmot to the interpreter.

"We shall want one to feed our army," said Swinton, laughing, "or our sheep will soon be devoured."

The Caffres were all immediately in motion, running down to the bank of the river, about a quarter of a mile distant; they swam across, and there remained waiting till our travellers should give the word.

The animals lay on a muddy bank, at a turn of the river, like so many swine asleep, some of them out, and some partly in and partly out of the water. As they were huddled together, they looked more like masses of black rock than anything else. Two lay considerably apart from the others, and it was toward these two that the Caffres, who had crossed the river, crept until they were in the high reeds, but a few yards from them. Henderson and Wilmot, with some of the Hottentots, descended the ravine on their side of the river, opposite to where the animals lay, and as soon as they were on the bank, being then within one hundred yards of them, they levelled and fired. At the report, all the animals started up from their beds as if astonished at the noise, which they had not been accustomed to. Three or four instantly plunged into the deep water, but the others, apparently half asleep, stood for a few seconds, as if not knowing what course to take: two of them were evidently wounded, as they rushed into the water; for they did not remain below, but rose to the surface immediately, as if in great agony. They appeared anxious to get out of the water altogether, and tried so to do, but fearing the people on the river's bank, they darted in again. In the meantime, at the first report of the guns, the two which lay apart from the others with their heads toward the river, as soon as they rose on their legs, were pierced with several assegais by the concealed Caffres, and plunged into the water with the spears remaining in their bodies. These also rose, and floundered like the others; and as their heads appeared above, they were met with the unerring rifle of the Major and whole volleys from Wilmot and

85

the Hottentots, till, exhausted from loss of blood, they floated dead upon the surface.

The Caffres waited till the bodies had been borne some hundred yards down the stream, that they might not be attacked when in the water by the remainder of the herd, and then swam off, and pushed the bodies on shore. This was a very seasonable supply of provisions for so large a band of people; but those who belonged to the caravan were not the only parties who benefited: all the Caffres of the surrounding hamlets hastened to the river, and carried off large quantities of the flesh of the animals; there was, however, more than enough for all, and for the wolves and hyenas after they had taken what they chose. It was so late before the animals were cut up, that they decided upon remaining where they were that night; for now that they had the Caffre warriors with them, they had no fear as to losing their oxen, the king having stated that his men should be responsible for them.

Large fires were lighted, and the Caffres and Hottentots, all mingled together, were busy roasting, boiling, and frying the flesh of the hippopotamus, and eating it as fast as it was cooked, so that they were completely gorged before they lay down to sleep; Wilmot had also given them a ration of tobacco each, which had added considerably to the delight of the feast.

"It is not bad eating by any means," said the Major, as they were at supper.

"No; it is something like old veal," replied Swinton. "Now, what is Omrah about? He is after some mischief, by the way he creeps along."

"A monkey is a fool to that boy," observed the Major, "and he appears to know how to imitate every animal he has ever heard."

"Did you hear the dance he led some of the Hottentots on Sunday evening, when we were at the Mission?"

"No; what was that?"

"Bremen told me of it; I thought he would have died with laughing. You are aware that there is a species of bird here which they call the honey-bird,—by naturalists, the *Cuculus indicator;* do you not remember I showed you a specimen which I was preserving?"

"You have showed us so many specimens, that I really forget."

"Well, I should have given you at the same time the natural history of the bird. It is very partial to honey, upon which it lives as much as it can; but as the bees make their hives in the trunks of old decayed trees, and the hole they enter by is very small, the bird cannot obtain it without assistance. Its instinct induces it to call in the aid of man, which it does by a peculiar note, like cher-cher-cher, by which it gives notice that it has found out a beehive. The natives of Africa well know this, and as soon as the bird flies close to them, giving out this sound, they follow it; the bird leads them on, perching every now and then, to enable them to keep up with it, until it arrives · at the tree, over which it flutters without making any more noise."

"How very curious!"

"Little Bushman knows this as well as the Hottentots, and hearing that they were going out in search of honey he went before them into the wood, concealing himself, and imitating the note of the bird so exactly, that the Hottentots went on following it for several miles, wondering how it was that the bird should lead them such a distance, but unwilling to give up the pursuit. About sunset, he had brought them back to the very edge of the wood from whence they had started, when he showed himself about one hundred yards ahead of them, dancing, capering, and tumbling so like Begum, that they thought it was her before them, and not him. He gained the caravan again without their knowing who played them the trick; but he told Swanevelt, who speaks his language, and Swanevelt told Bremen."

"Capital!" said the Major; "well, he is after some trick now, depend upon it."

"He has a great talent for drawing," observed Alexander.

"A very great one; I have given him a pencil and occasionally a piece of paper, and he draws all the birds, so that I can recognise them; but you must know that all the Bushmen have that talent, and that their caves are full of the sketches of all sorts of animals, remarkably characteristic.

The organ of imitation is very strongly developed in the Bushmen, which accounts for their talents as draftsmen, and Omrah's remarkable imitative powers."

"Do you then believe in phrenology, Swinton?" said Alexander.

"I neither believe nor disbelieve in that and many more modern discoveries of the same kind; I do not think it right to reject them or to give blind credence. Not a day passes but some discovery excites our wonder and admiration, and points out to us how little we do know. The great fault is, that when people have made a discovery to a certain extent, they build upon it, as if all their premises were correct; whereas, they have, in fact, only obtained a mere glimmering to light them to a path which may some future day lead to knowledge. That the general principles of phrenology are correct may be fairly assumed, from the examination of the skulls of men and animals, and of different men; but I give no credence to all the divisions and subdivisions which have, in my opinion, been most presumptuously marked out by those who profess, and of course fully believe, the full extent of these supposed discoveries."

"And mesmerism?" said Alexander.

"I make the same reply; there is *something* in it, that is certain, but nothing yet sufficiently known to warrant any specific conclusion to be drawn."

"There is a great deal of humbug in it," said the Major.

"So there is in all sciences; when truth fails them and they are at fault, they fill up the hiatus with supposition; which is, as you term it, humbug."

"Well, I vote that we return to our waggons; everybody appears fast asleep except us three."

Such was not, however, the case; for they had not been half-an-hour on their mattresses, before they were awakened by loud cries of "help," which made them seize their guns and jump out of the waggons without waiting for their clothes.

The Hottentots and Caffres were so full of hippopotamus flesh, that the noise did not awake but a small portion of them, and these only turned round and stared about without getting up, with the exception of Bremen, who

88

was on his feet and, with his gun in his hand, running in the direction of the cries. He was followed by our travellers, and they soon came up with the object of their search, which proved to be no other than Big Adam, the Hottentot; and as soon as they perceived his condition, which they could do by the light of the fires still burning, they all burst out laughing so excessively that they could not help him.

That it was the work of little Omrah there was no doubt, for Big Adam had not forgotten the former trick the boy had played him, and had more than once, when he caught the boy, given him a good cuffing. Big Adam was on the ground, dragged away by two of the largest dogs. Omrah had taken the bones he could find with most flesh upon them belonging to the hippopotamus, and had tied them with leathern thongs to the great toes of Big Adam as he lay snoring after his unusual repast. He had then waited till all were asleep, and had let loose the two largest dogs, which were always tied with the others under the waggons, and not over-fed, to make them more watchful.

The dogs had prowled about for food, and had fallen in with these large bones, which they immediately seized, and were dragging away, that they might make their repast without interruption; but in attempting to drag away the bones, they had dragged Big Adam some yards by his great toes, and the pain and fright—for the Hottentot thought they were hyenas or wolves—had caused him thus to scream for help. Bremen divided the thongs with his knife, and the dogs ran off growling with the bones, and Adam stood again upon his feet, still so much terrified as not to be able to comprehend the trick which had been played him. Our travellers, having indulged their mirth, retired once more to their resting-places. The Major found Omrah and Begum both in their corners of the waggon, the former pretending to be fast asleep, while the latter was chattering and swearing at the unusual disturbance.

At daylight next morning they resumed their journey. Big Adam walked rather stiff, and looked very sulky. Omrah had perched himself on a tilt of the baggage-

89

waggon with Begum, and was quite out of the Hottentot's reach; for Bremen had told the others what had happened, and there had been a general laugh against Big Adam, who vowed vengeance against little Omrah. The country was now very beautiful and fertile, and the Caffre hamlets were to be seen in all directions. Except visits from the Caffres, who behaved with great decorum when they perceived that the caravan was escorted by the king's warriors, and who supplied them nearly every day with a bullock for the use of the people, no adventure occurred for four days, when they crossed the Bashee or St. John's River, to which the territories of Hinza extended; but although the tribes beyond did not acknowledge his authority, they respected the large force of the caravan, and were much pleased at receiving small presents of tobacco and snuff.

Milk, in baskets, was constantly brought in by the women; for the Caffres weave baskets of so close a texture that they hold any liquid, and are the only utensil used for that purpose. At the Bashee River, after they had passed the ford, they remained one day to hunt the hippopotami, and were successful; only Major Henderson, who was not content to hunt during the day, but went out at night, had a narrow escape. He was in one of the paths, and had wounded a female, and was standing watching the rising to the surface of the wounded animal, for it was bright moonlight, when the male, which happened to be feeding on the bank above, hearing the cry of the female, rushed right down the path upon the Major. Fortunately for him, the huge carcass of the animal gave it such an ungovernable degree of velocity, as to prevent it turning to the right hand or left. It passed within a yard of the Major, sweeping the bushes and underwood, so as to throw him down as it passed. The Major got up again, it may be truly said, more frightened than hurt; but at all events he had had enough of hippopotamus-hunting for that night, for he recovered his gun, and walked back to the waggon, thanking Heaven for his providential escape.

The next morning, Swanevelt and Bremen went down the banks of the river, and discovered the body of the

hippopotamus, which they dragged on shore, and, returning to the waggons, sent the Caffres to cut it up; but
before the Caffres belonging to the caravan could arrive
there, they found that the work had been done for them
by the natives, and that nothing was left but the bones
of the animal; but this is always considered fair in the
Caffre-land; every one helps himself when an elephant
or other large animal is killed, although he may have
had no hand in its destruction. The number of elephant-
paths now showed them that they were surrounded by
these animals, and the Caffres of the country said that there
were large herds close to them.

It was therefore proposed by the Major that they
should have a grand elephant-hunt, at which all the
Caffres of their own party and the natives of the country
should assist. This proposal was joyfully received by
all, especially the natives, who were delighted at such an
opportunity of having the assistance of the white men's
guns; and the next day was appointed for the sport. By
the advice of the natives, the caravan proceeded some
miles down to the eastward, to the borders of a very thick
forest, where they stated that the elephants were to be
found.

They arrived at the spot in the afternoon, and every one
was busy in making preparations for the following day. The
Hottentots, who had been used to the sport, told long stories
to those who had not, and, among the rest, Big Adam
spoke much of his prowess and dexterity. Uncommonly
large fires were lighted that night, for fear that the elephants
should break into the camp. All night their cries were to
be heard in the forest, and occasionally the breaking of the
branches of the trees proved that they were close to the
caravan. Begum, who was particularly alive to danger,
crept to Major Henderson's bed, and would remain there
all night, although he several times tried to drive her away.
Notwithstanding continued alarms, the caravan was, however, unmolested.

CHAPTER XIII

*Look out—The signal—The Major's nerve—Charge upon the
camp — Hottentots drunk — Begum's uneasiness — Signs of
danger—Lions' sagacity—Anecdotes.*

AT daylight the following morning, there was a large concourse of Caffres in the camp, all waiting till our travellers
were ready for the sport. Having made a hasty breakfast,
they, by the advice of the Çaffres, did not mount their
horses, but started on foot, as the Caffres stated that the
elephants were on the side of the hill. Ascending by an
elephant-path, in less than half-an-hour they arrived at the
top of the hill, when a grand and magnificent panorama
was spread before them. From the crown of the hill they
looked down upon a valley studded with clumps of trees,
which divided the cleared ground, and the whole face of
the valley was covered with elephants. There could not
have been less than nine hundred at one time within the
scope of their vision.

Every height, every green knoll, was dotted with groups
of six or seven, some of their vast bodies partly concealed
by the trees upon which they were browsing, others walking in the open plain, bearing in their trunks a long
branch of a tree, with which they evidently protected
themselves from the flies. The huge bodies of the animals,
with the corresponding magnitude of the large timber-trees
which surrounded them, gave an idea of nature on her
grandest scale.

After a few minutes' survey, they turned to the party
who were collected behind them, and gave notice that
they were to commence immediately. The head men of
the Caffres gave their orders, and the bands of natives
moved silently away in every direction, checking any
noise from the dogs, which they had brought with them
in numerous packs. Our travellers were to leeward of
the herd on the hill where they stood, and as it was the
intention of the natives to drive the animals toward

92

them, the Caffre warriors as well as the Hottentots all took up positions on the hill ready to attack the animals as they were driven that way.

About an hour passed away, when the signal was given by some of the native Caffres, who had gained the side of the valley to westward of the elephants. Perched up at various high spots, they shouted with stentorian lungs, and their shouts were answered by the rest of the Caffres on every side of the valley, so that the elephants found themselves encompassed on all sides, except on that where the hill rose from the valley. As the Caffres closed in, their shouts reverberating from the rocks, and mixed up with the savage howlings of the dogs, became tremendous; and the elephants, alarmed, started first to one side of the valley, then to the other, hastily retreating from the clamour immediately raised as they approached, shaking their long ears and trumpeting loudly, as with uplifted trunks they trotted to and fro.

At last, finding no other avenue of escape, the herd commenced the ascent of the hill, cracking the branches and boughs, and rolling the loose stones down into the valleys, as they made their ascent, and now adding their own horrid shrieks to the din which had been previously created. On they came, bearing everything down before them, carrying havoc in their rage to such an extent, that the forest appeared to bow down before them; while large masses of loose rock leaped and bounded and thundered down into the valley, raising clouds of dust in their passage.

"This is tremendously grand," whispered Alexander to the Major.

"It is most awfully so; I would not have missed the sight for anything; but here they come—look at that tall tree borne down by the weight of the whole mass."

"See the great bull leader," said Swinton; "let us all fire upon him—what a monster!"

"Look out," said the Major, whose rifle was discharged as he spoke, and was quickly followed by those of Alexander and Swinton.

"He's down; be quick and load again. Omrah, give me the other rifle."

"Take care! take care!" was now cried on all sides,

for the fall of the leading elephant and the volleys of musketry from the Hottentots had so frightened the herd, that they had begun to separate and break off two or three together, or singly in every direction. The shrieks and trumpetings, and the crashing of the boughs so near to them, were now deafening; and the danger was equally great. The Major had but just levelled his other rifle when the dense foliage close to him opened as if by magic, and the head of a large female presented itself within four yards of him.

Fortunately the Major was a man of great nerve, and his rifle brought her down at his feet, when so near to him that he was compelled to leap away out of the reach of her trunk, for she was not yet dead. Another smaller elephant followed so close, that it tumbled over the carcass of the first, and was shot by Alexander as it was recovering its legs.

"Back, sirs, or you will be killed," cried Bremen, running to them; "this way—the whole herd is coming right upon you." They ran for their lives, following the Hottentot, who brought them to a high rock which the elephants could not climb, and where they were safe.

They had hardly gained it when the mass came forward in a cloud of dust, and with a noise almost inconceivable, scrambling and rolling to and fro as they passed on in a close-wedged body. Many were wounded and tottering, and as they were left behind, the Caffres, naked, with their assegais in their hands, leaping forward and hiding, as required, running with the greatest activity close up to the rear of the animals, either pierced them with their assegais, or hamstrung them with their sharp-cutting weapons, crying out in their own tongue to the elephants, "Great captain! don't kill us—don't tread upon us, mighty chief!"—supplicating, strangely enough, the mercy of those to whom they were showing none. As it was almost impossible to fire without a chance of hitting a Caffre, our travellers contented themselves with looking on, till the whole herd had passed by, and had disappeared in the jungle below.

"They have gone right in the direction of the waggons," said Swinton.

"Yes, sir," replied the Hottentot, Bremen; "but we must not interfere with them any more; they are now so scattered in the jungle, that it would be dangerous. We must let them go away as fast as they can."

They remained for a few minutes more, till every elephant and Caffre had disappeared, and then went back cautiously to the spot from whence they had first fired, and where they had such a fine prospect of the valley. Not an elephant was to be seen in it; nothing but the ravages which the herd had committed upon the trees, many of which, of a very large size, had been borne to the ground by the enormous strength of these animals. They then proceeded to the spot where the great bull elephant had fallen by the rifle of Major Henderson.

They found that the ball had entered just under the eye. It was a monster that must have stood sixteen feet high by Bremen's calculation, and it had two very fine tusks. While they were standing by the carcass of the animal, the armed Hottentots returned from the pursuit, and stated that seven elephants had been despatched, and others were so wounded that they could not live. They now set to work to take the teeth out of the animal, and were very busy when a Hottentot came running up, and reported that the herd of elephants in their retreat had dashed through the camp, and done a good deal of mischief; that a male elephant had charged the waggon of Major Henderson, and had forced his tusk through the side; that the tusk had pierced one of the casks of liquor, which was running out, although not very fast, and that the waggon must be unloaded to get out the cask and save the rest of the liquor.

Several Hottentots immediately hurried back with him to help in unloading the waggon, and by degrees they all slipped away except Bremen, Swanevelt, who was cutting out the tusks, and Omrah, who remained perched upon the huge carcass of the animal, imitating the trumpeting and motions of the elephant, and playing all sorts of antics. A party of Caffres soon afterward came up and commenced cutting up the carcass, and then our travellers walked away in the direction of the camp, to ascertain what mischief had been done.

On their return, which, as they stopped occasionally to examine the other animals that had fallen, must have taken an hour, they found that the Hottentots had not commenced unloading the waggon; although they had put tubs to catch the running liquor, of which they had taken so large a quantity that some were staggering about, and the rest lying down in a state of senseless intoxication.

"I thought they were very officious in going back to assist," observed the Major; "a pretty mess we should be in, if we were in an enemy's country, and without our Caffre guard."

"Yes, indeed," replied Alexander, turning over the tub of liquor, and spilling it on the ground, much to the sorrow of the Hottentots who were not yet insensible; "however, we will now let the cask run out, and watch that they get no more."

As the Caffres were busy with the carcasses of the elephants, and most of the Hottentots dead drunk, it was useless to think of proceeding until the following day. Indeed, the oxen and horses were all scattered in every direction, by the elephants breaking into the caravan, and it would be necessary to collect them, which would require some time. Our travellers, therefore, gave up the idea of proceeding further that day, and taking their guns, walked on to the forest, in the direction where most of the elephants killed had fallen. They passed by three carcasses, upon which the Caffres were busily employed, and then they came to a fourth, when a sight presented itself which quite moved their sympathy. It was the carcass of a full-grown female, and close to it was an elephant calf, about three feet and a half high, standing by the side of its dead mother.

The poor little animal ran round and round the body with every demonstration of grief, piping sorrowfully, and trying in vain to raise it up with its tiny trunk. When our travellers arrived, it ran up to them, entwining its little proboscis round their legs, and showing its delight at finding somebody. On the trees round the carcass were perched a number of vultures, waiting to make a meal of the remains, as soon as the hunters had cut it up, for their beaks could not penetrate the tough hide. Our travellers remained there for more than an hour, watching the motions and playing with the young elephant, which made several attempts to induce its prostrate mother to take notice of it. Finding, however, that all its efforts were ineffectual, when our travellers quitted the spot to go back, it voluntarily followed them to the caravans, where it remained, probably quite as much astonished to find all the Hottentots lying about as insensible as its mother.

It may be as well here to observe, that the little animal did not live beyond a very few days after, from want of its necessary food.

In the evening, Bremen and Swanevelt returned with tusks of the bull elephant, which were very large, and the Caffre warriors also came in; the other Caffres belonging to the country were too busy eating for the present. The chief of the Caffre warriors brought in the tufts of the other elephants' tails and the teeth, and the men were loaded with the flesh. As soon as the Caffres found that the oxen and horses had been frightened away, and perceived that the Hottentots were not in a situation to go after them, they threw down their meat and went in pursuit. Before dark the cattle were all brought back; the fires were lighted, and the Caffres did not give over their repast until near midnight.

Our travellers did not think it advisable, as the Hottentots were now no protection, to go to bed; they made up a large fire, and remained by it, talking over the adventures of the day. While they were conversing, Begum, who had been sitting by her master, showed signs of uneasiness, and at last clung round the Major with an evident strong fear.

"Why, what can be the matter with the Princess?" said the Major; "something has frightened her."

"Yes, that is evident; perhaps there is an elephant near; shall we waken Bremen and Swanevelt, who are close to us?"

Begum chattered, and her teeth also chattered with fear, as she clung closer and closer. Little Omrah, who was sitting by, looked very earnestly at the baboon, and at last touching the shoulder of Alexander to attract his attention, he first pointed to the baboon, imitating its fright, and then going on his hands and feet, imitated the motions and growl of an animal.

"I understand," cried the Major, seizing his gun; "the lad means that there is a lion near, and that is what frightens the baboon."

"Lion!" said the Major to Omrah.

But Omrah did not understand him; but pulling out his paper and pencil, in a second almost he drew the form of a lion.

"Clever little fellow! Wake them all, and get your guns ready," said the Major, starting on his legs; "it can't be far off; confound the monkey, she won't let go," continued he, tearing off Begum and throwing her away. Begum immediately scampered to the waggon and hid herself.

They had just awakened up the two Hottentots, when a roar was given so loud and tremendous, that it appeared like thunder, and was reverberated from the rocks opposite for some seconds.

No one but those who have been in the country, and have fallen in with this animal in its wild and savage state, can have any idea of the appalling effect of a lion's roar. What is heard in a menagerie is weak, and can give but a faint conception of it. In the darkness of the night it is almost impossible to tell from what quarter the sound proceeds; this arises from the habit which the animal has of placing his mouth close to the ground when he roars, so that his voice rolls over the earth, as it were like a breaker, and the sound is carried along with all its tremendous force. It is indeed a most awful note of preparation, and so thought Alexander, who had never heard one before.

The Caffres had wakened up at the noise, and our travellers and the Hottentots now fired their guns off in every direction to scare away the animal. Repeated discharges had this effect, and in the course of half-an-hour everything was again quiet.

"Well," observed Alexander, "this is the first time that I ever heard the roar of a lion in its wild state; and I can assure you that I shall never forget it as long as I live."

It is not the first time I have heard it," replied the

Major; "but I must say, what with the darkness and still-ness of the night, and the reverberation, I never heard it so awful before. But you, Swinton, who have travelled in the Namaqua-land, have, of course."

"Yes, I have, but very seldom."

"But it is rather singular that we have not heard the lion before this, is it not?" said Alexander.

"The lion is often near without giving you notice," replied Swinton; "but I do not think that there are many lions in the country we have traversed; it is too populous. On the other side of the mountains, if we return that way, we shall find them in plenty. Wherever the antelopes are in herds, wherever you find the wild horse, zebra, and giraffe, you will as certainly find the lion, for he preys upon them."

"I know very well, Swinton, that you are closely atten-tive to the peculiar habits of animals, and that they form a portion of your study. Have you much knowledge of the lion? and if so, suppose you tell us something about them."

"I have certainly studied the habits of the lion, and what I have gathered from my own observation and the information I received from others, I shall be most happy to communicate. The lion undoubtedly does not kill wantonly—of that I have had repeated instances. I recollect one which is rather remarkable, as it showed the sagacity of the noble brute. A man who belonged to one of the Mission stations, on his return home from a visit to his friends, took a circuitous route to pass a pool of water, at which he hoped to kill an antelope. The sun had risen to some height when he arrived there, and as he could not perceive any game, he laid his gun down on a low shelving rock, the back part of which was covered with some brushwood. He went down to the pool and had a hearty drink, returned to the rock, and after smoking his pipe, feeling weary, he lay down and fell fast asleep.

"In a short time, the excessive heat reflected from the rock awoke him, and opening his eyes he perceived a large lion about a yard from his feet, crouched down, with his eyes glaring on his face. For some minutes he remained motionless with fright, expecting every moment that he would be in the jaws of the monster; at last he recovered his presence of mind, and casting his eye towards his gun, moved his hand slowly towards it; upon which the lion raised up his head and gave a tremendous roar, which induced him hastily to withdraw his hand. With this the lion appeared satisfied, and crouched with his head between his fore-paws as before. After a little while the man made another attempt to possess himself of his gun. The lion raised his head and gave another roar, and the man desisted; another and another attempt were at intervals made, but always with the same anger shown on the part of the lion."

"Why, the lion must have known what he wanted the gun for."

"Most certainly he did, and therefore would not allow the man to touch it. It is to be presumed that the sagacious creature had been fired at before; but you observe that he did not wish to harm the man. He appeared to say—You are in my power; you shall not go away: you shall not take your musket to shoot me with, or I will tear you to pieces."

"It certainly was very curious. Pray, how did it end?"

"Why, the heat of the sun on the rock was so over-powering, that the man was in great agony; his naked feet were so burned, that he was compelled to keep moving them, placing one upon the other and changing them every minute. The day passed, and the night also; the lion never moved from the spot. The sun rose again, and the heat became so intense that the poor man's feet were past all feeling. At noon, on that day, the lion rose and walked to the pool, which was only a few yards distant, looking behind him every moment to see if the man moved; the man once more attempted to reach his gun, and the lion, perceiving it, turned in rage, and was on the point of springing upon him; the man withdrew his hand, and the beast was pacified."

"How very strange!"

"The animal went to the water and drank; it then returned and lay down at the same place as before, about a yard from the man's feet. Another night passed away, and the lion kept at his post. The next day, in the forenoon, the animal again went to the water, and while there looked as if he heard a noise in an opposite quarter, and then disappeared in the bushes.

"Perceiving this, the man made an effort, and seized his gun, but in attempting to rise he found it not in his power, as the strength of his ankles was gone. With his gun in his hand, he crept to the pool and drank, and, looking at his feet, he discovered that his toes had been quite roasted and the skin torn off as he crawled through the grass. He sat at the pool for a few minutes expecting the lion's return, and resolved to send the contents of his gun through his head; but the lion did not return, so the poor fellow tied his gun on his back and crawled away on his hands and knees as well as he could. He was quite exhausted, and could have proceeded no further, when providentially a person fell in with him and assisted him home; but he lost his toes, and was a cripple for life."

"What makes this story more remarkable is," observed the Major, "that the lion, as it is rational to suppose, must have been hungry after watching the man for sixty hours, even admitting that he had taken a meal but a short time before."

"I know many other curious and well-authenticated anecdotes about this noble animal," observed Swinton, "which I shall be happy to give you; but I must look at my memorandum-book, or I may not be quite correct in my story. One fact is very remarkable, and as I had it from Mr. ———, the missionary, who stated that he had several times observed it himself, I have no hesitation in vouching for its correctness, the more so, as I did once perceive a similar fact myself; it is, that the fifth commandment is observed by lions — they honour their father and mother.

"If an old lion is in company with his children, as the natives call them, although they are in size equal to himself, or if a number of lions meet together in quest of game, there is always one who is admitted by them to be the oldest and ablest, and who leads. If the game is come up with, it is this one who creeps up to it, and seizes it, while the others lie crouched upon the grass; if the old

10.

lion is successful, which he generally is, he retires from his victim, and lies down to breathe himself and rest for perhaps a quarter of an hour. The others in the meantime draw round and lie down at a respectful distance, but never presume to go near the animal which the old lion has killed. As soon as the old lion considers himself sufficiently rested, he goes up to the prey and commences at the breast and stomach, and after eating a considerable portion he will take a second rest, none of the others presuming to move.

"Having made a second repast, he then retires; the other lions watch his motions, and all rush to the remainder of the carcass, which is soon devoured. I said that I witnessed an instance myself in corroboration of this statement, which I will now mention. I was sitting on a rock after collecting some plants, when below me I saw a young lion seize an antelope; he had his paw upon the dead animal, when the old lion came up,—upon which the young one immediately retired till his superior had dined first, and then came in for the remainder. Mercy on us! what is that?"

"I thought it was the lion again," said Alexander, "but it is thunder; we are about to have a storm."

"Yes, and a fierce one too," said the Major; "I am afraid that we must break up our party and retire under cover. We have some large drops of rain already."

A flash of lightning now dazzled them, and was followed by another, and an instantaneous peal of thunder.

"There is no mistake in this," said Swinton; "and I can tell you that we shall have it upon us in less than a minute, so I am for my waggon."

"At all events it will wash these Hottentots sober," observed the Major, as they all walked away to their separate waggons for shelter.

CHAPTER XIV

A storm—Sober again—Elephant steak—Omrah's tricks—Man-eaters—A horrible adventure—The sleepers awakened.

THEY had scarcely gained the waggons before the thunder and lightning became incessant, and so loud as to be deafening. It appeared as if they were in the very centre of the contending elements, and the wind rose and blew with terrific force, while the rain poured down as if the flood-gates of heaven were indeed opened. The lightning was so vivid, that for the second that it lasted you could see the country round to the horizon almost as clear as day; the next moment all was terrific gloom accompanied by the stunning reports of the thunder, which caused every article in the waggons, and the waggons themselves, to vibrate from the concussion. A large tree, not fifty yards from the caravan, was struck by the lightning, and came down with an appalling crash. The Caffres had all roused up, and had sheltered themselves under the waggons.

The Hottentots had also begun to move, but had not yet recovered their senses—indeed, they were again stupefied by the clamour of the elements. The storm lasted about an hour, and then as suddenly cleared up again; the stars again made their appearance in the sky above, and the red tinge of the horizon announced the approach of daylight. When the storm ceased, our travellers, who had not taken off their clothes, came out from their shelter, and met each other by the side of the extinguished fire.

"Well," said Alexander, "I have been made wise on two points this night; I now know what an African storm is, and also the roar of an African lion. Have you heard if there is any mischief done, Bremen?" continued Alexander to the Hottentot, who stood by.

"No, sir; but I am afraid it will take us a long while to collect the cattle; they will be dispersed in all directions, and we may have lost some of them. It will soon be day-light, and then we must set off after them."

"Are those fellows quite sober now?"

"Yes, sir," replied Bremen, laughing; "water has washed all the liquor out of them."

"Well, you may tell them, as a punishment, I shall stop their tobacco for a week."

"Better not now, sir," said Bremen thoughtfully; "the men don't like to go further up the country, and they may be troublesome."

"I think so too," said Swinton; "you must recollect that the cask was running out, and the temptation was too strong. I should overlook it this time. Give them a severe reprimand, and let them off."

"I believe it will be the best way," replied Alexander; "not that I fear their refusing to go on, for if they do, I will dismiss them, and go on with the Caffres; they dare not go back by themselves, that is certain."

"Sir," said Bremen, "that is very true; but you must not trust the Caffres too much—Caffres always try to get guns and ammunition: Caffre king, Hinza, very glad to get the waggons and what is in them: make him rich man, and powerful man, with so many guns. Caffre king will not rob in his own country, because he is afraid of the English; but if the waggon's robbed, and you are killed in this country, which is not his, then he make excuses, and say, 'I know nothing about it.' Say that their people do it, not his people."

"Bremen talks very sensibly," said the Major; "we must keep the Hottentots as a check to the Caffres, and the Caffres as a check to the Hottentots."

"That is our policy, depend upon it," replied Swinton.

"You are right, and we will do so; but the day is break-ing; so, Bremen, collect the people together to search for the cattle; and, Omrah, tell Mahomed to come here."

"By-the-bye, Swinton," said Major Henderson, "those elephants' tusks lying by the waggon remind me of a question I want to put to you:—In Ceylon, where I have often hunted the elephant, they have no tusks; and in India the tusks are not common, and in general very small. How do you account for this variety?"

104

"It has been observed before; and it is but a fair surmise, that Providence, ever attentive to the wants of the meanest animals, has furnished such large tusks to the African elephant for the necessity which requires them. In Ceylon there is plenty of grass, and an abundant supply of water all the year round; and further, in Ceylon, the elephant has no enemy to defend himself against. Here, in Africa, the rivers are periodical torrents, which dry up, and the only means which an elephant has of obtaining water during the dry season is to dig with his tusks into the bed of the river, till he finds the water, which he draws up with his trunk. Moreover, he has to defend himself against the rhinoceros, which is a formidable antagonist, and often victorious. He requires tusks also for his food in this country, for the elephant digs up the mimosa here with his tusks, that he may feed upon the succulent roots of the tree. Indeed, an elephant in Africa without his tusks could not well exist."

"Thank you for your explanation, which appears very satisfactory and conclusive; and now let us go to breakfast, for Mahomed, I perceive, is ready, and Omrah has displayed our teacups, and is very busy blowing into the spout of the teapot, a Bushman way of ascertaining if it is stopped up. However, we must not expect to make a London footman out of a 'Child of the Desert.'"

"Where is his adversary and antagonist, the valiant Big Adam?"

"He was among those who indulged in the liquor yesterday afternoon, and I believe was worse than any one of them. The little Bushman did not fail to take advantage of his defenceless state, and has been torturing him in every way he could imagine during the whole night. I saw him pouring water into the Hottentot's mouth as he lay on his back with his mouth wide open, till he nearly choked him. To get it down faster, Omrah had taken the big tin funnel, and had inserted one end into his mouth, which he filled till the water ran out; after that he was trying what he could do with fire, for he began putting hot embers between Big Adam's toes; I daresay the fellow cannot walk to-day."

"I fear that some day he will kill Omrah, or do him

some serious injury; the boy must be cautioned," said Alexander.

"I am afraid it will be of no use, and Omrah must take his chance: he is aware of Big Adam's enmity as well as you are, and is always on his guard; but as for persuading him to leave off his tricks, or to reconcile them to each other, it is impossible," said Swinton—"you don't know a Bushman."

"Then pray tell us something about them," said the Major, "as soon as you have finished that elephant-steak, which you appear to approve of. Of what race are the Bushmen?"

"I will tell you when I have finished my breakfast," replied Swinton, "and not before: if I begin to talk, you will eat all the steak, and that won't do."

"I suspect that we shall not leave this to-day," said Alexander. "If, as Bremen says, the cattle have strayed very far, it will be too late to go in the afternoon, and to-morrow you recollect is Sunday, and that, we have agreed, shall be kept as it ought to be."

"Very true," said the Major; "then we must make Swinton entertain us by telling us more about the lions, for he had not finished when the storm came on."

"No," replied Swinton; "I had a great deal more to say, and I shall be very happy at any seasonable time, Major, to tell you what I know—but not just now."

"My dear fellow," said the Major, putting another piece of elephant-steak upon Swinton's plate, "pray don't entertain the idea that I want you to talk on purpose that I may eat your share and my own too; only ascribe my impatience to the true cause—the delight I have in receiving instruction and amusement from you."

"Well, Swinton, you have extorted a compliment from the Major."

"Yes, and an extra allowance of steak, which is a better thing," replied Swinton, laughing. "Now I have finished my breakfast, I will tell what I know about Omrah's people.

"The Bushmen are originally a Hottentot race—of that I think there is little doubt; but I believe they are a race of people produced by circumstances, if I may use the

106

expression. The Hottentot on the plains lives a nomad life, pasturing and living upon his herds. The Bushman may be considered as the Hottentot driven out of his fertile plains, deprived of his cattle, and compelled to resort to the hills for his safety and subsistence—in short, a Hill Hottentot: impelled by hunger and by injuries, he has committed depredations upon the property of others until he has had a mark set upon him; his hand has been against every man, and he has been hunted like a wild beast, and compelled to hide himself in the caves of almost inaccessible rocks and hills.

"Thus, generation after generation, he has suffered privation and hunger, till the race has dwindled down to the small size which it is at present. Unable to contend against force, his only weapons have been his cunning and his poisoned arrows, and with them he has obtained his livelihood—or rather, it may be said, has contrived to support life, and no more. There are, however, many races mixed up with the Bushmen; for runaway slaves, brought from Madagascar, Malays, and even those of the mixed white breed, when they have committed murder or other penal crimes, have added to the race and incorporated themselves with them; they are called the Children of the Desert, and they are literally such."

"Have you seen much of them?"

"Yes, when I was in the Namaqua-land and in the Bechuana territory I saw a great deal of them. I do not think that they are insensible to kindness, and moreover, I believe that they may often be trusted; but you run a great risk."

"Have they ever shown any gratitude?"

"Yes; when I have killed game for them, they have followed me on purpose to show me the pools of water, without which we should have suffered severely, if we had not perished. We were talking about lions; it is an old-received opinion, that the jackal is the lion's provider; it would be a more correct one to say that the lion is the Bushman's provider."

"Indeed!"

"I once asked a Bushman, 'How do you live?' His reply was, 'I live by the lions.' I asked him to explain to me. He said, 'I will show what I do: I let the lions follow the game and kill it and eat till they have their bellies full, then I go up to where the lion is sitting down by the carcass, and I go pretty near to him; I cry out, What have you got there, cannot you spare me some of it? Go away and let me have some meat, or I'll do you some harm. Then I dance and jump about and shake my skin-dress, and the lion looks at me, and he turns round and walks away; he growls very much, but he don't stay, and then I eat the rest.'"

"And is that true?"

"Yes, I believe it, as I have had it confessed by many others. The fact is, the lion is only dangerous when he is hungry—that is, if he is not attacked; and if, as the Bushman said, the lion has eaten sufficiently, probably not wishing to be disturbed, after his repast, by the presence and shouts of the Bushman, the animal retires to some other spot. I was informed that a very short time afterwards, this Bushman, who told me what I have detailed to you, was killed by a lioness, when attempting to drive it away from its prey by shouting as he was used to do. The fact was, that he perceived a lioness devouring a wild horse, and went up to her as usual; but he did not observe that she had her whelps with her: he shouted; she growled savagely, and before he had time to retreat, she sprang upon him and tore him to pieces."

"The lion does not prey upon men, then, although he destroys them?"

"Not generally; but the Namaqua people told me that, if a lion once takes a fancy to men's flesh—and they do, after they have in their hunger devoured one or two —they become doubly dangerous, as they will leave all other game and hunt man only; but this I cannot vouch for being the truth, although it is very probable."

"If we judge from analogy, it is," replied the Major. "The Bengal tigers in India, it is well known, if they once taste human flesh, prefer it to all other, and they are well known to the natives, who term them man-eaters. Strange to say, it appears that human flesh is not wholesome for them; for their skins become mangy after they have taken to eating that alone. I have shot a 'man-eater' from the back of an elephant, and I found that the skin was not worth taking."

"The Namaquas," replied Swinton, "told me that a lion, once enamoured of human flesh, would, in order to obtain it, so far overcome his caution, that he would leap through a fire to seize a man. I once went to visit a Namaqua chief, who had been severely wounded by a lion of this description —a man-eater, as the Major terms them—and he gave me the following dreadful narrative, which certainly corroborates what they assert of the lion who had once taken a fancy to human flesh.

"The chief told me that he had gone out with a party of his men to hunt: they had guns, bows and arrows, and assegais. On the first day, as they were pursuing an elephant, they came across some lions who attacked them, and they were obliged to save their lives by abandoning a horse, which the lions devoured. They then made hiding-places of thick bushes by a pool, where they knew the elephant and rhinoceros would come to drink.

"As they fired at a rhinoceros, a lion leaped into their inclosure, took up one of the men in his mouth and carried him off, and all that they afterwards could find of him the next day was one of the bones of his leg. The next night, as they were sitting by a fire inside of their inclosure of bushes, a lion came, seized one of the men, dragged him through the fire, and tore out his back. One of the party fired, but missed; upon which, the lion, dropping his dying victim, growled at the men across the fire, and they durst not repeat the shot; the lion then took up his prey in his mouth, and went off with it.

"Alarmed at such disasters, the Namaquas collected together in one strong inclosure, and at night sent out one of the slaves for water. He had no sooner reached the pool than he was seized by a lion; he called in vain for help, but was dragged off through the woods, and the next day his skull only was found, clean licked by the rough tongue of the lion.

"Having now lost three men in three days, the chief and his whole party turned out to hunt and destroy lions only. They followed the spoor or track of the one which had taken the slave, and they soon found two lions, one of which, the smallest, they shot; and then, having taken their breakfast, they went after the other, and largest, which was recognised as the one which had devoured the man.

"They followed the animal to a patch of reeds, where it had intrenched itself; they set fire to the reeds and forced it out, and as it was walking off it was severely wounded by one of the party, when it immediately turned back, and, with a loud roar, charged right through the smoke and the burning reeds. The monster dashed in among them and seized the chief's brother by the back, tearing out his ribs and exposing his lungs.

"The chief rushed to the assistance of his expiring brother; his gun burned priming. He dashed it down, and in his desperation seized the lion by the tail. The lion let go the body, and turned upon the chief, and with a stroke of his fore-paw tore a large piece of flesh off the chief's arm; then struck him again and threw him on the ground. The chief rose instantly, but the lion then seized him by the knee, threw him down again, and there held him, mangling his left arm.

"Torn and bleeding, the chief in a feeble voice called to his men to shoot the animal from behind, which was at last done with a ball which passed through the lion's brain. After this destruction of four men in four days, the hunting was given over; the body of the chief's brother was buried, and the party went home, bearing with them their wounded chief."

"Well, that is the most horrible lion-adventure I have yet heard," said the Major. "Heaven preserve us from a man-eating lion!"

"It really has almost taken away my breath," said Alexander.

"Well, then, I will tell you one more amusing, and not so fatal in its results; I was told it by a Bushman," said Swinton. "A Bushman was following a herd of zebras, and had just succeeded in wounding one with his arrow, when he discovered that he had been interfering with a lion, who was also in chase of the same animals. As the lion appeared very angry at this interference with his rights as lord of the manor, and evidently inclined to punish the Bushman as a poacher upon his preserves, the latter, perceiving a tree convenient, climbed up into it as fast as he could. The lion allowed the herd of zebras to go away, and turned his attention to the Bushman. He walked round and round the tree, and every now and then he growled as he looked up at the Bushman.

"At last the lion lay down at the foot of the tree, and there he kept watch all night. The Bushman kept watch also, but towards morning, feeling very tired, he was overcome by sleep, and as he slept, he dreamed, and what do you think that he dreamed?—he dreamed that he fell from the tree into the jaws of the lion. Starting up in horror from the effects of his dream, he lost his hold, and falling from the branch, down he came with all his weight right on the back of the lion. The lion, so unexpectedly saluted, sprang up with a loud roar, tossing off the Bushman, and running away as fast as he could; and the Bushman, recovering his legs and his senses, also took to his heels in a different direction; and thus were the 'sleepers awakened,' and the dream became true."

"Besiegers retreating and fort evacuated both at the same time," cried the Major, laughing.

"Well, I think you have had enough of the lion now," said Swinton.

"No, we had quite enough of him last night, if you choose," replied Alexander. "But your lions are not quite so near as he was."

CHAPTER XV

Quah! quah!—Alexander's and the Major's danger—A critical situation—Omrah's presence of mind—Divine worship—Instruction of Caffres—Advance of the enemy—Panic of the natives—Refusal to proceed—The tables turned—The council —Submission—Arrangements.

IT was not until the evening that the Caffres and Hottentots returned with the cattle, which they had great difficulty in collecting; two or three of the oxen were not brought back till late at night, so frightened had the animals been by the approach of the lion. In the afternoon, as it was too late to think of proceeding, our travellers, with their guns on their shoulders, and accompanied by Omrah and Begum, who would always follow the Major if she was not tied up, strolled away from the camp to amuse themselves. At first they walked to the hill from which they had such a splendid view of the valley covered with elephants, and, proceeding to where the male elephant had fallen, found that his flesh had, by the Caffres, the wolves, and the vultures, been completely taken off his bones, and it lay there a beautiful skeleton for a museum.

As, however, they had no room for such weighty articles in their waggons, they left it, after Swinton had made some observations upon the structure of the animal. Begum would not go near the skeleton, but appeared to be frightened at it. They then proceeded to the rock which had been their place of refuge when the herd of elephants had charged upon them; and as they stood under it, they were suddenly saluted with a loud noise over their heads, sounding like quah, quah!

As soon as Begum heard it, she ran up to the Major with every sign of trepidation, holding fast to his skin trousers.

"What was that?" said Alexander; "I see nothing."

"I know what it is," said the Major; "it is a herd of baboons; there they are; don't you see their heads over the rocks?"

112

"Let them show themselves a little more, and we'll have a shot at them," replied Alexander, cocking his gun.

"Not for your life," cried Swinton; "you will be skinned and torn to pieces, if they are numerous, and you enrage them. You have no idea what savage and powerful creatures they are. Look at them now; they are coming down gradually; we had better be off."

"I think so too," said the Major; "they are very angry; they have seen Begum, and imagine that we have one of their herd in our possession. Pray don't fire, Wilmot, unless it is for your life; we are too few to make them afraid of us. Here they come; there are a hundred of them at least; let us walk away slowly—it won't do to run, for that would make them chase us at once."

The baboons, some of which were of gigantic size, were now descending from the rock, grunting, grinning, springing from stone to stone, protruding their mouths, shaking their heads, drawing back the skin of their foreheads, and showing their formidable tusks, advancing nearer and nearer, and threatening an attack. Some of the largest males advanced so close as to make a snatch at Omrah. As for Begum, she kept behind the Major, hiding herself as much as possible. At last one or two advanced so close, rising on their hind-legs, that the Major was obliged to ward them off with his gun. "Point your guns at them," said Swinton, "if they come too close; but do not fire, I beg you. If we only get from off this rocky ground to the plain below, we shall probably get rid of them."

The ground on which they were formed a portion of the rocky hill upon which they had taken shelter the day of the elephant hunt; and within twenty-five yards of them there was an abrupt descent of about four feet, which joined it to the plain. They had gained half-way, parrying the animals off as well as they could, as they retreated backward, when some of the baboons came down from the other side of the rock, so as to attempt to cut off their retreat, their object evidently being to gain possession of Begum, whom they considered as belonging to them—and a captive.

Their situation now became more critical; for the whole herd were joining the foremost; and the noise they made, and the anger they expressed, were much greater than before.

"We must fire, I really believe," said the Major, when they heard a deep, hollow growl, followed up by a roar of some animal, apparently not very far off. At this sound the baboons halted, and listened in silence: again the growl was repeated, and followed up by the roar, and the baboons, at a shriek given by one on the rock, turned round and took to their heels, much to the delight of our travellers, who had felt the peculiar difficulty and danger of their situation.

"What animal was that which has frightened them off?" said the Major.

"It was the growl of a leopard," replied Swinton; "we must keep a sharp look-out; it can't be far off. The leopard is the great enemy of the baboons. But where is Omrah?"

They all looked round, but the boy was not to be seen. At last he showed his head above the foot of the rocky hill, where there was a descent of four feet, as we have mentioned, then sprang up the rock, and began capering, and imitating the baboons as they came on to the attack.

As they were laughing at him, all at once he stopped, and putting his hands to his mouth he gave the growl and roar of a leopard, which they had heard, and then set off running away baboon fashion.

"It was the Bushman, then, that frightened them off; he is a clever little fellow."

"And I am not sure that he has not saved our lives," replied Swinton; "but he has been brought up among them, one may say, and knows their habits well. If he had not hid himself below the rocks before he imitated the leopard, it would have been of no use, for they would not have been frightened, hearing the growl proceeding from him. I admire the boy's presence of mind."

"I thought at one time that the baboons had an idea that Omrah was one of them. What a snatch they made at him!"

"It would not have been the first time that these animals have carried off a boy," said Swinton; "I saw one at Latakoo, who had lived two years with the baboons, which had carried him off."

"How did they treat him?"

'Very well indeed; but they kept him a prisoner. When they found that he would not eat the coarse food which they did, they brought him other things; and they invariably allowed him to drink first at the pools."

"Well, that was homage to our superiority. Confound their quahs, I shall not get them out of my head for a week. What terrible large tusks they have!"

"Yes, their incisors are very strong. They often destroy the leopard when they meet it in numbers; but if one happens to be away from the herd, he has, of course, no chance with such an animal. Begum did not appear at all willing to renew her connection."

"None of the monkey tribe, after they have lived with man, ever are; indeed it is a question, if they had taken possession of her, whether they would not have torn her to pieces immediately, or have worried her to death some way or other."

"Well, at all events, Swinton, you have been rewarded for your kindness to that poor little Bushman, and we have reaped the benefit of it," observed Alexander. "But here come some of the oxen; I hope we shall be able to start early on Monday. The native Caffres say that the waggons cannot proceed much further."

"No, not further than to the banks of the Umtata River; but you will then be not a great way from your destination. Daaka is the chief's name, is it not?"

"Yes, that is his name; and if he is as supposed to be, he is my first cousin. How strange it sounds to me, as I look around me in this savage and wild country, that I should be within forty miles of a blood-relation, who is an inhabitant of it!"

"Well, we shall soon know the truth; but I must say, if it is only to end in a morning call, you have come a long way for the purpose," replied the Major.

"I have come to ascertain a fact, which, from what I now know of the country and its inhabitants, will be the source of anything but pleasure if it be established. My only hope is that it may prove otherwise than we suppose; and there is little chance of that, I fear."

"At all events, come what may," observed Swinton, "you will have done your duty."

On their return, they found all the men and cattle collected, and that night they increased the number of their fires, and tied the oxen to the waggons, that they might not be scattered by the return of the lion. The latter did not, however, make his appearance, and the night was passed without any disturbance. The following day being Sunday, the Hottentots were assembled, and desired not to start from the camp, as they would be expected to attend to prayers and Divine service; and as no hunting expedition was proposed, the Caffre warriors, as well as the native Caffres, who came in with their baskets of milk and other articles for sale and barter, also remained. Before dinner-time, the bell which had been brought with them from the Cape, to ring in case of any one having strayed from the camp, that he might be guided to return, was tolled by Bremen, and the Hottentots were assembled. Prayers and a portion of the Bible were then read.

The Caffre warriors, who had been told that the white men were going to pray to their God, were very silent and attentive, although they could not understand what was said; and the native Caffres, men, women, and children, sat down and listened. As soon as the service was over, the Caffre head man of the warriors asked the interpreter to inquire of our travellers why they struck the bell? was it to let God know that they were about to pray, and did He hear what they said?

Swinton replied, that their God heard all that they said, and listened to the prayers of those who trusted in Him.

A great many other questions were put by the Caffres, all of which were replied to with great caution by Mr. Swinton, as he was fearful that they might not otherwise be understood by the Caffres; but they were, as it was

116

proved by the questions which followed in consequence. A great portion of the afternoon was passed away in explaining and replying to the interrogatories of these people, and our travellers felt convinced that by having kept the Sabbath in that savage land they had done some good by the example; for, as Swinton truly observed—

"The missionaries come into the land to spread the gospel of Christ; they tell the natives that such is the religion and belief of the white men, and that such are the doctrines which are inculcated. Now white men come here as traders, or are occasionally seen here as travellers; and if the natives find, as they have found, that these white men, stated by the missionaries to hold the same belief, not only show no evidence of their belief, but are guilty of sins expressly forbidden by the religion preached, is not the work of the missionary nearly destroyed?

"I have often thought that the behaviour of the Dutch boors toward the natives must have had such an effect; indeed I may say that the colony has been founded upon very opposite principles to those of 'doing unto others as you would they should do unto you.' I believe that there never yet was an intercourse between Christians nominal and savages, in any portion of the globe, but that the savages have with great justice thrown in the Christians' teeth, that they preached one thing but did another. Unfortunately the taunt is but too true. Even those who had left their country for religious persecution have erred in the same way. The conduct of the Puritans who landed at Salem was as barbarous towards the Indians as that of Pizarro and his followers towards the Mexicans. In either case the poor aborigines were hunted to death."

On Monday they started at daylight, and proceeded on the journey; but they made little progress, on account of the difficulty of travelling with the waggons in a country consisting of alternate precipices and ravines, without any roads. The second day proved to be one of greater difficulty; they were obliged to cut down trees, fill up holes, remove large pieces of rock, and with every precaution the waggons were often out of order, aud they were obliged to halt for repairs.

At night they were about ten miles from the Umtata River, and it was doubtful, from the accounts received from the natives of the country, if they would be able to go further with the waggons than to its bank. But in the evening, news was brought that the Amaquibi, the nation of warriors which were governed by Quetoo, and which had come from the north, had been attacked by two of the native tribes, aided by some white men with guns; that the white men had all been destroyed, and that the hostile army were marching south.

The native Caffres appeared to be in a panic, and this panic was soon communicated to the Hottentots. At first, murmurings were heard as they sat round the fire, and at last they broke out into open mutiny. Big Adam, with three others, came up to the fire where our travellers were sitting, and intimated that they must return immediately, as they would proceed no further; that if it was decided to go on, the Hottentots would not, as they had no intention of being murdered by the savages who were advancing. Swinton, who could speak the Dutch language, having consulted with Alexander and the Major, replied that it was very true that the army of Quetoo was to the northward; but that the report of the defeat of the Caffres and of the army advancing was not confirmed. It was only a rumour, and might all be false; that even if true, it did not follow they were advancing in the direction in which they themselves were about to proceed; that it would be sufficient time for them to retreat when they found out what were the real facts, which would be the case in a few days at the furthest. But the Hottentots would not listen to anything that he said; they declared that they would proceed no further.

By this time all the other Hottentots had joined the first who came up to our travellers, and made the same demand, stating their determination not to proceed a mile further. Only Bremen and Swanevelt opposed the rest, and declared that they would follow their masters wherever they chose to lead them. Alexander now sent

118

for the interpreter and the chief of the Caffre warriors, lent him by Hinza, and desired the interpreter to ask the Caffre whether he and his band would follow them. The Caffre answered that they would; Hinza had given them in charge, and they could not return and say that they, had left them because there was an enemy at hand. Hinza would kill them all if they did; they must bring back the travellers safe, or lose their lives in their defence.

"Well, then," said the Major, "now we can do without these cowardly fellows, who are no use to us but to eat and drink; so now let us discharge them at once, all but Bremen and Swanevelt."

"I agree with you, Major," said Alexander; "what do you think, Swinton?"

"Yes, let us discharge them, for then they will be in a precious dilemma. We will discharge them without arms, and desire them to go home; that they dare not do, so they will remain. But let us first secure their muskets, which lie round their fire, before we dismiss them; or they will not, perhaps, surrender them, and we may be in an awkward position. I will slip away, and while I am away, do you keep them in talk until I return, which I shall not do until I have locked up all the guns in the store-waggon."

As Swinton rose, the Major addressed the Hottentots. "Now, my lads," said he, "here are Bremen and Swanevelt who consent to follow us; all the Caffre warriors agree to follow us; and here are about twenty of you who refuse. Now I cannot think that you will leave us; you know that we have treated you well, and have given you plenty of tobacco; you know that you will be punished as soon as you return to the Cape. Why then are you so foolish? Now look you: I am sure that upon reflection you will think better of it. Let me understand clearly your reasons for not proceeding with us; I wish to hear them again, and let each man speak for himself."

The Hottentots immediately began to state over again their reasons for not going on; and thus the Major, who made each give his reason separately, gained their attention, and the time which was required. Before they all had spoken, Swinton came back and took his seat by the fire.

"All's safe," said he; "Bremen and Swanevelt's guns have been locked up with the others." Our travellers had their own lying by them. The Caffre warriors, who were standing behind the Hottentots, had all their assegais in their hands; but their shields, as usual, were hanging to the sides of the waggons. The Major allowed the whole of the Hottentots to speak, and when they were done, he said, "Now, Wilmot, turn the tables on them."

Alexander then got up with his gun in his hand, the Major and Swinton did the same, and then Alexander told the Hottentots that they were a cowardly set of fellows; that with Bremen and Swanevelt, and the band of Caffre warriors, he could do without them; that since they did not choose to proceed, they might now leave the camp immediately, as they should get neither food nor anything else from them in future. "So now be off, the whole of you; and if I find one to-morrow morning in sight of the camp, or if one of you dares to follow us, I will order the Caffres to run him through. You are dismissed, and to-morrow we leave without you."

Alexander then called the chief of the Caffre warriors, and desired him, in the presence of the Hottentots, to give particular charge of the cattle, horses, and sheep, to his warriors during the night; and if any one attempted to touch them, to run him through the body. "Do this immediately," said Alexander to the chief, who without delay spoke to his men, and they went off in obedience to his orders.

The Hottentots, who had heard all this, now retreated to their waggon, but were struck with consternation when they found that their guns had been removed; for they trusted to their guns and ammunition to enable them to procure food and protect themselves on their return. They consulted together in a low voice; they looked round and perceived that our three travellers had quitted the fire, and were keeping guard with their guns upon the waggons, to prevent any attempt of breaking them open, on the part of the Hottentots. Moreover, ten of the Caffres, with their spears, had, since the breaking up of the conference, been put in charge of the waggons by the chief, at the request of the Major. The Hottentots now perceived their forlorn position.

How could they, without arms and ammunition, and without provisions, return to the Cape, such a number of miles distant? How could they exist, if they remained where they were? When they insisted upon our travellers returning, they had quite overlooked the circumstance that these could protect themselves with the Caffre warriors, and that they were not in a condition to enforce their demand.

After a long conversation, they did what all Hottentots will do under any emergency,—they lay down by the fire, and fell fast asleep. Swinton, having ascertained that they were really asleep, proposed that they themselves should retire to the waggon, and leave the Caffres on guard, which they did; as they well knew that a Hottentot once fast asleep is not easily roused up even to "treason, stratagem, or spoil."

Shortly after break of day, Bremen came to them, stating that he found the waggons could proceed no further, as he had walked on, and discovered that a mile before them there was a ravine so deep that it would be difficult for the cattle to go down, and for the waggons impossible; that at a distance of three miles below he could see the river, which was also so embedded in rocks, as to be impassable by the waggons.

The Major immediately went with Bremen, to satisfy himself of the truth of this, and returned, stating that further progress with waggons was impossible.

"Well, then, we must now hold a council," said Swinton. "Of course, proceed you will, Wilmot, that is decided; the only question is, as we must now proceed on horseback, what force you will take with you, and what shall be left in charge of the waggons?"

"I think we can trust the Caffres, do not you?"

"Yes, I do; but I wish from my heart that the Hottentots had not rebelled; for although in some respects cowardly fellows, yet with their muskets they are brave, and their muskets keep the natives in order."

"To the Caffres, the contents of the waggons would prove a temptation; but these are not temptations to the Hottentots, whose object is to get back safe, and receive their wages. Thus we play them off against each other."

"Here are all the Hottentots coming up to us," said the Major; "I hope it is to make submission; it is very desirable that they should do so before they know that the waggons proceed no further."

The surmise of the Major was correct: the Hottentots had again canvassed the matter over, and, perceiving the helplessness of their position, had come in a body to beg forgiveness, and to offer to accompany our travellers wherever they pleased to take them.

It was a long while before Alexander would consent to receive them again, and not until they had made promise upon promise, that he seemed at last to be mollified. Swinton then interceded for them, and at last Alexander consented, upon their future good behaviour, to overlook their conduct. This matter having been satisfactorily arranged, the former question was resumed.

"One of you, I fear, must remain with the waggons," observed Alexander; "or both of you, if you please. I have no right to ask you to go upon any wild-goose chase, and run into danger for nothing."

"That one should remain with the waggons will be necessary," said Swinton; "and I think that the Major, if he does not object, is the proper person. The party who are left must provide themselves with food by their guns; and it will require more military tact than I possess to arrange that and to defend the waggons. I will accompany you, Wilmot, as I can speak better Dutch, and the interpreter will not get on well without me."

"Will you have the kindness to take charge of the waggons, Major, during our absence?"

"I think, perhaps, it will be as well; although I had rather have gone with you," replied the Major. "I propose that you take thirty of the Caffres, Bremen, and eight Hottentots with you; leave me Swanevelt and the other Hottentots."

"Yes, that will do very well; we will leave the Caffre head man with you."

"No; he must go with the larger portion of his party; he could not well be separated from them. I will find a proper place for the waggons, and stockade myself regularly in; that will be a good job for the Hottentots, and I dare say I shall do very well."

"I shall not leave you Omrah, 'Major," said Swinton; "for, as we shall take four horses with us, I wish him to ride one, and he can attend upon us, as you have Mahomed."

"You may have Begum to ride the other," replied the Major, "if you please; then you will each have a groom."

"No, no, it would be a pity to part you and her; however, there is no time to be lost, for if this great chief and warrior Quetoo is advancing, it may be as well to be ready for a retreat; the sooner we are off, the sooner we shall be back; so now to pack up."

CHAPTER XVI

An expedition—Rumours of war—Judicious advice—Daaka's hut—The interview with Daaka—Explanations—Remains of the Grosvenor—*The mystery solved—Alexander's joy—The waggons again—The Major's fortress—Plans for the future.*

THE first step taken by Alexander was to send for the Hottentots, and, after again reproving them for their former behaviour, he asked who were ready to volunteer to proceed with him, as he had decided to leave the waggons with Major Henderson, and proceed on horseback the short distance of his journey which remained to be accomplished.

Several of the Hottentots immediately came forward; the heads of the mutiny held back, and thus proved to Alexander that the men who had come forward were persuaded into it by the others, and regretted what they had done. He therefore immediately accepted their services, and their muskets were returned to them. Alexander then stated his intentions to the Caffre head man, who selected the thirty warriors that were required, and in the course of three hours everything was ready for their departure.

It was arranged that in case of danger arising to either party, they should, if possible, fall back to the newly-established Mission of Morley, on the sea-coast; but otherwise, the waggons would remain where they were till Alexander's return. Having packed up all they required in small packages, to be carried by the Caffres, they bade farewell to the Major, and set off, having no baggage but what we have mentioned; for Alexander would not be encumbered with a load of heavy articles which must prevent rapid progress, or rapid retreat if necessary.

In two hours they arrived by difficult passes at the banks of the Umtata River, which they crossed, and soon afterward falling in with a Caffre kraal, they were informed that Daaka, the chief whom they sought, did not reside more than twenty miles distant; and they easily procured a guide to show them the way.

The reports of the advance of the Amaquibi army were here fully confirmed, and the natives were preparing to leave the kraal with all their cattle. It appeared, however, that at present the army was stationary; the warriors carousing and enjoying themselves after the victory which they had gained over the Caffres. As these had been assisted by white men and their guns, the spirits of the Amaquibi were raised to an extraordinary degree, and they were intending to carry their arms to the southward, as soon as Quetoo, their chief, had somewhat recovered from his wounds received in the late action. Indeed, it was the wounded state of their chief which was the principal cause of the army not having immediately proceeded to the southward.

Having obtained this information, the travellers resumed their journey along the banks of the Umtata, over a country of surprising beauty, the deep river being full of hippopotami, which were lying on the banks or snorting in the stream. They could not wait to kill one during the daytime, but promised the men they would allow them to make the attempt in the evening, after their day's march was over. Towards sunset, they stopped on the banks of the river on a rising ground, and the Hottentots and some Caffres were then directed to go down to the river in chase of the hippopotami, as it was advisable to save their provisions as much as possible.

Before night they had succeeded, and the carcass of the animal was hauled on shore. As soon as the party had taken as much as they required, the native Caffres carried off the remainder of the flesh. As they were sitting down carousing by the fire which had been lighted, the Caffre head warrior came up to the interpreter, and told Alexander and Swinton not to say that they were Hinza's warriors if asked where they came from. On being asked why, he told them that Hinza had married a daughter of the chief of this country, and after a time had sent her back again to her father, and that this had created ill blood between the tribes, although no war had taken place. Alexander and Swinton, who perceived that the advice was judicious, told him that they would not, and after partaking of the hippopotamus flesh they all lay down to repose under the far spreading branches of a large tree.

The next morning they set off, and after an hour's journey the guide told them that they were at the kraal of Daaka, the descendant of the Europeans. The bellowing of the cattle and noise of the calves soon directed them to the spot, and they entered a kraal consisting of several very wretched huts. On inquiring for Daaka, a woman pointed out a hut at a little distance, and, as they dismounted and walked up, he came out to meet them. Swinton and Alexander shook hands with the chief, and said that they were very glad to see him, and that they had come far to pay him a visit. The chief ordered a hut to be swept out for their accommodation, which they took possession of.

"You have no idea, Swinton," said Alexander, "how much I am excited already by this interview."

"I can imagine it, my dear Wilmot," said Swinton; "it is but natural, for he is your kinsman by all report, and certainly, although a Caffre in his habits and manners, his countenance and features are strikingly European."

"That I have observed myself, and it has fully convinced me of the truth of the statement. I am most anxious to examine him—we must call the interpreter."

The chief entered the hut soon afterwards, and took his seat; the interpreter was sent for, and the conversation was begun by Daaka, who like most of the Caffre chiefs, with the hope of obtaining presents, stated himself to be very poor, his cattle to be dying, and his children without milk. Our travellers allowed him to go on for some time in this manner, and then sent for a present of beads and tobacco, which they gave him. They then commenced their inquiries, and the first question they asked was, why he resided so near the sea.

"Because the sea is my mother," replied he; "I came from the sea, and the sea feeds me when I am hungry."

"In that reply he evidently refers to the wreck of the ship," observed Swinton; "and I presume, from the fish-bones which we have seen about the kraal, that these Caffres feed on fish, which the other tribes do not, and therefore it is that he says his mother feeds him."

"Was your mother white?" inquired Alexander.

"Yes," replied Daaka, "her skin was white as yours; her hair was just like yours, long and dark; but before she died it was quite white."

"What was your mother's name?"

"Kuma," replied the chief.

"Had you any brothers and sisters?"

"Yes, I had; I have one sister alive now."

"What is her name?" inquired Swinton.

"Bess," replied the chief.

"This is very confirmatory," said Alexander; "my aunt's name was Elizabeth; she must have called her child after herself."

"Whom did your mother marry?"

"She first married my uncle, and had no children; and then she married my father; both were chiefs and I am a chief; she had five children by my father."

126

A long conversation took place after this, the substance of which we may as well communicate to our reader in few words. From the children of Kuma, supposed to be Elizabeth, the aunt of Alexander, were produced a numerous race of the European blood, who were celebrated in the Caffre land for their courage ; they were continually engaged in war, as their alliance was eagerly sought, and in consequence had nearly all perished. Daaka himself was renowned for warlike exploits, but he was now a very old man. In the evening the chief took his leave, and went to his own hut.

As soon as they were alone, Alexander said to Swinton, "I have now so far fulfilled my promise to my worthy relation that I have seen this descendant of his child ; but what am I to do? An old man like him is not very likely to consent to go to England, and as for his sister Bess, he states that she is equally infirm ; the progeny of the rest of the family are scattered about, and he himself knows nothing about them ; to collect them would be impossible, and if collected, equally impossible to remove them, for they would not leave. My old relative fancies, in his mind's eye, his daughter weeping over her captivity, and longing to be restored to her country and her relations ; still retaining European feelings and sympathies, and miserable in her position ; her children brought up by her with the same ideas, and some day looking forward to their emancipation from this savage state of existence : I think if he were here, and saw old Daaka, he would soon divest himself of all these romantic ideas."

"I think so too ; but there is one thing which has struck me very forcibly, Alexander, which is, if this Daaka is the son of your aunt how comes it that he is so old? When was the *Grosvenor* lost?"

"In the year 1782."

"And we are now in 1829. Your aunt you stated to have been ten or twelve years old at the time of the wreck. Allowing her to marry at the earliest age, Daaka could not well be more than forty-eight years old ; and surely he is more than that."

"He looks much older, certainly ; but who can tell the

age of a savage, who has been living a life of constant
privation, and who has been so often wounded as his scars
show that he has been? Wounds and hardship will soon
make a man look old."

"That is very true, but still he appears to me to be older
than the dates warrant."

"I think his stating that his sister was named Bess is
full corroboration."

"It is rather circumstantial evidence, Wilmot: now what
do you propose to do?"

"I hardly know; but I wish to be in Daaka's company
some time longer, that I may gain more intelligence; and
I think of proposing to him that we should go down to
visit the remains of the wreck of his mother, as he terms
it. I should like to see a spot so celebrated for misfortune, and behold the remains of the ill-fated vessel;
I should like to have to tell my good old uncle all I can,
and he will wish that I should be able to give him every
information."

"Well, I think it is a good plan of yours, and we will
propose it to him to-morrow morning."

"And I should like to visit his sister Bess—indeed, I must
do so. He says she is much younger than he is."

"He did, and therefore I think his age does not correspond
with our dates, as I observed before," replied Swinton; "but,
as you say, you must see his sister."

Daaka had sent an old cow as a present to Alexander,
which was a very seasonable supply, as the hippopotamus-
flesh had all been eaten. The next morning they proposed
that he should accompany them to where the *Grosvenor* had
been wrecked.

Daaka did not at first appear to know what they wished,
and inquired, through the interpreter, whether they meant
the ship that was wrecked on the sea-coast, pointing to
the eastward. On receiving an answer in the affirmative,
he agreed to set off with them that afternoon, saying that
it was about forty miles off, and that they could not get
there until the next day.

About noon they set off on their journey, and as they
made but slow progress over a rugged although most
beautiful country, they stopped at night at a kraal about

" All that remained of the unfortunate *Grosvenor*."

half-way. Early the next morning they were led by
Daaka and some Caffres who accompanied him to the
sea-shore, and when they had arrived at the beach, it
being then low water, Daaka pointed to a reef, upon
which were to be seen the guns, ballast, and a portion
of the keelson of a ship—all that remained of the unfortunate *Grosvenor*.

As the sea washed over the reef, now covering and now
exposing these mementoes of misery and suffering, Alexander
and Swinton remained for some time without speaking; at
last Alexander said—

"Swinton, you have read the history of this unfortunate
vessel, I know, for you asked me for it to read. What a
succession of scenes of horror do these remains, which from
their solid weight only have defied the power of the winds
and waves, conjure up at this moment in my mind. I think
I now behold the brave vessel dashed upon the reefs—the
scream of despair from all on board—the heart-rending
situation of the women and children — their wonderful
escape and landing on shore, only to be subjected to greater
suffering. See, Swinton, that must have been the rock
which they all gained, and upon which they remained
shivering through the night."

"It is, I have no doubt, from its position," said Swinton.

"Yes, it must have been. I think I see them all—men,
women, and helpless children — huddled together, half-
clothed and suffering, quitting that rock by this only path
from it, and setting off upon their mad and perilous journey;
the scattering of the parties—their perils and hunger—
their conflicts with the natives—their sufferings from heat
and from thirst—their sinking down one by one into the
welcome arms of death, or torn to pieces by the wolves
and hyenas as they lagged behind the others. How much
more fortunate those who never gained the shore."

"Yes, indeed," replied Swinton; "except the eight
who reached the Cape, and the five that Daaka asserts
were saved, all the rest must have perished in that dreadful
manner."

Alexander remained for some time in painful thought; at
last he turned to Daaka and said, as he pointed to the
remains of the wreck, " And this, then, is your mother?"

Daaka looked at him and shook his head. "No, not my mother this," replied he; "my mother down there," pointing out in a northerly direction.

"What does he mean, Swinton? he says this is not his mother."

"I will speak to him, Wilmot; you are too much agitated," replied Swinton.

"Is not that the vessel which your mother was lost in?" said Swinton, through the interpreter.

"No," replied Daaka; "my mother came on shore in a vessel up the little river out there; I was a boy when this large ship was wrecked; and got some iron from her to make assagais."

"Merciful Heaven! what joy I feel; I trust it is true what he says."

"I have no doubt of it, Wilmot; I told you he was too old a man," replied Swinton; "but let me question him further."

Our readers may imagine the impatience of Alexander while the questions of Swinton were being answered, and by which it appears that Daaka's mother was lost at the mouth of the Lauwanbaz, a small river some miles to the eastward of the Zemsooboo. An old Caffre, who had come down with Daaka, now gave a particular account of the wreck of the *Grosvenor*, corroborating all Daaka's assertions.

"Were there none of the *Grosvenor's* people left in the country?" inquired Swinton.

"None," replied the old man; "they all went to the southward."

"Did you hear what became of them?"

"Some lay down and died, some fought the natives and were killed; the wolves ate the rest; not one left alive; they all perished."

"Were none of the women and children saved and kept as slaves?"

"No, not one; they had no meat, no milk, and they all died."

After some other inquiries, the old man, who at first did not reply willingly, stated that he had, with other Caffres, followed the last party; had seen them all dead,

130

and had taken off their clothes, and that as they died they were buried by those who still survived.

"A better fate, cruel as it was, than living as they must have lived," said Swinton.

"Yes, truly," replied Alexander; "you don't know, Swinton, what a load has been removed from my mind, and how light-hearted I feel, notwithstanding this recital of their sufferings. My poor uncle! God grant that he may live till my return with this distinct intelligence, with the assurance that he has no grandchildren living the life of a heathen, and knowing no God. What a relief will it prove to him; how soothing will it be to his last days! How grateful am I to God, that I have had so happy an issue to my mission! Now, Swinton, we will return as soon as you please; as soon as we arrive at Daaka's kraal, I will take down in writing the statement of these people, and then we will hasten back to the Major."

"And I daresay," said Swinton, as he remounted his horse, "that you will make old Daaka a more handsome present, for proving himself no relation to you, than if he had satisfactorily established himself as your own first cousin."

"You may be sure that my gratitude towards him is much greater than ever could have been my kindred feeling from friendship. I am so light-hearted, Swinton, and so grateful to God, that I almost wish to dismount in my anxiety to return my thanks; but I do so in my heart of hearts, at all events."

On the following day they arrived at Daaka's kraal, and then Alexander took down very carefully in writing the statements made by Daaka and the other Caffres. They all agreed on the one point, which was, that the European descendants now living in the country were wrecked in another vessel many years before the loss of the *Grosvenor*, and that not one of the *Grosvenor's* people—men, women, or children—had survived, except the few who arrived at the Cape.

Having obtained these satisfactory documents, they made a handsome present to Daaka and the other Caffres, and immediately set out upon their return to the waggons. As they journeyed back to the westward, they found the Caffres quitting their huts, and driving away the cattle, that they might not fall into the power of the army of Quetoo, which it was said was now in motion, and scattering the tribes before them. As our travellers were not at all anxious to have any communication with these savage invaders, in two days they crossed the Umtata, and towards the evening were within sight of the waggons. A shout from the Hottentots and Caffres gave notice of their approach. The shout was returned, and in a few minutes they were shaking hands with the Major, who was delighted to see them.

"I did not expect you back so soon," replied the Major; "and as I perceive that you are unaccompanied, I presume that your Caffre relations would not quit their kraals."

"You shall know all about it, Major, very soon; it will be enough at present to let you know that we have nothing but good news."

"That I rejoice to hear; but it was well you came back as you did, for I have been making every preparation, and had you not returned in a few days, I should have retreated; the invaders are close at hand."

"We know it, and, if they are told that there are waggons here well loaded, they will come on quickly, with the hopes of plunder, so we must delay no longer," replied Alexander; "to-morrow we will yoke and set off. We can determine upon our route as we are travelling, but the first point is to retreat from this quarter."

"Exactly; the oxen are in prime order and can make a long day's march, and we know our country for some days, at all events; but enter my fortress, dismount, and let us go into the tent which I have pitched. You shall then tell me your adventures, while Mahomed fries a delicate piece of elephant's flesh for you."

"Have you killed an elephant?"

"Yes, but not without much difficulty and some danger, I assure you; I wanted your help sadly, for these Hottentots are too much alarmed to take good aim, and I had only my own rifle to trust to; but I have done very well considering, and I shall prove to our commander-in-chief that I have supplied the garrison without putting him to any expense during his absence. We have been feeding upon green monkeys for three days, and very good eating they are, if you do not happen upon a very old one."

When they entered the enclosure made by the Major, they were surprised at the state of defence in which he had put it. His hedge of thorns upon rocks piled up was impregnable, and the waggons were in the centre, drawn up in a square; the entrance would only admit one person at a time, and was protected by bars at night.

"Why, Major, you might have held out against the whole force of the Amaquibi in this position."

"Yes, provided I had provisions and water," replied the Major; "but I fear they would soon have starved me out; however, it was as well to be prepared against any sudden night-attack, and therefore I fortified my camp: now come in, and welcome back again."

The news which they had to impart to the Major was soon given, and he was highly delighted at the intelligence: "And now," said he, "what do you mean to do, Wilmot?—go back again, of course, but by what route?"

"Why, Major, you and Swinton have been so kind in coming with me thus far, and I have been so successful in my expedition, that I shall now leave you to decide as you please. I have effected all that I wished, my business is over, and I am ready to meet you in any way you choose; anything you decide upon I shall agree to willingly and join in heartily, so now speak your wishes."

"Well, I will speak mine very frankly," replied the Major. "We have had some sport in this country, it is true, but not so much as I could have wished; for game is rather scarce, with the exception of elephants and sea-cows. Now I should like to cross the mountains, and get into the Bechuana and Bushman country, where game is as plentiful as I believe water is scarce; we can return that way, if you please, almost as well as we can through the Caffre country—what say you, Swinton?"

"Well, I am of your opinion. As Wilmot says, business is over and we have nothing to do but to amuse ourselves. I am very anxious to pass through this country, as I shall add greatly to my collections, I have no doubt; but it must not be expected that we shall fare as well as we have done in this: it will be the dry season, and we may be in want of water occasionally."

"I am equally desirous of going through that country, where I hope to shoot a giraffe,—that is my great ambition," replied Wilmot; "therefore we may consider that we are all agreed, and the affair is settled; but the question is, how shall we proceed back? We must return to Hinza's territory and send back the Caffres. Shall we return to Butterworth?"

"I think that must depend upon circumstances, and we can talk it over as we go along: the first point to ascertain is the best passage over the mountains; and it appears to me that we shall be diverging much too far to the eastward if we return to Butterworth; but the Caffres will soon give us the necessary information."

"I wonder if the quarrel between Hinza and Voosani has been made up," said Alexander; "for we must pass through the Tambookie tribe if we cross the mountains, and if there is war between them we may meet with difficulty."

"We shall hear as soon as we have crossed the Bashee River," replied Swinton; "and then we must decide accordingly. All that can be settled now is, that to-morrow we start on our return, and that we will cross the mountains, if we possibly can."

"Yes, that is decided," replied Alexander.

"Well, then, as soon as you have finished your elephant-steak, Wilmot, we will get out a bottle of wine, drink the first half of it to congratulate you upon the success of your mission, and the other half shall be poured out in bumpers to a happy return."

134

CHAPTER XVII

THE RETURN

*Quetoo's movements—Destruction of his army—The return—
Plenty of sport—The warriors rewarded—Precautions—Antelopes—The victim—A large meal.*

THE delight of the Hottentots at the announcement of
the return of the expedition was not to be concealed;
and now that they knew that they were retreating from
the danger, as they were further removed they became
proportionately brave. We must not include all the
Hottentots in this observation, as Bremen, Swanevelt, and
one or two more were really brave men; but we do refer
to the principal portion of them, with Big Adam at their
head, who now flourished and vapoured about, as if he
could by himself kill and eat the whole army of the dreaded
Quetoo.

As it was the intention of our travellers to pass over the
Mambookei chain of mountains, into the Bushman and
Koranna territory, they did not return the same route by
which they came, but more to the westward through the
territory of the Tambookie Caffres, not any one time
entering upon the territory of the Amakosas, the tribe of
Caffres governed by Hinza, who had lent them his warriors.

Voosani, the chief of the Tambookies, was very friendly,
and had offered no opposition to their passage through
a portion of his domains on their advance. They now lost
no time, but continued their journey as fast as they could,
although during the day they saw a great quantity of game,
and were almost every night saluted with the roaring of
the lions.

In a week they found themselves on the banks of the
White Kae River, and not far from the foot of the mountains which they intended to pass. Here they halted, with
the intention of remaining some few days, that they might
unload and rearrange the packing of their waggons, repair
what was necessary, and provide themselves with more oxen

135

and sheep for their journey in the sterile territory of the Bushmen.

During their route, the rumours relative to the army of Quetoo were incessant. He had attacked and murdered Lieutenant Farewell and his people, who were on a trading expedition in the interior, and taken possession of and plundered their waggons. Flushed with success over white people armed with muskets, Quetoo had now resolved to turn his army to the southward, and attack the tribes of the Amaponda Caffres, governed by Fakoo, and the missionary station of Morley, lately established near the coast, between the St. John and the Umtata rivers.

To effect this, Quetoo commenced his ravages upon all the lesser tribes tributary to Fakoo, and having put them to indiscriminate slaughter, driven away their cattle, and burned their kraals, his army advanced to the missionary station, which the missionaries were compelled to desert, and fall back upon the St. John River.

One of the men belonging to the tribe near Morley came to the caravan where our travellers had halted, and, on being questioned as to the loss they had experienced, cried out, "Ask not how many are killed, but how many are saved: our wives, where are they? and our children, do you see any of them?"

But Fakoo, the chief of the Amapondas, had roused himself and collected his army. He resolved upon giving battle to the enemy. He found the Amaquibi encamped in a forest, and he surrounded them with a superior army; he then contrived, by attacking and retreating, to lead them into a position from which there was no escape but by the pass by which they had entered, and which he completely blocked up with his own forces.

The Amaquibi could not retreat, and a furious conflict took place, which ended in the destruction of the whole of Quetoo's army. Quetoo himself was not present, as he still remained confined with the wound he had received in the prior engagement, in which he had been victorious. A portion of Fakoo's army was sent against him, and he fled with the loss of all the cattle and treasures he had collected; and thus was the invading force at last totally dispersed and not heard of any more.

This news was very satisfactory to our travellers, as they did not know whether they would have had time to make their arrangements, if Quetoo's army had been victorious; and it was still more pleasing to the Hottentots, who were now even braver than before, all lamenting that they had not remained on the banks of the Umtata River, where the combat took place, that they might have assisted at the destruction of the invaders.

It was towards the end of August before our travellers had made their preparations and were ready for a start. They had decided to try the pass through the Mamboo-kei chain of mountains, to the eastward of the one named Stormbergen, and as they expected to meet with some difficulties, it was decided that the Caffre warriors should not be dismissed till they had arrived at the Bushman territory; they proposed then to turn to the N.W., so as to fall in with that portion of the Orange River which was known by the name of the Vaal or Yellow River, crossing the Black or Cradock River, which is also another branch of the Orange River.

This arrangement was made, that they might get into the country more abounding with game, and better furnished with water than any other portion of the sterile deserts which they had to pass through.

Having, as usual, kept holy the Lord's day, on the Monday morning they started in high spirits, and with their cattle in excellent order. The passage through the ravine was very difficult; they had to fill up holes, roll away stones, and very often put double teams to drag the waggons.

They made but ten miles on the first day, and found the night cold, after the heat to which they had been subjected. The second day was also one of toil and danger, but on the third they found that they had commenced the descent, and the whole Bushman country was spread before them. But the descent was even more perilous than the ascent, and it was not without great exertion that they saved their waggons from falling over the precipices.

On the fourth evening they had crossed the mountains, and were now at the foot of them on the western side.

It was with difficulty that they collected wood enough to make their fires for the night, and the continual roaring told them that they were now in the domain of the lion and his satellites.

At break of day they all rose, that they might view the country which they were about to traverse. It was one wild desert of sand and stones, interspersed with small shrubs, and here and there a patch of bushes; apparently one vast, dry, arid plain, with a haze over it, arising from the heat. Our travellers, however, did not at first notice this change: their eyes were fixed upon the groups of quaggas and various antelopes which were strewed over the whole face of the country; and, as soon as they had taken their breakfast, they mounted their horses in pursuit. It had been their intention to have dismissed the Caffres on that morning, but the chief of the band pointed out that it would be as well that they should kill some game, to provide them with food for their journey back; and our travellers approved of the suggestion, as it would save their sheep.

Alexander and the Major set off with Bremen, Swanevelt, and Omrah on horseback, while the Caffres on foot kept well up with them. The other Hottentots were ordered to remain with Swinton at the encampment, as they had to repair the damages done to the waggons in crossing the mountains.

Omrah had shown himself so useful, that he had been permitted to practice with a fowling-piece carrying ball, and had proved himself very expert. He now was mounted on the Major's spare horse; that in case the Major's was knocked up, he might change it, for Omrah's weight was a mere nothing.

The plan of the chase was, that the Caffres should spread in a half-circle, and conceal themselves as much as possible, while those on horseback should turn the animals and drive them in their direction. As they advanced on the plain, they discovered what the haze had prevented their seeing at early dawn, that the plain was covered with a variety of beautiful flowers, of the amaryllis and other tribes, and with the hills of ants and ant-eater's holes, which latter were very dangerous to the horses.

The sun was now up in the heavens, and blazed fiercely, the heat was intense, although still early in the day. When they turned their heads towards the mountains which they had passed, they were struck with astonishment at the grandeur of the scene: rocks and cliffs in wild chaos, barren ridges and towering peaks, worn by time into castellated fortresses and other strange shapes, calling to their fancy the ruins of a former world. With the exception of a pool of water, near to which the caravan had halted, not a vestige of that element was to be seen in any direction; all was one plain, ending only in the horizon, without a tree, the line only broken by the groups of animals and the long necks of the packs of ostriches in the distance.

If, however, the vegetable kingdom was deficient, the animal was proportionably abundant, and Alexander and the Major were soon at their speed after a troop of quaggas and zebras, which they succeeded in turning towards the Caffres. As soon as the animals had entered the radius of the half-circle, and were within distance, they checked their horses and opened their fire upon them; at the same time the Caffres showed themselves, and the animals were for a time confounded by finding themselves so nearly surrounded.

During their hesitation, and while they attempted to break through here and there, and then turned again, several were brought to the ground by the guns of the mounted party, till at last, as if they had summoned up their resolution, the whole herd, led by a splendid male, burst away in a direction close to the horsemen, and made their escape from the circle in a cloud of dust, scattering the stones behind them as they fled.

The Caffres ran up to the animals which lay wounded, and put them out of their misery by inserting the point of their assagais into the spine, which caused immediate death. Seven animals were killed, three zebras and four quaggas; and as Swinton had requested that they might not be cut up till he had ascertained if he required their skins, Omrah was sent back to bring him to where they were lying.

Swinton soon came, and Alexander said to him, " Now,

139

Swinton, let us know if you want any of the skins of these animals to preserve."

"No," replied Swinton, "I have them already; I just thought it possible that you might have killed a zebra."

"Well, have we not? there are three of them."

"No, my good fellow, they are not of the real zebra species; they belong to a class described by Burchell, the traveller, which is termed the striped quagga. The quagga and striped quagga, as you may see, have the ears of a horse, while the zebra has those of the ass. The true zebra hardly ever descends upon the plains, but lives altogether upon the mountainous regions; occasionally it may be found, it is true, and that is the reason why I came to see."

"Are they good eating, these animals?"

"The quagga is very indifferent food, but the striped quagga is very passable; so if you intend to save any for our dinner, pray let it be some of the latter. Have you done hunting to-day?"

"Yes," replied the Major, "if Wilmot is of my opinion, I think we had better not work our horses any more just now; the plain is so full of large holes—ant-eaters' holes, Bremen says they are."

"Yes, they are ant-eaters' holes, and very dangerous; I have seen them several feet deep. If we do not start to-day, I will ask the Hottentots to try and procure one for me to-night, as I wish to have a stuffed specimen."

"We do not intend to start till to-morrow morning," replied Alexander; "we must dismiss the Caffres to-night, that they may be also ready to go home to-morrow. They will now have provisions enough."

Our travellers now rode back to the caravan, leaving the Caffres to bring home the flesh. As soon as they had dined, the chief of the warriors was desired to come with all his men, and Alexander then made every man a handsome present, consisting of tobacco, snuff, cloth, knives and beads. To the chief of the band he gave three times as much as the others, and then, having delivered to him a very liberal collection of articles for their king Hinza, Alexander told the chief to acquaint the king that he had been very much pleased with the conduct of the men, and thanked his Majesty for the loan of them, and requested that his Majesty would accept of the packet of articles which he had selected for him.

He then thanked the men for their good conduct, told them to take all the flesh that they wished for the journey, and stated that they were at liberty to depart that evening or the next morning, as they thought proper. The Caffres were perfectly satisfied with Alexander's liberality, and the chief of the warriors, making a short speech in reply, retired with his men.

"Well, I'm very sorry that these fine fellows are leaving," said the Major.

"And so am I; but I could not well detain them, and they said that they could not go further with us without the king's permission," replied Alexander.

"Of course not," replied the Major; "but that does not lessen my regret at their departure; they have been both steady and brave, as well as active and willing, and I do not expect that our Hottentots will serve us so well."

"You are right not to expect it, Major," replied Swinton; "if you did, you would be miserably disappointed. If they knew now where we were going, they would desert us. The only hold that we have upon the greater number of them is their fear; they go forward because they are afraid to go back; but if they could get hold of our horses, with their guns and ammunition, they would leave us as soon as we advanced in the desert."

"Very true, I fear; but we have a few stanch fellows among them, and two at least whom we can depend upon—Bremen and Swanevelt."

"How far is it from here to the Black River, Swinton?"

"About forty miles; not so much perhaps to the river's bed, but at least that, if not more, before we shall fall in with any water at this season of the year."

"We must not fail to fill our water-kegs before we leave this."

"No, for we shall have no water to-night, that is certain. We cannot travel more than twenty miles over such a country as this; for turning here and there to avoid the holes and ant-hills, the twenty miles will be at least thirty," said Swinton; "but now I must go and tell

141

the Hottentots to find me what I want: a pound of tobacco will procure it, I have no doubt."

"But I have mine," observed the Major, after Swinton was gone; "we are too near the pool, and we shall be surrounded with lions to-night; the Hottentots may pretend that they will go, but they will not."

"One cannot well blame them; I'm sure a pound of tobacco would not persuade me to put my head into a lion's mouth; but I agree with you, we are too near the pool, and as we must collect the cattle to secure them during the night, I think we had better fill our water-kegs, and then yoke and take up a position for the night about half a mile further off. But here comes Swinton, who can give us his advice."

As Swinton agreed with them, they yoked the oxen, and drove forward about a mile from the pool; they then secured them to the waggons and lighted large fires round the caravan.

The Major was correct as regarded the Hottentots' procuring an ant-eater for Swinton; they would not leave the fires, and the continual approach of the lions during the night proved that they were wise in so doing. There was no occasion for the lions to roar; the moaning of Begum, and her clinging to the Major, the trembling of the dogs, and the uneasiness of the cattle, invariably gave notice of lions being at hand. Shots were fired off during the night, to keep them at a distance, but otherwise the night passed away undisturbed.

They started the following morning about daybreak, and at the same time the Caffres took their departure to their own country. The ground over which the caravan travelled was stony and sandy at intervals, and they had not proceeded far before they again discovered a great variety of game dispersed over the level plain. They did not, however, attempt to pursue them, as they were anxious to go on as far as possible, so as to give the oxen an opportunity of picking up what little food they could during the middle of the day, at which time the Major and Alexander proposed that they should go in pursuit of game. But before they had travelled three hours, they were surprised at a cloud of dust, which obscured the horizon, in the direction they were proceeding.

"What can that be ?" said Alexander.

"I think it is springbok," said Bremen the Hottentot.

"Springbok! why, there must be thousands and thou.. sands of them."

"I believe that Bremen is right," said Swinton; "it must be one of the migratory herds of springboks; I have never seen them, but I have often been told of them."

The body of antelopes now advanced towards them, keeping on a straight path; and to state their numbers would have been impossible : there might have been fifty or a hundred thousand, or more. As far as the eye could see in any direction, it was one moving mass covering the whole plain. As they approached the caravan, those nearest huddled on one side and occasionally bounded away with the remarkable springs made by this animal, and from which it has its name, alighting not upon the earth, but, for want of room, upon the backs of its companions, and then dropping in between the ranks.

A hazy vapour arose from these countless herds as they moved on, and more than once the Hottentots, who were standing on the waggons, which had been stopped as the herd came up to them, pointed out a lion which was journeying with the crowds to feast at his leisure. The animals appeared very tame, and several were killed close to the wheels of the waggons, for the evening's supper. Notwithstanding that the herd moved at a rapid pace, it was more than two hours before the whole had passed by.

"Well," observed Alexander, "I can now say that I have seen no want of game in Africa. Where will they go to ?"

"They will go directly on to the southward," replied Swinton; "the migration of these animals is one of the most remarkable proofs of the fecundity of animal life. Like the ants, they devour everything before them; and if we journey in the direction they have come from, we shall find no food for the cattle until after the rains. After the rains fall, these animals will return to their former pastures. It is the want of food which has brought them so far to the southward."

"Their track is evidently from the north and eastward," said the Major; "had we not better change our course more to the northward?"

"No, I should think not; they have probably travelled on this side of the Nu Gareip or Black River. We shall have neither water nor food for the cattle to-night, and therefore I think we had better go on as we are going, so as to make sure of water for them to-morrow, at all events. It's useless now stopping to feed the cattle, we had better continue right on till the evening; we shall sooner arrive at the river, and so gain by it."

It was but half-an-hour before dark that they unyoked the tired oxen. Water or grass there was none; and, what was another misfortune, they could not find sufficient wood of any kind to keep up the necessary fires during the night. All they could collect before dark was but enough for one fire, and they considered it better, therefore, that only one should be lighted.

The waggons were drawn up so as to form a square, inside of which were tied the horses; the sheep were driven underneath, and the oxen were tied up outside. They feasted well themselves upon the delicate meat of the springboks, but the poor animals had neither food nor water after their hard day's journey.

As soon as they had supped they retired to their waggons, and the Hottentots remained by the side of the fire, which was but frugally supplied, that it might last till morning; but that there were lions prowling in the vicinity was evident from the restlessness of the oxen, who tried to break the leathern thongs with which they were fastened.

The moon had just risen, and showed an imperfect light, when they perceived the bodies of some animals between them and the horizon. They appeared very large, as they always do in an imperfect light, and the Hottentots soon made out that they were five or six lions not forty yards distant. The truth of this supposition was confirmed by an angry roar from one of them, which induced most of the Hottentots to seize their guns, and some to creep under the waggons.

The oxen now struggled furiously to escape, for the roar of the lions had spread consternation.

Our travellers heard it in their waggons, and were out with their guns in a minute. At last one of the oxen broke loose, and, as it was running behind its companions, as if seeking a more secure shelter, being not more than three or four yards from them, another roar was followed by a spring of one of the lions, which bore the animal to the earth.

The Major and Wilmot were advancing before the fire to the attack, when the animal for a moment let go his prey, and was about to spring upon them. Bremen called out for them to retreat, which they did, as the animal advanced step by step towards them.

Satisfied with their retiring, the lion then went to his prey, and dragged it to a distance of about fifty yards, where it commenced its meal; and they distinctly heard, although they could not plainly distinguish, the tearing of the animal's flesh and the breaking of its bones by the lion, while its bellowings were most pitiful.

They all now fired in the direction where they heard the noise; the lion replied to the volley by a tremendous roar, and rushed up within twenty yards of the waggons, so as to be distinctly visible. Bremen begged our travellers not to molest the animal, as it was evidently very hungry and very angry, and would certainly make a spring upon them, which must be attended with disastrous effects.

The other lions were also now moving round and round the camp; they therefore reloaded their guns, and remained still, looking at the lion tearing and devouring his prey.

"We must be quiet here," said Bremen to Alexander; "there are many lions round us, and our fire is not sufficient to scare them away, and they may attack us."

"Would it not be better to fire our guns,—that would frighten them?"

"Yes, sir, it would frighten the other lions, perhaps, but it would enrage this one so near to us, and he would certainly make a charge. We had better throw a little gunpowder upon some ashes now and then, as we have but a small fire: the flash will drive them away for the time."

In the meantime the lion was making his meal upon the poor ox, and when any other of the hungry lions approached him, he would rush at them, and pursue them for some paces with a horrible growl, which made not only the poor oxen, but the men also, to shudder as they heard it.

In this manner was the night passed away, every one with his gun in his hand, expecting an immediate attack; but the morning at last dawned, to the great relief of them all. The lions had disappeared, and they walked out to where the old lion had made his meal, and found that he had devoured nearly the whole of the ox; and such was the enormous strength of his jaws, that the rib-bones were all demolished, and the bones of the legs, which are known as the marrow-bones, were broken as if by a hammer.

"I really," observed the Major, "have more respect for a lion, the more I become intimate with his feline majesty."

"Well, but he is off," observed Swinton, "and I think we had better be off too."

CHAPTER XVIII

Conversation—Gnoos—Five lions—Thirst quenched—Ferocity of the hyena—Anecdotes—Preparations for a chase.

THE oxen were yoked, and the caravan proceeded at slow pace to gain the wished-for river. As our travellers walked their horses—for the poor animals had been without food or water for twenty-four hours, and all idea of chasing the various herds of animals which were to be seen in their path was abandoned for the present—Swinton remarked, "We are not far from the track of the Mantatees, when they made their irruption upon the Caffres about eighteen months back."

"I was intending to ask you for some information on that point, Swinton. There has been more than one irruption into the country from the natives to the north-

146

ward. Mr. Fairburn gave me a very fair idea of the
history of the Cape colony, but we were both too much
engaged after our arrival in Cape Town for me to obtain
further information."

"I will, you may be assured, tell you all I know,"
replied Swinton; "but you must not expect to find in
me a Mr. Fairburn. I may as well remark, that Africa
appears to be a country not able to afford support to a
dense population, like Europe; and the chief cause of this
is the great want of water, occasionally rendered more trying
by droughts of four or five year's continuance."

"I grant that such is the case at present," observed the
Major; "but you well know that it is not that there is
not a sufficient quantity of rain, which falls generally
once a year, but because the water which falls is carried
off so quickly. Rivers become torrents, and in a few
weeks pour all their water into the sea, leaving, I may
say, none for the remainder of the year."

"That is true," replied Swinton.

"And so it will be until the population is not only
dense, but, I may add, sufficiently enlightened and industrious. Then, I presume, they will take the same measures
for securing a supply of water throughout the year which
have been so long adopted in India, and were formerly in
South America by the Mexicans. I mean that of digging
large tanks, from which the water cannot escape, except by
evaporation."

"I believe that it will be the only remedy."

"Not only the remedy, but more than a remedy; for
tanks once established, vegetation will flourish, and the
vegetation will not only husband the water in the country,
but attract more."

"All that is very true," replied Swinton, "and I trust
the time will come, when not only this land may be well
watered with the dew of heaven, but that the rivers of
grace may flow through it in every direction, and the tree
of Christ may flourish."

"Amen," replied Alexander.

"But to resume the thread of my discourse," continued Swinton; "I was about to say that the increase
of population, and I may add the increase of riches,—

147

for in these nomadic tribes cattle are the only riches,—is the great cause of these descents from the north; for the continued droughts which I have mentioned of four or five years compel them to seek for pasture elsewhere, after their own is burned up. At all events, it appears that the Caffre nations have been continually sustaining the pressure from without, both from the northward and the southward, for many years.

"When the Dutch settled at the Cape, they took possession of the country belonging to the Hottentot tribes, driving the few that chose to preserve their independence into the Bushman and Namaqua lands, increasing the population in those countries, which are only able to afford subsistence to a very scattered few. Then, again, they encroached upon the Caffres, driving them first beyond the great Fish River, and afterwards still more to the northward. The Bushman tribes of hill Hottentots, if we may so term them, have also been increased by various means, notwithstanding the constant massacres of these unhappy people by the Dutch boors; moreover, we have by our injudicious colonial regulations added another and a new race of people, who are already considerable in their numbers."

"Which do you refer to?"

"To the people now known by the name of Griquas, from their having taken possession of the Griqua country. They are the mixed race between the Hottentots and the whites. By the Dutch colonial law, these people could not hold possession of any land in the colony; and this act of injustice and folly has deprived us of a very valuable race of men, who might have added much to the prosperity of the colony. Brave and intelligent, industrious to a great degree, they, finding themselves despised on account of the Hottentot blood in their veins, have migrated from the colony and settled beyond the boundaries. Being tolerably well provided with fire-arms, those who are peaceably inclined can protect themselves, while those who are otherwise commit great depredations upon the poor savages, following the example shown them by the colonists, and sweeping off their cattle and their property, in defiance of law and justice.

148

You now perceive, Alexander, how it is that there has been a pressure from the southward."

"That is very evident," replied the Major.

"Perhaps I had better proceed to the northward by degrees, and make some mention of the Caffre tribes, which are those who have suffered from being, as it were, pressed between encroachments from the north and the south. The Caffre race is very numerous. The origin of the general term Caffre, which means Infidel, and no more, is not known, any more than is that of the term Hottentot."

"A proof of what we found out at school," observed the Major, "that nicknames, as they are termed, stick longer than real ones."

"Precisely," replied Swinton; "our acquaintance is mostly with the more southern Caffres, who occupy the land bordering on the east coast of Africa, from the Cape boundary to Port Natal. These are the Amakosa tribe, whose warriors have just left us; the Tambookies, whose territory we have recently quitted, and to the northward of them by Port Natal, the Hambonas. These are the Eastern Caffres.

"On the other side of the Mambookei chain of mountains, and in the central portion of Africa, below the tropic, are the Bechuanas, who inhabit an extent of country as yet imperfectly known to us. These may be termed the Central Caffres.

"On the western side of the African coast, and above Namaqualand, whose inhabitants are probably chiefly of the Hottentot race, we have the Damaras, who may be classed as the Western Caffres; with these we have had little or no communication.

"All these tribes speak the Bechuana or Caffre language, with very slight variations; they are all governed by chiefs or kings, and subdivided into numerous bodies; but they are all Caffres. Of their characters I have only to observe, that as far as we have experienced, the Caffres of the eastern coast, which we have just left, are very superior to the others in courage and in every other good quality. Now, have I made myself intelligible, Alexander?"

"Most clearly so."

"I nevertheless wish we were sitting down in some safe place instead of travelling on horseback over this withered tract, and that I had the map before me to make you understand better."

"I will refer to the map as soon as I can," replied Alexander; "but I have studied the map a great deal, and therefore do not so much require it."

"All these Caffre tribes live much the same life; their wealth is in cattle; they are partly husbandmen, partly herdsmen, and partly hunters; and their continual conflicts with the wild beasts of the country prepare them for warriors. The Eastern Caffres, from whom we have lately parted, are the most populous; indeed, now that we have taken from them so much of their country, they have scarcely pasturage for their cattle. I have said that the Eastern Caffres' territory extends as far as the latitude of Port Natal, but it formerly extended much further to the northward, as it did to the southward, before we drove them from their territory; indeed as far north as Delagoa Bay; all the country between Port Natal and Delagoa Bay being formerly inhabited by tribes of Caffres. I believe, Alexander, that Mr. Fairburn gave you a history of the celebrated monarch Chaka, the king of the Zulus ?"

"Yes, he did."

"Well, it was Chaka who overran that country I am now speaking of, and drove out all the tribes who occupied it, as well as a large portion of the Bechuana tribes who inhabited lands more to the northward. Now the irruptions we have had into the Caffre and Bechuana country bordering upon the colony have been wholly brought about by the devastations committed by Chaka. Of course I refer to those irruptions which have taken place since our knowledge and possession of the Cape. I have no doubt that such irruptions have been continued, and that they have occurred once in every century for ages. They have been brought about by a population increasing beyond the means of subsistence, and have taken place as soon as the overplus have required it.

"The migration of the springboks, which we witnessed yesterday, may be more frequent, but are not more certain than those of the central population of Africa. The Caffres themselves state that they formerly came from the northward, and won their territory by conquest; and the Hottentots have the same tradition as regards themselves.

"The invasion of the Mantatees, as they are called (and by the Eastern Caffres Ficani), was nothing more than that of a people dispossessed of their property, and driven from the territory by the Zulus, under Chaka; and, indeed, this last army under Quetoo, which has been destroyed within this month, may be considered as invading from a similar cause. Having separated from Chaka, Quetoo could find no resting-place, and he therefore came to the southward with the intention of wresting the territory from the Caffres, in which he has failed. Had he not failed, and been cut off by the Caffres, he would have destroyed them, and thus made room for his own people."

"Of course; for the end of all these invasions and migrations must be in such a sacrifice of human life as to afford sustenance and the means of subsistence to those who remain," observed the Major.

"Precisely; and such must continue to be the case on this continent, until the arts and civilisation have taught men how to increase the means of subsistence. To produce this, Christianity must be introduced; for Christianity and civilisation go hand in hand."

"But the Mantatees or Ficani, who are they?"

"I have already said they were northern Caffre tribes, dispossessed of their territory by Chaka. The names of the tribes we do not know. Mantatee, in the Caffre language, signifies an invader, and Ficani also, marauders; both terms applicable to the people, but certainly not the names of the tribes.

"I believe, now, I have said enough on the subject to allow me to enter upon the history of this last invasion; but, to tell the truth, the heat is so overpowering, and I feel my tongue so parched, that you must excuse me for deferring this account till another opportunity. As. soon as we are a little more at our ease, I will give you the history of the Mantatees."

"We are much obliged to you for what you have told us, Swinton, and will spare you for the present," replied Alexander. "What animals are those?—look!"

"They are gnoos," replied Swinton. "There are two varieties of them, the common gnoo and the brindled gnoo. They form an intermediate link between the antelope family and the bovine or ox, and they are very good eating."

"Then, I wish we were able to go after them. They do not seem to be afraid of us, but approach nearer at every gallop which they make."

"Yes, although shy, they have a great deal of curiosity," replied Swinton. "Watch them now."

The animals bounded away again, as Swinton spoke, and then returned to gaze upon the caravan, stirring up the dust with their hoofs, tossing their manes, and lashing their sides with their long tails, as they curvetted and shook their heads, sometimes stamping as if in defiance, and then flying away like the wind, as if from fear.

"They are safe this time," observed Major Henderson; "but another day we will try their mettle."

"You will find them fierce and dangerous when wounded, sir," said Bremen, who had ridden up. "We are not many miles from the river, for the cattle begin to sniff."

"I am delighted to hear you say so; for then there must be water near. But the haze and glare together are so great that we cannot distinguish above two miles, if so much."

"No, sir," replied the Hottentot; "but I can see well enough to see *them*," continued he, pointing with his finger to a rising ground about a hundred yards off, on the right of them. "One, two, three—there are five of them."

"What are they?" said the Major, looking in the direction pointed out. "I see; they are lions."

"Yes, sir; but we must take no notice of them, and they will not annoy us. They are not hungry."

"You are right," said Swinton, "we must go right on,
152

neither stopping nor hastening our speed. Let the driver look to the oxen; for, tired as they are, the smell of the lions is sufficient to give them ungovernable strength for the moment."

"Well," said the Major, "bring us our guns, Bremen. I am willing to accept the armed neutrality, if they will consent to it.

The caravan passed on; the lions remaining crouched where they were, eyeing them, it is true, but not rising from their beds. The oxen, however, either through fear of the lions, or the scent of water near, became more brisk in their motions, and in half-an-hour they perceived a line of trees before them, which told them that they were near the bed of the Nu Gareip or Cradock River.

The poor animals redoubled their exertions, and soon arrived at the banks. Bremen had ridden forward and reported that there still was water in the river, but only in pools. As the herbage was destroyed on the side where they were, they would have crossed the bed of the river before they unyoked, but that they found impossible. The animals were so impatient for the water, that, had they not been released, they would have broken the waggons.

Horses, oxen, and sheep all plunged into the pools together, and for some minutes appeared as though they would never be satisfied. They at last went out, but soon returned again, till their sides were distended with the quantity of the element which they had imbibed.

An hour was allowed for the animals to rest and enjoy themselves, and then they were again yoked to drag the waggons to the other side of the river, where there was a sufficiency of pasturage and of wood to make up their fires.

As it was their intention to remain there for a day or two, the waggons were drawn up at some distance from the river, so as not to interfere with the path by which the wild animals went down to drink. The spoors or tracks of the lions and buffaloes and other animals were so abundant, as to show that this precaution was necessary.

As soon as the waggons were arranged in the usual manner, the cattle were permitted to graze till the evening, when they were brought in and secured, as usual, inside and round the waggons. They supped off the remainder of the springbok, which was not very sweet; but the horses and men were both too much exhausted with the fatiguing journey to hunt until the following day.

That night they were not disturbed by lions, but the hyenas contrived to crawl under the waggons, and, having severely bitten one of the oxen, succeeded in carrying off one of the sheep. They had been so often annoyed by these animals, that we have never mentioned them; but on the following morning it was found that the ox had been so seriously injured that the leg-bone was broken, and they were obliged to destroy the animal.

"Were the courage of the hyena equal to his strength, it would be a most formidable animal," observed Swinton; "but the fact is, it seldom or never attacks mankind, although there may be twenty in a troop. At the same time, among the Caffres they very often do enter the huts of the natives, and occasionally devour children and infirm people. But this is greatly owing to the encouragement they receive from the custom of the Caffres leaving their dead to be devoured by these animals, which gives them a liking for human flesh, and makes them more bold to obtain it."

"They must have a tremendous power in their jaw," observed Alexander.

"They have, and it is given them for all-wise purposes. The hyena and the vulture are the scavengers of the tropical regions. The hyena devours what the vulture leaves, which is the skin and bones of a dead carcass. Its power of jaw is so great that it breaks the largest bone with facility."

"Are there many varieties of them?"

"In Africa there are four :—The common spotted hyena, or wolf of the colonists, whose smell is so offensive that dogs leave it with disgust after it is killed; its own fellows will, however, devour it immediately. The striped or ferocious hyena, called the shard-wolf, and another which the colonists call the bay-wolf, and which I believe to be the one known as the laughing hyena. There is another variety, which is a sort of link between the hyena and the dog, called the venatica. It hunts in packs, and the colonists term it the wild honde. It was first classed by Burchell the traveller. This last is smaller, but much fiercer, than the others."

"I know that there are leopards in the country, but we have never yet fallen in with one. Are they dangerous?"

"The leopard shuns any conflict with man, but when driven to desperation it becomes a formidable antagonist. I recollect very well two boors having attacked a leopard, and the animal, being hotly pressed by them and wounded, turned round and sprang upon the one nearest, pulling him to the ground, biting his shoulder, and tearing him with his claws. The other, seeing the danger of his comrade, sprang from his horse and attempted to shoot the animal through the head. He missed, and the leopard left the first man, sprang upon *him*, and, striking him on the face, tore his scalp down over his eyes. The hunter grappled with the animal, and at last they rolled together down a steep cliff. As soon as the first hunter could reload his gun, he rushed after them to save his friend, but it was too late. The animal had seized him by the throat, and mangled him so dreadfully that death was inevitable, and all that the man could do was to avenge his comrade's death by shooting the leopard."

"That proves the leopard is not to be trifled with."

"No animal is, when it stands at bay, or is driven to desperation; and, in confirmation of this, I once witnessed one of these animals—the quaggas—which, being pressed to the edge of a precipice by a mounted hunter, seized the man's foot with its teeth, aud actually tore it off, so that, although medical aid was at hand, the man died from loss of blood."

"One would hardly expect such a tragical issue to the chase of a wild jackass," observed the Major.

"No; but 'in the midst of life we are in death,' and we never know from whence the blow may come. Until it occurred, such an event was supposed impossible, and the very idea would have created nothing but ridicule. By-the-bye, one of our good missionaries was very near losing his life by a leopard. He went to save a Hottentot who had been seized, and was attacked by the leopard

which, as in the former instance, left his first antagonist to
meet his second. Fortunately Mr. S. was a very powerful
man, and assistance was sooner given him than in the
former instance. Neither he nor the Hottentot, however,
escaped without severe wounds, which confined them for
many weeks."

"Is there more than one variety of leopard, Swinton?"

"Yes, there is the common leopard and the hunting
leopard; besides, I think, two or three smaller varieties,
as the tiger-cat and wild cat. What do you propose doing
to-day? Do you stay here, or advance, Wilmot?"

"Why, the Major wishes to have a shot at the gnoos;
he has never killed one yet; and as I am of his opinion,
that a day's rest will recover the oxen, and we are in no
hurry, I think we may as well stop and provision our camp
for a few days."

"With all my heart. I am sorry that the hyena has
added to our store, by obliging us to kill the poor ox; however, it cannot be helped. There is a large body of gnoos
and quaggas under that small hill to the westward; but
there are better animals for the table when we get a little
further to the northward."

"Which are those?"

"The eland, the largest of the antelope species, and
sometimes weighing more than a thousand pounds; moreover, they are very fat, and very easy to run down. They
are excellent eating. When I was in the Namaquas' land,
we preferred them to any other food; but I see another
variety of game on the plain there."

"What?"

Omrah pointed them out. "They are either Bushmen
(tame Bushmen, as they are called, in contradistinction to
the others), or else Korannas; most probably the latter.
They are coming right towards us; but Mahomed says
breakfast is ready."

By the time that breakfast was finished, a party of
twelve Korannas had joined the caravan. They made signs
that they were hungry, pointing to the straps which confined their stomachs. The interpreter told them that they
were about to hunt, and that they should have some of the
game, at which they were much pleased.

"Do you know what those straps are called, round their waists, Wilmot?" said Swinton. "They are called the belts of famine. All the natives wear them when hard pressed by hunger, and they say that they are a great relief. I have no doubt but such is the fact."

"Well," said the Major, "I hope soon to enable the poor fellows to loosen their belts, and fill their stomachs till they are as tight as a drum. Saddle the horses, Bremen. Omrah, you ride my spare horse and carry my spare rifle."

Omrah, who now understood English, although he spoke but few words, gave a nod of the head and went off to the waggon for the Major's rifle.

CHAPTER XIX

A practical joke—A lucky escape—History of the Mantatees— Mantatee courage—A final slaughter—Discussions—Swinton's account of Africaner.

As soon as the horses were ready, our travellers set out in chase of the gnoos and quaggas, which were collected to the westward of the caravan. Bremen, Swanevelt, and Omrah were mounted, and ten of the Hottentots followed with their guns, and the Korannas on foot; among the others, Big Adam, who had been explaining to those who had never seen the gnoos the manner in which he used to kill them.

The herd permitted them to approach within two hundred yards of them, and then, after curvetting and prancing, and galloping in small circles, they stood still at about the same distance, looking, with curiosity and anger mixed, at the horsemen. After a time, they took to their heels and scoured the plain for about two miles, when they again stopped, tossing their heads and manes, and stamping as if in defiance.

The mounted party remained quiet till those on foot had again drawn near, and the Hottentots, firing their guns, drove the herd within shot of our travellers' guns, and three of the gnoos fell, while the others bounded off to a greater distance; but as they neared the caravan, they again started back, and were again closed in by the whole party.

The Hottentots now advanced cautiously, creeping as near as they could to the animals, whose attention was directed to the horsemen. The Hottentots were nearly within range, when Omrah, who was mounted on the Major's spare horse, fastened to the ramrod of the Major's rifle a red bandanna handkerchief, which he usually wore round his head, and separating quickly from the rest of the horsemen, walked his horse to where Big Adam was creeping along to gain a shot, and stationed himself behind him, waving the red handkerchief at the animals. Omrah was well aware that a gnoo is as much irritated at a red handkerchief as a bull, and as soon as he commenced waving it, one of the largest males stepped out in that direction, pawing the ground and preparing for a charge.

Big Adam, who had no idea that Omrah was so occupied behind him, now rose to have a shot, and just as he rose the gnoo made his charge, and Big Adam, being between the gnoo and the horse which Omrah rode, was of course the party against whom the animal's choler was raised.

Omrah, as soon as the animal charged, had wheeled round and galloped away, while in the meantime Big Adam, perceiving the animal rushing at him, lost all presence of mind, his gun went off without effect, and he turned tail; the horns of the gnoo were close upon him, when of a sudden, to the surprise of those who were looking on, Big Adam disappeared, and the gnoo passed over where he had been.

"Why, what has become of him?" said Alexander, laughing.

"I don't know, but I think he has had a wonderful escape," replied the Major: "he has disappeared like a ghost through a trap-door."

"But I see his heels," cried Swinton, laughing; "he has fallen into an ant-eater's hole, depend upon it; that mischievous little urchin might have caused his death."

"It was only to make him prove his steady aim which he was boasting so much about," replied the Major; "but stop a moment; I will bring down that gallant little animal, and then we will look for Big Adam."

But before the Major could get near enough to the gnoo, which was still tearing up the ground and looking for his adversary, Omrah, who had put by the handkerchief, advanced with the Major's rifle, and brought the animal down. A volley was at the same time discharged at the herd by the Hottentots, and three more fell, after which the remainder scampered away, and were soon out of sight.

They then rode up to where Big Adam had disappeared, and found him, as Swinton had supposed, in a deep ant-eater's hole, head downward, and bellowing for help. His feet were just above the surface, and that was all; the Hottentots helped him out, and Big Adam threw himself on his back, and seemed exhausted with fright and having been so long in a reversed position, and was more vexed at the laugh which was raised against him.

The gnoos were soon cut up, and when the Hottentots had taken away as much as they required, the rest of the carcasses were made over to the hungry Korannas. Swinton shook his head at Omrah, who pretended that he did not understand why, until the laughter of Alexander and the Major was joined in by Swinton himself.

As they had pretty well fatigued their horses in the chase, they resolved to return to the caravan, and keep them as fresh as they could for future service. They dined and supped on the flesh of the gnoos, which was approved of, and after supper Alexander said — "And now, Swinton, if you feel inclined, the Major and I will be very glad to hear your history of the Mantatees."

"With pleasure," replied Swinton. "The assemblage of tribes known as the Mantatees or Invaders, according to the best authorities we can collect, inhabited the countries to the westward of the Zulu territory, in the same latitude, which is that of Delagoa Bay. As all these tribes subsist almost entirely upon the flesh and the milk of their cattle, if deprived of them, they are driven to desperation, and must either become robbers in their turn, or perish by hunger. Such was the case of the Mantatees. Unable to withstand the attacks of the Zulus, they were driven from their country, and joined their forces with others who had shared the same fate.

"Such was the origin of the Mantatees, who, although they had not courage to withstand the attacks of the Zulus, were stimulated by desperation and famine to a most extraordinary courage in the attacks which they made upon others.

"Forming an immense body, now that they were collected together, accompanied by their wives and children, and unable to procure the necessary subsistence, it is certain that their habits were so far changed that they at last became cannibals, and were driven to prey upon the dead bodies of their enemies, or the flesh of their comrades who fell in the combats.

"The Bechuana tribes, who are the Caffres of the interior, were the first assailed, their towns sacked and burned, and their cattle seized and devoured. They proceeded on to the Wankeets, one of the Damara tribes, who inhabit the western coast to the northward of the Namaqualand; but the Wankeets were a brave people, and prepared for them, and the Mantatees were driven back with great slaughter. Astounded at their defeat, they turned to the southward, and invaded the Bechuana country.

"At that time our missionaries had established themselves at Koranna, and when the report of the Mantatees advancing was brought to them, the Bechuanas were in a great consternation; for although finer-looking men than the eastern Caffres, they are not by any means so brave and warlike.

"As the advance of these people would have been the ruin of the mission, as well as the destruction of the tribe, who were afraid to encounter them, Mr. M., the missionary, determined upon sending for the assistance of the Griquas, the people whom I have before mentioned, and who had not only horses, but were well armed. The Griquas came under their chief, Waterboer, and marched against the enemy, accompanied by a large army of Bechuanas, who, encouraged by the presence of the Griquas, now went forth to the combat.

"The Mantatees had at that time advanced as far, and had taken possession of Litakoo, a Bechuana town containing 16,000 inhabitants; and I will now give, as nearly as I can recollect it, the account of Mr. M., the missionary at Kuruman, who accompanied the Griquas, to propose and effect, if it were possible, an amicable arrangement with the invaders.

"He told me that as they proceeded with a small party, ahead of the Griqua force, to effect their purpose, they passed by numbers of the enemy, who had advanced to the pools to drink, and had there sunk down and expired from famine. As they neared the mass of the enemy, they found that all the cattle which they had captured were enclosed in the centre of a vast multitude. They attempted a parley, but the enemy started forward and hurled their spears with the most savage fury, and they were compelled to retreat, finding no hopes of obtaining a parley.

"The next day it was decided that the Griquas should advance. They numbered about one hundred well-mounted and well-armed men. The enemy flew at them with terrible howls, hurling their javelins and clubs; their black dismal appearance, their savage fury, and their hoarse loud voices producing a strange effect. The Griquas, to prevent their being surrounded, very wisely retreated.

"It was at last decided that the Griquas should fire, and it was hoped that as the Mantatees had never seen the effects of firearms they would be humbled and alarmed, and thus further bloodshed might be prevented. Many of the Mantatees fell; but, although the survivors looked with astonishment upon the dead and their wounded warriors writhing in the dust, they flew with lion-like vengeance at the horsemen, wrenching the weapons from the hands of their dying companions to replace those which they had already discharged at their antagonists.

"As those who thus stepped out from the main body to attack the Griquas were the chiefs of the Mantatees, and many of them were killed, their deaths, one after the other, disheartened the whole body.

"After the Griquas had commenced the attack, the Bechuana army came up and assisted with their poisoned arrows, with which they plied the enemy; but a small body of the fierce Mantatees, sallying out, put the whole of the Bechuanas to flight.

"After a combat of two hours and a half, the Griquas, finding their ammunition failing, determined, at great risk, to charge the whole body. They did so, and the Mantatees gave way, and fled in a westerly direction; but they were intercepted by the Griquas, and another charge being made, the whole was pell-mell and confusion.

"Mr. M. says that the scene which now presented itself was most awful, and the state of suspense most cruel. The undulating country around was covered with warriors — Griquas, Mantatees, and Bechuanas, all in motion — so that it was impossible to say who were enemies and who were friends. Clouds of dust rose from the immense masses, some flying, others pursuing; and to their screams and yells were added the bellowing of the oxen, the shouts of the yet unvanquished warriors, the groans of the dying, and the wails of women and of children. At last the enemy retreated to the town, which they set in flames, to add to the horror of the scene.

"Then another desperate struggle ensued; the Mantatees attempted to enclose the Griquas in the burning town, but not succeeding, they fled precipitately. Strange to say, the Mantatee forces were divided into two parts, and during the time that the Griquas engaged the one, the other remained in the town, having such confidence in the former that they did not come to their assistance.

"When the town was set on fire both armies united, and retreated together to the northward, in a body of not less than 40,000 warriors. As soon as the Mantatees retreated, the Bechuanas commenced the work of slaughter. Women and children were butchered without mercy; but as for the wounded Mantatees, it appeared as if nothing would make them yield. There were many instances of an individual being surrounded by fifty Bechuanas, but as long as life remained he fought.

"Mr. M. says that he saw more than one instance of a Mantatee fighting wildly against numbers, with ten or

162

twelve arrows and spears pierced in his body. Struggling with death, the men would rally, raise themselves from the ground, discharge their weapons, and fall dead, their revengeful and hostile spirit only ceasing when life was extinct."

"And yet these same people permitted their own country to be taken from them by the Zulus."

"Yes, it was so; but want and necessity had turned them into desperate warriors."

"I wonder they never thought of going back and recovering their own country. They would have been a match for the Zulus. Is that the end of their history, Swinton?"

"No, not quite. But perhaps you are tired?"

"Oh no. Pray go on."

"The Mantatees, although defeated by the Griquas, soon recovered their courage, and intelligence came that they were about to make a descent upon Kuruman, where the missionaries had their station. The Mantatees, having been informed that the Griquas had gone home, now determined to revenge themselves upon the Bechuanas, whom they considered but as the dust under their feet.

"On this information, Mr. M. wrote to Waterboer, who commanded the Griquas, requesting his immediate return; but Waterboer replied that an immense body of Mantatees were coming down upon the Griquas by the Val or Yellow River, and that they were forced to remain, to defend their own property, advising Mr. M. to retreat with his family to the Griqua town, and put themselves under their protection.

"As they could no longer remain, the mission station was abandoned, and the missionaries, with their wives and families, retreated to Griqua town. They had not, however, been long at Griqua town before news arrived that both the bodies of Mantatees had altered their routes. One portion of them went eastward, towards the country from which they had been driven by the Zulus, and another, it appears, took possession of the country near the sources of the Orange River, where for many years they carried on a predatory warfare with the tribes in that

163

district. At last a portion of them were incorporated, and settled down on that part which is now known as the Mantatee new country; the remainder made an irruption into the eastern Caffre country, where they were known as the Ficani."

"And what became of them?"

"They defeated one or two of the Caffre chiefs, and the Caffres implored the assistance of the English colonists, which was granted, and a large armed force was sent out against the invaders. They were found located —for they had built a town—near the sources of the Umtata River. The Caffres joined with all their forces, and the Ficani were surprised. A horrid slaughter took place; muskets, artillery, and Congreve rockets were poured upon the unfortunate wretches, who were hemmed in on all sides by the Caffres, and the unfortunate Ficani may be said to have been exterminated, for the Caffres spared neither man, woman, nor child. Such is the history of the Mantatees; their destruction was horrible, but perhaps unavoidable."

"Very true," observed Alexander; "I cannot help thinking that desolating contests like these are permitted by a controlling Providence as chastisements, yet with a gracious end; for, surely it was better that they should meet with immediate death, than linger till famine put an end to their misery. This is certain, that they must have been destroyed, or others destroyed to make room for them. In either case a great sacrifice of life was to be incurred. War, dreadful as it is in detail, appears to be one of the necessary evils of human existence, and a means by which we do not increase so rapidly as to devour each other.

"I don't know whether you have made the observation, but it appears to me the plague and cholera are almost necessary in the countries where they break out; and it is very remarkable that the latter disease never made its appearance in Europe (at least not for centuries, I may say) until after peace had been established, and the increase of population was so rapid.

"During the many years that Europe was devastated and the population thinned by war, we had no cholera,

164

and but little of one or two other epidemics which have since been very fatal. What I mean to infer is, that the hand of Providence may be seen in all this. Thus sanguinary wars and the desolating ravages of disease, which are in themselves afflictive visitations, and probably chastisements for national sins, may nevertheless have the effect, in some cases, of preventing the miseries which result from an undue increase of population."

"You may be quite right, Alexander," observed Swinton; "the ways of Heaven are inscrutably mysterious, and when we offer up prayers for the removal of what may appear to be a heavy calamity, we may be deprecating that which in the end may prove a mercy."

"One thing I could not help remarking in your narrative, Swinton," observed the Major, "which is the position of the missionaries during this scene of terror. You passed it slightly over, but it must have been most trying."

"Most surely it was."

"And yet I have not only read but heard much said against them, and strong opposition made to subscriptions for their support."

"I grant it, but it is because people know that a great deal of money has been subscribed, and do not know the uses to which it is applied. They hear reports read, and find perhaps that the light of the Gospel has but as yet glimmered in one place or another; that in other places all labour has hitherto been thrown away. They forget that it is the grain of mustard-seed which is to become a great tree, and spread its branches; they wish for immoderate returns, and are therefore disappointed. Of course I cannot give an opinion as to the manner in which the missions are conducted in other countries; but as I have visited most of the missions in these parts, I can honestly assert, and I think you have already yourself seen enough to agree with me, that the money entrusted to the societies is not thrown away or lavishly expended; the missionaries labour with their own hands, and almost provide for their own support."

"There I agree with you, Swinton," replied Alexander; "but what are the objections raised against them? for now

165

that I have seen them with my own eyes, I cannot imagine what they can be."

"The objections which I have heard, and have so often attempted to refute, are, that the generality of missionaries are a fanatical class of men, who are more anxious to inculcate the peculiar tenets of their own sects and denominations than the religion of our Saviour; that most of them are uneducated and vulgar men—many of them very intemperate and very injudicious—some few of them of bad moral character; and that their exertions, if they have used them—whether to civilise or to Christianise the people among whom they are sent—have not been followed by any commensurate results."

"And now let us have your replies to these many objections."

"It is no doubt true that the missionaries who are labouring among the savages of the interior are, many, if not most of them, people of limited education. Indeed, the major portion of them have been brought up as mechanics. But I much question whether men of higher attainments and more cultivated minds would be better adapted to meet the capacities of unintellectual barbarians. A highly educated man may be appreciated among those who are educated themselves; but how can he be appreciated by the savage? On the contrary, the savage looks with much more respect upon a man who can forge iron, repair his weapons, and excite his astonishment by his cunning workmanship; for then the savage perceives and acknowledges his superiority, which in the man of intellect he would never discover.

"Besides, admitting that it would be preferable to employ persons of higher mental attainments, where are they to be found? Could you expect, when so many labourers are required in the vineyard, a sufficient number of volunteers among the young men brought up at the universities? Would they be able to submit to those privations, and incur those hardships to which the African missionaries are exposed? Would they be able to work hard and labour for their daily bread, or be willing to encounter such toil and such danger as must be encountered by those who are sent here? I fear not

166

And allow me here to remark, that at the first preaching of Christianity it was not talented and educated men who were selected by our Saviour; out of the twelve, the Apostle Paul was the only one who had such claims.

"If we had beheld the Galilean fishermen mending their nets, should we have ever imagined that those humble labourers were to be the people who should afterwards regenerate the world?—should overthrow the idolatries and crumble the superstitions of ancient empires and kingdoms?—and that what they—uneducated, but, we admit, divinely inspired and supported—had taught should be joyfully received, as it is now, we may say, from the rising to the setting of the sun, to the utmost boundaries of the earth?"

"Most truly and most admirably argued, Swinton," replied Alexander. "The Almighty, as if to prove how insignificant in His sight is all human power, has often made use of the meanest instruments to accomplish the greatest ends. Who knows but that even our keeping holy the Sabbath-day in the desert may be productive of some good, and be the humble means of advancing the Divine cause? We must ever bear in mind the counsel, 'In the morning sow thy seed, and in the evening withhold not thy hand; for thou knowest not whether shall prosper, either this or that, or whether they both shall be alike good.'"

"Surely so," replied Swinton; "the natives consider us as a superior race; they see our worship, and they are led to think that must be right which they perceive is done by those to whom they look up as their superiors. It may induce them to inquire and to receive information—eventually to be enrolled among the followers of our Saviour. It is, however, not to be denied that in some few instances persons have been chosen for the office of missionaries who have proved themselves unworthy; but that must and will ever be the case where human agents are employed. But it argues no more against the general respectability and utility of the missionaries as a body, than the admission of the traitor Judas among the apostles. To the efficacy of their works, and their zeal in the cause, I myself, having visited the station, have no hesitation in bearing testimony. Indeed I cannot but admire the exemplary fortitude, the wonderful patience and perseverance, which the missionaries have displayed.

"These devoted men are to be found in the remotest deserts, accompanying the wild and wandering savages from place to place, suffering from hunger and from thirst, destitute of almost every comfort, and at times without even the necessaries of life. Some of them have without murmuring spent their whole lives in such service; and yet their zeal is set down as fanaticism by those who remain at home, and assert that the money raised for their equipment is thrown away. Happily, they have not looked for their reward in this world, but have built their hopes upon that which is to come."

"That the people who joined the mission stations have become more civilised, and that they are very superior to their countrymen, is certain," observed the Major; "but have you seen any proof of Christianity having produced any remarkably good effect among the natives?—I mean one that might be brought forward as convincing evidence to those who have shown themselves inimical or lukewarm in the cause."

"Yes," replied Swinton, "the history of Africaner is one; and there are others, although not so prominent as that of the party to whom I refer."

"Well, Swinton, you must now be again taxed. You must give us the history of Africaner."

"That I will, with pleasure, that you may be able to narrate it, when required, in support of the missions. Africaner was a chief, and a descendant of chiefs of the Hottentot nation, who once pastured their own flocks and herds on their own native hills, within a hundred miles of Cape Town. As the Dutch colonists at the Cape increased, so did they, as Mr. Fairburn has stated to Alexander, dispossess the Hottentots of their lands, and the Hottentots, unable to oppose their invaders, gradually found themselves more and more remote from the possessions of their forefathers.

"After a time Africaner and his diminished clan

found themselves compelled to join and take service under a Dutch boor, and for some time proved himself a most faithful shepherd in looking after and securing the herds of his employer. Had the Dutch boor behaved with common humanity, not to say gratitude, towards those who served him so well, he might now have been alive; but, like all the rest of his countrymen, he considered the Hottentots as mere beasts of burden, and at any momentary anger they were murdered and hunted down as if they were wild animals.

"Africaner saw his clan daily diminished by the barbarity of his feudal master, and at last resolved upon no further submission. As the Bushmen were continually making attempts upon the cattle of the boor, Africaner and his people had not only been well trained to fire-arms, but had them constantly in their possession. His assumed master, having an idea that there would be a revolt, resolved upon sending a portion of Africaner's people to a distant spot, where he intended to secure them, and by their destruction weaken the power of the clan.

"This, as he was a sort of magistrate, he had the power to enforce; but Africaner, suspecting his views, resolved to defeat them. Order after order was sent to the huts of Africaner and his people. They positively refused to comply. They requested to be paid for their long services, and be permitted to retire further into the interior. This was sternly denied, and they were ordered to appear at the house of the boor. Fearful of violence, yet accustomed to obey his order, Africaner and his brothers went up; but one of his brothers concealed his gun under his cloak. On their arrival, the boor came out and felled Africaner to the ground. His brother immediately shot the boor with his gun, and thus did the miscreant meet with the just reward of his villainies and murder.

"The wife, who had witnessed the murder of her husband, shrieked and implored mercy; they told her that she need not be alarmed, but requested that the guns and ammunition in the house should be delivered up to them, which was immediately done. Africaner then hastened back to his people, collected them and all his cattle, with

169

what effects they could take with them, and directed his course to the Orange River.

"He was soon out of the reach of his pursuers, for it required time in so scattered a district to collect a sufficient force. Africaner fixed his abode upon the banks of the Orange River, and afterwards a chief ceding to him his dominion in Great Namaqualand, the territory became his by right as well as by conquest. I think I had better leave off now; it is getting late, and we must to bed, if we are to start early to-morrow morning."

"We will have mercy upon you, Swinton, and defer our impatience," said the Major. "Good-night to you, and may you not have a lion's serenade."

"No, I hope not; their music is too loud to be agreeable;—good-night."

CHAPTER XX

Omrah's intelligence—Lion-hunting—Silence and caution—An unpleasant surprise—Self-sacrifice of a gemsbok—Swinton's story continued — Conversation on lions — Anecdotes — Big Adam punished.

HAVING filled their water-kegs, the next morning at daylight they yoked the oxen and left the banks of the Cradock or Black River, to proceed more to the northward, through the Bushmen's country; but as they were aware that there was no water to be procured, if they quitted the stream altogether, till they arrived at the Val or Yellow River, they decided upon following the course of the Black River to the westward for some time, before they struck off for the Val or Yellow River, near to which they expected to fall in with plenty of game, and particularly the giraffe and rhinoceros.

Although at that season of the year the river was nearly dry, still there was a scanty herbage on and near its bank, intermixed with beds of rushes and high reeds; this was sufficient for the pasture of the cattle, but it was infested with lions and other animals, which at the dry season of the year kept near the river-bank for a supply of water.

By noon they had proceeded about fifteen miles to the westward, and as they advanced they found that the supply of water in the river was more abundant; they then unyoked the cattle to allow them to feed till the evening, for it was too dangerous to turn them loose at night. As they were in no hurry, they resolved that they would only travel for the future from daylight till noon; the afternoon and evening were to be spent in hunting, and at night they were to halt the caravan and secure everything as before, by enclosing the horses and sheep, and tying up the oxen.

By this arrangement the cattle would not be exhausted with their labour, and they would have time to follow the object of their journey—that of hunting the wild animals with which the country abounded, and also of procuring a constant supply of food for themselves and their attendants.

Having now travelled as far as they wished, they stopped at the foot of a rising ground, about a quarter of a mile from the river's bank, and which was on the outskirts of a large clump of mimosa and other trees. As soon as the cattle were unyoked and had gone down to the river to drink, our travellers ordered their horses to be saddled, and as the banks of the river on that side were low, they rode up to the rising ground to view the country beyond, and to ascertain what game might be in sight.

When they arrived at the summit, and were threading their way through the trees, Omrah pointed to a broken branch, and said, "Elephant here not long ago."

Bremen said that Omrah was right, and that the animals could not have left more than a week, and that probably they had followed the course of the stream. The print of another foot was observed by Omrah, and he pointed it out; but not knowing the name to give the animal in English or Dutch, he imitated its motions.

"Does he mean a gnoo?" said Alexander.

Omrah shook his head, and, raising his hands up, motioned that the animal was twice as big.

"Come here, Bremen; what print of a hoof is this?" said Swinton.

"Buffalo, sir,—fresh print—was here last night."

"That's an animal that I am anxious to slay," said the Major.

"You must be very careful that he does not slay *you*," replied Swinton; "for it is a most dangerous beast, almost as much so as a lion."

"Well, we must not return without one, at all events," said Alexander; "nor without a lion also, as soon as we can find one alone; but those we have seen in the day-time have always been in threes and fours, and I think the odds too great with our party; but the first single lion we fall in with, I vote we try for his skin."

"Agreed," replied the Major; "what do you say, Swinton?"

"Why, I say agreed also; but as I came here to look for other things rather than lions, I should say, as far as I am concerned, that the best part of valour would be discretion. However, depend upon it, if you go after a lion I shall be with you: I have often been at the destruction of them when with Dutch boors; but then recollect we have no horses to spare, and therefore we must not exactly follow their method."

"How do they hunt the lions, then?" inquired Alexander.

"They hunt them more for self-defence than for pleasure," replied Swinton; "but on the outskirts of the colony the lions are so destructive to the herds, that the colonists must destroy them. They generally go out, ten or twelve of them, with their long guns, not fewer if possible; and you must recollect that these boors are not only very cool, brave men, but most excellent shots. I fear you will not find that number among our present party, as, with the exception of our three selves and Bremen and Swanevelt, I do not believe that there is one man here who would face a lion; so that when we do attack one it will be at a disadvantage.

"The Dutch boors, as soon as they have ascertained where the lion lies, approach the bushes to within a moderate distance, and then alighting, they make all their horses fast together with their bridles and halters. In this there is danger, as sometimes the lion will spring out upon them at once, and, if so, probably not only horses but men are sacrificed. If the lion remains quiet, which is usually the case, they advance towards him within thirty paces or thereabouts, as they know that he generally makes a spring at half that distance ; but as they advance, they back their horses towards him, as a shield in front of them, knowing that the lion will spring upon the horses.

"As they move forward, the lion at first looks at them very calmly, and very often wags his tail as if in a playful humour; but when they approach nearer, he growls, as if to warn them off. Then, as they continue to approach, he gradually draws up his hind legs under his body, ready for a spring at them as soon as they are within distance, and you see nothing of him except his bristling mane and his eyes glaring like fire ; for he is then fully enraged, and in the act of springing the next moment.

"This is the critical moment, and the signal is given for half the party to fire. If they are not successful in laying him dead on the spot with this first volley, he springs like a thunderbolt upon the horses. The remainder of the party then fire, and seldom fail to put an end to him; but generally one or more of the horses are either killed or so wounded as to be destroyed in consequence ; and sometimes, although rarely, one or more of the hunters share the same fate. So you observe that, with every advantage, it is a service of danger, and therefore should not be undertaken without due precaution."

"Very true, Swinton ; but it will never do to return to the Cape without having killed a lion."

"As you please ; but even that would be better than being killed yourself by a lion, and not returning at all. However, my opinion is that you will have to kill a lion before you have travelled much further, without going in quest of him. There are hundreds of them here ; as many as there are in Namaqualand."

"Look, master!" said Bremen, pointing to seven or eight splendid antelopes about a mile distant.

"I see," replied the Major. "What are they ?"

"Gemsbok," said Swinton. "Now, I will thank you for a specimen of that beautiful creature, if you can get it for me. We must dismount, leave our horses here,

173

and crawl along from tree to tree, and bush to bush, till we get within shot."

"They are, indeed, noble animals. Look at that large male, which appears to be the leader and master of the herd. What splendid horns!" cried Alexander.

"Give the horses to Omrah and Swanevelt. Bremen shall go with us. Hist! not a word; they are looking in this direction," said the Major.

"Recollect to try for the large male. I want him most particularly," said Swinton.

"Master," said Bremen, "we must creep till we get those bushes between us and the game. Then we can crawl through the bushes and get a good shot."

"Yes, that will be the best plan," said Swinton. "As softly as we can, for they are very shy animals."

They followed one another for two or three hundred yards, creeping from one covert to another, till they had placed the bushes on the plain between them and the herd. They then stopped a little and reconnoitred. The herd of antelopes had left off feeding, and now had all their heads turned towards the bushes, and in the direction where they were concealed; the large male rather in advance of the others, with his long horns pointing forward, and his nose close to the ground. Our party kept silence for some time, watching the animals; but none of them moved much from their positions; and as for the male, he remained as if he were a statue.

"They must have scented us," whispered Alexander.

"No, sir," said Bremen; "the wind blows from them to us. I can't think what they are about. But perhaps they may have seen us."

"At all events, we shall gain nothing by remaining here; we shall be more concealed as we descend and approach them," observed the Major.

"That is true; so come along. Creep like mice," said Swinton.

They did so, and at last arrived at the patch of brushwood which was between them and the antelopes, and were now peeping and creeping to find out an opening to fire through, when they heard a rustling within. Bremen touched the sleeve of the Major and beckoned a retreat, and motioned to the others; but before they could decide, as they did not know why the Hottentot proposed it, for he did not speak himself, and put his hand to his mouth as a hint to them to be silent, a roar like thunder came from the bushes within three yards of them, accompanied with a rushing noise which could not be mistaken. It was the roar and spring of the lion; and they looked round amazed and stunned, to ascertain who was the victim.

"Merciful Heaven!" exclaimed Alexander, "and no one hurt!"

"No, master; lion spring at antelope. Now we shall find him on other side of the bush, and kill him easy, when his eyes are shut."

Bremen led the way round the copse, followed by our travellers; they soon arrived on the other side of it, with their guns all ready; but on their arrival, to their astonishment they perceived the lion and the male gemsbok lying together. The antelope was dead, but the lion still alive; though the horns of the gemsbok had passed through his body. At the sight of the hunters, the lion, pierced through as he was, raised his head with a loud roar, and struck out with his paw, as he twisted towards them, his eyes glowing like hot coals, and showing his tremendous fangs. Alexander was the first who fired, and the ball penetrating the brain of the noble animal, it fell down dead upon the body of the antelope.

"This is the finest sight I ever witnessed," observed Swinton. "I have heard that the gemsboks' horns are sometimes fatal to the lion, but I could hardly credit it. They have passed nearly through his body; the points are under the skin."

"Now we know, master, why gemsbok have his nose to the ground and his horn pointed," said Bremen; "he saw the lion, and fought him to save his herd."

"I am quite stunned yet," observed Alexander. "What a noble animal it is! Well, at all events I can say that I have shot a lion, which is more than you can, Major."

"I only wish that when I shoot one I may have no more danger to incur," replied the Major. "What a different idea does one have of a lion in a menagerie and one in its free and native state. Why, the menagerie lions can't roar at all; they are nothing but overgrown cats, compared to the lion of the desert."

"That is very true," observed Swinton; "however, I am delighted, for now I have not only my gemsbok, which is a gem above price, but also as fine a lion as I have ever seen. I should like to have them stuffed and set up just as they were before Alexander killed them. His rage and agony combined were most magnificent. After all, the lion is the king of beasts. Bremen, send Swanevelt to the caravan for some of the men. I must have both skin and skeleton of the antelope, and the skin of the lion."

Our travellers were quite satisfied with the sport of the day, and after waiting for some time, while the Hottentots disentangled the animals and took off the skins, they returned to the caravan, Omrah having secured a portion of the flesh of the gemsbok for their supper.

As they were returning, they observed a herd of buffaloes at a great distance, and proposed to themselves the hunting of them after they had halted on the following day, if the animals were at any reasonable distance from them. At supper the flesh of the antelope was pronounced better than that of the gnoo; and after supper, as soon as the cattle had been all secured, and the fires lighted, Alexander proposed that Swinton should finish his history of Africaner.

"If I remember right, I left off where Africaner and his people had escaped to Namaqualand, where he became a chief. Attempts were made to take him prisoner and bring him to the colony, but without success. Expedition after expedition failed, and Africaner dared them to approach his territories. At last, the colonists had recourse to the Griquas, and offered them a large reward if they would bring Africaner in.

"The Griquas, commanded by a celebrated chief of the name of Berend, made several attempts, and in consequence a cruel war was carried on between Berend and Africaner, in which neither party gained the advantage. Africaner, discovering that the colonists had bribed

176

Berend to make war against him, now turned his wrath against them. A Dutch boor fell a victim to his fury, and he carried off large quantities of their cattle, and eventually Africaner became the terror of the colony. The natives also who resided in Namaqualand commenced depredations upon Africaner, but he repaid them with such interest that at last every tribe fled at his approach, and his name carried dismay into their solitary wastes. The courage and intrepidity shown by Africaner and his brothers in their various combats were most remarkable; but to narrate all his adventures would occupy too much time. It is certain that he not only became dreaded, but in consequence of his forbearance on several occasions he was respected.

"It was in 1810 that the missionaries came into the Namaqualand, and it unfortunately happened that a dispute arose about some of Africaner's property which was seized, and at the same time Africaner lost some cattle. The parties who were at variance with Africaner lived near to the mission station, and very unwisely the people at the mission station were permitted to go to their assistance.

"This roused the anger of Africaner, who vowed vengeance on the mission and the people collected around it or connected with it. As Africaner had commenced his attacks upon the Namaquas, and was advancing towards the mission, the missionaries were compelled to abandon the station and return to the colony. The mission station was soon afterwards taken possession of by Africaner, and the houses burnt to the ground.

"A curious circumstance occurred during this affair: his followers were seeking everywhere for plunder, when some of them entered the burial ground, and one of them, treading on an apparently new-made grave, was astonished by soft notes of music proceeding from the ground beneath.

"Superstitious as the natives are, and having most of them, in former days, heard something of the Christian doctrines, they started and stood transfixed with astonishment, expecting the dead to arise, as they had been once told. One of them mustered courage to put his foot again

177   M

upon the spot, and the reply was soft and musical as before. Away they all started to Africaner, to inform him that there was life and music in the grave.

"The chief, who feared neither the living nor the dead, went to the burial-ground with his men, and jumped upon the spot, which immediately gave out the soft note as before. Africaner ordered an immediate exhumation, when the source of the mystery proved to be the piano-forte of the missionary's wife, which being too cumbrous an article to take away, had been buried there, with the hope of being one day able to recover it. Never having seen such an instrument before, Africaner had it dissected for the sake of the brass wires; and thus the piano was destroyed."

"I doubt if it would ever have been dug up in Caffreland," observed Alexander.

"I am convinced it never would have been, but have remained as a wonder and object of fear as long as it held together," replied Swinton; "but to proceed—

"The mission station having been for some time broken up by this attack of Africaner, Mr. C., a missionary, anxious to restore it, wrote a letter to Africaner on the subject, and received a favourable reply, and a Mr. E. was sent to the residence of Africaner himself. After a short time, Africaner and his two brothers, with a number of others, were baptized.

"At first it must be admitted that their profession of Christianity did not greatly improve their conduct; but this was very much to be ascribed to the circumstance that the duties of the station had devolved upon one who ought not to have been selected for the task. Upon his removal, and a more fitting minister of the Gospel taking his place, a great change was soon observable in Africaner; and, from having been one of the most remorseless pursuers of his vengeance—a firebrand spreading discord, war, and animosity among the neighbouring tribes — he would now make every concession and any sacrifice to prevent collision and bloodshed between contending parties.

"Although his power was so great that he might have raised his arm and dared them to lift a spear or draw
178

a bow, he would entreat them as a suppliant to be reconciled.

"'Look at me,' he would say, 'how many battles have I fought; how much cattle have I taken; but what has it done for me, but make me full of shame and sorrow?'

"In short, from that time till he died, he became a peacemaker and a Christian, both in word and deed. His whole life was devoted to acts of kindness and charity —to instructing and exhorting, and following the precepts of Him in whose faith eventually he lived and died."

"Well, Swinton, you have indeed given us a remarkable proof that the missionary labours are not always thrown away, and we thank you for your compliance with our request."

"It is a remarkable instance, if you only consider how many hundreds of lives might have been sacrificed, if Africaner had continued his career of slaughter and of plunder; and how many lives, I may add, have been also saved by his interference as a peacemaker, instead of being, as he formerly was, a promoter of war and bloodshed."

"Swinton," said Alexander, "I wanted to ask you a question which I had nearly forgotten. Do you recollect what Bremen said to us, that the lion had seized the gemsbok, and that now the lion would shut his eyes, and that he would shoot him?"

"Yes, I do; and he was correct in what he stated, for I have witnessed it myself. When a lion seizes a large animal like an ox or horse, or the animal he fell a martyr to this afternoon, he springs upon it, seizes it by the throat with his terrible fangs, and holds it down with his paws till it expires. From the moment the lion seizes his prey he shuts his eyes, and never opens them again until the life of his prey is extinct. I remember a Hottentot, when a lion had seized an ox in this way, running up to him with his gun and firing within a few yards' distance. The lion, however, did not deign to notice the report of the gun, but continued to hold fast his prey. The Hottentot loaded again, fired, and again missed; reloaded again, and then shot the lion through the head."

"How very strange!"

"It is, and I cannot give any reason for it; but that it is so, I well know to be a fact. Perhaps it may be that the animal, after long fasting, is quite absorbed with the grateful taste of the blood flowing into his mouth, while the animal is writhing under his clutches. But there are many singular points about the lion, which is a much more noble and intelligent animal than most people have any idea of; I have collected a number of facts relative to his Majesty which would surprise you. The Bushmen know the animal and his habits so well, that they seldom come to any accident from their inhabiting a country in which I really believe the population of lions exceeds that of Bushmen."

"Is it true that the lion, as well as other animals, is afraid of the eye of man?" said the Major; "can you reply to that question?"

"Yes, I can," answered Swinton; "I was about to say that he is and is not, but a better answer will be to give you what has come to my knowledge: I consider that the lion is a much more dangerous animal in this country, and indeed in any other where there are no firearms, than where the occupants are possessed of them.

"It may appear strange, but it is my fixed opinion that the lion has an idea of the deadly nature of firearms, and that he becomes in consequence more afraid of man. You remember a story I told you of a lion watching a man for two days without destroying him, but never permitting him to lay hold of his gun. Now it is satisfactorily proved that a lion will pass a man who has a gun in his hand without attacking him, provided that he does not attempt to level the gun; but the moment that he does he will spring upon him.

"An instance of that occurred to the great lion-hunter Diedrich Muller, who mentioned it to me. He had been alone hunting in the wilds, when he came suddenly upon a large lion, which, instead of giving way as they usually do, seemed disposed, from the angry attitude which he assumed, to dispute his progress.

"Muller instantly alighted, and, confident of his unerring aim, levelled his gun at the forehead of the lion, which

180

had crouched in the act to spring, within sixteen paces of him; but as he fired, his horse, whose bridle was round his arm, started back, and, jerking him aside, caused him to miss; the lion bounded forward, but stopped within a few paces, confronting Muller, who stood defenceless, as his gun was discharged, and his horse had galloped off.

"The man and the beast stood looking each other in the face for a short time. At length the lion moved backward, as if to go away. Muller began loading his gun; the lion looked over his shoulder, growled, and immediately returned to his former position within a few paces of Muller. Muller stood still, with his eyes fixed on the animal. The lion again moved cautiously off; when he was at a certain distance, Muller proceeded to ram down his bullet. The lion again looked back and growled angrily. Muller again was quiet, and the animal continued turning and growling as it moved off, till at last it bounded away."

"You imagine, then, that the lion is aware of the fatal effects of firearms?" said the Major.

"It would appear so, not only on account of their being so angry if presented at them, or being touched even when they are close to them, but also from the greater respect the lion pays to man where firearms are in use. The respect that he pays to men in the colony is not a general custom of the animal.

"As I said before, the lion is more dangerous in this Bushman country; because, in the first place, his awe of man has been removed, from his invariably successful rencounters with those who have no weapons of force with which to oppose him; and, secondly, because he has but too often tasted human flesh, after which a lion becomes more partial to it than any other food.

"It is asserted that when a lion has once succeeded in snatching some unfortunate Bushman from his cave, he never fails to return regularly every night, in hopes of another meal, until the horde is so harassed that they are compelled to seek some other shelter. From apprehension of such attacks, it is also asserted that the Bushmen are in the habit of placing their aged and infirm people at the entrance of the cave during the night, that, should the lion come, the least valuable and most useless of their community may first fall a prey to the animal."

"Of course, if permitted to help himself in that way, the lion cannot have much fear of man," observed Wilmot; "and his lurking abroad in the night takes away much from the nobleness of disposition which you are inclined to attribute to him."

"By no means," continued Swinton. "That a lion generally lurks and lies in wait to seize his prey is certain, but this is the general characteristic of the feline tribe, of which he may be considered as the head; and it is for this mode of hunting that nature has fitted him.

"The wolf, the hound, and others, are furnished with an acute scent, and are enabled to tire down their prey by a long chase. The feline tribe are capable of very extraordinary efforts of activity and speed for a very short time; if they fail to seize their prey at the first spring, or after a few tremendous bounds, they generally abandon the pursuit.

"The lion can spring from nine to twelve yards at a leap, and for a few seconds can repeat these bounds with such activity and velocity as to outstrip the movements of the quickest horse; but he cannot continue these amazing efforts, and does not attempt it. In fact, the lion is no more than a gigantic cat, and he must live by obtaining his prey in the same manner as a cat.

"In these countries, his prey is chiefly of the antelope species, the swiftest animals on earth; and what chance would he have, if he were to give one of his magnanimous roars to announce his approach? He knows his business better; he crouches in the rank grass and reeds by the sides of the paths made by the animals to descend to the rivers and pools to drink, and as they pass he makes his spring upon them.

"Now I do not consider that his obtaining his food as nature has pointed out to him is any argument against vhat I consider the really noble disposition of the lion, which is, that he does not kill for mere cruelty, and that he is really generous, unless compelled by hunger to destroy, as I have already shown by one or two examples."

"We are convinced, my dear Swinton," said Alexander; "but now let us have your opinion as to his being afraid to meet the eye of man."

"I consider that the lion will generally retreat before the presence of man; but he does not retreat cowardly, like the leopard or hyena, and others. He never slinks away, he appears calmly to survey his opponent, as apparently measuring his prowess. I should say that the lion seems to have a secret impression that man is not his natural prey, and although he will not always give place to him, he will not attack him, if, in the first place, the man shows no sign of fear, and in the second, no signs of hostility.

"But this instinctive deference to man is not to be reckoned upon. He may be very angry, he may be very hungry, he may have been just disappointed in taking his prey, or he may be accompanied by the female and cubs; in short, the animal's temper may have been ruffled, and in this case he becomes dangerous.

"An old Namaqua chief with whom I was conversing, and who had been accustomed to lions from childhood, fully corroborated these opinions, and also that there is that in the eye of man before which the lion quails. He assured me that the lion very seldom attacks a man, if not provoked; but he will approach him within a few paces and survey him steadily. Sometimes he attempts to get behind him, as if he could not stand his look, but was desirous of springing upon him unawares. He said that if a man in such a case attempted to fly, he would run the greatest danger, but that if he had presence of mind to confront the animal, it would in almost every instance after a short time retire.

"Now I have already brought forward the instance of Muller and the lion, as a proof of the effect of a man's eye upon the lion. I will now give another, still more convincing, as the contact was still closer, and the lion had even tasted blood.

"A boor of the name of Gyt was out with one of his neighbours hunting. Coming to a fountain, surrounded as usual with tall reeds and rushes, Gyt gave his gun to his comrade, and alighted to see if there was any water

183

remaining in it; but as he approached the fountain, an enormous lion started up close at his side, and seized him by the left arm. Gyt, although thus taken by surprise, stood motionless and without struggling, for he was aware that the least attempt to escape would occasion his immediate destruction. The animal also remained motionless, holding Gyt fast by the arm with his fangs, but without biting it severely, at the same time shutting his eyes, as if he could not withstand the eyes of his victim fixed upon him."

"What a terrible position!"

"Yes; but I may here observe that the lion was induced to seize the man in consequence of their coming so completely in contact, and, as it were, for self-defence. Had they been further apart, the lion would, as usually is the case, have walked away; and, moreover, the eye of the man being so close to him had, at the same time, more power over the lion, so as to induce him to shut his own. But to continue—

"As they stood in this position, Gyt recovered his presence of mind, and beckoned to his comrade to advance with his gun and shoot the lion through the head. This might easily have been done, as the animal continued still with his eyes closed, and Gyt's body concealed any object approaching. But his comrade was a cowardly scoundrel, and, instead of coming to Gyt's assistance, he cautiously crawled up a rock to secure himself from any danger. For a long while Gyt continued earnestly to entreat his comrade by signs to come to his assistance —the lion continuing all this while perfectly quiet—but in vain."

"How my blood boils at the conduct of this scoundrel," said the Major; "admitting his first impulse to have been fear, yet to allow his comrade to remain in that position so long a while covers him with infamy."

"I think if Gyt escaped, he must have felt very much inclined to shoot the wretch himself."

"The lion-hunters affirm that, if Gyt had but persevered a little longer, the animal would have at last released his hold and left Gyt uninjured; that the grip of the lion was more from fear that the man would hurt him, than

184

from any wish to hurt the man; and such is my opinion. But Gyt, indignant at the cowardice of his comrade, and losing patience with the lion, at last drew his hunting-knife, which all the boors invariably carry at their side, and with all the power of his right arm thrust it into the lion's breast.

"The thrust was a deadly one, for it was aimed with judgment, and Gyt was a bold and powerful man; but it did not prove effectual so as to save Gyt's life, for the enraged lion, striving in his death agonies to grapple with Gyt,—held at arm's length by the strength of desperation on the part of the boor,—so dreadfully lacerated with his talons the breast and arms of poor Gyt, that his bones were left bare.

"At last the lion fell dead, and Gyt fell with him. His cowardly companion, who had witnessed this fearful struggle from the rock, now took courage to advance, and carried the mangled body of Gyt to the nearest house. Medical aid was at hand, but vainly applied, as on the third day he died of a locked jaw. Such was the tragical end of this rencounter, from the sheer cowardice of Gyt's companion.

"I could mention many other instances in which lions have had men in their power and have not injured them, if they have neither attempted to escape nor to assault; but I think I have given enough already, not only to prove the fact of his general forbearance towards man, but also that there is something in the eye of man at which the lion and other animals, I believe, will quail."

"I can myself give an instance that this fascinating effect, or whatever it may be, of the human eye, is not confined wholly to the lion," said the Major.

"One of our officers in India, having once rambled into a jungle adjoining the British encampment, suddenly encountered a Bengal tiger. The meeting was evidently most unexpected on both sides, and both parties made a dead halt, earnestly gazing at each other. The officer had no firearms with him, although he had his regulation sword by his side; but that he knew would be of no defence if he had to struggle for life with such a fearful antagonist. He was, however, a man of undaunted courage, and he had heard that even a Bengal tiger might be checked by looking him steadily in the face.

"His only artillery being, like a lady's, that of his eyes, he directed them point blank at the tiger. He would have infinitely preferred a rifle, as he was not at all sure but that his eyes might miss fire. However, after a few minutes, during which the tiger had been crouched ready for his spring, the animal appeared disturbed and irresolute, slunk on one side, and then attempted to crawl round behind the officer.

"This, of course, the officer would not permit, and he turned to the tiger as the tiger turned, with the same constancy that, Tom Moore says, the 'sunflower turns to the sun.'

"The tiger then darted into the thicket, and tried to catch him by coming suddenly upon him from another quarter, and taking him by surprise; but our officer was wide awake, as you may suppose, and the tiger, finding that it was no go, at last went off himself, and the officer immediately went off too, as fast as he could, to the encampment."

"I am glad to have heard your narrative, Major," replied Swinton; "for many doubts have been thrown upon the question of the power of the human eye, and your opinion is a very corroborative one."

"Do not you imagine that the lion-tamers, who exhibit in Europe, have taken advantage of this peculiar fact?"

"I have no doubt but that it is one of their great helps; but I think that they resort to other means, which have increased the instinctive fear that the animals have of them. I have witnessed these exhibitions, and always observed that the man never for a moment took his eyes off the animal which he was playing with or commanding."

"I have observed that also; but what are the other means to which you allude?"

"I cannot positively say, but I can only express an opinion. The most painful and most stunning effects of a blow upon any part of the body, not only of man but of brutes, is a blow on the nose. Many animals, such as the

186

seal and others, are killed by it immediately, and there is no doubt but a severe blow on that tender part will paralyse almost any beast for the time and give him a dread for the future. I believe that repeated blows upon the nose will go further than any other means to break the courage of any beast, and I imagine that these are resorted to: but it is only my opinion, recollect, and it must be taken for just as much as it is worth."

"Do not you think that animals may be tamed by kindness, if you can produce in them the necessary proportion of love and fear?"

"Yes, I was about to say every animal, but I believe some must be excepted; and this is from their having so great a fear of man, rather than from any other cause. If their fear could be overcome, they might be tamed. Of course there are some animals which have not sufficient reasoning power to admit of their being tamed; for instance, who would ever think of taming a scorpion?"

"I believe that there is one animal which, although taken as a cub, has resisted every attempt to tame it in the slightest degree,—this is the grizzly bear of North America."

"I have heard so too," replied Swinton; "at all events, up to the present time they have been unsuccessful. It is an animal of most unamiable disposition, that is certain; and I would rather encounter ten lions, if all that they say of it is true. But it is time for us to go to bed. Those fires are getting rather low. Who has the watch?"

The Major rose and walked round to find the Hottentot who was on that duty, and found him fast asleep. After sundry kicks in the ribs, the fellow at last woke up.

"Is it your watch?"

"Yaw, Mynher," replied Big Adam, rolling out of his kaross.

"Well, then, you keep it so well, that you will have no tobacco next time it is served out."

"Gentlemen all awake and keep watch, so I go to sleep a little," replied Adam, getting up on his legs.

"Look to your fires, sir," replied the Major, walking to his waggon.

187

CHAPTER XXI

Interview with Bushmen—A shrewd surmise—A herd of buf-faloes—A providential escape—A scene—Swanevelt in danger —Conversation—A story.

As they fully expected to fall in with a herd of buffaloes as they proceeded, they started very early on the following morning. They had now the satisfaction of finding that the water was plentiful in the river, and, in some of the large holes which they passed, they heard the snorting and blowing of the hippopotami, to the great delight of the Hottentots, who were very anxious to procure one, being very partial to its flesh.

As they travelled that day, they fell in with a small party of Bushmen; they were shy at first, but one or two of the women at last approached, and receiving some presents of snuff and tobacco, the others soon joined; and as they understood from Omrah and the Hottentots that they were to hunt in the afternoon, they followed the caravan, with the hopes of obtaining food.

They were a very diminutive race, the women, although very well formed, not being more than four feet high. Their countenances were pleasing,—that is, the young ones; and one or two of them would have been pretty, had they not been so disfigured with grease and dirt. Indeed, the effluvia from them was so unpleasant, that our travellers were glad that they should keep at a distance; and Alexander said to Swinton, "Is it true that the lion and other animals prefer a black man to a white, as being of a higher flavour, Swinton, or is it only a joke?"

"I should think there must be some truth in the idea," observed the Major; "for they say that the Bengal tiger will always take a native in preference to a European."

"It is, I believe, not to be disputed," replied Swinton, 'that for one European devoured by the lion or other animals, he feasts upon ten Hottentots or Bushmen, perhaps more; but I ascribe the cause of his so doing, not exactly to his perceiving any difference in the flesh of a black and

188

white man, and indulging his preference. The lion, like many other beasts of prey, is directed to his game by his scent as well as by his eye; that is certain. Now, I appeal to you, who have got rid of these Bushmen, and who know so well how odoriferous is the skin of a Hottentot, whether a lion's nose is not much more likely to be attracted by one of either of these tribes of people, than it would by either you or me. How often, in travelling, have we changed our position, when the wind has borne down upon us the effluvia of the Hottentot who was driving?—why that effluvia is borne down with the wind for miles, and is as savoury to the lion, I have no doubt, as a beefsteak is to us."

"There can, I think, be no doubt of that," said Alexander; "but it is said that they will select a Hottentot from white men."

"No doubt of it, because they follow up the scent right to the party from whence it emanates. I can give you an instance of it. I was once travelling with a Dutch farmer, with his waggon and Hottentots. We unyoked and lay down on the sand for the night; there were the farmer and I, two Hottentot men and a woman—by-the-bye, a very fat one, and who consequently was more heated by the journey. During the night a lion came and carried away the woman from among us all, and by his tracks, as we found on the following morning, he had passed close to the farmer and myself."

"Was the woman killed?"

"The night was so dark that we could see nothing; we were roused by her shrieks, and seized our guns, but it was of no use. I recollect another instance which was not so tragical. A Hottentot was carried off by a lion during the night, wrapped up in his sheep-skin kaross, sleeping, as they usually do, with his face to the ground. As the lion trotted away with him, the fellow contrived to wriggle out of his kaross, and the lion went off with only his mantle."

"Well, I should think one of the karosses must be a very savoury morsel for a hungry lion," said the Major;—"but I imagine it is almost time to unyoke; we must have travelled nearly twenty miles, and these forests promise well for the game we are in search of."

"I suspect that they contain not only buffaloes, but elephants; however, we shall soon find out by examining the paths down to the river, which they make in going for water."

"I think that yonder knoll would be a good place to fix our encampment, Swinton," said the Major; "it is well shaded with mimosas, and yet clear of the main forest."

"Well, you are quartermaster-general, and must decide."

The Major ordered Bremen to arrange the waggons as usual, and turn the cattle out to feed. As soon as this had been accomplished, they saddled their horses, and awaited the return of Swanevelt, who had gone to reconnoitre. Shortly afterwards he returned, with the report that there were the tracks of elephants, buffaloes, and lions, in every direction by the river's banks; and as the dogs would now be of use, they were ordered to be let loose, which they seldom were, unless the game was large and to be regularly hunted down. Our travellers mounted and proceeded into the forest, accompanied by all the Hottentots except the cattle-keepers and the Bushmen; Bremen, Swanevelt, and Omrah only being on horseback, as well as themselves. As they rode forward slowly and cautiously at the outset, Swinton asked the Major whether he had ever shot buffaloes.

"Yes, in India," replied the Major; "and desperate animals they are in that country."

"I was about to say that you will find them such here; and, Alexander, you must be very careful. In the first place, a leaden bullet is of little use against their tough hides, and, I may almost say, impenetrable foreheads. The best shot is under the fore-shoulder."

"Our balls are hardened with tin," observed Alexander.

"I know that," replied Swinton; "but still they are most dangerous animals, especially if you fall in with a single buffalo. It is much safer to attack a herd; but we have no time to talk over the matter now, only, as I say, be very careful, and whatever you do, do not approach one which is wounded, even if he be down on his knees. But here comes Bremen with news."

The Hottentot came up and announced that there was

190

a large herd of buffaloes on the other side of the hill, and proposed that they should take a sweep round them, so as to drive them towards the river.

This proposal was considered good, and was acted upon; and, after riding about a mile, they gained the position which seemed the most desirable. The dogs were then let loose, and the Hottentots on foot, spread themselves on every side, shouting so as to drive the animals before them. The herd collected together and for a short while stood at bay with the large bulls in front, and then set off through the forest towards the river, followed by all the hunters on horse and on foot. In a quarter of an hour the whole herd had taken refuge in a large pool in the river, which, with the reeds and rushes, and small islands in the centre, occupied a long slip of ground.

The Major, with Swanevelt and two other Hottentots, proceeded further up the river, that they might cross it before the attack commenced, and the others agreed to wait until the signal was given by the Major's firing. As soon as they heard the report of the Major's rifle, Swinton and Alexander, with their party, advanced to the banks of the river. They plunged in, and were soon up to the horses' girths, with the reeds far above their heads. They could hear the animals forcing their way through the reeds, but could not see them; and after some severe labour, Swinton said—"Alexander, it will be prudent for us to go back; we can do nothing here, and we shall stand a chance of being shot by our own people, who cannot see us. We must leave the dogs to drive them out, or the Hottentots and Bushmen; but we must regain the banks."

Just as Swinton said this, a loud rushing was heard through the reeds. "Look out!" cried he; but he could say no more before the reeds opened and a large hippopotamus rushed upon them, throwing over Alexander's horse on his side, and treading Alexander and his horse both deep under the water as he passed over them and disappeared. Although the water was not more than four feet in depth, it was with difficulty that the horse and rider could extricate themselves from the reeds, among which they had been jammed and entangled; and Alex-

191

ander's breath was quite gone when he at last emerged. Bremen and Swinton hastened to give what assistance they could, and the horse was once more on his legs. "My rifle," cried Alexander; "it is in the water."

"We will find it!" said Swinton: "haste up to the banks as fast as you can, for you are defenceless."

Alexander thought it advisable to follow Swinton's advice, and with some difficulty regained the bank, where he was soon afterwards followed by Swinton and Bremen, who had secured his rifle. Alexander called Omrah, and sent him to the caravan for another rifle, and then for the first time he exclaimed, "Oh, what a brute! It was lucky the water was deep, or he would have jammed me on the head, so that I never should have risen up again."

"You have indeed had a providential escape, Alexander," replied Swinton; "is your horse hurt?"

"He must be, I should think," said Alexander, "for the animal trod upon him; but he does not appear to show it at present."

In the meantime several shots were fired from the opposite side of the river by the Major and his party, and occasionally the head or horns of the buffalo were seen above the reeds by the Hottentots, who remained with Swinton and Alexander: but the animals still adhered to their cover. Omrah having brought another rifle, Bremen then proposed that the Hottentots, Bushmen, and dogs should force their way through the reeds and attempt to drive the animals out; in which there would be no danger, as the animals could not charge with any effect in the deep water and thick rushes.

"Provided they don't meet with a hippopotamus," said Alexander, laughing.

"Won't say a word about him, sir," replied Bremen, who then went and gave the directions.

The Hottentots and Bushmen, accompanied by the dogs, then went into the reeds, and their shouting and barking soon drove out some of the buffaloes on the opposite side, and the reports of the guns were heard.

At last one came out on that side of the river where Alexander and Swinton were watching; Swinton fired, and the animal fell on its knees; a shot from Alexander brought it down dead and turned on its side. One of the Bushmen ran up to the carcass, and was about to use his knife, when another buffalo charged from the reeds, caught the Bushman on his horns, and threw him many yards in the air. The Bushman fell among the reeds behind the buffalo, which in vain looked about for his enemy, when a shot from Bremen brought him to the ground.

Shortly afterwards the Bushman made his appearance from the reeds; he was not at all hurt, with the exception of a graze from the horns of the animal, and a contusion of the ribs.

The chase now became warm; the shouting of the Hottentots, the barking of the dogs, and the bellowing of the herd, which were forcing their way through the reeds before them, were very exciting. By the advice of Swinton, they took up their position on a higher ground, where the horses had good footing, in case the buffaloes should charge.

As soon as they arrived there, they beheld a scene on the other side of the river, about one hundred yards from them, which filled them with anxiety and terror; the Major's horse was galloping away, and the Major not to be seen. Under a large tree, Swanevelt was in a sitting posture, holding his hands to his body as if severely wounded, his horse lying by his side, and right before him an enormous bull buffalo, standing motionless; the blood was streaming from the animal's nostrils, and it was evidently tottering from weakness and loss of blood; at last it fell.

"I fear there is mischief done," cried Swinton; "where can the Major be, and the two Hottentots who were with him! Swanevelt is hurt and his horse killed, that is evident. We had better call them off, and let the buffaloes remain quiet, or escape as they please."

"There is the Major," said Alexander, "and the Hottentots too; they are not hurt, don't you see them?—they were up the trees; thank God."

They now observed the Major run up to Swanevelt, and presently the two Hottentots went in pursuit of the Major's horse. Shortly afterwards, Swanevelt, with the assistance of the Major, got upon his legs, and, taking up his gun, walked slowly away.

"No great harm done, after all," said Alexander; "God be praised: but here come the whole herd, Swinton."

"Let them go, my good fellow," replied Swinton, "we have had enough of buffalo-hunting for the present."

The whole herd had now broken from the reeds about fifty paces from where they were stationed, and with their tails raised, tossing with their horns, and bellowing with rage and fear, darted out of the reeds, dripping with slime and mud, and rushed off towards the forest. In a few seconds they were out of sight.

"A good riddance," said Swinton; "I hope the Major is now satisfied with buffalo-hunting."

"I am, at all events," replied Alexander. "I feel very sore and stiff. What a narrow escape that Bushman had."

"Yes, he had indeed; but, Alexander, your horse is not well: he can hardly breathe. You had better dismount."

Alexander did so, and unloosed his girths. Bremen got off his horse, and, offering it to Alexander, took the bridle of the other and examined him.

"He has his ribs broken, sir," said the Hottentot,— "two of them, if not more."

"No wonder, poor fellow; lead him gently, Bremen. Oh, here comes the Major. Now we shall know what has occurred; and there is Swanevelt and the two men."

"Well, Major, pray tell us your adventures, for you have frightened us dreadfully."

"Not half so much as I have been frightened myself," replied the Major; "we have all had a narrow escape, I can assure you, and Swanevelt's horse is dead."

"Is Swanevelt hurt?"

"No, he was most miraculously preserved; the horn of the buffalo has grazed the whole length of the body, and yet not injured him. But let us go to the caravan and have something to drink, and then I will tell you all about it—I am quite done up, and my tongue cleaves to the roof of my mouth."

As soon as they had arrived at the caravan and dismounted, the Major drank some water, and then gave
his narrative. "We had several shots on our side of the
river, for the buffaloes had evidently an intention of
crossing over, had we not turned them. We had killed
two, when a bull buffalo charged from the reeds upon
Swanevelt, and before he could turn his horse and put
him to his speed, the horns of the buffalo had ripped up
the poor animal, and he fell with Swanevelt under him.
The enraged brute disengaged himself from the horse,
and made a second charge upon Swanevelt; but he
twisted on one side, and the horn only grazed him, as I
have mentioned. I then fired and wounded the animal.
He charged immediately, and I turned my horse, but
from fright he wheeled so suddenly that I lost my
stirrups, and my saddle turned round.

"I found that I could not recover my seat, and that I
was gradually sliding under the horse's belly, when he
passed under a tree, and I caught a branch and swung
myself on to it, just as the buffalo, which was close behind us, come up to me. As he passed under, his back
hit my leg; so you may imagine it was 'touch and go.'
The animal, perceiving that the horse left him, and I was
not on it, quitted his pursuit, and came back bellowing
and roaring, and looking everywhere for me.

"At last it perceived Swanevelt, who had disengaged
himself from the dead horse, and was sitting under the
tree, apparently much hurt, as he is, poor fellow, although
not seriously. It immediately turned back to him, and
would certainly have gored him to death, had not Kloet,
who was up in a tree, fired at the animal and wounded
him mortally—for his career was stopped as he charged
towards Swanevelt, and was not ten yards from him. The
animal could proceed no further, and there he stood until
he fell dead."

"We saw that portion of the adventure ourselves,
Major," said Swinton; "and now we will tell you our
own, which has been equally full of incident and danger."
Swinton having related what had passed on his side of
the river, the Major observed:

"You may talk about lions, but I'd rather go to ten

195

lion-hunts than one more buffalo-hunt. I have had enough of buffaloes for all my life."

"I am glad to hear you say so," replied Swinton, "for they are most ferocious and dangerous animals, as you may now acknowledge, and the difficulty of giving them a mortal wound renders the attack of them very hazardous. I have seen and heard enough of buffalo-hunting to tell you that you have been fortunate, although you have lost one horse and have another very much hurt;—but here come the spoils of the chase; at all events, we will benefit by the day's sport, and have a good meal."

"I can't eat now," said Alexander; "I am very stiff. I shall go and lie down for an hour or two."

"And so shall I," said the Major; "I have no appetite."

"Well, then, we will all meet at supper," said Swinton. "In the meantime I shall see if I can be of any use to Swanevelt. Where's Omrah?"

"I saw him and Begum going out together just now," said the Major. "What for, I do not know."

"Oh! I told him to get some of the Bushman roots," said Alexander; "they are as good as potatoes when boiled; and he has taken the monkey to find them."

The Major and Alexander remained on their beds till supper-time, when Mahomed woke them up. They found themselves much refreshed by their sleep, and also found that their appetites had returned. Buffalo-steaks and fried Bushman roots were declared to be a very good substitute for beefsteaks and fried potatoes; and after they had made a hearty meal, Alexander inquired of Swinton what he had seen of buffalo-hunting when he had been at the Cape before.

"I have only been once or twice engaged in a buffalo-hunt; but I can tell you what I have heard, and what I have collected from my own knowledge, as to the nature of the animal, of which indeed to-day you have had a very good proof. I told you this morning that a single buffalo was more dangerous than a herd; and the reason is this: at the breeding season, the fiercest bulls drive the others away from the herd, in the same manner as the elephants do; and these solitary buffaloes are extremely dangerous, as they do not wait to be attacked, but will attack a man without any provocation. They generally conceal themselves, and rush out upon you unawares, which makes it more difficult to escape from them. They are so bold, that they do not fear the lion himself; and I have been told by the Dutch boors, that when a buffalo has killed one of their comrades by goring and tossing him, it will not leave its victim for hours, but continue to trample on him with his hoofs, crushing the body with its knees as an elephant does, and with its rough tongue stripping off the skin as far as it can. It does not do all this at one time, but it leaves the body, and returns again, as if to glut its vengeance."

"What a malicious brute!"

"Such is certainly its character. I recollect a history of a buffalo-hunting adventure, told me by a Dutch farmer, who was himself an eye-witness to the scene. He had gone out with a party to hunt a herd of buffaloes which were grazing on a piece of marshy ground, sprinkled with a few mimosa trees. As they could not get within shot of the herd, without crossing a portion of the marsh, which was not safe for horses, they agreed to leave their steeds in charge of two Hottentots, and to advance on foot; thinking that, in case any of the buffaloes should charge them, it would be easy to escape by running back to the marsh, which would bear the weight of a man, but not of a horse, much less that of a buffalo.

"They advanced accordingly over the marsh, and being concealed by some bushes, they had the good fortune to bring down with the first volley three of the fattest of the herd; and also so severely wounded the great bull, which was the leader of the herd, that he dropped down on his knees, bellowing most furiously. Thinking that the animal was mortally wounded, the foremost of the huntsmen walked out in front of the bushes from which they had fired, and began to reload his musket as he advanced, in order to give the animal a finishing shot. But no sooner did the enraged animal see the man advancing, than he sprang up and charged headlong at him. The man threw down his gun, and ran towards the marsh; but the beast was so close upon him, that he despaired of escaping by that direction, and turning suddenly round

197

a clump of copsewood, began to climb an old mimosa tree which stood close to it.

"The buffalo was, however, too quick for him. Bounding forward with a roar, which the farmer told me was one of the most hideous and appalling sounds that he ever heard, he caught the poor fellow with his terrible horns, just as he had nearly got out of reach, and tossed him in the air with such force, that after whirling round and round to a great height, the body fell into the fork of the branches of the tree. The buffalo went round the tree roaring, and looking for the man, until, exhausted by wounds and loss of blood, it again fell down on its knees. The other hunters then attacked and killed him; but they found their comrade, who was still hanging in the tree, quite dead."

"Well, I have no doubt but that such would have been the fate of Swanevelt or of me had the brute got hold of us," said the Major; "I never saw such a malignant,diabolical expression in any animal's countenance as there was upon that buffalo's. A lion is, I should say, a gentleman and a man of honour compared to such an evil-disposed ruffian."

"Well, Major, you have only to let them alone: recollect, you were the aggressor," said Swinton, laughing.

"Very true; I never wish to see one again."

"And I never wish to be in the way of a hippopotamus again, I can assure you," said Alexander, "for a greater want of politeness I never met with."

During this conversation the Hottentots and Bushmen at the other fires had not been idle. The Hottentots had fried and eaten, and fried and eaten, till they could hold no more; and the Bushmen, who in the morning looked as thin and meagre as if they had not had a meal for a month, were now so stuffed that they could hardly walk, and their lean stomachs were distended as round as balls. The Bushman who had been tossed by the buffalo came up and asked for a little tobacco, at the same time smiling and patting his stomach, which was distended to a most extraordinary size.

"Yes, let us give them some," said Alexander; "it will complete their day's happiness. Did you ever see a fellow so stuffed? I wonder he does not burst."

"It is their custom. They starve for days, and then gorge in this way when an opportunity offers, which is but seldom. Their calendar, such as it is, is mainly from recollections of feasting; and I will answer for it, that if one Bushman were on some future day to ask another when such a thing took place, he would reply, just before or just after the white men killed the buffaloes."

"How do they live in general?"

"They live upon roots at certain seasons of the year; upon locusts when a flight takes place; upon lizards, beetles—anything. Occasionally they procure game, but not very often. They are obliged to lie in wait for it, and wound it with their poisoned arrows, and then they follow its track and look for it the next day. Subtle as the poison is they only cut out the part near the wound, and eat the rest of the animal. They dig pit-holes for the hippopotamus and rhinoceros, and occasionally take them. They poison the pools for the game also; but their living is very precarious, and they often suffer the extremities of hunger."

"Is that the cause, do you imagine, of their being so diminutive a race, Swinton?"

"No doubt of it. Continual privation and hardships from generation to generation have, I have no doubt, dwindled them down to what you see."

"How is it that these Bushmen are so familiar? I thought that they were savage and irreclaimable."

"They are what are termed tame Bushmen; that is, they have lived near the farmers, and have by degrees become less afraid of the Europeans. Treated kindly, they have done good in return to the farmers by watching their sheep, and performing other little services, and have been rewarded with tobacco. This has given them confidence to a certain degree. But we must expect to meet with others that are equally wild, and who will be very mischievous; attempting to drive off our cattle, and watching in ambush all round our caravan, ready for any pilfering that they can successfully accomplish; and then we shall discover that we are in their haunts without even seeing them."

"How so?"

"Because it will only be by their thefts that we shall find it out. But it is time for bed, and as to-morrow is Sunday you will have a day of rest, which I think you both require."

"I do," replied Alexander, "so good-night to you both."

CHAPTER XXII

Overpowering heat—Divine service—An intrusion—The poisoned lion—Discussion on venomous reptiles—Lizard shot—Swinton's information to his companions.

As arranged, they did not travel on the Sunday. Early in the morning the oxen and horses and sheep were turned out to pasture; all except the horse which had been ridden by Alexander on the preceding day, and which was found to be suffering so much that they took away a large quantity of blood from him before he was relieved.

The Bushmen still remained with them, and were likely to do so as long as there was any prospect of food. The four buffaloes which had been killed, as well as the horse which had been gored to death, were found picked clean to the bones on the following day, by the hyenas and other animals which were heard prowling during the whole night. But as large quantities of the buffalo-flesh had been cut off, and hung upon the trees near the caravan, there was more than sufficient for a second feast for the Bushmen and Hottentots, and there was nothing but frying and roasting during the whole of the day.

The sun was intensely hot, and Alexander and the Major both felt so fatigued from the exertions of the day before, that after breakfast they retired to their waggons, and Swinton did not attempt to disturb them, as they were in a sound sleep till the evening, when they were much refreshed and very hungry. Swinton said he had thought it better that they should not be awakened, as the heat was so overpowering, and they could perform Divine service in the evening, if they thought proper, when it would be cooler. This was agreed to, and after an early supper they summoned all the Hottentots, who, although gorged, were still unwilling to leave their fires, as they said the Bushmen would devour all the flesh that was left, in their absence.

This remonstrance was not listened to, and they all assembled. The prayers were read and the service gone through by the light of a large fire, for it was very dark before the service was finished. The Bushmen, as the Hottentots prophesied, had taken advantage of their absence to help themselves very liberally; and as Swinton read the prayers, the eyes of the Hottentots were continually turning round to their own fires, where the Bushmen were throwing on large pieces of buffalo-flesh, and, before they were even heated through, were chewing them and tearing them to pieces with their teeth.

Never perhaps was there a congregation whose attention was so divided, and who were more anxious for the conclusion of the service. This uneasiness shown by the Hottentots appeared at last to be communicated to the oxen, which were tied up round the waggons. The fire required replenishing, but none of the Hottentots moved to perform the office: perhaps they thought that if Swinton could no longer see, the service must conclude; but Swinton knew it by heart, and continued reading the Commandments, which was the last portion which he read, and Alexander and the Major repeated the responses. The Major, whose face was towards the cattle, had observed their uneasiness, and guessed the cause, but did not like to interrupt the service, as it was just over. Begum began clinging to him in the way she always did when she was afraid; Swinton had just finished, and the Major was saying, "Swinton, depend upon it," when a roar like thunder was heard, and a dark mass passed over their heads.

The bellowing and struggling of the oxen was almost instantaneously succeeded by a lion, with an ox borne on his shoulder, passing right through the whole congregation, sweeping away the remnants of the fire and the Hottentots right and left, and vanishing in a moment from their sight. As may be imagined, all was confusion and alarm. Some screamed, some shouted and ran for their guns; but it was too late. On examination, it was found that the lion had seized the ox which had been tied up near to where they were sitting; their fire being nearly extinguished, and the one which should have been kept alight next to it altogether neglected by the Hottentots, in their anxiety to keep up those on which they had been broiling their buffalo-steaks.

The leather thongs by which the ox had been tied up were snapped like threads, and many of the other oxen had, in their agony of fear, broken their fastenings and escaped. As the lion bounded away through the assembled party, it appeared as if the ox was not a feather's weight to him. He had, however, stepped rather roughly upon two of the Hottentots, who lay groaning, as if they had been severely hurt; but upon examination it was found that they had only been well scratched and covered with ashes. The Bushmen, however, had left their meal, and with their bows and small poisoned arrows had gone in pursuit. Bremen and one or two of the Hottentots proposed also to go, but our travellers would not permit them. About an hour afterwards the Bushmen returned, and Omrah had communication with them; and through Bremen they learned that the Bushmen had come up with the lion about a mile distant, and had discharged many of their arrows at him, and, they were convinced, with effect, as a heavy growl or an angry roar was the announcement when he was hit; but, although he was irritated, he continued his repast. Omrah then said, "Lion dead to-morrow—Bushmen find him."

"Well," said Alexander, as they went to their waggons, which, in consequence of this event, and their having to make up large fires before they went to bed, they did not do till late, "I believe this is the first time that Divine service was ever wound up by such intrusion."

"Perhaps so," replied Swinton; "but I think it proves that we have more cause for prayer, surrounded as we are by such danger. The lion might have taken one of us, and by this time we should have suffered a horrid death."

"I never felt the full force of the many similes and comparisons in the Scriptures, where the lion is so often introduced, till now," observed Alexander.

"It was indeed a most awful sermon after the prayers," said the Major: "I trust never to hear such a one again; but is it not our own fault? This is the second time that one of our oxen has been carried off by a lion, from the circle of fires not being properly attended to. It is the neglect of the Hottentots, certainly; but if they are so neglectful, we should attend to them ourselves."

"It will be as well to punish them for their neglect," said Swinton, "by stopping their tobacco for the week; for if they find that we attend to the fires ourselves, they will not keep one in, that you may depend upon. However, we will discuss that point to-morrow, so good-night."

Omrah came to the Major the next morning, before the oxen were yoked, to say that the Bushmen had found the lion, and that he was not yet dead, but nearly so; that the animal had dragged away that portion of the ox that he did not eat, about half a mile further; that there he had lain down, and he was so sick that he could not move.

At this intelligence they mounted their horses, and, guided by the Bushmen, arrived at the bush where the lion lay. The Bushmen entered at once, for they had previously reconnoitered, and were saluted with a low snarl, very different from the roar of the preceding night. Our travellers followed, and found the noble creature in his last agonies, his strength paralysed, and his eyes closed. One or two of the small arrows of the Bushmen were still sticking in his hide, and did not appear to have entered more than half an inch; but the poison was so subtle, that it had rapidly circulated through his whole frame; and while they were looking down upon the noble beast, it dropped its jaws and expired.

As our travellers turned back to join the caravan, Alexander observed: "Those Bushmen, diminutive as they are in size, and contemptible as their weapons appear, must be dangerous enemies, when the mere prick of one of their small arrows is certain death. What is their poison composed of?"

"Of the venom extracted from snakes, which is mixed up with the juice of the euphorbia, and boiled down till it becomes of the consistency of glue. They then dip the heads of the arrows into it, and let it dry on."

"Is, then, the venom of snakes so active after it has been taken away from the animal?"

"Yes, for a considerable time after. I remember a story, which is, I believe, well authenticated, of a man who had been bitten through his boot by a rattlesnake in America. The man died, and shortly afterwards his two sons died one after the other, with just the same symptoms as their father, although they had not been bitten by snakes. It was afterwards discovered that upon the father's death the sons had one after the other taken possession of and put on his boots, and the boots being examined, the fang of the rattlesnake was discovered to have passed through the leather and remained there. The fang had merely grazed the skin of the two sons when they put on the boots, and had thus caused their death."

"Are the snakes here as deadly in their poison as the rattlesnake of America?"

"Equally so,—that is, two or three of them; some are harmless. The most formidable is the cobra capella (not the same as the Indian snake of the same name). It is very large, being usually five feet long; but it has been found six and even seven feet. This snake has been known to dart at a man on horseback, and with such force as to overshoot his aim. His bite is certain death, I believe, as I never heard of a man recovering from the wound."

"Well, that is as bad as can be. What is the next?"

"The next is what they call the puff adder. It is a very heavy, sluggish animal, and very thick in proportion to its length, and when attacked in front, it cannot make any spring. It has, however, another power, which, if you are not prepared for it, is perhaps equally dangerous —that of throwing itself backwards in a most surprising manner. This is, however, only when trod upon or provoked; but its bite is very deadly. Then two of the mountain adders are among the most dangerous snakes here. The mountain adder is small, and, from its not being so easily seen and so easily avoided, is very dangerous, and its bite as fatal as the others."

"I trust that is the end of your catalogue?"

"Not exactly; there is another, which I have specimens of, but whose faculties I have never seen put to the test, which is called the spirting snake. It is about three feet long, and its bite, although poisonous, is not fatal. But it has a faculty, from which its name is derived, of spirting its venom into the face of its assailant, and if the venom enters the eye, at which the animal darts it, immediate blindness ensues. There are a great many other varieties, some of which we have obtained possession of during our journey. Many of them are venomous, but not so fatal as the first three I have mentioned.

"Indeed, it is a great blessing that the Almighty has not made the varieties of snakes aggressive or fierce,—which they are not. Provided, as they are, with such dreadful powers, if they were so, they would indeed be formidable; but they only act in self-defence, or when provoked. I may as well here observe, that the Hottentots, when they kill any of the dangerous snakes, invariably cut off the head and bury it; and this they do, that no one may by chance tread upon it, as they assert that the poison of the fangs is as potent as ever, not only for weeks but months afterwards."

"That certainly is a corroboration of the story that you told us of the rattlesnake's fang in the boot."

"It is so; but although there are so many venomous snakes in this country, it is remarkable how very few accidents or deaths occur from them. I made an inquiry at the Moravian Mission, where these venomous snakes are very plentiful, how many people they had lost by their bites, and the missionaries told me, that out of eight hundred Hottentots belonging to the mission, they had only lost two men by the bites of snakes during a space of seven years; and in other places where I made the same inquiry, the casualties were much less in proportion to the numbers."

"Is the boa-constrictor found in this part of Africa?"

"Not so far south as we now are, but it is a few degrees

more to the northward. I have never seen it, but I believe there is no doubt of its existence."

"The South American Indians have a very subtle poison with which they kill their game. Are you aware, Swinton, of its nature? Is it like the Bushmen's poison?"

"I know the poison well; it was brought over by Mr. Waterton, whose amusing works you may have read. It is called the wourali poison, and is said to be extracted from a sort of creeping vine, which grows in the country. The natives, however, add the poison of snakes to the extract; and the preparation is certainly very fatal, as I can bear witness to."

"Have you ever seen it tried?"

"Yes, I have tried it myself. When I was in Italy I became acquainted with Mr. W., and he gave two or three of us, who were living together, a small quantity, not much more than two grains of mustard-seed in size. We purchased a young mule to make the experiment upon; an incision was made in its shoulder, and the poison inserted under the skin. I think in about six or seven minutes the animal was dead. Mr. W. said that the effects would have been instantaneous, if the virtue of the poison had not somewhat deteriorated from its having been kept so long."

"The wourali poison only acts upon the nerves, I believe?" said the Major.

"Only upon the nerves; and although so fatal, if immediate means are resorted to, a person who is apparently dead from it may be brought to life again by the same process as is usual in the recovery of drowned or suffocated people. A donkey upon which the poison had acted was restored in this manner, and for the remainder of his days permitted to run in Sir Joseph Banks's park. But the poison of snakes acts upon the blood, and therefore occasions death without remedy."

"But there are remedies, I believe, for even the most fatal poisons?"

"Yes, in His provident mercy God has been pleased to furnish remedies at hand, and where the snake exists the remedy is to be found. The rattlesnake root is a cure, if taken and applied immediately; and it is well known that the ichneumon when bitten by the cobra capella, in his attack upon it, will hasten to a particular herb and eat it immediately, to prevent the fatal effect of the animal's bite."

"I once saw a native of India," said the Major, "who for a small sum would allow himself to be bitten by a cobra capella. He was well provided with the same plant used by the ichneumon, which he swallowed plentifully, and also rubbed on the wound. It is impossible to say, but, so far as I could judge, there was no deception."

"I think it very possible; if the plant will cure the ichneumon, why not a man? I have no doubt but that there are many plants which possess virtues of which we have no knowledge. Some few, and perhaps some of the most valuable, we have discovered; but our knowledge of the vegetable kingdom, as far as its medicinal properties are known, is very slight; and perhaps many which were formerly known have, since the introduction of mineral antidotes, been lost sight of."

"Why, yes; long before chemistry had made any advances, we do hear in old romances of balsams of most sovereign virtues," said Alexander, laughing.

"Which, I may observe, is almost a proof that they did in reality exist; and the more so, because you will find that the knowledge of these sovereign remedies was chiefly in the hands of the Jews, the oldest nation upon the earth; and from their constant communication with each other, most likely to have transmitted their knowledge from generation to generation."

"We have also reason to believe that not only they had peculiar *remedies* in their times, but also—if we are to credit what has been handed down to us—that the art of *poisoning* was much better understood," said the Major.

"At all events, they had not the knowledge of chemistry which now leads to its immediate detection," replied Swinton. "But, Alexander, there are three hippopotami lying asleep on the side of the river. Have you a mind to try your skill?"

"No, not particularly," replied Alexander; "I have had

enough of hippopotami. By-the-bye, the river is much wider than it was."

"Yes, by my calculation we ought to travel no more to the westward after to-day. We must now cut across to the Yellow or Val River. We shall certainly be two days without water or pasturage for the cattle, but they are in such good condition that they will not much feel it. There is a river which we shall cross near its head, but the chance of water is very small; indeed, I believe we shall find it nowhere, except in these great arteries, if I may so call them."

"Well, I was thinking so myself, Swinton, as I looked at the map yesterday, when I lay in my waggon," said the Major; "so then to-morrow for a little variety; that is, a desert."

"Which it will most certainly be," replied Swinton; "for, except on the banks of the large rivers, there are no hopes of vegetation in this country at this season of the year; but in another month we may expect heavy falls of rain."

"The Bushmen have left us, I perceive," said Alexander.

"Yes, they have probably remained behind to eat the lion."

"What, will they eat it now that it has been poisoned?"

"That makes no difference to them; they merely cut out the parts wounded, and invariably eat all the carcases of the animals which they kill, and apparently without any injury. There is nothing which a Bushman will not eat. A flight of locusts is a great feast to him."

"I cannot imagine them to be very palatable food."

"I have never tasted them," replied Swinton; "but I should think not. They do not, however, eat them raw; they pull off their wings and legs, and dry their bodies; they then beat them into a powder."

"Do you suppose that St. John's fare of locusts and wild honey was the locust which we are now referring to?"

"I do not know, but I should rather think not, and for one reason, which is, that although a person in the wilderness might subsist upon these animals, if always to be procured, yet the flights of locusts are very uncertain. Now there is a tree in the country where St. John retired,

208

which is called the locust-tree, and produces a large sweet
bean, shaped like the common French bean, but nearly a
foot long, which is very palatable and nutritious. It is
even now given to cattle in large quantities; and I imagine that this was the locust referred to; and I believe
many of the commentators on the holy writings have
been of the same opinion. I think we have now gone far
enough for to-day; we may as well halt there. Do you
intend to hunt, Major? I see some animals there at a
distance."

"I should say not," said Alexander; "if we are to
cross a desert tract to-morrow we had better not fatigue
our horses."

"Certainly not. No, Swinton, we will remain quiet, unless
game comes to us."

"Yes, and look after our water-kegs being filled, and
the fires lighted to-night," said Alexander; "and I trust
we may have no more sermons from lions, although
Shakespeare does say, 'sermons from stones, and good in
everything.'"

They halted their caravan upon a rising ground, and
having taken the precaution to see the water-kegs filled
and the wood collected, they sat down to dinner upon
fried ham and cheese; for the Hottentots had devoured
all the buffalo-flesh, and demanded a sheep to be killed
for supper. This was consented to although they did not
deserve it; but as their tobacco had been stopped for
their neglect of providing fuel and keeping up the fires,
it was considered politic not to make them too discontented.

Alexander had been walking by the side of the river
with the Major, while the Hottentots were arranging the
camp, and Swinton was putting away some new specimens in natural history which he had collected, when
Omrah, who was with them, put his finger to his lips and
stopped them. As they perfectly understood what he
required they stood still and silent. Omrah then pointed
to something which was lying on the low bank, under a
tuft of rushes; but they could not distinguish it, and
Omrah asked by signs for the Major's rifle, took aim, and
fired. A loud splashing was heard in the water, and

they pushed their way through the high grass and reeds, until they arrived at the spot, where they perceived an animal floundering in the agonies of death."

"An alligator!" exclaimed the Major; "well, I had no idea that there were any here inland. They said that there were plenty at the mouths of the rivers, on the coast of the Eastern Caffres, but I am astonished to find one here."

"What did you fire at?" asked Swinton, who now joined them.

"An alligator, and he is dead. I am afraid that he won't be very good eating," replied the Major.

"That's not an alligator, Major," said Swinton, "and it is very good eating. It is a large lizard of the guana species, which is found about these rivers; it is amphibious, but perfectly harmless, subsisting upon vegetables and insects. I tell you it is a great delicacy, ugly as it looks. It is quite dead, so let us drag it out of the water, and send it up to Mahomed by Omrah."

The animal, which was about four feet long, was dragged out of the water by the tail, and Omrah took it to the camp.

"Well, I really thought it was a small alligator," said the Major; "but now I perceive my mistake. What a variety of lizards there appears to be in this country."

"A great many from the chameleon upward," replied Swinton. "By-the-bye, there is one which is said to be very venomous. I have heard many well-authenticated stories of the bite being not only very dangerous, but in some instances fatal. I have specimens of the animal in my collection. It is called here the geitje."

"Well, it is rather remarkable, but we have in India a small lizard, called the gecko by the natives, which is said to be equally venomous. I presume it must be the same animal, and it is singular that the names should vary so little. I have never seen an instance of its poisonous powers, but I have seen a whole company of sepoys run out of their quarters because they have heard the animal make its usual cry in the thatch of the building; they say that it drops down upon people from the roof."

"Probably the same animal; and a strong corrobora-tion that the report of its being venomous is with good foundation."

"And yet if we were to make the assertion in England we should in all probability not be believed."

"Not by many, I grant—not by those who only know a little; but by those who are well informed, you probably would be. The fact is, from a too ready credulity, we have now turned to almost a total scepticism, unless we have ocular demonstration. In the times of Marco Polo, Sir John Mandeville, and others,—say in the fifteenth century, when there were but few travellers and but little education, a traveller might assert almost anything and gain credence; latterly a traveller hardly dare assert anything. Le Vaillant and Bruce, who travelled in the South and North of Africa, were both stigmatised as liars, when they published their accounts of what they had seen, and yet every tittle has since been proved to be correct. However, as people are now better informed, they do not reject so positively; for they have certain rules to guide them between the possible and the impossible."

"How do you mean?"

"I mean, for instance, that if a person was to tell me that he had seen a mermaid, with the body of a woman and the scaly tail of a fish, I should at once say that I could not believe him. And why? because it is contrary to the laws of nature. The two component parts of the animal could not be combined, as the upper portion would belong to the mammalia, and be a hot-blooded animal, the lower to a cold-blooded class of natural history. Such a junction would, therefore, be impossible. But there are, I have no doubt, many animals still undiscovered, or rather still unknown to Europeans, the description of which may at first excite suspicion, if not doubt. But as I have before observed, the account would, in all probability, not be rejected by a naturalist, although it might be by people without much knowledge of the animal kingdom, who would not be able to judge by comparison whether the existence of such an animal was credible. Even fabulous animals have had their origin from existing ones. The unicorn is, no doubt, the gemsbok antelope; for when you look at the animal at a

211

distance, its two horns appear as if they were only one, and the Bushmen have so portrayed the animal in their caves. The dragon is also not exactly imaginary; for, the *Lacerta volans,* or flying lizard of Northern Africa, is very like a small dragon in miniature. So that even what has been considered as fabulous has arisen from exaggeration or mistake."

"You think, then, Swinton, that we are bound to believe all that travellers tell us?"

"Not so; but not to reject what they assert, merely because it does not correspond with our own ideas on the subject. The most remarkable instance of unbelief was relative to the aërolites or meteoric stones formed during a thunder-storm in the air, and falling to the earth. Of course you have heard that such have occurred?"

"I have," replied the Major, "and I have seen several in India."

"This was treated as a mere fable not a century back; and when it was reported (and not the first time) that such a stone had fallen in France, the *savans* were sent in deputation to the spot. They heard the testimony of the witnesses that a loud noise was heard in the air; that they looked up and beheld an opaque body descending; that it fell on the earth with a force which nearly buried it in the ground, and was so hot at the time that it could not be touched with the hand. It afterward became cold. Now, the *savans* heard all this, and pronounced that it could not be; and for a long while every report of the kind was treated with contempt. Now every one knows, and every one is fully satisfied of the fact, and not the least surprise is expressed when they are told of the circumstance. As Shakespeare makes Hamlet observe very truly—'There are more things in heaven and earth, Horatio, than are dreamt of in your philosophy.'"

CHAPTER XXIII

A good shot—Water scarce—Omrah in trouble—Turtle soup—
Sufferings—Sufferings at an end—An earthly paradise.

THERE was no alarm during the night, and the next morning they yoked the oxen and changed their course to the northward. The whole of the cattle had been led down to the river to drink, and allowed two hours to feed before they started; for they were about to pass through a sterile country of more than sixty miles, where they did not expect to find either pasturage or water. They had not left the river more than three miles behind them when the landscape changed its appearance. As far as the eye could scan the horizon all vestiges of trees had disappeared, and now the ground was covered with low stunted bushes and large stones. Here and there were to be seen small groups of animals, the most common of which were the quaggas. As our travellers were in the advance, they started six or seven ostriches which had been sitting, and a ball from the Major's rifle brought one to the ground, the others running off at a velocity that the fastest horse could scarcely have surpassed.

"That was a good shot, Major," said Alexander.

"Yes," replied Swinton; "but take care how you go too near the bird; you have broken his thigh, and he may be dangerous. They are very fierce. As I thought, here is the nest. Let Bremen kill the bird,—he understands them, Major. It is the male, and those which have escaped are all females."

"What a quantity of eggs!" said Alexander. "Is the nest a joint concern?"

"Yes," replied Swinton. "All those which are in the centre of the nest with their points upward are the eggs for hatching. There are, let me see, twenty-six of them, and you observe that there are as many more round about the nest. Those are for the food of the young ostriches as soon as they are born. However, we will save them that trouble. Bremen must take the eggs outside the nest

213

for us, and the others the people may have. They are not very particular whether they are fresh or not."

"This is a noble bird," said the Major, "and has some beautiful feathers. I suppose we may let Bremen take the feathers out and leave the body!"

"Yes; I do not want it; but Bremen will take the skin, I daresay. It is worth something at the Cape."

As soon as the Hottentots had secured the eggs, and Bremen had skinned the ostrich, which did not occupy many minutes, they rode on, and Swinton then said—

"The male ostrich generally associates with from three to seven females, which all lay in the same nest. He sits as well as the females, and generally at night, that he may defend the eggs from the attacks of the hyenas and other animals!"

"You do not mean to say that he can fight these animals!"

"And kill them also. The ostrich has two powerful weapons; its wing, with which it has often been known to break a hunter's leg, the blow from it is so violent; and what is more fatal, its foot, with the toe of which it strikes and kills both animals and men. I once myself, in Namaqualand, saw a Bushman who had been struck on the chest by the foot of the ostrich, and it had torn open his chest and stomach, so that his entrails were lying on the ground. I hardly need say that the poor wretch was dead."

"I could hardly have credited it," observed Alexander.

"The Bushmen skin the ostrich, and spread the skin upon a frame of wicker-work; the head and neck are supported by a skin thrust through them. The skin they fix on one of their sides, and carry the head and neck in one of their hands, while the other holds the bow and arrows. In this disguise—of course with the feathered side of him presented to the bird or beast he would get near to—he walks along, pecking with the head at the bushes, and imitating the motions of the ostrich. By this stratagem he very often is enabled to get within shot of the other ostriches, or the quaggas and gnoos which consort with these birds."

"I should like to see that very much," said the Major.

"You would be surprised at the close imitation, as I have

been. I ought to have said that the Bushman whitens his legs with clay. It is, however, a service of danger, for I have, as I told you, known a man killed by the male ostrich; and the natives say that it is by no means uncommon for them to receive very serious injury."

"Hold hard," said the Major, "there is a lion; what a terrible black mane he has got! What do you say, Swinton? He is by himself."

Swinton looked at the animal, which was crossing about three hundred yards ahead of them; he was on a low hill with his head close to the ground.

"I certainly say not. Let him pass, by all means; and I only hope he will take no notice of us. I must give you the advice which an old Namaqua chief gave me. He said—'Whenever you see a lion moving in the middle of the day, you may be certain that he is in great want of food and very angry. Never attack one then, for they are very dangerous and most desperate.' If, therefore, Major, you wish a very serious affair, and one or two lives lost, you will attack that animal. But you must expect that what I say will happen."

"Indeed, my dear Swinton, I neither wish to lose my own life, nor to risk those of others, and therefore we will remain here till his majesty has had time to get out of our way; and I hope he may soon find a dinner."

By this time the caravan had come up with them, and they then proceeded. The face of the country became even more sterile, and at last not an animal of any description was to be seen. As there was nothing for the oxen to feed upon they continued their route during the whole of the day, and at night they halted and secured the cattle to the waggons. Wood for fires they were not able to procure, and therefore they made one half of the Hottentots watch during the night with their muskets to scare off wild beasts. But, as Swinton observed, there was little chance of their being disturbed by lions or other animals, as they were so distant from water, and there was no game near them upon which the wild beasts prey; and so it proved, for during the whole night they did not even hear the cry of a hyena or a jackal.

At the first gleaming of light the oxen were again yoked,

with the hopes of their being able to gain the Val River by night. The relay oxen were now put to, to relieve those which appeared to suffer most. At noon the heat was dreadful, and the horses, which could not support the want of water as the oxen could, were greatly distressed. They continued for about two hours more, and then perceived a few low trees. Begum, who had been kept without water, that she might exert herself to find it, started off as fast as she could, followed by Omrah. After running to the trees they altered their course to the eastward, toward some ragged rocks. The caravan arrived at the trees, which they found were growing on the banks of the river Alexandria, which they knew they should pass; but not a drop of water was to be discovered; even the pools were quite dry. As they searched about, all of a sudden Begum came running back screaming, and with every mark of terror, and clung, as usual, to the Major when frightened.

"Where is the Bushboy?" said Bremen.

"Something has happened," cried Swinton; "come all of you with your guns."

The whole party, Hottentots and all, hastened toward the rocks where Omrah and Begum had been in search of water. As soon as they reached within fifty paces, quite out of breath with their haste, they were saluted with the quah, quah, of a herd of baboons, which were perched at the edge of the rocks, and which threatened them in their usual way, standing on their fore-legs, and making as if they would fly at them.

"Now, then, what is to be done?" said the Major. "Shall we fire? Do you think that they have possession of the boy?"

"If they have, they will let him go. Yes, we are too numerous for them now, and they will not show fight, depend upon it. Let us all take good aim and fire a volley right into them."

"Well, then, I'll take that venerable old chap that appears to be the leader, and the great-grandfather of them all," said the Major. "Are you all ready?—then fire."

The volley had its effect; three or four of the animals were killed, many were wounded, and the whole herd went

216

scampering off with loud shrieks and cries, the wounded trailing themselves after the others as well as they could.

The whole party then ascended the crags to look after Omrah—all but Begum, who would not venture. They had hardly gained the summit when they heard Omrah's voice below, but could not see him. "There he is, sir," said Swanevelt, "down below there." Swinton and the Major went down again, and at last, guided by the shouts of the boy, they came to a narrow cleft in the rock, about twenty feet deep, at the bottom of which they heard, but could not see, the boy. The cleft was so narrow that none of the men could squeeze down it. Swinton sent one of them back for some leathern thongs or a piece of rope to let down to him.

During the delay Bremen inquired of Omrah if he was hurt, and received an answer in the negative. When the rope came, and was lowered down to him, Omrah seized it and was hauled up by the Hottentots. He appeared to have suffered a little, as his hair was torn out in large handfuls, and his shirt was in ribbons; but with the exception of some severe scratches from the nails of the baboons, he had no serious injury. Omrah explained to the Hottentots, who could talk his language, that Begum and he had come to the cleft, and had discovered that there was water at the bottom of it; that Begum had gone down, and that he was following, when the baboons, which drank in the chasm, had come upon them. Begum had sprung up and escaped, but he could not; and that the animals had followed him down, until he was so jammed in the cleft that he could descend no further; and that there they had pulled out his hair and torn his shirt, as they saw. Having heard Omrah's story, and satisfied themselves that he had received no serious injury, they then went to where the baboons had been shot. Two were dead; but the old one, which the Major had fired at, was alive, although severely wounded, having received two shots, one in his arm and the other in his leg, which was broken by the ball. All the poor old creature's fierceness appeared to have left him. It was evidently very weak from the loss of blood, and sat down leaning against the rock. Every now and then it would raise itself, and look down upon the wound in its leg,

217

examining the hole where the bullet had passed through; then it would hold up its wounded arm with its other hand, and look them in the face inquiringly, as much as to say, "What have you done this for?"

"Poor creature," said Alexander; "how much its motions are those of a human being. Its mute expostulation is quite painful to witness."

"Very true," said the Major; "but still, if it had not those wounds, it would tear you to pieces if it could."

"That it certainly would," said Swinton; "but still it is an object of pity. It cannot recover, and we had better put it out of its misery."

Desiring Bremen to shoot the animal through the head, our travellers then walked back to the caravan. As they returned by the banks of the river they perceived Begum very busy, scraping up the baked mud at the bottom of a pool.

"What is the princess about?" said Alexander.

"I know," cried Omrah, who immediately ran to the assistance of the baboon; and after a little more scraping, he pulled out a live tortoise about a foot long.

"I have heard that when the pools dry up the tortoises remain in the mud till the pools are filled up again," said Swinton.

"Are they good eating, Swinton?"

"Excellent."

"Turtle soup in the desert, that's something unexpected."

The Hottentots now set to work and discovered five or six more, which they brought out. They then tried in vain to get at the water in the deep cleft, but finding it impossible, the caravan continued its course.

"How much more of this desert have we to traverse," said Alexander, "before we come to the river?"

"I fear that we shall not arrive there before to-morrow night," said Swinton, "unless we travel on during the night, which I think will be the best plan; for fatiguing as it will be to the animals they will be even more exhausted if they pass another day under the sun without water, and at night they will bear their work better. We gain nothing by stopping, as the longer they are on the journey, the more they will be exhausted."

"I am really fearful for the horses, they suffer so much."

"At night we will wash their mouths with a sponge full of water; we can spare so much for the poor creatures."

"In the deserts of Africa you have always one of three dangers to encounter," said Swinton; "wild men, wild beasts, and want of water."

"And the last is the worst of the three," replied the Major. "We shall have a moon to-night for a few hours."

"Yes, and if we had not it would be of no consequence; the stars give light enough, and we have little chance of wild beasts here. We now want water; as soon as we get rid of that danger, we shall then have the other to encounter."

The sun went down at last; the poor oxen toiled on with their tongues hanging out of their mouths. At sunset the relay oxen were yoked, and they continued their course by the stars. The horses had been refreshed, as Swinton had proposed; but they were too much exhausted to be ridden, and our travellers, with their guns on their shoulders, and the dogs loose, to give notice of any danger, now walked by the sides of the waggons over the sandy ground. The stars shone out brilliantly, and even the tired cattle felt relief, from the comparative coolness of the night air. All was silent, except the creaking of the wheels of the waggons and the occasional sighs of the exhausted oxen, as they thus passed through the desert.

"Well," observed the Major, after they had walked about an hour without speaking, "I don't know what your thoughts may have been all this while, but it has occurred to me that a party of pleasure may be carried to too great lengths; and I think that I have been very selfish in persuading Wilmot to undergo all that we have undergone, and are likely to undergo, merely because I wished to shoot a giraffe."

"I presume that I must plead guilty also," replied Swinton, "in having assisted to induce him; but you know a naturalist is so ardent in his pursuit that he thinks of nothing else."

"I do not think that you have either of you much to answer for," replied Alexander; "I was just as anxious to go as you were; and as far as I am concerned, have not the slightest wish to turn back again, till we have executed our proposed plans. We none of us undertook this journey with the expectation of meeting with no difficulties or no privations; and I fully anticipate more than we have yet encountered, or are encountering now. If I get back on foot, and without a sole left to my shoe, I shall be quite content; at the same time, I will not continue it if you both wish to return."

"Indeed, my dear fellow, I have no wish but to go on; but I was afraid that we were running you into dangers which we have no right to do."

"You have a right, allowing that I did not myself wish to proceed," replied Alexander. "You escorted me safe through the country to ascertain a point in which you had not the slightest interest, and it would indeed be rewarding you very ill if I were now to refuse to gratify you: but the fact is, I am gratifying myself at the same time."

"Well, I am very glad to hear you say so," replied the Major, "as it makes my mind at ease; what time do you think it is, Swinton?"

"It is about three o'clock; we shall soon have daylight, and I hope with daylight we shall have some sight to cheer us. We have travelled well, and cannot by my reckoning be far from the Val River. Since yesterday morning we have made sixty miles or thereabouts; and if we have not diverged from our course, the poor animals will soon be relieved."

They travelled on another weary hour, when Begum gave a cry, and started off ahead of the waggons; the oxen raised their heads to the wind, and those which were not in the yokes after a short while broke from the keepers, and galloped off, followed by the horses, sheep, and dogs. The oxen in the yokes also became quite unruly, trying to disengage themselves from the traces.

"They have smelt the water; it is not far off, sir," said Bremen; "we had better unyoke them all, and let them go."

"Yes, by all means," said Alexander.

So impatient were the poor beasts that it was very difficult to disengage them, and many broke loose before it could be effected; as soon as they were freed they followed their companions at the same rapid pace.

"At all events we shall know where to find them," said the Major, laughing: "well, I really so felt for the poor animals that I am as happy as if I was as thirsty as they are, and was now quenching my thirst. It's almost daylight."

As the day dawned, they continued to advance in the direction that the animals had taken, and they then distinguished the trees that bordered the river, which was about two miles distant. As soon as it was broad daylight, they perceived that the whole landscape had changed in appearance. Even where they were walking there was herbage, and near to the river it appeared most luxuriant. Tall mimosa-trees were to be seen in every direction, and in the distance large forests of timber. All was verdant and green, and appeared to them as a paradise after the desert in which they had been wandering on the evening before. As they arrived at the river's banks they were saluted with the lively notes of the birds hymning forth their morning praise, and found the cattle, after slaking their thirst, were now quietly feeding upon the luxuriant grass which surrounded them.

"Well may the Psalmist and prophets talk of the beauty of flowing rivers," said Alexander; "now we feel the truth and beauty of the language; one would almost imagine that the sacred writings were indited in these wilds."

"If not in these they certainly were in the Eastern countries, which assimilate strongly with them," said Swinton; "but, as you truly say, it is only by having passed through the country that you can fully appreciate their beauties. We never know the real value of anything till we have felt what it is to be deprived of it; and in a temperate climate, with a pump in every house, people can not truly estimate the value of 'flowing rivers.'"

The Hottentots having now arrived, the cattle were driven back to the waggons and yoked, that they might be brought up to a spot which had been selected for their encampment. In the meantime our travellers, who were tired with their night's walk, lay down under a large mimosa-tree, close to the banks of the river.

"We shall stay here a day or two, of course," said the Major.

"Yes, for the sake of the cattle; the poor creatures deserve a couple of days' rest."

"Do you observe how the mimosas are torn up on the other side of the river?" said Swinton; "the elephants have been very numerous there lately."

"Why do they tear the trees up?" said Alexander.

"To feed upon the long roots, which are very sweet; they destroy an immense number of the smaller trees in that manner."

"Well, we must have another elephant-hunt," said the Major.

"We may have hunts of every kind, I expect, here," replied Swinton; "we are now in the very paradise of wild animals, and the further we go the more we shall find."

"What a difference there is in one day's journey in this country," observed Alexander; "yesterday morning there was not a creature to be seen, and all was silent as death. Now listen to the noise of the birds, and as for beasts, I suspect we shall not have far to look for them."

"No, for there is a hippopotamus just risen; and now he's down again—there's food for a fortnight at one glance," cried the Major.

"How the horses and sheep are enjoying themselves —they are making up for lost time; but here come the waggons."

"Well, then, I must get up and attend to my department," said the Major. "I presume that we must expect our friends the lions again now."

"Where there is food for lions, you must expect lions, Major," said Swinton.

"Very true, and fuel to keep them off; by-the-bye, turtle soup for dinner, recollect; tell Mahomed."

"I'll see to it," said Alexander; "but we must have something for breakfast, as soon as I have had a wash at the river's side. I would have a bath, only I have such a respect for the hippopotami."

"Yes, you will not forget them in a hurry," said Swinton, laughing.

"Not as long as I have breath in my body, for they took all the breath out of it. Come, Swinton, will you go with me, and make your toilet at the river's banks?"

"Yes, and glad to do so; for I am covered with the sand of the desert."

CHAPTER XXIV

Aspect of the country—Chase of a rhinoceros—Omrah's plan succeeds—A lion's leap—Account of a rhinoceros-hunt—Elands shot—A lioness attacked—The lion's skin awarded—An expiring effort.

OUR travellers remained very quiet that day and the next. The horses had suffered so much, that they required two days of rest, and they themselves were not sorry to be inactive after their fatiguing journey over the desert. The cattle enjoyed the luxuriant pasture, and although the tracks of the lions were discovered very near to them, yet, as they had plenty of fuel and attended themselves to the fires, they had not any visits from them during the night. The Hottentots had been out to reconnoitre, and found a profusion of game, in a large plain, about two miles distant; and it was decided that they would rest where they were for a day or two, if the game were not frightened away. The river had been crossed by Swanevelt, who stated that there was a large herd of elephants on the other side, and the tracks of the rhinoceros were to be seen on both sides of the river.

On the third morning after their arrival at the Val, they set off, accompanied by the Hottentots, to the plain which they had spoken of; riding through magnificent groups of acacia or camelthorn trees, many of which were covered with the enormous nests of the social grosbeaks. As they descended to the plain they perceived large herds of brindled gnoos, quaggas, and antelopes covering the whole face of the country as far as the eye could reach, moving about in masses to and fro, joining each other and separating, so that the whole plain seemed alive with them.

"Is not this splendid?" cried the Major. "Such a sight

is worth all the trouble and labour which we have undergone. What would they say in England, if they could but behold this scene?"

"There must be thousands and thousands," said Alexander. "Tell me, Swinton, what beautiful animals are those of a purple colour?"

"They are called the purple sassabys," replied Swinton; "one of the most elegant of the antelope tribe."

"And those red and yellow out there?"

"They are the harte beests. I wish to have male and female specimens of both, if I can."

"See!" said the Major, "there is a fine flock of ostriches. We are puzzled where to begin. Come, we have surveyed the scene long enough; now forward,—to change it."

They rode down, and were soon within shot of the animals, and the rifles began their work. The Hottentots commenced firing from various points, and, alarmed by the report of the guns, the animals now fled away in every direction, and the whole place was one cloud of dust. Our travellers put their horses to their speed, and soon came up with them again, as their numbers impeded the animals in their flight. Every shot told, for it was hardly possible to miss; and the Hottentots who followed on foot, put those who were wounded out of their misery. At last the horses were too fatigued and too much out of wind to continue the pursuit, and they reined up.

"Well, Alexander, this has been sport, has it not?" said the Major.

"Yes, a grand battue, on a grand scale, indeed."

"There were three animals which you did not observe," said Swinton; "but it was impossible to get at them, they were so far off; but we must try for them another time."

"What were they?"

"The elands, the largest of the antelope tribe," replied Swinton, "and the best eating of them all. Sometimes they are nineteen hands high at the chest, and will weigh nearly 2000 lbs. It has the head of an antelope, but the body is more like that of an ox. It has magnificent straight horns, but they are not dangerous. They are easily run down, for, generally speaking, they are very fat and incapable of much exertion."

"We will look out for them to-morrow," said the Major. "See how the vultures are hovering over us; they know there will be bones for them to pick this night."

"More than bones," replied Alexander; "for what can we do with so many carcasses? There is provision for a month, if it would keep. What a prodigious variety of animals there appears to be in this country."

"Yes, they are congregated here, because the country, from want of rain, may be considered as barren. But within eight or nine degrees of latitude from the Cape, we find the largest and most minute of creation. We have the ostrich and the little creeper among the birds. Among the beasts we have the elephant, weighing 4000 lbs., and the black specked mouse, weighing a quarter of an ounce. We have the giraffe, seventeen feet high, and the little viverra, a sort of weasel, of three inches. I believe there are thirty varieties of antelopes known and described; eighteen of them are found in this country, and there are the largest and smallest of the species; for we have the eland, and we have the pigmy antelope, which is not above six inches high. We see here also the intermediate links of many genera, such as the eland and the gnoo; and as we find the elephant, the rhinoceros, and Wilmot's friend, the hippopotamus, we certainly have the bulkiest animals in existence."

Bremen now came up to say that they had discovered a rhinoceros close to the riverside, concealed in the bushes underneath a clump of acacia. The Major and Alexander having declared their intention of immediately going in pursuit, Swinton advised them to be cautious, as the charge of a rhinoceros was a very awkward affair, if they did not get out of the way. They rode down to the clump of trees and bushes where the animal was said to be hid, and, by the advice of Bremen, sent for the dogs to worry the animal out. Bremen, who was on foot, was desired by the Major to take the horse which Omrah rode, that he might be more expeditious, and our travellers remained with a clear space of two hundred yards between them and the bushes where the animal was concealed. The Hottentots had also followed them, and were ordered on no account to fire till they had taken their positions, and the dogs were sent in to drive the animal out.

When Bremen was but a short distance from them with
the dogs, Swinton advised that they should dismount and
take possession of a small clump of trees which grew very
close together, as they would be concealed from the animal.
They called Omrah to take the horses, but he was not to
be seen; so they gave them to one of the Hottentots, to
lead them to some distance out of harm's way.

"The vision of the rhinoceros is so limited," observed
Swinton, "that it is not difficult to get out of his way on
his first charge; but at his second he is generally prepared
for your manœuvre. A ball in the shoulder is the most
fatal. Look out, Bremen has turned in the dogs." The
barking of the dogs, which commenced as soon as they
entered the bushes, did not continue more than a minute,
when a female rhinoceros of the black variety burst out of
the thicket in pursuit of the retreating dogs. Several shots
were fired by the Hottentots, who were concealed in different quarters, without effect; the animal rushing along and
tearing up the ground with its horns, looking out for its
enemies. At last it perceived a Hottentot, who showed
himself from a bush near to where our travellers were concealed. The animal charged immediately, and in charging
was brought down on its knees by a shot from Alexander.
The Hottentots rushed out, regardless of Swinton's calling
out to them to be careful, as the animal was not dead, and
had surrounded it within a few yards, when it rose again
and fiercely charged Swanevelt, who narrowly escaped. A
shot from the Major put an end to its career, and they then
walked to where the animal lay, when a cry from Omrah,
who was standing near the river, attracted their notice, and
they perceived that the male rhinoceros, of whose presence
they were not aware, had just burst out of the same covert,
and was charging towards them.

Every one immediately took to his heels; many of the
Hottentots in their fear dropping their muskets, and fortunately the distance they were from the covert gave
them time to conceal themselves in the thickets before
the animal had time to come up with them. A shot from
Swinton turned the assailant, who now tore up the earth
in his rage, looking everywhere round with its sharp flashing
eye for a victim. At this moment, while it seemed hesitat-

"The rhinoceros, the moment that the boy caught his eye, rushed
furiously towards him."

ing and peering about, to the astonishment of the whole party, Omrah showed himself openly on the other side of the rhinoceros, waving his red handkerchief, which he had taken off his head. The rhinoceros, the moment that the boy caught his eye, rushed furiously towards him. "The boy's lost," cried Swinton; but hardly had the words gone from his mouth, when to their astonishment the rhinoceros disappeared, and Omrah stood capering and shouting with delight. The fact was that Omrah, when he had left our travellers, had gone down towards the river, and as he went along had with his light weight passed over what he knew full well to be one of the deep pits dug by the Bushmen to catch those animals. Having fully satisfied himself that it was so, he had remained by the side of it, and when the rhinoceros rushed at him, had kept the pit between himself and the animal. His object was to induce the animal to charge at him, which it did, and when within four yards of the lad, had plunged into the pit dug for him. The success of Omrah's plan explained the whole matter at once, and our travellers hastened up to where the rhinoceros was impounded, and found that a large stake, fixed upright in the centre of the pit, had impaled the animal. A shot from the Major put an end to the fury and agony of the animal.

"I never was more excited in my life; I thought the boy was mad and wanted to lose his life," said Alexander.

"And so did I," replied Swinton; "and yet I ought to have known him better. It was admirably done; here we have an instance of the superiority of man endowed with reasoning power over brutes. A rhinoceros will destroy the elephant; the lion can make no impression on him, and flies before him like a cat. He is, in fact, the most powerful of all animals; he fears no enemy, not even man, when he is provoked or wounded; and yet he has fallen by the cleverness of that little monkey of a Bushboy. I think, Major, we have done enough now, and may go back to the caravan."

"Yes, I am well satisfied with our day's sport, and am not a little hungry. We may now let the Hottentots bring home as much game as they can. You have taken care to give directions about your specimens, Swinton?"

"Yes, Bremen knows the animals I require, and is now after them. Omrah, run and tell that fellow to bring our horses here."

"Swinton, can birds and beasts talk, or can they not?" said the Major. "I ask that question because I am now looking at the enormous nests of the grosbeaks. It is a regular town, with some hundreds of houses. These birds, as well as those sagacious animals, the beaver, the ant, and the bee, not to mention a variety of others, must have some way of communicating their ideas."

"That there is no doubt of," replied Swinton, laughing; "but still I believe that man only is endowed with speech."

"Well, we know that; but if not with speech, they must have some means of communication which answers as well."

"As far as their wants require it, no doubt," replied Swinton, "but to what extent is hidden from us. Animals have instinct and reasoning powers, but not reason."

"Where is the difference?"

"The reasoning powers are generally limited to their necessities; but with animals who are the companions of man, they appear to be more extended."

"We have a grand supper to-night," said Alexander; "what shall I help you to—harte-beest, sassaby, or rhinoceros?"

"Thank you," replied the Major, laughing; "I'll trouble you for a small piece of that rhinoceros steak—underdone, if you please."

"How curious that would sound in Grosvenor Square."

"Not if you shot the animals in Richmond Park," said Swinton.

"Those rascally Hottentots will collect no fuel to-night if we do not make them do it now," said the Major. "If they once begin to stuff it will be all over with them."

"Very true; we had better set them about it before the feast begins. Call Bremen, Omrah."

Having given their directions, our party finished their supper, and then Alexander asked Swinton whether he had ever known any serious accidents resulting from the hunting of the rhinoceros.

"Yes," replied Swinton; "I once was witness to the death of a native chief."

"Then pray tell us the story," said the Major. "By hearing how other people have suffered, we learn how to take care of ourselves."

"Before I do so, I will mention what was told me by a Namaqua chief about a lion; I am reminded of it by the Major's observations as to the means animals have of communicating with each other. Once when I was travelling in Namaqualand, I observed a spot which was imprinted with at least twenty spoors or marks of a lion's paw; and as I pointed them out a Namaqua chief told me that a lion had been practising his leap. On demanding an explanation, he said that if a lion sprang at an animal, and missed it by leaping short, he would always go back to where he sprang from, and practise the leap so as to be successful on another occasion; and he then related to me the following anecdote, stating that he was an eye-witness to the incident:

"'I was passing near the end of a craggy hill from which jutted out a smooth rock of from ten to twelve feet high, when I perceived a number of zebras galloping round it, which they were obliged to do, as the rock beyond was quite steep. A lion was creeping towards the rock to catch the male zebra, which brought up the rear of the herd. The lion sprang and missed his mark; he fell short, with only his head over the edge of the rock, and the zebra galloped away, switching his tail in the air. Although the object of his pursuit was gone, the lion tried the leap on the rock a second and a third time, till he succeeded. During this two more lions came up and joined the first lion. They seemed to be talking, for they roared a great deal to each other; and then the first lion led them round the rock again and again. Then he made another grand leap, to show them what he and they must do another time. The chief added, 'They evidently were talking to each other, but I could not understand a word of what they said, although they talked loud enough; but I thought it was as well to be off, or they might have some talk about me.'"

"Well, they certainly do not whisper," said the Major, laughing. "Thank you for that story, Swinton, and now for the rhinoceros hunt."

"I was once out hunting with a Griqua of the name of

Henrick and two or three other men; we had wounded a springbok, and were following its track, when we came upon the footing of a rhinoceros, and shortly afterwards we saw a large black male in the bush."

"You mention a black rhinoceros. Is there any other?"

"Yes, there is a white rhinoceros, as it is called, larger than the black, but not so dangerous. It is, in fact, a stupid sort of animal. The black rhinoceros, as you are aware, is very fierce. Well, to continue: Henrick slipped down behind a bush, fired, and wounded the animal severely in the foreleg. The rhinoceros charged, we all fled, and the animal, singling out one of our men, closely pursued him; but the man, stopping short, while the horn of the rhinoceros ploughed up the ground at his heels, dexterously jumped on one side. The rhinoceros missed him and passed on in full speed, and before the brute could recover himself and change his course, the whole of us had climbed up into trees. The rhinoceros, limping with his wound, went round and round, trying to find us out by the scent, but he tried in vain. At last one of the men, who had only an assegai, said, 'Well, how long are we going to stay here? Why don't you shoot?'

"'Well,' said Henrick, 'if you are so anxious to shoot, you may if you please. Here is my powder-and-shot belt, and my gun lies under the tree. The man immediately descended from the tree, loaded the gun, and approaching the rhinoceros he fired and wounded it severely in the jaw. The animal was stunned, and dropped on the spot. Thinking that it was dead, we all descended fearlessly and collected round it; and the man who had fired was very proud, and was giving directions to the others, when of a sudden the animal began to recover, and kicked with his hind legs. Henrick told us all to run for our lives, and set us the example. The rhinoceros started up again, and singling out the unfortunate man who had got down and fired at it, roaring and snorting with rage, thundered after him.

"The man, perceiving that he could not outrun the beast, tried the same plan as the other hunter did when the rhinoceros charged him: stopping short, he jumped on one side, that the animal might pass him; but the brute was not to be balked a second time; he caught the man on his horn under the left thigh, and cutting it open as if it had been done with an axe, tossed him a dozen yards up in the air. The poor fellow fell facing the rhinoceros, with his legs spread; the beast rushed at him again, and ripped up his body from his stomach to almost his throat, and again tossed him in the air. Again he fell heavily to the ground. The rhinoceros watched his fall, and running up to him trod upon him and pounded him to a mummy. After this horrible tragedy, the beast limped off into a bush. Henrick then crept up to the bush; the animal dashed out again, and would certainly have killed another man if a dog had not turned it. In turning short round upon the dog, the bone of its foreleg, which had been half broken through by Henrick's first shot, snapped in two, and it fell, unable to recover itself, and was then shot dead."

"A very awkward customer, at all events," observed the Major. "I presume a leaden bullet would not enter?"

"No, it would flatten against most parts of his body. By-the-bye, I saw an instance of a rhinoceros having been destroyed by that cowardly brute the hyena."

"Indeed!"

"Yes, patience and perseverance on the hyena's part effected the work. The rhinoceros takes a long while to turn round, and the hyena attacked him behind, biting him with his powerful jaws above the joint of the hind leg, and continued so to do, till he had severed all the muscles, and the animal, forced from pain to lie down, was devoured as you may say alive from behind; the hyena still tearing at the same quarter, until he arrived at the vital parts. By the track which was marked by the blood of the rhinoceros, the hyena must have followed the animal for many miles, until the rhinoceros was in such pain that it could proceed no further.—But if you are to hunt to-morrow at daybreak, it is time to go to sleep; so good-night."

At daybreak the next morning, they took a hasty meal, and started again for the plain. Swinton, having to prepare his specimens, did not accompany them. There was a heavy fog on the plain when they arrived at it, and they waited for a short time, skirting the south side of it, with the view of drawing the animals towards the encampment. At last the fog vanished, and discovered the whole country, as before, covered with every variety of wild animals. But as their object was to obtain the eland antelope, they remained stationary for some time, seeking for those animals among the varieties which were scattered in all directions. At last Omrah, whose eyes were far keener than even the Hottentots', pointed out three at a distance, under a large acacia thorn. They immediately rode at a trot in that direction, and the various herds of quaggas, gnoos, and antelopes scoured away before them; and so numerous were they, and such was the clattering of hoofs, that you might have imagined that it was a heavy charge of cavalry. The objects of their pursuit remained quiet until they were within three hundred yards of them, and then they set off at a speed, notwithstanding their heavy and unwieldy appearance, which for a short time completely distanced the horses. But this speed could not be continued, and the Major and Alexander soon found themselves rapidly coming up. The poor animals exerted themselves in vain; their sleek coats first turned to a blue colour, and then white with foam and perspiration, and at last they were beaten to a standstill, and were brought down by the rifles of our travellers, who then dismounted their horses, and walked up to the quarry.

"What magnificent animals!" exclaimed Alexander.

"They are enormous, certainly," said the Major. "Look at the beautiful dying eye of that noble beast. Is it not speaking?"

"Yes, imploring for mercy, as it were, poor creature."

"Well, these three beasts, that they say are such good eating, weigh more than fifty antelopes."

"More than fifty springboks, I grant. Well, what shall we do now?"

"Let our horses get their wind again, and then we will see if we can fall in with some new game."

"I saw two or three antelopes of a very different sort from the sassabys and harte-beests towards that rising ground. We will go that way as soon as the Hottentots come up and take charge of our game."

"Does Swinton want to preserve one of these creatures?"

"I believe not, they are so very bulky. He says we shall find plenty as we go on, and that he will not encumber the waggons with a skin until we leave the Val River, and turn homeward. Now, Bremen and Omrah, come with us."

The Major and Alexander then turned their horses' heads, and rode slowly towards the hill which they had noticed, and the antelopes which the Major had observed were now seen among the bushes which crowned the hill. Bremen said that he did not know the animals, and the Major was most anxious to obtain one to surprise Swinton with. As soon as they came within two hundred yards of the bushes on the other side of which the antelopes were seen, the Major gave his horse to Omrah and advanced alone very cautiously, that he might bring one down with his rifle. He gained the bushes without alarming the animals, and the party left behind were anxiously watching his motions, expecting him every moment to fire, when the Major suddenly turned round and came back at a hurried pace.

"What is the matter?" said Alexander.

"Matter enough to stop my growth for all my life," replied the Major. "If ever my heart was in my mouth, it was just now. I was advancing softly, and step by step, towards the antelopes, and was just raising my rifle to fire, when I heard something flapping the ground three or four yards before me. I looked down, and it was the tail of a lioness, which fortunately was so busy watching the antelopes with her head the other way, that she did not perceive my being near her; whereupon I beat a retreat, as you have witnessed."

"Well, what shall we do now?"

"Wait a little till I have recovered my nerves," said the Major, "and then I'll be revenged upon her. Swinton is not here to preach prudence, and have a lion-hunt I will."

"With all my heart," replied Alexander. "Bremen, we are going to attack the lioness."

"Yes, sir," said Bremen; "then we had better follow Cape fashion. We will back the horses towards her, and Omrah will hold them while we will attack her. I think one only had better fire, so we keep two guns in reserve."

"You are right, Bremen," said Alexander. "Then you

and I will reserve our fire, and the Major shall try his rifle upon her."

With some difficulty the horses were backed towards the bush, until the Major could again distinguish where the lioness lay, at about sixty paces' distance. The animal appeared still occupied with the game in front of her, watching her opportunity to spring, for her tail and hind-quarters were towards them. The Major fired, and the animal bounded off with a loud roar; while the antelopes flew away like the wind. The roar of the lioness was answered by a deep growl from another part of the bush, and immediately afterwards a lion bolted out, and bounded from the bushes across the plain, to a small mimosa grove about a quarter of a mile off.

"What a splendid animal!" said Alexander; "look at his black mane, it almost sweeps the ground."

"We must have him," cried the Major, jumping on his horse.

Alexander, Bremen, and Omrah did the same, and they followed the lion, which stood at bay under the mimosas, measuring the strength of the party, and facing them in a most noble and imposing manner. It appeared, however, that he did not like their appearance, or was not satisfied with his own position, for as they advanced he retreated at a slow pace, and took up his position on the summit of a stony hill close by, the front of which was thickly dotted with low thorn-bushes. The thorn-bushes extended about 200 yards from where the lion stood disdainfully surveying the party as they approached towards him, and appearing, with a conscious pride in his own powers, to dare them to approach him.

They dismounted from their horses as soon as they arrived at the thorn-bushes, and the Major fired. The rifle-ball struck the rock close to the lion, who replied with an angry growl. The Major then took the gun from Omrah and fired, and again the ball struck close to the animal's feet. The lion now shook his mane, gave another angry roar; and by the glistening of his eyes, and the impatient switching of his tail, it was evident that he would soon become the attacking party.

"Load both your guns again," said Alexander, "and then let me have a shot, Major."

As soon as the Major's guns were loaded, Alexander took aim and fired. The shot broke the lion's foreleg, which he raised up with a voice of thunder, and made a spring from the rock towards where our party stood.

"Steady now," cried the Major to Bremen, at the same time handing his spare rifle to Alexander.

The rush of the angry animal was heard through the bushes advancing nearer and nearer; and they all stood prepared for the encounter. At last out the animal sprang, his mane bristling on end, his tail straight out, and his eye-balls flashing rage and vengeance. He came down upon the hind-quarters of one of the horses, which immediately started off, overthrowing and dragging Omrah to some distance. One of the lion's legs being broken, had occasioned the animal to roll off on the side of the horse, and he now remained on the ground ready for a second spring, when he received a shot through the back from Bremen, who stood behind him. The lion, with another dreadful roar, attempted to spring upon the Major, who was ready with his rifle to receive him; but the shot from Bremen had passed through his spine and paralysed his hind-quarters, and he made the attempt in vain, a second and a third time throwing his fore-quarters up in the air, and then falling down again, when a bullet from the Major passed through his brain. The noble beast sunk down, gnawing the ground and tearing it with the claws of the leg which had not been wounded, and then, in a few seconds, breathed his last.

"I am glad that is over, Alexander," said the Major; "it was almost too exciting to be pleasant."

"It was very awful for the time, I must acknowledge," replied Alexander. "What an enormous brute! I think I never saw such a magnificent skin.

"It is yours by the laws of war," said the Major.

"Nay," replied Alexander, "it was you that gave him his *coup de grace*."

"Yes, but if you had not broken his leg, he might have given some of us our *coup de grace*. No, no, the skin is yours. Now the horses are off, and we cannot send for the Hottentots. They have got rid of Omrah, who is coming back with his shirt torn into tatters."

"The men will catch the horses and bring them here, depend upon it, sir," said Bremen, "and then they can take off the skin."

"Well, if I am to have the lion's skin, I must have that of the lioness also, Major; so we must finish our day's hunting with forcing her to join her mate."

"Very good, with all my heart."

"Better wait till the men come with the horses, sir," said Bremen; "three guns are too few to attack a lion—very great danger indeed."

"Bremen is right, Alexander; we must not run such a risk again. Depend upon it, if the animal's leg had not been broken, we should not have had so easy a conquest. Let us sit down quietly till the men come up."

In about half-an-hour, as Bremen had conjectured, the Hottentots, perceiving the horses loose, and suspecting that something had happened, went in chase of them, and as soon as they had succeeded in catching them, brought them in the direction to which they had seen our travellers ride. They were not a little astonished at so small a party having ventured to attack a lion, and gladly prepared for the attack of the lioness. Three of the dogs having accompanied them, it was decided that they should be put into the bushes where the lioness was lying when the Major fired at her, so as to discover where she now was; and leaving the lion for the present, they all set off for the first jungle.

The dogs could not find the lioness in the bushes, and it was evident that she had retreated to some other place; and Swanevelt, who was an old lion-hunter, gave his opinion that she would be found in the direction near to where the lion was killed. They went therefore in that direction, and found that she was in the clump of mimosas to which the lion had first retreated. The previous arrangement of backing the horses towards where she lay was attempted, but the animals had been too much frightened in the morning by the lion's attack to be persuaded. They reared and plunged in such a manner as to be with difficulty prevented from breaking loose; it was therefore necessary to abandon that plan, and trust to themselves and their numbers. The clump of trees was surrounded by the party, and the dogs encouraged to go in, which they did, every now and then rushing back from the paws of the lioness. The Hottentots now fired into the clump at random, and their volleys were answered by the loud roars of the animal, which would not, however, show herself, and half-an-hour was passed away in this manner.

At last she was perceived at one side of the jungle by Swanevelt, who fired with effect, for the animal gave a loud roar, and then bounded out, not attempting to rush upon any person, but to make her escape from her assailants. A volley was fired at her, and one shot took effect, for she fell with her head to the ground, and tumbled right over; but immediately after she recovered herself, and made off for the bushes where she had been first discovered.

"She was hit hard that time, at all events," said the Major.

"Yes, sir," said Bremen, "that was her deathshot, I should think; but she is not dead yet, and may give us a great deal of trouble."

They followed her as fast as they could on foot, and the dogs were soon upon her again; the animal continued to roar, and always from the same spot; so that it was evident she was severely wounded. Alexander and the Major reserved their fire, and approached to where the dogs were baying, not twenty yards from the jungle. Another roar was given, and suddenly the body of the lioness rushed through the air, right in the direction where they stood; she passed, however, between them, and when she reached the ground, she fell on her side quite dead. It was her last expiring effort, and she died in the attempt. Alexander and the Major, who were both ready to fire, lowered their rifles when they perceived that she was dead.

"Well," said the Major, "I will say that when I first saw her tail, I was more frightened than I was just now, when she made the spring; I was so taken by surprise."

"I don't doubt it. She is a very large animal, and will make a handsome companion to the lion. If we live and do well, and get home to England again, I will have her stuffed along with him, and put them in the same case."

"I trust you will, and that I shall come and see them," replied the Major.

"I am sure I do, from my heart, my good fellow. I am very much pleased at our having killed both these beasts, without Swinton being with us, as he would have been persuading us to leave them alone."

"And he would have done very right," replied the Major. "We are two naughty boys, and shall be well scolded when we go back."

"Which I vote we do now. I think we have done quite enough for to-day."

"Yes, indeed," replied the Major, mounting his horse; "enough to talk of all our lives. Now let us gallop home, and say nothing about having killed the lions until the Hottentots bring them to the caravan."

CHAPTER XXV

Swinton's astonishment—A dialogue—Maternal affection—An alarm—Griquas fallen in with—The message to Moselekatsee —Fire!—The Matabili king—Expectations.

"WELL, what sport have you had?" was Swinton's first question when he was joined by Alexander and the Major. Replied the latter—"Pretty well; we saw an antelope quite new to us, which we. tried very hard to shoot, but were prevented by an unexpected meeting with a lioness." The Major then gave an account of his perceiving the tail of the lioness, and his rapid retreat.

"I am very glad to hear that you were so prudent, Major; it would have been a very rash thing to attack a lioness with only three guns. So the antelopes escaped?"

"Yes, but we have the elands, which you say are such good eating. Do we stay here any longer, or do we proceed up the river?"

"You must ask Wilmot to decide that point," said Swinton.

"It is just as you please," said Alexander; "but they say that the more you go to the northward, the more plentiful is the game."

238

"Yes, and we shall fall in with the giraffe," said the Major, "which is now the great object of my ambition. I have killed the rhinoceros and elephant, and now I must have the giraffe; they can kill the two first animals in India, but the other is only to be had in this country."

"And when you meet again your Indian friends, you wish to say that you have killed what they have not?"

"Certainly; what is the good of travelling so far, if one has not something to boast of when one returns? If I say I have hunted and killed the rhinoceros and elephant, they may reply to me, 'So have we;' but if I add the giraffe, that will silence them; don't you observe, Swinton, I then remain master of the field? But here come the Hottentots with our game; come, Swinton, leave your preparations for a little while, and see what our morning's sport has been."

Swinton put aside the skin of the sassaby that he was cleaning, and walked with them to where the men were assembled, and was not a little surprised when he saw the skins and jaws of the lion and lioness. He was still more so when the Major recounted how they had been shot.

"You certainly have run a great risk," said he, "and I am glad that you have been so successful. You are right in saying that I should have persuaded you not to attempt it; you are like two little boys who have taken advantage of the absence of their tutor to run into mischief. However, I am glad that it has been done, as I now hope your desire to kill a lion will not again lead you into unnecessary danger."

"No, indeed," replied Alexander; "having once accomplished the feat, and being fully aware of the great risk that is run, we shall be more prudent in future."

"That is all I ask of you," said Swinton, "for I should be unhappy if we did not all three return safe to the Cape. I never saw a finer lion's skin: I will arrange it for you, that it shall arrive at the Cape in good order."

As usual, the afternoon was by the Hottentots devoted to eating as much as they could possibly contrive to get down their throats; the flesh of the eland was pronounced excellent by our travellers, and there was much more than

they could possibly consume. The Hottentots were only
allowed to bring a certain quantity into the camp, that
they might not attract the wild beasts. They would have
brought it all in, although they never could have eaten it.
The cattle were driven up in the evening, the fires lighted,
and the night passed quietly away.

At daylight they turned the cattle out to graze for a
couple of hours, and then yoked and proceeded on their
journey, keeping as near as they could to the banks of the
river. They saw many hippopotami, snorting and rising
for a moment above the water, but they passed by them
without attempting to shoot at them, as they did not wish
to disturb the other game. As they advanced, the variety
of flowers which were in bloom attracted the notice of
Alexander, who observed—

"Does not this plain put you in mind of a Turkey carpet,
Major; so gay with every variety of colour?"

"Yes, and as scentless," replied the Major; "they are
all very brilliant in appearance; but one modest English
violet is, to my fancy, worth them all."

"I agree with you," replied Swinton; "but still you
must acknowledge that this country is beautiful beyond
description,—these grassy meads so spangled with numerous
flowers, and so broken by the masses of grove and forest!
Look at these aloes blooming in profusion, with their coral
tufts—in England what would they pay for such an exhibition?—and the crimson and lilac hues of these poppies and
amaryllis blended together: neither are you just in saying
that there is no scent in this gay parterre. The creepers
which twine up those stately trees are very sweetly scented;
and how picturesque are the twinings of those vines upon
the mimosas. I cannot well imagine the Garden of Eden
to have been more beautiful."

"And in another respect there is a resemblance," said
the Major, laughing; "the serpent is in it."

"Yes, I grant that," replied Swinton.

"Well, I can feel no real pleasure without security; if
I am to be ever on the alert, and turning my eyes in every
direction, that I may not tread upon a puff adder, or avoid
the dart of the cobra capella, I can feel little pleasure in
looking at the rich hues of those flowers which conceal them.

As I said before, give me the violet and the rose of England, which I can pick and smell in security."

"I agree with you, Major," said Alexander; "but," continued he, laughing, "we must make allowance for Swinton, as a naturalist. A puff adder has a charm for him, because it adds one more to the numerous specimens to be obtained; and he looks upon these flowers as a botanist, rejoicing as he adds to his herbal, or gathers seeds and bulbs to load his waggon with. You might as well find fault with a husbandman for rejoicing in a rich harvest."

"Or with himself for being so delighted at the number and the variety of the animals which fall to his rifle," replied Swinton, smiling. "There I have you, Major."

"I grant it," replied the Major; "but what is that in the river—the back of a hippopotamus?"

"No, it is the back of an elephant, I should rather think; but the reeds are so high, that it is difficult to ascertain. There may be a herd bathing in the river, nothing more likely."

"Let us stop the caravan; the creaking of these wheels would drive away anything," replied the Major; "we will then ride forward and see what it is. It is not more than half a mile from us."

"Be it so," replied Swinton. "Omrah, get the rifles, and tell Bremen to come here. Now, Major, is it to be a regular hunt, or only a passing shot at them; for I now perceive through my glass that they are elephants?"

"Well, I think a passing shot will be best; for if we are to hunt, we must send a party on the opposite side of the river, and that will be a tedious affair."

"I think myself it will be better to proceed," said Swinton; "so now, then, to scatter the enemy."

They soon arrived at that part of the river where they had at a distance discovered the elephants bathing; but as they approached, the high reeds prevented them from seeing the animals, although they could hear them plainly. At last, as they proceeded a little further up the river, they discovered a female with its young one by its side; the mother playing with its offspring, pouring water over it with its trunk, and now and then pressing it into the water, so as to compel it to swim. They watched the motions of the animals for some time, and the Major first broke silence by saying.

"I really have not the heart to fire at the poor creature ; its maternal kindness, and the playing of the little one, are too interesting. It would be cruel, now that we do not want meat, for an eland is to be killed every ten minutes."

"I am glad to hear you say so," replied Swinton. "Let us fire over them, and set them all in motion."

"Agreed," said the Major; "this is to start them," and he fired off his rifle in the air.

The noise that ensued was quite appalling ; the shrieks and cries of the elephants, and the treading down and rushing through the reeds, the splashing and floundering in the mud, for a few seconds, was followed by the bounding out of the whole herd on the opposite bank of the river, tossing their trunks, raising up their ears, roaring wildly, and starting through the bushes into the forest from which they had descended. Two large males only were to be perceived among the whole herd, the rest were all females and their young ones, who scrambled away after the males, crowding together, but still occasionally looking behind after their young ones, till they had all disappeared in the forest, the cracking and crushing of the bushes in which were heard for many minutes afterward.

"That was a splendid scene," said Alexander.

"Yes, it was a living panorama, which one must come to Africa to behold."

"I do not think that I shall ever become a true elephant-hunter," said the Major. "I feel a sort of repugnance to destroy so sagacious an animal, and a degree of remorse when one lies dead. At the same time, if once accustomed to the fearful crashing and noise attending their movements, I do not consider them very dangerous animals to pursue."

"Not if people are cool and collected. We have had several famous elephant-hunters among the Dutch farmers. I remember that one of them, after a return from a successful chase, made a bet that he would go up to a wild elephant and pluck eight hairs out of his tail. He did so, and won his bet, for the elephant cannot see behind him, and is not

very quick in turning round. However, a short time afterward he made the same attempt, and being foolhardy from
success, the animal was too quick for him, and he was crushed
to death."

Bremen now came up to them, to say that there was a
party of people to the eastward, and he thought that there
was a waggon. On examination with their telescopes they
found that such was the case; and our travellers turned
their horses' heads in the direction, to ascertain who they
might be, leaving the caravan to proceed by the banks of
the river. In about an hour they came close to them, and
Swinton immediately recognised them as Griquas, or mixed
European and Hottentot races. Of course they met in the
most friendly manner, and the Griquas said that they had
come to hunt the elephant, eland, and other animals; the
former for their ivory, and the latter for their flesh. Their
waggon, which was a very old one, was loaded with flesh,
cut in long strips, and hanging to dry; and they had a great
many hundred-weight of ivory, which they had already
collected. As soon as our travellers had explained to them
their own motions, the Griquas said that they would bring
their waggon down in the evening and encamp with them.
Our travellers then returned to the caravan.

As they promised, the Griquas joined them late in the
afternoon. They were a party of sixteen; all stout fellows,
and armed with the long guns used by the Dutch boors.
They said that they had been two months from Griqua-
town, and were thinking of returning very soon, as their
waggon was loaded to the extent that it would bear. The
Major stating that it was their intention to hunt the giraffe,
the Griquas informed them that they would not find the
animal to the southward of the Val River, and they would
have to cross over into the territories of the king Moselekatsee, who ruled over the Bechuana country, to the northward of the river; and that it would be very dangerous to
attempt so to do without his permission; indeed, that there
would be danger in doing so, even with it.

"Do you know anything of this person, Swinton?"

"Yes, I have heard of him, but I did not know that he
had extended his conquests so low down as to the Val
River."

"Who is he?"

"You have heard of Chaka, the king of the Zulus, who conquered the whole country, as far as Port Natal to the eastward?"

"Yes," replied Alexander, "we have heard of him."

"Well, Moselekatsee was a chief of two or three tribes, who, when hard pressed by his enemies, took refuge with Chaka, and became one of his principal warrior chiefs. After a time he quarrelled with Chaka, about the distribution of some cattle they had taken, and aware that he had no mercy to expect from the tyrant, he revolted from him with a large force, and withdrew to the Bechuana country. There he conquered all the tribes, enrolled them in his own army, and gradually became as formidable as Chaka himself. In the arrangements of his army he followed the same plans as Chaka, and has now become a most powerful monarch, and, they do say, is almost as great a tyrant and despot as Chaka himself was. I believe that the Griquas are right in saying there would be danger in passing through his dominions without his permission."

"But," said Alexander, "I suppose if we send a message to him and presents, there will be no difficulty?"

"Perhaps not, except that our caravan may excite his cupidity, and he may be induced to delay us to obtain possession of its contents. However, we had better put this question to the Griquas, who probably can answer it better."

The Griquas, on being questioned, replied that the best plan would be to send a message to the Matabili capital, where Moselekatsee resided, requesting permission to hunt in the country, and begging the monarch to send some of his principal men to receive the presents which they had to offer;—that it would not take long to receive an answer, as it would only be necessary to deliver the message to the first officer belonging to Moselekatsee, at the advanced post. That officer would immediately despatch a native with the message, who would arrive much sooner than any one they could send themselves. Bremen and three other Hottentots offered to take the message, if our travellers wished it. This was agreed to, and that afternoon they mounted their horses, and crossed the river. By the advice of the Griquas the camp was shifted about a mile further up the river, on account of the lions.

The weather now threatened a change; masses of clouds accumulated, but were again dispersed. The next day the weather was again threatening; thunder pealed in the distant mountains, and the forked lightning flew in every direction; but the rain, if any, was expended on the neighbouring hills.

A strong wind soon blew up so as to try the strength of the canvas awning of their waggons, and they found it difficult to keep their fires in at night. They had encamped upon a wide plain covered with high grass, and abounding with elands and other varieties of antelopes: here they remained for five days, waiting the reply of the king of the Matabili, and went out every day to procure game. On the Sabbath-day, after they had, as usual, performed divine service, they observed a heavy smoke to windward, which, as the wind was fresh, soon bore down upon them and inconvenienced them much.

Swanevelt stated that the high grass had been fired by some means or another, and as it threatened to come down upon the encampment, the Hottentots and Griquas were very busy beating down the grass round about them. When they had so done, they went to windward some hundred yards and set fire to the grass in several places; the grass burned quickly, till it arrived at where it had been beaten down, and the fire was extinguished. That this was a necessary precaution was fully proved, for as the night closed in, the whole country for miles was on fire, and the wind bore the flames down rapidly toward them.

The sky was covered with clouds, and the darkness of the night made the flames appear still more vivid; the wind drove them along with a loud crackling noise, sweeping over the undulating ground, now rising and now disappearing in the hollows, the whole landscape lighted up for miles.

As our travellers watched the progress of the flames, and every now and then observed a terrified antelope spring from its lair, and appearing like a black figure in a phantasmagoria, suddenly the storm burst upon them, and the rain poured down in torrents, accompanied with large hailstones and thunder and lightning. The wind was instantly lulled, and after the first burst of the storm a deathlike silence succeeded to the crackling of the flames. A deluge of rain descended, and in an instant every spark of the conflagration was extinguished, and the pitchy darkness of the night was unbroken by even a solitary star.

The next morning was bright and clear, and after breakfast, they perceived the Hottentots who had been sent on their message to Moselekatsee on the opposite bank of the river, accompanied by three of the natives; they soon crossed the river and came to the encampment. The natives, who were Matabili, were tall, powerful men, well proportioned, and with regular features; their hair was shorn, and surmounted with an oval ring attached to the scalp, and the lobe of their left ears was perforated with such a large hole, that it contained a small gourd, which was used as a snuff-box. Their dress was a girdle of strips of cat-skins, and they each carried two javelins and a knobbed stick for throwing.

They were heartily welcomed by our travellers, who placed before them a large quantity of eland-steaks, and filled their boxes with snuff. As soon as they had finished eating, and drawn up a large quantity of snuff into their nostrils, they explained through the Griquas, who could speak their language, that they had come from the greatest of all monarchs in the world, Moselekatsee, who wished to know who the strangers were, what they wanted of him, and what presents they had brought.

Swinton, who was spokesman, returned for answer that they were hunters, and not traders; that they had come to see the wonders of the country belonging to so great a monarch, and that hearing that his Majesty had animals in his country which were not to be found elsewhere, they wanted permission to kill some, to show upon their return to their own people what a wonderful country it was that belonged to so great a monarch; that they had brought beads and copper wire, and knives, and boxes for making fire, and snuff and tobacco, all of which they wished to present to the great monarch; a part as soon as they had received his permission to enter his territory, and another part when they were about to leave it. A handsome present of the above articles was then produced, and the messengers of the king, having surveyed the articles with some astonishment, declared that their king would feel very glad when he saw all these things, and that he had desired them to tell our travellers that they might come into his dominions with safety, and kill all the animals that they pleased. That his Majesty had commanded one of them to remain with the party, and that as soon as he had received his presents, he would send a chief to be answerable for their safety. The Matabili then packed up the articles presented, and two of them set off at full speed on their return to the king. The third, who remained, assured our travellers that they might cross the river and enter the Matabili country as soon as they pleased.

A debate now ensued as to whether they should go with their whole force or not. The Matabili had informed them that in three days' journey they would fall in with the giraffe, which they were in search of, and as there would be some risk in crossing the river, and they had every reason to expect that it would soon rise, the question was whether it would be prudent to take over even one of the waggons. The opinion of the Griquas was asked, and it was ultimately arranged that they should take over Alexander's waggon only, with fifteen pair of oxen, and that some of the Griquas should accompany them, with Swanevelt, Omrah, and Mahomed;—that Bremen and the Hottentots should remain where they were, with the other three waggons and the rest of the Griquas, until our travellers should return.

This arrangement was not at all disagreeable to the Hottentots, who did not much like the idea of entering the Matabili country, and were very happy in their present quarters, as they were plentifully provided with good meat. Alexander's waggon was therefore arranged so as to carry the bedding and articles they might require, all other things being removed to the other waggons. Their best oxen were selected, and eight of the fleetest of their horses, and on the following morning, having ascertained from the Matabili the best place to cross the river, our travellers set off, and in an hour were on the other side.

There was no change in the country during the first

247

day's journey; the same variety and brilliancy of flowers were everywhere to be seen. The eland and the other antelopes were plentiful, and they were soon joined by parties of the natives, who requested them to shoot the animals for them, which they did in quantities even sufficient to satisfy them. Indeed, if they found them troublesome, our travellers had only to bring down an eland, and the natives were immediately left behind, that they might devour the animal, which was done in an incredibly short space of time. The Matabili who had conducted them proved to be a chief, and if he gave any order it was instantly obeyed; so that our travellers had no trouble with the natives except their begging and praying for snuff, which was incessant, both from the men and women. Neither did they fear any treachery from the Matabili king, as they were well armed, and the Griquas were brave men, and the superiority of their weapons made them a match for a large force. Every precaution, however, was taken when they halted at night, which they invariably did in the centre of an open plain, to prevent any surprise; and large fires were lighted round the waggon.

They travelled on in this way for two days more, when in the evening they arrived at a large plain sprinkled with mimosa trees, and abutting on the foot of a low range of hills. The Matabili told them that they would find the giraffes on these plains, and the Major, who was very anxious, kept his telescope to his eyes, looking round in every direction till nightfall, but did not succeed in descrying any of the objects of his search. They retired that night with anxious expectation for the following morning, when they anticipated that they should fall in with these remarkable animals. Their guns were examined and every precaution taken, and having lighted their fires and set the watch, they went to bed; and, after commending themselves to the care of Providence, were soon fast asleep.

CHAPTER XXVI

Chase of a giraffe—Proposed retreat—The Major's object attained —Treachery—Treachery defeated—Omrah's scheme—Hopes of water disappointed.

WITH the exception of three lions coming very near to the encampment and rousing up the Griquas, nothing occurred during the night. In the morning they yoked the oxen and had all the horses saddled ready for the chase; but they were disappointed for nearly the whole day; as, although they saw a variety of game, no giraffe appeared in sight. In the afternoon, as they passed by a clump of mimosas, they were charged by a rhinoceros, which nearly threw down Alexander's best horse; but a volley from the Griquas laid him prostrate. It was a very large animal, but not of the black or ferocious sort, being what is termed the white rhinoceros. Within the last two days they had also observed that the gnoo was not of the same sort as the one which they had seen so long, but a variety which Swinton told them was called the brindled gnoo; it was, however, in every other respect the same animal, as to its motions and peculiarities. Toward the evening the Matabili warrior who accompanied them pointed to a mimosa at a distance, and made signs to the Major that there was a giraffe.

"I cannot see him—do you, Alexander?" said the Major; "he points to that mimosa with the dead stump on the other side of it, there. Yes, it is one, I see the stump, as I called it, move; it must be the neck of the animal. Let loose the dogs, Swanevelt," cried the Major, starting off at full speed, and followed by Alexander, and Omrah, with the spare horse. In a minute or two the giraffe was seen to get clear of the mimosa, and then set off in an awkward, shambling kind of gallop; but awkward as the gallop appeared, the animal soon left the Major behind. It sailed along with incredible velocity, its long, swan-like neck keeping time with its legs, and its black tail curled above its back.

"Push on, Alexander," cried the Major; "if ever there were seven-league boots, that animal has a pair of them on. He goes like the wind; but he cannot keep it up long, depend upon it, and our horses are in capital condition."

Alexander and the Major were now neck and neck, close to each other, at full speed, when of a sudden the Major's horse stumbled, and fell upon an ostrich, which was sitting on her nest; Alexander's horse also stumbled and followed after the Major; and there they were, horses and riders, all rolling together among the ostrich-eggs; while the ostrich gained her legs, and ran off as fast as the giraffe.

As soon as they had got on their legs again, and caught the bridles of their horses, they looked round, but could not distinguish the giraffe, which was out of sight among the mimosa trees; while Omrah was very busy picking up their rifles, and laughing in a very disrespectful manner. The Major and Alexander soon joined in the laugh. No bones were broken, and the horses had received no injury. All they had to do was to return to the caravan looking very foolish.

"Your first essay in giraffe-hunting has been very successful," said Swinton, laughing, as they came up to him.

"Yes, we both threw very pretty summersets, did we not?" said Alexander. "However, we have got some ostrich-eggs for supper, and that is better than nothing. It will soon be dark, so we had better encamp for the night, had we not?"

"I was about to propose it," said Swinton.

"Did you ever hunt the giraffe, Swinton?" inquired Alexander, as they were making their supper on roasted ostrich-eggs; each of them holding one between his knees, and dipping out with a large spoon.

"Never," replied Swinton; "I have often seen them in Namaqualand, but never killed one. I remember, however, a circumstance connected with the giraffe, which would have been incredible to me, if I had not seen the remains of the lion. You are well aware how long and strong are the thorns of the mimosa (or kamel tree, as the Dutch call it, from the giraffe browsing upon it), and how the boughs of these trees lie like an umbrella, close upon one another. A

250

native chief informed me that he witnessed a lion attacking a giraffe. The lion always springs at the head or neck, and seizes the animal by that part, riding him, as it were. The giraffe sets off at full speed with its enemy, and is so powerful as often to get rid of him; for I have seen giraffes killed which had the marks of the lion's teeth and claws upon them. In this instance the lion made a spring, but the giraffe at that very moment turning sharp round, the lion missed his aim, and by the blow it received was tossed in the air, so that he fell upon the boughs of the mimosa on his back. The boughs were not only compact enough to bear his weight, but the thorns that pierced through his body were so strong as to hold the enormous animal where he lay. He could not disengage himself; and they pointed out to me the skeleton on the boughs of the tree, as a corroboration of the truth of the story."

"It does really approach to the marvellous," observed the Major; "but, as you say, seeing is believing. I trust that we shall be more fortunate to-morrow."

"I have gained a piece of information from Swanevelt," said Swinton, "which makes me very anxious that we should leave this as soon as possible; which is, that the Matabili king had no idea that we had Griquas in our company, and still less that we were to come into his country with only the Griquas as attendants. You are not perhaps aware that Moselekatsee is the deadly enemy of the Griquas, with whom he has had several severe conflicts, and that we are not very safe on that account?"

"Why did not the Griquas say so?" replied Alexander.

"Because they do not care for the Matabili, and I presume are glad to come into the country, that they may know something of it, in case of their making an attack upon it. Depend upon it, as soon as the king hears of it, we shall be looked upon as spies, and he may send a party to cut us off."

"Have you said anything to the Griquas?"

"Yes, and they laughed, and said that they should not care if we went right up to the principal town, where Moselekatsee resides."

"Well, they are bold enough, and so far are good travelling companions; but we certainly did not come here to fight,"

251

observed the Major. "But does the Matabili with us know that they are Griquas?"

"He did not; he supposed that they were Cape people whom we had brought with us; but he has found it out by the Hottentots, I suppose. Swanevelt says that the very first body of Matabili that we fell in with, he sent a runner off immediately, I presume to give the information. I think, therefore, that the sooner we can get away the better."

"Well, I agree with you, Swinton," replied Alexander. "We will try for the giraffe to-morrow, and when the Major has had the satisfaction of killing one, we will re-trace our steps, for should we be attacked it will be impossible to defend ourselves long against numbers. So now to bed."

They rose early the next morning, and, leaving the waggon where it was, again proceeded on horseback in search of giraffes. They rode at a slow pace for four or five miles, before they could discover any. At last a herd of them were seen standing together browsing on the leaves of the mimosa. They made a long circuit to turn them, and drive them toward the camp, and in this they succeeded. The animals set off at their usual rapid pace, but did not keep it up long, as there were several not full grown among them, which could not get over the ground so fast as the large male of the preceding day. After a chase of three miles they found that the animals' speed was rapidly decreasing, and they were coming up with them. When within a hundred yards Alexander fired and wounded a female which was in the rear. The Major pushed on with the dogs after a large male, and it stopped at bay under a mimosa, kicking most furiously at the dogs. The Major levelled his rifle, and brought the animal down with his first shot. It rose again, however, and for a hundred yards went away at a fast pace; but it again fell, to rise no more. The female which Alexander had wounded received another shot, and was then also prostrated."

"I have killed a *giraffe*," said the Major, standing by the side of the one he had killed. "It has been a long way to travel, and there have been some dangers to encounter for the sake of performing this feat; but we have all our follies, and are eager in pursuit of just as great trifles through life; so that in this I am not perhaps more foolish than the rest of mankind. I have obtained my wishes—I have killed a giraffe; and now I don't care how soon we go back again."

"Nor do I," replied Alexander; "for I can say with you, when we arrive in England, I too have killed a giraffe; so you will not be able to boast over me. By Swinton's account, if we stay here much longer, we shall have to kill Matabili, which I am not anxious to do; therefore, I now say with you, I don't care how soon we go back to the Cape."

As they were not more than two miles from the waggon, they rode back, and sent the Griquas to bring in the flesh of the animals; Swinton not caring for the skins, as he had already procured some in Namaqualand, and the weight of them would be so very great for the waggon. On their return they had some conversation with the Griquas, who candidly acknowledged that it was very likely that the Matabili king would attempt to cut them off, although they appeared not at all afraid of his making the attempt. They, however, readily consented to return the next morning. That night a messenger arrived to the Matabili chief who was escorting them. What was the communication of course our travellers could not tell; but their suspicions were confirmed by the behaviour of the man. When he found that, on the following morning, they yoked the oxen and retraced their steps, he begged them not to go, but to advance into the interior of the country, where they would find plenty of game; told them that the king would be very angry if they left so soon; and if he did not see them his heart would be very sad. But our travellers had made up their mind, and travelled back during the whole of that day. The Matabili despatched the messenger who had come to him, and who again set off at all speed; at night he urged our travellers not to go back, saying that the king would be very angry with him. But as the Griquas were now equally convinced that treachery was intended, they paid no attention to the Matabili chief, and continued their route, shooting elands by the way for their sustenance. Late in the evening of the third day they found themselves on the borders of the Val River. It was still two hours before dark, and as the Matabili pressed them to encamp where they were, they were satisfied that they had better not, and therefore they forded the river, and rejoined the caravan, under charge of Bremen, just as night closed in.

The Griquas said, that from the Matabili wishing them to remain on the other side of the river, they were persuaded that a force would arrive during that night or the following morning, and that it would be necessary to be on the look-out; although probably the enemy would not venture to attack them without further orders, now that they were no longer in Moselekatsee's dominions. Every preparation was therefore made : the Griquas and Hottentots were all supplied with ammunition, and mustered with their guns in their hands. The waggons were arranged, the fires lighted, and four men were posted as sentinels round the encampment. What added still more to their suspicions was, that, about an hour after dark, the Matabili chief was not to be found.

"My opinion is," said the Major, "that we ought to steal a march upon them. Our oxen are in excellent condition and may travel till to-morrow evening without feeling it. Let us yoke and be off at once, now that it is dark. The moon will rise about two o'clock in the morning, but before that the waggons will be twelve or fifteen miles off. Alexander and I, with Bremen, will remain here with our horses and wait till the moon rises, to see if we can discover anything : and we can easily join the waggons by daybreak. We will keep the fires up, to allow them to suppose that we are still encamped, that they may not pursue."

"And also to keep off the lions," observed Alexander, "which are not enemies to be despised."

"I think it is a very good plan; but why not have more men with you? We have plenty of horses, and so have the Griquas."

"Well then, let us talk to the Griquas."

The Griquas approved of the plan; and, having their own horses, six of them agreed to remain with Alexander and the Major, and Swanevelt and two more of the Hottentots were also mounted to remain; which made a force of twelve men, well mounted and well armed. The remainder of the caravan yoked the oxen to the waggons, and, under the direction of Swinton, set off in a southerly direction, across the desert, instead of going by the banks of the Val River, as before.

This had been arranged previously to any expected attack from the Matabili, as it would considerably shorten the distance on returning, although they knew that they would find much difficulty in procuring water for a few days. After the caravan had departed, it was found that Omrah had helped himself to a horse and a gun, and had remained in the camp; but as he was always useful, his so doing was passed over without notice. In half-an-hour the waggons were out of sight, and the noise of their wheels was no longer to be heard.

They fastened their horses in the centre of the fires, and sat down by them till the moon rose, when they directed their eyes to the opposite bank of the river; but for some time nothing was discovered to confirm their suspicions. When the moon was about an hour high, they perceived a body of men coming down toward the banks, and the moon shone upon their shields, which were white. As soon as they arrived at the bank of the river they all sat down, without making any noise. Shortly afterward another body, with dark-coloured shields, made their appearance, who came down and joined the first.

"We were not wrong in our suspicions, at all events," said the Major; "I should say that there are not less than a thousand men in these two parties which have already appeared. Now, what shall we do? Shall we remain here, or shall we be off, and join the waggons?"

"I really can hardly decide which would be the best," replied Alexander; "let us have a consultation with Bremen and the Griquas."

"If we were to go away now," said Bremen, "the fires would soon be out, and they might suspect something, and come over to reconnoitre. When they found that we were gone, they would perhaps follow us, and overtake the waggons; but if we remain here, and keep the fires up till daybreak, the waggons will have gained so much more distance."

The Griquas were of the same opinion; and it was decided that they would remain there till daybreak, and then set off.

"But," said Alexander, "shall we leave this before they can see us, or allow them to see us?"

The Griquas said that it would be better that the enemy should see them, as then they would know that the fires had been kept up to deceive them, and that the waggons were probably a long way off.

This having been agreed upon, a careful watch was kept upon the enemy during the remainder of the night. Although the moon had discovered the approach of the Matabili to the party, the spot where the camp had been pitched was in the shade, so that from the opposite side of the river only the fires could be distinguished. A little before dawn, some one was heard approaching, and they were all prepared to fire, when they discovered that it was Omrah, who, unknown to them, had crawled down to the banks of the river to reconnoitre the enemy.

Omrah, who was out of breath with running, stated that some of the Matabili were crossing the river, and that six had landed on this side, before he came up to give the information. He pointed to a clump of trees about three hundred yards off, and said that they had gone up in that direction, and were probably there by that time.

"Then we had better saddle and mount," said the Major, "and ride away gently to the wood on this side of the camp. We shall then be able to watch their motions without being seen."

This advice was good, and approved by all. They led out their horses without noise, and as soon as they had done so, they went back, and threw more fuel on the fires. They then retreated to the wood, which was about the same distance from the camp, on the other side, as the clump of trees where the Matabili were secreted.

They had hardly concealed themselves before the Matabili in the clump, surprised at not seeing the awnings of the waggons, and suspecting that they had been deceived, came out from their ambuscade; first crawling on all-fours, and as they arrived at the camp, and found only fires burning, rising up one after another. After remaining about a minute in

256

consultation, two of the party were sent back to the river to communicate this intelligence to the main body, while the others searched about in every direction. Alexander, with the Major and their party, remained where they were, as it was their intention to cross through the wood, until they came to the open ground, about a quarter of a mile to the southward, and then show themselves to the enemy, before they went to join the waggons.

In a few minutes it was daylight, and they now perceived that the whole body of the Matabili were crossing the river.

"They intend to pursue us, then," said Alexander.

Omrah now pointed to the side of the river, in the direction which the waggons had travelled when they came up by its banks, saying, "When go away—ride that way first—same track waggon go that way back—same way waggon come."

"The boy is right," said the Major; "when we start from the wood, we will keep by the riverside, in the track by which the waggons came; and when we are concealed from them by the hills or trees, we will then start off to the southward after the waggons."

"I see," replied Alexander; "they will probably take the marks of the waggon-wheels coming here, for those of the waggons going away, and will follow them; presuming, as we go that way, that our waggons have gone also. But here they come up the banks; it is time for us to be off."

"Quite time," said the Major; "so now let us show ourselves, and then trust to our heels."

The Matabili force was now within four hundred yards of the camp. It was broad daylight; and, with their white and red shields and short spears in their hands, they presented a very formidable appearance.

There was no time to be lost, so the party rode out of the end of the wood nearest the river, and as soon as they made their appearance, were received by a yell from the warriors, who dashed forward in the direction where they stood. The Major had directed that no one should fire, as he and Alexander did not wish that any blood should be shed unnecessarily. They therefore waved their hands, and turning

257   R

their horses' heads galloped off by the banks of the river, keeping in the tracks made by the waggons when they came up.

As soon as they galloped a quarter of a mile they pulled up, and turned their horses' heads to reconnoitre. They perceived that the Matabili force was pursuing them at the utmost speed; but as they had no horsemen, that speed was of course insufficient to overtake the well-mounted party in advance. As soon as they were near, our party again galloped off and left them behind. Thus they continued for four or five miles, the Matabili force pursuing them, or rather following the tracks of the waggons, when they observed a belt of trees before them about a mile off; this the Major considered as a good screen to enable them to alter their course without being perceived by the enemy. They there-fore galloped forward, and as soon as they were hidden by the trees, turned off in a direction by which they made certain to fall in with the track which the waggons had made on their departure during the night.

They had ridden about two miles, still concealed in the wood, when they had the satisfaction of perceiving the Matabili force still following at a rapid pace the tracks of the waggons on the riverside. Having watched them for half-an-hour, as they now considered that all was safe, they again continued their course, so as to fall in with the waggons.

" I think we are clear of them now," said the Major; "they have evidently fallen into the trap proposed by that clever little fellow Omrah."

" He is a very intelligent boy," observed Alexander, "and, travelling in this country, worth his weight in gold."

" I wish Swinton would make him over to me," said the Major; " but, Alexander, do you observe what a change there is already in the country?"

" I do indeed," replied Alexander; "and all ahead of us it appears to be still more sterile and bare."

" Yes, when you leave the rivers, you leave vegetation of all kinds almost. There is no regular rainy season at all here, Swinton says; we may expect occasional torrents of rain during three months, but they are now very uncertain; the mountains attract the greater portion of the rain, and

258

sometimes there will not be a shower on the plains for the whole year."

"How far shall we have to travel before we fall in with water again?" inquired Alexander.

"Swinton says there may be water in a river about sixty miles from where we started last night; if not, we shall have to proceed about thirty miles further, to the Gykoup or Vet River. After that we shall have to depend for many days upon the water we may find in the holes, which, as the season is now coming on, may probably be filled by the rain."

Alexander and his party rode for seven or eight miles before they fell in with the tracks of the caravan; they then pulled up their jaded horses, and proceeded at a more leisurely pace, so that it was not till late in the evening that they discovered the waggons at some distance, having passed the dry bed of Salt River ahead of them. During the whole day their horses had had neither food nor water, and the animals were much exhausted when they came up with the waggons. The oxen also were fatigued with so long a journey, having made nearly fifty miles since they started the evening before.

The country was now stony and sterile; a little vegetation was to be found here and there, but not sufficient to meet the wants of the animals, and water there was none. During the day but little game had been seen—a few zebras and ostriches only; all other varieties had disappeared. There was of course no wood to light the fires round the encampment: a sufficiency for cooking their victuals had been thrown into the waggons, and two sheep were killed to supply a supper for so numerous a party. But the absence of game also denoted the absence of lions, and they were not disturbed during the night. In the morning the Griquas parted company with them, on the plea that their oxen and horses were in too poor a condition to pass over the desert, and that they must make a direct course for the Val River and return by its banks.

Our travellers gave them a good supply of ammunition, the only thing that they wished for, and the Griquas, yoking their oxen to the crazy old waggon, set off in a westerly direction.

The route of the caravan was now directed more to

the south-west, and they passed over an uninterrupted plain strewed with small land-tortoises, and covered with a profusion of the gayest flowers. About noon, after a sultry journey of nine hours, they fortunately arrived at a bog, in which they found a pool of most fetid water, which nothing but necessity could have compelled either them or the exhausted animals to drink. Near this pool in the desert they found several wild animals, and they obtained three gnoos for a supply of provision; the little wood that they had in the waggon for fuel was all used up in cooking their supper.

A heavy dew fell during the night, and in the morning, before the sun rose, they were enveloped in a thick fog. As the fog dispersed, they perceived herds of quaggas in all directions, but at a great distance. They again yoked the oxen and proceeded on their journey; the country was now covered with herbage and flowers of every hue, and looked like a garden.

"How strange that the ground should be covered with flowers where there is no rain or water to be found," observed Alexander.

"It is the heavy dews of the night which support them," said Swinton, "and perhaps the occasional rains which fall."

A line of trees to the southward told them that they were now approaching an unnamed river, and the tired oxen quickened their pace; but on their arrival they found that the bed of the river was dry, and not even a drop of water was to be found in the pools. The poor animals, which had been unyoked, snuffed and smelt at the wet, damp earth, and licked it with their tongues, but could obtain no relief. The water which they had had in the casks for their own drinking was now all gone; and there were no hopes of obtaining any till they arrived at the Vet River, at least twenty-five to thirty miles distant. Two of the oxen lay down to rise no more, the countenances of the Hottentots were dejected and sullen, and our travellers felt that their situation was alarming.

While they were still searching and digging for water, the sky became overcast, thunder and lightning were seen and heard in the distance, and the clouds came rolling in volumes toward them. Hope was now in every face; they already anticipated the copious showers which were to succeed; their eyes ever fixed upon the coming storm; even the cattle appeared to be conscious that relief was at hand. All the day the clouds continued to gather, and the lightning to gleam. Night closed in, but the rain had not yet fallen; the wind rose up, and in less than an hour all the clouds had passed away, the stars shone out brightly, and they were left in a state of suffering and disappointment.

CHAPTER XXVII

Further progress—The horses and oxen break away—The pursuit—Hopes and fears—The caravan lost—Intense heat—Omrah's courage—A temporary relief—Despair—Water at last obtained—Swinton's signals answered.

As our travellers were sitting together, each occupied with his own melancholy thoughts, after the dispersion of the clouds and the anticipated relief, the Major said—

"It is useless our remaining here; we must all perish if we do not proceed, and it would be better for us to yoke and travel by night; the animals will bear the journey better, and the people will not be so inclined to brood over their misfortunes when on the march as when thus huddled together here, and communicating their lamentations to dishearten each other. It is now nine o'clock; let us yoke and push on as far as we can."

"I agree with you, Major," said Alexander; "what do you say, Swinton?"

"I am convinced that it will be the best plan, so let us rouse up the people at once. There is the roar of a lion at some distance, and we have no fires to scare them off."

"The creaking of the waggon-wheels will be better than nothing," replied the Major.

The Hottentots were roused, and the orders given to yoke: the poor fellows were all sound asleep; for a Hottentot, when he hungers or thirsts, seeks refuge from all his miseries in sleep. The oxen were yoked, and they proceeded; but hardly had they gone a mile, when the roar of three or four lions, close upon them, caused such alarm to the horses and the oxen which were not yoked, that they started off in full gallop in a northerly direction.

Alexander, the Major, and Omrah, who were the best mounted, immediately set off in pursuit of them, desiring Swinton to proceed with the caravan, and they would drive on the cattle and join him. They galloped off as well as the horses could gallop, and perceived the stray horses and oxen still at full speed, as if they were chased by the lions. They followed in the direction, but it was now so dark that they were guided only by the clatter of their hoofs and their shoes in the distance; and after a chase of four or five miles they had lost all vestiges of them, and pulled up their panting steeds.

"We may as well go back again," said Alexander; "the animals must have made a circuit."

"I suppose so," said the Major; "but my horse trembles so, that I had better dismount for a little while, that he may recover himself; indeed, so had you too and Omrah, for the animals are completely worn out."

"The clouds are rising again," said Alexander; "I trust that we may not be disappointed a second time."

"Yes, and there is lightning again in the horizon—may the Almighty help us in our distress," exclaimed the Major.

The horses, exhausted from want of water, continued to pant so fearfully, that it was nearly half-an-hour before they ventured to mount, that they might return to the caravan. In the meantime the heavens had become wholly obscured by the clouds, and there was every prospect of a heavy shower; at last a few drops did fall.

"Thank God!" exclaimed Alexander, as he lifted his face up to the heavens to feel the drops as they fell. "Now let us return."

They mounted their horses and set off, but the stars were no longer visible to guide them, and they proceeded on at a slow pace, uncertain whether they were right or wrong. This they cared little about; their thoughts were upon the coming rain, which they so anxiously awaited. For more than three hours they were tantalised by the lightning flashing and the thunder pealing, every moment expecting the flood-gate of the heavens to be opened; but, as before, they were doomed to disappointment. Before the morning dawned the clouds had again retreated; and when the sky was clear, they found by the stars that their horses' heads were turned to the northward and eastward.

They altered their course in silence, for they were worn out and despondent; they suffered dreadfully from thirst, and it was pitiable to see the tongues of the poor horses hanging out of their mouths. Day dawned, and there were no signs of the caravan. A thick vapour was rising from every quarter, and they hoped that when it cleared up they would be more fortunate; but no, there was the same monotonous landscape, the same carpet of flowers without perfume. The sun was now three hours high, and the heat was intense; their tongues clove to the roofs of their mouths, while still they went on over flowery meads; but neither forest nor pool, nor any trees which might denote the bed of the river, caught their earnest gaze.

"This is dreadful," said Alexander at last, speaking with difficulty.

"We are lost, that is certain," said the Major; "but we must trust in God."

"Yes, we may now say, Lord help us, or we perish," replied Alexander.

At this moment little Omrah, who had been behind, rode up to them, and offered them one of the Hottentots' pipes, which he had lighted, saying, "Smoke,—not feel so bad." Alexander took it, and after a few whiffs found that it had the effect of producing a little saliva, and he handed it to the Major, who did the same, and felt immediate relief.

They continued to walk their horses in a southerly direction; but the heat was now so great, that it became almost insufferable, and at last the horses stood still. They dismounted and drove their horses slowly before them over the glowing plain; and now the mirage deluded and tanta-lised them in the strangest manner. At one time Alexander pointed with delight (for he could not speak) to what he imagined to be the waggons; they pushed on, and found that it was a solitary quagga, magnified thus by the mirage.

Sometimes they thought that they saw lakes of water in the distance, and hastened on to them; and then they fancied they were close to rivers and islands, covered with luxuriant foliage, but still were doomed to disappointment; as all was the result of the highly-rarefied air, and the refraction of the sun's rays on the sultry plain. What would they have given for a bush even to afford them any shelter from the noonday sun, for the crowns of their heads appeared as if covered with live coal, and their minds began to wander. The poor horses moved at the slowest pace, and only when driven on by Omrah, who appeared to suffer much less than his masters. Every now and then he handed to them the pipe, but at last even that had no longer any relief. Speech had been for some hours totally lost. Gradually the sun sunk down to the horizon, and as his scorching rays became less intense they to a certain degree recovered their wandering senses.

At night they sat down by the side of the horses, and, worn out with fatigue and exhaustion, fell into a troubled sleep; a sleep which, if it relieved their worn-out frames, condemned them to the same tantalising feelings as had been created by the mirage during the day. They dreamed that they were in the bowers of paradise, hearing heavenly music; passing from crystal stream to stream, slaking their thirst at each, and reclining on couches of verdant green. Everything that was delightful appeared to them in their dreams; they were in the abodes of bliss; and thus did they remain for an hour or two, when they were wakened up by the roar of a lion, which reminded them that they were without food or water in the desert.

They awoke speechless with thirst, their eyes inflamed, and their whole bodies burning like a coal, and the awful roar of the lion still reverberated along the ground. They started on their legs, and found Omrah close to them, holding the bridles of the horses, which were attempting to escape. They were still confused, when they were fully restored to their waking senses by a second roar of the lion still nearer to them; and by the imperfect light of the stars they could now distinguish the beast at about one hundred yards' distance. Omrah put the bridles of their two horses in their hands, and motioned them to go on in the

direction opposite to where the lion was. They did so
without reflection, mechanically obeying the directions of
the man-child, and not perceiving that Omrah did not
follow them. They had advanced about one hundred yards
with the terrified animals, when another loud roar was
followed up by the shriek of the other horse, announcing
that he had become a victim to the savage animal. They
both started, and dropping the reins of their horses, hastened
with their rifles to the help of Omrah, cf whose absence
they now for the first time were aware; but they were
met half-way by the boy, who contrived to say with difficulty, " Lion want horse, not little Bushman." They waited
a few seconds, but the cries of the poor animal, and the
crushing and cracking of its bones, were too painful to hear;
and they hastened on and rejoined the other horses,
which appeared paralysed with fear, and had remained
stationary.

They again led their horses on for an hour, when they
arrived at a small pile of rocks; there they again lay down,
for they were quite exhausted and careless of life. Not
even the roar of a lion would have aroused them now, or
if it had roused them they would have waited for the
animal to come and put an end to their misery. But another
and a softer noise attracted the quick ear of Omrah, and he
pushed Alexander, and put his finger up to induce him to
listen.

Having listened a little longer, Omrah made signs to
Alexander and the Major to follow him. The noise which
Omrah had heard was the croaking of a frog, which denoted
water at hand, and the sniffing of the horses confirmed him
in his supposition. Omrah led the way through the rocks,
descending lower and lower; and ever and anon listening
to the noise of the animal, till he perceived the stars of
heaven above reflected in a small pool, which he pointed
out to Alexander and the Major. Down they dropped to
earth and drank, and as soon as their thirst was satisfied
they rose, and pushed Omrah forward to make him drink
also; and as the boy who had saved their lives was drinking,
they kneeled down and prayed—not loud, for they had
not yet recovered their speech; but if ever grateful prayers
were offered up to the Almighty throne, they were by our

two travellers, as they kneeled by the side of this small pool. They rose and hastened to their horses, and led them down to the water, when the poor animals filled themselves almost to bursting, walked away, and returned to drink more. They also repeated their draught several times, and then lay down, and would have fallen asleep by the side of the pool had not Omrah, who could now speak freely, said, "No, no; lion come here for water; up the rock again and sleep there—I bring horses." This good advice was followed, and when they had gained the summit of the rising ground they again lay down and slept till daylight.

When they awoke they found themselves much refreshed, but they now felt—what they had not done during their extreme suffering from thirst—the craving pangs of hunger. Omrah was fast asleep, and the horses picking among the herbage about two hundred yards off.

"We have much to thank God for," said Alexander to the Major.

"We have indeed, and next to Divine aid, we have to thank that poor boy. We have been as children in his hands, and we are indebted to him and his resources for our lives this night. I could not speak yesterday, nor could you; but his courage in remaining with the horse as an offering to the lion I shall not forget."

"He is a child of the desert," replied Alexander; "he has been brought up among lions, and where there is scarcity of water, and he has most wonderfully guided us in our path; but we are still in the desert, and have lost our companions. What must we do? Shall we attempt to regain the caravan, or push off to the westward, to fall in with the river again?"

"We will talk of this an hour hence," replied the Major; "let us now go down to the pool, and as soon as I have had a drink I will try if I cannot kill something for a meal. My hunger is now almost as great as was my thirst."

"And mine too, so I will go with you; but we must be careful how we approach the water, as we may fall in with some animal to make a meal of."

"Or with a lion, ready to make a meal of us," replied

266

the Major; "so in either instance we must approach it cautiously."

As they walked to the pool, they discovered the head of an antelope just above a rock. The Major fired, and the animal fell. The report of the rifle was answered by a roar; three lions bounded away from the rock, and went at a quick canter over the plain.

"Both our suppositions have proved correct," observed Alexander, as they walked up to where the antelope lay dead; "but how are we to cook the animal?"

"Any dry stuff will serve for a fire, if we can only get enough, and a very little cooking will serve us just now. Here comes Omrah. Let us carry the game up to where we slept last night, as soon as we have had a drink."

They went to the pool, and were surprised to behold the filthy puddle which had appeared to them so like nectar the night before. They were not sufficiently thirsty to overcome their disgust, and they turned away from it.

Omrah now began collecting dried grass, and herbs, and lichen from the rocks, and had soon a sufficiency to make a small fire; they struck a light, and cutting off steaks from the antelope, were in a short time very busy at the repast. When their hunger was appeased, they found that their thirst was renewed, and they went down to the pool, and shutting their eyes drank plentifully. Omrah cooked as much of the meat as the small fire would permit, that they might not want for the next twenty-four hours; and the horses being again led to the water to drink, they mounted, and proceeded to the southward, followed by Omrah on foot. Another day was passed in searching for the caravan without success. No water was to be found. The heat was dreadful; and at night they threw themselves down on the ground, careless of life; and had it not been sinful they would have prayed for death. The next morning they arose in a state of dreadful suffering; they could not speak, but they made signs, and resolved once more to attempt to join the caravan.

They proceeded during the whole of the forenoon in the direction by which they hoped to discover the tracks of the waggons. The heat was overpowering, and they felt all the agony of the day before. At last the horses could proceed no farther; they both lay down, and our travellers had little hopes of their ever rising again. The scorching of the sun's rays was so dreadful, that they thrust their heads into some empty ant-hills to keep off the heat, and there they lay in as forlorn and hopeless a state as the horses. Speak they could not; their parched tongues rattled like boards against the roofs of their mouths; their lips were swollen and bloated, and their eyes inflamed and starting from the sockets. As Alexander afterwards said to Swinton, he then recollected the thoughts which had risen in his mind on his departure from the English shore, and the surmise whether he might not leave his bones bleaching in the desert; and Alexander now believed that such was to be the case, and he prayed mentally and prepared for death. The Major was fully possessed of the same idea; but as they lay at some yards' distance, with their heads buried in the ant-hills, they could not communicate with each other even by signs. At last they fell into a state of stupor and lost all recollection. But an Almighty Providence watched over them, and during their state of insensibility the clouds again rose and covered the firmament, and this time they did not rise in mockery; for before the day was closed, torrents descended from them and deluged the whole plain.

Omrah, who had held up better than his masters, crawled out of the ant-hill into which he had crept; and as soon as the rain descended, he contrived to pull the heads of the Major and Alexander, who still remained senseless, from out of the ant-hills, and to turn their blackened and swollen faces to the sky. As their clothes became saturated with the rain, and the water poured into their mouths, they gradually revived, and at last were completely restored. The wind now rose and blew fresh, and before morning they were shivering with cold, and when they attempted to get up found their limbs were cramped.

Soon after daylight the rain ceased, and they were glad to bask in the then cheering rays of the sun, which had nearly destroyed them on the day before. The horses had recovered their legs and were feeding close to them; and the flesh of the antelope, which had been untasted, was now greedily devoured. Most devoutly did they return thanks for their preservation, and the hopes which were now held out to them of ultimately regaining the colony; for they had abandoned all hopes of reaching the caravan, as they considered the risk of crossing the desert too great. They made up their minds to push for the Val River as fast as they could, and proceed back by its banks.

They had two horses, and Omrah could ride behind one of them, when he was tired; they had guns and ammunition, and although they were fully aware of the dangers to which they would be exposed, they thought lightly of them after what they had suffered. They now mounted their horses, and proceeded at a slow pace toward the westward, for the poor animals were still very weak. At sunset they had travelled about ten miles, and looked out for a spot to pass the night. Wood to light fires they had none, but they hoped, if their horses were not taken away by the lions, to reach a branch of the river by the following evening. There was now no want of water, as they repeatedly passed by small pools, which, for a day or two at least, would not be evaporated by the heat of the sun. But they knew that by that time, if no more rain fell, they would have again to undergo the former terrible privations, and therefore resolved upon continuing their course towards the river as their safest plan, now that they had lost the caravan.

As they were seated on a rising ground which they had chosen for their night's rest, and occasionally firing off their rifles to drive away the lions which were heard prowling about; all of a sudden Omrah cried out, and pointed to the northward; our travellers turned and perceived a rocket ascending the firmament, and at last breaking out into a group of brilliant stars.

"It is the caravan," exclaimed the Major; "Swinton has remembered that I put some rockets into my waggon.'

"We must have passed it," said Alexander, springing on his feet. "God be praised for all His mercies."

"Amen," replied the Major devoutly.

Omrah ran after the horses, which were feeding close to them, for their instinctive fear of the lions made them keep as close as possible to their masters. They were soon mounted, with Omrah behind the Major, and set off at all the speed that they could obtain from the animals. After an interval another rocket was seen, and by its light they discovered that they were not a mile from the waggons. The horses appeared to be sensible of this, and went off at a quicker pace; and in a few minutes they had rushed in among the cattle, and Alexander and the Major were received into the arms of Swinton, and surrounded by the Hottentots, who were loud in their congratulations at their return.

As soon as Alexander and the Major had made known their perils and sufferings to Swinton, the latter informed them that about three hours after they had left the caravan in pursuit of the cattle, the animals had returned, and that of course he had fully expected them to follow. Finding that they did not arrive, he had decided upon remaining where he was, at all events, for another day; but that the cattle were by that time so exhausted, that it was with difficulty they were moved, and he could not proceed with them more than ten miles, when they lay down in their yokes. Thirteen had died, and the others must have shared their fate, if it had not been for the providential rain, which had restored them.

Swinton stated that he had been in a great state of alarm for them, and that he had almost satisfied himself that they had perished, although he had used every means that he could think of. When he fired the rockets off, he had scarcely a hope of thus bringing them back to the caravan.

"However," observed Swinton, "it shows that we should never despair, and never leave a chance untried, even in the most desperate circumstances. You are back again, and I thank the Almighty for it with all my heart and all my soul and all my strength, most fervently and most sincerely. I have been very, very miserable, I can assure you, my dear fellows. The idea of returning to the Cape without you was dreadful. Indeed, I never would have left the country until I had found you, or had some clue to your deaths."

"Our preservation has indeed been miraculous," replied the Major; "I never thought to have raised my head out of the ant-hill again."

"Nor I," replied Alexander; "and next to the Almighty, we certainly owe our lives to little Omrah. There is nothing that I would not do for that boy, if you will only give him over to my care."

"Or mine, Swinton," replied the Major.

"Depend upon it," replied Swinton, "I will do all for him that ought to be done; I owe him a debt of gratitude for preserving my friends, and will not forget to repay it."

"Well, then, you must allow us to help him as well," replied the Major. "How far are we now from the Modder River?"

"About forty miles, I should think, and we had better push on as fast as we can; for although the river will contain water, the pools in the desert between us and the river will soon be dried up. The cattle, however, are still very weak, and, as I have stated, we have lost all our relays. But you must long to have a good night's rest, so go to your waggons, and we will watch and keep off the wild beasts. We have been obliged to fire our guns all night long since your absence, and have burned one of the spare poles of the waggons to cook our victuals."

Everything is comparative. When our travellers first took up their night's lodgings in the waggons they found their resting-places hard, after sleeping in comfortable beds at Cape Town; but now, after having passed their nights in the wild desert, their mattresses in the waggons were a luxury that was fully appreciated. Returning thanks to Heaven for their preservation, Alexander and the Major slept soundly till morning, notwithstanding that the latter was often half roused by the importunities of Begum, who appeared delighted at the return of her master.

At daylight the oxen were yoked, and they proceeded on their journey. There was no want of game; indeed, they were so plentiful that they shot them from the caravan as they passed. At night they had made twenty-five miles, and before they had unyoked, a deluge of rain again fell, and they passed a very uncomfortable night, as it was very cold, and they could light no fires, from want of fuel. Anything, however, was better than the want of water; and early in the morning they again yoked their oxen, and, after a hard day's toil, were rejoiced to perceive at a distance the trees which lined the banks of the Modder River. The sight was hailed with joy by the Hottentots, who shouted aloud; for they considered their dangers and difficulties to be over, now that they were approaching to the boundaries of the colony.

CHAPTER XXVIII

*Panic produced by a lion—Omrah's and Big Adam's predica-
ment—A lion's mode of stimulating his appetite—A meeting
with Bushmen — Cattle stolen—Recovery attempted — Oxen
poisoned—Death of Piets—Arrival at Cape Town.*

As the cattle required some repose, after the sufferings
they had gone through, our travellers resolved to remain a
few days on the banks of the Modder River. The pasturage
was fine and the game abundant. Gnoos and springboks
were to be seen in every direction, and quaggas, bonteboks,
and several other varieties of antelopes were in profusion
over the now undulating country. Neither were our
travellers sorry to have some repose for themselves, although
every mile that they drew nearer to the Cape made them
more anxious to return.

As usual, the caravan was halted on a rising ground, at
some distance from the river, to avoid the wild beasts, which
during the day were concealed, and during the night
prowled on its banks, to spring upon the animals which
came down for water. As there was now plenty of wood,
the fires were again lighted at night, and the oxen driven
in and tied up. During the day the animals revelled on the
luxurious pasture, and in a week had become quite sleek and
in good condition.

Every day our travellers went out to hunt for a supply
of provisions, and never returned without more than was
sufficient. Swinton was anxious to possess one or two more
specimens of the oryx, or gemsbok. This antelope, we
have before observed, from having very straight horns,
which at a distance appear as one, has given rise to the
fabulous animal the unicorn, which is now one of the
supporters of the royal arms. It is a very formidable
animal; being the one that our travellers found with its
horns pierced through the lion which had attacked it. The
horses being now fresh and in good heart, Alexander and
the Major went in pursuit of this animal very often, but
without success, as the chase was continually interrupted

by the herds of ostriches and other game which fell in their way.

One morning, having discovered with the telescope that three of these gemsbok were some miles distant on a rising ground, they set off, accompanied by a portion of the Hottentots on foot, who were desired to go round, so as to drive the animals toward the camp. Bremen and Big Adam were of the party, and they had made a circuit of three or four miles, so as to get on the other side of the game, which now darted down from the high ground, and, descending on the plain, stopped for a while looking at their pursuers, while the horsemen advanced toward them in the opposite direction. A shot from Alexander at last brought one of these splendid animals to the ground, while the others fled off to a distance, so as to give no hopes of again coming up with them; and the party on foot, as well as the horsemen, now proceeded to the spot where the gemsbok lay dead.

As Swinton wanted the animal for a specimen, it was placed on the back of the horse which Omrah rode as usual, and one of the Hottentots went off with it to the camp, which was not more than three miles distant. They were debating whether they should make an attempt to get near to the other gemsbok, which were still in sight at a distance, or try for some other game, when they perceived three lions not far from them on a rising ground; and suddenly the horses, from which they had dismounted to give them time to recover their wind, broke loose from the Hottentots who held the bridles, and galloped away toward the camp. The cause of the panic was now evident, for a very large male lion had detached himself from the other two, and was advancing slowly toward the party.

As soon as they perceived the approach of the lion, which they had not at first, they all seized their guns; but being wholly unprepared for such a sudden attack, there was a great deal of confusion; the Major crying out, "Let no one fire till I tell him," only produced more alarm among the Hottentots, all of whom, except Bremen, appeared to be at their wits' ends. When within fifty yards the lion made one or two bounds, and in a moment was among them all, before they could bring their guns to their shoulders: the retreat was general in every direction, and not a shot was fired.

All, however, did not escape; Big Adam had started back, and coming with all his force against Omrah, who was standing behind him, had fallen over the boy, and they were both flat on their backs, when the lion made his spring. The lion was standing up, looking proudly at his flying enemies, when Big Adam, who was close to him, attempted to rise and gain his feet; but perceiving this, the animal, with a blow of its fore-paw, laid him prostrate again, set its foot upon his breast, and in this attitude again looked proudly round him, as if confident of his superiority.

Omrah, who had sense enough to lie still, had yet his eyes sufficiently opened to see what was going on; and as the lion appeared to be looking at the scattered party, in a direction away from him, Omrah made one or two turns over, so as to get further off, hoping that he might escape unperceived. The lion, however, heard the rustling, and turning round growled at him, and Omrah remained still again. As Big Adam's feet were turned toward Omrah, the lion now took up his position, deliberately lying down at full length upon Big Adam's body, with his hind-quarters upon the Hottentot's face, so that he not only secured his prisoner, but watched Omrah, who lay about three yards from him.

In the meantime the anxiety of the other party may be imagined; they considered that Big Adam and Omrah must be sacrificed. It was proposed to fire with good aim, so as, if possible, to bring the animal's attention and indignation upon themselves; but Swinton cried out not to fire on any account. "The animal is not hungry or even angry," said Swinton. "If let alone, he will probably walk away without doing them injury. At all events, our firing will be the signal for their destruction."

The advice of Swinton was considered good, especially as it was backed by that of Bremen, who also said that the lion was not hungry, and that, by the way in which he moved his tail, he was evidently more inclined to play than anything else.

But in the meantime the pressure of the lion, whose weight was enormous, was not only more than Big Adam could bear, but the hind-quarters of the animal being over his face prevented him from breathing; and at last he was

compelled to struggle to get his head clear. The consequence of his struggling was a severe bite on the leg inflicted on poor Adam; not, however, in a furious manner;
for the lion merely caught at him as a cat would at a mouse,
to prevent its escape, or because it was not quite dead.
However, Big Adam had so far disengaged his head that
he could now breathe; and as the party kept crying out
to him to lie still, he continued so to do, although nearly
suffocated with the enormous weight of the animal.

Omrah, who had remained still during all this time, perceiving that the lion was licking the blood which flowed
from the wound in Big Adam's leg, thought that he might
as well try another roll over, and being on his back, he
turned over on his face away from the lion. Thereupon
the lion rose from off Big Adam, walked up to Omrah, and,
to the horror of our travellers, took up the boy by his
waistcloth, and, carrying him like a small bundle in his
mouth, went back to Big Adam, and laying Omrah close
down to the Hottentot's head, again took up his position
on his body; now, however, with his paws upon the Hottentot's breast, so that he might keep Omrah in view before
him. Little Omrah had sense enough not to move during
the time that the lion carried him, or after he was laid
down.

The change in the position of the lion occasioned our
travellers and the party to walk round, so as to be able to
watch the countenance of the animal, as everything depended upon the temper he might be in. The Major and
Alexander became very impatient, and were for advancing to
the attack, but Swinton persuaded them not to do so until
the last moment.

The lion now put its fore-paw upon the Hottentot's
mouth, and again stopped his breath; this occasioned another struggle on the part of Big Adam, which was followed
by the animal seizing him by the arm and biting him
severely; but in so doing the lion removed its paw, and
the man could breathe again. The taste of blood appeared
pleasant to the lion, for it continued biting the arm, descending from the shoulder to the hand, and as the blood flowed
from the wounds on its paws the lion licked it off. Again
and again it licked its paw clean, and then, with its glaring

eyes fixed intently upon the Hottentot's face, it smelt him first on one side and then on the other, and appeared only to be waiting for a return of appetite to commence a deliberate meal upon the poor fellow's body.

·In the meantime our travellers were standing about seventy yards distant, waiting for the signal to attack, when Bremen observed to Swinton—

" He won't wait much longer, sir; the blood has given him an appetite. We must now drive him away, or they will both be killed."

"I think so too," replied Swinton; "let us first try if we can disturb him without making him angry; that will be the best way. We must go back out of springing distance, and then all shout together, and keep hallooing at him."

This advice was followed; they retreated a hundred yards, and then all shouted at once, and after that the Hottentots hallooed and bawled to the lion. This had the effect intended: the lion rose from the bodies and advanced toward the party, who stood still hallooing at him, but not attempting to irritate him by presenting their guns. The lion looked steadfastly at them for some time, and then turned away. After retreating a few steps, it turned back to face them; the whole party continued on the same spot, neither advancing so as to irritate him, nor retreating so as to let the animal suppose that they were afraid of him. When the lion had continued for a few minutes this course of retreating and advancing, he turned right round, and went away at a hand canter, and our travellers immediately hastened to the spot where Big Adam and Omrah were still lying.

Omrah, who was not at all hurt, instantly jumped on his legs, and, if he had been afraid, appeared to have quite recovered his courage, as he cut all manner of capers and laughed immoderately; but Big Adam was greatly exhausted and could not move, as much from the immense pressure of the lion's enormous body, as from the blood that he had lost by the wounds which he had received. On examination, the bite in his leg was found to be much the most serious, as the bone was injured; the wounds on his arm were all flesh-wounds, and although very painful, were not dangerous.

He was at present unable to speak, and was carried by his comrades to the camp. Our travellers followed the Hottentots, as they all had enough of hunting for that day. As soon as they arrived, Big Adam's wounds were dressed by Swinton, and the poor fellow was accommodated with a bed made up for him in the baggage-waggon. They remained two days more on the banks of the Modder River, and then they forded it and continued their journey.

On the second day they perceived some small human figures on the summit of a hill at some distance, which the Hottentots declared to be Bushmen, of which people there were numerous hordes in this part of the country. An attempt was made to open a communication with them, but in vain, as when any of the party advanced on horseback toward them, the Bushmen made a precipitate retreat. As they were now in the neighbourhood of these plunderers, every care was taken of the cattle, which were tied up before dark to prevent their being stolen.

On the following day they very unexpectedly fell in with a party of nine of the Bushmen, who were very busy devouring a quagga which they had killed. They replied to questions put to them with much fear and trembling, and, having been presented with some tobacco, they made a precipitate retreat. On that night the fires of the Bushmen were to be seen on several of the surrounding hills. They continued their course on the following day, when they fell in with about twenty women of the race we have just mentioned, who approached the caravan without fear, requesting tobacco and food; the former was given to them in small quantities, and a shot from the Major's rifle soon procured them the latter. They were now without water again, and had no chance of procuring any, except from the pools, until they arrived at the Nu Gariep, or Black River, which they had crossed when they came out from the Caffre Land.

Having travelled till dark, they halted under a hill, and were soon afterward joined by a party of Bushwomen, who continued with them in spite of all their attempts to get rid of them. They were very small in person, well made, and the young were rather pretty in their features, but their ornaments were enough to disgust any one but a Hottentot; for they were smeared with grease and red ochre, and were adorned ·with the entrails of animals as necklaces. The Hottentots, however, appeared to think this very delightful, and were pleased with their company, and as the women showed them a pool of water, where the oxen could drink, it was not considered advisable to drive them away. But Swinton observed that it would be necessary to keep a very sharp lookout, as the women were invariably sent by the Bushmen as spies, that they might watch the opportunity for stealing cattle.

They now resumed their former plan; starting at a very early hour, and travelling till afternoon, when the cattle were allowed several hours to feed, and were then tied up for the night to the waggons. Indeed the lions were now not so numerous as they had been, and they had more to fear from the Bushmen and the hyenas, which were very plentiful.

The next day fully proved the truth of this, for the oxen, having been unyoked as usual to feed, about two o'clock in the afternoon, had been led to a hollow of luxuriant pasture by the cattle-keepers, where they could not be seen from the caravan, although they were not half a mile off. Toward dusk, when it was time to drive them in and tie them up to the waggons, it was found that the cattle-keepers, who had been in company with the Bushwomen, had neglected their charge, and they were not to be found.

The keepers came running in, stating that a lion had scared the cattle, and that the animals had galloped off to a great distance. But Omrah, who had gone to where the cattle had been feeding, returned to the camp and told Swinton that it was not lions but Bushmen who had stolen them; and, bringing the horses ready saddled to the Major and Alexander, said, that if they did not follow them immediately, the cattle would be all killed. It was also observed that the Bushwomen had all disappeared.

Swinton, who was well aware of the customs of the Bushmen, immediately proposed that they should mount as many as they could, and go in chase, as there was not an hour to be lost. In half-an-hour a party, consisting of our three travellers, Bremen, Omrah, and three of the most trusty of the Hottentots, who were all that they could mount, set off in the direction which they knew must have been taken, so

278

as to conceal the cattle from the sight of those in the caravan ; and it being a fine moonlight night the keen eyes of Omrah tracked them for more than five miles, where they were at fault, as the traces of their hoofs were no longer to be seen.

" What shall we do now ? " said the Major.

" We must trust to Omrah," replied Swinton, " he knows the habits of his people well, and they will not deceive him."

Omrah, who had been very busy kneeling on the ground, and striking a light every now and then with a flint and steel, to ascertain the track more distinctly, now came up and made them comprehend that the Bushmen had turned back upon the very track they had gone upon, and that they must return and find where they diverged from it again.

This created considerable delay, as they had to walk the horses back for more than a mile, when they again found the footing of the cattle diverging from the track to the south-ward and eastward, in the direction of some hills.

They now made all the haste that they could, and pro-ceeded so rapidly on the track, that in about an hour they perceived the whole herd of oxen driven up the side of a hill by a party of Bushmen. They put spurs to their horses and galloped as fast as they could in pursuit, and soon came up with them ; when a discharge of rifles left three Bushmen on the ground and put all the rest to flight. The cattle, which were much frightened, were with some difficulty turned and driven back toward the encampment. In the meantime the disappointed Bushmen had turned upon those near, and were letting fly their arrows from the bushes where they were concealed and continued thus to assail them until the party arrived at the open plain. One of the Hottentots was wounded by an arrow in the neck ; but that was the only accident which occurred to any of the party, and this was not known to our travellers until after their arrival at the en-campment, when it was almost daybreak ; and then, tired with the fatigues of the night, all were glad to obtain a few hours' rest.

When they rose the next morning, Swanevelt informed them that nine of the oxen were so wounded with the poisoned arrows of the Bushmen, that they could not live ; and also, that Piets the Hottentot had been badly wounded in the neck with one of the arrows. Swinton immediately ordered the man to be brought to him, as he was well aware of the fatal effects of a wound from a Bushman's arrow.

It appeared that Piets had pulled the arrow out of his neck, but that some pieces of the barb had remained in the wound, and that these his companions had been extracting with their knives, and the wound was very much inflamed in consequence. Swinton immediately cut out as much of the affected part as he could, applied ammonia to the wound, and gave him laudanum to mitigate the pain, which was very acute; but the poor fellow lay groaning during the whole of the day.

They now examined the wounded oxen, which were already so swollen with the poison that there were no hopes of saving them, and they were immediately put out of their pain. Several others were found slightly hurt, but not so as to lose all hopes of their recovery; but this unfortunate circumstance prevented them from continuing their journey for two days; as the whole of the oxen had been much harassed and cut by the Bushmen, although not wounded by poisoned arrows. During this delay the poor Hottentot became hourly worse; his head and throat were much swollen, and he said that he felt the poison working within him.

After many hours of suffering, during which swellings appeared in various parts of his body, the poor fellow breathed his last; and the next day being Sunday, they remained as usual, and the body of the unfortunate man was consigned to a grave. This event threw a cloud over the whole caravan, and whenever any of the Bushwomen made their appearance at a distance and made signs that they wished to come into the camp, an angry bullet was sent instantly over their heads, which made them take to their heels.

On the Monday morning they again started with their reduced trains, for now they had barely sufficient cattle to drag the waggons. Fortunately they were but a few miles from the Nu Gariep, and they arrived at its banks before evening. The next day they crossed it with difficulty, putting all the oxen to two of the waggons and then returning for the others.

They were now once more in the colony, and their dangers and difficulties were now to be considered over. It was

not, however, till a week afterward that they succeeded
in crossing the Sweenberg and arriving at Graff Reynet.
At this beautiful spot they remained for a few days, to
make arrangements and to procure horses, that they might
proceed to Cape Town as fast as possible, leaving Bremen
in charge of the waggons, which he was to bring down to
them as soon as he could. We shall pass over the remainder
of their journey on horseback, as there was nothing remarkable to be related. Suffice it to say, that on the 11th of
January 1830, they arrived safe and sound at Cape Town,
and were warmly congratulated by Mr. Fairburn and their
many friends, after all the dangers and difficulties which
they had encountered.

CHAPTER XXIX

*Parting scenes—Alexander and the Major embark—Alexander's
arrival at home—He relates his adventures—Sir Charles's
health gradually declines—His presents to Swinton and the
Major—His death—Conclusion.*

ALEXANDER WILMOT again took possession of the
apartments in Mr. Fairburn's house, and was not sorry once
more to find himself surrounded by all the comforts and
luxuries of civilisation. He could scarcely believe where
he was when he woke up the first morning, and found that
he had slept the whole night without being disturbed by
the roar of a lion or the cries of the hyena and jackal:
and after the habit to which he had been so long accustomed,
of eating his meals in the open air with his plate on his
knees, he could hardly reconcile himself for a few days
to a well laid-out table. The evenings were passed in
narrating their adventures to Mr. Fairburn, who was truly
glad of the result of the mission to Port Natal, as it would
be so satisfactory to old Sir Charles.

Alexander was now most anxious to return to England,
and resolved to take his passage in the first ship which
sailed after the arrival of the waggon with his effects. In
the meantime his mornings were chiefly passed with Swinton

and the Major, the latter of whom intended to go to England by the same vessel as Alexander. In three weeks· after their return to the Cape the four waggons arrived, and excited much curiosity, as they were filled with every variety of the animal kingdom which was indigenous to the country. Swinton's treasures were soon unloaded and conveyed to his house, and our naturalist was as happy as an enthusiastic person could be in the occupation that they gave him. Alexander only selected a few things, among which were the skins of the lion and lioness. As for the Major he had had all his pleasure in the destruction of the animals.

Bremen reported that all the Hottentots had behaved very well, and that Big Adam had nearly recovered, and was able to limp about a little, although it would be a long while before he would regain the perfect use of his leg. Alexander now sent for them all, and paid them their wages, with an extra sum as a gratuity for their good conduct. To Bremen and Swanevelt, who had invariably conducted themselves faithfully, and who had been the leading and most trustworthy men, he gave to each a waggon and span of ten oxen as a present by which they might in future obtain their livelihood, and the poor fellows considered themselves as rich as the king of England. The other waggons and cattle of every description were left with Swinton to be disposed of.

The Major pressed Swinton very hard to part with little Omrah, but Swinton would not consent. The Major therefore presented Omrah with one of his best rifles, and accoutrements to correspond, as a mark of his attachment; and Alexander desired that all the money which was realised by the sale of the remaining waggons and other articles, as well as the cattle and horses, should be put by for Omrah's benefit. As a keepsake, Alexander gave the lad his telescope, with which he knew that Omrah would be highly pleased.

We may here as well observe, that, a few months after Alexander and the Major left the Cape, Omrah, who had been placed at a school by Swinton, was admitted into the church, and baptized by the name of Alexander Henderson Omrah; Alexander and the Major being his sponsors by proxies. He turned out a very clever scholar and remains with Swinton at this moment. He has more than once accompanied him into the interior, and has done much in reclaiming his countrymen, the bushmen, from their savage way of life, and has been of great service to the missionaries as interpreter of the Word to his heathen brethren.

About a fortnight after the return of the waggons to Cape Town a free trader cast anchor in Table Bay to take in water, and Alexander and the Major secured a passage in her to England. Alexander parted with great regret from Mr. Fairburn and Swinton, with whom he promised to correspond, and they sailed with a fair wind for St. Helena, where they remained for a few days, and took that opportunity of visiting the tomb of Napoleon, the former Emperor of the French. A seven week's passage brought them into the Channel, and they once more beheld the white cliffs of England.

Alexander's impatience to see his uncle, from whom he had found a letter waiting for him on his return to the Cape, stating that he was in tolerable health, induced him to leave the ship in a pilot-boat and land at Falmouth. Taking leave for a time of the Major, who preferred going on to Portsmouth, Alexander travelled with all possible speed, and on the second day arrived at his uncle's.

"Is my uncle quite well!" said Alexander, as he leaped out of the chaise, to the old butler who was at the door.

"No, sir, not quite well: he has been in bed for this last week, but there is nothing serious the matter, I believe."

Alexander hastened upstairs and was once more in the arms of Sir Charles Wilmot, who embraced him warmly, and then, exhausted with the emotion, sank back on his pillow.

"Leave me for a little while, my dear boy, till I recover myself a little," said Sir Charles. "I have no complaint, but I am very weak and feeble. I will send for you very soon."

Alexander, who was himself much affected, was not sorry to withdraw for a while, and sent the housekeeper, who attended his aged relative, into the room. In about an hour a message arrived requesting that he would return to his uncle.

"And now, my dear, kind boy, tell me everything. I am indeed overjoyed to see you back again; I have not had one line from you since you left the Cape, and I really think that the worry and anxiety that I have felt have been the cause of my taking to my bed. Now you are back I shall be quite well again. Now, tell me all, and I will not interrupt you."

Alexander sat down on the bed, and entered into a full detail of the results of his expedition to Port Natal; reading over all the memoranda which they had collected, and satisfactorily proving that the descendants of the Europeans then existing could not by any possibility be from those who had been lost in the *Grosvenor* East Indiaman.

Sir Charles Wilmot listened in silence to all Alexander had to say, and then, joining his hands above the bed-clothes, exclaimed, "Gracious Lord, I thank Thee that this weight has been removed from my mind." He then for some minutes prayed in silence, and when he had finished, he requested Alexander to leave him till the evening.

The physician having called shortly after Alexander left his uncle, Alexander requested his opinion as to Sir Charles's state of health. The former replied—

"He has but one complaint, my dear sir, which all the remedies in the world are not very likely to remove: it is the natural decay of nature, arising from old age. I do not consider that he is in any immediate danger of dissolution. I think it very likely that he may never rise from his bed again; but, at the same time, he may remain bedridden for months. He sinks very gradually, for he has had naturally a very strong constitution. I believe the anxiety of his mind, arising from your absence, and the blame he laid on himself for having allowed you to undertake your expedition, have worn him more than anything else; but now that you have returned, I have no doubt, after the first excitement is over that he will rally. Still man is born to die, Mr. Wilmot, and your uncle has already lived beyond the three-score years and ten allotted to the average age of man. Depend upon it, every-

"They once more beheld the white cliffs of England."

thing shall be done which can protract a life so dear to you."

Alexander thanked the physician, and the latter then went upstairs to Sir Charles. On his return he informed Alexander that Sir Charles's pulse was stronger, but something must be allowed for the excitement which he had undergone.

When Alexander saw his uncle in the evening, the latter again thanked him for having undertaken the expedition, and having brought back such satisfactory accounts.

"I am much your debtor, my dear boy," said he; "and if it is any satisfaction to you (which I am sure it must be from your kind heart) to know that you have smoothed the death-bed of one who loves you, you have your reward. I feel quite strong now; and if it will not be too much trouble, I should like you to give me a narrative of the whole expedition; not all at once, but a little now and then. You shall begin now, and mind you enter into every little detail, —everything will interest me."

Alexander commenced his narrative, as his uncle requested, stating to him how they were fitted out; the names of all the people; describing Swinton and the Major, and giving a much closer narrative of what passed than we have done in these pages. After an hour or so, during which Alexander had not got so far in his narrative as to have quitted the Cape for Algoa Bay, he left off, that he might not weary his uncle, and wished him good-night.

For many weeks did the narrative, and the conversation produced by it, serve to amuse and interest the old gentleman, who still remained in his bed. But long before it was finished Major Henderson had arrived at the hall, and had been introduced to Sir Charles, who was much pleased with him, and requested him to remain as long as he found it agreeable. The Major, at Alexander's request, had the lion and lioness set up in Leadbeater's best style, and the case had now arrived at the hall, and was brought up into Sir Charles's room, that he might have some idea of the animals with which they had had to contend; and there it remained, for the old gentleman would not allow it to be taken away.

"I must send out a present to that little Omrah," said

Sir Charles, one morning, as he was conversing with the Major; "what shall it be?"

"Well, sir, I hardly know; but I think the best present for him would be a watch."

"Then, Major, order one of the best gold watches that can be made, when you go to town, and send it out to him; and, Major,—I am sorry to give you that trouble, but I am an old bedridden man, and that must be my excuse,—take the keys from the dressing-table, and open the small drawer of that cabinet, and you will find two morocco cases in it, which I will thank you to bring to me."

The Major did so, and Sir Charles, raising himself on his pillow, opened the cases, which contained each a massive ring in which was set a diamond of great value.

"These two rings were presented me by Eastern princes, Major, at the time that I was resident in their country. There is little difference in their value, but you would find it difficult to match the stones, even in England. I will shut the cases up again, and now that I have shut them up in my hands, take one out for me. Thank you, Major; that one is a present from me to our friend Swinton, and you must send it out to him with the watch for the Bush-boy. The other, Major, I hope you will not refuse to accept as a testimony of my gratitude to you, for having accompanied my dear boy on his expedition."

Sir Charles put the other case into the Major's hands.

"I certainly will not refuse anything as a remembrance from you, Sir Charles," replied the Major; "I accept your splendid present with many thanks, and so will Swinton, I am certain; but he will be more pleased with the kind attention than he will be with its great value; and I trust you will believe me when I add that such is also my own feeling."

"I only hope you may have both as much pleasure in receiving as I have in giving them," replied Sir Charles; "so put them in your pocket and say no more about them. There is Alexander coming up, I know his tread; I hope you do not mean to desert him now that the shooting season is coming on; he will be very lonely, poor fellow, without you."

"I have good news, my dear uncle," said Alexander, as he entered; "Swinton is coming home; I have a letter from him, and he will be here, he trusts, a fortnight after his letter."

"I shall be most happy to shake hands with him," said Sir Charles. "Pray write for him to come down immediately he arrives."

Three weeks after this announcement Swinton made his appearance, and we hardly need say was most warmly welcomed. Omrah he would not bring with him, as he wished him to continue his education; but the Major declared that he had left the boy because he was afraid of his being taken from him. Our travellers were thus all reunited, and they agreed among themselves that it was quite as comfortable at the hall as it was at the Bechuana country; and that if the sporting was not quite so exciting, at all events it was not quite so dangerous.

Swinton and the Major remained with Alexander till the opening of the next year, and then they both left at the same time, and sailed in the same ship; the Major to rejoin his regiment in India, Swinton to his favourite locality in Africa, to obtain some more specimens in natural history.

As the physician had declared, Sir Charles never rose from his bed again; but he sunk so gradually that it was almost imperceptible, and it was not until the summer of that year that he slept with his fathers, dying without pain, and in perfect possession of his senses.

Alexander now came into possession of the estates and title, and certainly he entered upon them without any reproach as to his conduct toward his uncle, who died blessing him. And now my tale is ended, and I wish my young readers farewell.

THE END

www.ingramcontent.com/pod-product-compliance
Lightning Source LLC
Chambersburg PA
CBHW030919020726
47498CB00001B/25